THE CHAMBER

"GRISHAM'S BEST

"FASCINATING . . . ABSORBING . . . Represents both growth and departure for [Grisham] . . . I'd bet that even Faulkner would have been proud of the hometown boy."—*The Philadelphia Inquirer*

"ONE OF HIS BEST! . . . CHILLING."
—*The Detroit News*

"WOW! Grisham never stacks the deck or cheats. The suspense level in *The Chamber* is surprisingly high . . . I COULD NOT PUT THIS BOOK ASIDE."
—*The Flint Journal* (Mich.)*

"*THE CHAMBER* DOES GRAB HOLD AND IT DOESN'T LET GO. Part of its power comes from suspense. . . . More of it comes from Grisham's unflinching gaze on the conditions in Mississippi's penitentiary."
—*The Boston Globe*

"SUBSTANTIAL . . . THIS IS SERIOUS STUFF . . . He clearly wants the novel to provoke debate . . . a complex novel about a painful, confusing topic."
—*The Houston Chronicle*

Please turn the page for more extraordinary acclaim. . . .

"RIVETING . . . The story is told documentary style, much like Truman Capote's *In Cold Blood*. It has a chilling ring of reality that keeps the reader enthralled." —*The Baton Rouge Advocate*

"*THE CHAMBER* . . . shows [Grisham] is maturing as a writer and as a storyteller, leaving this reader waiting eagerly to see in what direction this former lawyer will head next." —*Bangor Daily News* (Me.)

"MASTERFUL . . . A novel that is at once a searing, disturbing, critical look at capital punishment and a heart-wrenching story of escalating tension. With sharp, clear prose, magnificent characterizations, and an eloquent evocation of time, place, and milieu, he has written his most provocative, most dramatic and best novel yet." —*The Buffalo News*

"Is *The Chamber* worth all this hoopla? YES! . . . SUSPENSEFUL . . . ENGROSSING . . . CREDIBLE CHARACTERS . . . CRISP DIALOGUE . . . GRITTY." —*Richmond Times-Dispatch*

"PROVOCATIVE . . . GRIPPING . . . All the elements that have made Grisham a successful writer are here: fine writing, believable characters, social comment, courtroom drama, and legal maneuvers a layman can figure out." —*The Christian Science Monitor*

Books by John Grisham

A TIME TO KILL
THE FIRM
THE PELICAN BRIEF
THE CLIENT
THE CHAMBER
THE RAINMAKER
THE RUNAWAY JURY
THE PARTNER
THE STREET LAWYER
THE TESTAMENT

John Grisham

The Chamber

Island
BOOKS

ISLAND BOOKS
Published by
Dell Publishing
a division of
Bantam Doubleday Dell Publishing Group, Inc.
1540 Broadway
New York, New York 10036

All characters in this book are fictitious, and any resemblance to actual persons, living or dead, is purely coincidental.

The trademark Dell® is registered in the U.S. Patent and Trademark Office.

ISBN: 0-440-22060-2

Reprinted by arrangement with Doubleday, a division of Bantam Doubleday Dell

Printed in the United States of America
Published simultaneously in Canada

May 1995

44   43

OPM

ACKNOWLEDGMENTS

I was a lawyer once, and represented people charged with all sorts of crimes. Fortunately, I never had a client convicted of capital murder and sentenced to death. I never had to go to death row, never had to do the things the lawyers do in this story.

Since I despise research, I did what I normally do when writing a novel. I found lawyers with expertise, and I befriended them. I called them at all hours and picked their brains. And it is here that I thank them.

Leonard Vincent has been the attorney for the Mississippi Department of Corrections for many years, and he opened his office to me. He helped me with the law, showed me his files, took me to death row, and toured me around the vast state penitentiary known simply as Parchman. He told me many stories that somehow found their way into this one. Leonard and I are still struggling with the moral perplexities of the death penalty, and I suspect we always will. Thanks also to his staff, and to the guards and personnel at Parchman.

Jim Craig is a man of great compassion and a fine lawyer. As the Executive Director of the Mississippi Capital Defense Resource Center, he's the official attorney for most of the inmates on death row. He deftly steered me through the impenetrable maze of postconviction appeals and habeas corpus warfare. The inevitable mistakes are mine, not his.

I went to law school with Tom Freeland and Guy Gillespie, and I thank them for their ready assistance. Marc Smirnoff is a friend and the editor of The Oxford

American, and, as usual, worked on the manuscript before I sent it to New York.

Thanks also to Robert Warren and William Ballard for their help. And, as always, a very special thanks to my best friend, Renee, who still reads each chapter over my shoulder.

ONE

THE DECISION to bomb the office of the radical Jew lawyer was reached with relative ease. Only three people were involved in the process. The first was the man with the money. The second was a local operative who knew the territory. And the third was a young patriot and zealot with a talent for explosives and an astonishing knack for disappearing without a trail. After the bombing, he fled the country and hid in Northern Ireland for six years.

The lawyer's name was Marvin Kramer, a fourth-generation Mississippi Jew whose family had prospered as merchants in the Delta. He lived in an antebellum home in Greenville, a river town with a small but strong Jewish community, a pleasant place with a history of little racial discord. He practiced law because commerce bored him. Like most Jews of German descent, his family had assimilated nicely into the culture of the Deep South, and viewed themselves as nothing but typical Southerners who happened to have a different religion. Anti-Semitism rarely surfaced. For the most part, they blended with the rest of established society and went about their business.

Marvin was different. His father sent him up North to Brandeis in the late fifties. He spent four years there, then three years in law school at Columbia, and when he returned to Greenville in 1964 the civil rights movement had center stage in Mississippi. Marvin got in the thick of it. Less than a month after opening his little law office, he was arrested along with two of his Brandeis classmates for attempting to register black voters. His father was furious. His family was embarrassed, but Marvin couldn't have cared less. He received his first death threat at the age of twenty-five, and started carrying a gun. He bought a pistol for his wife, a Memphis girl, and instructed their black maid to keep one in her purse. The Kramers had twin two-year-old sons.

The first civil rights lawsuit filed in 1965 by the law offices of Marvin B. Kramer and Associates (there were no associates yet) alleged a multitude of discriminatory voting practices by local officials. It made headlines around the state, and Marvin got his picture in the papers. He also got his name on a Klan list of Jews to harass. Here was a radical Jew lawyer with a beard and a bleeding heart, educated by Jews up North and now marching with and representing Negroes in the Mississippi Delta. It would not be tolerated.

Later, there were rumors of Lawyer Kramer using his own money to post bail for Freedom Riders and civil rights workers. He filed lawsuits attacking whites-only facilities. He paid for the reconstruction of a black church bombed by the Klan. He was actually seen welcoming Negroes into his home. He made speeches before Jewish groups up North and urged them to get involved in the struggle. He wrote sweeping letters to newspapers, few of which were printed. Lawyer Kramer was marching bravely toward his doom.

The presence of a nighttime guard patrolling benignly around the flower beds prevented an attack upon the Kramer home. Marvin had been paying the guard for two years. He was a former cop and he was heavily armed, and the Kramers let it be known to all of Greenville that they were protected by an expert marksman. Of course, the Klan knew about the guard, and the Klan knew to leave him alone. Thus, the decision was made to bomb Marvin Kramer's office, and not his home.

The actual planning of the operation took very little time, and this was principally because so few people were involved in it. The man with the money, a flamboyant redneck prophet named Jeremiah Dogan, was at the time the Imperial Wizard for the Klan in Mississippi. His predecessor had been loaded off to prison, and Jerry Dogan was having a wonderful time orchestrating the bombings. He was not stupid. In fact, the FBI later admitted Dogan was quite effective as a terrorist because he delegated the dirty work to small, autonomous groups of hit men who worked completely independent of one another. The FBI had become expert at infiltrating the Klan with informants, and Dogan trusted no one but family and a handful of accomplices. He owned the largest used car lot in Meridian, Mississippi, and had made plenty of money on all sorts of shady deals. He sometimes preached in rural churches.

The second member of the team was a Klansman by the name of Sam Cayhall from Clanton, Mississippi, in Ford County, three hours north of Meridian and an hour south of Memphis. Cayhall was known to the FBI, but his connection to Dogan was not. The FBI considered him to be harmless because he lived in an area of the state with almost no Klan activity. A few crosses had been burned in Ford County recently, but no bombings, no killings. The FBI knew that Cayhall's father had been a Klansman, but on the whole the family appeared to be rather passive. Dogan's recruitment of Sam Cayhall was a brilliant move.

The bombing of Kramer's office began with a phone call on the night of April 17, 1967. Suspecting, with good reason, that his phones were tapped, Jeremiah Dogan waited until midnight and drove to a pay phone at a gas station south of Meridian. He also suspected he was being followed by the FBI, and he was correct. They watched him, but they had no idea where the call was going.

Sam Cayhall listened quietly on the other end, asked a question or two, then hung up. He returned to his bed, and told his wife nothing. She knew better than to ask. The next morning he left the house early and drove into the town of Clanton. He ate his daily breakfast at The Coffee Shop, then placed a call on a pay phone inside the Ford County Courthouse.

Two days later, on April 20, Cayhall left Clanton at dusk and drove two hours to Cleveland, Mississippi, a Delta college town an hour from Greenville. He waited for forty minutes in the parking lot of a busy shopping center, but saw no sign of a green Pontiac. He ate fried chicken in a cheap diner, then drove to Greenville to scout the law offices of Marvin B. Kramer and Associates. Cayhall had spent a day in Greenville two weeks earlier, and knew the city fairly well. He found Kramer's office, then drove by his stately home, then found the synagogue again. Dogan said the synagogue might be next, but first they needed to hit the Jew lawyer. By eleven, Cayhall was back in Cleveland, and the green Pontiac was parked not at the shopping center but at a truck stop on Highway 61, a secondary site. He found the ignition key under the driver's floor mat, and took the car for a drive through the rich farm fields of the Delta. He turned onto a farm road and opened the trunk. In a cardboard box covered with newspapers, he found fifteen sticks of dynamite, three blasting caps, and a fuse. He drove into town and waited in an all-night café.

At precisely 2 A.M., the third member of the team walked into the crowded truck stop and sat across from Sam Cayhall. His name was Rollie Wedge, a young man of no more than twenty-two, but a trusted veteran of the civil rights war. He said he was from Louisiana, now lived somewhere in the mountains where no one could find him, and though he never boasted, he had told Sam Cayhall several times that he fully expected to be killed in the struggle for white supremacy. His father was a Klansman and a demolition contractor, and from him Rollie had learned how to use explosives.

Sam knew little about Rollie Wedge, and didn't believe much of what he said. He never asked Dogan where he found the kid.

They sipped coffee and made small talk for half an hour. Cayhall's cup shook occasionally from the jitters, but Rollie's was calm and steady. His eyes never blinked. They had done this together several times now, and Cayhall marveled at the coolness of one so young. He had reported to Jeremiah Dogan that the kid never got excited, not even when they neared their targets and he handled the dynamite.

Wedge's car was a rental from the Memphis airport. He retrieved a small bag from the backseat, locked the car, and left it at the truck stop. The green Pontiac with Cayhall behind the wheel left Cleveland and headed south on Highway 61. It was almost 3 A.M., and there was no traffic. A few miles south of the village of Shaw, Cayhall turned onto a dark gravel road and stopped. Rollie instructed him to stay in the car while he inspected the explosives. Sam did as he was told. Rollie took his bag with him to the trunk where he inventoried the dynamite, the blasting caps, and the fuse. He left his bag in the trunk, closed it, and told Sam to head to Greenville.

They drove by Kramer's office for the first time around 4 A.M. The street was deserted, and dark, and

Rollie said something to the effect that this would be their easiest job yet.

"Too bad we can't bomb his house," Rollie said softly as they drove by the Kramer home.

"Yeah. Too bad," Sam said nervously. "But he's got a guard, you know."

"Yeah, I know. But the guard would be easy."

"Yeah, I guess. But he's got kids in there, you know."

"Kill 'em while they're young," Rollie said. "Little Jew bastards grow up to be big Jew bastards."

Cayhall parked the car in an alley behind Kramer's office. He turned off the ignition, and both men quietly opened the trunk, removed the box and the bag, and slid along a row of hedges leading to the rear door.

Sam Cayhall jimmied the rear door of the office and they were inside within seconds. Two weeks earlier, Sam had presented himself to the receptionist under the ruse of asking for directions, then asked to use the rest room. In the main hallway, between the rest room and what appeared to be Kramer's office, was a narrow closet filled with stacks of old files and other legal rubbish.

"Stay by the door and watch the alley," Wedge whispered coolly, and Sam did exactly as he was told. He preferred to serve as the watchman and avoid handling the explosives.

Rollie quickly sat the box on the floor in the closet, and wired the dynamite. It was a delicate exercise, and Sam's heart raced each time as he waited. His back was always to the explosives, just in case something went wrong.

They were in the office less than five minutes. Then they were back in the alley strolling nonchalantly to the green Pontiac. They were becoming invincible. It was all so easy. They had bombed a real estate office in

Jackson because the realtor had sold a house to a black couple. A Jewish realtor. They had bombed a small newspaper office because the editor had uttered something neutral on segregation. They had demolished a Jackson synagogue, the largest in the state.

They drove through the alley in the darkness, and as the green Pontiac entered a side street its headlights came on.

In each of the prior bombings, Wedge had used a fifteen-minute fuse, one simply lit with a match, very similar to a firecracker. And as part of the exercise, the team of bombers enjoyed cruising with the windows down at a point always on the outskirts of town just as the explosion ripped through the target. They had heard and felt each of the prior hits, at a nice distance, as they made their leisurely getaways.

But tonight would be different. Sam made a wrong turn somewhere, and suddenly they were stopped at a railroad crossing staring at flashing lights as a freighter clicked by in front of them. A rather long freight train. Sam checked his watch more than once. Rollie said nothing. The train passed, and Sam took another wrong turn. They were near the river, with a bridge in the distance, and the street was lined with run-down houses. Sam checked his watch again. The ground would shake in less than five minutes, and he preferred to be easing into the darkness of a lonely highway when that happened. Rollie fidgeted once as if he was becoming irritated with his driver, but he said nothing.

Another turn, another new street. Greenville was not that big a city, and if he kept turning Sam figured he could work his way back to a familiar street. The next wrong turn proved to be the last. Sam hit the brakes as soon as he realized he had turned the wrong way on a one-way street. And when he hit the brakes, the engine quit. He yanked the gearshift into park, and turned the ignition. The engine turned perfectly, but it just wouldn't start. Then, the smell of gasoline.

"Dammit!" Sam said through clenched teeth. "Dammit!"

Rollie sat low in his seat and stared through the window.

"Dammit! It's flooded!" He turned the key again, same result.

"Don't run the battery down," Rollie said slowly, calmly.

Sam was near panic. Though he was lost, he was reasonably sure they were not far from downtown. He breathed deeply, and studied the street. He glanced at his watch. There were no other cars in sight. All was quiet. It was the perfect setting for a bomb blast. He could see the fuse burning along the wooden floor. He could feel the jarring of the ground. He could hear the roar of ripping wood and sheetrock, brick and glass. Hell, Sam thought as he tried to calm himself, we might get hit with debris.

"You'd think Dogan would send a decent car," he mumbled to himself. Rollie did not respond, just kept his gaze on something outside his window.

At least fifteen minutes had passed since they had left Kramer's office, and it was time for the fireworks. Sam wiped rows of sweat from his forehead, and once again tried the ignition. Mercifully, the engine started. He grinned at Rollie, who seemed completely indifferent. He backed the car a few feet, then sped away. The first street looked familiar, and two blocks later they were on Main Street. "What kind of fuse did you use?" Sam finally asked, as they turned onto Highway 82, less than ten blocks from Kramer's office.

Rollie shrugged as if it was his business and Sam shouldn't ask. They slowed as they passed a parked police car, then gained speed on the edge of town. Within minutes, Greenville was behind them.

"What kind of fuse did you use?" Sam asked again with an edge to his voice.

"I tried something new," Rollie answered without looking.

"What?"

"You wouldn't understand," Rollie said, and Sam did a slow burn.

"A timing device?" he asked a few miles down the road.

"Something like that."

THEY DROVE to Cleveland in complete silence. For a few miles, as the lights of Greenville slowly disappeared across the flat land, Sam half-expected to see a fireball or hear a distant rumble. Nothing happened. Wedge even managed to catch a little nap.

The truck stop café was crowded when they arrived. As always, Rollie eased from his seat and closed the passenger door. "Until we meet again," he said with a smile through the open window, then walked to his rental car. Sam watched him swagger away, and marveled once more at the coolness of Rollie Wedge.

It was by now a few minutes after five-thirty, and a hint of orange was peeking through the darkness to the east. Sam pulled the green Pontiac onto Highway 61, and headed south.

THE HORROR of the Kramer bombing actually began about the time Rollie Wedge and Sam Cayhall parted ways in Cleveland. It started with the alarm clock on a nightstand not far from Ruth Kramer's pillow. When it erupted at five-thirty, the usual hour, Ruth knew instantly that she was a very sick woman. She had a slight fever, a vicious pain in her temples, and she was quite nauseated. Marvin helped her to the bathroom not far away where she stayed for thirty minutes. A nasty flu bug had been circulating through Greenville for a month, and had now found its way into the Kramer home.

The maid woke the twins, Josh and John, now five years old, at six-thirty, and quickly had them bathed, dressed, and fed. Marvin thought it best to take them to nursery school as planned and get them out of the house and, he hoped, away from the virus. He called a doctor friend for a prescription, and left the maid twenty dollars to pick up the medication at the pharmacy in an hour. He said good-bye to Ruth, who was lying on the floor of the bathroom with a pillow under her head and an icepack over her face, and left the house with the boys.

Not all of his practice was devoted to civil rights litigation; there was not enough of that to survive on in Mississippi in 1967. He handled a few criminal cases and other generic civil matters: divorces, zoning, bankruptcy, real estate. And despite the fact that his father barely spoke to him, and the rest of the Kramers barely uttered his name, Marvin spent a third of his time at the office working on family business. On this particular morning, he was scheduled to appear in court at 9 A.M. to argue a motion in a lawsuit involving his uncle's real estate.

The twins loved his law office. They were not due at nursery school until eight, so Marvin could work a little before delivering the boys and heading on to court. This happened perhaps once a month. In fact, hardly a day passed without one of the twins begging Marvin to take them to his office first and then to nursery school.

They arrived at the office around seven-thirty, and once inside, the twins went straight for the secretary's desk and the thick stack of typing paper, all waiting to be cut and copied and stapled and folded into envelopes. The office was a sprawling structure, built over time with additions here and there. The front door opened into a small foyer where the receptionist's desk sat almost under a stairway. Four chairs for waiting clients hugged the wall. Magazines were scattered under the chairs. To the right and left of the foyer were small offices for lawyers—Marvin now had three associates working for him. A hallway ran directly from the foyer through the center of the downstairs, so from the front door the rear of the building could be seen some eighty feet away. Marvin's office was the largest room downstairs, and it was the last door on the left, next to the cluttered closet. Just across the hall from the closet was Marvin's secretary's office. Her name was Helen, a shapely young woman Marvin had been dreaming about for eighteen months.

Upstairs on the second floor were the cramped offices of another lawyer and two secretaries. The third floor had no heat or air conditioning, and was used for storage.

He normally arrived at the office between seven-thirty and eight because he enjoyed a quiet hour before the rest of the firm arrived and the phone started ringing. As usual, he was the first to arrive on Friday, April 21.

He unlocked the front door, turned on the light switch, and stopped in the foyer. He lectured the twins about making a mess on Helen's desk, but they were off down the hallway and didn't hear a word. Josh already had the scissors and John the stapler by the time Marvin stuck his head in for the first time and warned them. He smiled to himself, then went to his office where he was soon deep in research.

At about a quarter to eight, he would recall later from the hospital, Marvin climbed the stairs to the third floor to retrieve an old file which, he thought at the time, had some relevance to the case he was preparing. He mumbled something to himself as he bounced up the steps. As things evolved, the old file saved his life. The boys were laughing somewhere down the hall.

The blast shot upward and horizontally at several thousand feet per second. Fifteen sticks of dynamite in the center of a wooden framed building will reduce it to splinters and rubble in a matter of seconds. It took a full minute for the jagged slivers of wood and other debris to return to earth. The ground seemed to shake like a small earthquake, and, as witnesses would later describe, bits of glass sprinkled downtown Greenville for what seemed like an eternity.

Josh and John Kramer were less than fifteen feet from the epicenter of the blast, and fortunately never knew what hit them. They did not suffer. Their mangled bodies were found under eight feet of rubble by local firemen. Marvin Kramer was thrown first against the ceiling of the third floor, then, unconscious, fell along with the remnants of the roof into the smoking crater in the center of the building. He was found twenty minutes later and rushed to the hospital. Within three hours, both legs were amputated at the knees.

The time of the blast was exactly seven forty-six, and this in itself was somewhat fortunate. Helen, Marvin's secretary, was leaving the post office four blocks away and felt the blast. Another ten minutes, and she would have been inside making coffee. David Lukland, a young associate in the law firm, lived three blocks away, and had just locked his apartment door when he heard and felt the blast. Another ten minutes, and he would've been picking through his mail in his second-floor office.

A small fire was ignited in the office building next door, and though it was quickly contained it added greatly to the excitement. The smoke was heavy for a few moments, and this sent people scurrying.

There were two injuries to pedestrians. A three-foot section of a two-by-four landed on a sidewalk a hundred yards away, bounced once, then hit Mrs. Mildred Talton square in the face as she stepped away from her parked car and looked in the direction of the explosion. She received a broken nose and a nasty laceration, but recovered in due course.

The second injury was very minor but very significant. A stranger by the name of Sam Cayhall was walking slowly toward the Kramer office when the ground shook so hard he lost his footing and tripped on a street curb. As he struggled to his feet, he was hit once in the neck and once in the left cheek by flying glass. He ducked behind a tree as shards and pieces rained around him. He gaped at the devastation before him, then ran away.

Blood dripped from his cheek and puddled on his shirt. He was in shock and did not remember much of this later. Driving the same green Pontiac, he sped away from downtown, and would most likely have made it safely from Greenville for the second time had he been thinking and paying attention. Two cops in a patrol car were speeding into the business district to respond to the bombing call when they met a green Pontiac which, for some reason, refused to move to the shoulder and yield. The patrol car had sirens blaring, lights flashing, horns blowing, and cops cursing, but the green Pontiac just froze in its lane of traffic and wouldn't budge. The cops stopped, ran to it, yanked open the door, and found a man with blood all over him. Handcuffs were slapped around Sam's wrists. He was shoved roughly into the rear seat of the police car, and taken to jail. The Pontiac was impounded.

* * *

THE BOMB that killed the Kramer twins was the crudest of sorts. Fifteen sticks of dynamite wrapped tightly together with gray duct tape. But there was no fuse. Rollie Wedge had used instead a detonating device, a timer, a cheap windup alarm clock. He had removed the minute hand from the clock, and drilled a small hole between the numbers seven and eight. Into the small hole he had inserted a metal pin which, when touched by the sweeping hour hand, would complete the circuit and detonate the bomb. Rollie wanted more time than a fifteen-minute fuse could provide. Plus, he considered himself an expert and wanted to experiment with new devices.

Perhaps the hour hand was warped a bit. Perhaps the dial of the clock was not perfectly flat. Perhaps Rollie in his enthusiasm had wound it too tight, or not tight enough. Perhaps the metal pin was not flush with the dial. It was, after all, Rollie's first effort with a timer. Or perhaps the timing device worked precisely as planned.

But whatever the reason or whatever the excuse, the bombing campaign of Jeremiah Dogan and the Ku Klux Klan had now spilled Jewish blood in Mississippi. And, for all practical purposes, the campaign was over.

TWO

ONCE THE BODIES were removed, the Greenville police sealed off the area around the ruins and kept the crowd away. Within hours, the premises were given to an FBI team from Jackson, and before dark a demolition unit was sifting through the rubble. Dozens of FBI agents solemnly began the tedious task of picking up every tiny piece, examining it, showing it to someone else, then packing it away to be fitted together on another day. An empty cotton warehouse on the edge of town was leased and became the repository for the Kramer rubble.

With time, the FBI would confirm what it initially assumed. Dynamite, a timer, and a few wires. Just a basic bomb hooked together by a hack lucky enough not to have killed himself.

Marvin Kramer was quickly flown to a fancier hospital in Memphis, and listed as critical but stable for three days. Ruth Kramer was hospitalized for shock, first in Greenville, then driven in an ambulance to the same hospital in Memphis. They shared a room, Mr. and Mrs. Kramer, and also shared a sufficient quantity of sedatives. Countless doctors and relatives stood vigil. Ruth was born and raised in Memphis, so there were plenty of friends to watch her.

AS THE DUST WAS SETTLING around Marvin's office, the neighbors, some of them storekeepers and others office clerks, swept glass from the sidewalks and whispered to one another as they watched the police and rescue people start the digging. A mighty rumor swept downtown Greenville that a suspect was already in custody. By noon on the day of the bombing, it was common knowledge among the clusters of onlookers that the man's name was Sam Cayhall, from Clanton, Mississippi, that he was a member of the Klan, and that he was somehow injured in the attack. One report provided ghastly details of other Cayhall bombings with all sorts of gruesome injuries and disfigured corpses, all involving poor Negroes, though. Another report told of the brilliant heroics of the Greenville police in tracking down this madman within seconds of the blast. On the news at noon, the Greenville TV station confirmed what was already known, that the two little boys were dead, their father was severely injured, and that Sam Cayhall was in custody.

Sam Cayhall came within moments of being released on thirty dollars' bond. By the time he was rushed to the police station, he had regained his senses and had apologized sufficiently to the angry cops for not yielding as they wished. He was booked on a very minor charge, and sent to a holding room to be further processed and released. The two arresting officers sped away to inspect the blast.

A janitor who doubled as the jail medic approached Sam with a battered first aid kit, and washed the dried blood from his face. The bleeding had stopped. Sam repeated again that he'd been in a fight in a bar. Rough night. The medic left, and an hour later an assistant jailer appeared in the sliding window of the holding room with more papers. The charge was failure to yield to an emergency vehicle, the maximum fine was thirty dollars, and if Sam could post this sum in cash then he would be free to go as soon as the paperwork cleared and the car was released. Sam paced nervously around the room, glancing at his watch, softly rubbing the wound to his cheek.

He would be forced to disappear. There was a record of this arrest, and it wouldn't be long before these yokels put his name and the bombing together, and then, well, he needed to run away. He'd leave Mississippi, maybe team up with Rollie Wedge and leave for Brazil or someplace. Dogan would give them the money. He'd call Dogan as soon as he left Greenville. His car was sitting at the truck stop in Cleveland. He would swap vehicles there, then head on to Memphis and catch a Greyhound bus.

That's what he would do. He was an idiot for returning to the scene, but, he thought, if he just kept his cool these clowns would release him.

Half an hour passed before the assistant jailer arrived with another form. Sam handed him thirty dollars cash, and received a receipt. He followed the man through a narrow hallway to the front desk of the jail where he was given a summons to appear in Greenville Municipal Court in two weeks. "Where's the car?" he asked as he folded the summons.

"They're bringing it. Just wait here."

Sam checked his watch and waited for fifteen minutes. Through a small window in a metal door he watched cars come and go in the parking lot in front of the jail. Two drunks were dragged to the desk by a husky cop. Sam fidgeted, and waited.

From somewhere behind him a new voice called slowly, "Mr. Cayhall." He turned and came face-to-face with a short man in a badly faded suit. A badge was waved under Sam's nose.

"I'm Detective Ivy, Greenville P.D. Need to ask you a few questions." Ivy waved at a row of wooden doors along a hallway, and Sam obediently followed.

* * *

FROM THE MOMENT he first sat across the dirty
desk from Detective Ivy, Sam Cayhall had little to say.
Ivy was in his early forties but gray and heavily wrinkled around the eyes. He lit an unfiltered Camel, offered one to Sam, then asked how his face got cut. Sam
played with the cigarette but did not light it. He'd
given up smoking years earlier, and though he felt the
urge to start puffing at this critical moment, he just
thumped it gently on the table. Without looking at Ivy,
he said that maybe he'd been in a fight.

Ivy sort of grunted with a short smile as if he expected this type of reply, and Sam knew he was facing
a pro. He was scared now, and his hands began shaking. Ivy, of course, noticed all this. Where was the
fight? Who were you fighting with? When did it happen? Why were you fighting here in Greenville when
you live three hours away? Where did you get the car?

Sam said nothing. Ivy peppered him with questions,
all unanswerable by Sam because the lies would lead to
more lies and Ivy would have him tied in knots in seconds.

"I'd like to talk to an attorney," Sam finally said.

"That's just wonderful, Sam. I think that's exactly
what you should do." Ivy lit another Camel and blew
thick smoke at the ceiling.

"We had a little bomb blast this morning, Sam. Do
you know that?" Ivy asked, his voice rising slightly in a
mocking tone.

"No."

"Tragic. A local lawyer by the name of Kramer got
his office blown to bits. Happened about two hours
ago. Probably the work of Kluckers, you know. We
don't have any Kluckers around here, but Mr. Kramer
is a Jewish fellow. Let me guess—you know nothing
about it, right?"

"That's right."

"Really, really sad, Sam. You see, Mr. Kramer had two little boys, Josh and John, and, as fate would have it, they were in the office with their daddy when the bomb went off."

Sam breathed deeply and looked at Ivy. Tell me the rest of it, his eyes said.

"And these two little boys, twins, five years old, just cute as can be, got blown to bits, Sam. Deader than hell, Sam."

Sam slowly lowered his head until his chin was an inch off his chest. He was beaten. Murder, two counts. Lawyers, trials, judges, juries, prison, everything hit at once and he closed his eyes.

"Their daddy might get lucky. He's at the hospital now in surgery. The little boys are at the funeral home. A real tragedy, Sam. Don't suppose you know anything about the bomb, do you, Sam?"

"No. I'd like to see a lawyer."

"Of course." Ivy slowly stood and left the room.

THE PIECE OF GLASS in Sam's face was extracted by a physician and sent to an FBI lab. The report contained no surprises—same glass as the front windows of the office building. The green Pontiac was quickly traced to Jeremiah Dogan in Meridian. A fifteen-minute fuse was found in the trunk. A deliveryman came forward and explained to the police that he had seen the car near Mr. Kramer's office around 4 A.M.

The FBI made sure the press immediately knew Mr. Sam Cayhall was a longtime member of the Klan, and that he was the prime suspect in several more bombings. The case was cracked, they felt, and they heaped accolades upon the Greenville police. J. Edgar Hoover himself issued a statement.

Two days after the bombing, the Kramer twins were laid to rest in a small cemetery. At the time, 146 Jews

lived in Greenville, and with the exception of Marvin
Kramer and six others, every one attended the service.
And they were outnumbered two to one by reporters
and photographers from all over the country.

SAM SAW THE PICTURES and read the stories in his
tiny cell the next morning. The assistant jailer, Larry
Jack Polk, was a simpleton who by now was a friend
because, as he had whispered to Sam early on, he had
cousins who were Klansmen and he'd always wanted
to join but his wife wouldn't stand for it. He brought
Sam fresh coffee and newspapers each morning. Larry
Jack had already confessed his admiration for Sam's
bombing skills.

Other than the few bare words needed to keep Larry
Jack manipulated, Sam said virtually nothing. The day
after the bombing he had been charged with two
counts of capital murder, so the gas chamber scenario
occupied his thoughts. He refused to say a word to Ivy
and the other police; same for the FBI. The reporters
asked, of course, but didn't make it past Larry Jack.
Sam phoned his wife and told her to stay in Clanton
with the doors locked. He sat alone in his cinder-block
cell and began a diary.

If Rollie Wedge was to be discovered and linked to
the bombing, then he would have to be found by the
cops. Sam Cayhall had taken an oath as a Klansman,
and to him the oath was sacred. He would never, never
squeal on a Klansman. He fervently hoped Jeremiah
Dogan felt the same about his oath.

Two days after the bombing, a shady lawyer with a
swirling hairdo named Clovis Brazelton made his first
appearance in Greenville. He was a secret member of
the Klan, and had become quite notorious around
Jackson representing all sorts of thugs. He wanted to
run for governor, said his platform would stand for the

preservation of the white race, that the FBI was satanic, that blacks should be protected but not mixed with whites, and so on. He was sent by Jeremiah Dogan to defend Sam Cayhall, and more important, to make sure Cayhall kept his mouth shut. The FBI was all over Dogan because of the green Pontiac, and he feared an indictment as a co-conspirator.

Co-conspirators, Clovis explained to his new client right off the bat, are just as guilty as the ones who actually pull the trigger. Sam listened, but said little. He had heard of Brazelton, and did not yet trust him.

"Look, Sam," Clovis said as if explaining things to a first grader, "I know who planted the bomb. Dogan told me. If I count correctly, that makes four of us—me, you, Dogan, and Wedge. Now, at this point, Dogan is almost certain that Wedge will never be found. They haven't talked, but the kid's brilliant and he's probably in another country by now. That leaves you and Dogan. Frankly, I expect Dogan to be charged anytime now. But the cops'll have a hard time nailing him unless they can prove that ya'll conspired to blow up the Jew's office. And the only way they can prove this is if you tell them."

"So I take the fall?" Sam asked.

"No. You just keep quiet about Dogan. Deny everything. We'll fabricate a story about the car. Let me worry about that. I'll get the trial moved to another county, maybe up in the hills or someplace where they don't have Jews. Get us an all-white jury, and I'll hang it up so fast it'll make heroes out of both of us. Just let me handle it."

"You don't think I'll be convicted?"

"Hell no. Listen, Sam, take my word for it. We'll get us a jury full of patriots, your kind of people, Sam. All white. All worried about their little children being forced to go to schools with little nigger kids. Good people, Sam. We'll pick twelve of 'em, put 'em in the jury box, and explain to 'em how these stinkin' Jews have encouraged all this civil rights nonsense. Trust me, Sam, it'll be easy." With that, Clovis leaned across the shaky table, patted Sam on the arm, and said, "Trust me, Sam, I've done it before."

Later that day, Sam was handcuffed, surrounded by Greenville city policemen, and led to a waiting patrol car. Between the jail and the car, he had his picture taken by a small army of photographers. Another group of these assertive people were waiting at the courthouse when Sam arrived with his entourage.

He appeared before the municipal judge with his new lawyer, the Honorable Clovis Brazelton, who waived the preliminary hearing and performed a couple of other quiet and routine legal maneuvers. Twenty minutes after he'd left the jail, Sam was back. Clovis promised to return in a few days to start plotting strategy, then he wandered outside and performed admirably for the reporters.

IT TOOK A FULL MONTH for the media frenzy to subside in Greenville. Both Sam Cayhall and Jeremiah Dogan were indicted for capital murder on May 5, 1967. The local district attorney proclaimed loudly that he would seek the death penalty. The name of Rollie Wedge was never mentioned. The police and FBI had no idea he existed.

Clovis, now representing both defendants, successfully argued for a change of venue, and on September 4, 1967, the trial began in Nettles County, two hundred miles from Greenville. It turned into a circus. The Klan set up camp on the front lawn of the courthouse and staged noisy rallies almost on the hour. They shipped in Klansmen from other states, even had a list of guest speakers. Sam Cayhall and Jeremiah Dogan were seized as symbols of white supremacy, and their beloved names were called a thousand times by their hooded admirers.

The press watched and waited. The courtroom was filled with reporters and journalists, so the less fortunate were forced to wait under the shade trees on the front lawn. They watched the Klansmen and listened to the speeches, and the more they watched and photographed the longer the speeches became.

Inside the courtroom, things were going smoothly for Cayhall and Dogan. Brazelton worked his magic and seated twelve white patriots, as he preferred to call them, on the jury, then began poking rather significant holes in the prosecution's case. Most importantly, the evidence was circumstantial—no one actually saw Sam Cayhall plant the bomb. Clovis preached this loudly in his opening statement, and it found its mark. Cayhall was actually employed by Dogan, who'd sent him to Greenville on an errand, and he just happened to be near the Kramer building at a most unfortunate moment. Clovis almost cried when he thought of those two precious little boys.

The dynamite fuse in the trunk had probably been left there by its previous owner, a Mr. Carson Jenkins, a dirt contractor from Meridian. Mr. Carson Jenkins testified that he handled dynamite all the time in his line of work, and that he evidently had simply left the fuse in the trunk when he sold the car to Dogan. Mr. Carson Jenkins was a Sunday school teacher, a quiet, hardworking salt-of-the-earth little man who was completely believable. He was also a member of the Ku Klux Klan, but the FBI didn't know it. Clovis orchestrated this testimony without a flaw.

The fact that Cayhall's car had been left at the truck stop in Cleveland was never discovered by the police or FBI. During his first phone call from jail, he had instructed his wife to get his son, Eddie Cayhall, and drive to Cleveland immediately for the car. This was a significant piece of luck for the defense.

But the strongest argument presented by Clovis Brazelton was simply that no one could prove that his clients conspired to do anything, and how in the world can you, the jurors of Nettles County, send these two men to their deaths?

After four days of trial, the jury retired to deliberate. Clovis guaranteed his clients an acquittal. The prosecution was almost certain of one. The Kluckers smelled victory, and increased the tempo on the front lawn.

There were no acquittals, and there were no convictions. Remarkably, two of the jurors boldly dug in their heels and pressed to convict. After a day and a half of deliberations, the jury reported to the judge that it was hopelessly deadlocked. A mistrial was declared, and Sam Cayhall went home for the first time in five months.

THE RETRIAL took place six months later in Wilson County, another rural area four hours from Greenville and a hundred miles from the site of the first trial. There were complaints of Klan harassment of prospective jurors in the first trial, so the judge, for reasons that were never made clear, changed venue to an area crawling with Kluckers and their sympathizers. The jury again was all-white and certainly non-Jewish. Clovis told the same stories with the same punch lines. Mr. Carson Jenkins told the same lies.

The prosecution changed strategy a bit, to no avail. The district attorney dropped the capital charges and pressed for a conviction for murder only. No death penalty, and the jury could, if it so chose, find Cayhall and Dogan guilty of manslaughter, a much lighter charge but a conviction nonetheless.

The second trial had something new. Marvin Kramer sat in a wheelchair by the front row and glared at the jurors for three days. Ruth had tried to watch the first trial, but went home to Greenville where she was hospitalized again for emotional problems. Marvin had been in and out of surgery since the bombing, and his doctors would not allow him to watch the show in Nettles County.

For the most part, the jurors could not stand to look at him. They kept their eyes away from the spectators, and, for jurors, paid remarkable attention to the witnesses. However, one young lady, Sharon Culpepper, mother of twin boys, could not help herself. She glanced at Marvin repeatedly, and many times their eyes locked. He pleaded with her for justice.

Sharon Culpepper was the only one of the twelve who initially voted to convict. For two days she was verbally abused and harangued by her peers. They called her names and made her cry, but she doggedly held on.

The second trial ended with a jury hung eleven to one. The judge declared a mistrial, and sent everybody home. Marvin Kramer returned to Greenville, then to Memphis for more surgery. Clovis Brazelton made a spectacle of himself with the press. The district attorney made no promises of a new trial. Sam Cayhall went quietly to Clanton with a solemn vow to avoid any more dealings with Jeremiah Dogan. And the Imperial Wizard himself made a triumphant return to Meridian where he boasted to his people that the battle for white supremacy had just begun, good had defeated evil, and on and on.

The name of Rollie Wedge had been uttered only once. During a lunch break in the second trial, Dogan whispered to Cayhall that a message had been received from the kid. The messenger was a stranger who spoke to Dogan's wife in a hallway outside the courtroom. And the message was quite clear and simple. Wedge was nearby, in the woods, watching the trial, and if Dogan or Cayhall mentioned his name, their homes and families would be bombed to hell and back.

THREE

RUTH AND MARVIN KRAMER separated in 1970. He was admitted to a mental hospital later that year, and committed suicide in 1971. Ruth returned to Memphis and lived with her parents. In spite of their problems, they had pressed hard for a third trial. In fact, the Jewish community in Greenville was highly agitated and vocal when it became apparent that the district attorney was tired of losing and had lost his enthusiasm for prosecuting Cayhall and Dogan.

Marvin was buried next to his sons. A new park was dedicated to the memory of Josh and John Kramer, and scholarships were established. With time, the tragedy of their deaths lost some of its horror. Years passed, and Greenville talked less and less about the bombing.

Despite pressure from the FBI, a third trial did not materialize. There was no new evidence. The judge would no doubt change venue again. A prosecution looked hopeless, but still the FBI did not quit.

With Cayhall unwilling and Wedge unavailable, Dogan's bombing campaign fizzled. He continued to wear his robe and make his speeches, and began to fancy himself as a major political force. Journalists up North were intrigued by his blatant race-baiting, and he was always willing to put on his hood and give outrageous interviews. He was mildly famous for a brief period, and he enjoyed it immensely.

But by the late 1970s, Jeremiah Dogan was just another thug with a robe in a rapidly declining organization. Blacks were voting. The public schools were desegregated. Racial barriers were being struck down by federal judges throughout the South. Civil rights had arrived in Mississippi, and the Klan had proven pitifully inept in keeping Negroes where they belonged. Dogan couldn't draw flies to a cross-burning.

In 1979, two significant events occurred in the open but inactive Kramer bombing case. The first was the election of David McAllister as the district attorney in Greenville. At twenty-seven he became the youngest D.A. in the state's history. As a teenager he had stood in the crowd and watched the FBI pick through the rubble of Marvin Kramer's office. Shortly after his election, he vowed to bring the terrorists to justice.

The second event was the indictment of Jeremiah Dogan for income tax evasion. After years of successfully dodging the FBI, Dogan got sloppy and ran afoul of the IRS. The investigation took eight months and resulted in an indictment that ran for thirty pages. According to it, Dogan had failed to report over a hundred thousand dollars between 1974 and 1978. It contained eighty-six counts, and carried a maximum of twenty-eight years in prison.

Dogan was dead guilty, and his lawyer (not Clovis Brazelton) immediately began exploring the possibility of a plea bargain. Enter the FBI.

Through a series of heated and angry meetings with Dogan and his lawyer, a deal was offered by the government whereby Dogan would testify against Sam Cayhall in the Kramer case, and in return he would serve no time in jail for tax evasion. Zero days behind bars. Heavy probation and fines, but no jail. Dogan had not spoken to Cayhall in over ten years. Dogan was not active in the Klan anymore. There were lots of reasons to consider the deal, not the least of which was the issue of remaining a free man or spending a decade or so in prison.

To prod him along, the IRS attached all of his assets, and planned a nice little fire sale. And to help with his decision, David McAllister convinced a grand jury in Greenville to indict him and his pal Cayhall once again for the Kramer bombing.

Dogan caved in and jumped at the deal.

AFTER TWELVE YEARS of living quietly in Ford County, Sam Cayhall once again found himself indicted, arrested, and facing the certainty of a trial and the possibility of the gas chamber. He was forced to mortgage his house and small farm to hire a lawyer. Clovis Brazelton had gone on to bigger things, and Dogan was no longer an ally.

Much had changed in Mississippi since the first two trials. Blacks had registered to vote in record numbers, and these new voters had elected black officials. All-white juries were rare. The state had two black trial judges, two black sheriffs, and black lawyers could be spotted with their white brethren roaming the courthouse hallways. Officially, segregation was over. And many white Mississippians were beginning to look back and wonder what all the fuss was about. Why had there been such resistance to basic rights for all people? Though it had a long way to go, Mississippi was a far different place in 1980 than in 1967. And Sam Cayhall understood this.

He hired a skilled trial advocate from Memphis named Benjamin Keyes. Their first tactic was to move to dismiss the indictment on the grounds that it was unfair to try him again after such a delay. This proved to be a persuasive argument, and it took a decision by the Mississippi Supreme Court to settle the matter. By a vote of six to three, the court ruled that the prosecution could proceed.

And proceed it did. The third and final trial of Sam Cayhall began in February of 1981, in a chilly little courthouse in Lakehead County, a hill county in the northeastern corner of the state. Much could be said about the trial. There was a young district attorney, David McAllister, who performed brilliantly but had the obnoxious habit of spending all his spare time with the press. He was handsome and articulate and compassionate, and it became very clear that this trial had a purpose. Mr. McAllister had political ambitions on a grand scale.

There was a jury of eight whites and four blacks. There were the glass sample, the fuse, the FBI reports, and all the other photos and exhibits from the first two trials.

And then, there was the testimony of Jeremiah Dogan, who took the stand in a denim workshirt and with a humble countenance solemnly explained to the jury how he conspired with Sam Cayhall sitting over there to bomb the office of Mr. Kramer. Sam glared at him intensely and absorbed every word, but Dogan looked away. Sam's lawyer berated Dogan for half a day, and forced him to admit that he'd cut a deal with the government. But the damage was done.

It was of no benefit to the defense of Sam Cayhall to raise the issue of Rollie Wedge. Because to do so would be to admit that Sam in fact had been in Greenville with the bomb. Sam would be forced to admit that he was a co-conspirator, and under the law he would be just as guilty as the man who planted the dynamite. And to present this scenario to the jury, Sam would be forced to testify, something neither he nor his attorney wanted. Sam could not withstand a rigorous cross-examination, because Sam would be forced to tell one lie to cover the last.

And, at this point, no one would believe a sudden tale of a mysterious new terrorist who'd never been mentioned before, and who came and went without being seen. Sam knew the Rollie Wedge angle was futile, and he never mentioned the man's name to his own lawyer.

AT THE CLOSE of the trial, David McAllister stood before the jury in a packed courtroom and presented his closing argument. He talked of being a youngster in Greenville and having Jewish friends. He didn't know they were different. He knew some of the Kramers, fine folks who worked hard and gave back to the town. He also played with little black kids, and learned they made wonderful friends. He never understood why they went to one school and he went to another. He told a gripping story of feeling the earth shake on the morning of April 21, 1967, and running in the direction of downtown where smoke was drifting upward. For three hours, he stood behind the police barricades and waited. He saw the firemen scurry about when they found Marvin Kramer. He saw them huddle in the debris when they found the boys. Tears dripped down his cheeks when the little bodies, covered in white sheets, were carried slowly to an ambulance.

It was a splendid performance, and when McAllister finished the courtroom was silent. Several of the jurors dabbed at their eyes.

ON FEBRUARY 12, 1981, Sam Cayhall was convicted on two counts of capital murder and one count of attempted murder. Two days later, the same jury in the same courtroom returned with a sentencing verdict of death.

He was transported to the state penitentiary at Parchman to begin waiting for his appointment with the gas chamber. On February 19, 1981, he first set foot on death row.

FOUR

THE LAW FIRM of Kravitz & Bane had almost three hundred lawyers peacefully coexisting under the same roof in Chicago. Two hundred and eighty-six to be exact, though it was difficult for anyone to keep score because at any given moment there were a dozen or so leaving for a multitude of reasons, and there were always two dozen or so shiny, fresh new recruits trained and polished and just itching for combat. And though it was huge, Kravitz & Bane had failed to play the expansion game as quickly as others, had failed to gobble up weaker firms in other cities, had been slow to raid clients from its competitors, and thus had to suffer the distinction of being only the third-largest firm in Chicago. It had offices in six cities, but, much to the embarrassment of the younger partners, there was no London address on the letterhead.

Though it had mellowed some, Kravitz & Bane was still known as a vicious litigation firm. It had tamer departments for real estate, tax, and antitrust, but its money was made in litigation. When the firm recruited it sought the brightest third-year students with the highest marks in mock trials and debate. It wanted young men (a token female here and there) who could be instantly trained in the slash-and-attack style perfected long ago by Kravitz & Bane litigators.

There was a nice though small unit for plaintiffs' personal injury work, good stuff from which they took 50 percent and allowed their clients the remainder. There was a sizable section for white-collar criminal defense, but the white-collar defendant needed a sizable net worth to strap on Kravitz & Bane. Then there were the two largest sections, one for commercial litigation and one for insurance defense. With the exception of the plaintiffs' work, and as a percentage of gross it was almost insignificant, the firm's money was earned by billable hours. Two hundred bucks per hour for insurance work; more if the traffic could stand it. Three hundred bucks for criminal defense. Four hundred for a big bank. Even five hundred dollars an hour for a rich corporate client with lazy in-house lawyers who were asleep at the wheel.

Kravitz & Bane printed money by the hour and built a dynasty in Chicago. Its offices were fashionable but not plush. They filled the top floors of, fittingly, the third-tallest building downtown.

Like most large firms, it made so much money it felt obligated to establish a small pro bono section to fulfill its moral responsibility to society. It was quite proud of the fact that it had a full-time pro bono partner, an eccentric do-gooder named E. Garner Goodman, who had a spacious office with two secretaries on the sixty-first floor. He shared a paralegal with a litigation partner. The firm's gold-embossed brochure made much of the fact that its lawyers were encouraged to pursue pro bono projects. The brochure proclaimed that last year, 1989, Kravitz & Bane lawyers donated almost sixty thousand hours of their precious time to clients who couldn't pay. Housing project kids, death row inmates, illegal aliens, drug addicts, and, of course, the firm was deeply concerned with the plight of the homeless. The brochure even had a photograph of two young lawyers, jackets off, sleeves rolled up, ties loosened about the neck, sweat in the armpits, eyes filled with compassion, as they performed some menial chore in the midst of a group of minority children in what appeared to be an urban landfill. Lawyers saving society.

Adam Hall had one of the brochures in his thin file as he eased slowly along the hallway on floor sixty-one, headed in the general direction of the office of E. Garner Goodman. He nodded and spoke to another young lawyer, one he'd never seen before. At the firm Christmas party name tags were distributed at the door. Some of the partners barely knew each other. Some of the associates saw each other once or twice a year. He opened a door and entered a small room where a secretary stopped typing and almost smiled. He asked for Mr. Goodman, and she nodded properly to a row of chairs where he was to wait. He was five minutes early for a 10 A.M. appointment, as if it mattered. This was pro bono now. Forget the clock. Forget billable hours. Forget performance bonuses. In defiance of the rest of the firm, Goodman allowed no clocks on his walls.

Adam flipped through his file. He chuckled at the brochure. He read again his own little résumé—college at Pepperdine, law school at Michigan, editor of the law review, case note on cruel and unusual punishment, comments on recent death penalty cases. A rather short résumé, but then he was only twenty-six. He'd been employed at Kravitz & Bane for all of nine months now.

He read and made notes from two lengthy U.S. Supreme Court decisions dealing with executions in California. He checked his watch, and read some more. The secretary eventually offered coffee, which he politely declined.

THE OFFICE of E. Garner Goodman was a stunning study in disorganization. It was large but cramped, with sagging bookshelves on every wall and stacks of dusty files covering the floor. Little piles of papers of all sorts and sizes covered the desk in the center of the office. Refuse, rubbish, and lost letters covered the rug under the desk. If not for the closed wooden blinds, the large window could have provided a splendid view of Lake Michigan, but it was obvious Mr. Goodman spent no time at his window.

He was an old man with a neat gray beard and bushy gray hair. His white shirt was painfully starched. A green paisley bow tie, his trademark, was tied precisely under his chin. Adam entered the room and cautiously weaved around the piles of papers. Goodman did not stand but offered his hand with a cold greeting.

Adam handed the file to Goodman, and sat in the only empty chair in the room. He waited nervously while the file was studied, the beard was gently stroked, the bow tie was tinkered with.

"Why do you want to do pro bono work?" Goodman mumbled after a long silence. He did not look up from the file. Classical guitar music drifted softly from recessed speakers in the ceiling.

Adam shifted uncomfortably. "Uh, different reasons."

"Let me guess. You want to serve humanity, give something back to your community, or, perhaps, you feel guilty because you spend so much time here in this sweatshop billing by the hour that you want to cleanse your soul, get your hands dirty, do some honest work, and help other people." Goodman's beady blue eyes darted at Adam from above the black-framed reading spectacles perched on the tip of his rather pointed nose. "Any of the above?"

"Not really."

Goodman continued scanning the file. "So you've been assigned to Emmitt Wycoff?" He was reading a letter from Wycoff, Adam's supervising partner.

"Yes sir."

"He's a fine lawyer. I don't particularly care for him, but he's got a great criminal mind, you know. Probably one of our top three white-collar boys. Pretty abrasive, though, don't you think?"

"He's okay."

"How long have you been under him?"

"Since I started. Nine months ago."

"So you've been here for nine months?"

"Yes sir."

"What do you think of it?" Goodman closed the file and stared at Adam. He slowly removed the reading glasses and stuck one stem in his mouth.

"I like it, so far. It's challenging."

"Of course. Why did you pick Kravitz & Bane? I mean, surely with your credentials you could've gone anywhere. Why here?"

"Criminal litigation. That's what I want, and this firm has a reputation."

"How many offers did you have? Come on, I'm just being curious."

"Several."

"And where were they?"

"D.C. mainly. One in Denver. I didn't interview with New York firms."

"How much money did we offer you?"

Adam shifted again. Goodman was, after all, a partner. Surely he knew what the firm was paying new associates. "Sixty or so. What are we paying you?"

This amused the old man, and he smiled for the first time. "They pay me four hundred thousand dollars a year to give away their time so they can pat themselves on the back and preach about lawyers and about social responsibility. Four hundred thousand, can you believe it?"

Adam had heard the rumors. "You're not complaining, are you?"

"No. I'm the luckiest lawyer in town, Mr. Hall. I get paid a truckload of money for doing work I enjoy, and I punch no clock and don't worry about billing. It's a lawyer's dream. That's why I still bust my ass sixty hours a week. I'm almost seventy, you know."

The legend around the firm was that Goodman, as a younger man, succumbed to the pressure and almost killed himself with liquor and pills. He dried out for a year while his wife took the kids and left him, then he convinced the partners he was worth saving. He just needed an office where life did not revolve around a clock.

"What kind of work are you doing for Emmitt Wycoff?" Goodman asked.

"Lot of research. Right now he's defending a bunch of defense contractors, and that takes most of my time. I argued a motion in court last week." Adam said this with a touch of pride. Rookies were usually kept chained to their desks for the first twelve months.

"A real motion?" Goodman asked, in awe.

"Yes sir."

"In a real courtroom?"

"Yes sir."

"Before a real judge?"

"You got it."

"Who won?"

"Judge ruled for the prosecution, but it was close. I really tied him in knots." Goodman smiled at this, but the game was quickly over. He opened the file again.

"Wycoff sends along a pretty strong letter of recommendation. That's out of character for him."

"He recognizes talent," Adam said with a smile.

"I assume this is a rather significant request, Mr. Hall. Just what is it you have in mind?"

Adam stopped smiling and cleared his throat. He was suddenly nervous, and decided to recross his legs. "It's, uh, well, it's a death penalty case."

"A death penalty case?" Goodman repeated.

"Yes sir."

"Why?"

"I'm opposed to the death penalty."

"Aren't we all, Mr. Hall? I've written books about it. I've handled two dozen of these damned things. Why do you want to get involved?"

"I've read your books. I just want to help."

Goodman closed the file again and leaned on his desk. Two pieces of paper slid off and fluttered to the floor. "You're too young and you're too green."

"You might be surprised."

"Look, Mr. Hall, this is not the same as counseling winos at a soup kitchen. This is life and death. This is high pressure stuff, son. It's not a lot of fun."

Adam nodded but said nothing. His eyes were locked on to Goodman's, and he refused to blink. A phone rang somewhere in the distance, but they both ignored it.

"Any particular case, or do you have a new client for Kravitz & Bane?" Goodman asked.

"The Cayhall case," Adam said slowly.

Goodman shook his head and tugged at the edges of his bow tie. "Sam Cayhall just fired us. The Fifth Circuit ruled last week that he does indeed have the right to terminate our representation."

"I've read the opinion. I know what the Fifth Circuit said. The man needs a lawyer."

"No he doesn't. He'll be dead in three months with or without one. Frankly, I'm relieved to have him out of my life."

"He needs a lawyer," Adam repeated.

"He's representing himself, and he's pretty damned

good, to be perfectly honest. Types his own motions and briefs, handles his own research. I hear he's been giving advice to some of his buddies on death row, just the white ones though."

"I've studied his entire file."

E. Garner Goodman twirled his spectacles slowly and thought about this. "That's a half a ton of paper. Why'd you do it?"

"I'm intrigued by the case. I've watched it for years, read everything written about the man. You asked me earlier why I chose Kravitz & Bane. Well, the truth is that I wanted to work on the Cayhall case, and I think this firm has handled it pro bono for, what, eight years now?"

"Seven, but it seems like twenty. Mr. Cayhall is not the most pleasant man to deal with."

"Understandable, isn't it? I mean, he's been in solitary for almost ten years."

"Don't lecture me about prison life, Mr. Hall. Have you ever seen the inside of a prison?"

"No."

"Well, I have. I've been to death row in six states. I've been cursed by Sam Cayhall when he was chained to his chair. He's not a nice man. He's an incorrigible racist who hates just about everybody, and he'd hate you if you met him."

"I don't think so."

"You're a lawyer, Mr. Hall. He hates lawyers worse than he hates blacks and Jews. He's been facing death for almost ten years, and he's convinced he's the victim of a lawyer conspiracy. Hell, he tried to fire us for two years. This firm spent in excess of two million dollars in billable time trying to keep him alive, and he was more concerned with firing us. I lost count of the number of times he refused to meet with us after we traveled all the way to Parchman. He's crazy, Mr. Hall.

Find yourself another project. How about abused kids or something?"

"No thanks. My interest is in death penalty cases, and I'm somewhat obsessed with the story of Sam Cayhall."

Goodman carefully returned the spectacles to the tip of his nose, then slowly swung his feet onto the corner of the desk. He folded his hands across the starched shirt. "Why, may I ask, are you so obsessed with Sam Cayhall?"

"Well, it's a fascinating case, don't you think? The Klan, the civil rights movement, the bombings, the tortured locale. The backdrop is such a rich period in American history. Seems ancient, but it was only twenty-five years ago. It's a riveting story."

A ceiling fan spun slowly above him. A minute passed.

Goodman lowered his feet to the floor and rested on his elbows. "Mr. Hall, I appreciate your interest in pro bono, and I assure you there's much to do. But you need to find another project. This is not a mock trial competition."

"And I'm not a law student."

"Sam Cayhall has effectively terminated our services, Mr. Hall. You don't seem to realize this."

"I want the chance to meet with him."

"For what?"

"I think I can convince him to allow me to represent him."

"Oh really."

Adam took a deep breath, then stood and walked deftly around the stacks of files to the window. Another deep breath. Goodman watched, and waited.

"I have a secret for you, Mr. Goodman. No one else knows but Emmitt Wycoff, and I was sort of forced to tell him. You must keep it confidential, okay?"

"I'm listening."

"Do I have your word?"

"Yes, you have my word," Goodman said slowly, biting a stem.

Adam peeked through a slit in the blinds and watched a sailboat on Lake Michigan. He spoke quietly. "I'm related to Sam Cayhall."

Goodman did not flinch. "I see. Related how?"

"He had a son, Eddie Cayhall. And Eddie Cayhall left Mississippi in disgrace after his father was arrested for the bombing. He fled to California, changed his name, and tried to forget his past. But he was tormented by his family's legacy. He committed suicide shortly after his father was convicted in 1981."

Goodman now sat with his rear on the edge of his chair.

"Eddie Cayhall was my father."

Goodman hesitated slightly. "Sam Cayhall is your grandfather?"

"Yes. I didn't know it until I was almost seventeen. My aunt told me after we buried my father."

"Wow."

"You promised not to tell."

"Of course." Goodman moved his butt to the edge of his desk, and placed his feet in the chair. He stared at the blinds. "Does Sam know—"

"No. I was born in Ford County, Mississippi, a town called Clanton, not Memphis. I was always told I was born in Memphis. My name then was Alan Cayhall, but I didn't know this until much later. I was three years old when we left Mississippi, and my parents never talked about the place. My mother believes that there was no contact between Eddie and Sam from the day we left until she wrote him in prison and told him his son was dead. He did not write back."

"Damn, damn, damn," Goodman mumbled to himself.

"There's a lot to it, Mr. Goodman. It's a pretty sick family."

"Not your fault."

"According to my mother, Sam's father was an active Klansman, took part in lynchings and all that. So I come from pretty weak stock."

"Your father was different."

"My father killed himself. I'll spare you the details, but I found his body, and I cleaned up the mess before my mother and sister returned home."

"And you were seventeen?"

"Almost seventeen. It was 1981. Nine years ago. After my aunt, Eddie's sister, told me the truth, I became fascinated with the sordid history of Sam Cayhall. I've spent hours in libraries digging up old newspaper and magazine stories; there is quite a lot of material. I've read the transcripts of all three trials. I've studied the appellate decisions. In law school I began studying this firm's representation of Sam Cayhall. You and Wallace Tyner have done exemplary work."

"I'm glad you approve."

"I've read hundreds of books and thousands of articles on the Eighth Amendment and death penalty litigation. You've written four books, I believe. And a number of articles. I know I'm just a rookie, but my research is impeccable."

"And you think Sam will trust you as his lawyer?"

"I don't know. But he's my grandfather, like it or not, and I have to go see him."

"There's been no contact—"

"None. I was three when we left, and I certainly don't remember him. I've started a thousand times to write him, but it never happened. I can't tell you why."

"It's understandable."

"Nothing's understandable, Mr. Goodman. I do not understand how or why I'm standing here in this office at this moment. I always wanted to be a pilot, but I went to law school because I felt a vague calling to help society. Someone needed me, and I suppose I felt that someone was my demented grandfather. I had four job offers, and I picked this firm because it had the guts to represent him for free."

"You should've told someone up front about this, before we hired you."

"I know. But nobody asked if my grandfather was a client of this firm."

"You should've said something."

"They won't fire me, will they?"

"I doubt it. Where have you been for the past nine months?"

"Here, working ninety hours a week, sleeping on my desk, eating in the library, cramming for the bar exam, you know, the usual rookie boot camp you guys designed for us."

"Silly, isn't it?"

"I'm tough." Adam opened a slit in the blinds for a better view of the lake. Goodman watched him.

"Why don't you open these blinds?" Adam asked. "It's a great view."

"I've seen it before."

"I'd kill for a view like this. My little cubbyhole is a mile from any window."

"Work hard, bill even harder, and one day this will all be yours."

"Not me."

"Leaving us, Mr. Hall?"

"Probably, eventually. But that's another secret, okay? I plan to hit it hard for a couple of years, then move on. Maybe open my own office, one where life does not revolve around a clock. I want to do public interest work, you know, sort of like you."

"So after nine months you're already disillusioned with Kravitz & Bane."

"No. But I can see it coming. I don't want to spend my career representing wealthy crooks and wayward corporations."

"Then you're certainly in the wrong place."

Adam left the window and walked to the edge of the desk. He looked down at Goodman. "I am in the wrong place, and I want a transfer. Wycoff will agree to send me to our little office in Memphis for the next few months so I can work on the Cayhall case. Sort of a leave of absence, with full pay of course."

"Anything else?"

"That's about it. It'll work. I'm just a lowly rookie, expendable around here. No one will miss me. Hell, there are plenty of young cutthroats just eager to work eighteen hours a day and bill twenty."

Goodman's face relaxed, and a warm smile appeared. He shook his head as if this impressed him. "You planned this, didn't you? I mean, you picked this firm because it represented Sam Cayhall, and because it has an office in Memphis."

Adam nodded without a smile. "Things have worked out. I didn't know how or when this moment would arrive, but, yes, I sort of planned it. Don't ask me what happens next."

"He'll be dead in three months, if not sooner."

"But I have to do something, Mr. Goodman. If the firm won't allow me to handle the case, then I'll probably resign and try it on my own."

Goodman shook his head and jumped to his feet. "Don't do that, Mr. Hall. We'll work something out. I'll need to present this to Daniel Rosen, the managing partner. I think he'll approve."

"He has a horrible reputation."

"Well deserved. But I can talk to him."

"He'll do it if you and Wycoff recommend it, won't he?"

"Of course. Are you hungry?" Goodman was reaching for his jacket.

"A little."

"Let's go out for a sandwich."

THE LUNCH CROWD at the corner deli had not arrived. The partner and the rookie took a small table in the front window overlooking the sidewalk. Traffic was slow and hundreds of pedestrians scurried along, just a few feet away. The waiter delivered a greasy Reuben for Goodman and a bowl of chicken soup for Adam.

"How many inmates are on death row in Mississippi?" Goodman asked.

"Forty-eight, as of last month. Twenty-five black, twenty-three white. The last execution was two years ago, Willie Parris. Sam Cayhall will probably be next, barring a small miracle."

Goodman chewed quickly on a large bite. He wiped his mouth with the paper napkin. "A large miracle, I would say. There's not much left to do legally."

"There are the usual assortment of last ditch motions."

"Let's save the strategy talks for later. I don't suppose you've ever been to Parchman."

"No. Since I learned the truth, I've been tempted to return to Mississippi, but it hasn't happened."

"It's a massive farm in the middle of the Mississippi Delta, not too far from Greenville, ironically. Something like seventeen thousand acres. Probably the hottest place in the world. It sits on Highway 49, just like a little hamlet off to the west. Lots of buildings and houses. The front part is all administration, and it's not enclosed by fencing. There are about thirty different camps scattered around the farm, all fenced and secured. Each camp is completely separate. Some are miles apart. You drive past various camps, all enclosed by chain link and barbed wire, all with hundreds of prisoners hanging around, doing nothing. They wear different colors, depending on their classification. It seemed as if they were all young black kids, just loitering about, some playing basketball, some just sitting on the porches of the buildings. An occasional white face. You drive in your car, alone and very slowly, down a gravel road, past the camps and the barbed wire until you come to a seemingly innocuous little building with a flat roof. It has tall fences around it with guards watching from the towers. It's a fairly modern facility. It has an official name of some sort, but everyone refers to it simply as the Row."

"Sounds like a wonderful place."

"I thought it would be a dungeon, you know, dark and cold with water dripping from above. But it's just a little flat building out in the middle of a cotton field. Actually, it's not as bad as death rows in other states."

"I'd like to see the Row."

"You're not ready to see it. It's a horrible place filled with depressing people waiting to die. I was sixty years old before I saw it, and I didn't sleep for a week afterward." He took a sip of coffee. "I can't imagine how you'll feel when you go there. The Row is bad enough when you're representing a complete stranger."

"He is a complete stranger."

"How do you intend to tell him—"

"I don't know. I'll think of something. I'm sure it'll just happen."

Goodman shook his head. "This is bizarre."

"The whole family is bizarre."

"I remember now that Sam had two children, seems like one is a daughter. It's been a long time. Tyner did most of the work, you know."

"His daughter is my aunt, Lee Cayhall Booth, but she tries to forget her maiden name. She married into old Memphis money. Her husband owns a bank or two, and they tell no one about her father."

"Where's your mother?"

"Portland. She remarried a few years ago, and we talk about twice a year. Dysfunctional would be a mild term."

"How'd you afford Pepperdine?"

"Life insurance. My father had trouble keeping a job, but he was wise enough to carry life insurance. The waiting period had expired years before he killed himself."

"Sam never talked about his family."

"And his family never talks about him. His wife, my grandmother, died a few years before he was convicted. I didn't know this, of course. Most of my genealogical research has been extracted from my mother, who's done a great job of forgetting the past. I don't know how it works in normal families, Mr. Goodman, but my family seldom gets together, and when two or more of us happen to meet the last thing we discuss is the past. There are many dark secrets."

Goodman was nibbling on a chip and listening closely. "You mentioned a sister."

"Yes, I have a sister, Carmen. She's twenty-three, a bright and beautiful girl, in graduate school at Berkeley. She was born in L.A., so she didn't go through the name change like the rest of us. We keep in touch."

"She knows?"

"Yes, she knows. My aunt Lee told me first, just after my father's funeral, then, typically, my mother asked me to tell Carmen. She was only fourteen at the time. She's never expressed any interest in Sam Cayhall. Frankly, the rest of the family wishes he would quietly just go away."

"They're about to get their wish."

"But it won't be quietly, will it, Mr. Goodman?"

"No. It never is. For one brief but terrible moment, Sam Cayhall will be the most talked about man in the country. We'll see the same old footage from the bomb blast, and the trials with the Klan marching around the courthouses. The same old debate about the death penalty will erupt. The press will descend upon Parchman. Then, they'll kill him, and two days later it'll all be forgotten. Happens every time."

Adam stirred his soup and carefully picked out a sliver of chicken. He examined it for a second, then returned it to the broth. He was not hungry. Goodman finished another chip, and touched the corners of his mouth with the napkin.

"I don't suppose, Mr. Hall, that you're thinking you can keep this quiet."

"I had given it some thought."

"Forget it."

"My mother begged me not to do it. My sister wouldn't discuss it. And my aunt in Memphis is rigid with the remote possibility that we'll all be identified as Cayhalls and forever ruined."

"The possibility is not remote. When the press finishes with you, they'll have old black-and-whites of you sitting on your granddaddy's knee. It'll make great print, Mr. Hall. Just think of it. The forgotten grandson charging in at the last moment, making a heroic effort to save his wretched old grandfather as the clock ticks down."

"I sort of like it myself."

"Not bad, really. It'll bring a lot of attention to our beloved little law firm."

"Which brings up another unpleasant issue."

"I don't think so. There are no cowards at Kravitz & Bane, Adam. We have survived and prospered in the rough and tumble world of Chicago law. We're known as the meanest bastards in town. We have the thickest skins. Don't worry about the firm."

"So you'll agree to it."

Goodman placed his napkin on the table and took another sip of coffee. "Oh, it's a wonderful idea, assuming your gramps will agree to it. If you can sign him up, or re-sign him I should say, then we're back in business. You'll be the front man. We can feed you what you need from up here. I'll always be in your shadow. It'll work. Then, they'll kill him and you'll never get over it. I've watched three of my clients die, Mr. Hall, including one in Mississippi. You'll never be the same."

Adam nodded and smiled and looked at the pedestrians on the sidewalk.

Goodman continued. "We'll be around to support you when they kill him. You won't have to bear it alone."

"It's not hopeless, is it?"

"Almost. We'll talk strategy later. First, I'll meet with Daniel Rosen. He'll probably want a long conference with you. Second, you'll have to see Sam and have a little reunion, so to speak. That's the hard part. Third, if he agrees to it, then we'll get to work."

"Thanks."

"Don't thank me, Adam. I doubt if we'll be on speaking terms when this is over."

"Thanks anyway."

FIVE

THE MEETING was organized quickly. E. Garner Goodman made the first phone call, and within an hour the necessary participants had been summoned. Within four hours they were present in a small, seldom used conference room next to Daniel Rosen's office. It was Rosen's turf, and this disturbed Adam more than a little.

By legend, Daniel Rosen was a monster, though two heart attacks had knocked off some of the edge and mellowed him a bit. For thirty years he had been a ruthless litigator, the meanest, nastiest, and without a doubt one of the most effective courtroom brawlers in Chicago. Before the heart attacks, he was known for his brutal work schedule—ninety-hour weeks, midnight orgies of work with clerks and paralegals digging and fetching. Several wives had left him. As many as four secretaries at a time labored furiously to keep pace. Daniel Rosen had been the heart and soul of Kravitz & Bane, but no longer. His doctor restricted him to fifty hours a week, in the office, and prohibited any trial work.

Now, Rosen, at the age of sixty-five and getting heavy, had been unanimously selected by his beloved colleagues to graze the gentler pastures of law office management. He had the responsibility of overseeing the rather cumbersome bureaucracy that ran Kravitz & Bane. It was an honor, the other partners had explained feebly when they bestowed it upon him.

So far the honor had been a disaster. Banished from

the battlefield he desperately loved and needed, Rosen
went about the business of managing the firm in a
manner very similar to the preparation of an expensive
lawsuit. He cross-examined secretaries and clerks over
the most trivial of matters. He confronted other partners and harangued them for hours over vague issues
of firm policy. Confined to the prison of his office, he
called for young associates to come visit him, then
picked fights to gauge their mettle under pressure.

He deliberately took the seat directly across the
small conference table from Adam, and held a thin file
as if it possessed a deadly secret. E. Garner Goodman
sat low in the seat next to Adam, twiddling his bow tie
and scratching his beard. When he telephoned Rosen
with Adam's request, and broke the news of Adam's
lineage, Rosen had reacted with predictable foolish-
ness.

Emmitt Wycoff stood at one end of the room with a
matchbox-sized cellular phone stuck to his ear. He was
almost fifty, looked much older, and lived each day in
a fixed state of panic and telephones.

Rosen carefully opened the file in front of Adam and
removed a yellow legal pad. "Why didn't you tell us
about your grandfather when we interviewed you last
year?" he began with clipped words and a fierce stare.

"Because you didn't ask me," Adam answered.
Goodman had advised him the meeting might get
rough, but he and Wycoff would prevail.

"Don't be a wiseass," Rosen growled.

"Come on, Daniel," Goodman said, and rolled his
eyes at Wycoff who shook his head and glanced at the
ceiling.

"You don't think, Mr. Hall, that you should've informed us that you were related to one of our clients?
Certainly you believe we have a right to know this,

don't you, Mr. Hall?" His mocking tone was one usually reserved for witnesses who were lying and trapped.

"You guys asked me about everything else," Adam replied, very much under control. "Remember the security check? The fingerprints? There was even talk of a polygraph."

"Yes, Mr. Hall, but you knew things we didn't. And your grandfather was a client of this firm when you applied for employment, and you damned sure should've told us." Rosen's voice was rich, and moved high and low with the dramatic flair of a fine actor. His eyes never left Adam.

"Not your typical grandfather," Adam said quietly.

"He's still your grandfather, and you knew he was a client when you applied for a job here."

"Then I apologize," Adam said. "This firm has thousands of clients, all well heeled and paying through the nose for our services. I never dreamed one insignificant little pro bono case would cause any grief."

"You're deceitful, Mr. Hall. You deliberately selected this firm because it, at the time, represented your grandfather. And now, suddenly, here you are begging for the file. It puts us in an awkward position."

"What awkward position?" Emmitt Wycoff asked, folding the phone and stuffing it in a pocket. "Look, Daniel, we're talking about a man on death row. He needs a lawyer, dammit!"

"His own grandson?" Rosen asked.

"Who cares if it's his own grandson? The man has one foot in the grave, and he needs a lawyer."

"He fired us, remember?" Rosen shot back.

"Yeah, and he can always rehire us. It's worth a try. Lighten up."

"Listen, Emmitt, it's my job to worry about the image of this firm, and the idea of sending one of our new associates down to Mississippi to have his ass kicked and his client executed does not appeal to me. Frankly, I think Mr. Hall should be terminated by Kravitz & Bane."

"Oh wonderful, Daniel," Wycoff said. "Typical hard-nose response to a delicate issue. Then who'll represent Cayhall? Think about him for a moment. The man needs a lawyer! Adam may be his only chance."

"God help him," Rosen mumbled.

E. Garner Goodman decided to speak. He locked his hands together on the table and glared at Rosen. "The image of this firm? Do you honestly think we're viewed as a bunch of underpaid social workers dedicated to helping people?"

"Or how about a bunch of nuns working in the projects?" Wycoff added helpfully, with a sneer.

"How could this possibly hurt the image of our firm?" Goodman asked.

The concept of retreat had never entered Rosen's mind. "Very simple, Garner. We do not send our rookies to death row. We may abuse them, try to kill them, expect them to work twenty hours a day, but we do not send them into battle until they are ready. You know how dense death penalty litigation is. Hell, you wrote the books. How can you expect Mr. Hall here to be effective?"

"I'll supervise everything he does," Goodman answered.

"He's really quite good," Wycoff added again. "He's memorized the entire file, you know, Daniel."

"It'll work," Goodman said. "Trust me, Daniel, I've been through enough of these things. I'll keep my finger on it."

"And I'll set aside a few hours to help," Wycoff added. "I'll even fly down if necessary."

Goodman jerked and stared at Wycoff. "You! Pro bono?"

"Sure. I have a conscience."

Adam ignored the banter and stared at Daniel Rosen. Go ahead and fire me, he wanted to say. Go ahead, Mr. Rosen, terminate me so I can go bury my grandfather, then get on with the rest of my life.

"And if he's executed?" Rosen asked in the direction of Goodman.

"We've lost them before, Daniel, you know that. Three, since I've run pro bono."

"What are his chances?"

"Quite slim. Right now he's holding on by virtue of a stay granted by the Fifth Circuit. The stay should be lifted any day now, and a new execution date will be set. Probably late summer."

"Not long, then."

"Right. We've handled his appeals for seven years, and they've run their course."

"Of all the people on death row, how'd we come to represent this asshole?" Rosen demanded.

"It's a very long story, and at this moment it's completely irrelevant."

Rosen made what appeared to be serious notes on his legal pad. "You don't think for a moment you'll keep this quiet, do you?"

"Maybe."

"Maybe, hell. Just before they kill him, they'll make him a celebrity. The media will surround him like a pack of wolves. You'll be discovered, Mr. Hall."

"So?"

"So, it'll make great copy, Mr. Hall. Can't you see the headlines—LONG-LOST GRANDSON RETURNS TO SAVE GRAMPS."

"Knock it off, Daniel," Goodman said.

But he continued. "The press will eat it up, don't you see, Mr. Hall? They'll expose you and talk about how crazy your family is."

"But we love the press, don't we, Mr. Rosen?" Adam asked coolly. "We're trial lawyers. Aren't we supposed to perform for the cameras? You've never—"

"A very good point," Goodman interrupted. "Daniel, perhaps you shouldn't advise this young man to ignore the press. We can tell stories about some of your stunts."

"Yes, please, Daniel, lecture the kid about everything else, but lay off the media crap," Wycoff said with a nasty grin. "You wrote the book."

For a brief moment, Rosen appeared to be embarrassed. Adam watched him closely.

"I rather like the scenario myself," Goodman said, twirling his bow tie and studying the bookshelves behind Rosen. "There's a lot to be said for it, actually. Could be great for us poor little pro bono folks. Think of it. This young lawyer down there fighting like crazy to save a rather famous death row killer. And he's our lawyer—Kravitz & Bane. Sure, there'll be a ton of press, but what will it hurt?"

"It's a wonderful idea, if you ask me," Wycoff added just as his mini-phone buzzed somewhere deep in a pocket. He stuck it to his jaw and turned away from the meeting.

"What if he dies? Don't we look bad?" Rosen asked Goodman.

"He's supposed to die, okay? That's why he's on death row," Goodman explained.

Wycoff stopped his mumbling and slid the phone into a pocket. "I gotta go," he said, moving toward the door, nervous now, in a hurry. "Where are we?"

"I still don't like it," Rosen said.

"Daniel, Daniel, always a hard-ass," Wycoff said as he stopped at the end of the table and leaned on it with both hands. "You know it's a good idea, you're just pissed because he didn't tell us up front."

"That's true. He deceived us, and now he's using us."

Adam took a deep breath and shook his head.

"Get a grip, Daniel. His interview was a year ago, in the past. It's gone, man. Forget about it. We have more pressing matters at hand. He's bright. He works very hard. Smooth on his feet. Meticulous research. We're lucky to have him. So his family's messed up. Surely we're not going to terminate every lawyer here with a dysfunctional family." Wycoff grinned at Adam. "Plus, all the secretaries think he's cute. I say we send him south for a few months, then get him back here as soon as possible. I need him. Gotta run." He disappeared and closed the door behind him.

The room was silent as Rosen scribbled on his pad, then gave it up and closed the file. Adam almost felt sorry for him. Here was this great warrior, the legendary Charlie Hustle of Chicago law, a great barrister who for thirty years swayed juries and terrified opponents and intimidated judges, now sitting here as a pencil pusher, trying desperately to agonize over the question of assigning a rookie to a pro bono project. Adam saw the humor, the irony, and the pity.

"I'll agree to it, Mr. Hall," Rosen said with much drama in his low voice, almost a whisper, as if terribly frustrated by all this. "But I promise you this: When the Cayhall matter is over, and you return to Chicago, I'll recommend your termination from Kravitz & Bane."

"Probably won't be necessary," Adam said quickly.

"You presented yourself to us under false pretenses," Rosen continued.

"I said I was sorry. Won't happen again."

"Plus, you're a smartass."

"So are you, Mr. Rosen. Show me a trial lawyer who's not a smartass."

"Real cute. Enjoy the Cayhall case, Mr. Hall, because it'll be your last bit of work for this firm."

"You want me to enjoy an execution?"

"Relax, Daniel," Goodman said softly. "Just relax. No one's getting fired around here."

Rosen pointed an angry finger at Goodman. "I swear I'll recommend his termination."

"Fine. All you can do is recommend, Daniel. I'll take it to the committee, and we'll just have a huge brawl. Okay?"

"I can't wait," Rosen snarled as he jumped to his feet. "I'll start lobbying now. I'll have my votes by the end of the week. Good day!" He stormed from the room and slammed the door.

They sat in silence next to each other, just staring across the table over the backs of the empty chairs to the rows of thick law books lined neatly on the wall, listening to the echo of the slamming door.

"Thanks," Adam finally said.

"He's not a bad guy, really," Goodman said.

"Charming. A real prince."

"I've known him a long time. He's suffering now, really frustrated and depressed. We're not sure what to do with him."

"What about retirement?"

"It's been considered, but no partner has ever been forced into retirement. For obvious reasons, it's a precedent we'd like to avoid."

"Is he serious about firing me?"

"Don't worry, Adam. It won't happen. I promise. You were wrong in not disclosing it, but it's a minor sin. And a perfectly understandable one. You're young, scared, naive, and you want to help. Don't worry about Rosen. I doubt if he'll be in this position three months from now."

"Deep down, I think he adores me."

"It's quite obvious."

Adam took a deep breath and walked around the table. Goodman uncapped his pen and began making notes. "There's not much time, Adam," he said.

"I know."

"When can you leave?"

"Tomorrow. I'll pack tonight. It's a ten-hour drive."

"The file weighs a hundred pounds. It's down in printing right now. I'll ship it tomorrow."

"Tell me about our office in Memphis."

"I talked to them about an hour ago. Managing partner is Baker Cooley, and he's expecting you. They'll have a small office and a secretary for you, and they'll help if they can. They're not much when it comes to litigation."

"How many lawyers?"

"Twelve. It's a little boutique firm we swallowed ten years ago, and no one remembers exactly why. Good boys, though. Good lawyers. It's the remnants of an old firm that prospered with the cotton and grain traders down there, and I think that's the connection to Chicago. Anyway, it looks nice on the letterhead. Have you been to Memphis?"

"I was born there, remember?"

"Oh yes."

"I've been once. I visited my aunt there a few years ago."

"It's an old river town, pretty laid back. You'll enjoy it."

Adam sat across the table from Goodman. "How can I possibly enjoy the next few months?"

"Good point. You should go to the Row as quickly as possible."

"I'll be there the day after tomorrow."

"Good. I'll call the warden. His name is Phillip Naifeh, Lebanese oddly enough. There are quite a few of them in the Mississippi Delta. Anyway, he's an old friend, and I'll tell him you're coming."

"The warden is your friend?"

"Yes. We go back several years, to Maynard Tole, a nasty little boy who was my first casualty in this war. He was executed in 1986, I believe, and the warden and I became friends. He's opposed to the death penalty, if you can believe it."

"I don't believe it."

"He hates executions. You're about to learn something, Adam—the death penalty may be very popular in our country, but the people who are forced to impose it are not supporters. You're about to meet these people: the guards who get close to the inmates; the administrators who must plan for an efficient killing; the prison employees who rehearse for a month beforehand. It's a strange little corner of the world, and a very depressing one."

"I can't wait."

"I'll talk to the warden, and get permission for the visit. They'll usually give you a couple of hours. Of course, it may take five minutes if Sam doesn't want a lawyer."

"He'll talk to me, don't you think?"

"I believe so. I cannot imagine how the man will react, but he'll talk. It may take a couple of visits to sign him up, but you can do it."

"When did you last see him?"

"Couple of years ago. Wallace Tyner and I went down. You'll need to touch base with Tyner. He was the point man on this case for the past six years."

Adam nodded and moved to the next thought. He'd been picking Tyner's brain for the past nine months.

"What do we file first?"

"We'll talk about it later. Tyner and I are meeting early in the morning to review the case. Everything's on hold, though, until we hear from you. We can't move if we don't represent him."

Adam was thinking of the newspaper photos, the black and whites from 1967 when Sam was arrested, and the magazine photos, in color, from the third trial in 1981, and the footage he'd pieced together into a thirty-minute video about Sam Cayhall. "What does he look like?"

Goodman left his pen on the table and fiddled with his bow tie. "Average height. Thin—but then you seldom see a fat one on the Row—nerves and lean food. He chain-smokes, which is common because there's not much else to do, and they're dying anyway. Some weird brand, Montclair, I believe, in a blue pack. His hair is gray and oily, as I recall. These guys don't get a shower every day. Sort of long in the back, but that was two years ago. He hasn't lost much of it. Gray beard. He's fairly wrinkled, but then he's pushing seventy. Plus, the heavy smoking. You'll notice the white guys on the Row look worse than the black ones. They're confined for twenty-three hours a day, so they sort of bleach out. Real pale, fair, almost sickly-looking. Sam has blue eyes, nice features. I suspect that at one time Sam Cayhall was a handsome fellow."

"After my father died, and I learned the truth about Sam, I had a lot of questions for my mother. She didn't have many answers, but she did tell me once that there was little physical resemblance between Sam and my father."

"Nor between you and Sam, if that's what you're getting at."

"Yeah, I guess."

"He hasn't seen you since you were a toddler, Adam. He will not recognize you. It won't be that easy. You'll have to tell him."

Adam stared blankly at the table. "You're right. What will he say?"

"Beats me. I expect he'll be too shocked to say much. But he's a very intelligent man, not educated, but well read and articulate. He'll think of something to say. It may take a few minutes."

"You sound as if you almost like him."

"I don't. He's a horrible racist and bigot, and he's shown no remorse for his actions."

"You're convinced he's guilty."

Goodman grunted and smiled to himself, then thought of a response. Three trials had been held to determine the guilt or innocence of Sam Cayhall. For nine years now the case had been batted around the appellate courts and reviewed by many judges. Countless newspaper and magazine articles had investigated the bombing and those behind it. "The jury thought so. I guess that's all that matters."

"But what about you? What do you think?"

"You've read the file, Adam. You've researched the case for a long time. There's no doubt Sam took part in the bombing."

"But?"

"There are a lot of buts. There always are."

"He had no history of handling explosives."

"True. But he was a Klan terrorist, and they were bombing like hell. Sam gets arrested, and the bombing stops."

"But in one of the bombings before Kramer, a witness claims he saw two people in the green Pontiac."

"True. But the witness was not allowed to testify at trial. And the witness had just left a bar at three in the morning."

"But another witness, a truck driver, claims he saw Sam and another man talking in a coffee shop in Cleveland a few hours before the Kramer bombing."

"True. But the truck driver said nothing for three years, and was not allowed to testify at the last trial. Too remote."

"So who was Sam's accomplice?"

"I doubt if we'll ever know. Keep in mind, Adam, this is a man who went to trial three times, yet never testified. He said virtually nothing to the police, very little to his defense lawyers, not a word to his juries, and he's told us nothing new in the past seven years."

"Do you think he acted alone?"

"No. He had help. Sam's carrying dark secrets, Adam. He'll never tell. He took an oath as a Klansman, and he has this really warped, romantic notion of a sacred vow he can never violate. His father was a Klansman too, you know?"

"Yeah, I know. Don't remind me."

"Sorry. Anyway, it's too late in the game to fish around for new evidence. If he in fact had an accomplice, he should've talked long ago. Maybe he should've talked to the FBI. Maybe he should've cut a deal with the district attorney. I don't know, but when you're indicted on two counts of capital murder and facing death, you start talking. You talk, Adam. You save your ass and let your buddy worry about his."

"And if there was no accomplice?"

"There was." Goodman took his pen and wrote a name on a piece of paper. He slid it across the table to Adam, who looked at it and said, "Wyn Lettner. The name is familiar."

"Lettner was the FBI agent in charge of the Kramer case. He's now retired and living on a trout river in the Ozarks. He loves to tell war stories about the Klan and the civil rights days in Mississippi."

"And he'll talk to me?"

"Oh sure. He's a big beer drinker, and he gets about half loaded and tells these incredible stories. He won't divulge anything confidential, but he knows more about the Kramer bombing than anyone. I've always suspected he knows more than he's told."

Adam folded the paper and placed it in his pocket. He glanced at his watch. It was almost 6 P.M. "I need to run. I have to pack and all."

"I'll ship the file down tomorrow. You need to call me as soon as you talk to Sam."

"I will. Can I say something?"

"Sure."

"On behalf of my family, such as it is—my mother who refuses to discuss Sam; my sister who only whispers his name; my aunt in Memphis who has disowned the name Cayhall—and on behalf of my late father, I would like to say thanks to you and to this firm for what you've done. I admire you greatly."

"You're welcome. And I admire you. Now get your ass down to Mississippi."

SIX

THE APARTMENT was a one-bedroom loft somewhere above the third floor of a turn-of-the-century warehouse just off the Loop, in a section of downtown known for crime but said to be safe until dark. The warehouse had been purchased in the mid-eighties by an S&L swinger who spent a bundle sanitizing and modernizing. He chopped it into sixty units, hired a slick realtor, and marketed it as yuppie starter condos. He made money as the place filled overnight with eager young bankers and brokers.

Adam hated the place. He had three weeks left on a six-month lease, but there was no place to go. He would be forced to renew for another six months because Kravitz & Bane expected eighteen hours a day, and there'd been no time to search for another apartment.

Nor had there been much time to purchase furniture, evidently. A fine leather sofa without arms of any kind sat alone on the wooden floor and faced an ancient brick wall. Two bean bags—yellow and blue—were nearby in the unlikely event a crowd materialized. To the left was a tiny kitchen area with a snack bar and three wicker stools, and to the right of the sofa was the bedroom with the unmade bed and clothes on the floor. Seven hundred square feet, for thirteen hundred bucks a month. Adam's salary, as a blue chip prospect nine months earlier, had begun at sixty thousand a year, and was now at sixty-two. From his gross pay of slightly over five thousand a month, fifteen hundred was withheld for state and federal income taxes. Another six hundred never reached his fingers but went instead into a Kravitz & Bane retirement fund guaranteed to relieve the pressure at age fifty-five, if they didn't kill him first. After rent, utilities, four hundred a month for a leased Saab, and incidentals such as frozen food and some nice clothes, Adam found himself with about seven hundred dollars to play with. Some of this remainder was spent on women, but the ones he knew were also fresh from college with new jobs and new credit cards and generally insistent on paying their own way. This was fine with Adam. Thanks to his father's faith in life insurance, he had no student loans. Even though there were things he wanted to buy, he doggedly plowed five hundred a month into mutual funds. With no immediate prospect of a wife and family, his goal was to work hard, save hard, and retire at forty.

Against the brick wall was an aluminum table with a television on it. Adam sat on the sofa, nude except for boxer shorts, holding the remote control. But for the colorless radiation from the screen, the loft was dark. It was after midnight. The video was one he'd pieced together over the years—*The Adventures of a Klan Bomber*, he called it. It started with a brief news report filed by a local crew in Jackson, Mississippi, on March 3, 1967, the morning after a synagogue was leveled by a bomb blast. It was the fourth known attack against Jewish targets in the past two months, the reporter said as a backhoe roared behind her with a bucketful of debris. The FBI had few clues, she said, and even fewer words for the press. The Klan's campaign of terror continues, she declared gravely, and signed off.

The Kramer bombing was next, and the story started with sirens screaming and police pushing people away from the scene. A local reporter and his cameraman were on the spot quickly enough to capture the initial

bedlam. People were seen running to the remains of
Marvin's office. A heavy cloud of gray dust hung above
the small oak trees on the front lawn. The trees were
battered and leafless, but standing. The cloud was still
and showed no signs of dissipating. Off camera, voices
yelled about a fire, and the camera rocked along and
stopped in front of the building next door where thick
smoke poured from a damaged wall. The reporter,
breathless and panting into the microphone, jabbered
incoherently about the entire shocking scene. He
pointed over here, then over there as the camera jerked
in belated response. The police pushed him away, but
he was too excited to care. Glorious pandemonium had
erupted in the sleepy town of Greenville, and this was
his grand moment.

Thirty minutes later, from a different angle, his voice
was somewhat calmer as he described the frantic removal of Marvin Kramer from the rubble. The police
extended their barricades and inched the crowd backward as the fire and rescue people lifted him and
worked the stretcher through the wreckage. The camera followed the ambulance as it sped away. Then, an
hour later and from still another angle, the reporter
was quite composed and somber as the two stretchers
with the covered little bodies were delicately handled
by the firemen.

The video cut from the footage of the bombing scene
to the front of the jail, and for the first time there was a
glimpse of Sam Cayhall. He was handcuffed and
ushered quickly into a waiting car.

As always, Adam pushed a button and replayed the
brief scene with the shot of Sam. It was 1967, twenty-
three years ago. Sam was forty-six years old. His hair
was dark and cut close, the fashion of the times. There
was a small bandage under his left eye, away from the
camera. He walked quickly, stride for stride with the

deputies because people were watching and taking pictures and yelling questions. He turned only once to their voices, and, as always, Adam froze the tape and stared for the millionth time into the face of his grandfather. The picture was black and white and not clear, but their eyes always met.

Nineteen sixty-seven. If Sam was forty-six, then Eddie was twenty-four, and Adam was almost three. He was known as Alan then. Alan Cayhall, soon to be a resident of a distant state where a judge would sign a decree giving him a new name. He had often watched this video and wondered where he was at the precise moment the Kramer boys were killed: 7:46 A.M., April 21, 1967. His family lived at that time in a small house in the town of Clanton, and he was probably still asleep not far from his mother's watch. He was almost three, and the Kramer twins were only five.

The video continued with more quick shots of Sam being led to and from various cars, jails, and courthouses. He was always handcuffed, and he developed the habit of staring at the ground just a few feet in front of him. His face bore no expression. He never looked at the reporters, never acknowledged their inquiries, never said a word. He moved quickly, darting out of doors and into waiting cars.

The spectacle of his first two trials was amply recorded by daily television news reports. Over the years, Adam had been able to retrieve most of the footage, and had carefully edited the material. There was the loud and blustering face of Clovis Brazelton, Sam's lawyer, holding forth for the press at every opportunity. But the clips of Brazelton had been edited quite heavily, with time. Adam despised the man. There were clear, sweeping shots of the courthouse lawns, with the crowds of silent onlookers, and the heavily armed state police, and the robed Klansmen with their coneheads and sinister masks. There were brief glimpses of Sam, always in a hurry, always shielding himself from the cameras by ducking along behind a beefy deputy. After the second trial and the second hung jury, Marvin Kramer stopped his wheelchair on the sidewalk in front of the Wilson County Courthouse, and with tears in his eyes bitterly condemned Sam Cayhall and the Ku Klux Klan and the hidebound justice system in Mississippi. As the cameras rolled, a pitiful incident unfolded. Marvin suddenly spotted two Klansmen in white robes not far away, and began screaming at them. One of them yelled back, but his reply was lost in the heat of the moment. Adam had tried everything to retrieve the Klansman's words from the air, but with no luck. The reply would be forever unintelligible. A couple of years earlier, while in law school at Michigan, Adam had found one of the local reporters who was standing there at the moment, holding a microphone not far from Marvin's face. According to the reporter, the reply from across the lawn had something to do with their desire to blow off the rest of Marvin's limbs. Something this crude and cruel appeared to be true because Marvin went berserk. He screamed obscenities at the Kluckers, who were easing away, and he spun the metal wheels of his chair, lunging in their direction. He was yelling and cursing and crying. His wife and a few friends tried to restrain him, but he broke free, his hands furiously working the wheels. He rolled about twenty feet, with his wife in chase, with the cameras recording it all, until the sidewalk ended and the grass began. The wheelchair flipped, and Marvin sprawled onto the lawn. The quilt around his amputated legs flung free as he rolled hard next to a tree. His wife and friends were on him immediately, and for a moment or two he disappeared into a small huddle on the ground. But he could still be heard. As the camera backed away and shot quickly at the two Klansmen, one doubled over with laughter and one frozen in place, an odd wailing erupted from the small crowd on the ground. Marvin was moaning, but in the shrill, high-pitched howl of a wounded madman. It was a sick sound, and after a few miserable seconds of it the video cut to the next scene.

Adam had tears in his eyes the first time he watched Marvin roll on the ground, howling and groaning, and though the images and sounds still tightened his throat, he had stopped crying long ago. This video was his creation. No one had seen it but him. And he'd watched it so many times that tears were no longer possible.

Technology improved immensely from 1968 to 1981, and the footage from Sam's third and last trial was much sharper and clearer. It was February of 1981, in a pretty little town with a busy square and a quaint courthouse of redbrick. The air was bitterly cold, and perhaps this kept away the crowds of on-lookers and demonstrators. One report from the first day of the trial had a brief shot of three behooded Klansmen huddled around a portable heater, rubbing their hands and looking more like Mardi Gras revelers than serious hoodlums. They were watched by a dozen or so state troopers, all in blue jackets.

Because the civil rights movement was viewed by this time as more of a historical event than a continuing struggle, the third trial of Sam Cayhall attracted more media than the first two. Here was an admitted Klansman, a real live terrorist from the distant era of Freedom Riders and church bombings. Here was a relic from those infamous days who'd been tracked down and was now being hauled to justice. The analogy to Nazi war criminals was made more than once.

Sam was not in custody during his last trial. He was

a free man, and his freedom made it even more difficult to catch him on camera. There were quick shots of him darting into various doors of the courthouse. Sam had aged gracefully in the thirteen years since trial number two. The hair was still short and neat, but half gray now. He appeared a bit heavier, but fit. He moved deftly along sidewalks and in and out of automobiles as the media gave chase. One camera caught him as he stepped from a side door of the courthouse, and Adam stopped the tape just as Sam stared directly into the camera.

Much of the footage of the third and final trial centered around a cocky young prosecutor named David McAllister, a handsome man who wore dark suits and a quick smile with perfect teeth. There was little doubt that David McAllister held grand political ambitions. He had the looks, the hair, the chin, the rich voice, the smooth words, the ability to attract cameras.

In 1989, eight short years after the trial, David McAllister was elected governor of the State of Mississippi. To no one's surprise, the widest planks in his platform had been more jails, longer sentences, and an unwavering affinity for the death penalty. Adam despised him too, but he knew that in a matter of weeks, maybe days, he would be sitting in the governor's office in Jackson, Mississippi, begging for a pardon.

The video ended with Sam, in handcuffs once again, being led from the courthouse after the jury condemned him to death. His face was expressionless. His lawyer appeared to be in shock and uttered a few unremarkable comments. The reporter signed off with the news that Sam would be transported to death row in a matter of days.

Adam pushed the rewind button and stared at the blank screen. Behind the armless sofa were three cardboard boxes that contained the rest of the story: the bulky transcripts of all three trials, which Adam had purchased while at Pepperdine; copies of the briefs and motions and other documents from the appellate warfare that had been raging since Sam's conviction; a thick and carefully indexed binder with neat copies of hundreds of newspaper and magazine stories about Sam's adventures as a Klansman; death penalty materials and research; notes from law school. He knew more about his grandfather than anyone alive.

Yet, Adam knew he had not scratched the surface. He pushed another button, and watched the video again.

SEVEN

THE FUNERAL for Eddie Cayhall occurred less than a month after Sam was sentenced to die. It was held in a small chapel in Santa Monica, and attended by few friends and even fewer family members. Adam sat on a front pew between his mother and sister. They held hands and stared at the closed casket just inches away. As always, his mother was stiff and stoic. Her eyes watered occasionally, and she was forced to dab them with a tissue. She and Eddie had separated and reconciled so many times the children had lost track of whose clothes were where. Though their marriage had never been violent, it had been lived in a continual state of divorce—threats of divorce, plans for divorce, solemn chats with the kids about divorce, negotiations for divorce, filings for divorce, retreats from divorce, vows to avoid divorce. During the third trial of Sam Cayhall, Adam's mother quietly moved her possessions back into their small house, and stayed with Eddie as much as possible. Eddie stopped going to work, and withdrew once again into his dark little world. Adam quizzed his mother, but she explained in a few short words that Dad was simply having another "bad time." The curtains were drawn; the shades were pulled; the lights were unplugged; the voices were lowered; the television was turned off as the family endured another of Eddie's bad times.

Three weeks after the verdict he was dead. He shot himself in Adam's bedroom, on a day when he knew Adam would be the first one home. He left a note on the floor with instructions for Adam to hurry and clean up the mess before the girls got home. Another note was found in the kitchen.

Carmen was fourteen at the time, almost three years younger than Adam. She had been conceived in Mississippi, but born in California after her parents' hasty migration westward. By the time she was born, Eddie had legally transformed his little family from Cayhalls to Halls. Alan had become Adam. They lived in East L.A., in a three-room apartment with dirty sheets on the windows. Adam remembered the sheets with the holes in them. It was the first of many temporary residences.

Next to Carmen on the front pew was a mysterious woman known as Aunt Lee. She had just been introduced to Adam and Carmen as Eddie's sister, his only sibling. As children they were taught not to ask questions about family, but occasionally Lee's name would surface. She lived in Memphis, had at one point married into a wealthy Memphis family, had a child, and had nothing to do with Eddie because of some ancient feud. The kids, Adam especially, had longed to meet a relative, and since Aunt Lee was the only one ever mentioned they fantasized about her. They wanted to meet her, but Eddie always refused because she was not a nice person, he said. But their mother whispered that Lee was indeed a good person, and that one day she would take them to Memphis to meet her.

Lee, instead, made the trip to California, and together they buried Eddie Hall. She stayed for two weeks after the funeral, and became acquainted with her niece and nephew. They loved her because she was pretty and cool, wore blue jeans and T-shirts, and walked barefoot on the beach. She took them shopping, and to the movies, and they went for long walks by the shore of the ocean. She made all sorts of excuses for not visiting sooner. She wanted to, she promised, but Eddie wouldn't allow it. He didn't want to see her because they had fought in the past.

And it was Aunt Lee who sat with Adam on the end of a pier, watching the sun sink into the Pacific, and finally talked of her father, Sam Cayhall. As the waves rocked gently beneath them, Lee explained to young Adam that he had a brief prior life as a toddler in a small town in Mississippi. She held his hand and at times patted his knee while she unveiled the forlorn history of their family. She laid out the barest details of Sam's Klan activities, and of the Kramer bombing, and of the trials that eventually sent him to death row in Mississippi. There were gaps in her oral history large enough to fill libraries, but she covered the high spots with a great deal of finesse.

For an insecure sixteen-year-old who'd just lost his father, Adam took the whole thing rather well. He asked a few questions as a cool wind found the coast and they huddled together, but for the most part he just listened, not in shock or anger, but with enormous fascination. This awful tale was oddly satisfying. There was a family out there! Perhaps he wasn't so abnormal after all. Perhaps there were aunts and uncles and cousins with lives to share and stories to tell. Perhaps there were old homes built by real ancestors, and land and farms upon which they settled. He had a history after all.

But Lee was wise and quick enough to recognize this interest. She explained that the Cayhalls were a strange and secret breed who kept to themselves and shunned outsiders. They were not friendly and warm people who gathered for Christmas and reunited on the Fourth of July. She lived just an hour away from Clanton, yet never saw them.

The visits to the pier at dusk became a ritual for the

next week. They would stop at the market and buy a
sack of red grapes, then spit seeds into the ocean until
well past dark. Lee told stories of her childhood in
Mississippi with her little brother Eddie. They lived on
a small farm fifteen minutes from Clanton, with ponds
to fish in and ponies to ride. Sam was a decent father;
not overbearing but certainly not affectionate. Her
mother was a weak woman who disliked Sam but
doted on her children. She lost a baby, a newborn,
when Lee was six and Eddie was almost four, and she
stayed in her bedroom for almost a year. Sam hired a
black woman to care for Eddie and Lee. Her mother
died of cancer, and it was the last time the Cayhalls
gathered. Eddie sneaked into town for the funeral, but
tried to avoid everyone. Three years later Sam was arrested for the last time and convicted.

Lee had little to say about her own life. She left
home in a hurry at the age of eighteen, the week after
high school graduation, and went straight to Nashville
to get famous as a recording artist. Somehow she met
Phelps Booth, a graduate student at Vanderbilt whose
family owned banks. They were eventually married
and settled into what appeared to be a miserable exis-
tence in Memphis. They had one son, Walt, who evidently was quite rebellious and now lived in Amsterdam. These were the only details.

Adam couldn't tell if Lee had transformed herself
into something other than a Cayhall, but he suspected
she had. Who could blame her?

Lee left as quietly as she had come. Without a hug or
a farewell, she eased from their home before dawn, and
was gone. She called two days later and talked to
Adam and Carmen. She encouraged them to write,
which they eagerly did, but the calls and letters from
her became further apart. The promise of a new relationship slowly faded. Their mother made excuses. She

said Lee was a good person, but she was nonetheless a Cayhall, and thus given to a certain amount of gloom and weirdness. Adam was crushed.

The summer after his graduation from Pepperdine, Adam and a friend drove across the country to Key West. They stopped in Memphis and spent two nights with Aunt Lee. She lived alone in a spacious, modern condo on a bluff overlooking the river, and they sat for hours on the patio, just the three of them, eating home-made pizza, drinking beer, watching barges, and talking about almost everything. Family was never mentioned. Adam was excited about law school, and Lee was full of questions about his future. She was vibrant and fun and talkative, the perfect hostess and aunt. When they hugged good-bye, her eyes watered and she begged him to come again.

Adam and his friend avoided Mississippi. They drove eastward instead, through Tennessee and the Smoky Mountains. At one point, according to Adam's calculations, they were within a hundred miles of Parchman and death row and Sam Cayhall. That was four years ago, in the summer of 1986, and he already had collected a large box full of material about his grandfather. His video was almost complete.

THEIR CONVERSATION on the phone last night had been brief. Adam said he would be living in Memphis for a few months, and would like to see her. Lee invited him to her condo, the same one on the bluff, where she had four bedrooms and a part-time maid. He would live with her, she insisted. Then he said he would be working in the Memphis office, working on Sam's case as a matter of fact. There was silence on the other end, then a weak offer to come on down anyway and they would talk about it.

Adam pushed her doorbell at a few minutes after

nine, and glanced at his black Saab convertible. The development was nothing but a single row of twenty units, all stacked tightly together with red-tiled roofs. A broad brick wall with heavy iron grating along the top protected those inside from the dangers of downtown Memphis. An armed guard worked the only gate. If not for the view of the river on the other side, the condos would be virtually worthless.

Lee opened the door and they pecked each other on the cheek. "Welcome," she said, looking at the parking lot, then locking the door behind him. "Are you tired?"

"Not really. It's a ten-hour drive but it took me twelve. I was not in a hurry."

"Are you hungry?"

"No. I stopped a few hours ago." He followed her into the den where they faced each other and tried to think of something appropriate to say. She was almost fifty, and had aged a lot in the past four years. The hair was now an equal mixture of gray and brunette, and much longer. She pulled it tightly into a ponytail. Her soft blue eyes were red and worried, and surrounded by more wrinkles. She wore an oversized cotton button-down and faded jeans. Lee was still cool.

"It's good to see you," she said with a nice smile.

"Are you sure?"

"Of course I'm sure. Let's sit on the patio." She took his hand and led him through the glass doors onto a wooden deck where baskets of ferns and bougainvillea hung from wooden beams. The river was below them. They sat in white wicker rockers. "How's Carmen?" she asked as she poured iced tea from a ceramic pitcher.

"Fine. Still in grad school at Berkeley. We talk once a week. She's dating a guy pretty serious."

"What's she studying now? I forget."

"Psychology. Wants to get her doctorate, then maybe teach." The tea was strong on lemon and short on sugar. Adam sipped it slowly. The air was still muggy and hot. "It's almost ten o'clock," he said. "Why is it so hot?"

"Welcome to Memphis, dear. We'll roast through September."

"I couldn't stand it."

"You get used to it. Sort of. We drink lots of tea and stay inside. How's your mother?"

"Still in Portland. Now married to a man who made a fortune in timber. I've met him once. He's probably sixty-five, but could pass for seventy. She's forty-seven and looks forty. A beautiful couple. They jet here and there, St. Barts, southern France, Milan, all the places where the rich need to be seen. She's very happy. Her kids are grown. Eddie's dead. Her past is tucked neatly away. And she has plenty of money. Her life is very much in order."

"You're too harsh."

"I'm too easy. She really doesn't want me around because I'm a painful link to my father and his pathetic family."

"Your mother loves you, Adam."

"Boy that's good to hear. How do you know so much?"

"I just know."

"Didn't realize you and Mom were so close."

"We're not. Settle down, Adam. Take it easy."

"I'm sorry. I'm wired, that's all. I need a stronger drink."

"Relax. Let's have some fun while you're here."

"It's not a fun visit, Aunt Lee."

"Just call me Lee, okay?"

"Okay. I'm going to see Sam tomorrow."

She carefully placed her glass on the table, then

stood and left the patio. She returned with a bottle of
Jack Daniel's, and poured a generous shot into both
glasses. She took a long drink and stared at the river in
the distance. "Why?" she finally asked.

"Why not? Because he's my grandfather. Because
he's about to die. Because I'm a lawyer and he needs
help."

"He doesn't even know you."

"He will tomorrow."

"So you'll tell him?"

"Yes, of course I'm going to tell him. Can you believe it? I'm actually going to tell a deep, dark, nasty
Cayhall secret. What about that?"

Lee held her glass with both hands and slowly shook
her head. "He'll die," she mumbled without looking at
Adam.

"Not yet. But it's nice to know you're concerned."

"I am concerned."

"Oh really. When did you last see him?"

"Don't start this, Adam. You don't understand."

"Fine. Fair enough. Explain it to me, then. I'm listening. I want to understand."

"Can't we talk about something else, dear? I'm not
ready for this."

"No."

"We can talk about this later, I promise. I'm just not
ready for it right now. I thought we'd just gossip and
laugh for a while."

"I'm sorry, Lee. I'm sick of gossip and secrets. I have
no past because my father conveniently erased it. I
want to know about it, Lee. I want to know how bad it
really is."

"It's awful," she whispered, almost to herself.

"Okay. I'm a big boy now. I can handle it. My father checked out on me before he had to face it, so I'm
afraid there's no one but you."

"Give me some time."

"There is no time. I'll be face-to-face with him tomorrow." Adam took a long drink and wiped his lips with his sleeve. "Twenty-three years ago, *Newsweek* said Sam's father was also a Klansman. Was he?"

"Yes. My grandfather."

"And several uncles and cousins as well."

"The whole damned bunch."

"*Newsweek* also said that it was common knowledge in Ford County that Sam Cayhall shot and killed a black man in the early fifties, and was never arrested for it. Never served a day in jail. Is this true?"

"Why does it matter now, Adam? That was years before you were born."

"So it really happened?"

"Yes, it happened."

"And you knew about it?"

"I saw it."

"You saw it!" Adam closed his eyes in disbelief. He breathed heavily and sunk lower into the rocker. The horn from a tugboat caught his attention, and he followed it downriver until it passed under a bridge. The bourbon was beginning to soothe.

"Let's talk about something else," Lee said softly.

"Even when I was a little kid," he said, still watching the river, "I loved history. I was fascinated by the way people lived years ago—the pioneers, the wagon trains, the gold rush, cowboys and Indians, the settling of the West. There was a kid in the fourth grade who claimed his great-great-grandfather had robbed trains and buried the money in Mexico. He wanted to form a gang and run away to find the money. We knew he was lying, but it was great fun playing along. I often wondered about my ancestors, and I remember being puzzled because I didn't seem to have any."

"What would Eddie say?"

"He told me they were all dead; said more time is wasted on family history than anything else. Every time I asked questions about my family, Mother would pull me aside and tell me to stop because it might upset him and he might go off into one of his dark moods and stay in his bedroom for a month. I spent most of my childhood walking on eggshells around my father. As I grew older, I began to realize he was a very strange man, very unhappy, but I never dreamed he would kill himself."

She rattled her ice and took the last sip. "There's a lot to it, Adam."

"So when will you tell me?"

Lee gently took the pitcher and refilled their glasses. Adam poured bourbon into both. Several minutes passed as they sipped and watched the traffic on Riverside Drive.

"Have you been to death row?" he finally asked, still staring at the lights along the river.

"No," she said, barely audible.

"He's been there for almost ten years, and you've never gone to see him?"

"I wrote him a letter once, shortly after his last trial. Six months later he wrote me back and told me not to come. Said he didn't want me to see him on death row. I wrote him two more letters, neither of which he answered."

"I'm sorry."

"Don't be sorry. I'm carrying a lot of guilt, Adam, and it's not easy to talk about. Just give me some time."

"I may be in Memphis for a while."

"I want you to stay here. We'll need each other." She hesitated and stirred the drink with an index finger. "I mean, he is going to die, isn't he?"

"It's likely."

"When?"

"Two or three months. His appeals are virtually exhausted. There's not much left."

"Then why are you getting involved?"

"I don't know. Maybe it's because we have a fighting chance. I'll work my tail off for the next few months and pray for a miracle."

"I'll be praying too," she said as she took another sip.

"Can we talk about something?" he asked, suddenly looking at her.

"Sure."

"Do you live here alone? I mean, it's a fair question if I'm going to be staying here."

"I live alone. My husband lives in our house in the country."

"Does he live alone? Just curious."

"Sometimes. He likes young girls, early twenties, usually employees at his banks. I'm expected to call before I go to the house. And he's expected to call before he comes here."

"That's nice and convenient. Who negotiated that agreement?"

"We just sort of worked it out over time. We haven't lived together in fifteen years."

"Some marriage."

"It works quite well, actually. I take his money, and I ask no questions about his private life. We do the required little social numbers together, and he's happy."

"Are you happy?"

"Most of the time."

"If he cheats, why don't you sue for divorce and clean him out? I'll represent you."

"A divorce wouldn't work. Phelps comes from a very proper, stiff old family of miserably rich people.

Old Memphis society. Some of these families have in-
termarried for decades. In fact, Phelps was expected to
marry a fifth cousin, but instead he fell under my
charms. His family was viciously opposed to it, and
a divorce now would be a painful admission that
his family was right. Plus, these people are proud
bluebloods, and a nasty divorce would humiliate them.
I love the independence of taking his money and living
as I choose."

"Did you ever love him?"

"Of course. We were madly in love when we married. We eloped, by the way. It was 1963, and the idea
of a large wedding with his family of aristocrats and
my family of rednecks was not appealing. His mother
would not speak to me, and my father was burning
crosses. At that time, Phelps did not know my father
was a Klansman, and of course I desperately wanted to
keep it quiet."

"Did he find out?"

"As soon as Daddy was arrested for the bombing, I
told him. He in turn told his father, and the word was
spread slowly and carefully through the Booth family.
These people are quite proficient at keeping secrets. It's
the only thing they have in common with us Cayhalls."

"So only a few know you're Sam's daughter?"

"Very few. I'd like to keep it that way."

"You're ashamed of—"

"Hell yes I'm ashamed of my father! Who wouldn't
be?" Her words were suddenly sharp and bitter. "I
hope you don't have some romanticized image of this
poor old man suffering on death row, about to be un-
justly crucified for his sins."

"I don't think he should die."

"Neither do I. But he's damned sure killed enough
people—the Kramer twins, their father, your father,

and God knows who else. He should stay in prison for the rest of his life."

"You have no sympathy for him?"

"Occasionally. If I'm having a good day and the sun is shining, then I might think of him and remember a small pleasant event from my childhood. But those moments are very rare, Adam. He has caused much misery in my life and in the lives of those around him. He taught us to hate everybody. He was mean to our mother. His whole damned family is mean."

"So let's just kill him, then."

"I didn't say that, Adam, and you're being unfair. I think about him all the time. I pray for him every day. I've asked these walls a million times why and how my father became such a horrible person. Why can't he be some nice old man right now sitting on the front porch with a pipe and a cane, maybe a little bourbon in a glass, for his stomach, of course? Why did my father have to be a Klansman who killed innocent children and ruined his own family?"

"Maybe he didn't intend to kill them."

"They're dead, aren't they? The jury said he did it. They were blown to bits and buried side by side in the same neat little grave. Who cares if he intended to kill them? He was there, Adam."

"It could be very important."

Lee jumped to her feet and grabbed his hand. "Come here," she insisted. They stepped a few feet to the edge of the patio. She pointed to the Memphis skyline several blocks away. "You see that flat building facing the river there. The nearest to us. Just over there, three or four blocks away."

"Yes," he answered slowly.

"The top floor is the fifteenth, okay. Now, from the right, count down six levels. Do you follow?"

"Yes." Adam nodded and counted obediently. The building was a showy high-rise.

"Now, count four windows to the left. There's a light on. Do you see it?"

"Yes."

"Guess who lives there."

"How would I know?"

"Ruth Kramer."

"Ruth Kramer! The mother?"

"That's her."

"Do you know her?"

"We met once, by accident. She knew I was Lee Booth, wife of the infamous Phelps Booth, but that was all. It was a glitzy fundraiser for the ballet or something. I've always avoided her if possible."

"This must be a small town."

"It can be tiny. If you could ask her about Sam, what would she say?"

Adam stared at the lights in the distance. "I don't know. I've read that she's still bitter."

"Bitter? She lost her entire family. She's never remarried. Do you think she cares if my father intended to kill her children? Of course not. She just knows they're dead, Adam, dead for twenty-three years now. She knows they were killed by a bomb planted by my father, and if he'd been home with his family instead of riding around at night with his idiot buddies, little Josh and John would not be dead. They instead would be twenty-eight years old, probably very well educated and married with perhaps a baby or two for Ruth and Marvin to play with. She doesn't care who the bomb was intended for, Adam, only that it was placed there and it exploded. Her babies are dead. That's all that matters."

Lee stepped backward and sat in her rocker. She rattled her ice again and took a drink. "Don't get me wrong, Adam. I'm opposed to the death penalty. I'm probably the only fifty-year-old white woman in the country whose father is on death row. It's barbaric, immoral, discriminatory, cruel, uncivilized—I subscribe to all the above. But don't forget the victims, okay. They have the right to want retribution. They've earned it."

"Does Ruth Kramer want retribution?"

"By all accounts, yes. She doesn't say much to the press anymore, but she's active with victims groups. Years ago she was quoted as saying she would be in the witness room when Sam Cayhall was executed."

"Not exactly a forgiving spirit."

"I don't recall my father asking for forgiveness."

Adam turned and sat on the ledge with his back to the river. He glanced at the buildings downtown, then studied his feet. Lee took another long drink.

"Well, Aunt Lee, what are we going to do?"

"Please drop the Aunt."

"Okay, Lee. I'm here. I'm not leaving. I'll visit Sam tomorrow, and when I leave I intend to be his lawyer."

"Do you intend to keep it quiet?"

"The fact that I'm really a Cayhall? I don't plan to tell anyone, but I'll be surprised if it's a secret much longer. When it comes to death row inmates, Sam's a famous one. The press will start some serious digging pretty soon."

Lee folded her feet under her and stared at the river. "Will it harm you?" she asked softly.

"Of course not. I'm a lawyer. Lawyers defend child molesters and assassins and drug dealers and rapists and terrorists. We are not popular people. How can I be harmed by the fact that he's my grandfather?"

"Your firm knows?"

"I told them yesterday. They were not exactly delighted, but they came around. I hid it from them, actually, when they hired me, and I was wrong to do so. But I think things are okay."

"What if he says no?"

"Then we'll be safe, won't we? No one will ever know, and you'll be protected. I'll go back to Chicago and wait for CNN to cover the carnival of the execution. And I'm sure I'll drive down one cool day in the fall and put some flowers on his grave, probably look at the tombstone and ask myself again why he did it and how he became such a lowlife and why was I born into such a wretched family, you know, the questions we've been asking for many years. I'll invite you to come with me. It'll be sort of a little family reunion, you know, just us Cayhalls slithering through the cemetery with a cheap bouquet of flowers and thick sunglasses so no one will discover us."

"Stop it," she said, and Adam saw the tears. They were flowing and were almost to her chin when she wiped them with her fingers.

"I'm sorry," he said, then turned to watch another barge inch north through the shadows of the river. "I'm sorry, Lee."

EIGHT

S O AFTER TWENTY-THREE YEARS, he was finally returning to the state of his birth. He didn't
particularly feel welcome, and though he wasn't
particularly afraid of anything he drove a cautious
fifty-five and refused to pass anyone. The road narrowed and sunk onto the flat plain of the Mississippi
Delta, and for a mile Adam watched as a levee snaked
its way to the right and finally disappeared. He eased
through the hamlet of Walls, the first town of any size
along 61, and followed the traffic south.

Through his considerable research, he knew that this
highway had for decades served as the principal con-
duit for hundreds of thousands of poor Delta blacks
journeying north to Memphis and St. Louis and Chicago and Detroit, places where they sought jobs and
decent housing. It was in these towns and farms, these
ramshackle shotgun houses and dusty country stores
and colorful juke joints along Highway 61 where the
blues was born and spread northward. The music
found a home in Memphis where it was blended with
gospel and country, and together they spawned rock
and roll. He listened to an old Muddy Waters cassette
as he entered the infamous county of Tunica, said to be
the poorest in the nation.

The music did little to calm him. He had refused
breakfast at Lee's, said he wasn't hungry but in fact
had a knot in his stomach. The knot grew with each
mile.

Just north of the town of Tunica, the fields grew vast

and ran to the horizon in all directions. The soybeans and cotton were knee high. A small army of green and red tractors with plows behind them crisscrossed the endless neat rows of leafy foliage. Though it was not yet nine o'clock, the weather was already hot and sticky. The ground was dry, and clouds of dust smoldered behind each plow. An occasional crop duster dropped from nowhere and acrobatically skimmed the tops of the fields, then soared upward. Traffic was heavy and slow, and sometimes forced almost to a standstill as a monstrous John Deere of some variety inched along as if the highway were deserted.

Adam was patient. He was not expected until ten, and it wouldn't matter if he arrived late.

At Clarksdale, he left Highway 61 and headed southeast on 49, through the tiny settlements of Mattson and Dublin and Tutwiler, through more soybean fields. He passed cotton gins, now idle but waiting for the harvest. He passed clusters of impoverished row houses and dirty mobile homes, all for some reason situated close to the highway. He passed an occasional fine home, always at a distance, always sitting majestically under heavy oaks and elms, and usually with a fenced swimming pool to one side. There was no doubt who owned these fields.

A road sign declared the state penitentiary to be five miles ahead, and Adam instinctively slowed his car. A moment later, he ran up on a large tractor puttering casually down the road, and instead of passing he chose to follow. The operator, an old white man with a dirty cap, motioned for him to come around. Adam waved, and stayed behind the plow at twenty miles per hour. There was no other traffic in sight. A random dirt clod flung from a rear tractor tire, and landed just inches in front of the Saab. He slowed a bit more. The operator twisted in his seat, and again waved for Adam to come around. His mouth moved and his face was angry, as if this were his highway and he didn't appreciate idiots following his tractor. Adam smiled and waved again, but stayed behind him.

Minutes later, he saw the prison. There were no tall chain-link fences along the road. There were no lines of glistening razor wire to prevent escape. There were no watchtowers with armed guards. There were no gangs of inmates howling at the passersby. Instead, Adam saw an entrance to the right and the words MISSISSIPPI STATE PENITENTIARY spanning from an arch above it. Next to the entrance were several buildings, all facing the highway and apparently unguarded.

Adam waved once again at the tractor operator, then eased from the highway. He took a deep breath, and studied the entrance. A female in uniform stepped from a guardhouse under the arch, and stared at him. Adam drove slowly to her, and lowered his window.

"Mornin'," she said. She had a gun on her hip and a clipboard in her hand. Another guard watched from inside. "What can we do for you?"

"I'm a lawyer, here to see a client on death row," Adam said weakly, very much aware of his shrill and nervous voice. Just calm down, he told himself.

"We ain't got nobody on death row, sir."

"I'm sorry?"

"Ain't no such place as death row. We got a bunch of 'em in the Maximum Security Unit, that's MSU for short, but you can look all over this place and you won't find no death row."

"Okay."

"Name?" she said, studying the clipboard.

"Adam Hall."

"And your client?"

"Sam Cayhall." He half-expected some sort of response to this, but the guard didn't care. She flipped a sheet, and said, "Stay right here."

The entrance became a driveway with shade trees and small buildings on each side. This wasn't a prison —this was a pleasant little street in a small town where any minute now a group of kids would appear on bicycles and roller skates. To the right was a quaint structure with a front porch and flower beds. A sign said this was the Visitors Center, as if souvenirs and lemonade were on sale for eager tourists. A white pickup with three young blacks in it and Mississippi Department of Corrections stenciled on the door passed by without slowing a bit.

Adam caught a glimpse of the guard standing behind his car. She was writing something on the clipboard as she approached his window. "Where'bouts in Illinois?" she asked.

"Chicago."

"Got any cameras, guns, or tape recorders?"

"No."

She reached inside and placed a card on his dash. Then she returned to her clipboard, and said, "Got a note here that you're supposed to see Lucas Mann."

"Who's that?"

"He's the prison attorney."

"I didn't know I was supposed to see him."

She held a piece of paper three feet from his face. "Says so right here. Take the third left, just up there, then wind around to the back of that redbrick building." She was pointing.

"What does he want?"

She snorted and shrugged at the same time, and walked to the guardhouse shaking her head. Dumbass lawyers.

Adam gently pressed the accelerator and eased by the Visitors Center and down the shaded drive. On both sides were neat white frame houses where, he learned later, prison guards and other employees lived with their families. He followed her instructions and parked in front of an aging brick building. Two trust-ees in blue prison pants with white stripes down the legs swept the front steps. Adam avoided eye contact and went inside.

He found the unmarked office of Lucas Mann with little trouble. A secretary smiled at him, and opened another door to a large office where Mr. Mann was standing behind his desk and talking on the phone.

"Just have a seat," the secretary whispered as she closed the door behind him. Mann smiled and waved awkwardly as he listened to the phone. Adam set his briefcase in a chair and stood behind it. The office was large and clean. Two long windows faced the highway and provided plenty of light. On the wall to the left was a large framed photo of a familiar face, a hand-some young man with an earnest smile and strong chin. It was David McAllister, governor of the State of Mississippi. Adam suspected identical photos were hung in every state government office, and also plas-tered in every hallway, closet, and toilet under the state's domain.

Lucas Mann stretched the phone cord and walked to a window, his back to the desk and Adam. He cer-tainly didn't appear to be a lawyer. He was in his mid-fifties with flowing dark gray hair, which he somehow pulled and kept situated on the back of his neck. His dress was the hippest of fraternity chic—severely starched khaki workshirt with two pockets and a mixed salad tie, still tied but hanging loose; top button unbuttoned to reveal a gray cotton tee shirt; brown chinos, likewise starched to the crunch with a perfect one-inch cuff falling just enough to allow a peek at white socks; loafers shined immaculately. It was obvious Lucas knew how to dress, and also obvious he was engaged in a different practice of law. If he'd had a small earring in his left lobe, he would have been the perfect aging hippie who in his later years was yielding to conformity.

The office was neatly furnished with government hand-me-downs: a worn wooden desk that seemed impeccably organized; three metal chairs with vinyl cushions; a row of mismatched file cabinets along one wall. Adam stood behind a chair and tried to calm himself. Could this meeting be required of all visiting attorneys? Surely not. There were five thousand inmates in Parchman. Garner Goodman had not mentioned a visit with Lucas Mann.

The name was vaguely familiar. Somewhere deep in one of his boxes of court files and newspaper clippings he had seen the name of Lucas Mann, and he desperately tried to remember if he was a good guy or a bad one. What exactly was his role in death penalty litigation? Adam knew for certain that the enemy was the state's Attorney General, but he couldn't fit Lucas into the scenario.

Mann suddenly hung up the phone and shoved a hand at Adam. "Nice to meet you, Mr. Hall. Please have a seat," he said softly in a pleasant drawl as he waved at a chair. "Thanks for stopping by."

Adam took a seat. "Sure. A pleasure to meet you," he replied nervously. "What's up?"

"A couple of things. First, I just wanted to meet you and say hello. I've been the attorney here for twelve years. I do most of the civil litigation that this place spews forth, you know, all kinds of crazy litigation filed by our guests—prisoners' rights, damage suits, that kind of stuff. We get sued every day, it seems. By statute, I also play a small role in the death cases, and I understand you're here to visit Sam."

"That's correct."

"Has he hired you?"

"Not exactly."

"I didn't think so. This presents a small problem. You see, you're not supposed to visit an inmate unless you actually represent him, and I know that Sam has successfully terminated Kravitz & Bane."

"So I can't see him?" Adam asked, almost with a trace of relief.

"You're not supposed to. I had a long talk yesterday with Garner Goodman. He and I go back a few years to the Maynard Tole execution. Are you familiar with that one?"

"Vaguely."

"Nineteen eighty-six. It was my second execution," he said as if he'd personally pulled the switch. He sat on the edge of his desk and looked down at Adam. The starch crackled gently in his chinos. His right leg swung from the desk. "I've had four, you know. Sam could be the fifth. Anyway, Garner represented Maynard Tole, and we got to know each other. He's a fine gentleman and fierce advocate."

"Thanks," Adam said because he could think of nothing else.

"I hate them, personally."

"You're opposed to the death penalty?"

"Most of the time. I go through stages, actually. Every time we kill someone here I think the whole world's gone crazy. Then, invariably, I'll review one of these cases and remember how brutal and horrible some of these crimes were. My first execution was Teddy Doyle Meeks, a drifter who raped, mutilated, and killed a little boy. There was not much sadness here when he was gassed. But, hey, listen, I could tell war stories forever. Maybe we'll have time for it later, okay?"

"Sure," Adam said without commitment. He could not envision a moment when he wanted to hear stories about violent murderers and their executions.

"I told Garner that I didn't think you should be permitted to visit Sam. He listened for a while, then he explained, rather vaguely I must say, that perhaps yours was a special situation, and that you should be allowed at least one visit. He wouldn't say what was so special about it, know what I mean?" Lucas rubbed his chin when he said this as if he had almost solved the puzzle. "Our policy is rather strict, especially for MSU. But the warden will do whatever I ask." He said this very slowly, and the words hung in the air.

"I, uh, really need to see him," Adam said, his voice almost cracking.

"Well, he needs a lawyer. Frankly, I'm glad you're here. We've never executed one unless his lawyer was present. There's all sorts of legal maneuvering up to the very last minute, and I'll just feel better if Sam has a lawyer." He walked around the desk and took a seat on the other side. He opened a file and studied a piece of paper. Adam waited and tried to breathe normally.

"We do a fair amount of background on our death inmates," Lucas said, still looking at the file. The statement had the tone of a solemn warning. "Especially when the appeals have run and the execution is looming. Do you know anything about Sam's family?"

The knot suddenly felt like a basketball in Adam's stomach. He managed to shrug and shake his head at the same time, as if to say he knew nothing.

"Do you plan to talk to Sam's family?"

Again, no response, just the same inept shrug of the shoulders, very heavy shoulders at this moment.

"I mean, normally, in these cases, there's quite a lot of contact with the condemned man's family as the execution gets closer. You'll probably want to contact these folks. Sam has a daughter in Memphis, a Mrs. Lee Booth. I have an address, if you want it." Lucas watched him suspiciously. Adam could not move. "Don't suppose you know her, do you?"

Adam shook his head, but said nothing.

"Sam had one son, Eddie Cayhall, but the poor guy committed suicide in 1981. Lived in California. Eddie left two children, a son born in Clanton, Mississippi, on May 12, 1964, which, oddly enough, is your birthday, according to my *Martindale-Hubbell Law Directory*. Says you were born in Memphis on the same day. Eddie also left a daughter who was born in California. These are Sam's grandchildren. I'll try and contact them, if you—"

"Eddie Cayhall was my father," Adam blurted out, and he took a deep breath. He sank lower in the chair and stared at the top of the desk. His heart pounded furiously, but at least he was breathing again. His shoulders were suddenly lighter. He even managed a very small smile.

Mann's face was expressionless. He thought for a long minute, then said with a hint of satisfaction, "I sort of figured that." He immediately started flipping papers as if the file possessed many other surprises. "Sam's been a very lonely man on death row, and I've often wondered about his family. He gets some mail, but almost none from his family. Virtually no visitors, not that he wants any. But it's a bit unusual for such a noted inmate to be ignored by his family. Especially a white one. I don't pry, you understand."

"Of course not."

Lucas ignored this. "We have to make preparations for the execution, Mr. Hall. For example, we have to know what to do with the body. Funeral arrangements and all. That's where the family comes in. After I talked to Garner yesterday, I asked some of our people in Jackson to track down the family. It was really quite easy. They also checked your paperwork, and immediately discovered that the State of Tennessee has no record of the birth of Adam Hall on May 12, 1964. One thing sort of led to another. It wasn't difficult."

"I'm not hiding anymore."

"When did you learn about Sam?"

"Nine years ago. My aunt, Lee Booth, told me after we buried my father."

"Have you had any contact with Sam?"

"No."

Lucas closed the file and reclined in his squeaky chair. "So Sam has no idea who you are or why you're here?"

"That's right."

"Wow." He whistled at the ceiling.

Adam relaxed a bit and sat up in his chair. The cat was now out of the bag, and had it not been for Lee and her fears of being discovered he would have felt completely at ease. "How long can I see him today?" he asked.

"Well, Mr. Hall—"

"Just call me Adam, okay?"

"Sure, Adam, we really have two sets of rules for the Row."

"Excuse me, but I was told by a guard at the gate that there was no death row."

"Not officially. You'll never hear the guards or other personnel refer to it as anything but Maximum Security or MSU or Unit 17. Anyway, when a man's time is about up on the Row we relax the rules quite a bit. Normally, a visit with the lawyer is limited to an hour a day, but in Sam's case you can have all the time you need. I suspect you'll have a lot to talk about."

"So there's no time limit?"

"No. You can stay all day if you like. We try to

make things easy in the last days. You can come and go as you please as long as there's no security risk. I've been to death row in five other states, and, believe me, we treat them the best. Hell, in Louisiana they take the poor guy out of his unit and place him in what's called the Death House for three days before they kill him. Talk about cruel. We don't do that. Sam will be treated special until the big day."

"The big day?"

"Yeah. It's four weeks from today, you know? August 8." Lucas reached for some papers on the corner of his desk, then handed them to Adam. "This came down this morning. The Fifth Circuit lifted the stay late yesterday afternoon. The Mississippi Supreme Court just set a new execution date for August 8."

Adam held the papers without looking at them. "Four weeks," he said, stunned.

"Afraid so. I took a copy of it to Sam about an hour ago, so he's in a foul mood."

"Four weeks," Adam repeated, almost to himself. He glanced at the court's opinion. The case was styled *State of Mississippi v. Sam Cayhall.* "I guess I'd better go see him, don't you think?" he said without thinking.

"Yeah. Look, Adam, I'm not one of the bad guys, okay?" Lucas slowly eased to his feet and walked to the edge of his desk where he gently placed his rear. He folded his arms and looked down at Adam. "I'm just doing my job, okay. I'll be involved because I have to watch this place and make sure things are done legally, by the book. I won't enjoy it, but it'll get crazy and quite stressful, and everybody will be ringing my phone —the warden, his assistants, the Attorney General's office, the governor, you, and a hundred others. So I'll be in the middle of it, though I don't want to. It's the most unpleasant thing about this job. I just want you to realize that I'm here if you need me, okay? I'll always be fair and truthful with you."

"You're assuming Sam will allow me to represent him."

"Yes. I'm assuming this."

"What are the chances of the execution taking place in four weeks?"

"Fifty-fifty. You never know what the courts will do at the last minute. We'll start preparing in a week or so. We have a rather long checklist of things to do to get ready for it."

"Sort of a blueprint for death."

"Something like that. Don't think we enjoy it."

"I guess everybody here is just doing their job, right?"

"It's the law of this state. If our society wants to kill criminals, then someone has to do it."

Adam placed the court opinion in his briefcase and stood in front of Lucas. "Thanks, I guess, for the hospitality."

"Don't mention it. After you visit with Sam, I'll need to know what happened."

"I'll send you a copy of our representation agreement, if he signs it."

"That's all I need."

They shook hands and Adam headed for the door.

"One other thing," Lucas said. "When they bring Sam into the visiting room, ask the guards to remove the handcuffs. I'll make sure they do. It'll mean a lot to Sam."

"Thanks."

"Good luck."

NINE

THE TEMPERATURE had risen at least ten degrees when Adam left the building and walked past the same two trustees sweeping the same dirt in the same languid motions. He stopped on the front steps, and for a moment watched a gang of inmates gather litter along the highway less than a hundred yards away. An armed guard on a horse in a ditch watched them. Traffic zipped along without slowing. Adam wondered what manner of criminals were these who were allowed to work outside the fences and so close to a highway. No one seemed to care about it but him.

He walked the short distance to his car, and was sweating by the time he opened the door and started the engine. He followed the drive through the parking lot behind Mann's office, then turned left onto the main prison road. Again, he was passing neat little white homes with flowers and trees in the front yard. What a civilized little community. An arrow on a road sign pointed left to Unit 17. He turned, very slowly, and within seconds was on a dirt road that led quickly to some serious fencing and razor wire.

The Row at Parchman had been built in 1954, and officially labeled the Maximum Security Unit, or simply MSU. An obligatory plaque on a wall inside listed the date, the name of the governor then, the names of various important and long-forgotten officials who were instrumental in its construction, and, of course, the names of the architect and contractor. It was state

of the art for that period—a single-story flat roof building of red brick stretching in two long rectangles from
the center.

Adam parked in the dirt lot between two other cars
and stared at it. No bars were visible from the outside.
No guards patrolled around it. If not for the fences and
barbed wire, it could almost pass for an elementary
school in the suburbs. Inside a caged yard at the end of
one wing, a solitary inmate dribbled a basketball on a
grassless court and flipped it against a crooked back-
board.

The fence in front of Adam was at least twelve feet
high, and crowned at the top with thick strands of
barbed wire and a menacing roll of shiny razor wire. It
ran straight and true to the corner where it joined a
watchtower where guards looked down. The fence en-
compassed the Row on all four sides with remarkable
symmetry, and in each corner an identical tower stood
high above with a glass-enclosed guard station at the
top. Just beyond the fence the crops started and seemed
to run forever. The Row was literally in the middle of a
cotton field.

Adam stepped from his car, felt suddenly claustro-
phobic, and squeezed the handle of his thin briefcase as
he glared through the chain link at the hot, flat little
building where they killed people. He slowly removed
his jacket, and noticed his shirt was already spotted
and sticking to his chest. The knot in his stomach had
returned with a vengeance. His first few steps toward
the guard station were slow and awkward, primarily
because his legs were unsteady and his knees were
shivering. His fancy tasseled loafers were dusty by the
time he stopped under the watchtower and looked up.
A red bucket, the type one might use to wash a car,
was being lowered on a rope by an earnest woman in a
uniform. "Put your keys in the bucket," she explained

efficiently, leaning over the railing. The barbed wire on the top of the fence was five feet below her.

Adam quickly did as she instructed. He carefully laid his keys in the bucket where they joined a dozen other key rings. She jerked it back and he watched it rise for a few seconds, then stop. She tied the rope somehow, and the little red bucket hung innocently in the air. A nice breeze would have moved it gently, but at the moment, in this stifling vacuum, there was scarcely enough air to breathe. The winds had died years ago.

The guard was finished with him. Someone somewhere pushed a button or pulled a lever, Adam had no idea who did it, but a humming noise kicked in, and the first of two bulky chain-link gates began to slide a few feet so he could enter. He walked fifteen feet along the dirt drive, then stopped as the first gate closed behind him. He was in the process of learning the first basic rule of prison security—every protected entrance has either two locked doors or gates.

When the first gate stopped behind him and locked itself into place, the second one dutifully snatched itself free and rolled along the fence. As this was happening, a very stocky guard with arms as big as Adam's legs appeared at the main door of the unit and began to amble along the brick path to the entrance. He had a hard belly and a thick neck, and he sort of waited for Adam as Adam waited for the gates to secure everything.

He eased forward an enormous black hand, and said, "Sergeant Packer." Adam shook it and immediately noticed the shiny black cowboy boots on Sergeant Packer's feet.

"Adam Hall," he said, trying to manage the hand.

"Here to see Sam," Packer stated as a fact.

"Yes sir," Adam said, wondering if everyone here referred to him simply as Sam.

"Your first visit here?" They began a slow walk toward the front of the building.

"Yeah," Adam said, looking at the open windows along the nearest tier. "Are all death row inmates here?" he asked.

"Yep. Got forty-seven as of today. Lost one last week."

They were almost to the main door. "Lost one?"

"Yeah. The Big Court reversed. Had to move him in with the general population. I have to frisk you." They were at the door, and Adam glanced around nervously to see just exactly where it was that Packer wished to conduct the frisk.

"Just spread your legs a little," Packer said, already taking the briefcase and placing it on the concrete. The fancy tasseled loafers were now stuck in place. Though he was dizzy and momentarily without the use of all his faculties, Adam could not at this horrible moment remember anyone ever asking him to spread his legs, even just a little.

But Packer was a pro. He patted expertly around the socks, moved up quite delicately to the knees, which were more than a little wobbly, then around the waist in no time flat. Adam's first frisk was mercifully finished just seconds after it started when Sergeant Packer made a rather cursory pass under both arms as if Adam might be wearing a shoulder harness with a small pistol inside it. Packer deftly stuck his massive right hand into the briefcase, then handed it back to Adam. "Not a good day to see Sam," he said.

"So I've heard," Adam replied, slinging his jacket once again over his shoulder. He faced the iron door as if it was now time to enter the Row.

"This way," Packer mumbled as he stepped down onto the grass and headed around the corner. Adam obediently followed along yet another little redbrick trail until they came to a plain, nondescript door with weeds growing beside it. The door was not marked or labeled.

"What's this?" Adam asked. He vaguely recalled Goodman's description of this place, but at the moment all details were fuzzy.

"Conference room." Packer produced a key and unlocked the door. Adam glanced around before he entered and tried to gather his bearings. The door was next to the central section of the unit, and it occurred to Adam that perhaps the guards and their administrators didn't want the lawyers underfoot and poking around. Thus, the outside entrance.

He took a deep breath and stepped inside. There were no other lawyers visiting their clients, and this was particularly comforting to Adam. This meeting could become tumultuous and perhaps emotional, and he preferred to do it in private. At least for the moment the room was empty. It was large enough for several lawyers to visit and counsel, probably thirty feet long and twelve feet wide with a concrete floor and bright fluorescent lighting. The wall on the far end was red-brick with three windows high at the top, just like the exterior of the unit's tiers. It was immediately obvious that the conference room had been added as an afterthought.

The air conditioner, a small window unit, was snarling angrily and producing much less than it should. The room was divided neatly by a solid wall of brick and metal; the lawyers had their side and the clients had theirs. The partition was made of brick for the first three feet, then a small counter provided the lawyers a place to set their mandatory legal pads and take their pages of mandatory notes. A bright green screen of thick metal grating sat solidly on the counter and ran up to the ceiling.

Adam walked slowly to the end of the room, sidestepping a varied assortment of chairs—green and gray government throwaways, folding types, narrow cafeteria seats.

"I'm gonna lock this door," Packer said as he stepped outside. "We'll get Sam." The door slammed, and Adam was alone. He quickly picked out a place at the end of the room just in case another lawyer arrived, at which time the other lawyer would undoubtedly take a position far to the other end and they could plot strategy with some measure of privacy. He pulled a chair to the wooden counter, placed his jacket on another chair, removed his legal pad, unscrewed his pen, and began chewing his fingernails. He tried to stop the chewing, but he couldn't. His stomach flipped violently, and his heels twitched out of control. He looked through the screen and studied the inmates' portion of the room—the same wooden counter, the same array of old chairs. In the center of the screen before him was a slit, four inches by ten, and it would be through this little hole that he would come face-to-face with Sam Cayhall.

He waited nervously, telling himself to be calm, take it easy, relax, he could handle this. He scribbled something on the legal pad, but honestly couldn't read it. He rolled up his sleeves. He looked around the room for hidden microphones and cameras, but the place was so simple and modest he couldn't imagine anyone trying to eavesdrop. If Sergeant Packer was any indication, the staff was laid-back, almost indifferent.

He studied the empty chairs on both sides of the screen, and wondered how many desperate people, in the last hours of their lives, had met here with their attorneys and listened for words of hope. How many urgent pleas had passed through this screen as the clock ticked steadily away? How many lawyers had sat where he was now sitting and told their clients that there was nothing left to do, that the execution would proceed? It was a somber thought, and it calmed Adam quite a bit. He was not the first to be here, and he would not be the last. He was a lawyer, well trained, blessed with a quick mind, and arriving here with the formidable resources of Kravitz & Bane behind him. He could do his job. His legs slowly became still, and he quit chewing his fingernails.

A door bolt clicked, and he jumped through his skin. It opened slowly, and a young white guard stepped into the inmates' side. Behind him, in a bright red jumpsuit, hands cuffed behind, was Sam Cayhall. He glowered around the room, squinting through the screen, until his eyes focused on Adam. A guard pulled at his elbow and led him to a spot directly across from the lawyer. He was thin, pale, and six inches shorter than both guards, but they seemed to give him plenty of room.

"Who are you?" He stared at Adam, who at the moment had a fingernail between his teeth.

One guard pulled a chair behind Sam, and the other guard sat him in it. He stared at Adam. The guards backed away, and were about to leave when Adam said, "Could you remove the handcuffs, please?"

"No sir. We can't."

Adam swallowed hard. "Just take them off, okay. We're gonna be here for a while," he said, mustering a degree of forcefulness. The guards looked at each other as if this request had never been heard. A key was quickly produced, and the handcuffs were removed.

Sam was not impressed. He glared at Adam through the opening in the screen as the guards made their noisy departure. The door slammed, and the deadbolt clicked.

They were alone, the Cayhall version of a family reunion. The air conditioner rattled and spewed, and for a long minute it made the only sounds. Though he tried valiantly, Adam was unable to look Sam in the eyes for more than two seconds. He busied himself with important note taking on the legal pad, and as he numbered each line he could feel the heat of Sam's stare.

Finally, Adam stuck a business card through the opening. "My name is Adam Hall. I'm a lawyer with Kravitz & Bane. Chicago and Memphis."

Sam patiently took the card and examined it front and back. Adam watched every move. His fingers were wrinkled and stained brown with cigarette smoke. His face was pallid, the only color coming from the salt and pepper stubble of five days' growth. His hair was long, gray, and oily, and slicked back severely. Adam decided quickly that he looked nothing like the frozen images from the video. Nor did he resemble the last known photos of himself, those from the 1981 trial. He was quite an old man now, with pasty delicate skin and layers of tiny wrinkles around his eyes. Deep furrows of age and misery cut through his forehead. The only attractive feature was the set of piercing indigo eyes that lifted themselves from the card. "You Jew boys never quit, do you?" he said in a pleasant, even tone. There was no hint of anger.

"I'm not Jewish," Adam said, successfully returning the stare.

"Then how can you work for Kravitz & Bane?" he asked as he set the card aside. His words were soft, slow, and delivered with the patience of a man who'd spent nine and a half years alone in a six-by-nine cell.

"We're an equal opportunity employer."

"That's nice. All proper and legal, I presume. In full compliance with all civil rights decisions and federal do-gooder laws."

"Of course."

"How many partners are in Kravitz & Bane now?"

Adam shrugged. The number varied from year to year. "Around a hundred and fifty."

"A hundred and fifty partners. And how many are women?"

Adam hesitated as he tried to count. "I really don't know. Probably a dozen."

"A dozen," Sam repeated, barely moving his lips. His hands were folded and still, and his eyes did not blink. "So, less than ten percent of your partners are women. How many nigger partners do you have?"

"Could we refer to them as blacks?"

"Oh sure, but of course that too is an antiquated term. They now want to be called African-Americans. Surely you're politically correct enough to know this."

Adam nodded but said nothing.

"How many African-American partners do you have?"

"Four, I believe."

"Less than three percent. My, my. Kravitz & Bane, that great bastion of civil justice and liberal political action, does, in fact, discriminate against African-Americans and Female-Americans. I just don't know what to say."

Adam scratched something illegible on his pad. He could argue, of course, that almost a third of the associates were female and that the firm made diligent efforts to sign the top black law students. He could explain how they had been sued for reverse discrimination by two white males whose job offers disappeared at the last moment.

"How many Jewish-American partners do you have? Eighty percent?"

"I don't know. It really doesn't matter to me."

"Well, it certainly matters to me. I was always embarrassed to be represented by such blatant bigots."

"A lot of people would find it appropriate."

Sam carefully reached into the only visible pocket of his jumpsuit, and removed a blue pack of Montclairs and a disposable lighter. The jumpsuit was unbuttoned halfway down the chest, and a thick matting of gray hair showed through the gap. The fabric was a very light cotton. Adam could not imagine life in this place with no air conditioning.

He lit the cigarette and exhaled toward the ceiling. "I thought I was through with you people."

"They didn't send me down here. I volunteered."

"Why?"

"I don't know. You need a lawyer, and—"

"Why are you so nervous?"

Adam jerked his fingernails from his teeth and stopped tapping his feet. "I'm not nervous."

"Sure you are. I've seen lots of lawyers around this place, and I've never seen one as nervous as you. What's the matter, kid? You afraid I'm coming through the screen after you?"

Adam grunted and tried to smile. "Don't be silly. I'm not nervous."

"How old are you?"

"Twenty-six."

"You look twenty-two. When did you finish law school?"

"Last year."

"Just great. The Jewish bastards have sent a greenhorn to save me. I've known for a long time that they secretly wanted me dead, now this proves it. I killed some Jews, now they want to kill me. I was right all along."

"You admit you killed the Kramer kids?"

"What the hell kind of question is that? The jury

said I did. For nine years, the appeals courts have said
the jury was right. That's all that matters. Who the hell
are you, asking me questions like that?"

"You need a lawyer, Mr. Cayhall. I'm here to help."

"I need a lot of things, boy, but I damned sure don't
need an eager little tenderfoot like you to give me advice. You're dangerous, son, and you're too ignorant to
know it." Again, the words came deliberately and
without emotion. He held the cigarette between the index and middle finger of his right hand, and casually
flipped ashes in an organized pile in a plastic bowl. His
eyes blinked occasionally. His face showed neither feeling nor sentiment.

Adam took meaningless notes, then tried again to
stare through the slit into Sam's eyes. "Look, Mr.
Cayhall, I'm a lawyer, and I have a strong moral conviction against the death penalty. I am well educated,
well trained, well read on Eighth Amendment issues,
and I can be of assistance to you. That's why I'm here.
Free of charge."

"Free of charge," Sam repeated. "How generous. Do
you realize, son, that I get at least three offers a week
now from lawyers who want to represent me for free?
Big lawyers. Famous lawyers. Rich lawyers. Some real
slimy snakes. They're all perfectly willing to sit where
you're now sitting, file all the last minute motions and
appeals, do the interviews, chase the cameras, hold my
hand in the last hours, watch them gas me, then do yet
another press conference, then sign a book deal, a
movie deal, maybe a television mini-series deal about
the life and times of Sam Cayhall, a real Klan murderer. You see, son, I'm famous, and what I did is now
legendary. And since they're about to kill me, then I'm
about to become even more famous. Thus, the lawyers
want me. I'm worth a lot of money. A sick country,
right."

Adam was shaking his head. "I don't want any of that, I promise. I'll put it in writing. I'll sign a complete confidentiality agreement."

Sam chuckled. "Right, and who's going to enforce it after I'm gone?"

"Your family," Adam said.

"Forget my family," Sam said firmly.

"My motives are pure, Mr. Cayhall. My firm has represented you for seven years, so I know almost everything about your file. I've also done quite a lot of research into your background."

"Join the club. I've had my underwear examined by a hundred half-ass reporters. There are many people who know much about me, it seems, and all this combined knowledge is of absolutely no benefit to me right now. I have four weeks. Do you know this?"

"I have a copy of the opinion."

"Four weeks, and they gas me."

"So let's get to work. You have my word that I will never talk to the press unless you authorize it, that I'll never repeat anything you tell me, and that I will not sign any book or movie deal. I swear it."

Sam lit another cigarette and stared at something on the counter. He gently rubbed his right temple with his right thumb, the cigarette just inches from his hair. For a long time the only sound was the gurgling of the overworked window unit. Sam smoked and contemplated. Adam doodled on his pad and was quite proud that his feet were motionless and his stomach was not aching. The silence was awkward, and he figured, correctly, that Sam could sit and smoke and think in utter silence for days.

"Are you familiar with *Barroni*?" Sam asked quietly.

"*Barroni*?"

"Yes, *Barroni*. Came down last week from the Ninth Circuit. California case."

Adam racked his brain for a trace of *Barroni*. "I might have seen it."

"You might have seen it? You're well trained, well read, et cetera, and you might have seen *Barroni*? What kind of half-ass lawyer are you?"

"I'm not a half-ass lawyer."

"Right, right. What about *Texas v. Eekes*? Surely you've read that one?"

"When did it come down?"

"Within six weeks."

"What court?"

"Fifth Circuit."

"Eighth Amendment?"

"Don't be stupid," Sam grunted in genuine disgust. "Do you think I'd spend my time reading freedom of speech cases? This is my ass sitting over here, boy, these are my wrists and ankles that will be strapped down. This is my nose the poison will hit."

"No. I don't remember *Eekes*."

"What do you read?"

"All the important cases."

"Have you read *Barefoot*?"

"Of course."

"Tell me about *Barefoot*."

"What is this, a pop quiz?"

"This is whatever I want it to be. Where was *Barefoot* from?" Sam asked.

"I don't remember. But the full name was *Barefoot v. Estelle*, a landmark case in 1983 in which the Supreme Court held that death row inmates cannot hold back valid claims on appeal so they can save them for later. More or less."

"My, my, you have read it. Does it ever strike you as odd how the same court can change its mind whenever it wants to? Think about it. For two centuries the U.S. Supreme Court allowed legal executions. Said they were constitutional, covered nicely by the Eighth Amendment. Then, in 1972 the U.S. Supreme Court read the same, unchanged Constitution and outlawed the death penalty. Then, in 1976 the U.S. Supreme Court said executions were in fact constitutional after all. Same bunch of turkeys wearing the same black robes in the same building in Washington. Now, the U.S. Supreme Court is changing the rules again with the same Constitution. The Reagan boys are tired of reading too many appeals, so they declare certain avenues to be closed. Seems odd to me."

"Seems odd to a lot of people."

"What about *Dulaney*?" Sam asked, taking a long drag. There was little or no ventilation in the room and a cloud was forming above them.

"Where's it from?"

"Louisiana. Surely you've read it."

"I'm sure I have. In fact, I've probably read more cases than you, but I don't always bother to memorize them unless I plan to use them."

"Use them where?"

"Motions and appeals."

"So you've handled death cases before. How many?"

"This is the first."

"Why am I not comforted by this? Those Jewish-American lawyers at Kravitz & Bane sent you down here to experiment on me, right? Get yourself a little hands-on training so you can stick it on your résumé."

"I told you—they didn't send me down here."

"How about Garner Goodman? Is he still alive?"

"Yes. He's your age."

"Then he doesn't have long, does he? And Tyner?"

"Mr. Tyner's doing well. I'll tell him you asked."

"Oh please do. Tell him I really miss him, both of

them, actually. Hell, it took me almost two years to fire them."

"They worked their butts off for you."

"Tell them to send me a bill." Sam chuckled to himself, his first smile of the meeting. He methodically stubbed out the cigarette in the bowl, and lit another. "Fact is, Mr. Hall, I hate lawyers."

"That's the American way."

"Lawyers chased me, indicted me, prosecuted me, persecuted me, screwed me, then sent me to this place. Since I've been here, they've hounded me, screwed me some more, lied to me, and now they're back in the form of you, a rookie zealot without a clue of how to find the damned courthouse."

"You might be surprised."

"It'll be a helluva surprise, son, if you know your ass from a hole in the ground. You'll be the first clown from Kravitz & Bane to possess such information."

"They've kept you out of the gas chamber for the past seven years."

"And I'm supposed to be thankful? There are fifteen residents of the Row with more seniority than me. Why should I be next? I've been here for nine and a half years. Treemont's been here for fourteen years. Of course, he's an African-American and that always helps. They have more rights, you know. It's much harder to execute one of them because whatever they did was someone else's fault."

"That's not true."

"How the hell do you know what's true? A year ago you were still in school, still wearing faded blue jeans all day long, still drinking beer at happy hours with your idealistic little buddies. You haven't lived, son. Don't tell me what's true."

"So you're in favor of swift executions for African-Americans?"

"Not a bad idea, really. In fact, most of these punks deserve the gas."

"I'm sure that's a minority opinion on death row."

"You could say that."

"And you, of course, are different and don't belong here."

"No, I don't belong here. I'm a political prisoner, sent here by an egomaniac who used me for his own political purposes."

"Can we discuss your guilt or innocence?"

"No. But I didn't do what the jury said I did."

"So you had an accomplice? Someone else planted the bomb?"

Sam rubbed the deep furrows in his forehead with his middle finger, as if he were flipping the bird. But he wasn't. He was suddenly in a deep and prolonged trance. The conference room was much cooler than his cell. The conversation was aimless, but at least it was conversation with someone other than a guard or the invisible inmate next door. He would take his time, make it last as long as possible.

Adam studied his notes and pondered what to say next. They had been chatting for twenty minutes, sparring really, with no clear direction. He was determined to confront their family's history before he left. He just didn't know how to do it.

Minutes passed. Neither looked at the other. Sam lit another Montclair.

"Why do you smoke so much?" Adam finally said.

"I'd rather die of lung cancer. It's a common desire on death row."

"How many packs a day?"

"Three or four."

Another minute passed. Sam slowly finished the cigarette, and kindly asked, "Where'd you go to school?"

"Law school at Michigan. Undergrad at Pepperdine."

"Where's that?"

"California."

"Is that where you grew up?"

"Yeah."

"How many states have the death penalty?"

"Thirty-eight. Most of them don't use it, though. It seems to be popular only in the Deep South, Texas, Florida, and California."

"You know our esteemed legislature has changed the law here. Now we can die by lethal injection. It's more humane. Ain't that nice? Doesn't apply to me, though, since my conviction was years ago. I'll get to sniff the gas."

"Maybe not."

"You're twenty-six?"

"Yeah."

"Born in 1964."

"That's right."

Sam removed another cigarette from the pack and tapped the filter on the counter. "Where?"

"Memphis," Adam replied without looking at him.

"You don't understand, son. This state needs an execution, and I happen to be the nearest victim. Louisiana, Texas, and Florida are killing them like flies, and the law-abiding people of this state can't understand why our little chamber is not being used. The more violent crime we have, the more people beg for executions. Makes 'em feel better, like the system is working hard to eliminate murderers. The politicians openly campaign with promises of more prisons and tougher sentences and more executions. That's why those clowns in Jackson voted for lethal injection. It's supposed to be more humane, less objectionable, thus easier to implement. You follow?"

Adam nodded his head slightly.

"It's time for an execution, and my number is up. That's why they're pushing like hell. You can't stop it."

"We can certainly try. I want the opportunity."

Sam finally lit the cigarette. He inhaled deeply, then whistled the smoke through a small opening in his lips. He leaned forward slightly on his elbows and peered through the hole in the screen. "What part of California are you from?"

"Southern. L.A." Adam glanced at the piercing eyes, then looked away.

"Your family still there?"

A wicked pain shot through Adam's chest, and for a second his heart froze. Sam puffed his cigarette and never blinked.

"My father's dead," he said with a shaky voice, and sank a few inches in his chair.

A long minute passed as Sam sat poised on the edge of his seat. Finally, he said, "And your mother?"

"She lives in Portland. Remarried."

"Where's your sister?" he asked.

Adam closed his eyes and dropped his head. "She's in college," he mumbled.

"I believe her name is Carmen, right?" Sam asked softly.

Adam nodded. "How'd you know?" he asked through gritted teeth.

Sam backed away from the screen and sank into the folding metal chair. He dropped his current cigarette on the floor without looking at it. "Why did you come here?" he asked, his voice much firmer and tougher.

"How'd you know it was me?"

"The voice. You sound like your father. Why'd you come here?"

"Eddie sent me."

Their eyes met briefly, then Sam looked away. He

slowly leaned forward and planted both elbows on both knees. His gaze was fixed on something on the floor. He grew perfectly still.

Then he placed his right hand over his eyes.

TEN

PHILLIP NAIFEH was sixty-three years old, and nineteen months away from retirement. Nineteen months and four days. He had served as superintendent of the State Department of Corrections for twenty-seven years, and in doing so had survived six governors, an army of state legislators, a thousand prisoners' lawsuits, countless intrusions by the federal courts, and more executions than he cared to remember.

The warden, as he preferred to be called (although the title was officially nonexistent under the terminology of the Mississippi Code), was a full-blooded Lebanese whose parents had immigrated in the twenties and settled in the Delta. They had prospered with a small grocery store in Clarksdale where his mother had become somewhat famous for her homemade Lebanese desserts. He was educated in the public schools, went off to college, returned to the state, and, for reasons long forgotten, had become involved in criminal justice.

He hated the death penalty. He understood society's yearning for it, and long ago he had memorized all the sterile reasons for its necessity. It was a deterrent. It removed killers. It was the ultimate punishment. It was biblical. It satisfied the public's need for retribution. It relieved the anguish of the victim's family. If pressed, he could make these arguments as persuasively as any prosecutor. He actually believed one or two of them.

But the burden of the actual killing was his, and he

despised this horrible aspect of his job. It was Phillip Naifeh who walked with the condemned man from his cell to the Isolation Room, as it was called, to suffer the last hour before death. It was Phillip Naifeh who led him next door to the Chamber Room, and supervised the strapping of the legs, arms, and head. "Any last words?" he had uttered twenty-two times in twenty-seven years. It was left to him to tell the guards to lock the chamber door, and it was left to him to nod to the executioner to pull the levers to mix the deadly gas. He had actually watched the faces of the first two as they died, then decided it was best to watch the faces of the witnesses in the small room behind the chamber. He had to select the witnesses. He had to do a hundred things listed in a manual of how to legally kill death row inmates, including the pronouncing of death, the removal of the body from the chamber, the spraying of it to remove the gas from the clothing, and on and on.

He had once testified before a legislative committee in Jackson, and given his opinions about the death penalty. He had a better idea, he had explained to deaf ears, and his plan would keep condemned killers in the Maximum Security Unit in solitary confinement where they couldn't kill, couldn't escape, and would never be eligible for parole. They would eventually die on death row, but not at the hands of the state.

This testimony made headlines and almost got him fired.

Nineteen months and four days, he thought to himself as he gently ran his fingers through his thick gray hair and slowly read the latest opinion from the Fifth Circuit. Lucas Mann sat across the desk and waited.

"Four weeks," Naifeh said, putting the opinion aside. "How many appeals are left?" he asked in a gentle drawl.

"The usual assortment of last ditch efforts," Mann replied.

"When did this come down?"

"Early this morning. Sam will appeal it to the Supreme Court, where it will probably be ignored. This should take a week or so."

"What's your opinion, counselor?"

"The meritorious issues have all been presented at this point. I'd give it a fifty percent chance of happening in four weeks."

"That's a lot."

"Something tells me this one might go off."

In the interminable workings of death penalty roulette, a 50 percent chance was close to a certainty. The process would have to be started. The manual would have to be consulted. After years of endless appeals and delays, the last four weeks would be over in the blink of an eye.

"Have you talked to Sam?" the warden asked.

"Briefly. I took him a copy of the opinion this morning."

"Garner Goodman called me yesterday, said they were sending down one of their young associates to talk to Sam. Did you take care of it?"

"I talked to Garner, and I talked to the associate. His name is Adam Hall, and he's meeting with Sam as we speak. Should be interesting. Sam's his grandfather."

"His what!"

"You heard me. Sam Cayhall is Adam Hall's paternal grandfather. We were doing a routine background on Adam Hall yesterday, and noticed a few gray spots. I called the FBI in Jackson, and within two hours they had plenty of circumstantial evidence. I confronted him this morning, and he confessed. I don't think he's trying to hide it."

"But he has a different name."

"It's a long story. They haven't seen each other since Adam was a toddler. His father fled the state after Sam was arrested for the bombing. Moved out West, changed names, drifted around, in and out of work, sounds like a real loser. Killed himself in 1981. Anyway, Adam here goes to college and makes perfect grades. Goes to law school at Michigan, a Top Ten school, and is the editor of the law review. Takes a job with our pals at Kravitz & Bane, and he shows up this morning for the reunion with his grandfather."

Naifeh now raked both hands through his hair and shook his head. "How wonderful. As if we needed more publicity, more idiotic reporters asking more asinine questions."

"They're meeting now. I am assuming Sam will agree to allow the kid to represent him. I certainly hope so. We've never executed an inmate without a lawyer."

"We should do some lawyers without the inmates," Naifeh said with a forced smile. His hatred for lawyers was legendary, and Lucas didn't mind. He understood. He had once estimated that Phillip Naifeh had been named as a defendant in more lawsuits than anyone else in the history of the state. He had earned the right to hate lawyers.

"I retire in nineteen months," he said, as if Lucas had never heard this. "Who's next after Sam?"

Lucas thought a minute and tried to catalog the voluminous appeals of forty-seven inmates. "No one, really. The Pizza Man came close four months ago, but he got his stay. It'll probably expire in a year or so, but there are other problems with his case. I can't see another execution for a couple of years."

"The Pizza Man? Forgive me."

"Malcolm Friar. Killed three pizza delivery boys in a

week. At trial he claimed robbery was not the motive, said he was just hungry."

Naifeh raised both hands and nodded. "Okay, okay, I remember. He's the nearest after Sam?"

"Probably. It's hard to say."

"I know." Naifeh gently pushed away from his desk and walked to a window. His shoes were somewhere under the desk. He thrust his hands in his pockets, pressed his toes into the carpet, and thought deeply for a while. He had been hospitalized after the last execution, a mild heart flutter as his doctor preferred to call it. He'd spent a week in a hospital bed, watching his little flutter on a monitor, and promised his wife he would never suffer through another execution. If he could somehow survive Sam, then he could retire at full pension.

He turned and stared at his friend Lucas Mann. "I'm not doing this one, Lucas. I'm passing the buck to another man, one of my subordinates, a younger man, a good man, a man who can be trusted, a man who's never seen one of these shows, a man who's just itching to get blood on his hands."

"Not Nugent."

"That's the man. Retired Colonel George Nugent, my trusted assistant."

"He's a nut."

"Yes, but he's our nut, Lucas. He's a fanatic for details, discipline, organization, hell, he's the perfect choice. I'll give him the manual, tell him what I want, and he'll do a marvelous job of killing Sam Cayhall. He'll be perfect."

George Nugent was an assistant superintendent at Parchman. He had made a name for himself by implementing a most successful boot camp for first offenders. It was a brutal six-week ordeal in which Nugent strutted and swaggered around in black boots, cursing like a drill instructor and threatening gang rape for the slightest infraction. The first offenders rarely came back to Parchman.

"Nugent's crazy, Phillip. It's a matter of time before he hurts someone."

"Right! Now you understand. We're going to let him hurt Sam, just the way it should be done. By the book. Heaven knows how much Nugent loves a book to go by. He's the perfect choice, Lucas. It'll be a flawless execution."

It really mattered little to Lucas Mann. He shrugged, and said, "You're the boss."

"Thanks," Naifeh said. "Just watch Nugent, okay. I'll watch him on this end, and you watch the legal stuff. We'll get through it."

"This will be the biggest one yet," Lucas said.

"I know. I'll have to pace myself. I'm an old man."

Lucas gathered his file from the desk and headed for the door. "I'll call you after the kid leaves. He's supposed to check in with me before he goes."

"I'd like to meet him," Naifeh said.

"He's a nice kid."

"Some family, huh."

THE NICE KID and his condemned grandfather had spent fifteen minutes in silence, the only sound in the room the uneasy rattling of the overworked AC unit. At one point, Adam had walked to the wall and waved his hand before the dusty vents. There was a trace of cool air. He leaned on the counter with his arms folded and stared at the door, as far away from Sam as possible. He was leaning and staring when the door opened and the head of Sergeant Packer appeared. Just checking to see if things were okay, he said, glancing first at Adam then down the room and through the screen at

Sam, who was leaning forward in his chair with a hand over his face.

"We're fine," Adam said without conviction.

"Good, good," Packer said, and hurriedly closed the door. It locked, and Adam slowly made his way back to his chair. He pulled it close to the screen and rested on his elbows. Sam ignored him for a minute or two, then wiped his eyes with a sleeve and sat up. They looked at each other.

"We need to talk," Adam said quietly.

Sam nodded but said nothing. He wiped his eyes again, this time with the other sleeve. He removed a cigarette and put it between his lips. His hand shook as he flicked the lighter. He puffed quickly.

"So you're really Alan," he said in a low, husky voice.

"At one time, I guess. I didn't know it until my father died."

"You were born in 1964."

"Correct."

"My first grandson."

Adam nodded and glanced away.

"You disappeared in 1967."

"Something like that. I don't remember it, you know. My earliest memories are from California."

"I heard Eddie went to California, and that there was another child. Someone told me later her name was Carmen. I would hear bits and pieces over the years, knew y'all were somewhere in Southern California, but he did a good job of disappearing."

"We moved around a lot when I was a kid. I think he had trouble keeping a job."

"You didn't know about me?"

"No. The family was never mentioned. I found out about it after his funeral."

"Who told you?"

"Lee."

Sam closed his eyes tightly for a moment, then puffed again. "How is she?"

"Okay, I guess."

"Why'd you go to work for Kravitz & Bane?"

"It's a good firm."

"Did you know they represented me?"

"Yes."

"So you've been planning this?"

"For about five years."

"But why?"

"I don't know."

"You must have a reason."

"The reason is obvious. You're my grandfather, okay. Like it or not, you're who you are and I'm who I am. And I'm here now, so what are we going to do about it?"

"I think you should leave."

"I'm not leaving, Sam. I've been preparing for this a long time."

"Preparing for what?"

"You need legal representation. You need help. That's why I'm here."

"I'm beyond help. They're determined to gas me, okay, for lots of reasons. You don't need to get involved in it."

"Why not?"

"Well, for one, it's hopeless. You're gonna get hurt if you bust your ass and you're unsuccessful. Second, your true identity will be revealed. It'll be very embarrassing. Life for you will be much better if you remain Adam Hall."

"I am Adam Hall, and I don't plan to change it. I'm also your grandson, and we can't change that, can we? So what's the big deal?"

"It'll be embarrassing for your family. Eddie did a great job of protecting you. Don't blow it."

"My cover's already blown. My firm knows it. I told Lucas Mann, and—"

"That jerk'll tell everybody. Don't trust him for a minute."

"Look, Sam, you don't understand. I don't care if he tells. I don't care if the world knows that I'm your grandson. I'm tired of these dirty little family secrets. I'm a big boy now, I can think for myself. Plus, I'm a lawyer, and my skin is getting thick. I can handle it."

Sam relaxed a bit in his chair and looked at the floor with a pleasant little smirk, the kind grown men often give to little boys who are acting bigger than their years. He grunted at something and very slowly nodded his head. "You just don't understand, kid," he said again, now in a measured, patient tone.

"So explain it to me," Adam said.

"It would take forever."

"We have four weeks. You can do a lot of talking in four weeks."

"Just exactly what is it that you want to hear?"

Adam leaned even closer on his elbows, pen and pad ready. His eyes were inches from the slit in the screen. "First, I want to talk about the case—appeals, strategies, the trials, the bombing, who was with you that night—"

"No one was with me that night."

"We can talk about it later."

"We're talking about it now. I was alone, do you hear me?"

"Okay. Second, I want to know about my family."

"Why?"

"Why not? Why keep it buried? I want to know about your father and his father, and your brothers and cousins. I may dislike these people when it's all over, but I have the right to know about them. I've been deprived of this information all of my life, and I want to know."

"It's nothing remarkable."

"Oh really. Well, Sam, I think it's pretty remarkable that you've made it here to death row. This is a pretty exclusive society. Throw in the fact that you're white, middle class, almost seventy years old, and it becomes even more remarkable. I want to know how and why you got here. What made you do those things? How many Klansmen were in my family? And why? How many other people were killed along the way?"

"And you think I'll just spill my guts with all this?"

"Yeah, I think so. You'll come around. I'm your grandson, Sam, the only living, breathing relative who gives a damn about you anymore. You'll talk, Sam. You'll talk to me."

"Well, since I'll be so talkative what else will we discuss?"

"Eddie."

Sam took a deep breath and closed his eyes. "You don't want much, do you?" he said softly. Adam scribbled something meaningless on his pad.

It was now time for the ritual of another cigarette, and Sam performed it with even more patience and care. Another blast of blue smoke joined the fog well above their heads. His hands were steady again. "When we get finished with Eddie, who do you want to talk about?"

"I don't know. That should keep us busy for four weeks."

"When do we talk about you?"

"Anytime." Adam reached into his briefcase and removed a thin file. He slid a sheet of paper and a pen through the opening. "This is an agreement for legal representation. Sign at the bottom."

Without touching it, Sam read it from a distance. "So I sign up again with Kravitz & Bane."

"Sort of."

"What do you mean, sort of? Says right here I agree to let those Jews represent me again. It took me forever to fire them, and, hell, I wasn't even paying them."

"The agreement is with me, Sam, okay. You'll never see those guys unless you want to."

"I don't want to."

"Fine. I happen to work for the firm, and so the agreement must be with the firm. It's easy."

"Ah, the optimism of youth. Everything's easy. Here I sit less than a hundred feet from the gas chamber, clock ticking away on the wall over there, getting louder and louder, and everything's easy."

"Just sign the damned paper, Sam."

"And then what?"

"And then we go to work. Legally, I can't do anything for you until we have that agreement. You sign it, we go to work."

"And what's the first bit of work you'd like to do?"

"Walk through the Kramer bombing, very slowly, step by step."

"It's been done a thousand times."

"We'll do it again. I have a thick notebookful of questions."

"They've all been asked."

"Yeah, Sam, but they haven't been answered, have they?"

Sam stuck the filter between his lips.

"And they haven't been asked by me, have they?"

"You think I'm lying."

"Are you?"

"No."

"But you haven't told the whole story, have you?"

"What difference does it make, counselor? You've read *Bateman*."

"Yeah, I've memorized *Bateman*, and there are a number of soft spots in it."

"Typical lawyer."

"If there's new evidence, then there are ways to present it. All we're doing, Sam, is trying to create enough confusion to make some judge somewhere give it a second thought. Then a third thought. Then he grants a stay so he can learn more."

"I know how the game is played, son."

"Adam, okay, it's Adam."

"Yeah, and just call me Gramps. I suppose you plan to appeal to the governor."

"Yes."

Sam inched forward in his chair and moved close to the screen. With the index finger of his right hand, he began pointing at a spot somewhere in the center of Adam's nose. His face was suddenly harsh, his eyes narrow. "You listen to me, Adam," he growled, finger pointing back and forth. "If I sign this piece of paper, you are never to talk to that bastard. Never. Do you understand?"

Adam watched the finger but said nothing.

Sam decided to continue. "He is a bogus son of a bitch. He is vile, sleazy, thoroughly corrupt, and completely able to mask it all with a pretty smile and a clean haircut. He is the only reason I'm sitting here on death row. If you contact him in any way, then you're finished as my lawyer."

"So I'm your lawyer."

The finger dropped and Sam relaxed a bit. "Oh, I may give you a shot, let you practice on me. You know, Adam, the legal profession is really screwed up. If I was a free man, just trying to make a living, minding my own business, paying my taxes, obeying the laws and such, then I couldn't find a lawyer who'd take the time to spit on me unless I had money. But here I am, a convicted killer, condemned to die, not a penny to my name, and I've got lawyers all over the country begging to represent me. Big, rich lawyers with long names preceded with initials and followed by numerals, famous lawyers with their own jets and television shows. Can you explain this?"

"Of course not. Nor do I care about it."

"It's a sick profession you've gotten yourself in."

"Most lawyers are honest and hardworking."

"Sure. And most of my pals here on death row would be ministers and missionaries if they hadn't been wrongly convicted."

"The governor might be our last chance."

"Then they might as well gas me now. That pompous ass'll probably want to witness my execution, then he'll hold a press conference and replay every detail for the world. He's a spineless little worm who's made it this far because of me. And if he can milk me for a few more sound bites, then he'll do it. Stay away from him."

"We can discuss it later."

"We're discussing it now, I believe. You'll give me your word before I sign this paper."

"Any more conditions?"

"Yeah. I want something added here so that if I decide to fire you, then you and your firm won't fight me. That should be easy."

"Let me see it."

The agreement was passed through the slit again, and Adam printed a neat paragraph at the bottom. He handed it back to Sam, who read it slowly and laid it on the counter.

"You didn't sign it," Adam said.

"I'm still thinking."

"Can I ask some questions while you're thinking?"

"You can ask them."

"Where did you learn to handle explosives?"

"Here and there."

"There were at least five bombings before Kramer, all with the same type, all very basic—dynamite, caps, fuses. Kramer, of course, was different because a timing device was used. Who taught you how to make bombs?"

"Have you ever lit a firecracker?"

"Sure."

"Same principle. A match to the fuse, run like crazy, and boom."

"The timing device is a bit more complicated. Who taught you how to wire one?"

"My mother. When do you plan to return here?"

"Tomorrow."

"Good. Here's what we'll do. I need some time to think about this. I don't want to talk right now, and I damned sure don't want to answer a bunch of questions. Let me look over this document, make some changes, and we'll meet again tomorrow."

"That's wasting time."

"I've wasted almost ten years here. What's another day?"

"They may not allow me to return if I don't officially represent you. This visit is a favor."

"A great bunch of guys, aren't they? Tell them you're my lawyer for the next twenty-four hours. They'll let you in."

"We have a lot of ground to cover, Sam. I'd like to get started."

"I need to think, okay. When you spend over nine years alone in a cell, you become real good at thinking and analyzing. But you can't do it fast, understand? It takes longer to sort things out and place them in order.

I'm sort of spinnin' right now, you know. You've hit me kinda hard."

"Okay."

"I'll be better tomorrow. We can talk then. I promise."

"Sure." Adam placed the cap on his pen and stuck it in his pocket. He slid the file into the briefcase, and relaxed in his seat. "I'll be staying in Memphis for the next couple of months."

"Memphis? I thought you lived in Chicago."

"We have a small office in Memphis. I'll be working out of there. The number's on the card. Feel free to call anytime."

"What happens when this thing is over?"

"I don't know. I may go back to Chicago."

"Are you married?"

"No."

"Is Carmen?"

"No."

"What's she like?"

Adam folded his hands behind his head and examined the thin fog above them. "She's very smart. Very pretty. Looks a lot like her mother."

"Evelyn was a beautiful girl."

"She's still beautiful."

"I always thought Eddie was lucky to get her. I didn't like her family, though."

And she certainly didn't like Eddie's, Adam thought to himself. Sam's chin dropped almost to his chest. He rubbed his eyes and pinched the bridge of his nose. "This family business will take some work, won't it?" he said without looking.

"Yep."

"I may not be able to talk about some things."

"Yes you will. You owe it to me, Sam. And you owe it to yourself."

"You don't know what you're talking about, and you wouldn't want to know all of it."

"Try me. I'm sick of secrets."

"Why do you want to know so much?"

"So I can try and make some sense of it."

"That'll be a waste of time."

"I'll have to decide that, won't I?"

Sam placed his hands on his knees, and slowly stood. He took a deep breath and looked down at Adam through the screen. "I'd like to go now."

Their eyes met through the narrow diamonds in the partition. "Sure," Adam said. "Can I bring you anything?"

"No. Just come back."

"I promise."

ELEVEN

PACKER CLOSED THE DOOR and locked it, and together they stepped from the narrow shadow outside the conference room into the blinding midday sun. Adam closed his eyes and stopped for a second, then fished through his pockets in a desperate search for sunglasses. Packer waited patiently, his eyes sensibly covered with a pair of thick imitation Ray·Bans, his face shielded by the wide brim of an official Parchman cap. The air was suffocating and almost visible. Sweat immediately covered Adam's arms and face as he finally found the sunglasses in his briefcase and put them on. He squinted and grimaced, and once able to actually see, he followed Packer along the brick trail and baked grass in front of the unit.

"Sam okay?" Packer asked. His hands were in his pockets and he was in no hurry.

"I guess."

"You hungry?"

"No," Adam replied as he glanced at his watch. It was almost one o'clock. He wasn't sure if Packer was offering prison food or something else, but he was taking no chances.

"Too bad. Today's Wednesday, and that means turnip greens and corn bread. Mighty good."

"Thanks." Adam was certain that somewhere deep in his genes he was supposed to crave turnip greens and corn bread. Today's menu should make his mouth drool and his stomach yearn. But he considered himself a Californian, and to his knowledge had never seen turnip greens. "Maybe next week," he said, hardly believing he was being offered lunch on the Row.

They were at the first of the double gates. As it opened, Packer, without removing his hands from his pockets, said, "When you coming back?"

"Tomorrow."

"That soon?"

"Yeah. I'm going to be around for a while."

"Well, nice to meet you." He grinned broadly and walked away.

As Adam walked through the second gate, the red bucket began its descent. It stopped three feet from the ground, and he rattled through the selection at the bottom until he found his keys. He never looked up at the guard.

A white mini-van with official markings on the door and along the sides was waiting by Adam's car. The driver's window came down, and Lucas Mann leaned out. "Are you in a hurry?"

Adam glanced at his watch again. "Not really."

"Good. Hop in. I need to talk to you. We'll take a quick tour of the place."

Adam didn't want a quick tour of the place, but he was planning to stop by Mann's office anyway. He opened the passenger's door and threw his coat and briefcase on a rear seat. Thankfully, the air was at full throttle. Lucas, cool and still impeccably starched, looked odd sitting behind the wheel of a mini-van. He eased away from MSU and headed for the main drive.

"How'd it go?" he asked. Adam tried to recall Sam's exact description of Lucas Mann. Something to the effect that he could not be trusted.

"Okay, I guess," he replied, carefully vague.

"Are you going to represent him?"

"I think so. He wants to dwell on it tonight. And he wants to see me tomorrow."

"No problem, but you need to sign him up tomorrow. We need some type of written authorization from him."

"I'll get it tomorrow. Where are we going?" They turned left and headed away from the front of the prison. They passed the last of the neat white houses with shade trees and flower beds, and now they were driving through fields of cotton and beans that stretched forever.

"Nowhere in particular. Just thought you might want to see some of our farm. We need to cover a few things."

"I'm listening."

"The decision of the Fifth Circuit hit the wire at mid-morning, and we've already had at least three phone calls from reporters. They smell blood, of course, and they want to know if this might be the end for Sam. I know some of these people, dealt with them before on other executions. A few are nice guys, most are obnoxious jerks. But anyway, they're all asking about Sam and whether or not he has a lawyer. Will he represent himself to the very end? You know, that kind of crap."

In a field to the right was a large group of inmates in white pants and without shirts. They were working the rows and sweating profusely, their backs and chests drenched and glistening under the scorching sun. A guard on a horse watched them with a rifle. "What are these guys doing?" Adam asked.

"Chopping cotton."

"Are they required to?"

"No. All volunteers. It's either that or sit in a cell all day."

"They wear white. Sam wears red. I saw a gang by the highway in blue."

"It's part of the classification system. White means these guys are low risk."

"What were their crimes?"

"Everything. Drugs, murder, repeat offenders, you name it. But they've behaved since they've been here, so they wear white and they're allowed to work."

The mini-van turned at an intersection, and the fences and razor wire returned. To the left was a series of modern barracks built on two levels and branching in all directions from a central hub. If not for the barbed wire and guard towers, the unit could pass for a badly designed college dormitory. "What's that?" Adam asked, pointing.

"Unit 30."

"How many units are there?"

"I'm not sure. We keep building and tearing down. Around thirty."

"It looks new."

"Oh yes. We've been in trouble with the federal courts for almost twenty years, so we've been doing lots of building. It's no secret that the real superintendent of this place has been a federal judge."

"Can the reporters wait until tomorrow? I need to see what Sam has on his mind. I'd hate to talk to them now, and then things go badly tomorrow."

"I think I can put them off a day. But they won't wait long."

They passed the last guard tower and Unit 30 disappeared. They drove at least two miles before the gleaming razor wire of another compound peeked above the fields.

"I talked to the warden this morning, after you got here," Lucas said. "He said he'd like to meet you. You'll like him. He hates executions, you know. He was hoping to retire in a couple of years without going through another, but now it looks doubtful."

"Let me guess. He's just doing his job, right?"

"We're all doing our jobs here."

"That's my point. I get the impression that everybody here wants to pat me on the back and speak to me in sad voices about what's about to happen to poor old Sam. Nobody wants to kill him, but you're all just doing your jobs."

"There are plenty of people who want Sam dead."

"Who?"

"The governor and the Attorney General. I'm sure you're familiar with the governor, but the AG is the one you'd better watch. He, of course, wants to be governor one day. For some reason we've elected in this state a whole crop of these young, terribly ambitious politicians who just can't seem to sit still."

"His name's Roxburgh, right?"

"That's him. He loves cameras, and I expect a press conference from him this afternoon. If he holds true to form, he'll take full credit for the victory in the Fifth Circuit, and promise a diligent effort to execute Sam in four weeks. His office handles these things, you know. And then it wouldn't surprise me if the governor himself doesn't appear on the evening news with a comment or two. My point is this, Adam—there will be enormous pressure from above to make sure there are no more stays. They want Sam dead for their own political gain. They'll milk it for all they can get."

Adam watched the next camp as they drove by. On a concrete slab between two buildings, a game of basketball was in full force with at least a dozen players on each side. All were black. Next to the court, a row of barbells was being pumped and jerked around by some heavy lifters. Adam noticed a few whites.

Lucas turned onto another road. "There's another reason," he continued. "Louisiana is killing them right and left. Texas has executed six already this year. Florida, five. We haven't had an execution in over two years. We're dragging our feet, some people say. It's time to show these other states that we're just as serious about good government as they are. Just last week in Jackson a legislative committee held hearings on the issue. There were all sorts of angry statements by our leaders about the endless delays in these matters. Not surprisingly, it was decided that the federal courts are to blame. There's lots of pressure to kill somebody. And Sam happens to be next."

"Who's after Sam?"

"Nobody, really. It could be two years before we get this close again. The buzzards are circling."

"Why are you telling me this?"

"I'm not the enemy, okay? I'm the attorney for the prison, not the State of Mississippi. And you've never been here before. I thought you'd want to know these things."

"Thanks," Adam said. Though the information was unsolicited, it was certainly useful.

"I'll help in any way I can."

The roofs of buildings could be seen on the horizon. "Is that the front of the prison?" Adam asked.

"Yes."

"I'd like to leave now."

THE MEMPHIS OFFICE of Kravitz & Bane occupied two floors of a building called Brinkley Plaza, a 1920s edifice on the corner of Main and Monroe in downtown. Main Street was also known as the Mid-America Mall. Cars and trucks had been banished when the city attempted to revitalize its downtown and converted asphalt into tiles, fountains, and decorative trees. Only pedestrian traffic was permitted on the Mall.

The building itself had been revitalized and renewed tastefully. Its main lobby was marble and bronze. The

K&B offices were large and richly decorated with antiques and oak-paneled walls and Persian rugs.

Adam was escorted by an attractive young secretary to the corner office of Baker Cooley, the managing partner. They introduced themselves, shook hands, and admired the secretary as she left the room and closed the door. Cooley leered a bit too long and seemed to hold his breath until the door was completely closed and the glimpse was over.

"Welcome south," Cooley said, finally exhaling and sitting in his posh burgundy leather swivel chair.

"Thanks. I guess you've talked to Garner Goodman."

"Yesterday. Twice. He gave me the score. We've got a nice little conference room at the end of this hall with a phone, computer, plenty of room. It's yours for the, uh, duration."

Adam nodded and glanced around the office. Cooley was in his early fifties, a neat man with an organized desk and a clean room. His words and hands were quick, and he bore the gray hair and dark circles of a frazzled accountant. "What kind of work goes on here?" Adam asked.

"Not much litigation, and certainly no criminal work," he answered quickly as if criminals were not allowed to set their dirty feet on the thick carpeting and fancy rugs of this establishment. Adam remembered Goodman's description of the Memphis branch —a boutique firm of twelve good lawyers whose acquisition years earlier by Kravitz & Bane was now a mystery. But the additional address looked nice on the letterhead.

"Mostly corporate stuff," Cooley continued. "We represent some old banks, and we do a lot of bond work for local governmental units."

Exhilarating work, Adam thought.

"The firm itself dates back a hundred and forty years, the oldest in Memphis, by the way. Been around since the Civil War. It split up and spun off a few times, then merged with the big boys in Chicago."

Cooley delivered this brief chronicle with pride, as if the pedigree had a damned thing to do with practicing law in 1990.

"How many lawyers?" Adam asked, trying to fill in the gaps of a conversation that had started slow and was going nowhere.

"A dozen. Eleven paralegals. Nine clerks. Seventeen secretaries. Miscellaneous support staff of ten. Not a bad operation for this part of the country. Nothing like Chicago, though."

You're right about that, Adam thought. "I'm looking forward to visiting here. I hope I won't be in the way."

"Not at all. I'm afraid we won't be much help, though. We're the corporate types, you know, office practitioners, lots of paperwork and all. I haven't seen a courtroom in twenty years."

"I'll be fine. Mr. Goodman and those guys up there will help me."

Cooley jumped to his feet and rubbed his hands as if he wasn't sure what else to do with them. "Well, uh, Darlene will be your secretary. She's actually in a pool, but I've sort of assigned her to you. She'll give you a key, give you the scoop on parking, security, phones, copiers, the works. All state of the art. Really good stuff. If you need a paralegal, just let me know. We'll steal one from one of the other guys, and—"

"No, that won't be necessary. Thanks."

"Well, then, let's go look at your office."

Adam followed Cooley down the quiet and empty hallway, and smiled to himself as he thought of the offices in Chicago. There the halls were always filled with harried lawyers and busy secretaries. Phones rang incessantly, and copiers and faxes and intercoms beeped and buzzed and gave the place the atmosphere of an arcade. It was a madhouse for ten hours a day. Solitude was found only in the alcoves of the libraries, or maybe in the corners of the building where the partners worked.

This place was as quiet as a funeral parlor. Cooley pushed open a door and flipped on a switch. "How's this?" he asked, waving his arm in a broad circle. The room was more than adequate, a long narrow office with a beautiful polished table in the center and five chairs on each side. At one end, a makeshift workplace with a phone, computer, and executive's chair had been arranged. Adam walked along the table, glancing at the bookshelves filled with neat but unused law books. He peeked through the curtains of the window. "Nice view," he said, looking three floors below at the pigeons and people on the Mall.

"Hope it's adequate," Cooley said.

"It's very nice. It'll work just fine. I'll keep to myself and stay out of your way."

"Nonsense. If you need anything, just give me a call." Cooley was walking slowly toward Adam. "There is one thing, though," he said with his eyebrows suddenly serious.

Adam faced him. "What is it?"

"Got a call a couple of hours ago from a reporter here in Memphis. Don't know the guy, but he said he's been following the Cayhall case for years. Wanted to know if our firm was still handling the case, you know. I suggested he contact the boys in Chicago. We, of course, have nothing to do with it." He pulled a scrap of paper from his shirt pocket and handed it to Adam. It had a name and a phone number.

"I'll take care of it," Adam said.

Cooley took a step closer and crossed his arms on

his chest. "Look, Adam, we're not trial lawyers, you know. We do the corporate work. Money's great. We're very low key, and we avoid publicity, you know."

Adam nodded slowly but said nothing.

"We've never touched a criminal case, certainly nothing as huge as this."

"You don't want any of the dirt to rub off on you, right?"

"I didn't say that. Not at all. No. It's just that things are different down here. This is not Chicago. Our biggest clients happen to be some rather staid and proper old bankers, been with us for years, and, well, we're just concerned about our image. You know what I mean?"

"No."

"Sure you do. We don't deal with criminals, and, well, we're very sensitive about the image we project here in Memphis."

"You don't deal with criminals?"

"Never."

"But you represent big banks?"

"Come on, Adam. You know where I'm coming from. This area of our practice is changing rapidly. Deregulation, mergers, failures, a real dynamic sector of the law. Competition is fierce among the big law firms, and we don't want to lose clients. Hell, everybody wants banks."

"And you don't want your clients tainted by mine?"

"Look, Adam, you're from Chicago. Let's keep this matter where it belongs, okay? It's a Chicago case, handled by you guys up there. Memphis has nothing to do with it, okay?"

"This office is part of Kravitz & Bane."

"Yeah, and this office has nothing to gain by being connected to scum like Sam Cayhall."

"Sam Cayhall is my grandfather."

"Shit!" Cooley's knees buckled and his arms dropped from his chest. "You're lying!"

Adam took a step toward him. "I'm not lying, and if you object to my presence here, then you need to call Chicago."

"This is awful," Cooley said as he retreated and headed for the door.

"Call Chicago."

"I might do that," he said, almost to himself, as he opened the door and disappeared, mumbling something else.

Welcome to Memphis, Adam said as he sat in his new chair and stared at the blank computer screen. He placed the scrap of paper on the table and looked at the name and phone number. A sharp hunger pain hit, and he realized he hadn't eaten in hours. It was almost four. He was suddenly weak and tired and hungry.

He gently placed both feet on the table next to the phone, and closed his eyes. The day was a blur, from the anxiety of driving to Parchman and seeing the front gate of the prison, from the unexpected meeting with Lucas Mann, to the horror of stepping onto the Row, to the fear of confronting Sam. And now the warden wanted to meet him, the press wanted to inquire, the Memphis branch of his firm wanted it all hushed up. All this, in less than eight hours.

What could he expect tomorrow?

THEY SAT next to each other on the deep cushioned sofa with a bowl of microwave popcorn between them. Their bare feet were on the coffee table amid a half dozen empty cartons of Chinese food and two bottles of wine. They peered over their toes and watched the television. Adam held the remote control. The room was dark. He slowly ate popcorn.

Lee hadn't moved in a long time. Her eyes were wet, but she said nothing. The video started for the second time.

Adam pushed the Pause button as Sam first appeared, in handcuffs, being rushed from the jail to a hearing. "Where were you when you heard he was arrested?" he asked without looking at her.

"Here in Memphis," she said quietly but with a strong voice. "We had been married for a few years. I was at home. Phelps called and said there had been a bombing in Greenville, at least two people were dead. Might be the Klan. He told me to watch the news at noon, but I was afraid to. A few hours later, my mother called and told me they had arrested Daddy for the bombing. She said he was in jail in Greenville."

"How'd you react?"

"I don't know. Stunned. Scared. Eddie got on the phone and told me that he and Mother had been instructed by Sam to sneak over to Cleveland and retrieve his car. I remember Eddie kept saying that he'd finally done it, he'd finally done it. He'd killed someone else. Eddie was crying and I started crying, and I remember it was horrible."

"They got the car."

"Yeah. No one ever knew it. It never came out during any of the trials. We were scared the cops would find out about it, and make Eddie and my mother testify. But it never happened."

"Where was I?"

"Let me see. You guys lived in a little white house in Clanton, and I'm sure you were there with Evelyn. I don't think she was working at the time. But I'm not sure."

"What kind of work was my father doing?"

"I don't remember. At one time he worked as a manager in an auto parts store in Clanton, but he was always changing jobs."

The video continued with clips of Sam being escorted to and from the jail and the courthouse, then there was the report that he had been formally indicted for the murders. He paused it. "Did any one of you visit Sam in jail?"

"No. Not while he was in Greenville. His bond was very high, a half a million dollars, I think."

"It was a half a million."

"And at first the family tried to raise the money to bail him out. Mother, of course, wanted me to convince Phelps to write a check. Phelps, of course, said no. He wanted no part of it. We fought bitterly, but I couldn't really blame him. Daddy stayed in jail. I remember one of his brothers trying to borrow against some land, but it didn't work. Eddie didn't want to go to jail to see him, and Mother wasn't able. I'm not sure Sam wanted us there."

"When did we leave Clanton?"

Lee leaned forward and took her wineglass from the table. She sipped and thought for a moment. "He'd been in jail about a month, I believe. I drove down one day to see Mother, and she told me Eddie was talking about leaving. I didn't believe it. She said he was embarrassed and humiliated and couldn't face people around town. He'd just lost his job and he wouldn't leave the house. I called him and talked to Evelyn. Eddie wouldn't get on the phone. She said he was depressed and disgraced and all that, and I remember telling her that we all felt that way. I asked her if they were leaving, and she distinctly said no. About a week later, Mother called again and said you guys had packed and left in the middle of the night. The landlord was calling and wanting rent, and no one had seen Eddie. The house was empty."

"I wish I remembered some of this."

"You were only three, Adam. The last time I saw you, you were playing by the garage of the little white house. You were so cute and sweet."

"Gee thanks."

"Several weeks passed, then one day Eddie called me and told me to tell Mother that you guys were in Texas and doing okay."

"Texas?"

"Yeah. Evelyn told me much later that y'all sort of drifted westward. She was pregnant and anxious to settle down someplace. He called again and said y'all were in California. That was the last call for many years."

"Years?"

"Yeah. I tried to convince him to come home, but he was adamant. Swore he'd never return, and I guess he meant it."

"Where were my mother's parents?"

"I don't know. They were not from Ford County. Seems like they lived in Georgia, maybe Florida."

"I've never met them."

He pushed the button again and the video continued. The first trial started in Nettles County. The camera panned the courthouse lawn with the group of Klansmen and rows of policemen and swarms of onlookers.

"This is incredible," Lee said.

He stopped it again. "Did you go to the trial?"

"Once. I sneaked into the courthouse and listened to the closing arguments. He forbade us to watch any of his three trials. Mother was not able. Her blood pressure was out of control, and she was taking lots of medication. She was practically bedridden."

"Did Sam know you were there?"

"No. I sat in the back of the courtroom with a scarf over my head. He never saw me."

"What was Phelps doing?"

"Hiding in his office, tending to his business, praying no one would find out Sam Cayhall was his father-in-law. Our first separation occurred not long after this trial."

"What do you remember from the trial, from the courtroom?"

"I remember thinking that Sam got himself a good jury, his kind of people. I don't know how his lawyer did it, but they picked twelve of the biggest rednecks they could find. I watched the jurors react to the prosecutor, and I watched them listen carefully to Sam's lawyer."

"Clovis Brazelton."

"He was quite an orator, and they hung on every word. I was shocked when the jury couldn't agree on a verdict and a mistrial was declared. I was convinced he would be acquitted. I think he was shocked too."

The video continued with reactions to the mistrial, with generous comments from Clovis Brazelton, with another shot of Sam leaving the courthouse. Then the second trial began with its similarities to the first. "How long have you worked on this?" she asked.

"Seven years. I was a freshman at Pepperdine when the idea hit. It's been a challenge." He fast-forwarded through the pathetic scene of Marvin Kramer spilling from his wheelchair after the second trial, and stopped with the smiling face of a local anchorwoman as she chattered on about the opening of the third trial of the legendary Sam Cayhall. It was 1981 now.

"Sam was a free man for thirteen years," Adam said. "What did he do?"

"He kept to himself, farmed a little, tried to make ends meet. He never talked to me about the bombing or any of his Klan activities, but he enjoyed the attention in Clanton. He was somewhat of a local legend down there, and he was sort of smug about it. Mother's health declined, and he stayed at home and took care of her."

"He never thought about leaving?"

"Not seriously. He was convinced his legal problems were over. He'd had two trials, and walked away from both of them. No jury in Mississippi was going to convict a Klansman in the late sixties. He thought he was invincible. He stayed close to Clanton, avoided the Klan, and lived a peaceful life. I thought he'd spend his golden years growing tomatoes and fishing for bream."

"Did he ever ask about my father?"

She finished her wine and placed the glass on the table. It had never occurred to Lee that she would one day be asked to recall in detail so much of this sad little history. She had worked so hard to forget it. "I remember during the first year he was back home, he would occasionally ask me if I'd heard from my brother. Of course, I hadn't. We knew you guys were somewhere in California, and we hoped you were okay. Sam's a very proud and stubborn person, Adam. He would never consider chasing you guys down and begging Eddie to come home. If Eddie was ashamed of his family, then Sam felt like he should stay in California." She paused and sunk lower into the sofa. "Mother was diagnosed with cancer in 1973, and I hired a private investigator to find Eddie. He worked for six months, charged me a bunch of money, and found nothing."

"I was nine years old, fourth grade, that was in Salem, Oregon."

"Yeah. Evelyn told me later that you guys spent time in Oregon."

"We moved all the time. Every year was a different

school until I was in the eighth grade. Then we settled in Santa Monica."

"You were elusive. Eddie must've hired a good lawyer, because any trace of Cayhall was eliminated. The investigator even used some people out there, but nothing."

"When did she die?"

"Nineteen seventy-seven. We were actually sitting in the front of the church, about to start the funeral, when Eddie slid in a side door and sat behind me. Don't ask how he knew about Mother's death. He simply appeared in Clanton, then disappeared again. Never said a word to Sam. Drove a rental car so no one could check his plates. I drove to Memphis the next day, and there he was, waiting in my driveway. We drank coffee for two hours and talked about everything. He had school pictures of you and Carmen, everything was just wonderful in sunny Southern California. Good job, nice house in the suburbs, Evelyn was selling real estate. The American dream. Said he would never return to Mississippi, not even for Sam's funeral. After swearing me to secrecy, he told me about the new names, and he gave me his phone number. Not his address, just his phone number. Any breach of secrecy, he threatened, and he would simply disappear again. He told me not to call him, though, unless it was an emergency. I told him I wanted to see you and Carmen, and he said that it might happen, one day. At times he was the same old Eddie, and at times he was another person. We hugged and waved good-bye, and I never saw him again."

Adam flipped the remote and the video moved. The clear, modern images of the third and final trial moved by quickly, and there was Sam, suddenly thirteen years older, with a new lawyer as they darted through a side door of the Lakehead County Courthouse. "Did you go to the third trial?"

"No. He told me to stay away."

Adam paused the video. "At what point did Sam realize they were coming after him again?"

"It's hard to say. There was a small story in the Memphis paper one day about this new district attorney in Greenville who wanted to reopen the Kramer case. It was not a big story, just a couple of paragraphs in the middle of the paper. I remember reading it with horror. I read it ten times and stared at it for an hour. After all these years, the name Sam Cayhall was once again in the paper. I couldn't believe it. I called him, and, of course, he had read it too. He said not to worry. About two weeks later there was another story, a little larger this time, with David McAllister's face in the middle of it. I called Daddy, he said everything was okay. That's how it got started. Rather quietly, then it just steamrolled. The Kramer family supported the idea, then the NAACP got involved. One day it became obvious that McAllister was determined to push for a new trial, and that it was not going to go away. Sam was sickened by it, and he was scared, but he tried to act brave. He'd won twice he said, he could do it again."

"Did you call Eddie?"

"Yeah. Once it was obvious there would be a new indictment, I called him and broke the news. He didn't say much, didn't say much at all. It was a brief conversation, and I promised to keep him posted. I don't think he took it very well. It wasn't long before it became a national story, and I'm sure Eddie followed it in the media."

They watched the remaining segments of the third trial in silence. McAllister's toothsome face was everywhere, and more than once Adam wished he'd done a bit more editing. Sam was led away for the last time in handcuffs, and the screen went blank.

"Has anyone else seen this?" Lee asked.

"No. You're the first."

"How did you collect it all?"

"It took time, a little money, a lot of effort."

"It's incredible."

"When I was a junior in high school, we had this goofy teacher of political science. He allowed us to haul in newspapers and magazines and debate the issues of the day. Someone brought a front page story from the *L.A. Times* about the upcoming trial of Sam Cayhall in Mississippi. We kicked it around pretty good, then we watched it closely as it took place. Everyone, including myself, was quite pleased when he was found guilty. But there was a huge debate over the death penalty. A few weeks later, my father was dead and you finally told me the truth. I was horrified that my friends would find out."

"Did they?"

"Of course not. I'm a Cayhall, a master at keeping secrets."

"It won't be a secret much longer."

"No, it won't."

There was a long pause as they stared at the blank screen. Adam finally pushed the power button and the television went off. He tossed the remote control on the table. "I'm sorry, Lee, if this will embarrass you. I mean it. I wish there was some way to avoid it."

"You don't understand."

"I know. And you can't explain it, right? Are you afraid of Phelps and his family?"

"I despise Phelps and his family."

"But you enjoy their money."

"I've earned their money, okay? I've put up with him for twenty-seven years."

"Are you afraid your little clubs will ostracize you? That they'll kick you out of the country clubs?"

"Stop it, Adam."

"I'm sorry," he said. "It's been a weird day. I'm coming out of the closet, Lee. I'm confronting my past, and I guess I expect everyone to be as bold. I'm sorry."

"What does he look like?"

"A very old man. Lots of wrinkles and pale skin. He's too old to be locked up in a cage."

"I remember talking to him a few days before his last trial. I asked him why he didn't just run away, vanish into the night and hide in someplace like South America. And you know what?"

"What?"

"He said he thought about it. Mother had been dead for several years. Eddie was gone. He had read books about Mengele and Eichmann and other Nazi war criminals who disappeared in South America. He even mentioned São Paulo, said it was a city of twenty million and filled with refugees of all sorts. He had a friend, another Klansman I think, who could fix the paperwork and help him hide. He gave it a lot of thought."

"I wish he had. Maybe my father would still be with us."

"Two days before he went to Parchman, I saw him in the jail in Greenville. It was our last visit. I asked him why he hadn't run. He said he never dreamed he would get the death penalty. I couldn't believe that for years he'd been a free man and could've easily run away. It was a big mistake, he said, not running. A mistake that would cost him his life."

Adam placed the popcorn bowl on the table, and slowly leaned toward her. His head rested on her shoulder. She took his hand. "I'm sorry you're in the middle of this," she whispered.

"He looked so pitiful sitting there in a red death row jumpsuit."

TWELVE

CLYDE PACKER poured a generous serving of a strong brew into a cup with his name on it, and began filling out the morning's paperwork. He had worked the Row for twenty-one years, the last seven as the Shift Commander. For eight hours each morning, he would be one of four Tier Sergeants, in charge of fourteen condemned men, two guards, and two trustees. He completed his forms and checked a clipboard. There was a note to call the warden. Another note said that F. M. Dempsey was low on heart pills and wanted to see the doctor. They all wanted to see the doctor. He sipped the steaming coffee as he left the office for his morning inspection. He checked the uniforms of two guards at the front door and told the young white one to get a haircut.

MSU was not a bad place to work. As a general rule, death row inmates were quiet and well behaved. They spent twenty-three hours a day alone in their cells, separated from each other and thus unable to instigate trouble. They spent sixteen hours a day sleeping. They were fed in their cells. They were allowed an hour of outdoor recreation per day, their "hour out" as they called it, and they could have this time alone if they chose. Everyone had either a television or a radio, or both, and after breakfast the four tiers came to life with music and news and soap operas and quiet conversations through the bars. The inmates could not see their neighbors next door, but they conversed with little trouble. Arguments erupted occasionally over the volume of someone's music, but these little spats were quickly settled by the guards. The inmates had certain rights, and then they had certain privileges. The removal of a television or a radio was devastating.

The Row bred an odd camaraderie among those sentenced there. Half were white, half were black, and all had been convicted of brutal killings. But there was little concern about past deeds and criminal records, and generally no real interest in skin color. Out in the general prison population, gangs of all varieties did an effective job of classifying inmates, usually on the basis of race. On the Row, however, a man was judged by the way he handled his confinement. Whether they liked each other or not, they were all locked together in this tiny corner of the world, all waiting to die. It was a ragtag little fraternity of misfits, drifters, outright thugs, and cold-blooded killers.

And the death of one could mean the death of all. The news of Sam's new death sentence was whispered along the tiers and through the bars. When it made the noon news yesterday, the Row became noticeably quieter. Every inmate suddenly wanted to talk to his lawyer. There was a renewed interest in all matters legal, and Packer had noticed several of them plowing through their court files with televisions off and radios down.

He eased through a heavy door, took a long drink, and walked slowly and quietly along Tier A. Fourteen identical cells, six feet wide and nine feet deep, faced the hallway. The front of each cell was a wall of iron bars, so that at no time did an inmate have complete privacy. Anything he happened to be doing—sleeping, using the toilet—was subject to observation by the guards.

They were all in bed as Packer slowed in front of each little room and looked for a head under the sheets. The cell lights were off and the tier was dark. The hall man, an inmate with special privileges, would wake them, or rack-'em-up, at five. Breakfast would be served at six—eggs, toast, jam, sometimes bacon, coffee, and fruit juice. In a few minutes the Row would slowly come to life as forty-seven men shook off their sleep and resumed the interminable process of dying. It happened slowly, one day at a time, as another miserable sunrise brought another blanket of heat into their private little pockets of hell. And it happened quickly, as it had the day before, when a court somewhere rejected a plea or a motion or an appeal and said that an execution must happen soon.

Packer sipped coffee and counted heads and shuffled quietly along through his morning ritual. Generally, MSU ran smoothly when routines were unbroken and schedules were followed. There were lots of rules in the manual, but they were fair and easy to follow. Everyone knew them. But an execution had its own handbook with a different policy and fluctuating guidelines that generally upset the tranquility of the Row. Packer had great respect for Phillip Naifeh, but damned if he didn't rewrite the book before and after each execution. There was great pressure to do it all properly and constitutionally and compassionately. No two killings had been the same.

Packer hated executions. He believed in the death penalty because he was a religious man, and when God said an eye for an eye, then God meant it. He preferred, however, that they be carried out somewhere else by other people. Fortunately, they had been so rare in Mississippi that his job proceeded smoothly with little interference. He'd been through fifteen in twenty-one years, but only four since 1982.

He spoke quietly to a guard at the end of the tier. The sun was beginning to peek through the open win-

dows above the tier walkway. The day would be hot
and suffocating. It would also be much quieter. There
would be fewer complaints about the food, fewer demands to see the doctor, a scattering of gripes about
this and that, but on the whole they would be a docile
and preoccupied group. It had been at least a year and
maybe longer since a stay had been withdrawn this
close to an execution. Packer smiled to himself as he
searched for a head under the sheets. This day would
indeed be a quiet one.

During the first few months of Sam's career on the
Row, Packer had ignored him. The official handbook
prohibited anything other than necessary contact with
inmates, and Packer had found Sam an easy person to
leave alone. He was a Klansman. He hated blacks. He
said little. He was bitter and surly, at least in the early
days. But the routine of doing nothing for eight hours a
day gradually softens the edges, and with time they
reached a level of communication that consisted of a
handful of short words and grunts. After nine and a
half years of seeing each other every day, Sam could on
occasion actually grin at Packer.

There were two types of killers on the Row, Packer
had decided after years of study. There were the cold-
blooded killers who would do it again if given the
chance, and there were those who simply made mistakes and would never dream of shedding more blood.
Those in the first group should be gassed quickly.
Those in the second group caused great discomfort for
Packer because their executions served no purpose. Society would not suffer or even notice if these men were
released from prison. Sam was a solid member of the
second group. He could be returned to his home where
he would soon die a lonesome death. No, Packer did
not want Sam Cayhall executed.

He shuffled back along Tier A, sipping his coffee and

looking at the dark cells. His tier was the nearest to the
Isolation Room, which was next door to the Chamber
Room. Sam was in number six on Tier A, literally less
than ninety feet from the gas chamber. He had requested a move a few years back because of some silly
squabble with Cecil Duff, then his next-door neighbor.

Sam was now sitting in the dark on the edge of his
bed. Packer stopped, walked to the bars. "Mornin',
Sam," he said softly.

"Mornin'," Sam replied, squinting at Packer. Sam
then stood in the center of his room and faced the
door. He was wearing a dingy white T-shirt and baggy
boxer shorts, the usual attire for inmates on the Row
because it was so hot. The rules required the bright red
coveralls to be worn outside the cell, but inside they
wore as little as possible.

"It's gonna be a hot one," Packer said, the usual
early morning greeting.

"Wait till August," Sam said, the standard reply to
the usual early morning greeting.

"You okay?" Packer asked.

"Never felt better."

"Your lawyer said he was coming back today."

"Yeah. That's what he said. I guess I need lots of
lawyers, huh, Packer?"

"Sure looks that way." Packer took a sip of coffee
and glanced down the tier. The windows behind him
were to the south, and a trickle of sunlight was making
its way through. "See you later, Sam," he said, and
eased away. He checked the remaining cells and found
all his boys. The doors clicked behind him as he left
Tier A and returned to the front.

THE ONE LIGHT in the cell was above the stainless
steel sink—made of stainless steel so it couldn't be
chipped and then used as a weapon or suicide device.

Under the sink was a stainless steel toilet. Sam turned on his light and brushed his teeth. It was almost five-thirty. Sleep had been difficult.

He lit a cigarette and sat on the edge of his bed, studying his feet and staring at the painted concrete floor that somehow retained heat in the summer and cold in the winter. His only shoes, a pair of rubber shower shoes, which he loathed, were under the bed. He owned one pair of wool socks, which he slept in during the winter. His remaining assets consisted of a black and white television, a radio, a typewriter, six T-shirts with holes, five pairs of plain white boxer shorts, a toothbrush, comb, nail clippers, an oscillating fan, and a twelve-month wall calendar. His most valuable asset was a collection of law books he had gathered and memorized over the years. They were also placed neatly on the cheap wooden shelves across from his bunk. In a cardboard box on the floor between the shelves and the door was an accumulation of bulky files, the chronological legal history of *State of Mississippi v. Sam Cayhall*. It, too, had been committed to memory.

His balance sheet was lean and short, and other than the death warrant there were no liabilities. The poverty had bothered him at first, but those concerns were dispelled years ago. Family legend held that his great-grandfather had been a wealthy man with acreage and slaves, but no modern Cayhall was worth much. He had known condemned men who had agonized over their wills as if their heirs would brawl over their old televisions and dirty magazines. He was considering preparing his own Last Will and Testament and leaving his wool socks and dirty underwear to the State of Mississippi, or perhaps the NAACP.

To his right was J. B. Gullitt, an illiterate white kid who'd raped and killed a homecoming queen. Three years earlier, Gullitt had come within days of execution before Sam intervened with a crafty motion. Sam pointed out several unresolved issues, and explained to the Fifth Circuit that Gullitt had no lawyer. A stay was immediately granted, and Gullitt became a friend for life.

To his left was Hank Henshaw, the reputed leader of a long-forgotten band of thugs known as the Redneck Mafia. Hank and his motley gang had hijacked an eighteen-wheeler one night, planning only to steal its cargo. The driver produced a gun, and was killed in the ensuing shootout. Hank's family was paying good lawyers, and thus he was not expected to die for many years.

The three neighbors referred to their little section of MSU as Rhodesia.

Sam flipped the cigarette into the toilet and reclined on his bed. The day before the Kramer bombing he had stopped at Eddie's house in Clanton, he couldn't remember why except that he did deliver some fresh spinach from his garden, and he had played with little Alan, now Adam, for a few minutes in the front yard. It was April, and warm, he remembered, and his grandson was barefoot. He remembered the chubby little feet with a Band-Aid around one toe. He had cut it on a rock, Alan had explained with great pride. The kid loved Band-Aids, always had one on a finger or a knee. Evelyn held the spinach and shook her head as he proudly showed his grandfather a whole box of assorted adhesives.

That was the last time he had seen Alan. The bombing took place the next day, and Sam spent the next ten months in jail. By the time the second trial was over and he was released, Eddie and his family were gone. He had too much pride to give chase. There had been rumors and gossip of their whereabouts. Lee said they were in California, but she couldn't find them. Years later, she talked to Eddie and learned of the second child, a girl named Carmen.

There were voices at the end of the tier. Then the flush of a toilet, then a radio. Death row was creaking to life. Sam combed his oily hair, lit another Montclair, and studied the calendar on the wall. Today was July 12. He had twenty-seven days.

He sat on the edge of his bed and studied his feet some more. J. B. Gullitt turned on his television to catch the news, and as Sam puffed and scratched his ankles he listened to the NBC affiliate in Jackson. After the rundown of local shootings, robberies, and killings, the anchorman delivered the hot news that an execution was materializing up at Parchman. The Fifth Circuit, he reported eagerly, had lifted the stay for Sam Cayhall, Parchman's most famous inmate, and the date was now set for August 8. Authorities believe that Cayhall's appeals have been exhausted, the voice said, and the execution could take place.

Sam turned on his television. As usual, the audio preceded the picture by a good ten seconds, and he listened as the Attorney General himself predicted justice for Mr. Cayhall, after all these many years. A grainy face formed on the screen, with words spewing forth, and then there was Roxburgh smiling and frowning at the same time, deep in thought as he relished for the cameras the scenario of finally hauling Mr. Cayhall into the gas chamber. Back to the anchorperson, a local kid with a peach fuzz mustache, who wrapped up the story by blitzing through Sam's horrible crime while over his shoulder in the background was a crude illustration of a Klansman in a mask and pointed hood. A gun, a burning cross, and the letters KKK finished the depiction. The kid repeated the date, August 8, as if his viewers should cir-

cle their calendars and plan to take the day off. Then
they were on to the weather.

He turned off the television, and walked to the bars.

"Did you hear it, Sam?" Gullitt called out from next
door.

"Yep."

"It's gonna get crazy, man."

"Yep."

"Look on the bright side, man."

"What's that?"

"You've only got four weeks of it." Gullitt chuckled
as he hit this punch line, but he didn't laugh long. Sam
pulled some papers from the file and sat on the edge of
his bed. There were no chairs in the cell. He read
through Adam's agreement of representation, a two-
page document with a page and a half of language. On
all margins, Sam had made neat, precise notes with a
pencil. And he had added paragraphs on the backs of
the sheets. Another idea hit him, and he found room to
add it. With a cigarette in his right fingers, he held the
document with his left and read it again. And again.

Finally, Sam reached to his shelves and carefully
took down his ancient Royal portable typewriter. He
balanced it perfectly on his knees. He inserted a sheet
of paper, and began typing.

AT TEN MINUTES after six, the doors on the north
end of Tier A clicked and opened, and two guards entered the hallway. One pushed a cart with fourteen
trays stacked neatly in slots. They stopped at cell number one, and slid the metal tray through a narrow
opening in the door. The occupant of number one was
a skinny Cuban who was waiting at the bars, shirtless
in his drooping briefs. He grabbed the tray like a starv-
ing refugee, and without a word took it to the edge of
his bed.

This morning's menu was two scrambled eggs, four pieces of toasted white bread, a fat slice of bacon, two scrawny containers of grape jelly, a small bottle of prepackaged orange juice, and a large styrofoam cup of coffee. The food was warm and filling, and had the distinction of being approved by the federal courts.

They moved to the next cell where the inmate was waiting. They were always waiting, always standing by the door like hungry dogs.

"You're eleven minutes late," the inmate said quietly as he took his tray. The guards did not look at him.

"Sue us," one said.

"I've got my rights."

"Your rights are a pain in the ass."

"Don't talk to me that way. I'll sue you for it. You're abusive."

The guards rolled away to the next door with no further response. Just part of the daily ritual.

Sam was not waiting at the door. He was busy at work in his little law office when breakfast arrived.

"I figured you'd be typing," a guard said as they stopped in front of number six. Sam slowly placed the typewriter on the bed.

"Love letters," he said as he stood.

"Well, whatever you're typing, Sam, you'd better hurry. The cook's already talking about your last meal."

"Tell him I want microwave pizza. He'll probably screw that up. Maybe I'll just go for hot dogs and beans." Sam took his tray through the opening.

"It's your call, Sam. Last guy wanted steak and shrimp. Can you imagine? Steak and shrimp around this place."

"Did he get it?"

"No. He lost his appetite and they filled him full of Valium instead."

"Not a bad way to go."

"Quiet!" J. B. Gullitt yelled from the next cell. The guards eased the cart a few feet down the tier and stopped in front of J.B., who was gripping the bars with both hands. They kept their distance.

"Well, well, aren't we frisky this morning?" one said.

"Why can't you assholes just serve the food in silence? I mean, do you think we want to wake up each morning and start the day by listening to your cute little comments? Just give me the food, man."

"Gee, J.B. We're awful sorry. We just figured you guys were lonely."

"You figured wrong." J.B. took his tray and turned away.

"Touchy, touchy," a guard said as they moved away in the direction of someone else to torment.

Sam sat his food on the bed and mixed a packet of sugar in his coffee. His daily routine did not include scrambled eggs and bacon. He would save the toast and jelly and eat it throughout the morning. He would carefully sip the coffee, rationing it until ten o'clock, his hour of exercise and sunshine.

He balanced the typewriter on his knees, and began pecking away.

THIRTEEN

SAM'S VERSION of the law was finished by nine-thirty. He was proud of it, one of his better efforts in recent months. He munched on a piece of toast as he proofed the document for the last time. The typing was neat but outdated, the result of an ancient machine. The language was effusive and repetitive, flowery and filled with words never uttered by humble laymen. Sam was almost fluent in legalese and could hold his own with any lawyer.

A door at the end of the hallway banged open, then shut. Heavy footsteps clicked along properly, and Packer appeared. "Your lawyer's here, Sam," he said, removing a set of handcuffs from his belt.

Sam stood and pulled up his boxer shorts. "What time is it?"

"A little after nine-thirty. What difference does it make?"

"I'm supposed to get my hour out at ten."

"You wanna go outside, or you wanna see your lawyer?"

Sam thought about this as he slipped into his red jumpsuit and slid his feet into his rubber sandals. Dressing was a swift procedure on death row. "Can I make it up later?"

"We'll see."

"I want my hour out, you know."

"I know, Sam. Let's go."

"It's real important to me."

"I know, Sam. It's real important to everyone. We'll try and make it up later, okay?"

Sam combed his hair with great deliberation, then rinsed his hands with cold water. Packer waited patiently. He wanted to say something to J. B. Gullitt, something about the mood he was in this morning, but Gullitt was already asleep again. Most of them were asleep. The average inmate on death row made it through breakfast and an hour or so of television before stretching out for the morning nap. Though his study was by no means scientific, Packer estimated they slept fifteen to sixteen hours a day. And they could sleep in the heat, the sweat, the cold, and amid the noise of loud televisions and radios.

The noise was much lower this morning. The fans hummed and whined, but there was no yelling back and forth.

Sam approached the bars, turned his back to Packer, and extended both hands through the narrow slot in the door. Packer applied the handcuffs, and Sam walked to his bed and picked up the document. Packer nodded to a guard at the end of the hall, and Sam's door opened electronically. Then it closed.

Leg chains were optional in these situations, and with a younger prisoner, perhaps one with an attitude and a bit more stamina, Packer probably would have used them. But this was just Sam. He was an old man. How far could he run? How much damage could he do with his feet?

Packer gently placed his hand around Sam's skinny bicep and led him along the hall. They stopped at the tier door, a row of more bars, waited for it to open and close, and left Tier A. Another guard followed behind as they came to an iron door that Packer unlocked with a key from his belt. They walked through it, and there was Adam sitting alone on the other side of the green grating.

Packer removed the handcuffs and left the room.

ADAM READ IT SLOWLY the first time. During the second reading he took a few notes and was amused at some of the language. He'd seen worse work from trained lawyers. And he'd seen much better work. Sam was suffering the same affliction that hit most first-year law students. He used six words when one would suffice. His Latin was dreadful. Entire paragraphs were useless. But, on the whole, not bad for a non-lawyer.

The two-page agreement was now four, typed neatly with perfect margins and only two typos and one misspelled word.

"You do pretty good work," Adam said as he placed the document on the counter. Sam puffed a cigarette and stared at him through the opening. "It's basically the same agreement I handed you yesterday."

"It's basically a helluva lot different," Sam said, correcting him.

Adam glanced at his notes, then said, "You seem to be concerned about five areas. The governor, books, movies, termination, and who gets to witness the execution."

"I'm concerned about a lot of things. Those happen to be non-negotiable."

"I promised yesterday I would have nothing to do with books and movies."

"Good. Moving right along."

"The termination language is fine. You want the right to terminate my representation, and that of Kravitz & Bane, at any time and for any reason, without a fight."

"It took me a long time to fire those Jewish bastards last time. I don't want to go through it again."

"That's reasonable."

"I don't care whether you think it's reasonable, okay? It's in the agreement, and it's non-negotiable."

"Fair enough. And you want to deal with no one but me."

"That's correct. No one at Kravitz & Bane touches my file. That place is crawling with Jews, and they don't get involved, okay? Same for niggers and women."

"Look, Sam, can we lay off the slurs? How about we refer to them as blacks?"

"Ooops. Sorry. How about we do the right thing and call them African-Americans and Jewish-Americans and Female-Americans? You and I'll be Irish-Americans, and also White-Male-Americans. If you need help from your firm, try to stick with German-Americans or Italian-Americans. Since you're in Chicago, maybe use a few Polish-Americans. Gee, that'll be nice, won't it? We'll be real proper and multicultural and politically correct, won't we?"

"Whatever."

"I feel better already."

Adam made a check mark by his notes. "I'll agree to it."

"Damned right you will, if you want an agreement. Just keep the minorities out of my life."

"You're assuming they're anxious to jump in."

"I'm not assuming anything. I have four weeks to live, and I'd rather spend my time with people I trust."

Adam read again a paragraph on page three of Sam's draft. The language gave Sam the sole authority to select two witnesses at his execution. "I don't understand this clause about the witnesses," Adam said.

"It's very simple. If we get to that point, there will be about fifteen witnesses. Since I'm the guest of honor, I get to select two. The statute, once you've had a chance to review it, lists a few who must be present. The warden, a Lebanese-American by the way, has some discretion in picking the rest. They usually conduct a lottery with the press to choose which of the vultures are allowed to gawk at it."

"Then why do you want this clause?"

"Because the lawyer is always one of the two chosen by the gassee. That's me."

"And you don't want me to witness the execution?"

"That's correct."

"You're assuming I'll want to witness it."

"I'm not assuming anything. It's just a fact that the lawyers can't wait to see their poor clients gassed once it becomes inevitable. Then they can't wait to get in front of the cameras and cry and carry on and rail against injustice."

"And you think I'll do that?"

"No. I don't think you'll do that."

"Then, why this clause?"

Sam leaned forward with his elbows on the counter. His nose was an inch from the screen. "Because you will not witness the execution, okay?"

"It's a deal," he said casually, and flipped to another page. "We're not going to get that far, Sam."

"Attaboy. That's what I want to hear."

"Of course, we may need the governor."

Sam snorted in disgust and relaxed in his chair. He crossed his right leg on his left knee, and glared at Adam. "The agreement is very plain."

Indeed it was. Almost an entire page was dedicated to a venomous attack on David McAllister. Sam forgot about the law and used words like "scurrilous" and "egotistical" and "narcissistic" and mentioned more than once the insatiable appetite for publicity.

"So you have a problem with the governor," Adam said.

Sam snorted.

"I don't think this is a good idea, Sam."

"I really don't care what you think."

"The governor could save your life."

"Oh really. He's the only reason I'm here, on death row, waiting to die in the gas chamber. Why in hell would he want to save my life?"

"I didn't say he wanted to. I said that he could. Let's keep our options open."

Sam smirked for a long minute as he lit a cigarette. He blinked and rolled his eyes as if this kid were the dumbest human he'd encountered in decades. Then he leaned forward on his left elbow and pointed at Adam with a crooked right finger. "If you think David McAllister will grant me a last minute pardon, then you're a fool. But let me tell you what he will do. He'll use you, and me, to suck out all the publicity imaginable. He'll invite you to his office at the state capitol, and before you get there he'll tip off the media. He'll listen with remarkable sincerity. He'll profess grave reservations about whether I should die. He'll schedule another meeting, closer to the execution. And after you leave, he'll hold a couple of interviews and divulge everything you've just told him. He'll rehash the Kramer bombing. He'll talk about civil rights and all that radical nigger crap. He'll probably even cry. The closer I get to the gas chamber, the bigger the media circus will become. He'll try every way in the world to get in the middle of it. He'll meet with you every day, if we allow it. He'll take us to the wire."

"He can do this without us."

"And he will. Mark my word, Adam. An hour before I die, he'll hold a press conference somewhere— probably here, maybe at the governor's mansion—and he'll stand there in the glare of a hundred cameras and deny me clemency. And the bastard will have tears in his eyes."

"It won't hurt to talk to him."

"Fine. Go talk to him. And after you do, I'll invoke paragraph two and your ass'll go back to Chicago."

"He might like me. We could be friends."

"Oh, he'll love you. You're Sam's grandson. What a great story! More reporters, more cameras, more journalists, more interviews. He'd love to make your acquaintance so he can string you along. Hell, you might get him reelected."

Adam flipped another page, made some more notes, and stalled for a while in an effort to move away from the governor. "Where'd you learn to write like this?" he asked.

"Same place you did. I was taught by the same learned souls who provided your instruction. Dead judges. Honorable justices. Windy lawyers. Tedious professors. I've read the same garbage you've read."

"Not bad," Adam said, scanning another paragraph.

"I'm delighted you think so."

"I understand you have quite a little practice here."

"Practice. What's a practice? Why do lawyers practice? Why can't they just work like everyone else? Do plumbers practice? Do truck drivers practice? No, they simply work. But not lawyers. Hell no. They're special, and they practice. With all their damned practicing you'd think they'd know what the hell they were doing. You'd think they'd eventually become good at something."

"Do you like anyone?"

"That's an idiotic question."

"Why is it idiotic?"

"Because you're sitting on that side of the wall. And you can walk out that door and drive away. And tonight you can have dinner in a nice restaurant and sleep in a soft bed. Life's a bit different on this side. I'm treated like an animal. I have a cage. I have a death sentence that allows the State of Mississippi to kill me in four weeks, and so yes, son, it's hard to be loving and compassionate. It's hard to like people these days. That's why your question is foolish."

"Are you saying you were loving and compassionate before you arrived here?"

Sam stared through the opening and puffed on the cigarette. "Another stupid question."

"Why?"

"It's irrelevant, counselor. You're a lawyer, not a shrink."

"I'm your grandson. Therefore, I'm allowed to ask questions about your past."

"Ask them. They might not be answered."

"Why not?"

"The past is gone, son. It's history. We can't undo what's been done. Nor can we explain it all."

"But I don't have a past."

"Then you are indeed a lucky person."

"I'm not so sure."

"Look, if you expect me to fill in the gaps, then I'm afraid you've got the wrong person."

"Okay. Who else should I talk to?"

"I don't know. It's not important."

"Maybe it's important to me."

"Well, to be honest, I'm not too concerned about you right now. Believe it or not, I'm much more worried about me. Me and my future. Me and my neck. There's a big clock ticking somewhere, ticking rather loudly, wouldn't you say? For some strange reason, don't ask me why, but I can hear the damned thing and it makes me real anxious. I find it very difficult to worry about the problems of others."

"Why did you become a Klansman?"

"Because my father was in the Klan."

"Why did he become a Klansman?"

"Because his father was in the Klan."

"Great. Three generations."

"Four, I think. Colonel Jacob Cayhall fought with Nathan Bedford Forrest in the war, and family legend has it that he was one of the early members of the Klan. He was my great-grandfather."

"You're proud of this?"

"Is that a question?"

"Yes."

"It's not a matter of pride." Sam nodded at the counter. "Are you going to sign that agreement?"

"Yes."

"Then do it."

Adam signed at the bottom of the back page and handed it to Sam. "You're asking questions that are very confidential. As my lawyer, you cannot breathe a word."

"I understand the relationship."

Sam signed his name next to Adam's, then studied the signatures. "When did you become a Hall?"

"A month before my fourth birthday. It was a family affair. We were all converted at the same time. Of course, I don't remember."

"Why did he stick with Hall? Why not make a clean break and go with Miller or Green or something?"

"Is that a question?"

"No."

"He was running, Sam. And he was burning bridges as he went. I guess four generations was enough for him."

Sam placed the contract in a chair beside him, and methodically lit another cigarette. He exhaled at the ceiling and stared at Adam. "Look, Adam," he said slowly, his voice suddenly much softer. "Let's lay off the family stuff for a while, okay? Maybe we'll get around to it later. Right now I need to know what's about to happen to me. What are my chances, you know? Stuff like that. How do you stop the clock? What do you file next?"

"Depends on several things, Sam. Depends on how much you tell me about the bombing."

"I don't follow."

"If there are new facts, then we present them. There are ways, believe me. We'll find a judge who'll listen."

"What kind of new facts?"

Adam flipped to a clean page on his pad, and scribbled the date in the margin. "Who delivered the green Pontiac to Cleveland on the night before the bombing?"

"I don't know. One of Dogan's men."

"You don't know his name?"

"No."

"Come on, Sam."

"I swear. I don't know who did it. I never saw the man. The car was delivered to a parking lot. I found it. I was supposed to leave it where I found it. I never saw the man who delivered it."

"Why wasn't he discovered during the trials?"

"How am I supposed to know? He was just a minor accomplice, I guess. They were after me. Why bother with a gopher? I don't know."

"Kramer was bombing number six, right?"

"I think so." Sam leaned forward again with his face almost touching the screen. His voice was low, his words carefully chosen as if someone might be listening somewhere.

"You think so?"

"It was a long time ago, okay." He closed his eyes and thought for a moment. "Yeah, number six."

"The FBI said it was number six."

"Then that settles it. They're always right."

"Was the same green Pontiac used in one or all of the prior bombings?"

"Yes. In a couple, as I remember. We used more than one car."

"All supplied by Dogan?"

"Yes. He was a car dealer."

"I know. Did the same man deliver the Pontiac for the prior bombings?"

"I never saw or met anyone delivering the cars for the bombings. Dogan didn't work that way. He was extremely careful, and his plans were detailed. I don't know this for a fact, but I'm certain that the man delivering the cars didn't have a clue as to who I was."

"Did the cars come with the dynamite?"

"Yes. Always. Dogan had enough guns and explosives for a small war. Feds never found his arsenal either."

"Where'd you learn about explosives?"

"KKK boot camp and the basic training manual."

"Probably hereditary, wasn't it?"

"No, it wasn't."

"I'm serious. How'd you learn to detonate explosives?"

"It's very basic and simple. Any fool could pick it up in thirty minutes."

"Then with a bit of practice you're an expert."

"Practice helps. It's not much more difficult than lighting a firecracker. You strike a match, any match will do, and you place it at the end of a long fuse until the fuse lights. Then you run like hell. If you're lucky, it won't blow up for about fifteen minutes."

"And this is something that is just sort of absorbed by all Klansmen?"

"Most of the ones I knew could handle it."

"Do you still know any Klansmen?"

"No. They've abandoned me."

Adam watched his face carefully. The fierce blue eyes were steady. The wrinkles didn't move. There was no emotion, no feeling or sorrow or anger. Sam returned the stare without blinking.

Adam returned to his notepad. "On March 2, 1967, the Hirsch Temple in Jackson was bombed. Did you do it?"

"Get right to the point, don't you?"

"It's an easy question."

Sam twisted the filter between his lips and thought for a second. "Why is it important?"

"Just answer the damned question," Adam snapped. "It's too late to play games."

"I've never been asked that question before."

"Well, I guess today's your big day. A simple yes or no will do."

"Yes."

"Did you use the green Pontiac?"

"I think so."

"Who was with you?"

"What makes you think someone was with me?"

"Because a witness said he saw a green Pontiac speed by a few minutes before the explosion. And he said two people were in the car. He even made a tentative identification of you as the driver."

"Ah, yes. Our little friend Bascar. I read about him in the newspapers."

"He was near the corner of Fortification and State streets when you and your pal rushed by."

"Of course he was. And he'd just left a bar at three in the morning, drunk as a goat, and stupid as hell to begin with. Bascar, as I'm sure you know, never made it near a courtroom, never placed his hand on a Bible and swore to tell the truth, never faced a cross-examination, never came forward until after I was under arrest in Greenville and half the world had seen pictures of the green Pontiac. His tentative identification occurred only after my face had been plastered all over the papers."

"So he's lying?"

"No, he's probably just ignorant. Keep in mind, Adam, that I was never charged with that bombing. Bascar was never put under pressure. He never gave sworn testimony. His story was revealed, I believe, when a reporter with a Memphis newspaper dug through the honky-tonks and whorehouses long enough to find someone like Bascar."

"Let's try it this way. Did you or did you not have someone with you when you bombed the Hirsch Temple synagogue on March 2, 1967?"

Sam's gaze fell a few inches below the opening, then to the counter, then to the floor. He pushed away slightly from the partition and relaxed in his chair. Predictably, the blue package of Montclairs was produced from the front pocket, and he took forever selecting one, then thumping it on the filter, then inserting it just so between his moist lips. The striking of the match was another brief ceremony, but one that was finally accomplished and a fresh fog of smoke lifted toward the ceiling.

Adam watched and waited until it was obvious no quick answer was forthcoming. The delay in itself was an admission. He tapped his pen nervously on the legal pad. He took quick breaths and noticed an increase in his heartbeat. His empty stomach was suddenly jittery. Could this be the break? If there had been an accomplice, then perhaps they had worked as a team and perhaps Sam had not actually planted the dynamite that killed the Kramers. Perhaps this fact could be presented to a sympathetic judge somewhere who would listen and grant a stay. Perhaps. Maybe. Could it be?

"No," Sam said ever so softly but firmly as he looked at Adam through the opening.

"I don't believe you."

"There was no accomplice."

"I don't believe you, Sam."

Sam shrugged casually as if he couldn't care less. He crossed his legs and wrapped his fingers around a knee.

Adam took a deep breath, scribbled something routinely as if he'd been expecting this, and flipped to a clean page. "What time did you arrive in Cleveland on the night of April 20, 1967?"

"Which time?"

"The first time."

"I left Clanton around six. Drove two hours to Cleveland. So I got there around eight."

"Where'd you go?"

"To a shopping center."

"Why'd you go there?"

"To get the car."

"The green Pontiac?"

"Yes. But it wasn't there. So I drove to Greenville to look around a bit."

"Had you been there before?"

"Yes. A couple of weeks earlier, I had scouted the place. I even went in the Jew's office to get a good look."

"That was pretty stupid, wasn't it? I mean, his secretary identified you at trial as the man who came in asking for directions and wanting to use the rest room."

"Very stupid. But then, I wasn't supposed to get caught. She was never supposed to see my face again." He bit the filter and sucked hard. "A very bad move. Of course, it's awfully easy to sit here now and second-guess everything."

"How long did you stay in Greenville?"

"An hour or so. Then I drove back to Cleveland to get the car. Dogan always had detailed plans with several alternates. The car was parked in spot B, near a truck stop."

"Where were the keys?"

"Under the mat."

"What did you do?"

"Took it for a drive. Drove out of town, out through some cotton fields. I found a lonely spot and parked the car. I popped the trunk to check the dynamite."

"How many sticks?"

"Fifteen, I believe. I was using between twelve and twenty, depending on the building. Twenty for the synagogue because it was new and modern and built with concrete and stone. But the Jew's office was an old wooden structure, and I knew fifteen would level it."

"What else was in the trunk?"

"The usual. A cardboard box of dynamite. Two blasting caps. A fifteen-minute fuse."

"Is that all?"

"Yes."

"Are you sure?"

"Of course I'm sure."

"What about the timing device? The detonator?"

"Oh yeah. I forgot about that. It was in another, smaller box."

"Describe it for me."

"Why? You've read the trial transcripts. The FBI expert did a wonderful job of reconstructing my little bomb. You've read this, haven't you?"

"Many times."

"And you've seen the photos they used at trial. The ones of the fragments and pieces of the timer. You've seen all this, haven't you?"

"I've seen it. Where did Dogan get the clock?"

"I never asked. You could buy one in any drugstore.

It was just a cheap windup alarm clock. Nothing fancy."

"Was this your first job with a timing device?"

"You know it was. The other bombs were detonated by fuses. Why are you asking me these questions?"

"Because I want to hear your answers. I've read everything, but I want to hear it from you. Why did you want to delay the Kramer bomb?"

"Because I was tired of lighting fuses and running like hell. I wanted a longer break between planting the bomb and feeling it go off."

"What time did you plant it?"

"Around 4 A.M."

"What time was it supposed to go off?"

"Around five."

"What went wrong?"

"It didn't go off at five. It went off a few minutes before eight, and there were people in the building by then, and some of these people got killed. And that's why I'm sitting here in a red monkey suit wondering what the gas'll smell like."

"Dogan testified that the selection of Marvin Kramer as a target was a joint effort between the both of you; that Kramer had been on a Klan hit list for two years; that the use of a timing device was something you suggested as a way to kill Kramer, because his routine was predictable; that you acted alone."

Sam listened patiently and puffed on his cigarette. His eyes narrowed to tiny slits and he nodded at the floor. Then he almost smiled. "Well, I'm afraid Dogan went crazy, didn't he? Feds hounded him for years, and he finally caved in. He was not a strong man, you know." He took a deep breath and looked at Adam. "But some of it's true. Not much, but some."

"Did you intend to kill him?"

"No. We weren't killing people. Just blowing up buildings."

"What about the Pinder home in Vicksburg? Was that one of yours?"

Sam nodded slowly.

"The bomb went off at four in the morning while the entire Pinder family was sound asleep. Six people. Miraculously, only one minor injury."

"It wasn't a miracle. The bomb was placed in the garage. If I'd wanted to kill anyone, I'd have put it by a bedroom window."

"Half the house collapsed."

"Yeah, and I could've used a clock and wiped out a bunch of Jews as they ate their bagels or whatever."

"Why didn't you?"

"As I said, we weren't trying to kill people."

"What were you trying to do?"

"Intimidate. Retaliate. Keep the damned Jews from financing the civil rights movement. We were trying to keep the Africans where they belonged—in their own schools and churches and neighborhoods and rest rooms, away from our women and children. Jews like Marvin Kramer were promoting an interracial society and stirring up the Africans. Son of a bitch needed to be kept in line."

"You guys really showed him, didn't you?"

"He got what he deserved. I'm sorry about the little boys."

"Your compassion is overwhelming."

"Listen, Adam, and listen good. I did not intend to hurt anyone. The bomb was set to go off at 5 A.M., three hours before he usually arrived for work. The only reason his kids were there was because his wife had the flu."

"But you feel no remorse because Marvin lost both legs?"

"Not really."

"No remorse because he killed himself?"

"He pulled the trigger, not me."

"You're a sick man, Sam."

"Yeah, and I'm about to get a lot sicker when I sniff the gas."

Adam shook his head in disgust, but held his tongue. They could argue later about race and hatred; not that he, at this moment, expected to make any progress with Sam on these topics. But he was determined to try. Now, however, they needed to discuss facts.

"After you inspected the dynamite, what did you do?"

"Drove back to the truck stop. Drank coffee."

"Why?"

"Maybe I was thirsty."

"Very funny, Sam. Just try and answer the questions."

"I was waiting."

"For what?"

"I needed to kill a couple of hours. By then it was around midnight, and I wanted to spend as little time in Greenville as possible. So, I killed time in Cleveland."

"Did you talk to anyone in the café?"

"No."

"Was it crowded?"

"I really don't remember."

"Did you sit alone?"

"Yes."

"At a table?"

"Yes." Sam managed a slight grin because he knew what was coming.

"A truck driver by the name of Tommy Farris said he saw a man who greatly resembled you in the truck stop that night, and that this man drank coffee for a long time with a younger man."

"I never met Mr. Farris, but I believe he had a lapse of memory for three years. Not a word to anyone, as I recall, until another reporter flushed him out and he got his name in the paper. It's amazing how these mystery witnesses pop up years after the trials."

"Why didn't Farris testify in your last trial?"

"Don't ask me. I suppose it was because he had nothing to say. The fact that I drank coffee alone or with someone seven hours before the bombing was hardly relevant. Plus, the coffee drinking took place in Cleveland, and had nothing to do with whether or not I committed the crime."

"So Farris was lying?"

"I don't know what Farris was doing. Don't really care. I was alone. That's all that matters."

"What time did you leave Cleveland?"

"Around three, I think."

"And you drove straight to Greenville?"

"Yes. And I drove by the Kramers' house, saw the guard sitting on the porch, drove by his office, killed some more time, and around four or so I parked behind his office, slipped through the rear door, planted the bomb in a closet in the hallway, walked back to my car, and drove away."

"What time did you leave Greenville?"

"I had planned to leave after the bomb went off. But, as you know, it was several months before I actually made it out of town."

"Where did you go when you left Kramer's office?"

"I found a little coffee shop on the highway, a half mile or so from Kramer's office."

"Why'd you go there?"

"To drink coffee."

"What time was it?"

"I don't know. Around four-thirty or so."

"Was it crowded?"

"A handful of people. Just your run-of-the-mill all-night diner with a fat cook in a dirty T-shirt and a waitress who smacked her chewing gum."

"Did you talk to anybody?"

"I spoke to the waitress when I ordered my coffee. Maybe I had a doughnut."

"And you were having a nice cup of coffee, just minding your own business, waiting for the bomb to go off."

"Yeah. I always liked to hear the bombs go off and watch the people react."

"So you'd done this before?"

"A couple of times. In February of that year I bombed the real estate office in Jackson—Jews had sold a house to some niggers in a white section—and I had just sat down in a diner not three blocks away when the bomb went off. I was using a fuse then, so I had to hustle away and park real fast and find a table. The girl had just set my coffee down when the ground shook and everybody froze. I really liked that. It was four in the morning and the place was packed with truckers and deliverymen, even had a few cops over in a corner, and of course they ran to their cars and sped away with lights blazing. My table shook so hard that coffee spilled from my cup."

"And that gave you a real thrill?"

"Yes, it did. But the other jobs were too risky. I didn't have the time to find a café or diner, so I just sort of rode around for a few minutes waiting for the fun. I'd check my watch closely, so I always knew about when it would hit. If I was in the car, I liked to be on the edge of town, you know." Sam paused and took a long puff from his cigarette. His words were slow and careful. His eyes danced a bit as he talked about his adventures, but his words were measured. "I did watch the Pinder bombing," he added.

"And how'd you do that?"

"They lived in a big house in the suburbs, lots of trees, sort of in a valley. I parked on the side of a hill about a mile away, and I was sitting under a tree when it went off."

"How peaceful."

"It really was. Full moon, cool night. I had a great view of the street, and I could see almost all of the roof. It was so calm and peaceful, everyone was asleep, then, boom, blew that roof to hell and back."

"What was Mr. Pinder's sin?"

"Just overall general Jewishness. Loved niggers. Always embraced the radical Africans when they came down from the North and agitated everybody. He loved to march and boycott with the Africans. We suspected he was financing a lot of their activities."

Adam made notes and tried to absorb all of this. It was hard to digest because it was almost impossible to believe. Perhaps the death penalty was not such a bad idea after all. "Back to Greenville. Where was this coffee shop located?"

"Don't remember."

"What was it called?"

"It was twenty-three years ago. And it was not the kind of place you'd want to remember."

"Was it on Highway 82?"

"I think so. What are you gonna do? Spend your time digging for the fat cook and the tacky waitress? Are you doubting my story?"

"Yes. I'm doubting your story."

"Why?"

"Because you can't tell me where you learned to make a bomb with a timing detonator."

"In the garage behind my house."

"In Clanton?"

"Out from Clanton. It's not that difficult."

"Who taught you?"

"I taught myself. I had a drawing, a little booklet with diagrams and such. Steps one, two, three. It was no big deal."

"How many times did you practice with such a device before Kramer?"

"Once."

"Where? When?"

"In the woods not far from my house. I took two sticks of dynamite and the necessary paraphernalia, and I went to a little creek bed deep in the woods. It worked perfectly."

"Of course. And you did all this study and research in your garage?"

"That's what I said."

"Your own little laboratory."

"Call it whatever you want."

"Well, the FBI conducted a thorough search of your house, garage, and premises while you were in custody. They didn't find a trace of evidence of explosives."

"Maybe they're stupid. Maybe I was real careful and didn't leave a trail."

"Or maybe the bomb was planted by someone with experience in explosives."

"Nope. Sorry."

"How long did you stay in the coffee shop in Greenville?"

"A helluva long time. Five o'clock came and went. Then it was almost six. I left a few minutes before six and drove by Kramer's office. The place looked fine. Some of the early risers were out and about, and I didn't want to be seen. I crossed the river and drove to Lake Village, Arkansas, then returned to Greenville. It was seven by then, sun was up and people were moving around. No explosion. I parked the car on a side street, and walked around for a while. The damned thing wouldn't go off. I couldn't go in after it, you know. I walked and walked, listening hard, hoping the ground would shake. Nothing happened."

"Did you see Marvin Kramer and his sons go into the building?"

"No. I turned a corner and saw his car parked, and I thought dammit! I went blank. I couldn't think. But then I thought, what the hell, he's just a Jew and he's done many evil things. Then, I thought about secretaries and other people who might work in there, so I walked around the block again. I remember looking at my watch when it was twenty minutes before eight, and I had this thought that maybe I should make an anonymous phone call to the office and tell Kramer that there was a bomb in the closet. And if he didn't believe me, then he could go look at it, then he could haul ass."

"Why didn't you?"

"I didn't have a dime. I'd left all my change as a tip for the waitress, and I didn't want to walk into a store and ask for change. I have to tell you I was real nervous. My hands were shaking, and I didn't want to act suspicious in front of anybody. I was a stranger, right? That was my bomb in there, right? I was in a small town where everybody knows everyone, and they damned sure remember strangers when there's a crime. I remember walking down the sidewalk, just across the street from Kramer's, and in front of a barbershop there was a newspaper rack, and this man was fumbling in his pocket for change. I almost asked him for a dime so I could make a quick call, but I was too nervous."

"Why were you nervous, Sam? You just said you

didn't care if Kramer got hurt. This was your sixth bombing, right?"

"Yeah, but the others were easy. Light the fuse, hit the door, and wait a few minutes. I kept thinking about that cute little secretary in Kramer's office, the one who'd shown me to the rest room. The same one who later testified at trial. And I kept thinking about the other people who worked in his office, because when I went in that day I saw people everywhere. It was almost eight o'clock, and I knew the place opened in a few minutes. I knew a lot of people were about to get killed. My mind stopped working. I remember standing beside a phone booth a block away, staring at my watch, then staring at the phone, telling myself that I had to make the call. I finally stepped inside and looked up the number, but by the time I closed the book I'd forgotten it. So I looked it up again, and I started to dial when I remembered I didn't have a dime. So I made up my mind to go into the barbershop to get some change. My legs were heavy and I was sweatin' like hell. I walked to the barbershop, and I stopped at the plate glass window and looked in. It was packed. They were lined up against the wall, talking and reading papers, and there was a row of chairs, all filled with men talking at the same time. I remember a couple of them looked at me, then one or two more began to stare, so I walked away."

"Where did you go?"

"I'm not sure. There was an office next door to Kramer's, and I remember seeing a car park in front of it. I thought maybe it was a secretary or someone about to go into Kramer's, and I think I was walking toward the car when the bomb went off."

"So you were across the street?"

"I think so. I remember rocking on my hands and

knees in the street as glass and debris fell all around me. But I don't remember much after that."

There was a slight knock on the door from the outside, then Sergeant Packer appeared with a large styrofoam cup, a paper napkin, a stir stick, and creamer. "Thought you might need a little coffee. Sorry to butt in." He placed the cup and accessories on the counter.

"Thanks," Adam said.

Packer quickly turned and headed for the door.

"I'll take two sugars, one cream," Sam said from the other side.

"Yes sir," Packer snapped without slowing. He was gone.

"Good service around here," Adam said.

"Wonderful, just wonderful."

FOURTEEN

S AM, OF COURSE, was not served coffee. He knew this immediately, but Adam did not. And so after waiting a few minutes, Sam said, "Drink it." He himself lit another cigarette, and paced around a bit behind his chair while Adam stirred the sugar with the plastic stick. It was almost eleven, and Sam had missed his hour out, and he had no confidence that Packer would find the time to make it up. He paced and squatted a few times, performed a half dozen deep bends, knees cracking and joints popping as he rose and sank unsteadily. During the first few months of his first year on the Row, he had grown quite disciplined with his exercise. At one point, he was doing a hundred push-ups and a hundred sit-ups in his cell each day, every day. His weight fell to a perfect one hundred and sixty pounds as the low-fat diet took its course. His stomach was flat and hard. He had never been so healthy.

Not long afterward, however, came the realization that the Row would be his final home, and that the state would one day kill him here. What's the benefit of good health and tight biceps when one is locked up twenty-three hours a day waiting to die? The exercise slowly stopped. The smoking intensified. Among his comrades, Sam was considered a lucky man, primarily because he had outside money. A younger brother, Donnie, lived in North Carolina and once a month shipped to Sam a cardboard box packed neatly with ten cartons of Montclair cigarettes. Sam averaged between three and four packs a day. He wanted to kill himself before the state got around to it. And he preferred to go by way of some protracted illness or affliction, some disease that would require expensive treatment, which the State of Mississippi would be constitutionally bound to provide.

It looked as though he would lose the race.

The federal judge who had assumed control of Parchman through a prisoners' rights suit had issued sweeping orders overhauling fundamental correction procedures. He had carefully defined the rights of prisoners. And he had set forth minor details, such as the square footage of each cell on the Row and the amount of money each inmate could possess. Twenty dollars was the maximum. It was referred to as "dust," and it always came from the outside. Death row inmates were not allowed to work and earn money. The lucky ones received a few dollars a month from relatives and friends. They could spend it in a canteen located in the middle of MSU. Soft drinks were known as "bottle-ups." Candy and snacks were "zu-zus" and "wham-whams." Real cigarettes in packages were "tight-legs" and "ready-rolls."

The majority of the inmates received nothing from the outside. They traded, swapped, and bartered, and gathered enough coins to purchase loose leaf tobacco, which they rolled into thin papers and smoked slowly. Sam was indeed a lucky man.

He took his seat and lit another one.

"Why didn't you testify at trial?" his lawyer asked through the screen.

"Which trial?"

"Good point. The first two trials."

"Didn't need to. Brazelton picked good juries, all white, good sympathetic people who understood things. I knew I wouldn't be convicted by those people. There was no need to testify."

"And the last trial?"

"That's a little more complicated. Keyes and I discussed it many times. He at first thought it might help, because I could explain to the jury what my intentions were. Nobody was supposed to get hurt, et cetera. The bomb was supposed to go off at 5 A.M. But we knew the cross-examination would be brutal. The judge had already ruled that the other bombings could be discussed to show certain things. I would be forced to admit that I did in fact plant the bomb, all fifteen sticks, which of course was more than enough to kill people."

"So why didn't you testify?"

"Dogan. That lying bastard told the jury that our plan was to kill the Jew. He was a very effective witness. I mean, think about it, here was the former Imperial Wizard of the Mississippi Klan testifying for the prosecution against one of his own men. It was stout stuff. The jury ate it up."

"Why did Dogan lie?"

"Jerry Dogan went crazy, Adam. I mean, really crazy. The Feds pursued him for fifteen years—bugged his phones, followed his wife around town, harassed his kinfolks, threatened his children, knocked on his door at all hours of the night. His life was miserable. Someone was always watching and listening. Then, he got sloppy, and the IRS stepped in. They, along with the FBI, told him he was looking at thirty years. Dogan cracked under the pressure. After my trial, I heard he was sent away for a while. You know, to an institution. He got some treatment, returned home, and died not long after."

"Dogan's dead?"

Sam froze in mid-puff. Smoke leaked from his mouth and curled upward past his nose and in front of his eyes, which at the moment were staring in disbelief through the opening and into those of his grandson. "You don't know about Dogan?" he asked.

Adam's memory blitzed through the countless articles and stories that he'd collected and indexed. He shook his head. "No. What happened to Dogan?"

"I thought you knew everything," Sam said. "Thought you'd memorized everything about me."

"I know a lot about you, Sam. I really don't care about Jeremiah Dogan."

"He burned in a house fire. He and his wife. They were asleep one night when a gas line somehow began leaking propane. Neighbors said it was like a bomb going off."

"When did this happen?"

"Exactly one year to the day after he testified against me."

Adam tried to write this down, but his pen wouldn't move. He studied Sam's face for a clue. "Exactly a year?"

"Yep."

"That's a nice coincidence."

"I was in here, of course, but I heard bits and pieces of it. Cops ruled it accidental. In fact, I think there was a lawsuit against the propane company."

"So, you don't think he was murdered?"

"Sure I think he was murdered."

"Okay. Who did it?"

"In fact, the FBI came here and asked me some questions. Can you believe it? The Feds poking their noses around here. A couple of kids from up North. Just couldn't wait to visit death row and flash their badges and meet a real live Klan terrorist. They were so damned scared they were afraid of their shadows. They asked me stupid questions for an hour, then left. Never heard from anybody again."

"Who would murder Dogan?"

Sam bit the filter and extracted the last mouthful of smoke from the cigarette. He stubbed it in the ashtray while exhaling through the screen. Adam waved at the smoke with exaggerated motions, but Sam ignored him. "Lots of people," he mumbled.

Adam made a note in the margin to talk about Dogan later. He would do the research first, then spring it again in some future conversation.

"Just for the sake of argument," he said, still writing, "it seems as though you should've testified to counter Dogan."

"I almost did," Sam said with a trace of regret. "The last night of the trial, me and Keyes and his associate, I forget her name, stayed up until midnight discussing whether or not I should take the stand. But think about it, Adam. I would've been forced to admit that I planted the bomb, that it had a timing device set to go off later, that I had been involved in other bombings, and that I was across the street from the building when it blew. Plus, the prosecution had clearly proven that Marvin Kramer was a target. I mean, hell, they played those FBI phone tapes to the jury. You should've heard it. They rigged up these huge speakers in the courtroom, and they set the tape player on a table in front of the jury like it was some kind of a live bomb. And there was Dogan on the phone to Wayne Graves, his voice was scratchy but very audible, talking about bombing Marvin Kramer for this and for that, and bragging about how he would send his Group, as he called me, to Greenville to take care of matters. The voices on that tape sounded like ghosts from hell, and the jury hung on every word. Very effective. And, then, of course, there was Dogan's own testimony. I would've looked ridiculous at that moment trying to testify and convince the jury that I really wasn't a bad guy. McAllister would've eaten me alive. So we decided

I shouldn't take the stand. Looking back, it was a bad move. I should've talked."

"But on the advice of your attorney you didn't?"

"Look, Adam, if you're thinking about attacking Keyes on the grounds of ineffective assistance of counsel, then forget it. I paid Keyes good money, mortgaged everything I had, and he did a good job. A long time ago Goodman and Tyner considered going after Keyes, but they found nothing wrong with his representation. Forget it."

The Cayhall file at Kravitz & Bane had at least two inches of research and memos on the issue of Benjamin Keyes's representation. Ineffective assistance of trial counsel was a standard argument in death penalty appeals, but it had not been used in Sam's case. Goodman and Tyner had discussed it at length, bouncing long memos back and forth between their offices on the sixty-first and sixty-sixth floors in Chicago. The final memo declared that Keyes had done such a good job at trial that there was nothing to attack.

The file also included a three-page letter from Sam expressly forbidding any attack on Keyes. He would not sign any petition doing so, he promised.

The last memo, however, had been written seven years earlier at a time when death was a distant possibility. Things were different now. Issues had to be resurrected or even fabricated. It was time to grasp at straws.

"Where is Keyes now?" Adam asked.

"Last I heard he took a job in Washington. He wrote me about five years ago, said he wasn't practicing anymore. He took it pretty hard when we lost. I don't think either one of us expected it."

"You didn't expect to be convicted?"

"Not really. I had already beaten it twice, you know. And my jury the third time had eight whites, or Anglo-

Americans I should say. As bad as the trial went, I don't think I ever really believed they'd convict me."

"What about Keyes?"

"Oh, he was worried. We damned sure didn't take it lightly. We spent months preparing for the trial. He neglected his other clients, even his family, for weeks while we were getting ready. McAllister was popping off in the papers every day, it seemed, and the more he talked the more we worked. They released the list of potential jurors, four hundred of them, and we spent days investigating those people. His pretrial preparation was impeccable. We were not naive."

"Lee told me you considered disappearing."

"Oh, she did."

"Yeah, she told me last night."

He tapped the next cigarette on the counter, and admired it for a moment as if it might be his last. "Yeah, I thought about it. Almost thirteen years passed before McAllister came after me. I was a free man, hell I was forty-seven years old when the second trial ended and I returned home. Forty-seven years old, and I had been cleared by two juries, and all this was behind me. I was happy. Life was normal. I farmed and ran a sawmill, drank coffee in town and voted in every election. The Feds watched me for a few months, but I guess they became convinced I'd given up bombing. From time to time, a pesky reporter or journalist would show up in Clanton and ask questions, but nobody spoke to them. They were always from up North, dumb as hell, rude and ignorant, and they never stayed long. One came to the house one day, and wouldn't leave. Instead of getting the shotgun, I just turned the dogs loose on him and they chewed his ass up. Never came back." He chuckled to himself and lit the cigarette. "Not in my wildest dreams did I envision this. If I'd had the slightest inkling, the faintest clue that this might happen to me, then I would have been gone years ago. I was completely free, you understand, no restrictions. I would've gone to South America, changed my name, disappeared two or three times, then settled in some place like São Paulo or Rio."

"Like Mengele."

"Something like that. They never caught him, you know. They never caught a bunch of those guys. I'd be living right now in a nice little house, speaking Portuguese and laughing at fools like David McAllister." Sam shook his head and closed his eyes, and dreamed of what might have been.

"Why didn't you leave when McAllister started making noises?"

"Because I was foolish. It happened slowly. It was like a bad dream coming to life in small segments. First, McAllister got elected with all his promises. Then, a few months later Dogan got nailed by the IRS. I started hearing rumors and reading little things in the newspapers. But I simply refused to believe it could happen. Before I knew it, the FBI was following me and I couldn't run."

Adam looked at his watch and was suddenly tired. They had been talking for more than two hours, and he needed fresh air and sunshine. His head ached from the cigarette smoke, and the room was growing warmer by the moment. He screwed the cap on his pen and slid the legal pad into his briefcase. "I'd better go," he said in the direction of the screen. "I'll probably come back tomorrow for another round."

"I'll be here."

"Lucas Mann has given me the green light to visit anytime I want."

"A helluva guy, isn't he?"

"He's okay. Just doing his job."

"So's Naifeh and Nugent and all those other white folks."

"White folks?"

"Yeah, it's slang for the authorities. Nobody really wants to kill me, but they're just doing their jobs. There's this little moron with nine fingers who's the official executioner—the guy who mixes the gas and inserts the canister. Ask him what he's doing as they strap me in, and he'll say 'Just doing my job.' The prison chaplain and the prison doctor and the prison psychiatrist, along with the guards who'll escort me in and the medics who'll carry me out, well, they're nice folks, nothing really against me, but they're just doing their jobs."

"It won't get that far, Sam."

"Is that a promise?"

"No. But think positive."

"Yeah, positive thinking's real popular around here. Me and the boys are big on motivational shows, along with travel programs and home shopping. The Africans prefer 'Soul Train.' "

"Lee's worried about you, Sam. She wanted me to tell you she's thinking about you and praying for you."

Sam bit his bottom lip and looked at the floor. He nodded slowly but said nothing.

"I'll be staying with her for the next month or so."

"She's still married to that guy?"

"Sort of. She wants to see you."

"No."

"Why not?"

Sam carefully eased from his chair and knocked on the door behind him. He turned and looked at Adam through the screen. They watched each other until a guard opened the door and took Sam away.

FIFTEEN

"THE KID left an hour ago, with authorization, though I haven't seen it in writing," Lucas Mann explained to Phillip Naifeh, who was standing in his window watching a litter gang along the highway. Naifeh had a headache, a backache, and was in the middle of a generally awful day, which had included three early phone calls from the governor and two from Roxburgh, the Attorney General. Sam, of course, had been the reason for the calls.

"So he's got himself a lawyer," Naifeh said while gently pressing a fist in the center of his lower back.

"Yeah, and I really like this kid. He stopped by when he left and looked like he'd been run over by a truck. I think he and his grandfather are having a rough time of it."

"It'll get worse for the grandfather."

"It'll get worse for all of us."

"Do you know what the governor asked me? Wanted to know if he could have a copy of our manual on how to carry out executions. I told him no, that in fact he could not have a copy. He said he was the governor of this state and he felt as though he should have a copy. I tried to explain that it wasn't really a manual as such, just a loose-leaf little book in a black binder that gets heavily revised each time we gas someone. What's it called, he wanted to know. I said it's called nothing, actually, no official name because thankfully it's not used that much, but that on further thought I myself have referred to it as the little black book. He pushed a little harder, I got a little madder, we hung up, and fifteen minutes later his lawyer, that little hunchback fart with eyeglasses pinching his nose—"

"Larramore."

"Larramore called me and said that according to this code section and that code section he, the governor, has a right to a copy of the manual. I put him on hold, pulled the code sections, made him wait ten minutes, then we read the law together, and, of course, as usual, he's lying and bluffing and figuring I'm an imbecile. No such language in my copy of the code. I hung up on him. Ten minutes later the governor called back, all sugar and spice, told me to forget the little black book, that he's very concerned about Sam's constitutional rights and all, and just wants me to keep him posted as this thing unfolds. A real charmer." Naifeh shifted weight on his feet and changed fists in his back while staring at the window.

"Then, half an hour later Roxburgh calls, and guess what he wants to know? Wants to know if I've talked to the governor. You see, Roxburgh thinks he and I are real tight, old political pals, you know, and therefore we can trust each other. And so he tells me, confidentially of course, buddy to buddy, that he thinks the governor might try to exploit this execution for his own political gain."

"Nonsense!" Lucas hooted.

"Yeah, I told Roxburgh that I just couldn't believe he would think such a thing about our governor. I was real serious, and he got real serious, and we promised each other that we'd watch the governor real close and if we saw any sign that he was trying to manipulate this situation, then we'd call each other real quick. Roxburgh said there were some things he could do to neutralize the governor if he got out of line. I didn't dare ask what or how, but he seemed sure of himself."

"So who's the bigger fool?"

"Probably Roxburgh. But it's a tough call." Naifeh stretched carefully and walked to his desk. His shoes were off and his shirttail was out. He was in obvious pain. "Both have insatiable appetites for publicity. They're like two little boys scared to death that one will get a bigger piece of candy. I hate 'em both."

"Everybody hates them except the voters."

There was a sharp knock on the door, three solid raps delivered at precise intervals. "Must be Nugent," Naifeh said, and his pain suddenly intensified. "Come in."

The door opened quickly and Retired Colonel George Nugent marched into the room, pausing only slightly to close the door, and moved officially toward Lucas Mann, who did not stand but shook hands anyway. "Mr. Mann." Nugent greeted him crisply, then stepped forward and shook hands across the desk with Naifeh.

"Have a seat, George," Naifeh said, waving at an empty chair next to Mann. Naifeh wanted to order him to cut the military crap, but he knew it would do no good.

"Yes sir," Nugent answered as he lowered himself into the seat without bending his back. Though the only uniforms at Parchman were worn by guards and inmates, Nugent had managed to fashion one for himself. His shirt and pants were dark olive, perfectly matched and perfectly ironed with precise folds and creases, and they miraculously survived each day without the slightest wrinkling. The pants stopped a few inches above the ankles where they disappeared into a pair of black leather combat boots, shined and buffed at least twice a day to a state of perpetual sparkle. There had once been a weak rumor that a secretary or maybe a trustee had seen a spot of mud on one of the soles, but the rumor had not been confirmed.

The top button was left open to form an exact triangle which revealed a gray T-shirt. The pockets and sleeves were bare and unadorned, free of his medals and ribbons, and Naifeh had long suspected that this caused the colonel no small amount of humiliation. The haircut was strict military with bare skin above the ears and a thin layer of gray sprouts on top. Nugent was fifty-two, had served his country for thirty-four years, first as a buck private in Korea and later as a captain of some variety in Vietnam, where he fought the war from behind a desk. He'd been wounded in a jeep wreck and sent home with another ribbon.

For two years now Nugent had served admirably as an assistant superintendent, a trusted, loyal, and dependable underling of Naifeh's. He loved details and regulations and rules. He devoured manuals, and was constantly writing new procedures and directives and modifications for the warden to ponder. He was a significant pain in the warden's ass, but he was needed nonetheless. It was no secret that the colonel wanted Naifeh's job in a couple of years.

"George, me and Lucas have been talking about the Cayhall matter. Don't know how much you know about the appeals, but the Fifth Circuit lifted the stay and we're looking at an execution in four weeks."

"Yes sir," Nugent snapped, absorbing and itemizing every word. "I read about it in today's paper."

"Good. Lucas here is of the opinion that this one might come down, you know. Right, Lucas?"

"There's a good chance. Better than fifty-fifty." Lucas said this without looking at Nugent.

"How long have you been here, George?"

"Two years, one month."

The warden calculated something while rubbing his temples. "Did you miss the Parris execution?"

"Yes sir. By a few weeks," he answered with a trace of disappointment.

"So you haven't been through one?"

"No sir."

"Well, they're awful, George. Just awful. Worst part of this job, by far. Frankly, I'm just not up to it. I was hoping I'd retire before we used the chamber again, but now that looks doubtful. I need some help."

Nugent's back, though painfully stiff already, seemed to straighten even more. He nodded quickly, eyes dancing in all directions.

Naifeh delicately sat in his seat, grimacing as he eased onto the soft leather. "Since I'm just not up to it, George, Lucas and I were thinking that maybe you'd do a good job with this one."

The colonel couldn't suppress a smile. Then it quickly disappeared and was replaced with a most serious scowl. "I'm sure I can handle it, sir."

"I'm sure you can too." Naifeh pointed to a black binder on the corner of his desk. "We have a manual of sorts. There it is, the collected wisdom of two dozen visits to the gas chamber over the past thirty years."

Nugent's eyes narrowed and focused on the black book. He noticed that the pages were not all even and uniform, that an assortment of papers were actually folded and stuffed slovenly throughout the text, that the binder itself was worn and shabby. Within hours, he quickly decided, the manual would be transformed into a primer worthy of publication. That would be his first task. The paperwork would be immaculate.

"Why don't you read it tonight, and let's meet again tomorrow?"

"Yes sir," he said smugly.

"Not a word to anyone about this until we talk again, understood?"

"No sir."

Nugent nodded smartly at Lucas Mann, and left the office cradling the black book like a kid with a new toy. The door closed behind him.

"He's a nut," Lucas said.

"I know. We'll watch him."

"We'd better watch him. He's so damned gung-ho he might try to gas Sam this weekend."

Naifeh opened a desk drawer and retrieved a bottle of pills. He swallowed two without the assistance of water. "I'm going home, Lucas. I need to lie down. I'll probably die before Sam does."

"You'd better hurry."

THE PHONE CONVERSATION with E. Garner Goodman was brief. Adam explained with some measure of pride that he and Sam had a written agreement on representation, and that they had already spent four hours together though little had been accomplished. Goodman wanted a copy of the agreement, and Adam explained that there were no copies as of now, that the original was safely tucked away in a cell on death row, and, furthermore, there would be copies only if the client decided so.

Goodman promised to review the file and get to work. Adam gave him Lee's phone number and promised to check in every day. He hung up the phone and stared at two terrifying phone messages beside his computer. Both were from reporters, one from a Memphis newspaper and one from a television station in Jackson, Mississippi.

Baker Cooley had talked to both reporters. In fact, a TV crew from Jackson had presented itself to the firm's receptionist and left only after Cooley made threats.

All this attention had upset the tedious routine of the
Memphis branch of Kravitz & Bane. Cooley was not
happy about it. The other partners had little to say to
Adam. The secretaries were professionally polite, but
anxious to stay away from his office.

The reporters knew, Cooley had warned him
gravely. They knew about Sam and Adam, the grand-
son-grandfather angle, and while he wasn't sure how
they knew, it certainly hadn't come from him. He
hadn't told a soul, until, of course, word was already
out and he'd been forced to gather the partners and
associates together just before lunch and break the
news.

It was almost five o'clock. Adam sat at his desk with
the door shut, listening to the voices in the hall as
clerks and paralegals and other salaried staff made last
minute preparations to leave for the day. He decided
he would have nothing to say to the TV reporter. He
dialed the number for Todd Marks at the *Memphis
Press*. A recorded message guided him through the
wonders of voice mail, and after a couple of minutes,
Mr. Marks picked up his five-digit extension and said
hurriedly, "Todd Marks." He sounded like a teenager.

"This is Adam Hall, with Kravitz & Bane. I had a
note to call you."

"Yes, Mr. Hall," Marks gushed, instantly friendly
and no longer in a hurry. "Thanks for calling. I, uh,
well, we, uh, picked up a rumor about your handling
of the Cayhall case, and, uh, I was just trying to track
it down."

"I represent Mr. Cayhall," Adam said with measured words.

"Yes, well, that's what we heard. And, uh, you're
from Chicago?"

"I am from Chicago."

"I see. How, uh, did you get the case?"

"My firm has represented Sam Cayhall for seven years."

"Yes, right. But didn't he terminate your services recently?"

"He did. And now he's rehired the firm." Adam could hear keys pecking away as Marks gathered his words into a computer.

"I see. We heard a rumor, just a rumor, I guess, that Sam Cayhall is your grandfather."

"Where'd you hear this?"

"Well, you know, we have sources, and we have to protect them. Can't really tell you where it came from, you know."

"Yeah, I know." Adam took a deep breath and let Marks hang for a minute. "Where are you now?"

"At the paper."

"And where's that? I don't know the city."

"Where are you?" Marks asked.

"Downtown. In our office."

"I'm not far away. I can be there in ten minutes."

"No, not here. Let's meet somewhere else. A quiet little bar someplace."

"Fine. The Peabody Hotel is on Union, three blocks from you. There's a nice bar off the lobby called Mallards."

"I'll be there in fifteen minutes. Just me and you, okay?"

"Sure."

Adam hung up the phone. Sam's agreement contained some loose and ambiguous language that attempted to prevent his lawyer from talking to the press. The particular clause had major loopholes that any lawyer could walk through, but Adam did not wish to push the issue. After two visits, his grandfather was still nothing but a mystery. He didn't like lawyers and would readily fire another, even his own grandson.

* * *

MALLARDS was filling up quickly with young, weary professionals who needed a couple of stiff ones for the drive to the suburbs. Few people actually lived in downtown Memphis, so the bankers and brokers met here and in countless other bars and gulped beer in green bottles and sipped Swedish vodka. They lined the bar and gathered around the small tables to discuss the direction of the market and debate the future of the prime. It was a tony place, with authentic brick walls and real hardwood floors. A table by the door held trays of chicken wings and livers wrapped with bacon.

Adam spotted a young man in jeans holding a notepad. He introduced himself, and they went to a table in the corner. Todd Marks was no more than twenty-five. He wore wire-rimmed glasses and hair to his shoulders. He was cordial and seemed a bit nervous. They ordered Heinekens.

The notepad was on the table, ready for action, and Adam decided to take control. "A few ground rules," he said. "First, everything I say is off the record. You can't quote me on anything. Agreed?"

Marks shrugged as if this was okay but not exactly what he had in mind. "Okay," he said.

"I think you call it deep background, or something like that."

"That's it."

"I'll answer some questions for you, but not many. I'm here because I want you to get it right, okay?"

"Fair enough. Is Sam Cayhall your grandfather?"

"Sam Cayhall is my client, and he has instructed me not to talk to the press. That's why you can't quote me. I'm here to confirm or deny. That's all."

"Okay. But is he your grandfather?"

"Yes."

Marks took a deep breath and savored this incredible fact, which no doubt led to an extraordinary story. He could see the headlines.

Then he realized he should ask some more questions. He carefully took a pen from his pocket. "Who's your father?"

"My father is deceased."

A long pause. "Okay. So Sam is your mother's father?"

"No. Sam is my father's father."

"All right. Why do you have different last names?"

"Because my father changed his name."

"Why?"

"I don't want to answer that. I don't want to go into a lot of family background."

"Did you grow up in Clanton?"

"No. I was born there, but left when I was three years old. My parents moved to California. That's where I grew up."

"So you were not around Sam Cayhall?"

"No."

"Did you know him?"

"I met him yesterday."

Marks considered the next question, and thankfully the beer arrived. They sipped in unison and said nothing.

He stared at his notepad, scribbled something, then asked, "How long have you been with Kravitz & Bane?"

"Almost a year."

"How long have you worked on the Cayhall case?"

"A day and a half."

He took a long drink, and watched Adam as if he expected an explanation. "Look, uh, Mr. Hall—"

"It's Adam."

"Okay, Adam. There seem to be a lot of gaps here. Could you help me a bit?"

"No."

"All right. I read somewhere that Cayhall fired Kravitz & Bane recently. Were you working on the case when this happened?"

"I just told you I've been working on the case for a day and a half."

"When did you first go to death row?"

"Yesterday."

"Did he know you were coming?"

"I don't want to get into that."

"Why not?"

"This is a very confidential matter. I'm not going to discuss my visits to death row. I will confirm or deny only those things that you can verify elsewhere."

"Does Sam have other children?"

"I'm not going to discuss family. I'm sure your paper has covered this before."

"But it was a long time ago."

"Then look it up."

Another long drink, and another long look at the notepad. "What are the odds of the execution taking place on August 8?"

"It's very hard to say. I wouldn't want to speculate."

"But all the appeals have run, haven't they?"

"Maybe. Let's say I've got my work cut out for me."

"Can the governor grant a pardon?"

"Yes."

"Is that a possibility?"

"Rather unlikely. You'll have to ask him."

"Will your client do any interviews before the execution?"

"I doubt it."

Adam glanced at his watch as if he suddenly had to catch a plane. "Anything else?" he asked, then finished off the beer.

Marks stuck his pen in a shirt pocket. "Can we talk again?"

"Depends."

"On what?"

"On how you handle this. If you drag up the family stuff, then forget it."

"Must be some serious skeletons in the closet."

"No comment." Adam stood and offered a handshake. "Nice meeting you," he said as they shook hands.

"Thanks. I'll give you a call."

Adam walked quickly by the crowd at the bar, and disappeared through the hotel lobby.

SIXTEEN

O F ALL THE SILLY, nitpicking rules imposed upon inmates at the Row, the one that irritated Sam the most was the five-inch rule. This little nugget of regulatory brilliance placed a limit on the volume of legal papers a death row inmate could possess in his cell. The documents could be no thicker than five inches when placed on end and squeezed together. Sam's file was not much different from the other inmates', and after nine years of appellate warfare the file filled a large cardboard box. How in hell was he supposed to research and study and prepare with such limitations as the five-inch rule?

Packer had entered his cell on several occasions with a yardstick that he waved around like a bandleader, then carefully placed against the papers. Each time Sam had been over the limit; once being caught, according to Packer's assessment, with twenty-one inches. And each time Packer wrote an RVR, a rules violation report, and some more paperwork went into Sam's institutional file. Sam often wondered if his file in the main administration building was thicker than five inches. He hoped so. And who cared? They'd kept him in a cage for nine and a half years for the sole purpose of sustaining his life so they could one day take it. What else could they do to him?

Each time Packer had given him twenty-four hours to thin his file. Sam usually mailed a few inches to his brother in North Carolina. A few times he had reluctantly mailed an inch or two to E. Garner Goodman.

At the present time, he was about twelve inches over.
And he had a thin file of recent Supreme Court cases
under his mattress. And he had two inches next door
where Hank Henshaw watched it on the bookshelf.
And he had about three inches next door in J. B. Gullitt's stack of papers. Sam reviewed all documents and
letters for Henshaw and Gullitt. Henshaw had a fine
lawyer, one purchased with family money. Gullitt had
a fool from a big-shot firm in D.C. who'd never seen a
courtroom.

The three-book rule was another baffling limitation
on what inmates could keep in their cells. This rule
simply said that a death row inmate could possess no
more than three books. Sam owned fifteen, six in his
cell, and nine scattered among his clients on the Row.
He had no time for fiction. His collection was solely
law books about the death penalty and the Eighth
Amendment.

He had finished a dinner of boiled pork, pinto beans,
and corn bread, and he was reading a case from the
Ninth Circuit in California about an inmate who faced
his death so calmly his lawyers decided he must be
crazy. So they filed a series of motions claiming their
client was indeed too crazy to execute. The Ninth Circuit was filled with California liberals opposed to the
death penalty, and they jumped at this novel argument.
The execution was stayed. Sam liked this case. He had
wished many times that he had the Ninth Circuit looking down upon him instead of the Fifth.

Gullitt next door said, "Gotta kite, Sam," and Sam
walked to his bars. Flying a kite was the only method
of correspondence for inmates several cells away. Gullitt handed him the note. It was from Preacher Boy, a
pathetic white kid seven doors down. He had become a
country preacher at the age of fourteen, a regular hell-
fire-and-brimstoner, but that career was cut short and

perhaps delayed forever when he was convicted of the rape and murder of a deacon's wife. He was twenty-four now, a resident of the Row for three years, and had recently made a glorious return to the gospel. The note said:

Dear Sam, I am down here praying for you right now. I really believe God will step into this matter and stop this thing. But if he don't, I'm asking him to take you quickly, no pain or nothing, and take you home. Love, Randy.

How wonderful, thought Sam, they're already praying that I go quickly, no pain or nothing. He sat on the edge of his bed and wrote a brief message on a scrap of paper.

Dear Randy:
Thanks for the prayers. I need them. I also need one of my books. It's called Bronstein's *Death Penalty Review*. It's a green book. Send it down. Sam.

He handed it to J.B., and waited with his arms through the bars as the kite made its way along the tier. It was almost eight o'clock, still hot and muggy but mercifully growing dark outside. The night would lower the temperature to the high seventies, and with the fans buzzing away the cells became tolerable.

Sam had received several kites during the day. All had expressed sympathy and hope. All offered whatever help was available. The music had been quieter and the yelling that erupted occasionally when someone's rights were being tampered with had not occurred. For the second day, the Row had been a more peaceful place. The televisions rattled along all day and into the night, but the volume was lower. Tier A was noticeably calmer.

"Got myself a new lawyer," Sam said quietly as he leaned on his elbows with his hands hanging into the hallway. He wore nothing but his boxer shorts. He could see Gullitt's hands and wrists, but he could never see his face when they talked in their cells. Each day as Sam was led outside for his hour of exercise, he walked slowly along the tier and stared into the eyes of his comrades. And they stared at him. He had their faces memorized, and he knew their voices. But it was cruel to live next door to a man for years and have long conversations about life and death while looking only at his hands.

"That's good, Sam. I'm glad to hear it."

"Yeah. Pretty sharp kid, I think."

"Who is it?" Gullitt's hands were clasped together. They didn't move.

"My grandson." Sam said this just loud enough for Gullitt to hear. He could be trusted with secrets.

Gullitt's fingers moved slightly as he pondered this. "Your grandson?"

"Yep. From Chicago. Big firm. Thinks we might have a chance."

"You never told me you had a grandson."

"I hadn't seen him in twenty years. Showed up yesterday and told me he was a lawyer and wanted to take my case."

"Where's he been for the past ten years?"

"Growing up, I guess. He's just a kid. Twenty-six, I think."

"You're gonna let a twenty-six-year-old kid take your case?"

This irritated Sam a bit. "I don't exactly have a lot of choices at this moment in my life."

"Hell, Sam, you know more law than he does."

"I know, but it'll be nice to have a real lawyer out there typing up motions and appeals on real computers and filing them in the proper courts, you know. It'll be nice to have somebody who can run to court and argue with judges, somebody who can fight with the state on equal footing."

This seemed to satisfy Gullitt because he didn't speak for several minutes. His hands were still, but then he began rubbing his fingertips together and this of course meant something was bothering him. Sam waited.

"I've been thinking about something, Sam. All day long this has been eatin' at me."

"What is it?"

"Well, for three years now you've been right there and I've been right here, you know, and you're my best friend in the world. You're the only person I can trust, you know, and I don't know what I'm gonna do if they walk you down the hall and into the chamber. I mean, I've always had you right there to look over my legal stuff, stuff that I'll never understand, and you've always given me good advice and told me what to do. I can't trust my lawyer in D.C. He never calls me or writes me, and I don't know what the hell's going on with my case. I mean, I don't know if I'm a year away or five years away, and it's enough to drive me crazy. If it hadn't been for you, I'd be a nut case by now. And what if you don't make it?" By now his hands were jumping and thrusting with all sorts of intensity. His words stopped and his hands died down.

Sam lit a cigarette and offered one to Gullitt, the only person on death row with whom he'd share. Hank Henshaw, to his left, did not smoke. They puffed for a moment, each blowing clouds of smoke at the row of windows along the top of the hallway.

Sam finally said, "I'm not going anywhere, J.B. My lawyer says we've got a good chance."

"Do you believe him?"

"I think so. He's a smart kid."

"That must be weird, man, having a grandson as your lawyer. I can't imagine." Gullitt was thirty-one, childless, married, and often complained about his wife's jody, or free world boyfriend. She was a cruel woman who never visited and had once written a short letter with the good news that she was pregnant. Gullitt pouted for two days before admitting to Sam that he had beaten her for years and chased lots of women himself. She wrote again a month later and said she was sorry. A friend loaned her the money for an abortion, she explained, and she didn't want a divorce after all. Gullitt couldn't have been happier.

"It's somewhat strange, I guess," Sam said. "He looks nothing like me, but he favors his mother."

"So the dude just came right out and told you he was your long-lost grandson?"

"No. Not at first. We talked for a while and his voice sounded familiar. Sounded like his father's."

"His father is your son, right?"

"Yeah. He's dead."

"Your son is dead?"

"Yeah."

The green book finally arrived from Preacher Boy with another note about a magnificent dream he had just two nights ago. He had recently acquired the rare spiritual gift of dream interpretation, and couldn't wait to share it with Sam. The dream was still revealing itself to him, and once he had it all pieced together he would decode it and untangle it and illustrate it for Sam. It was good news, he already knew that much.

At least he's stopped singing, Sam said to himself as he finished the note and sat on his bed. Preacher Boy had also been a gospel singer of sorts and a songwriter on top of that, and periodically found himself seized with the spirit to the point of serenading the tier at full volume and at all hours of the day and night. He was an untrained tenor with little pitch but incredible volume, and the complaints came fast and furious when he belted his new tunes into the hallway. Packer himself usually intervened to stop the racket. Sam had even threatened to step in legally and speed up the kid's execution if the caterwauling didn't stop, a sadistic move that he later apologized for. The poor kid was just crazy, and if Sam lived long enough he planned to use an insanity strategy that he'd read about from the California case.

He reclined on his bed and began to read. The fan ruffled the pages and circulated the sticky air, but within minutes the sheets under him were wet. He slept in dampness until the early hours before dawn when the Row was almost cool and the sheets were almost dry.

SEVENTEEN

THE AUBURN HOUSE had never been a house or a home, but for decades had been a quaint little church of yellow brick and stained glass. It sat surrounded by an ugly chain-link fence on a shaded lot a few blocks from downtown Memphis. Graffiti littered the yellow brick and the stained glass windows had been replaced with plywood. The congregation had fled east years ago, away from the inner city, to the safety of the suburbs. They took their pews and songbooks, and even their steeple. A security guard paced along the fence ready to open the gate. Next door was a crumbling apartment building, and a block behind was a deteriorating federal housing project from which the patients of Auburn House came.

They were all young mothers, teenagers without exception whose mothers had also been teenagers and whose fathers were generally unknown. The average age was fifteen. The youngest had been eleven. They drifted in from the project with a baby on a hip and sometimes another one trailing behind. They came in packs of three and four and made their visits a social event. They came alone and scared. They gathered in the old sanctuary, which was now a waiting room where paperwork was required. They waited with their infants while their toddlers played under the seats. They chatted with their friends, other girls from the project who'd walked to Auburn House because cars were scarce and they were too young to drive.

Adam parked in a small lot to the side and asked the

security guard for directions. He examined Adam closely, then pointed to the front door where two young girls were holding babies and smoking. He entered between them, nodding and trying to be polite, but they only stared. Inside, he found a half dozen of the same mothers sitting in plastic chairs with children swarming at their feet. A young lady behind a desk pointed at a door and told him to take the hallway on the left.

The door to Lee's tiny office was open and she was talking seriously to a patient. She smiled at Adam. "I'll be five minutes," she said, holding something that appeared to be a diaper. The patient did not have a child with her, but one was due very shortly.

Adam eased along the hallway and found the men's room. Lee was waiting for him in the hall when he came out. They pecked each other on the cheek. "What do you think of our little operation?" she asked.

"What exactly do you do here?" They walked through the narrow corridor with worn carpet and peeling walls.

"Auburn House is a nonprofit organization staffed with volunteers. We work with young mothers."

"It must be depressing."

"Depends on how you look at it. Welcome to my office." Lee waved at her door and they stepped inside. The walls were covered with colorful charts, one showing a series of babies and the foods they eat; another listed in large, simple words the most common ailments of newborns; another cartoonish illustration hailed the benefits of condoms. Adam took a seat and assessed the walls.

"All of our kids come from the projects, so you can imagine the postnatal instruction they receive at home. None of them are married. They live with their mothers or aunts or grandmothers. Auburn House was founded by some nuns twenty years ago to teach these kids how to raise healthy babies."

Adam nodded at the condom poster. "And to prevent babies?"

"Yes. We're not family planners, don't want to be, but it doesn't hurt to mention birth control."

"Maybe you should do more than mention it."

"Maybe. Sixty percent of the babies born in this county last year were out of wedlock, and the numbers go up each year. And each year there are more cases of battered and abandoned children. It'll break your heart. Some of these little fellas don't have a chance."

"Who funds it?"

"It's all private. We spend half our time trying to raise money. We operate on a very lean budget."

"How many counselors like you?"

"A dozen or so. Some work a few afternoons a week, a few Saturdays. I'm lucky. I can afford to work here full-time."

"How many hours a week?"

"I don't know. Who keeps up with them? I get here around ten and leave after dark."

"And you do this for free?"

"Yeah. You guys call it pro bono, I think."

"It's different with lawyers. We do volunteer work to justify ourselves and the money we make, our little contribution to society. We still make plenty of money, you understand. This is a little different."

"It's rewarding."

"How'd you find this place?"

"I don't know. It was a long time ago. I was a member of a social club, a hot-tea-drinkers club, and we'd meet once a month for a lovely lunch and discuss ways to raise a few pennies for the less fortunate. One day a nun spoke to us about Auburn House, and we adopted it as our beneficiary. One thing led to another."

"And you're not paid a dime?"

"Phelps has plenty of money, Adam. In fact, I donate a lot of it to Auburn House. We have an annual fund-raiser now at the Peabody, black tie and champagne, and I make Phelps lean on his banker buddies to show up with their wives and fork over the money. Raised over two hundred thousand last year."

"Where does it go?"

"Some goes to overhead. We have two full-time staffers. The building is cheap but it still costs. The rest goes for baby supplies, medicine, and literature. There's never enough."

"So you sort of run the place?"

"No. We pay an administrator. I'm just a counselor."

Adam studied the poster behind her, the one with a bulky yellow condom snaking its way harmlessly across the wall. He gathered from the latest surveys and studies that these little devices were not being used by teenagers, in spite of television campaigns and school slogans and MTV spots by responsible rock stars. He could think of nothing worse than sitting in this cramped little room all day discussing diaper rashes with fifteen-year-old mothers.

"I admire you for this," he said, looking at the wall with the baby food poster.

Lee nodded but said nothing. Her eyes were tired and she was ready to go. "Let's go eat," she said.

"Where?"

"I don't know. Anywhere."

"I saw Sam today. Spent two hours with him."

Lee sunk in her seat, and slowly placed her feet on the desk. As usual, she was wearing faded jeans and a button-down.

"I'm his lawyer."

"He signed the agreement?"

"Yes. He prepared one himself, four pages. We both signed it, and so now it's up to me."

"Are you scared?"

"Terrified. But I can handle it. I talked to a reporter with the *Memphis Press* this afternoon. They've heard the rumor that Sam Cayhall is my grandfather."

"What did you tell him?"

"Couldn't really deny it, could I? He wanted to ask all kinds of questions about the family, but I told him little. I'm sure he'll dig around and find some more."

"What about me?"

"I certainly didn't tell him about you, but he'll start digging. I'm sorry."

"Sorry about what?"

"Sorry that maybe they'll expose your true identity. You'll be branded as the daughter of Sam Cayhall, murderer, racist, anti-Semite, terrorist, Klansman, the oldest man ever led to the gas chamber and gassed like an animal. They'll run you out of town."

"I've been through worse."

"What?"

"Being the wife of Phelps Booth."

Adam laughed at this, and Lee managed a smile. A middle-aged lady walked to the open door and told Lee she was leaving for the day. Lee jumped to her feet and quickly introduced her handsome young nephew, Adam Hall, a lawyer from Chicago, who was visiting for a spell. The lady was sufficiently impressed as she backed out of the office and disappeared down the hall.

"You shouldn't have done that," Adam said.

"Why not?"

"Because my name will be in the paper tomorrow—Adam Hall, lawyer from Chicago, and grandson."

Lee's mouth dropped an inch before she caught it. She then gave a shrug as if she didn't care, but Adam saw the fear in her eyes. What a stupid mistake, she was telling herself. "Who cares?" she said as she picked up her purse and briefcase. "Let's go find a restaurant."

THEY WENT to a neighborhood bistro, an Italian family place with small tables and few lights in a converted bungalow. They sat in a dark corner and ordered drinks, iced tea for her and mineral water for him. When the waiter left, Lee leaned over the table and said, "Adam, there's something I need to tell you."

He nodded but said nothing.

"I'm an alcoholic."

His eyes narrowed then froze. They'd had drinks together the last two nights.

"It's been about ten years now," she explained, still low over the table. The nearest person was fifteen feet away. "There were a lot of reasons, okay, some of which you could probably guess. I went through recovery, came out clean, and lasted about a year. Then, rehab again. I've been through treatment three times, the last was five years ago. It's not easy."

"But you had a drink last night. Several drinks."

"I know. And the night before. And today I emptied all the bottles and threw away the beer. There's not a drop in the apartment."

"That's fine with me. I hope I'm not the reason."

"No. But I need your help, okay. You'll be living with me for a couple of months, and we'll have some bad times. Just help me."

"Sure, Lee. I wish you'd told me when I arrived. I don't drink much. I can take it or leave it."

"Alcoholism is a strange animal. Sometimes I can watch people drink and it doesn't bother me. Then I'll see a beer commercial and break into a sweat. I'll see an ad in a magazine for a wine I used to enjoy, and the craving is so intense I'll become nauseated. It's an awful struggle."

The drinks arrived and Adam was afraid to touch his mineral water. He poured it over the ice and stirred it with a spoon. "Does it run in the family?" he asked, almost certain that it did.

"I don't think so. Sam would sneak around and drink a little when we were kids, but he kept it from us. My mother's mother was an alcoholic, so my mother never touched the stuff. I never saw it in the house."

"How'd it happen to you?"

"Gradually. When I left home I couldn't wait to give it a try because it was taboo when Eddie and I were growing up. Then I met Phelps, and he comes from a family of heavy social drinkers. It became an escape, and then it became a crutch."

"I'll do whatever I can. I'm sorry."

"Don't be sorry. I've enjoyed having a drink with you, but it's time to quit, okay. I've fallen off the wagon three times, and it all starts with the idea that I can have a drink or two and keep it under control. I went a month one time sipping wine and limiting myself to a glass a day. Then it was a glass and a half, then two, then three. Then rehab. I'm an alcoholic, and I'll never get over it."

Adam lifted his glass and touched it to hers. "Here's to the wagon. We'll ride it together." They gulped their soft drinks.

The waiter was a student with a quick idea of what they should eat. He suggested the chef's baked ravioli because it was simply the best in town and would be on the table in ten minutes. They agreed.

"I often wondered what you did with your time but I was afraid to ask," Adam said.

"I had a job once. After Walt was born and started

school I got bored, so Phelps found me a job with one of his friend's companies. Big salary, nice office. I had my own secretary who knew much more about my job than I did. I quit after a year. I married money, Adam, so I'm not supposed to work. Phelps's mother was appalled that I would draw a salary."

"What do rich women do all day long?"

"Carry the burdens of the world. They must first make sure hubby is off to work, then they must plan the day. The servants have to be directed and supervised. The shopping is divided into at least two parts—morning and afternoon—with the morning usually consisting of several rigorous phone calls to Fifth Avenue for the necessities. The afternoon shopping is sometimes actually done in person, with the driver waiting in the parking lot, of course. Lunch takes up most of the day because it requires hours to plan and at least two hours to execute. It's normally a small banquet attended by more of the same harried souls. Then there's the social responsibility part of being a rich woman. At least three times a week she attends tea parties in the homes of her friends where they nibble on imported biscuits and whimper about the plight of abandoned babies or mothers on crack. Then, it's back home in a hurry to freshen up for hubby's return from the office wars. She'll sip her first martini with him by the pool while four people prepare their dinner."

"What about sex?"

"He's too tired. Plus, he probably has a mistress."

"This is what happened to Phelps?"

"I guess, although he couldn't complain about the sex. I had a baby, I got older, and he's always had a steady supply of young blondes from his banks. You wouldn't believe his office. It's filled with gorgeous women with impeccable teeth and nails, all with short skirts and long legs. They sit behind nice desks and talk on the phone, and wait for his beck and call. He has a small bedroom next to a conference room. The man's an animal."

"So you gave up the hard life of a rich woman and moved out?"

"Yeah. I was not a very good rich woman, Adam. I hated it. It was fun for a very short while, but I didn't fit in. Not the right blood type. Believe it or not, my family was not known in the social circles of Memphis."

"You must be kidding."

"I swear. And to be a proper rich woman with a future in this city you have to come from a family of rich fossils, preferably with a great-grandfather who made money in cotton. I just didn't fit in."

"But you still play the social game."

"No. I still make appearances, but only for Phelps. It's important for him to have a wife who's his age but with a touch of gray, a mature wife who looks nice in an evening dress and diamonds and can hold her own while gabbing with his boring friends. We go out three times a year. I'm sort of an aging trophy wife."

"Seems to me like he'd want a real trophy wife, one of the slinky blondes."

"No. His family would be crushed, and there's a lot of money in trust. Phelps walks on eggshells around his family. When his parents are gone, then he'll be ready to come out of the closet."

"I thought his parents hated you."

"Of course they do. It's ironic that they're the reason we're still married. A divorce would be scandalous."

Adam laughed and shook his head in bewilderment. "This is crazy."

"Yes, but it works. I'm happy. He's happy. He has his little girls. I fool around with whomever I want. No questions are asked."

"What about Walt?"

She slowly sat her glass of tea on the table and looked away. "What about him?" she said, without looking.

"You never talk about him."

"I know," she said softly, still watching something across the room.

"Let me guess. More skeletons in the closet. More secrets."

She looked at him sadly, then gave a slight shrug as if to say, what the hell.

"He is, after all, my first cousin," Adam said. "And to my knowledge, and barring any further revelations, he's the only first cousin I have."

"You wouldn't like him."

"Of course not. He's part Cayhall."

"No. He's all Booth. Phelps wanted a son, why I don't know. And so we had a son. Phelps, of course, had little time for him. Always too busy with the bank. He took him to the country club and tried to teach him golf, but it didn't work. Walt never liked sports. They went to Canada once to hunt pheasants, and didn't speak to each other for a week when they came home. He wasn't a sissy, but he wasn't athletic either. Phelps was a big prep school jock—football, rugby, boxing, all that. Walt tried to play, but the talent just wasn't there. Phelps drove him even harder, and Walt rebelled. So, Phelps, with the typical heavy hand, sent him away to boarding school. My son left home at the age of fifteen."

"Where did he go to college?"

"He spent one year at Cornell, then dropped out."

"He dropped out?"

"Yes. He went to Europe after his freshman year, and he's been there ever since."

Adam studied her face and waited for more. He

sipped his water, and was about to speak when the waiter appeared and rapidly placed a large bowl of green salad between them.

"Why did he stay in Europe?"

"He went to Amsterdam and fell in love."

"A nice Dutch girl?"

"A nice Dutch boy."

"I see."

She was suddenly interested in the salad, which she served on her plate and began cutting into small pieces. Adam did likewise, and they ate in silence for a while as the bistro filled up and became noisier. An attractive couple of tired yuppies sat at the small table next to them and ordered strong drinks.

Adam smeared butter on a roll, took a bite, then asked, "How did Phelps react?"

She wiped the corners of her mouth. "The last trip Phelps and I took together was to Amsterdam to find our son. He'd been gone for almost two years. He'd written a few times and called me occasionally, but then all correspondence stopped. We were worried, of course, so we flew over and camped out in a hotel until we found him."

"What was he doing?"

"Working as a waiter in a café. Had an earring in each ear. His hair was chopped off. Weird clothes. He was wearing those damned clogs with wool socks. Spoke perfect Dutch. We didn't want to make a scene, so we asked him to come to our hotel. He did. It was horrible. Just horrible. Phelps handled it like the idiot he is, and the damage was irreparable. We left and came home. Phelps made a big production of redoing his will and revoking Walt's trust."

"He's never come home?"

"Never. I meet him in Paris once a year. We both arrive alone, that's the only rule. We stay in a nice hotel and spend a week together, roaming the city, eating the food, visiting the museums. It's the highlight of my year. But he hates Memphis."

"I'd like to meet him."

Lee watched him carefully, then her eyes watered. "Bless you. If you're serious, I'd love for you to go with me."

"I'm serious. I don't care if he's gay. I'd enjoy meeting my first cousin."

She took a deep breath and smiled. The ravioli arrived on two heaping plates with steam rising in all directions. A long loaf of garlic bread was placed along the edge of the table, and the waiter was gone.

"Does Walt know about Sam?" Adam asked.

"No. I've never had the guts to tell him."

"Does he know about me and Carmen? About Eddie? About any of our family's glorious history?"

"Yes, a little. When he was a little boy, I told him he had cousins in California, but that they never came to Memphis. Phelps, of course, told him that his California cousins were of a much lower social class and therefore not worthy of his attention. Walt was groomed by his father to be a snob, Adam, you must understand this. He attended the most prestigious prep schools, hung out at the nicest country clubs, and his family consisted of a bunch of Booth cousins who were all the same. They're all miserable people."

"What do the Booths think of having a homosexual in the family?"

"They hate him, of course. And he hates them."

"I like him already."

"He's not a bad kid. He wants to study art and paint. I send him money all the time."

"Does Sam know he has a gay grandson?"

"I don't think so. I don't know who would tell him."

"I probably won't tell him."

"Please don't. He has enough on his mind."

The ravioli cooled enough to eat, and they enjoyed it in silence. The waiter brought more water and tea. The couple next to them ordered a bottle of red wine, and Lee glanced at it more than once.

Adam wiped his mouth and rested for a moment. He leaned over the table. "Can I ask you something personal?" he said quietly.

"All your questions seem to be personal."

"Right. So can I ask you one more?"

"Please do."

"Well, I was just thinking. Tonight you've told me you're an alcoholic, your husband's an animal, and your son is gay. That's a lot for one meal. But is there anything else I should know?"

"Lemme see. Yes, Phelps is an alcoholic too, but he won't admit it."

"Anything else?"

"He's been sued twice for sexual harassment."

"Okay. Forget about the Booths. Any more surprises from our side of the family?"

"We haven't scratched the surface, Adam."

"I was afraid of that."

EIGHTEEN

A LOUD THUNDERSTORM rolled across the Delta before dawn, and Sam was awakened by the crack of lightning. He heard raindrops dropping hard against the open windows above the hallway. Then he heard them drip and puddle against the wall under the windows not far from his cell. The dampness of his bed was suddenly cool. Maybe today would not be so hot. Maybe the rain would linger and shade the sun, and maybe the wind would blow away the humidity for a day or two. He always had these hopes when it rained, but in the summer a thunderstorm usually meant soggy ground, which under a glaring sun meant nothing but more suffocating heat.

He raised his head and watched the rain fall from the windows and gather on the floor. The water flickered in the reflected light of a distant yellow bulb. Except for this faint light, the Row was dark. And it was silent.

Sam loved the rain, especially at night and especially in the summer. The State of Mississippi, in its boundless wisdom, had built its prison in the hottest place it could find. And it designed its Maximum Security Unit along the same lines as an oven. The windows to the outside were small and useless, built that way for security reasons, of course. The planners of this little branch of hell also decided that there would be no ventilation of any sort, no chance for a breeze getting in or the dank air getting out. And after they built what they considered to be a model penal facility, they decided they would not air condition it. It would sit proudly beside the soybeans and cotton, and absorb the same heat and moisture from the ground. And when the land was dry, the Row would simply bake along with the crops.

But the State of Mississippi could not control the weather, and when the rains came and cooled the air, Sam smiled to himself and offered a small prayer of thanks. A higher being was in control after all. The state was helpless when it rained. It was a small victory.

He eased to his feet and stretched his back. His bed consisted of a piece of foam, six feet by two and a half, four inches thick, otherwise known as a mattress. It rested on a metal frame fastened securely to the floor and wall. It was covered with two sheets. Sometimes they passed out blankets in the winter. Back pain was common throughout the Row, but with time the body adjusted and there were few complaints. The prison doctor was not considered to be a friend of death row inmates.

He took two steps and leaned on his elbows through the bars. He listened to the wind and thunder, and watched the drops bounce along the windowsill and splatter on the floor. How nice it would be to step through that wall and walk through the wet grass on the other side, to stroll around the prison grounds in the driving rain, naked and crazy, soaking wet with water dripping from his hair and beard.

The horror of death row is that you die a little each day. The waiting kills you. You live in a cage and when you wake up you mark off another day and you tell yourself that you are now one day closer to death.

Sam lit a cigarette and watched the smoke float upward toward the raindrops. Weird things happen with our absurd judicial system. Courts rule this way one day and the other way the next. The same judges reach different conclusions on familiar issues. A court will ignore a wild motion or appeal for years, then one day embrace it and grant relief. Judges die and they're replaced by judges who think differently. Presidents come and go and they appoint their pals to the bench. The Supreme Court drifts one way, then another.

At times, death would be welcome. And if given the choice of death on one hand, or life on death row on the other, Sam would quickly take the gas. But there was always hope, always the slight glimmering promise that something somewhere in the vast maze of the judicial jungle would strike a chord with someone, and his case would be reversed. Every resident of the Row dreamed of the miracle reversal from heaven. And their dreams sustained them from one miserable day to the next.

Sam had recently read that there were almost twenty-five hundred inmates sentenced to die in America, and last year, 1989, only sixteen were executed. Mississippi had executed only four since 1977, the year Gary Gilmore insisted on a firing squad in Utah. There was safety in those numbers. They fortified his resolve to file even more appeals.

He smoked through the bars as the storm passed and the rain stopped. He took his breakfast as the sun rose, and at seven o'clock he turned on the television for the morning news. He had just bitten into a piece of cold toast when suddenly his face appeared on the screen behind a Memphis morning anchorperson. She eagerly reported the thrilling top story of the day, the bizarre case of Sam Cayhall and his new lawyer. Seems his new lawyer was his long-lost grandson, one Adam Hall, a young lawyer from the mammoth Chicago firm of Kravitz & Bane, the outfit who'd represented Sam for the past seven years or so. The photo of Sam was at least ten years old, the same one they used every time his name was mentioned on TV or in print. The photo of Adam was a bit stranger. He obviously had not posed for it. Someone had snapped it outdoors while he wasn't looking. She explained with wild eyes that the *Memphis Press* was reporting this morning that Adam Hall had confirmed that he was in fact the grandson of Sam Cayhall. She gave a fleeting sketch of Sam's crime, and twice gave the date of his pending execution. More on the story later, she promised, perhaps maybe as soon as the "Noon Report." Then she was off on the morning summary of last night's murders.

Sam threw the toast on the floor next to the bookshelves and stared at it. An insect found it almost immediately and crawled over and around it a half dozen times before deciding it wasn't worth eating. His lawyer had already talked to the press. What do they teach these people in law school? Do they give instruction on media control?

"Sam, you there?" It was Gullitt.

"Yeah. I'm here."

"Just saw you on channel four."

"Yeah. I saw it."

"You pissed?"

"I'm okay."

"Take a deep breath, Sam. It's okay."

Among men sentenced to die in the gas chamber, the expression "Take a deep breath" was used often and considered nothing more than an effort at humor. They said it to each other all the time, usually when one was angry. But when used by the guards it was far from funny. It was a constitutional violation. It had been mentioned in more than one lawsuit as an example of the cruel treatment dispensed on death row.

Sam agreed with the insect and ignored the rest of his breakfast. He sipped coffee and stared at the floor.

AT NINE-THIRTY, Sergeant Packer was on the tier looking for Sam. It was time for his hour of fresh air. The rains were far away and the sun was blistering the Delta. Packer had two guards with him and a pair of leg irons. Sam pointed at the chains, and asked, "What are they for?"

"They're for security, Sam."

"I'm just going out to play, aren't I?"

"No, Sam. We're taking you to the law library. Your lawyer wants to meet you there so y'all can talk amongst the law books. Now turn around."

Sam stuck both hands through the opening of his door. Packer cuffed them loosely, then the door opened and Sam stepped into the hall. The guards dropped to their knees and were securing the leg irons when Sam asked Packer, "What about my hour out?"

"What about it?"

"When do I get it?"

"Later."

"You said that yesterday and I didn't get my rec time. You lied to me yesterday. Now you're lying to me again. I'll sue you for this."

"Lawsuits take a long time, Sam. They take years."

"I want to talk to the warden."

"And I'm sure he wants to talk to you too, Sam. Now, do you want to see your lawyer or not?"

"I have a right to my lawyer and I have a right to my rec time."

"Get off his ass, Packer!" Hank Henshaw shouted from less than six feet away.

"You lie, Packer! You lie!" J. B. Gullitt added from the other side.

"Down, boys," Packer said coolly. "We'll take care of old Sam, here."

"Yeah, you'd gas him today if you could," Henshaw yelled.

The leg irons were in place, and Sam shuffled into his cell to get a file. He clutched it to his chest and waddled down the tier with Packer at his side and the guards following.

"Give 'em hell, Sam," Henshaw yelled as they walked away.

There were other shouts of support for Sam and catcalls at Packer as they left the tier. They were cleared through a set of doors and Tier A was behind them.

"The warden says you get two hours out this afternoon, and two hours a day till it's over," Packer said as they moved slowly through a short hallway.

"Till what's over?"

"This thang."

"What thang?"

Packer and most of the guards referred to an execution as a thang.

"You know what I mean," Packer said.

"Tell the warden he's a real sweetheart. And ask him if I get two hours if this thang doesn't go off, okay? And while you're at it, tell him I think he's a lying son of a bitch."

"He already knows."

They stopped at a wall of bars and waited for the door to open. They passed through it and stopped again by two guards at the front door. Packer made quick notes on a clipboard, and they walked outside where a white van was waiting. The guards took Sam by the arms and lifted him and his chains into the side door. Packer sat in the front with the driver.

"Does this thing have air conditioning?" Sam snapped at the driver, whose window was down.

"Yep," the driver said as they backed away from the front of MSU.

"Then turn the damned thing on, okay."

"Knock it off, Sam," Packer said without conviction.

"It's bad enough to sweat all day in a cage with no air conditioning, but it's pretty stupid to sit here and suffocate. Turn the damned thing on. I've got my rights."

"Take a deep breath, Sam," Packer drawled, and winked at the driver.

"That'll cost you, Packer. You'll wish you hadn't said that."

The driver hit a switch and the air started blowing. The van was cleared through the double gates and slowly made its way down the dirt road away from the Row.

Though he was handcuffed and shackled, this brief journey on the outside was refreshing. Sam stopped the bitching and immediately ignored the others in the van. The rains had left puddles in the grassy ditches beside the road, and they had washed the cotton plants, now more than knee-high. The stalks and leaves were dark green. Sam remembered picking cotton as a boy, then quickly dismissed the thought. He had trained his mind to forget the past, and on those rare occasions when a childhood memory flashed before him, he quickly snuffed it out.

The van crept along, and he was thankful for this. He stared at two inmates sitting under a tree watching a buddy lift weights in the sun. There was a fence around them, but how nice, he thought, to be outside walking and talking, exercising and lounging, never giving a thought to the gas chamber, never worrying about the last appeal.

*   *   *

THE LAW LIBRARY was known as the Twig because it was too small to be considered a full branch. The main prison law library was deeper into the farm, at another camp. The Twig was used exclusively by death row inmates. It was stuck to the rear of an administration building, with only one door and no windows. Sam had been there many times during the past nine years. It was a small room with a decent collection of current law books and up-to-date reporting services. A battered conference table sat in the center with shelves of books lining the four walls. Every now and then a trustee would volunteer to serve as the librarian, but good help was hard to find and the books were seldom where they were supposed to be. This irritated Sam immensely because he admired neatness and he despised the Africans, and he was certain that most if not all of the librarians were black, though he did not know this for a fact.

The two guards unshackled Sam at the door.

"You got two hours," Packer said.

"I got as long as I want," Sam said, rubbing his wrists as if the handcuffs had broken them.

"Sure, Sam. But when I come after you in two hours, I'll bet we load your gimpy little ass into the van."

Packer opened the door as the guards took their positions beside it. Sam entered the library and slammed the door behind him. He laid his file on the table and stared at his lawyer.

Adam stood at the far end of the conference table, holding a book and waiting for his client. He'd heard voices outside, and he watched Sam enter the room without guards or handcuffs. He stood there in his red jumpsuit, much smaller now without the thick metal screen between them.

They studied each other for a moment across the table, grandson and grandfather, lawyer and client, stranger and stranger. It was an awkward interval in which they sized each other up and neither knew what to do with the other.

"Hello, Sam," Adam said, walking toward him.

"Mornin'. Saw us on TV a few hours ago."

"Yeah. Have you seen the paper?"

"Not yet. It comes later."

Adam slid the morning paper across the table and Sam stopped it. He held it with both hands, eased into a chair, and raised the paper to within six inches of his nose. He read it carefully and studied the pictures of himself and Adam.

Todd Marks had evidently spent most of the evening digging and making frantic phone calls. He had verified that one Alan Cayhall had been born in Clanton, in Ford County, in 1964, and the father's name listed on the birth certificate was one Edward S. Cayhall. He checked the birth certificate for Edward S. Cayhall and found that his father was Samuel Lucas Cayhall, the same man now on death row. He reported that Adam Hall had confirmed that his father's name had been changed in California, and that his grandfather was Sam Cayhall. He was careful not to attribute direct quotes to Adam, but he nonetheless violated their agreement. There was little doubt the two had talked.

Quoting unnamed sources, the story explained how Eddie and his family left Clanton in 1967 after Sam's arrest, and fled to California where Eddie later killed himself. The trail ended there because Marks obviously ran out of time late in the day and could confirm nothing from California. The unnamed source or sources didn't mention Sam's daughter living in Memphis, so Lee was spared. The story ran out of steam with a series of no-comments from Baker Cooley, Garner Goodman, Phillip Naifeh, Lucas Mann, and a lawyer with the Attorney General's office in Jackson. Marks finished strong, though, with a sensational recap of the Kramer bombing.

The story was on the front page of the *Press,* above the main headline. The ancient picture of Sam was to the right, and next to it was a strange photo of Adam from the waist up. Lee had brought the paper to him hours earlier as he sat on the terrace and watched the early morning river traffic. They drank coffee and juice, and read and reread the story. After much analysis, Adam had decided that Todd Marks had placed a photographer across the street from the Peabody Hotel, and when Adam left their little meeting yesterday and stepped onto the sidewalk, he got his picture taken. The suit and tie were definitely worn yesterday.

"Did you talk to this clown?" Sam growled as he placed the paper on the table. Adam sat across from him.

"We met."

"Why?"

"Because he called our office in Memphis, said he'd heard some rumors, and I wanted him to get it straight. It's no big deal."

"Our pictures on the front page is no big deal?"

"You've been there before."

"And you?"

"I didn't exactly pose. It was an ambush, you see. But I think I look rather dashing."

"Did you confirm these facts for him?"

"I did. We agreed it would be background, and he could not quote me on anything. Nor was he supposed to use me as a source. He violated our agreement, and ripped his ass with me. He also planted a photographer, so I've spoken for the first and last time to the *Memphis Press.*"

Sam looked at the paper for a moment. He was relaxed, and his words were as slow as ever. He managed a trace of a smile. "And you confirmed that you are my grandson?"

"Yes. Can't really deny it, can I?"

"Do you want to deny it?"

"Read the paper, Sam. If I wanted to deny it, would it be on the front page?"

This satisfied Sam, and the smile grew a bit. He bit his lip and stared at Adam. Then he methodically removed a fresh pack of cigarettes, and Adam glanced around for a window.

After the first one was properly lit, Sam said, "Stay away from the press. They're ruthless and they're stupid. They lie and they make careless mistakes."

"But I'm a lawyer, Sam. It's inbred."

"I know. It's hard, but try to control yourself. I don't want it to happen again."

Adam reached into his briefcase, smiled, and pulled out some papers. "I have a wonderful idea how to save your life." He rubbed his hands together, then removed a pen from his pocket. It was time for work.

"I'm listening."

"Well, as you might guess, I've been doing a lot of research."

"That's what you're paid to do."

"Yes. And I've come up with a marvelous little theory, a new claim that I intend to file on Monday. The theory is simple. Mississippi is one of only five states still using the gas chamber, right?"

"That's right."

"And the Mississippi Legislature in 1984 passed a law giving a condemned man the choice of dying by lethal injection or in the gas chamber. But the new law applies only to those convicted after July 1, 1984. Doesn't apply to you."

"That's correct. I think about half the guys on the Row will get their choice. It's years away, though."

"One of the reasons the legislature approved lethal injection was to make the killings more humane. I've studied the legislative history behind the law and there was a lot of discussion of problems the state's had with gas chamber executions. The theory is simple: Make the executions quick and painless, and there will be fewer constitutional claims that they are cruel. Lethal injections raise fewer legal problems, thus the killings are easier to carry out. Our theory, then, is that since the state has adopted lethal injection, it has in effect said that the gas chamber is obsolete. And why is it obsolete? Because it's a cruel way to kill people."

Sam puffed on this for a minute and nodded slowly. "Keep going," he said.

"We attack the gas chamber as a method of execution."

"Do you limit it to Mississippi?"

"Probably. I know there were problems with Teddy Doyle Meeks and Maynard Tole."

Sam snorted and blew smoke across the table. "Problems? You could say that."

"How much do you know?"

"Come on. They died within fifty yards of me. We sit in our cells all day long and think about death. Everyone on the Row knows what happened to those boys."

"Tell me about them."

Sam leaned forward on his elbows and stared absently at the newspaper in front of him. "Meeks was the first execution in Mississippi in ten years, and they didn't know what they were doing. It was 1982. I'd been here for almost two years, and until then we were living in a dream world. We never thought about the gas chamber and cyanide pellets and last meals. We were sentenced to die, but, hell, they weren't killing anyone, so why worry? But Meeks woke us up. They killed him, so they could certainly kill the rest of us."

"What happened to him?" Adam had read a dozen stories about the botched execution of Teddy Doyle Meeks, but he wanted to hear it from Sam.

"Everything went wrong. Have you seen the chamber?"

"Not yet."

"There's a little room off to the side where the executioner mixes his solution. The sulfuric acid is in a canister that he takes from his little laboratory to a tube running into the bottom of the chamber. With Meeks, the executioner was drunk."

"Come on, Sam."

"I didn't see him, okay. But everyone knows he was drunk. State law designates an official state executioner, and the warden and his gang didn't think about it until just a few hours before the execution. Keep in mind, no one thought Meeks would die. We were all waiting on a last minute stay, because he'd been through it twice already. But there was no stay, and they scrambled around at the last minute trying to locate the official state executioner. They found him, drunk. He was a plumber, I think. Anyway, his first batch of brew didn't work. He placed the canister into the tube, pulled a lever, and everyone waited for Meeks to take a deep breath and die. Meeks held his breath as long as he could, then inhaled. Nothing happened. They waited. Meeks waited. The witnesses waited. Everybody slowly turned to the executioner, who was also waiting and cussing. He went back to his little room, and fixed up another mix of sulfuric acid. Then he had to retrieve the old canister from the chute, and that took ten minutes. The warden and Lucas Mann and the rest of the goons were standing around waiting and fidgeting and cussing this drunk plumber, who finally plugged in the new canister and pulled the lever. This time the sulfuric acid landed where it was supposed to—in a bowl under the chair where Meeks was strapped. The executioner pulled the second lever dropping the cyanide pellets, which were also under the chair, hovering above the sulfuric acid. The pellets dropped, and sure enough, the gas drifted upward to where old Meeks was holding his breath again. You can see the vapors, you know. When he finally sucked in a noseful of it, he started shaking and jerking, and this went on quite a while. For some reason, there's a metal pole that runs from the top of the chamber to the bottom, and it's directly behind the chair. Just about the time Meeks got still and everybody thought he was dead, his head started banging back and forth, striking this pole, just beating it like hell. His eyes were rolled back, his lips were wide open, he was foaming at the mouth, and there he was beating the back of his head in on this pole. It was sick."

"How long did it take to kill him?"

"Who knows. According to the prison doctor, death was instant and painless. According to some of the eyewitnesses, Meeks convulsed and heaved and pounded his head for five minutes."

The Meeks execution had provided death penalty abolitionists with much ammunition. There was little doubt he had suffered greatly, and many accounts were written of his death. Sam's version was remarkably consistent with those of the eyewitnesses.

"Who told you about it?" Adam asked.

"A couple of the guards talked about it. Not to me, of course, but word spread quickly. There was a public outcry, which would've been even worse if Meeks hadn't been such a despicable person. Everyone hated him. And his little victim had suffered greatly, so it was hard to feel sympathetic."

"Where were you when he was executed?"

"In my first cell, Tier D, on the far side away from

the chamber. They locked everybody down that night, every inmate at Parchman. It happened just after midnight, which is sort of amusing because the state has a full day to carry out the execution. The death warrant does not specify a certain time, just a certain day. So these gung-ho bastards are just itching to do it as soon as possible. They plan every execution for one minute after midnight. That way, if there's a stay, then they have the entire day for their lawyers to get it lifted. Buster Moac went down that way. They strapped him in at midnight, then the phone rang and they took him back to the holding room where he waited and sweated for six hours while the lawyers ran from one court to the next. Finally, as the sun was rising, they strapped him in for the last time. I guess you know what his last words were."

Adam shook his head. "I have no idea."

"Buster was a friend of mine, a class guy. Naifeh asked him if he had any last words, and he said yes, as a matter of fact, he did have something to say. He said the steak they'd cooked for his last meal was a bit too rare. Naifeh mumbled something to the effect that he'd speak to the cook about it. Then Buster asked if the governor had granted a last minute pardon. Naifeh said no. Buster then said, 'Well, tell that son of a bitch he's lost my vote.' They slammed the door and gassed him."

Sam was obviously amused by this, and Adam was obliged to offer an awkward laugh. He looked at his legal pad while Sam lit another cigarette.

Four years after the execution of Teddy Doyle Meeks, the appeals of Maynard Tole reached a dead end and it was time for the chamber to be used again. Tole was a Kravitz & Bane pro bono project. A young lawyer named Peter Wiesenberg represented Tole, under the supervision of E. Garner Goodman. Both

Wiesenberg and Goodman witnessed the execution, which in many ways was dreadfully similar to Meeks's. Adam had not discussed the Tole execution with Goodman, but he'd studied the file and read the eyewitness accounts written by Wiesenberg and Goodman.

"What about Maynard Tole?" Adam asked.

"He was an African, a militant who killed a bunch of people in a robbery and, of course, blamed everything on the system. Always referred to himself as an African warrior. He threatened me several times, but for the most part he was just selling wolf."

"Selling wolf?"

"Yeah, that means a guy is talking bad, talking trash. It's common with the Africans. They're all innocent, you know. Every damned one of them. They're here because they're black and the system is white, and even though they've raped and murdered it's someone else's fault. Always, always someone else's fault."

"So you were happy when he went?"

"I didn't say that. Killing is wrong. It's wrong for the Africans to kill. It's wrong for the Anglos to kill. And it's wrong for the people of the State of Mississippi to kill death row inmates. What I did was wrong, so how do you make it right by killing me?"

"Did Tole suffer?"

"Same as Meeks. They found them a new executioner and he got it right the first time. The gas hit Tole and he went into convulsions, started banging his head on the pole just like Meeks, except Tole evidently had a harder head because he kept beating the pole with it. It went on and on, and finally Naifeh and the goon squad got real anxious because the boy wouldn't die and things were getting sloppy, so they actually made the witnesses leave the witness room. It was pretty nasty."

"I read somewhere that it took ten minutes for him to die."

"He fought it hard, that's all I know. Of course, the warden and his doctor said death was instant and painless. Typical. They did, however, make one slight change in their procedure after Tole. By the time they got to my buddy Moac, they had designed this cute little head brace made of leather straps and buckles and attached to that damned pole. With Moac, and later with Jumbo Parris, they belted their heads down so tight there was no way they could flop around and whip the pole. A nice touch, don't you think? That makes it easier on Naifeh and the witnesses because now they don't have to watch as much suffering."

"You see my point, Sam? It's a horrible way to die. We attack the method. We find witnesses who'll testify about these executions and we try to convince a judge to rule the gas chamber unconstitutional."

"So what? Do we then ask for lethal injection? What's the point? Seems kind of silly for me to say I prefer not to die in the chamber, but, what the hell, lethal injection will do just fine. Put me on the gurney and fill me up with drugs. I'll be dead, right? I don't get it."

"True. But we buy ourselves some time. We'll attack the gas chamber, get a temporary stay, then pursue it through the higher courts. We could jam this thing for years."

"It's already been done."

"What do you mean it's already been done?"

"Texas, 1983. Case called *Larson*. The same arguments were made with no result. The court said gas chambers have been around for fifty years, and they've proven themselves quite efficient at killing humanely."

"Yeah, but there's one big difference."

"What?"

"This ain't Texas. Meeks and Tole and Moac and Parris weren't gassed in Texas. And, by the way, Texas has already gone to lethal injection. They threw away their gas chamber because they found a better way to kill. Most gas chamber states have traded them in for better technology."

Sam stood and walked to the other end of the table. "Well, when it's my time, I damned sure want to go with the latest technology." He paced along the table, back and forth three or four times, then stopped. "It's eighteen feet from one end of this room to the other. I can walk eighteen feet without hitting bars. Do you realize what it's like spending twenty-three hours a day in a cell that's six feet by nine? This is freedom, man." He paced some more, puffing as he came and went.

Adam watched the frail figure bounce along the edge of the table with a trail of smoke behind him. He had no socks and wore navy-colored rubber shower shoes that squeaked when he paced. He suddenly stopped, yanked a book from a shelf, threw it hard on the table, and began flipping pages with a flourish. After a few minutes of intense searching, he found exactly what he was looking for and spent five minutes reading it.

"Here it is," he mumbled to himself. "I knew I'd read this before."

"What is it?"

"A 1984 case from North Carolina. The man's name was Jimmy Old, and evidently Jimmy did not want to die. They had to drag him into the chamber, kicking and crying and screaming, and it took a while to strap him in. They slammed the door and dropped the gas, and his chin crashed onto his chest. Then his head rolled back and began twitching. He turned to the witnesses who could see nothing but the whites of his eyeballs, and he began salivating. His head rocked and swung around forever while his body shook and his mouth foamed. It went on and on, and one of the witnesses, a journalist, vomited. The warden got fed up with it and closed the black curtains so the witnesses couldn't see anymore. They estimate it took fourteen minutes for Jimmy Old to die."

"Sounds cruel to me."

Sam closed the book and placed it carefully onto the shelf. He lit a cigarette and studied the ceiling. "Virtually every gas chamber was built long ago by Eaton Metal Products in Salt Lake City. I read somewhere that Missouri's was built by inmates. But our little chamber was built by Eaton, and they're all basically the same—made of steel, octagonal in shape with a series of windows placed here and there so folks can watch the death. There's not much room inside the actual chamber, just a wooden seat with straps all over it. There's a metal bowl directly under the chair, and just inches above the bowl is a little bag of cyanide tablets that the executioner controls with a lever. He also controls the sulfuric acid, which is introduced into the affair by means of the canister. The canister makes its way through a tube to the bowl, and when the bowl fills with acid, he pulls the lever and drops the cyanide pellets. This causes the gas, which of course causes death, which of course is designed to be painless and quick."

"Wasn't it designed to replace the electric chair?"

"Yes. Back in the twenties and thirties, everyone had an electric chair, and it was just the most marvelous device ever invented. I remember as a boy they had a portable electric chair that they simply loaded into a trailer and took around to the various counties. They'd pull up at the local jail, bring 'em out in shackles, line 'em up outside the trailer, then run 'em through. It was an efficient way to alleviate overcrowded jails." He shook his head in disbelief. "Anyway, they, of course, had no idea what they were doing, and there were some horrible stories of people suffering. This is capital punishment, right? Not capital torture. And it wasn't just Mississippi. Many states were using these old, half-ass rigged electric chairs with a bunch of jakelegs pulling the switches, and there were all sorts of problems. They'd strap in some poor guy, pull the switch, give him a good jolt but not good enough, guy was roasting on the inside but wouldn't die, so they'd wait a few minutes, and hit him again. This might go on for fifteen minutes. They wouldn't fasten the electrodes properly, and it was not uncommon for flames and sparks to shoot from the eyes and ears. I read an account of a guy who received an improper voltage. The steam built up in his head and his eyeballs popped out. Blood ran down his face. During an electrocution, the skin gets so hot that they can't touch the guy for a while, so in the old days they had to let him cool off before they could tell if he was dead. There are lots of stories about men who would sit still after the initial jolt, then start breathing again. So they would of course hit 'em with another current. This might happen four or five times. It was awful, so this Army doctor invented the gas chamber as a more humane way to kill people. It is now, as you say, obsolete because of lethal injection."

Sam had an audience, and Adam was captivated. "How many men have died in Mississippi's chamber?" he asked.

"It was first used here in 1954, or thereabouts. Between then and 1970, they killed thirty-five men. No women. After *Furman* in 1972, it sat idle until Teddy Doyle Meeks in 1982. They've used it three times since then, so that's a total of thirty-nine. I'll be number forty."

He began pacing again, now much slower. "It's a terribly inefficient way to kill people," he said, much like a professor in front of a classroom. "And it's dangerous. Dangerous of course to the poor guy strapped in the chair, but also to those outside the chamber. These damned things are old and they all leak to some degree. The seals and gaskets rot and crumble, and the cost of building a chamber that will not leak is prohibitive. A small leak could be deadly to the executioner or anyone standing nearby. There are always a handful of people—Naifeh, Lucas Mann, maybe a minister, the doctor, a guard or two—standing in the little room just outside the chamber. There are two doors to this little room, and they are always closed during an execution. If any of the gas leaked from the chamber into the room, it would probably hit Naifeh or Lucas Mann and they'd croak right there on the floor. Not a bad idea, come to think of it.

"The witnesses are also in a great deal of danger, and they don't have a clue. There's nothing between them and the chamber except for a row of windows, which are old and equally subject to leakage. They're also in a small room with the door closed, and if there's a gas leak of any size these gawking fools get gassed too.

"But the real danger comes afterward. There's a wire they stick to your ribs and it runs through a hole in the chamber to outside where a doctor monitors the heartbeat. Once the doctor says the guy is dead, they open a valve on top of the chamber and the gas is supposed to evaporate. Most of it does. They'll wait fifteen minutes or so, then open the door. The cooler air from the outside that's used to evacuate the chamber causes a problem because it mixes with the remaining gas and condenses on everything inside. It creates a death trap for anyone going in. It's extremely dangerous, and most of these clowns don't realize how serious it is. There's a residue of prussic acid on everything—walls, windows, floor, ceiling, door, and, of course, the dead guy.

"They spray the chamber and the corpse with ammonia to neutralize the remaining gas, then the removal team or whatever it's called goes in with oxygen masks. They'll wash the inmate a second time with ammonia or chlorine bleach because the poison oozes through the pores in the skin. While he's still strapped in the chair, they cut his clothes off, put them in a bag, and burn them. In the old days they allowed the guy to wear only a pair of shorts so their job would be easier. But now they're such sweethearts they allow us to wear whatever we want. So if I get that far, I'll have a hell of a time selecting my wardrobe."

He actually spat on the floor as he thought about this. He cursed under his breath and stomped around the far end of the table.

"What happens to the body?" Adam asked, somewhat ashamed to tread on such sensitive matters but nonetheless anxious to complete the story.

Sam grunted a time or two, then stuck the cigarette in his mouth. "Do you know the extent of my wardrobe?"

"No."

"Consists of two of these red monkey suits, four or five sets of clean underwear, and one pair of these cute little rubber shower shoes that look like leftovers from a nigger fire sale. I refuse to die in one of these red suits. I've thought about exercising my constitutional rights and parading into the chamber buck naked. Wouldn't that be a sight? Can you see those goons trying to shove me around and strap me in and trying like hell not to touch my privates. And when they get me strapped down, I'll reach over and take the little heart monitor gizmo and attach it to my testicles. Wouldn't the doctor love that? And I'd make sure the witnesses saw my bare ass. I think that's what I'll do."

"What happens to the body?" Adam asked again.

"Well, once it's sufficiently washed and disinfected, they dress it in prison garb, pull it out of the chair, then put it in a body bag. They place it on a stretcher that goes into the ambulance, which takes it to a funeral home somewhere. The family takes over at that point. Most families."

Sam was now standing with his back to Adam, talking to a wall and leaning on a bookshelf. He was silent for a long time, silent and still as he gazed into the corner and thought about the four men he'd known who had already gone to the chamber. There was an unwritten rule on the Row that when your time came you did not go to the chamber in a red prison suit. You did not give them the satisfaction of killing you in the clothes they'd forced you to wear.

Maybe his brother, the one who sent the monthly supply of cigarettes, would help with a shirt and a pair of pants. New socks would be nice. And anything but the rubber shower shoes. He'd rather go barefoot than wear those damned things.

He turned and walked slowly to Adam's end of the table and took a seat. "I like this idea," he said, very quiet and composed. "It's worth a try."

"Good. Let's get to work. I want you to find more cases like Jimmy Old from North Carolina. Let's dig up every wretched and botched gas chamber execution known to man. We'll throw 'em all in the lawsuit. I want you to make a list of people who might testify about the Meeks and Tole executions. Maybe even Moac and Parris."

Sam was already on his feet again, pulling books from shelves and mumbling to himself. He piled them on the table, dozens of them, then buried himself among the stacks.

NINETEEN

THE ROLLING WHEAT FIELDS stretched for miles, then grew steeper as the foothills began. The majestic mountains lined the farmland in the distance. In a sweeping valley above the fields, with a view for miles in front and with the mountains as a barrier to the rear, the Nazi compound lay sprawled over a hundred acres. Its barbed-wire fences were camouflaged with hedgerows and underbrush. Its firing ranges and combat grounds were likewise screened to prevent detection from the air. Only two innocuous log cabins sat above the ground, and if seen from the outside would appear only to be fishing lodges. But below them, deep in the hills, were two shafts with elevators that dropped into a maze of natural caverns and man-made caves. Large tunnels, wide enough for golf carts, ran in all directions and connected a dozen different rooms. One room had a printing press. Two stored weapons and ammunition. Three large ones were living quarters. One was a small library. The largest room, a cavern forty feet from top to bottom, was the central hall where the members gathered for speeches and films and rallies.

It was a state-of-the-art compound, with satellite dishes feeding televisions with news from around the world, and computers linked to other compounds for the quick flow of information, and fax machines, cellular phones, and every current electronic device in vogue.

No fewer than ten newspapers were received into the

compound each day, and they were taken to a table in a room next to the library where they were first read by a man named Roland. He lived in the compound most of the time, along with several other members who maintained the place. When the newspapers arrived from the city, usually around nine in the morning, Roland poured himself a large cup of coffee and started reading. It was not a chore. He had traveled the world many times, spoke four languages, and had a voracious appetite for knowledge. If a story caught his attention, he would mark it, and later he would make a copy of it and give it to the computer desk.

His interests were varied. He barely scanned the sports, and never looked at the want ads. Fashion, style, living, fanfare, and related sections were browsed with little curiosity. He collected stories about groups similar to his—Aryans, other Nazis, the KKK. Lately, he'd been flagging many stories from Germany and Eastern Europe, and was quite thrilled with the rise of fascism there. He spoke fluent German and spent at least one month a year in that great country. He watched the politicians, with their deep concern about hate crimes and their desire to restrict the rights of groups such as his. He watched the Supreme Court. He followed the trials of skinheads in the United States. He followed the tribulations of the KKK.

He normally spent two hours each morning absorbing the latest news and deciding which stories should be kept for future reference. It was routine, but he enjoyed it immensely.

This particular morning would be different. The first glimpse of trouble was a picture of Sam Cayhall buried deep in the front section of a San Francisco daily. The story had but three paragraphs, but sufficiently covered the hot news that the oldest man on death row in America would now be represented by his grandson.

Roland read it three times before he believed it, then marked the story to be saved. After an hour, he'd read the same story five or six times. Two papers had the snapshot of young Adam Hall that appeared on the front page of the Memphis paper the day before.

Roland had followed the case of Sam Cayhall for many years, and for several reasons. First, it was normally the type of case that would interest their computers—an aging Klan terrorist from the sixties biding his time on death row. The Cayhall printout was already a foot thick. Though he was certainly no lawyer, Roland shared the prevailing opinion that Sam's appeals had run their course and he was about to die. This suited Roland just fine, but he kept his opinion to himself. Sam Cayhall was a hero to white supremacists, and Roland's own little band of Nazis had already been asked to participate in demonstrations before the execution. They had no direct contact with Cayhall because he had never answered their letters, but he was a symbol and they wanted to make the most of his death.

Roland's last name, Forchin, was of Cajun extraction from down around Thibodaux. He had no Social Security number; never filed tax returns; did not exist, as far as the government was concerned. He had three beautifully forged passports, one of which was German and one allegedly issued by the Republic of Ireland. Roland crossed borders and cleared immigration with no worries.

One of Roland's other names, known only to himself and never divulged to a breathing soul, was Rollie Wedge. He had fled the United States in 1967 after the Kramer bombing, and had lived in Northern Ireland. He had also lived in Libya, Munich, Belfast, and Lebanon. He had returned to the United States briefly in 1967 and 1968 to observe the two trials of Sam

Cayhall and Jeremiah Dogan. By then, he was traveling effortlessly with perfect papers.

There had been a few other quick trips back to the United States, all required because of the Cayhall mess. But as time passed, he worried about it less. He had moved to this bunker three years earlier to spread the message of Nazism. He no longer considered himself a Klansman. Now he was a proud fascist.

When he finished his morning reading, he had found the Cayhall story in seven of the ten papers. He placed them in a metal basket, and decided to see the sun. He poured more coffee in his styrofoam cup, and rode an elevator eighty feet to a foyer in a log cabin. It was a beautiful day, cool and sunny, not a cloud to be seen. He walked upward along a narrow trail toward the mountains, and within ten minutes was looking at the valley below him. The wheat fields were in the distance.

Roland had been dreaming of Cayhall's death for twenty-three years. They shared a secret, a heavy burden that would be lifted only when Sam was executed. He admired the man greatly. Unlike Jeremiah Dogan, Sam had honored his oath and never talked. Through three trials, several lawyers, countless appeals, and millions of inquiries, Sam Cayhall had never yielded. He was an honorable man, and Roland wanted him dead. Oh sure, he'd been forced to deliver a few threats to Cayhall and Dogan during the first two trials, but that was so long ago. Dogan cracked under pressure, and he talked and testified against Sam. And Dogan died.

This kid worried him. Like everyone else, Roland had lost track of Sam's son and his family. He knew about the daughter in Memphis, but the son had disappeared. And now this—this nice-looking, well-educated young lawyer from a big, rich Jewish law firm had popped up from nowhere and was primed to save

his grandfather. Roland knew enough about executions to understand that in the waning hours the lawyers try everything. If Sam was going to crack, he
would do it now, and he would do it in the presence of
his grandson.

He tossed a rock down the hillside and watched it
bounce out of sight. He'd have to go to Memphis.

SATURDAY was typically just another day of hard labor at Kravitz & Bane in Chicago, but things were a
bit more laid-back at the Memphis branch. Adam arrived at the office at nine and found only two other
attorneys and one paralegal at work. He locked himself
in his room and closed the blinds.

He and Sam had worked for two hours yesterday,
and by the time Packer returned to the law library with
the handcuffs and the shackles they had managed to
cover the table with dozens of law books and legal
pads. Packer had waited impatiently as Sam slowly
reshelved the books.

Adam reviewed their notes. He entered his own research into the computer, and revised the petition for
the third time. He had already faxed a copy of it to
Garner Goodman, who in turn had revised it and sent
it back.

Goodman was not optimistic about a fair hearing on
the suit, but at this stage of the proceedings there was
nothing to lose. If by chance an expedited hearing was
held in federal court, Goodman was ready to testify
about the Maynard Tole execution. He and Peter
Wiesenberg had witnessed it. In fact, Wiesenberg had
been so sickened by the sight of a living person being
gassed that he resigned from the firm and took a job
teaching. His grandfather had survived the Holocaust;
his grandmother had not. Goodman promised to con-

tact Wiesenberg, and felt confident he too would testify.

By noon, Adam was tired of the office. He unlocked his door and heard no sounds on the floor. The other lawyers were gone. He left the building.

He drove west, over the river into Arkansas, past the truck stops and dog track in West Memphis, and finally through the congestion and into the farm country. He passed the hamlets of Earle and Parkin and Wynne, where the hills began. He stopped for a Coke at a country grocery where three old men in faded overalls sat on the porch swatting flies and suffering in the heat. He lowered the convertible top and sped away.

Two hours later he stopped again, this time in the town of Mountain View to get a sandwich and ask directions. Calico Rock was not far up the road, he was told, just follow the White River. It was a lovely road, winding through the foothills of the Ozarks, through heavy woods and across mountain streams. The White River snaked its way along to the left, and it was dotted with trout fishermen in jon boats.

Calico Rock was a small town on a bluff above the river. Three trout docks lined the east bank near the bridge. Adam parked by the river and walked to the first one, an outfitter called Calico Marina. The building floated on pontoons, and was held close to the bank by thick cables. A row of empty rental boats was strung together next to the pier. The pungent smell of gasoline and oil emanated from a solitary gas pump. A sign listed the rates for boats, guides, gear, and fishing licenses.

Adam walked onto the covered dock and admired the river a few feet away. A young man with dirty hands emerged from a back room and asked if he could be of assistance. He examined Adam from top to bottom, and apparently decided that he was no fisherman.

"I'm looking for Wyn Lettner."

The name Ron was stitched above the shirt pocket and slightly covered with a smudge of grease. Ron walked back to his room and yelled, "Mr. Lettner!" in the direction of a screen door that led to a small shop. Ron disappeared.

Wyn Lettner was a huge man, well over six feet tall with a large frame that was quite overloaded. Garner had described him as a beer drinker, and Adam remembered this as he glanced at the large stomach. He was in his late sixties, with thinning gray hair tucked neatly under an EVINRUDE cap. There were at least three newspaper photographs of Special Agent Lettner indexed away somewhere in Adam's files, and in each he was the standard G-man—dark suit, white shirt, narrow tie, military haircut. And he was much trimmer in those days.

"Yes sir," he said loudly as he walked through the screen door, wiping crumbs from his lips. "I'm Wyn Lettner." He had a deep voice and a pleasant smile.

Adam pushed forward a hand, and said, "I'm Adam Hall. Nice to meet you."

Lettner took his hand and shook it furiously. His forearms were massive and his biceps bulged. "Yes sir," he boomed. "What can I do for you?"

Thankfully the dock was deserted, with the exception of Ron, who was out of sight but making noises with a tool in his room. Adam fidgeted a bit, and said, "Well, I'm a lawyer, and I represent Sam Cayhall."

The smile grew and revealed two rows of strong yellow teeth. "Got your work cut out for you, don't you?" he said with a laugh, and slapped Adam on the back.

"I guess so," Adam said awkwardly as he waited for another assault. "I'd like to talk about Sam."

Lettner was suddenly serious. He stroked his chin with a beefy hand and studied Adam with narrow eyes. "I saw it in the papers, son. I know Sam's your grandfather. Must be tough on you. Gonna get tougher, too." Then he smiled again. "Tougher on Sam as well." His eyes twinkled as if he'd just delivered a side-splitting punch line and he wanted Adam to double over with laughter.

Adam missed the humor. "Sam has less than a month, you know," he said, certain that Lettner had also read about the execution date.

A heavy hand was suddenly on Adam's shoulder and was shoving him in the direction of the shop. "Step in here, son. We'll talk about Sam. You wanna beer?"

"No. Thanks." They entered a narrow room with fishing gear hanging from the walls and ceilings, with rickety wooden shelves covered with food—crackers, sardines, canned sausages, bread, pork and beans, cupcakes—all the necessities for a day on the river. A soft-drink cooler sat in one corner.

"Take a seat," Lettner said, waving to a corner near the cash register. Adam sat in a shaky wooden chair as Lettner fished through an ice chest and found a bottle of beer. "Sure you don't want one?"

"Maybe later." It was almost five o'clock.

He twisted the top, drained at least a third of the bottle with the first gulp, smacked his lips, then sat in a beaten leather captain's chair, which had no doubt been removed from a customized van. "Are they finally gonna get old Sam?" he asked.

"They're trying awfully hard."

"What're the odds?"

"Not good. We have the usual assortment of last minute appeals, but the clock's ticking."

"Sam's not a bad guy," Lettner said with a trace of remorse, then washed it away with another long drink. The floor creaked quietly as the dock shifted with the river.

"How long were you in Mississippi?" Adam asked.

"Five years. Hoover called me after the three civil rights workers disappeared. Nineteen sixty-four. We set up a special unit and went to work. After Kramer, the Klan sort of ran out of gas."

"And you were in charge of what?"

"Mr. Hoover was very specific. He told me to infiltrate the Klan at all costs. He wanted it busted up. To be truthful, we were slow getting started in Mississippi. Bunch of reasons for it. Hoover hated the Kennedys and they were pushing him hard, so he dragged his feet. But when those three boys disappeared, we got off our asses. Nineteen sixty-four was a helluva year in Mississippi."

"I was born that year."

"Yeah, paper said you were born in Clanton."

Adam nodded. "I didn't know it for a long time. My parents told me I was born in Memphis."

The door jingled and Ron entered the shop. He looked at them, then studied the crackers and sardines. They watched him and waited. He glanced at Adam as if to say "Keep talking. I'm not listening."

"What do you want?" Lettner snapped at him.

He grabbed a can of Vienna sausage with his dirty hand and showed it to them. Lettner nodded and waved at the door. Ron ambled toward it, checking the cupcakes and potato chips as he went.

"He's nosy as hell," Lettner said after he was gone. "I talked to Garner Goodman a few times. It was years ago. Now, that's a weird bird."

"He's my boss. He gave me your name, said you'd talk to me."

"Talk about what?" Lettner asked, then took another drink.

"The Kramer case."

"The Kramer case is closed. The only thing left is
Sam and his date with the gas chamber."

"Do you want him executed?"

Voices followed footsteps, then the door opened
again. A man and a boy entered and Lettner got to his
feet. They needed food and supplies, and for ten minutes they shopped and talked and decided where the
fish were biting. Lettner was careful to place his beer
under the counter while his customers were present.

Adam removed a soft drink from the cooler and left
the shop. He walked along the edge of the wooden
dock next to the river, and stopped by the gas pump.
Two teenagers in a boat were casting near the bridge,
and it struck Adam that he'd never been fishing in his
life. His father had not been a man of hobbies and
leisure. Nor had he been able to keep a job. At the
moment, Adam could not remember exactly what his
father had done with his time.

The customers left and the door slammed. Lettner
lumbered to the gas pump. "You like to trout fish?" he
asked, admiring the river.

"No. Never been."

"Let's go for a ride. I need to check out a spot two
miles downriver. The fish are supposed to be thick."

Lettner was carrying his ice chest, which he dropped
carefully into a boat. He stepped down from the dock,
and the boat rocked violently from side to side as he
grabbed the motor. "Come on," he yelled at Adam,
who was studying the thirty-inch gap between himself
and the boat. "And grab that rope," Lettner yelled
again, pointing to a thin cord hooked to a grapple.

Adam unhitched the rope and stepped nervously into
the boat, which rocked just as his foot touched it. He

slipped and landed on his head and came within inches of taking a swim. Lettner howled with laughter as he pulled the starter rope. Ron, of course, had watched this and was grinning stupidly on the dock. Adam was embarrassed but laughed as if it were all very funny. Lettner gunned the engine, the front of the boat jerked upward, and they were off.

Adam clutched the handles on both sides as they sped through the water and under the bridge. Calico Rock was soon behind them. The river turned and twisted its way through scenic hills and around rocky bluffs. Lettner navigated with one hand and sipped a fresh beer with the other. After a few minutes, Adam relaxed somewhat and managed to pull a beer from the cooler without losing his balance. The bottle was ice cold. He held it with his right hand and clutched the boat with his left. Lettner was humming or singing something behind him. The high-pitched roar of the motor prevented conversation.

They passed a small trout dock where a group of clean-cut city slickers were counting fish and drinking beer, and they passed a flotilla of rubber rafts filled with mangy teenagers smoking something and absorbing the sun. They waved at other fishermen who were hard at work.

The boat slowed finally and Lettner maneuvered it carefully through a bend as if he could see the fish below and had to position himself perfectly. He turned off the engine. "You gonna fish or drink beer?" he asked, staring at the water.

"Drink beer."

"Figures." His bottle was suddenly of secondary importance as he took the rod and cast to a spot toward the bank. Adam watched for a second, and when there was no immediate result he reclined and hung his feet over the water. The boat was not comfortable.

"How often do you fish?" he asked.

"Every day. It's part of my job, you know, part of my service to my customers. I have to know where the fish are biting."

"Tough job."

"Somebody has to do it."

"What brought you to Calico Rock?"

"Had a heart attack in '75, so I had to retire from the Bureau. Had a nice pension and all, but, hell, you get bored just sitting around. The wife and I found this place and found the marina for sale. One mistake led to another, and here I am. Hand me a beer."

He cast again as Adam dispensed the beer. He quickly counted fourteen bottles remaining in the ice. The boat drifted with the river, and Lettner grabbed a paddle. He fished with one hand, sculled the boat with the other, and somehow balanced a fresh beer between his knees. The life of a fishing guide.

They slowed under some trees, and the sun was mercifully shielded for a while. He made the casting look easy. He whipped the rod with a smooth wrist action, and sent the lure anywhere he wanted. But the fish weren't biting. He cast toward the middle of the river.

"Sam's not a bad guy." He'd already said this once.

"Do you think he should be executed?"

"That's not up to me, son. The people of the state want the death penalty, so it's on the books. The people said Sam was guilty and then said he should be executed, so who am I?"

"But you have an opinion."

"What good is it? My thoughts are completely worthless."

"Why do you say Sam's not a bad guy?"

"It's a long story."

"We have fourteen beers left."

Lettner laughed and the vast smile returned. He

gulped from the bottle and looked down the river, away from his line. "Sam was of no concern to us, you understand. He was not active in the really nasty stuff, at least not at first. When those civil rights workers disappeared, we went in with a fury. We spread money all over the place, and before long we had all sorts of Klan informants. These people were basically just ignorant rednecks who'd never had a dime, and we preyed on their craving for money. We'd have never found those three boys had we not dropped some cash. About thirty thousand, as I remember it, though I didn't deal directly with the informant. Hell, son, they were buried in a levee. We found them, and it made us look good, you understand. Finally, we'd accomplished something. Made a bunch of arrests, but the convictions were difficult. The violence continued. They bombed black churches and black homes so damned often we couldn't keep up. It was like a war down there. It got worse, and Mr. Hoover got madder, and we spread around more money.

"Listen, son, I'm not going to tell you anything useful, you understand?"

"Why not?"

"Some things I can talk about, some I can't."

"Sam wasn't alone when he bombed the Kramer office, was he?"

Lettner smiled again and studied his line. The rod was sitting in his lap. "Anyway, by late '65 and early '66, we had a helluva network of informants. It really wasn't that difficult. We'd learn that some guy was in the Klan, and so we'd tail him. We'd follow him home at night, flashing our lights behind him, parking in front of his house. It'd usually scare him to death. Then we'd follow him to work, sometimes we'd go talk to his boss, flash our badges around, act like we were about to shoot somebody. We'd go talk to his parents, show them our badges, let them see us in our dark suits, let them hear our Yankee accents, and these poor country people would literally crack up right in front of us. If the guy went to church, we'd follow him one Sunday, then the next day we'd go talk to his preacher. We'd tell him that we had heard a terrible rumor that Mr. Such and Such was an active member of the Klan, and did he know anything about it. We acted like it was a crime to be a member of the Klan. If the guy had teenage children, we'd follow them on dates, sit behind them at the movies, catch them parking in the woods. It was nothing but pure harassment, but it worked. Finally, we'd call the poor guy or catch him alone somewhere, and offer him some money. We'd promise to leave him alone, and it always worked. Usually, they were nervous wrecks by this time, they couldn't wait to cooperate. I saw them cry, son, if you can believe it. Actually cry when they finally came to the altar and confessed their sins." Lettner laughed in the direction of his line, which was quite inactive.

Adam sipped his beer. Perhaps if they drank it all it would eventually loosen his tongue.

"Had this guy one time, I'll never forget him. We caught him in bed with his black mistress, which was not unusual. I mean, these guys would go out burning crosses and shooting into black homes, then sneak around like crazy to meet their black girlfriends. Never could understand why the black women put up with it. Anyway, he had a little hunting lodge deep in the woods, and he used it for a love nest. He met her there one afternoon for a quickie, and when he was finished and ready to go, he opened the front door and we took his picture. Got her picture too, and then we talked to him. He was a deacon or an elder in some country church, a real pillar, you know, and we talked to him like he was a dog. We ran her off and sat him down inside the little lodge there, and before long he was crying. As it turned out, he was one of our best witnesses. But he later went to jail."

"Why?"

"Well, it seems that while he was sneaking around with his girlfriend, his wife was doing the same thing with a black kid who worked on their farm. Lady got pregnant, baby was half and half, so our informant goes to the hospital and kills mother and child. He spent fifteen years at Parchman."

"Good."

"We didn't get a lot of convictions back in those days, but harassed them to a point where they were afraid to do much. The violence had slowed considerably until Dogan decided to go after the Jews. That caught us off guard, I have to admit. We had no clue."

"Why not?"

"Because he got smart. He learned the hard way that his own people would talk to us, so he decided to operate with a small, quiet unit."

"Unit? As in more than one person?"

"Something like that."

"As in Sam and who else?"

Lettner snorted and chuckled at once, and decided the fish had moved elsewhere. He placed his rod and reel in the boat, and yanked on the starter cord. They were off, racing once again downstream. Adam left his feet over the side, and his leather moccasins and bare ankles were soon wet. He sipped the beer. The sun was finally beginning to disappear behind the hills, and he enjoyed the beauty of the river.

The next stop was a stretch of still water below a bluff with a rope hanging from it. Lettner cast and reeled, all to no effect, and assumed the role of interrogator. He asked a hundred questions about Adam and his family—the flight westward, the new identities, the suicide. He explained that while Sam was in jail they checked out his family and knew he had a son who had just left town, but since Eddie appeared to be harmless they did not pursue the investigation. Instead, they spent their time watching Sam's brothers and cousins. He was intrigued by Adam's youth, and how he was raised with virtually no knowledge of kinfolks.

Adam asked a few questions, but the answers were vague and immediately twisted into more questions about his past. Adam was sparring with a man who'd spent twenty-five years asking questions.

The third and final hot spot was not far from Calico Rock, and they fished until it was dark. After five beers, Adam mustered the courage to wet a hook. Lettner was a patient instructor, and within minutes Adam had caught an impressive trout. For a brief interlude, they forgot about Sam and the Klan and other nightmares from the past, and they simply fished. They drank and fished.

MRS. LETTNER'S FIRST NAME was Irene, and she welcomed her husband and his unexpected guest with grace and nonchalance. Wyn had explained, as Ron drove them home, that Irene was accustomed to dropins. She certainly seemed to be unruffled as they staggered through the front door and handed her a string of trout.

The Lettner home was a cottage on the river a mile north of town. The rear porch was screened to protect it from insects, and not far below it was a splendid view of the river. They sat in wicker rockers on the porch, and opened another round of brew as Irene fried the fish.

Putting food on the table was a new experience for Adam, and he ate the fish he'd caught with great gusto. It always tastes better, Wyn assured him as he chomped and drank, when you catch it yourself. About halfway through the meal, Wyn switched to Scotch. Adam declined. He wanted a simple glass of water, but machismo drove him to continue with the beer. He couldn't wimp out at this point. Lettner would certainly chastise him.

Irene sipped wine and told stories about Mississippi. She had been threatened on several occasions, and their children refused to visit them. They were both from Ohio, and their families worried constantly about their safety. Those were the days, she said more than once with a certain longing for excitement. She was extremely proud of her husband and his performance during the war for civil rights.

She left them after dinner and disappeared somewhere in the cottage. It was almost ten o'clock, and Adam was ready for sleep. Wyn rose to his feet while holding on to a wooden beam, and excused himself for a visit to the bathroom. He returned in due course with two fresh Scotches in tall glasses. He handed one to Adam, and returned to his rocker.

They rocked and sipped in silence for a moment, then Lettner said, "So you're convinced Sam had some help."

"Of course he had some help." Adam was very much aware that his tongue was thick and his words were slow. Lettner's speech was remarkably clear.

"And what makes you so certain?"

Adam lowered the heavy glass and vowed not to take another drink. "The FBI searched Sam's house after the bombing, right?"

"Right."

"Sam was in jail in Greenville, and you guys got a warrant."

"I was there, son. We went in with a dozen agents and spent three days."

"And found nothing."

"You could say that."

"No trace of dynamite. No trace of blasting caps, fuses, detonators. No trace of any device or substance used in any of the bombings. Correct?"

"That's correct. So what's your point?"

"Sam had no knowledge of explosives, nor did he have a history of using them."

"No, I'd say he had quite a history of using them. Kramer was the sixth bombing, as I recall. Those crazy bastards were bombing like hell, son, and we couldn't stop them. You weren't there. I was in the middle of it. We had harassed the Klan and infiltrated to a point where they were afraid to move, then all of a sudden another war erupted and bombs were falling everywhere. We listened where we were supposed to listen. We twisted familiar arms until they broke. And we were clueless. Our informants were clueless. It was like another branch of the Klan had suddenly invaded Mississippi without telling the old one."

"Did you know about Sam?"

"His name was in our records. As I recall, his father had been a Klucker, and maybe a brother or two. So we had their names. But they seemed harmless. They lived in the northern part of the state, in an area not known for serious Klan violence. They probably burned some crosses, maybe shot up a few houses, but nothing compared to Dogan and his gang. We had our hands full with murderers. We didn't have time to investigate every possible Klucker in the state."

"Then how do you explain Sam's sudden shift to violence?"

"Can't explain it. He was no choirboy, okay? He had killed before."

"Are you sure?"

"You heard me. He shot and killed one of his black

employees in the early fifties. Never spent a day in jail for it. In fact, I'm not sure, but I don't think he was ever arrested for it. There may have been another killing, too. Another black victim."

"I'd rather not hear it."

"Ask him. See if the old bastard has guts enough to admit it to his grandson." He took another sip. "He was a violent man, son, and he certainly had the capability to plant bombs and kill people. Don't be naive."

"I'm not naive. I'm just trying to save his life."

"Why? He killed two very innocent little boys. Two children. Do you realize this?"

"He was convicted of the murders. But if the killings were wrong, then it's wrong for the state to kill him."

"I don't buy that crap. The death penalty is too good for these people. It's too clean and sterile. They know they're about to die, so they have time to say their prayers and say good-bye. What about the victims? How much time did they have to prepare?"

"So you want Sam executed?"

"Yeah. I want 'em all executed."

"I thought you said he wasn't a bad guy."

"I lied. Sam Cayhall is a cold-blooded killer. And he's guilty as hell. How else can you explain the fact that the bombings stopped as soon as he was in custody?"

"Maybe they were scared after Kramer?"

"They? Who the hell is they?"

"Sam and his partner. And Dogan."

"Okay. I'll play along. Let's assume Sam had an accomplice."

"No. Let's assume Sam was the accomplice. Let's assume the other guy was the explosives expert."

"Expert? These were very crude bombs, son. The first five were nothing more than a few sticks wrapped together with a fuse. You light the match, run like hell, and fifteen minutes later, Boom! The Kramer bomb was nothing but a half-ass rig with an alarm clock wired to it. They were lucky it didn't go off while they were playing with it."

"Do you think it was deliberately set to go off when it did?"

"The jury thought so. Dogan said they planned to kill Marvin Kramer."

"Then why was Sam hanging around? Why was he close enough to the bomb to get hit with debris?"

"You'll have to ask Sam, which I'm sure you've already done. Does he claim he had an accomplice?"

"No."

"Then that settles it. If your own client says no, what the hell are you digging for?"

"Because I think my client is lying."

"Too bad for your client, then. If he wants to lie and protect the identity of someone, then why should you care?"

"Why would he lie to me?"

Lettner shook his head in frustration, then mumbled something and took a drink. "How the hell am I supposed to know? I don't want to know, okay? I honestly don't care if Sam's lying or if Sam's telling the truth. But if he won't level with you, his lawyer and his own grandson, then I say gas him."

Adam took a long drink and stared into the darkness. He actually felt silly at times digging around trying to prove his own client was lying to him. He'd give this another shot, then talk about something else. "You don't believe the witnesses who saw Sam with another person?"

"No. They were pretty shaky, as I recall. The guy at the truck stop didn't come forward for a long time. The other guy had just left a honky-tonk. They weren't credible."

"Do you believe Dogan?"

"The jury did."

"I didn't ask about the jury."

Lettner's breathing was finally getting heavy, and he appeared to be fading. "Dogan was crazy, and Dogan was a genius. He said the bomb was intended to kill, and I believe him. Keep in mind, Adam, they almost wiped out an entire family in Vicksburg. I can't remember the name—"

"Pinder. And you keep saying *they* did this and that."

"I'm just playing along, okay. We're assuming Sam had a buddy with him. They planted a bomb at the Pinder house in the middle of the night. An entire family could've been killed."

"Sam said he placed the bomb in the garage so no one would get hurt."

"Sam told you this? Sam admitted he did it? Then why in the hell are you asking me about an accomplice? Sounds like you need to listen to your client. Son of a bitch is guilty, Adam. Listen to him."

Adam took another drink and his eyelids grew heavier. He looked at his watch, but couldn't see it. "Tell me about the tapes," he said, yawning.

"What tapes?" Lettner asked, yawning.

"The FBI tapes they played at Sam's trial. The ones with Dogan talking to Wayne Graves about bombing Kramer."

"We had lots of tapes. And they had lots of targets. Kramer was just one of many. Hell, we had a tape with two Kluckers talking about bombing a synagogue while a wedding was in progress. They wanted to bolt the doors and shoot some gas through the heating ducts so the entire congregation would be wiped out. Sick bastards, man. It wasn't Dogan, just a couple of his idiots talking trash, and so we dismissed it. Wayne

Graves was a Klucker who was also on our payroll, and he allowed us to tap his phones. He called Dogan one night, said he was on a pay phone, and they got to talking about hitting Kramer. They also talked about other targets. It was very effective at Sam's trial. But the tapes did not help us stop a single bombing. Nor did they help us identify Sam."

"You had no idea Sam Cayhall was involved?"

"None whatsoever. If the fool had left Greenville when he should have, he'd probably still be a free man."

"Did Kramer know he was a target?"

"We told him. But by then he was accustomed to threats. He kept a guard at his house." His words were starting to slur a bit, and his chin had dropped an inch or two.

Adam excused himself and cautiously made his way to the bathroom. As he returned to the porch, he heard heavy snoring. Lettner had slumped in his chair and collapsed with the drink in his hand. Adam removed it, then left in search of a sofa.

TWENTY

THE LATE MORNING was warm but seemed downright feverish in the front of the Army surplus jeep, which lacked air conditioning and other essentials. Adam sweated and kept his hand on the handle of the door which he hoped would open promptly in the event Irene's breakfast came roaring up.

He had awakened on the floor beside a narrow sofa in a room which he had mistaken for the den, but was in fact the washroom beside the kitchen. And the sofa was a bench, Lettner had explained with much laughter, that he used to sit on to take off his boots. Irene had eventually found his body after searching the house, and Adam apologized profusely until they both asked him to stop. She had insisted on a heavy breakfast. It was their one day of the week to eat pork, a regular tradition around the Lettner cottage, and Adam had sat at the kitchen table guzzling ice water while the bacon fried and Irene hummed and Wyn read the paper. She also scrambled eggs and mixed bloody marys.

The vodka deadened some of the pain in his head, but it also did nothing to calm his stomach. As they bounced toward Calico Rock on the bumpy road, Adam was terrified that he would be sick.

Though Lettner had passed out first, he was remarkably healthy this morning. No sign of a hangover. He'd eaten a plate full of grease and biscuits, and he'd sipped only one bloody mary. He'd diligently read the paper and commented about this and that, and Adam figured he was one of those functional alcoholics who got plastered every night but shook it off easily.

The village was in view. The road was suddenly smoother and Adam's stomach stopped bouncing. "Sorry about last night," Lettner said.

"What?" Adam asked.

"About Sam. I was harsh. I know he's your grandfather and you're very concerned. I lied about something. I really don't want Sam to be executed. He's not a bad guy."

"I'll tell him."

"Yeah. I'm sure he'll be thrilled."

They entered the town and turned toward the bridge. "There's something else," Lettner said. "We always suspected Sam had a partner."

Adam smiled and looked through his window. They passed a small church with elderly people standing under a shade tree in their pretty dresses and neat suits.

"Why?" Adam asked.

"For the same reasons. Sam had no history with bombs. He had not been involved in Klan violence. The two witnesses, especially the truck driver in Cleveland, always bothered us. The trucker had no reason to lie, and he seemed awfully certain of himself. Sam just didn't seem like the type to start his own bombing campaign."

"So who's the man?"

"I honestly don't know." They rolled to a stop by the river, and Adam opened his door just in case. Lettner leaned on the steering wheel, and cocked his head toward Adam. "After the third or fourth bombing, I think maybe it was the synagogue in Jackson, some big Jews in New York and Washington met with LBJ, who in turn called in Mr. Hoover, who in turn called me. I went to D.C., where I met with Mr. Hoover and the President, and they pretty much crawled my ass. I returned to Mississippi with renewed determination. We came down hard on our informants. I mean, we hurt some people. We tried everything, but to no avail. Our sources simply did not know who was doing the bombing. Only Dogan knew, and it was obvious he wasn't telling anybody. But after the fifth bomb, which I think was the newspaper office, we got a break."

Lettner opened his door and walked to the front of the jeep. Adam joined him there, and they watched the river ease along through Calico Rock. "You wanna beer? I keep it cold in the bait shop."

"No, please. I'm half-sick now."

"Just kidding. Anyway, Dogan ran this huge used car lot, and one of his employees was an illiterate old black man who washed the cars and swept the floors. We had carefully approached the old man earlier, but he was hostile. But out of the blue he tells one of our agents that he saw Dogan and another man putting something in the trunk of a green Pontiac a couple of days earlier. He said he waited, then opened the trunk and saw it was dynamite. The next day he heard that there was another bombing. He knew the FBI was swarming all around Dogan, so he figured it was worth mentioning to us. Dogan's helper was a Klucker named Virgil, also an employee. So I went to see Virgil. I knocked on his door at three o'clock one morning, just beat it like hell, you know, like we always did in those days, and before long he turned on the light and stepped on the porch. I had about eight agents with me, and we all stuck our badges in Virgil's face. He was scared to death. I told him we knew he had delivered the dynamite to Jackson the night before, and that he was looking at thirty years. You could hear his wife crying through the screen door. Virgil was shaking and ready to cry himself. I left him my card with instructions to call me before noon that very day, and I threatened him if he told Dogan or anybody else. I told him we'd be watching him around the clock.

"I doubt if Virgil went back to sleep. His eyes were red and puffy when he found me a few hours later. We got to be friends. He said the bombings were not the work of Dogan's usual gang. He didn't know much, but he'd heard enough from Dogan to believe that the bomber was a very young man from another state. This guy had dropped in from nowhere, and was supposed to be very good with explosives. Dogan picked the targets, planned the jobs, then called this guy, who sneaked into town, carried out the bombings, then disappeared."

"Did you believe him?"

"For the most part, yes. It just made sense. It had to be someone new, because by then we had riddled the Klan with informants. We knew virtually every move they made."

"What happened to Virgil?"

"I spent some time with him, gave him some money, you know, the usual routine. They always wanted money. I became convinced he had no idea who was planting the bombs. He would never admit that he'd been involved, that he'd delivered the cars and dynamite, and we didn't press him. We weren't after him."

"Was he involved with Kramer?"

"No. Dogan used someone else for that one. At times, Dogan seemed to have a sixth sense about when to mix things up, to change routines."

"Virgil's suspect certainly doesn't sound like Sam Cayhall, does he?" Adam asked.

"No."

"And you had no suspects?"

"No."

"Come on, Wyn. Surely you guys had some idea."

"I swear. We did not. Shortly after we met Virgil, Kramer got bombed and it was all over. If Sam had a buddy, then the buddy left him."

"And the FBI heard nothing afterward?"

"Not a peep. We had Sam, who looked and smelled extremely guilty."

"And, of course, you guys were anxious to close the case."

"Certainly. And the bombings stopped, remember. There were no bombings after Sam got caught, don't forget that. We had our man. Mr. Hoover was happy. The Jews were happy. The President was happy. Then they couldn't convict him for fourteen years, but that was a different story. Everyone was relieved when the bombings stopped."

"So why didn't Dogan squeal on the real bomber when he squealed on Sam?"

They had eased down the bank to a point just inches above the water. Adam's car sat nearby. Lettner cleared his throat and spat into the river. "Would you testify against a terrorist who was not in custody?"

Adam thought for a second. Lettner smiled, flashed his big yellow teeth, then chuckled as he started for the dock. "Let's have a beer."

"No. Please. I need to go."

Lettner stopped, and they shook hands and promised to meet again. Adam invited him to Memphis, and Lettner invited him back to Calico Rock for more fishing and drinking. At the moment, his invitation was not well received. Adam sent his regards to Irene, apologized again for passing out in the washroom, and thanked him again for the chat.

He left the small town behind, driving gingerly around the curves and hills, still careful not to upset his stomach.

* * *

LEE WAS STRUGGLING with a pasta dish when he entered her apartment. The table was set with china and silver and fresh flowers. The recipe was for baked manicotti, and things were not going well in the kitchen. On more than one occasion in the past week she'd confessed to being a lousy cook, and now she was proving it. Pots and pans were scattered along the countertops. Her seldom used apron was covered with tomato sauce. She laughed as they kissed each other on the cheeks and said there was a frozen pizza if matters got worse.

"You look awful," she said, suddenly staring at his eyes.

"It was a rough night."

"You smell like alcohol."

"I had two bloody marys for breakfast. And I need another one now."

"The bar's closed." She picked up a knife and stepped to a pile of vegetables. A zucchini was the next victim. "What did you do up there?"

"Got drunk with the FBI man. Slept on the floor next to his washer and dryer."

"How nice." She came within a centimeter of drawing blood. She jerked her hand away from the chopping block and examined a finger. "Have you seen the Memphis paper?"

"No. Should I?"

"Yes. It's over there." She nodded to a corner of the snack bar.

"Something bad?"

"Just read it."

Adam took the Sunday edition of the *Memphis Press* and sat in a chair at the table. On the front page of the second section, he suddenly encountered his smiling face. It was a familiar photo, one taken not long ago when he was a second-year law student at Michigan.

The story covered half the page, and his photo was joined by many others—Sam, of course, Marvin Kramer, Josh and John Kramer, Ruth Kramer, David McAllister, the Attorney General, Steve Roxburgh, Naifeh, Jeremiah Dogan, and Mr. Elliot Kramer, father of Marvin.

Todd Marks had been busy. His narrative began with a succinct history of the case which took an entire column, then he moved quickly to the present and re-capped the same story he'd written two days earlier. He found a bit more biographical data on Adam—college at Pepperdine, law school at Michigan, law review editor, brief employment history with Kravitz & Bane. Naifeh had very little to say, only that the execution would be carried out according to the law. McAllister, on the other hand, was full of wisdom. He had lived with the Kramer nightmare for twenty-three years, he said gravely, thinking about it every day of his life since it happened. It had been his honor and privilege to prosecute Sam Cayhall and bring the killer to jus-tice, and only the execution could close this awful chapter of Mississippi's history. No, he said after much thought, the idea of clemency was out of the question. Just wouldn't be fair to the little Kramer boys. And on and on.

Steve Roxburgh had evidently enjoyed his interview too. He stood ready to fight the final efforts by Cayhall and his lawyer to thwart the execution. He and his staff were prepared to work eighteen hours a day to carry out the wishes of the people. This matter had dragged on long enough, he was quoted as saying more than once, and it was time for justice. No, he was not worried about the last ditch legal challenges of Mr. Cayhall. He had confidence in his skills as a lawyer, the people's lawyer.

Sam Cayhall refused to comment, Marks explained,

and Adam Hall couldn't be reached, as if Adam was eager to talk but simply couldn't be found.

The comments from the family were both interesting and disheartening. Elliot Kramer, now seventy-seven and still working, was described as spry and healthy in spite of heart trouble. He was also very bitter. He blamed the Klan and Sam Cayhall not only for killing his two grandsons, but also for Marvin's death. He'd been waiting twenty-three years for Sam to be executed, and it couldn't come a minute too soon. He lashed out at a judicial system that allows a convict to live for almost ten years after the jury gives him a death penalty. He was not certain if he would witness the execution, it would be up to his doctors, he said, but he wanted to. He wanted to be there and look Cayhall in the eyes when they strapped him in.

Ruth Kramer was a bit more moderate. Time had healed many of the wounds, she said, and she was unsure how she would feel after the execution. Nothing would bring back her sons. She had little to say to Todd Marks.

Adam folded the paper and placed it beside the chair. He suddenly had a knot in his fragile stomach, and it came from Steve Roxburgh and David McAllister. As the lawyer expected to save Sam's life, it was frightening to see his enemies so eager for the final battle. He was a rookie. They were veterans. Roxburgh in particular had been through it before, and he had an experienced staff which included a renowned specialist known as Dr. Death, a skilled advocate with a passion for executions. Adam had nothing but an exhausted file full of unsuccessful appeals, and a prayer that a miracle would happen. At this moment he felt completely vulnerable and hopeless.

Lee sat next to him with a cup of espresso. "You look worried," she said, stroking his arm.

"My buddy at the trout dock was of no help."

"Sounds like old man Kramer is hell-bent."

Adam rubbed his temples and tried to ease the pain. "I need a painkiller."

"How about a Valium?"

"Wonderful."

"Are you real hungry?"

"No. My stomach is not doing well."

"Good. Dinner has been terminated. A slight problem with the recipe. It's frozen pizza or nothing."

"Nothing sounds good to me. Nothing but a Valium."

TWENTY-ONE

$\mathbf{A}$DAM DROPPED HIS KEYS in the red bucket and watched it ascend to a point twenty feet off the ground where it stopped and spun slowly on the end of the rope. He walked to the first gate, which jerked before sliding open. He walked to the second gate, and waited. Packer emerged from the front door a hundred feet away, stretching and yawning as if he'd been napping on the Row.

The second gate closed behind him, and Packer waited nearby. "Good day," he said. It was almost two, the hottest time of the day. A morning radio forecaster had merrily predicted the first one-hundred-degree day of the year.

"Hello, Sergeant," Adam said as if they were old friends now. They walked along the brick path to the small door with the weeds in front of it. Packer unlocked it, and Adam stepped inside.

"I'll get Sam," Packer said, in no hurry, and disappeared.

The chairs on his side of the metal screen were scattered about. Two were flipped over, as if the lawyers and visitors had been brawling. Adam pulled one close to the counter at the far end, as far as possible from the air conditioner.

He removed a copy of the petition he'd filed at nine that morning. By law, no claim or issue could be raised in federal court unless it had first been presented and denied in state court. The petition attacking the gas chamber had been filed in the Mississippi Supreme

Court under the state's postconviction relief statutes. It was a formality, in Adam's opinion, and in the opinion of Garner Goodman. Goodman had worked on the claim throughout the weekend. In fact, he'd worked all day Saturday while Adam was drinking beer and trout fishing with Wyn Lettner.

Sam arrived as usual, hands cuffed behind his back, no expression on his face, red jumpsuit unbuttoned almost to the waist. The gray hair on his pale chest was slick with perspiration. Like a well-trained animal, he turned his back to Packer, who quickly removed the cuffs, then left through the door. Sam immediately went for the cigarettes, and made certain one was lit before he sat down and said, "Welcome back."

"I filed this at nine this morning," Adam said, sliding the petition through the narrow slit in the screen. "I talked to the clerk with the supreme court in Jackson. She seemed to think the court will rule on it with due speed."

Sam took the papers, and looked at Adam. "You can bet on that. They'll deny it with great pleasure."

"The state will be required to respond immediately, so we've got the Attorney General scrambling right now."

"Great. We can watch the latest on the evening news. He's probably invited the cameras into his office while they prepare their response."

Adam removed his jacket and loosened his tie. The room was humid and he was already sweating. "Does the name Wyn Lettner ring a bell?"

Sam tossed the petition onto an empty chair and sucked hard on the filter. He released a steady stream of exhaust at the ceiling. "Yes. Why?"

"Did you ever meet him?"

Sam thought about this for a moment, before speaking, and, as usual, spoke with measured words.

"Maybe. I'm not sure. I knew who he was at the time. Why?"

"I found him over the weekend. He's retired now, and runs a trout dock on the White River. We had a long talk."

"That's nice. And what exactly did you accomplish?"

"He says he still thinks you had someone working with you."

"Did he give you any names?"

"No. They never had a suspect, or so he says. But they had an informant, one of Dogan's people, who told Lettner that the other guy was someone new, not one of the usual gang. They thought he was from another state, and that he was very young. That's all Lettner knew."

"And you believe this?"

"I don't know what I believe."

"What difference does it make now?"

"I don't know. It could give me something to use as I try to save your life. Nothing more than that. I'm desperate, I guess."

"And I'm not?"

"I'm grasping for straws, Sam. Grasping and filling in holes."

"So my story has holes?"

"I think so. Lettner said he was always doubtful because they found no trace of explosives when they searched your house. And you had no history of using them. He said you didn't seem to be the type to initiate your own bombing campaign."

"And you believe everything Lettner says?"

"Yeah. Because it makes sense."

"Let me ask you this. What if I told you there was someone else? What if I gave you his name, address, phone number, blood type, and urine analysis? What would you do with it?"

"Start screaming like hell. I'd file motions and appeals by the truckload. I'd get the media stirred up, and make a scapegoat out of you. I'd try to sensationalize your innocence and hope someone noticed, someone like an appellate judge."

Sam nodded slowly as if this was quite ridiculous and exactly what he'd expected. "It wouldn't work, Adam," he said carefully, as if lecturing to a child. "I have three and a half weeks. You know the law. There's no way to start screaming John Doe did it, when John Doe has never been mentioned."

"I know. But I'd do it anyway."

"It won't work. Stop trying to find John Doe."

"Who is he?"

"He doesn't exist."

"Yes he does."

"Why are you so sure?"

"Because I want to believe you're innocent, Sam. It's very important to me."

"I told you I'm innocent. I planted the bomb, but I had no intention of killing anyone."

"But why'd you plant the bomb? Why'd you bomb the Pinder house, and the synagogue, and the real estate office? Why were you bombing innocent people?"

Sam just puffed and looked at the floor.

"Why do you hate, Sam? Why does it come so easy? Why were you taught to hate blacks and Jews and Catholics and anyone slightly different from you? Have you ever asked yourself why?"

"No. Don't plan to."

"So, it's just you, right. It's your character, your composition, same as your height and blue eyes. It's something you were born with and can't change. It was passed down in the genes from your father and grandfather, faithful Kluckers all, and it's something you'll proudly take to your grave, right?"

"It was a way of life. It was all I knew."

"Then what happened to my father? Why couldn't you contaminate Eddie?"

Sam thumped the cigarette onto the floor and leaned forward on his elbows. The wrinkles tightened in the corners of his eyes and across his forehead. Adam's face was directly through the slit, but he did not look at him. Instead, he stared down at the base of the screen. "So this is it. Time for our Eddie talk." His voice was much softer and his words even slower.

"Where did you go wrong with him?"

"This, of course, has not a damned thing to do with the little gas party they're planning for me. Does it? Nothing to do with issues and appeals, lawyers and judges, motions and stays. This is a waste of time."

"Don't be a coward, Sam. Tell me where you went wrong with Eddie. Did you teach him the word nigger? Did you teach him to hate little black kids? Did you try to teach him how to burn crosses or build bombs? Did you take him to his first lynching? What did you do with him, Sam? Where did you go wrong?"

"Eddie didn't know I was in the Klan until he was in high school."

"Why not? Surely you weren't ashamed of it. It was a great source of family pride, wasn't it?"

"It was not something we talked about."

"Why not? You were the fourth generation of Cayhall Klansmen, with roots all the way back to the Civil War, or something like that. Isn't that what you told me?"

"Yes."

"Then why didn't you sit little Eddie down and show him pictures from the family album? Why didn't you tell him bedtime stories of the heroic Cayhalls and how they rode around at night with masks on their brave faces and burned Negro shacks? You know, war stories. Father to son."

"I repeat, it was not something we talked about."

"Well, when he got older, did you try to recruit him?"

"No. He was different."

"You mean, he didn't hate?"

Sam jerked forward and coughed, the deep, scratchy hacking action of a chain-smoker. His face reddened as he struggled for breath. The coughing grew worse and he spat on the floor. He stood and leaned at the waist with both hands on his hips, coughing and hacking while shuffling around and trying to stop it.

Finally, a break. He stood straight and breathed rapidly. He swallowed and spat again, then relaxed and inhaled slowly. The seizure was over, and his red face was suddenly pale again. He took his seat across from Adam, and puffed mightily on the cigarette as if some other device or habit was to blame for the coughing. He took his time, breathing deeply and clearing his throat.

"Eddie was a tender child," he began hoarsely. "He got it from his mother. He wasn't a sissy. In fact, he was just as tough as other little boys." A long pause, another drag of nicotine. "Not far from our house was a nigger family—"

"Could we just call them blacks, Sam? I've asked you this already."

"Forgive me. There was an African family on our place. The Lincolns. Joe Lincoln was his name, and he'd worked for us for many years. Had a common-law wife and a dozen common-law children. One of the boys was the same age as Eddie, and they were inseparable, best of friends. It was not that unusual in those days. You played with whoever lived nearby. I even had little African buddies, believe it or not. When Eddie started school, he got real upset because he rode one bus and his African pal rode another. Kid's name was Quince. Quince Lincoln. They couldn't wait to get home from school and go play on the farm. I remember Eddie was always disturbed because they couldn't go to school together. And Quince couldn't spend the night in our house, and Eddie couldn't spend the night with the Lincolns. He was always asking me questions about why the Africans in Ford County were so poor, and lived in run-down houses, and didn't have nice clothes, and had so many children in each family. He really suffered over it, and that made him different. As he got older, he grew even more sympathetic toward the Africans. I tried to talk to him."

"Of course you did. You tried to straighten him out, didn't you?"

"I tried to explain things to him."

"Such as?"

"Such as the need to keep the races separate. There's nothing wrong with separate but equal schools. Nothing wrong with laws prohibiting miscegenation. Nothing wrong with keeping the Africans in their place."

"Where's their place?"

"Under control. Let 'em run wild, and look at what's happened. Crime, drugs, AIDS, illegitimate births, general breakdown in the moral fabric of society."

"What about nuclear proliferation and killer bees?"

"You get my point."

"What about basic rights, radical concepts like the right to vote, the right to use public rest rooms, the right to eat in restaurants and stay in hotels, the right not to be discriminated against in housing, employment, and education?"

"You sound like Eddie."

"Good."

"By the time he was finishing high school he was spouting off like that, talking about how badly the Africans were being mistreated. He left home when he was eighteen."

"Did you miss him?"

"Not at first, I guess. We were fighting a lot. He knew I was in the Klan, and he hated the sight of me. At least, he said he did."

"So you thought more of the Klan than you did your own son?"

Sam stared at the floor. Adam scribbled on a legal pad. The air conditioner rattled and faded, and for a moment seemed determined to finally quit. "He was a sweet kid," Sam said quietly. "We used to fish a lot, that was our big thing together. I had an old boat, and we'd spend hours on the lake fishing for crappie and bream, sometimes bass. Then he grew up and didn't like me. He was ashamed of me, and of course it hurt. He expected me to change, and I expected him to see the light like all the other white kids his age. It never happened. We drifted apart when he was in high school, then it seems like the civil rights crap started, and there was no hope after that."

"Did he participate in the movement?"

"No. He wasn't stupid. He might have been sympathetic, but he kept his mouth shut. You just didn't go around talking that trash if you were local. There were enough Northern Jews and radicals to keep things stirred up. They didn't need any help."

"What did he do after he left home?"

"Joined the Army. It was an easy way out of town, away from Mississippi. He was gone for three years, and when he came back he brought a wife. They lived in Clanton and we barely saw them. He talked to his mother occasionally, but didn't have much to say to me. It was the early sixties by then, and the African movement was getting cranked up. There were a lot of Klan meetings, a lot of activity, most to the south of us. Eddie kept his distance. He was very quiet, never had much to say anyway."

"Then I was born."

"You were born around the time those three civil rights workers disappeared. Eddie had the nerve to ask me if I was involved in it."

"Were you?"

"Hell no. I didn't know who did it for almost a year."

"They were Kluckers, weren't they?"

"They were Klansmen."

"Were you happy when those boys were murdered?"

"How the hell is that relevant to me and the gas chamber in 1990?"

"Did Eddie know it when you got involved with the bombing?"

"No one knew it in Ford County. We had not been too active. As I said, most of it was to the south of us, around Meridian."

"And you couldn't wait to jump in the middle of it?"

"They needed help. The Fibbies had infiltrated so deep hardly anyone could be trusted. The civil rights movement was snowballing fast. Something had to be done. I'm not ashamed of it."

Adam smiled and shook his head. "Eddie was ashamed, wasn't he?"

"Eddie didn't know anything about it until the Kramer bombing."

"Why did you involve him?"

"I didn't."

"Yes you did. You told your wife to get Eddie and drive to Cleveland and pick up your car. He was an accessory after the fact."

"I was in jail, okay. I was scared. And no one ever knew. It was harmless."

"Perhaps Eddie didn't think so."

"I don't know what Eddie thought, okay. By the time I got out of jail, he had disappeared. Y'all were gone. I never saw him again until his mother's funeral, and then he slipped in and out without a word to anyone." He rubbed the wrinkles on his forehead with his left hand, then ran it through his oily hair. His face was sad, and as he glanced through the slit Adam saw a trace of moisture in the eyes. "The last time I saw Eddie, he was getting in his car outside the church after the funeral service. He was in a hurry. Something told me I'd never see him again. He was there because his mother had died, and I knew that would be his last visit home. There was no other reason for him to come back. I was on the front steps of the church, Lee was with me, and we both watched him drive away. There I was burying my wife, and at the same time watching my son disappear for the last time."

"Did you try to find him?"

"No. Not really. Lee said she had a phone number, but I didn't feel like begging. It was obvious he didn't want anything to do with me, so I left him alone. I often wondered about you, and I remember telling your grandmother how nice it would be to see you. But I wasn't about to spend a lot of time trying to track y'all down."

"It would've been hard to find us."

"That's what I heard. Lee talked to Eddie occasionally, and she would report to me. It sounded like you guys were moving all over California."

"I went to six schools in twelve years."

"But why? What was he doing?"

"A number of things. He'd lose his job, and we'd move because we couldn't pay the rent. Then Mother

would find a job, and we'd move somewhere else. Then
Dad would get mad at my school for some vague reason, and he'd yank me out."

"What kind of work did he do?"

"Once he worked for the post office, until he got
fired. He threatened to sue them, and for a long time
he maintained this massive little war against the postal
system. He couldn't find a lawyer to take his case, so
he abused them with paperwork. He always had a
small desk with an old typewriter and boxes filled with
his papers, and they were his most valuable possessions. Every time we moved, he took great care with
his office, as he called it. He didn't care about anything
else, there wasn't much, but he protected his office
with his life. I can remember many nights lying in bed
trying to sleep and listening to that damned typewriter
pecking away at all hours. He hated the federal government."

"That's my boy."

"But for different reasons, I think. The IRS came after him one year, which I always found odd because he
didn't earn enough to pay three dollars in taxes. So he
declared war on the Infernal Revenue, as he called it,
and that raged for years. The State of California re-
voked his driver's license one year when he didn't renew, and this violated all sorts of civil and human
rights. Mother had to drive him for two years until he
surrendered to the bureaucracy. He was always writing
letters to the governor, the President, U.S. senators,
congressmen, anyone with an office and staff. He
would just raise hell about this and that, and when
they wrote him back he'd declare a small victory. He
saved every letter. He got in a fight one time with a
next-door neighbor, something to do with a strange
dog peeing on our porch, and they were yelling at each
other across the hedgerow. The madder they got, the

more powerful their friends became, and both were just minutes away from making phone calls to all sorts of hotshots who would instantly inflict punishment on the other. Dad ran in the house, and within seconds returned to the argument with thirteen letters from the governor of the State of California. He counted them loudly and waved them under the neighbor's nose, and the poor guy was crushed. End of argument. End of dog pissing on our porch. Of course, every one of the letters had asked him, in a nice way, to get lost."

Though they didn't realize it, they were both smiling by the end of this brief story.

"If he couldn't keep a job, how did y'all survive?" Sam asked, staring through the opening.

"I don't know. Mother always worked. She was very resourceful, and she sometimes kept two jobs. Cashier in a grocery store. Clerk in a pharmacy. She could do anything, and I remember a couple of pretty good jobs as a secretary. At some point, Dad got a license to sell life insurance, and that became a permanent part-time job. I guess he was good at it, because things improved as I got older. He could work his own hours and reported to no one. This suited him, although he said he hated insurance companies. He sued one for canceling a policy or something, I really didn't understand it, and he lost the case. Of course, he blamed it all on his lawyer, who made the mistake of sending Eddie a long letter full of strong statements. Dad typed for three days, and when his masterpiece was finished he proudly showed it to Mother. Twenty-one pages of mistakes and lies by the lawyer. She just shook her head. He fought with that poor lawyer for years."

"What kind of father was he?"

"I don't know. That's a hard question, Sam."

"Why?"

"Because of the way he died. I was mad at him for a

long time after his death, and I didn't understand how he could decide that he should leave us, that we didn't need him anymore, that it was time for him to check out. And after I learned the truth, I was mad at him for lying to me all those years, for changing my name and running away. It was terribly confusing for a young kid. Still is."

"Are you still angry?"

"Not really. I tend to remember the good things about Eddie. He was the only father I've had, so I don't know how to rate him. He didn't smoke, drink, gamble, do drugs, chase women, beat his kids, or any of that. He had trouble keeping a job, but we never went without food or shelter. He and Mother were constantly talking about divorce, but it didn't work out. She moved out several times, and then he would move out. It was disruptive, but Carmen and I became accustomed to it. He had his dark days, or bad times, as they were known, when he would withdraw to his room and lock the door and pull the shades. Mother would gather us around her and explain that he was not feeling well, and that we should be very quiet. No television or radios. She was very supportive when he withdrew. He would stay in his room for days, then suddenly emerge as if nothing happened. We learned to live with Eddie's bad times. He looked and dressed normal. He was almost always there if we needed him. We played baseball in the backyard and rode rides at the carnival. He took us to Disneyland a couple of times. I guess he was a good man, a good father who just had this dark, strange side that flared up occasionally."

"But you weren't close."

"No, we weren't close. He helped me with my homework and science projects, and he insisted on perfect report cards. We talked about the solar system and the environment, but never about girls and sex and cars. Never about family and ancestors. There was no intimacy. He was not a warm person. There were times when I needed him and he was locked up in his room."

Sam rubbed the corners of his eyes, then he leaned forward again on his elbows with his face close to the screen and looked directly at Adam. "What about his death?" he asked.

"What about it?"

"How'd it happen?"

Adam waited for a long time before answering. He could tell this story several ways. He could be cruel and hateful and brutally honest, and in doing so destroy the old man. There was a mighty temptation to do this. It needed to be done, he'd told himself many times before. Sam needed to suffer; he needed to be slapped in the face with the guilt of Eddie's suicide. Adam wanted to really hurt the old bastard and make him cry.

But at the same time he wanted to tell the story quickly, glossing over the painful parts and then moving on to something else. The poor old man sitting captive on the other side of the screen was suffering enough. The government was planning to kill him in less than four weeks. Adam suspected he knew more about Eddie's death than he let on.

"He was going through a bad time," Adam said, gazing at the screen but avoiding Sam. "He'd been in his room for three weeks, which was longer than usual. Mother kept telling us that he was getting better, just a few more days and he'd come out. We believed her, because he always seemed to bounce out of it. He picked a day when she was at work and Carmen was at a friend's house, a day when he knew I'd be the first one home. I found him lying on the floor of my bedroom, still holding the gun, a thirty-eight. One shot to the right temple. There was a neat circle of blood around his head. I sat on the edge of my bed."

"How old were you?"

"Almost seventeen. A junior in high school. Straight A's. I realized he'd carefully arranged a half dozen towels on the floor then placed himself in the middle of them. I checked the pulse in his wrist, and he was already stiff. Coroner said he'd been dead three hours. There was a note beside him, typed neatly on white paper. The note was addressed Dear Adam. Said he loved me, that he was sorry, that he wanted me to take care of the girls, and that maybe one day I would understand. Then he directed my attention to a plastic garbage bag, also on the floor, and said I should place the dirty towels in the garbage bag, wipe up the mess, then call the police. Don't touch the gun, he said. And hurry, before the girls get home." Adam cleared his throat and looked at the floor.

"And so I did exactly what he said, and I waited for the police. We were alone for fifteen minutes, just the two of us. He was lying on the floor, and I was lying on my bed looking down at him. I started crying and crying, asking him why and how and what happened and a hundred other questions. There was my dad, the only dad I would ever have, lying there in his faded jeans and dirty socks and favorite UCLA sweatshirt. From the neck down he could've been napping, but he had a hole in his head and the blood had dried in his hair. I hated him for dying, and I felt so sorry for him because he was dead. I remember asking him why he hadn't talked to me before this. I asked him a lot of questions. I heard voices, and suddenly the room was filled with cops. They took me to the den and put a blanket around me. And that was the end of my father."

Sam was still on his elbows, but one hand was now

over his eyes. There were just a couple more things Adam wanted to say.

"After the funeral, Lee stayed with us for a while. She told me about you and about the Cayhalls. She filled in a lot of gaps about my father. I became fascinated with you and the Kramer bombing, and I began reading old magazine articles and newspaper stories. It took about a year for me to figure out why Eddie killed himself when he did. He'd been hiding in his room during your trial, and he killed himself when it was over."

Sam removed his hand and glared at Adam with wet eyes. "So you blame me for his death, right, Adam? That's what you really want to say, isn't it?"

"No. I don't blame you entirely."

"Then how much? Eighty percent? Ninety percent? You've had time to do the numbers. How much of it's my fault?"

"I don't know, Sam. Why don't you tell me?"

Sam wiped his eyes and raised his voice. "Oh what the hell! I'll claim a hundred percent. I'll take full responsibility for his death, okay? Is that what you want?"

"Take whatever you want."

"Don't patronize me! Just add my son's name to my list, is that what you want? The Kramer twins, their father, then Eddie. That's four I've killed, right? Anyone else you want to tack on here at the end? Do it quick, old boy, because the clock is ticking."

"How many more are out there?"

"Dead bodies?"

"Yes. Dead bodies. I've heard the rumors."

"And of course you believe them, don't you? You seem eager to believe everything bad about me."

"I didn't say I believed them."

Sam jumped to his feet and walked to the end of the room. "I'm tired of this conversation!" he yelled from thirty feet away. "And I'm tired of you! I almost wish I had those damned Jew lawyers harassing me again."

"We can accommodate you," Adam shot back.

Sam walked slowly back to his chair. "Here I am worried about my ass, twenty-three days away from the chamber, and all you want to do is talk about dead people. Just keep chirping away, old boy, and real soon you can start talking about me. I want some action."

"I filed a petition this morning."

"Fine! Then leave, dammit. Just get the hell out and stop tormenting me!"

TWENTY-TWO

THE DOOR on Adam's side opened, and Packer entered with two gentlemen behind him. They were obviously lawyers—dark suits, frowns, thick bulging briefcases. Packer pointed to some chairs under the air conditioner, and they sat down. He looked at Adam, and paid particular attention to Sam, who was still standing on the other side. "Everything okay?" he asked Adam.

Adam nodded and Sam eased into his chair. Packer left and the two new lawyers efficiently went about their business of pulling heavy documents from fat files. Within a minute, both jackets were off.

Five minutes passed without a word from Sam. Adam caught a few glimpses from the lawyers on the other end. They were in the same room with the most famous inmate on the Row, the next one to be gassed, and they couldn't help but steal curious peeks at Sam Cayhall and his lawyer.

Then the door opened behind Sam, and two guards entered with a wiry little black man who was shackled and manacled and cuffed as if he might erupt any moment and kill dozens with his bare hands. They led him to a seat across from his lawyers, and went about the business of liberating most of his limbs. The hands remained cuffed behind his back. One of the guards left the room, but the other took a position halfway between Sam and the black inmate.

Sam glanced down the counter at his comrade, a nervous type who evidently was not happy with his lawyers. His lawyers did not appear to be thrilled either. Adam watched them from his side of the screen, and within minutes their heads were close together and they were talking in unison through the slit while their client sat militantly on his hands. Their low voices were audible, but their words were indecipherable.

Sam eased forward again, on his elbows, and motioned for Adam to do likewise. Their faces met ten inches apart with the opening between them.

"That's Stockholm Turner," Sam said, almost in a whisper.

"Stockholm?"

"Yeah, but he goes by Stock. These rural Africans love unusual names. He says he has a brother named Denmark and one named Germany. Probably does."

"What'd he do?" Adam asked, suddenly curious.

"Robbed a whiskey store, I think. Shot the owner. About two years ago he got a death warrant, and it went down to the wire. He came within two hours of the chamber."

"What happened?"

"His lawyers got a stay, and they've been fighting ever since. You can never tell, but he'll probably be the next after me."

They both looked toward the end of the room where the conference was raging in full force. Stock was off his hands and sitting on the edge of his chair and raising hell with his lawyers.

Sam grinned, then chuckled, then leaned even closer to the screen. "Stock's family is dirt poor, and they have little to do with him. It's not unusual, really, especially with the Africans. He seldom gets mail or visitors. He was born fifty miles from here, but the free world has forgotten about him. As his appeals were losing steam, Stock started worrying about life and death and things in general. Around here, if no one claims your body, then the state buries you like a pauper in some cheap grave. Stock got concerned about what would happen to his body, and he started asking all kinds of questions. Packer and some of the guards picked up on it, and they convinced Stock that his body would be sent to a crematorium where it would be burned. The ashes would be dropped from the air and spread over Parchman. They told him that since he'd be full of gas anyway, when they stuck a match to him he'd go off like a bomb. Stock was devastated. He had trouble sleeping and lost weight. Then he started writing letters to his family and friends begging them for a few dollars so he could have a Christian burial, as he called it. The money trickled in, and he wrote more letters. He wrote to ministers and civil rights groups. Even his lawyers sent money.

"When his stay was lifted, Stock had close to four hundred dollars, and he was ready to die. Or so he thought."

Sam's eyes were dancing and his voice was light. He told the story slowly, in a low voice, and savored the details. Adam was amused more by the telling than by the narrative.

"They have a loose rule here that allows almost unlimited visitation for seventy-two hours prior to the execution. As long as there's no security risk, they'll allow the condemned man to do damned near anything. There's a little office up front with a desk and phone, and that becomes the visiting room. It's usually filled with all sorts of people—grandmothers, nieces, nephews, cousins, aunties—especially with these Africans. Hell, they run 'em in here by the busload. Kinfolks who haven't spent five minutes thinking about the inmate suddenly show up to share his last moments. It almost becomes a social event.

"They also have this rule, it's unwritten I'm sure,

that allows one final conjugal visit with the wife. If there's no wife, then the warden in his boundless mercy allows a brief appointment with a girlfriend. One last little quickie before lover boy checks out." Sam glanced along the counter at Stock, then leaned even closer.

"Well, ole Stock here is one of the more popular residents of the Row, and he somehow convinced the warden that he had both a wife and a girlfriend, and that these ladies would agree to spend a few moments with him before he died. At the same time! All three of them, together! The warden allegedly knew something fishy was going on, but everyone likes Stock, and, well, they were about to kill him anyway, so what's the harm. So Stock here was sitting in the little room with his mother and sisters and cousins and nieces, a whole passel of Africans, most of whom hadn't uttered his name in ten years, and he was eating his last meal of steak and potatoes while everybody else was crying and grieving and praying. With about four hours to go, they emptied the room and sent the family to the chapel. Stock waited for a few minutes while another van brought his wife and his girlfriend here to the Row. They arrived with guards, and were taken to the little office up front where Stock was waiting, all wild-eyed and ready. Poor guy'd been on the Row for twelve years.

"Well, they brought in a little cot for this liaison, and Stock and his gals got it on. The guards said later that Stock had some fine-looking women, and the guards also said they commented at the time on how young they looked. Stock was just about to have a go with either his wife or his girlfriend, it didn't really matter, when the phone rang. It was his lawyer. And his lawyer was crying and out of breath as he yelled out the great news that the Fifth Circuit had issued a stay.

"Stock hung up on him. He had more important matters at hand. A few minutes passed, then the phone rang again. Stock grabbed it. It was his lawyer again, and this time he was much more composed as he explained to Stock the legal maneuvering that had saved his life, for the moment. Stock offered his appreciation, then asked his lawyer to keep it quiet for another hour."

Adam again glanced to his right, and wondered which of the two lawyers had called Stock while he was exercising his constitutional right of the last conjugal visit.

"Well, by this time, the Attorney General's office had talked to the warden, and the execution had been called off, or aborted as they like to say. Made no difference to Stock. He was proceeding as if he would never see another woman. The door to the room cannot be locked from the inside, for obvious reasons, so Naifeh, after waiting patiently, gently knocked on the door and asked Stock to come on out. Time to go back to your cell, Stock, he said. Stock said he needed just another five minutes. No, said Naifeh. Please, Stock begged, and suddenly there were noises again. So the warden grinned at the guards who grinned at the warden, and for five minutes they studied the floor while the cot rattled and bounced around the little room.

"Stock finally opened the door and strutted out like the heavyweight champ of the world. The guards said he was happier about his performance than he was about his stay. They quickly got rid of the women, who as it turned out, were not really his wife and girlfriend after all."

"Who were they?"

"A couple of prostitutes."

"Prostitutes!" Adam said a bit too loud, and one of the lawyers stared at him.

Sam leaned so close his nose was almost in the slit. "Yeah, local whores. His brother somehow arranged it for him. Remember the funeral money he worked so hard to raise."

"You're kidding."

"That's it. Four hundred bucks spent on whores, which at first seems a bit stiff, especially for local African whores, but it seems they were scared to death about coming to death row, which I guess makes sense. They took all Stock's money. He told me later he didn't give a damn how they buried him. Said it was worth every dime. Naifeh got embarrassed, and he threatened to prohibit the conjugal visits. But Stock's lawyer, that little dark-haired one over there, filed a lawsuit and got a ruling that ensures one last quickie. I think Stock's almost looking forward to his next one."

Sam leaned back in his chair and the smile slowly left his face. "Personally, I haven't given much thought to my conjugal visit. It's intended for husband and wife relations only, you know, that's what the term means. But the warden'll probably bend the rules for me. What do you think?"

"I really haven't thought about it."

"I'm just kidding, you know. I'm an old man. I'd settle for a back rub and a stiff drink."

"What about your last meal?" Adam asked, still very quietly.

"That's not funny."

"I thought we were kidding."

"Probably something gross like boiled pork and rubber peas. Same crap they've been feeding me for almost ten years. Maybe an extra piece of toast. I'd hate to give the cook the opportunity to prepare a meal fit for free world humans."

"Sounds delicious."

"Oh, I'll share it with you. I've often wondered why they feed you before they kill you. They also bring the doctor in and give you a preexecution physical. Can you believe it? Gotta make sure you're fit to die. And they have a shrink on staff here who examines you before the execution, and he must report to the warden in writing that you're mentally sound enough to gas. And they have a minister on the payroll who'll pray and meditate with you and make sure your soul is headed in the right direction. All paid for by the taxpayers of the State of Mississippi and administered by these loving people around here. Don't forget the conjugal visit. You can die with your lust satisfied. They think of everything. They're very considerate. Really concerned about your appetite and health and spiritual well-being. Right at the very last, they put a catheter in your penis and a plug up your ass so you won't make a mess. This is for their benefit, not yours. They don't wanna have to clean you afterward. So, they feed you real good, anything you want, then they plug you up. Sick, isn't it? Sick, sick, sick, sick."

"Let's talk about something else."

Sam finished the last cigarette and thumped it on the floor in front of the guard. "No. Let's stop talking. I've had enough for one day."

"Fine."

"And no more about Eddie, okay? It's really not fair to come in here and hit me with stuff like that."

"I'm sorry. No more about Eddie."

"Let's try to focus on me the next three weeks, okay? That's more than enough to keep us busy."

"It's a deal, Sam."

ALONG HIGHWAY 82 from the east, Greenville was growing in an unsightly sprawl, with its strip shopping centers filled with video rental and dinky liquor stores, and its endless fast-food franchises and drive-up motels with free cable and breakfast. The river blocked such progress to the west, and since 82 was the main corridor it had evidently become the developers' favorite territory.

In the past twenty-five years, Greenville had grown from a sleepy river town of thirty-five thousand to a busy river city of sixty thousand. It was prosperous and progressive. In 1990, Greenville was the fifth-largest city in the state.

The streets leading into the central district were shaded and lined with stately old homes. The center of the town was pretty and quaint, well preserved and apparently unchanged, Adam thought, in stark contrast to the thoughtless chaos along Highway 82. He parked on Washington Street, at a few minutes after five, as downtown merchants and their customers were busy preparing for the end of the day. He removed his tie and left it with his jacket in the car because the temperature was still in the nineties and showed no sign of relenting.

He walked three blocks, and found the park with the life-sized bronze statue of two little boys in the center. They were the same size with the same smile and the same eyes. One was running while the other one skipped, and the sculptor had captured them perfectly. Josh and John Kramer, forever five years old, frozen in time with copper and tin. A brass plate below them said simply:

JOSH AND JOHN KRAMER
DIED HERE ON APRIL 21, 1967
(MARCH 2, 1962–APRIL 21, 1967)

The park was a perfect square, half a city block that had once held Marvin's law office and an old building next to it. The land had been in the Kramer family for years, and Marvin's father gave it to the city to be used as a memorial. Sam had done a fine job of leveling the law office, and the city had razed the building next to it. Some money had been spent on Kramer Park, and a lot of thought had gone into it. It was completely fenced with ornamental wrought iron and an entrance on each side from the sidewalks. Perfect rows of oaks and maples followed the fencing. Lines of manicured shrubs met at precise angles, then encircled flower beds of begonias and geraniums. A small amphitheater sat in one corner under the trees, and across the way a group of black children sailed through the air on wooden swings.

It was small and colorful, a pleasant little garden amid the streets and buildings. A teenaged couple argued on a bench as Adam walked by. A bicycle gang of eight-year-olds roared around a fountain. An ancient policeman ambled by and actually tipped his hat to Adam as he said hello.

He sat on a bench and stared at Josh and John, less than thirty feet away. "Never forget the victims," Lee had admonished. "They have the right to want retribution. They've earned it."

He remembered all the gruesome details from the trials—the FBI expert who testified about the bomb and the speed at which it ripped through the building; the medical examiner who delicately described the little bodies and what exactly killed them; the firemen who tried to rescue but were much too late and were left only to retrieve. There had been photographs of the building and the boys, and the trial judges had used great restraint in allowing just a few of these to go to the jury. McAllister, typically, had wanted to show huge enlarged color pictures of the mangled bodies, but they were excluded.

Adam was now sitting on ground that had once been the office of Marvin Kramer, and he closed his eyes and tried to feel the ground shake. He saw the footage from his video of smoldering debris and the cloud of dust suspended over the scene. He heard the frantic voice of the news reporter, the sirens shrieking in the background.

Those bronze boys were not much older than he was when his grandfather killed them. They were five and he was almost three, and for some reason he kept up with their ages. Today, he was twenty-six and they would be twenty-eight.

The guilt hit hard and low in the stomach. It made him shudder and sweat. The sun hid behind two large oaks to the west, and as it flickered through the branches the boys' faces gleamed.

How could Sam have done this? Why was Sam Cayhall his grandfather and not someone else's? When did he decide to participate in the Klan's holy war against Jews? What made him change from a harmless cross-burner to a full-fledged terrorist?

Adam sat on the bench, stared at the statue, and hated his grandfather. He felt guilty for being in Mississippi trying to help the old bastard.

He found a Holiday Inn and paid for a room. He called Lee and reported in, then watched the evening news on the Jackson channels. Evidently, it had been just another languid summer day in Mississippi with little happening. Sam Cayhall and his latest efforts to stay alive were the hot topics. Each station carried somber comments by the governor and the Attorney General about the newest petition for relief filed by the defense this morning, and each man was just sick and tired of the endless appeals. Each would fight valiantly to pursue this matter until justice was realized. One station began its own countdown—twenty-three days until execution, the anchorperson rattled off, as if reciting the number of shopping days left until Christmas. The number 23 was plastered under the same overworked photo of Sam Cayhall.

Adam ate dinner in a small downtown café. He sat alone in a booth, picking at roast beef and peas, listening to harmless chatter around him. No one mentioned Sam.

At dusk, he walked the sidewalks in front of the shops and stores, and thought of Sam pacing along these same streets, on the same concrete, waiting for the bomb to go off and wondering what in the world had gone wrong. He stopped by a phone booth, maybe the same one Sam had tried to use to call and warn Kramer.

The park was deserted and dark. Two gaslight street-lamps stood by the front entrance, providing the only light. Adam sat at the base of the statue, under the boys, under the brass plate with their names and dates of birth and death. On this very spot, it said, they died.

He sat there for a long time, oblivious to the darkness, pondering imponderables, wasting time with fruitless considerations of what might have been. The bomb had defined his life, he knew that much. It had taken him away from Mississippi and deposited him in another world with a new name. It had transformed his parents into refugees, fleeing their past and hiding from their present. It had killed his father, in all likelihood, though no one could predict what might have happened to Eddie Cayhall. The bomb had played a principal role in Adam's decision to become a lawyer, a calling he'd never felt until he learned of Sam. He'd dreamed of flying airplanes.

And now the bomb had led him back to Mississippi

for an undertaking laden with agony and little hope. The odds were heavy that the bomb would claim its final victim in twenty-three days, and Adam wondered what would happen to him after that.

What else could the bomb have in store for him?

TWENTY-THREE

FOR THE MOST PART, death penalty appeals drag along for years at a snail's pace. A very old snail. No one is in a hurry. The issues are complicated. The briefs, motions, petitions, et cetera, are thick and burdensome. The court dockets are crowded with more pressing matters.

Occasionally, though, a ruling can come down with stunning speed. Justice can become terribly efficient. Especially in the waning days, when a date for an execution has been set and the courts are tired of more motions, more appeals. Adam received his first dose of quick justice while he was wandering the streets of Greenville Monday afternoon.

The Mississippi Supreme Court took one look at his petition for postconviction relief, and denied it around 5 P.M. Monday. Adam was just arriving in Greenville and knew nothing about it. The denial was certainly no surprise, but its speed certainly was. The court kept the petition less than eight hours. In all fairness, the court had dealt with Sam Cayhall off and on for over ten years.

In the final days of death cases, the courts watch each other closely. Copies of filings and rulings are faxed along so that the higher courts know what's coming. The denial by the Mississippi Supreme Court was routinely faxed to the federal district court in Jackson, Adam's next forum. It was sent to the Honorable F. Flynn Slattery, a young federal judge who was new

to the bench. He had not been involved with the
Cayhall appeals.

Judge Slattery's office attempted to locate Adam Hall
between 5 and 6 P.M. Monday, but he was sitting in
Kramer Park. Slattery called the Attorney General,
Steve Roxburgh, and at eight-thirty a brief meeting
took place in the judge's office. The judge happened to
be a workaholic, and this was his first death case. He
and his clerk studied the petition until midnight.

If Adam had watched the late news Monday, he
would have learned that his petition had already been
denied by the supreme court. He was, however, sound
asleep.

At six Tuesday morning, he casually picked up the
Jackson paper and learned that the supreme court had
turned him down, that the matter was now in federal
court, assigned to Judge Slattery, and that both the Attorney General and the governor were claiming another victory. Odd, he thought, since he hadn't yet officially filed anything in federal court. He jumped into
his car and raced to Jackson, two hours away. At nine,
he entered the federal courthouse on Capitol Street in
downtown, and met briefly with Breck Jefferson, an
unsmiling young man, fresh from law school and holding the important position of Slattery's law clerk.
Adam was told to return at eleven for a meeting with
the judge.

ALTHOUGH HE ARRIVED at Slattery's office at exactly eleven, it was obvious a meeting of sorts had been
in progress for some time. In the center of Slattery's
huge office was a mahogany conference table, long and
wide with eight black leather chairs on each side. Slattery's throne was at one end, near his desk, and before
him on the table were stacks of papers, legal pads, and
other effects. The side to his right was crowded with

young white men in navy suits, all bunched together along the table, with another row of eager warriors seated close behind. This side belonged to the state, with His Honor, the governor, Mr. David McAllister, sitting closest to Slattery. His Honor, the Attorney General, Steve Roxburgh, had been banished to the middle of the table in an obvious losing battle over turf. Each distinguished public servant had brought to the table his most trusted litigators and thinkers, and this squadron of strategists had obviously been meeting with the judge and plotting long before Adam arrived.

Breck, the clerk, swung the door open and greeted Adam pleasantly enough, then asked him to step inside. The room was instantly silent as Adam slowly approached the table. Slattery reluctantly rose from his chair and introduced himself to Adam. The handshake was cold and fleeting. "Have a seat," he said ominously, fluttering his left hand at the eight leather chairs on the defense side of the table. Adam hesitated, then picked one directly across from a face he recognized as belonging to Roxburgh. He placed his briefcase on the table, and sat down. Four empty chairs were to his right, in the direction of Slattery, and three to his left. He felt like a lonesome trespasser.

"I assume you know the governor and the Attorney General," Slattery said, as if everyone had personally met these two.

"Neither," Adam said, shaking his head slightly.

"I'm David McAllister, Mr. Hall, nice to meet you," the governor said quickly, ever the anxious glad-handing politician, with an incredibly rapid flash of flawless teeth.

"A pleasure," Adam said, barely moving his lips.

"And I'm Steve Roxburgh," said the Attorney General.

Adam only nodded at him. He'd seen his face in the newspapers.

Roxburgh took the initiative. He began talking and pointing at people. "These are attorneys from my criminal appeals division. Kevin Laird, Bart Moody, Morris Henry, Hugh Simms, and Joseph Ely. These guys handle all death penalty cases." They all nodded obediently while maintaining their suspicious frowns. Adam counted eleven people on the other side of the table.

McAllister chose not to introduce his band of clones, all of whom were suffering from either migraines or hemorrhoids. Their faces were contorted from pain, or perhaps from quite serious deliberation about legal matters at hand.

"Hope we haven't jumped the gun, Mr. Hall," Slattery said as he slipped a pair of reading glasses on his nose. He was in his early forties, one of the young Reagan appointees. "When do you expect to officially file your petition here in federal court?"

"Today," Adam said nervously, still astounded by the speed of it all. This was a positive development though, he'd decided while driving to Jackson. If Sam got any relief, it would be in federal court, not state.

"When can the state respond?" the judge asked Roxburgh.

"Tomorrow morning. Assuming the petition here raises the same issues as those raised in the supreme court."

"They're the same," Adam said to Roxburgh, then he turned to Slattery. "I was told to be here at eleven o'clock. What time did the meeting start?"

"The meeting started when I decided it would start, Mr. Hall," Slattery said icily. "Do you have a problem with that?"

"Yes. It's obvious this conference started some time ago, without me."

"What's wrong with that? This is my office, and I'll start meetings whenever I want."

"Yeah, but it's my petition, and I was invited here to discuss it. Seems as though I should've been here for the entire meeting."

"You don't trust me, Mr. Hall?" Slattery was easing forward on his elbows, thoroughly enjoying this.

"I don't trust anybody," Adam said, staring at His Honor.

"We're trying to accommodate you, Mr. Hall. Your client doesn't have much time, and I'm only trying to move things along. I thought you'd be pleased that we were able to arrange this meeting with such speed."

"Thank you," Adam said, and looked at his legal pad. There was a brief silence as the tension eased a bit.

Slattery held a sheet of paper. "Get the petition filed today. The state will file its response tomorrow. I'll consider it over the weekend and issue a ruling on Monday. In the event I decide to conduct a hearing, I need to know from both sides how long it will take to prepare. How about you, Mr. Hall? How long to get ready for a hearing?"

Sam had twenty-two days to live. Any hearing would have to be a hurried, concise affair with quick witnesses and, he hoped, a swift ruling by the court. Adding to the stress of the moment was the crucial fact that Adam had no idea how long it would take to prepare for a hearing, because he'd never tried such a matter. He'd participated in a few minor skirmishes in Chicago, but always with Emmitt Wycoff close by. He was just a rookie, dammit! He wasn't even certain where the courtroom was located.

And something told him that the eleven vultures examining him at this precise second knew full well he didn't know what the hell he was doing. "I can be ready in a week," he said with a steady poker face and as much faith as he could muster.

"Very well," Slattery said, as if this was fine, a good answer, Adam, good boy. A week was reasonable. Then Roxburgh whispered something to one of his warlocks, and the whole bunch thought it was funny. Adam ignored them.

Slattery scribbled something with an ink pen, then studied it. He gave it to Breck the clerk, who treasured it and raced off to do something else with it. His Honor looked along the wall of legal infantry to his right, then he dropped his gaze upon young Adam. "Now, Mr. Hall, there's something else I'd like to discuss. As you know, this execution is scheduled to take place in twenty-two days, and I would like to know if this court can expect any additional filings on behalf of Mr. Cayhall. I know this is an unusual request, but we're operating here in an unusual situation. Frankly, this is my first involvement with a death penalty case as advanced as this one, and I think it's best if we all work together here."

In other words, Your Honor, you want to make damned sure there are no stays. Adam thought for a second. It was an unusual request, and one that was quite unfair. But Sam had a constitutional right to file anything at any time, and Adam could not be bound by any promises made here. He decided to be polite. "I really can't say, Your Honor. Not now. Maybe next week."

"Surely you'll file the usual gangplank appeals," Roxburgh said, and the smirking bastards around him all looked at Adam with wondrous amazement.

"Frankly, Mr. Roxburgh, I'm not required to discuss my plans with you. Or with the court, for that matter."

"Of course not," McAllister chimed in for some reason, probably just his inability to stay quiet for more than five minutes.

Adam had noticed the lawyer sitting to Roxburgh's right, a methodical sort with steely eyes that seldom left Adam. He was young but gray, clean-shaven, and very neat. McAllister favored him, and had leaned to his right several times as if receiving advice. The others from the AG's office seemed to accede to his thoughts and movements. There was a reference in one of the hundred articles Adam had clipped and filed away about an infamous litigator in the AG's office known as Dr. Death, a clever bird with a penchant for pushing death penalty cases to their conclusion. Either his first or last name was Morris, and Adam vaguely recalled a Morris something or other mentioned moments earlier during Roxburgh's garbled introduction of his staff.

Adam assumed him to be the nefarious Dr. Death. Morris Henry was his name.

"Well, hurry up and file them then," Slattery said with a good dose of frustration. "I don't want to work around the clock as this thing goes down to the wire."

"No sir," Adam said in mock sympathy.

Slattery glared at him for a moment, then returned to the paperwork in front of him. "Very well, gentlemen, I suggest you stick by your telephones Sunday night and Monday morning. I'll be calling as soon as I've made a decision. This meeting is adjourned."

The conspiracy on the other side broke up in a flurry of papers and files snatched from the table and sudden mumbled conversations. Adam was nearest the door. He nodded at Slattery, offered a feeble "Good day, Your Honor," and left the office. He gave a polite grin to the secretary and was into the hallway when someone called his name. It was the governor, with two flunkies in tow.

"Can we talk a minute?" McAllister asked, out

thrusting a hand at Adam's waist. They shook for a second.

"What about?"

"Just five minutes, okay."

Adam looked at the governor's boys waiting a few feet away. "Alone. Private. And off the record," he said.

"Sure," McAllister said, then pointed to a set of double doors. They stepped inside a small empty courtroom with the lights off. The governor's hands were free. Someone else carried his briefcase and bags. He stuck them deep in his pockets and leaned against a railing. He was lean and well dressed, nice suit, fashionable silk tie, obligatory white cotton shirt. He was under forty and aging remarkably well. Only a touch of gray tinted his sideburns. "How's Sam?" he asked, feigning deep concern.

Adam snorted, looked away, then set his briefcase on the floor. "Oh, he's wonderful. I'll tell him you asked. He'll be thrilled."

"I'd heard he was in bad health."

"Health? You're trying to kill him. How can you be worried about his health?"

"Just heard a rumor."

"He hates your guts, okay? His health is bad, but he can hang on for another three weeks."

"Hate is nothing new for Sam, you know."

"What exactly do you want to talk about?"

"Just wanted to say hello. I'm sure we'll get together shortly."

"Look, Governor, I have a signed contract with my client that expressly forbids me from talking to you. I repeat, he hates you. You're the reason he's on death row. He blames you for everything, and if he knew we were talking now, he'd fire me."

"Your own grandfather would fire you?"

"Yes. I truly believe it. So if I read in tomorrow's paper that you met with me today and we discussed Sam Cayhall, then I'll be on my way back to Chicago, which will probably screw up your execution because Sam won't have a lawyer. Can't kill a man if he doesn't have a lawyer."

"Says who?"

"Just keep it quiet, okay?"

"You have my word. But if we can't talk, then how do we discuss the issue of clemency?"

"I don't know. I haven't reached that point yet."

McAllister's face was always pleasant. The comely smile was always in place or just beneath the surface. "You have thought about clemency, haven't you?"

"Yes. With three weeks to go, I've thought about clemency. Every death row inmate dreams of a pardon, Governor, and that's why you can't grant one. You pardon one convict, and you'll have the other fifty pestering you for the same favor. Fifty families writing letters and calling night and day. Fifty lawyers pulling strings and trying to get into your office. You and I both know it can't be done."

"I'm not sure he should die."

He said this while looking away, as if a change of heart was under way, as if the years had matured him and softened his zeal to punish Sam. Adam started to say something, then realized the magnitude of these last words. He watched the floor for a minute, paying particular attention to the governor's tasseled loafers. The governor was deep in thought.

"I'm not sure he should die, either," Adam said.

"How much has he told you?"

"About what?"

"About the Kramer bombing."

"He says he's told me everything."

"But you have doubts?"

"Yes."

"So do I. I always had doubts."

"Why?"

"Lots of reasons. Jeremiah Dogan was a notorious liar, and he was scared to death of going to prison. The IRS had him cold, you know, and he was convinced that if he went to prison he'd be raped and tortured and killed by gangs of blacks. He was the Imperial Wizard, you know. Dogan was also ignorant about a lot of things. He was sly and hard to catch when it came to terrorism, but he didn't understand the criminal justice system. I always thought someone, probably the FBI, told Dogan that Sam had to be convicted or they'd ship him off to prison. No conviction, no deal. He was a very eager witness on the stand. He desperately wanted the jury to convict Sam."

"So he lied?"

"I don't know. Maybe."

"About what?"

"Have you asked Sam if he had an accomplice?"

Adam paused for a second and analyzed the question. "I really can't discuss what Sam and I have talked about. It's confidential."

"Of course it is. There are a lot of people in this state who secretly do not wish to see Sam executed." McAllister was now watching Adam closely.

"Are you one of them?"

"I don't know. But what if Sam didn't plan to kill either Marvin Kramer or his sons? Sure Sam was there, right in the thick of it. But what if someone else possessed the intent to murder?"

"Then Sam isn't as guilty as we think."

"Right. He's certainly not innocent, but not guilty enough to be executed either. This bothers me, Mr. Hall. Can I call you Adam?"

"Of course."

"I don't suppose Sam has mentioned anything about an accomplice."

"I really can't discuss that. Not now."

The governor slipped a hand from a pocket and gave Adam a business card. "Two phone numbers on the back. One is my private office number. The other is my home number. All phone calls are confidential, I swear. I play for the cameras sometimes, Adam, it goes with the job, but I can also be trusted."

Adam took the card and looked at the handwritten numbers.

"I couldn't live with myself if I failed to pardon a man who didn't deserve to die," McAllister said as he walked to the door. "Give me a call, but don't wait too late. This thing's already heating up. I'm getting twenty phone calls a day."

He winked at Adam, showed him the sparkling teeth once again, and left the room.

Adam sat in a metal chair against the wall, and looked at the front of the card. It was gold-embossed with an official seal. Twenty calls a day. What did that mean? Did the callers want Sam dead or did they want him pardoned?

A lot of people in this state do not wish to see Sam executed, he'd said, as if he was already weighing the votes he'd lose against those he might gain.

TWENTY-FOUR

THE SMILE from the receptionist in the foyer was not as quick as usual, and as Adam walked to his office he detected a more somber atmosphere among the staff and the handful of lawyers. The chatter was an octave lower. Things were a bit more urgent.

Chicago had arrived. It happened occasionally, not necessarily for purposes of inspection, but more often than not to service a local client or to conduct bureaucratic little firm meetings. No one had ever been fired when Chicago arrived. No one had ever been cursed or abused. But it always provided for a few anxious moments until Chicago left and headed back North.

Adam opened his office door and nearly smacked into the worried face of E. Garner Goodman, complete with green paisley bow tie, white starched shirt, bushy gray hair. He'd been pacing around the room and happened to be near the door when it opened. Adam stared at him, then took his hand and shook it quickly.

"Come in, come in," Goodman said, closing the door as he invited Adam into his own office. He hadn't smiled yet.

"What are you doing here?" Adam asked, throwing his briefcase on the floor and walking to his desk. They faced each other.

Goodman stroked his neat gray beard, then adjusted his bow tie. "There's a bit of an emergency, I'm afraid. Could be bad news."

"What?"

"Sit down, sit down. This might take a minute."

"No. I'm fine. What is it?" It had to be horrible if he needed to take it sitting down.

Goodman tinkered with his bow tie, rubbed his beard, then said, "Well, it happened at nine this morning. You see, the Personnel Committee is made up of fifteen partners, almost all are younger guys. The full committee has several subcommittees, of course, one for recruiting, hiring, one for discipline, one for disputes, and on and on. And, as you might guess, there's one for terminations. The Termination Subcommittee met this morning, and guess who was there to orchestrate everything."

"Daniel Rosen."

"Daniel Rosen. Evidently, he's been working the Termination Subcommittee for ten days trying to line up enough votes for your dismissal."

Adam sat in a chair at the table, and Goodman sat across from him.

"There are seven members of the subcommittee, and they met this morning at Rosen's request. There were five members present, so they had a quorum. Rosen, of course, did not notify me or anyone else. Termination meetings are strictly confidential, for obvious reasons, so there was no requirement that he notify anyone."

"Not even me?"

"No, not even you. You were the only item on the agenda, and the meeting lasted less than an hour. Rosen had the deck stacked before he went in, but he presented his case very forcefully. Remember, he was a courtroom brawler for thirty years. They record all termination meetings, just in case there's litigation afterward, so Rosen made a complete record. He, of course, claims that you were deceitful when you applied for employment with Kravitz & Bane; that it presents the firm with a conflict of interest, and on and on. And he had copies of a dozen or so newspaper articles about you and Sam and the grandfather-grandson angle. His argument was that you had embarrassed the firm. He was very prepared. I think we underestimated him last Monday."

"And so they voted."

"Four to one to terminate you."

"Bastards!"

"I know. I've seen Rosen in tough spots before, and the guy can be brutally persuasive. He usually gets his way. He can't go to courtrooms anymore, so he's picking fights around the office. He'll be gone in six months."

"That's a small comfort at the moment."

"There's hope. Word finally filtered to my office around eleven, and luckily Emmitt Wycoff was in. We went to Rosen's office and had a terrible fight, then we got on the phone. Bottom line is this—the full Personnel Committee meets at eight o'clock in the morning to review your dismissal. You need to be there."

"Eight o'clock in the morning!"

"Yeah. These guys are busy. Many have court dates at nine. Some have depositions all day. Out of fifteen, we'll be lucky to have a quorum."

"How much is a quorum?"

"Two-thirds. Ten. And if there's no quorum, then we might be in trouble."

"Trouble! What do you call this?"

"It could get worse. If there's no quorum in the morning, then you have the right to request another review in thirty days."

"Sam will be dead in thirty days."

"Maybe not. At any rate, I think we'll have the meeting in the morning. Emmitt and I have commitments from nine of the members to be there."

"What about the four who voted against me this morning?"

Goodman grinned and glanced away. "Guess. Rosen made sure his votes can be there tomorrow."

Adam suddenly slapped the table with both hands. "I quit, dammit!"

"You can't quit. You've just been terminated."

"Then I won't fight it. Sonofabitches!"

"Listen, Adam—"

"Sonofabitches!"

Goodman retreated for a moment to allow Adam to cool. He straightened his bow tie and checked the growth of his beard. He tapped his fingers on the table. Then he said, "Look, Adam, we're in good shape in the morning, okay. Emmitt thinks so. I think so. The firm's behind you on this. We believe in what you're doing, and, frankly, we've enjoyed the publicity. There've been nice stories in the Chicago papers."

"The firm certainly appears to be supportive."

"Just listen to me. We can pull this off tomorrow. I'll do most of the talking. Wycoff's twisting arms right now. We've got other people twisting arms."

"Rosen's not stupid, Mr. Goodman. He wants to win, that's all. He doesn't care about me, doesn't care about Sam, or you, or anyone else involved. He simply wants to win. It's a contest, and I'll bet he's on the phone right now trying to line up votes."

"Then let's go fight his cranky ass, okay. Let's walk into that meeting tomorrow with a chip on our shoulder. Let's make Rosen the bad guy. Honestly, Adam, the man does not have a lot of friends."

Adam walked to the window and peeked through the shades. Foot traffic was heavy on the Mall below. It was almost five. He had close to five thousand dollars in mutual funds, and if he was frugal and if he made certain lifestyle changes the money might last for six months. His salary was sixty-two thousand, and replacing it in the very near future would be difficult. But he had never been one to worry about money, and he wouldn't start now. He was much more concerned about the next three weeks. After a ten-day career as a death penalty lawyer, he knew he needed help.

"What will it be like at the end?" he asked after a heavy silence.

Goodman slowly rose from his chair and walked to another window. "Pretty crazy. You won't sleep much the last four days. You'll be running in all directions. The courts are unpredictable. The system is unpredictable. You keep filing petitions and appeals knowing full well they won't work. The press will be dogging you. And, most important, you'll need to spend as much time as possible with your client. It's crazy work and it's all free."

"So I'll need some help."

"Oh yes. You can't do it alone. When Maynard Tole was executed, we had a lawyer from Jackson staked out at the governor's office, one at the supreme court clerk's office in Jackson, one in Washington, and two on death row. That's why you have to go fight tomorrow, Adam. You'll need the firm and its resources. You can't do it by yourself. It takes a team."

"This is a real kick in the crotch."

"I know. A year ago you were in law school, now you've been terminated. I know it hurts. But believe me, Adam, it's just a fluke. It won't stand. Ten years from now you'll be a partner in this firm, and you'll be terrorizing young associates."

"Don't bet on it."

"Let's go to Chicago. I've got two tickets for a seven-fifteen flight. We'll be in Chicago by eight-thirty, and we'll find a nice restaurant."

"I need to get some clothes."

"Fine. Meet me at the airport at six-thirty."

THE MATTER was effectively settled before the meeting began. Eleven members of the Personnel Committee were present, a sufficient number for a quorum. They gathered in a locked library on the sixtieth floor, around a long table with gallons of coffee in the center of it, and they brought with them thick files and portable Dictaphones and fatigued pocket schedules. One brought his secretary, and she sat in the hallway and worked furiously. These were busy people, all of them less than an hour away from another frantic day of endless conferences, meetings, briefings, depositions, trials, telephones, and significant lunches. Ten men, one woman, all in their late thirties or early forties, all partners of K&B, all in a hurry to return to their cluttered desks.

The matter of Adam Hall was a nuisance to them. The Personnel Committee, in fact, was a nuisance to them. It was not one of the more pleasant panels upon which to serve, but they'd been duly elected and no one dared decline. All for the firm. Go team, go!

Adam had arrived at the office at seven-thirty. He'd been gone for ten days, his longest absence yet. Emmitt Wycoff had shifted Adam's work to another young associate. There was never a shortage of rookies at Kravitz & Bane.

By eight o'clock he was hiding in a small, useless conference room near the library on the sixtieth floor. He was nervous, but worked hard at not showing it. He sipped coffee and read the morning papers. Parchman was a world away. And he studied the list of fifteen names on the Personnel Committee, none of whom he knew. Eleven strangers who would kick his future around for the next hour, then vote quickly and get on with more important matters. Wycoff checked in and said hello a few minutes before eight. Adam thanked him for everything, apologized for being so much trouble, and listened as Emmitt promised a speedy and satisfactory outcome.

Garner Goodman opened the door at five minutes after eight. "Looks pretty good," he said, almost in a whisper. "Right now there are eleven present. We have commitments from at least five. Three of Rosen's votes from the subcommittee are here, but it looks like he might be a vote or two shy."

"Is Rosen here?" Adam asked, knowing the answer but hoping that maybe the old bastard had died in his sleep.

"Yes, of course. And I think he's worried. Emmitt was still making phone calls at ten last night. We've got the votes, and Rosen knows it." Goodman eased through the door and was gone.

At eight-fifteen, the chairman called the meeting to order and declared a quorum. The termination of Adam Hall was the sole issue on the agenda, indeed the only reason for this special meeting. Emmitt Wycoff went first, and in ten minutes did a fine job of telling how wonderful Adam was. He stood at one end of the table in front of a row of bookshelves, and chatted comfortably as if trying to persuade a jury. At least half of the eleven did not hear a word. They scanned documents and juggled their calendars.

Garner Goodman spoke next. He quickly summarized the case of Sam Cayhall, and provided the honest assessment that, in all likelihood, Sam would be executed in three weeks. Then he bragged on Adam, said he might have been wrong in not disclosing his relationship with Sam, but what the hell. That was then, and this is now, and the present is a helluva lot more important when your client has only three weeks to live.

Not a single question was asked of either Wycoff or Goodman. The questions, evidently, were being saved for Rosen.

Lawyers have long memories. You cut one's throat today, and he'll wait patiently in the weeds for years until he can return the favor. Daniel Rosen had lots of favors lying around the hallways of Kravitz & Bane, and as managing partner he was in the process of collecting them. He'd stepped on people, his own people, for years. He was a bully, a liar, a thug. In his glory days, he'd been the heart and soul of the firm, and he knew it. No one would challenge him. He had abused young associates and tormented his fellow partners. He had run roughshod over committees, ignored firm policies, stolen clients from other lawyers at Kravitz & Bane, and now in the decline of his career he was collecting favors.

Two minutes into his presentation, he was interrupted for the first time by a young partner who rode motorcycles with Emmitt Wycoff. Rosen was pacing, as if playing to a packed courtroom in his glory days, when the question stopped him. Before he could think of a sarcastic answer, another question hit him. By the time he could think of an answer to either of the first two, a third came from nowhere. The brawl was on.

The three interrogators worked like an efficient tag team, and it was apparent that they had been practicing. They took turns needling Rosen with relentless questions, and within a minute he was cursing and throwing insults. They kept their collective cool. Each had a legal pad with what appeared to be long lists of questions.

"Where's the conflict of interest, Mr. Rosen?"

"Certainly a lawyer can represent a family member, right, Mr. Rosen?"

"Did the application for employment specifically ask Mr. Hall if this firm represented a member of his family?"

"Do you have something against publicity, Mr. Rosen?"

"Why do you consider the publicity to be negative?"

"Would you try to help a family member on death row?"

"What are your feelings about the death penalty, Mr. Rosen?"

"Do you secretly want to see Sam Cayhall executed because he killed Jews?"

"Don't you think you've ambushed Mr. Hall?"

It was not a pleasant sight. Some of the greatest courtroom victories in recent Chicago history belonged to Daniel Rosen, and here he was getting his teeth kicked in in a meaningless fight before a committee. Not a jury. Not a judge. A committee.

The idea of retreat had never entered his mind. He pressed on, growing louder and more caustic. His retorts and acid replies grew personal, and he said some nasty things about Adam.

This was a mistake. Others joined the fray, and soon Rosen was flailing like wounded prey, just a few steps in front of the wolf pack. When it was apparent that he could never reach a majority of the committee, he lowered his voice and regained his composure.

He rallied nicely with a quiet summation about ethical considerations and avoiding the appearance of impropriety, scriptures that lawyers learn in law school and spit at each other when fighting but otherwise ignore when convenient.

When Rosen finished, he stormed out of the room, mentally taking notes of those who'd had the nerve to

grill him. He'd write their names in a file the minute he
got to his desk, and one day, well, one day he'd just do
something about it.

Papers and pads and electronic equipment vanished
from the table, which was suddenly clean except for
the coffee and empty cups. The chairman called for a
vote. Rosen got five. Adam got six, and the Personnel
Committee adjourned itself immediately and disappeared in a rush.

"Six to five?" Adam repeated as he looked at the
relieved but unsmiling faces of Goodman and Wycoff.

"A regular landslide," Wycoff quipped.

"Could be worse," Goodman said. "You could be
out of a job."

"Why am I not ecstatic? I mean, one lousy vote and
I'd be history."

"Not really," Wycoff explained. "The votes were
counted before the meeting. Rosen had maybe two
solid votes, and the others stuck with him because they
knew you would win. You have no idea of the amount
of arm twisting that took place last night. This does it
for Rosen. He'll be gone in three months."

"Maybe quicker," added Goodman. "He's a loose
cannon. Everybody's sick of him."

"Including me," Adam said.

Wycoff glanced at his watch. It was eight forty-five,
and he had to be in court at nine. "Look, Adam, I've
gotta run," he said, buttoning his jacket. "When are
you going back to Memphis?"

"Today, I guess."

"Can we have lunch? I'd like to talk to you."

"Sure."

He opened the door, and said, "Great. My secretary
will give you a call. Gotta run. See you." And he was
gone.

Goodman suddenly glanced at his watch too. His

watch ran much slower than the real lawyers in the firm, but he did have appointments to keep. "I need to see someone in my office. I'll join you guys for lunch."

"One lousy vote," Adam repeated, staring at the wall.

"Come on, Adam. It wasn't that close."

"It certainly feels close."

"Look, we need to spend a few hours together before you leave. I wanna hear about Sam, okay? Let's start with lunch." He opened the door and was gone.

Adam sat on the table, shaking his head.

TWENTY-FIVE

I F BAKER COOLEY and the other lawyers in the Memphis office knew anything about Adam's sudden termination and its quick reversal, it was not apparent. They treated him the same, which was to say they kept to themselves and stayed away from his office. They were not rude to him, because, after all, he was from Chicago. They smiled when forced to, and they could muster a moment of small talk in the hallways if Adam was in the mood. But they were corporate lawyers, with starched shirts and soft hands that were unaccustomed to the dirt and grime of criminal defense. They did not go to jails or prisons or holding tanks to visit with clients, nor did they wrangle with cops and prosecutors and cranky judges. They worked primarily behind their desks and around mahogany conference tables. Their time was spent talking to clients who could afford to pay them several hundred dollars an hour for advice, and when they weren't talking to clients they were on the phone or doing lunch with other lawyers and bankers and insurance executives.

There'd been enough in the newspapers already to arouse resentment around the office. Most of the lawyers were embarrassed to see the name of their firm associated with a character such as Sam Cayhall. Most of them had no idea that he'd been represented by Chicago for seven years. Now friends were asking questions. Other lawyers were making wisecracks. Wives

were humiliated over garden club teas. In-laws were
suddenly interested in their legal careers.

Sam Cayhall and his grandson had quickly become a
pain in the ass for the Memphis office, but nothing
could be done about it.

Adam could sense it but didn't care. It was a temporary office, suitable for three more weeks and hopefully
not a day longer. He stepped from the elevator Friday
morning, and ignored the receptionist who was suddenly busy arranging magazines. He spoke to his secretary, a young woman named Darlene, and she handed
him a phone message from Todd Marks at the *Memphis Press*.

He took the pink phone message to his office and
threw it in the wastebasket. He hung his coat on a
hanger, and began covering the table with paper. There
were pages of notes he'd taken on the flights to and
from Chicago, and similar pleadings he'd borrowed
from Goodman's files, and dozens of copies of recent
federal decisions.

He was soon lost in a world of legal theories and
strategies. Chicago was a fading memory.

ROLLIE WEDGE entered the Brinkley Plaza building
through the front doors to the Mall. He had waited
patiently at a table of a sidewalk café until the black
Saab appeared, then turned into a nearby parking garage. He was dressed in a white shirt with a tie, seer-
sucker slacks, casual loafers. He sipped an iced tea
while watching Adam walk along the sidewalk and
enter the building.

The lobby was empty as Wedge scanned the directory. Kravitz & Bane had the third and fourth floors.
There were four identical elevators, and he rode one to
the eighth floor. He stepped into a narrow foyer. To
the right was a door with the name of a trust company

emblazoned in brass, and to the left was an adjoining hallway lined with doors to all kinds of enterprises. Next to the water fountain was a door to the stairway. He casually walked down eight flights, checking doors as he went. No one passed him in the stairwell. He reentered the lobby, then rode the other elevator, alone, to the third floor. He smiled at the receptionist, who was still busy with the magazines, and was about to ask directions to the trust company when the phone rang and she became occupied with it. A set of double glass doors separated the reception area from the entryway to the elevators. He rode to the fourth floor, and found an identical set of doors, but no receptionist. The doors were locked. On a wall to the right was a coded entry panel with nine numbered buttons.

He heard voices, and stepped into the stairwell. There was no lock on the door from either side. He waited for a moment, then eased through the door and took a long drink of water. An elevator opened, and a young man in khakis and blue blazer bounced out with a cardboard box under one arm and a thick book in his right hand. He headed for the Kravitz & Bane doors. He hummed a loud tune and did not notice as Wedge fell in behind him. He stopped and carefully balanced the law book on top of the box, freeing his right hand to punch the code. Seven, seven, three, and the panel beeped with each number. Wedge was inches away, peering over his shoulder and gathering the code.

The young man quickly grabbed the book, and was about to turn around when Wedge bumped into him slightly, and said, "Damn! Sorry! I wasn't—" Wedge took a step backward and looked at the lettering above the door. "This isn't Riverbend Trust," he said, dazed and bewildered.

"Nope. This is Kravitz & Bane."

"What floor is this?" Wedge asked. Something clicked and the door was free.

"Fourth. Riverbend Trust is on the eighth."

"Sorry," Wedge said again, now embarrassed and almost pitiful. "Must've got off on the wrong floor."

The young man frowned and shook his head, then opened the door.

"Sorry," Wedge said for the third time as he backed away. The door closed and the kid was gone. Wedge rode the elevator to the main lobby and left the building.

He left downtown, and drove east and north for ten minutes until he came to a section of the city filled with government housing. He pulled into the driveway beside the Auburn House, and was stopped by a uniformed guard. He was just turning around, he explained, lost again, and he was very sorry. As he backed into the street, he saw the burgundy Jaguar owned by Lee Booth parked between two subcompacts.

He headed toward the river, toward downtown again, and twenty minutes later parked at an abandoned redbrick warehouse on the bluffs. While sitting in his car, he quickly changed into a tan shirt with blue trim around the short sleeves and the name Rusty stitched above the pocket. Then he was moving swiftly but inconspicuously on foot around the corner of the building and down a slope through weeds until he stopped in the brush. A small tree provided shade as he caught his breath and hid from the scorching sun. In front of him was a small field of Bermuda grass, thick and green and obviously well tended, and beyond the grass was a row of twenty luxury condominiums hanging over the edge of the bluff. A fence of brick and iron presented a vexing problem, and he studied it patiently from the privacy of the brush.

One side of the condos was the parking lot with a closed gate leading to the only entrance and exit. A uniformed guard manned the small, boxlike, air-conditioned gatehouse. Few cars were in sight. It was almost 10 A.M. The outline of the guard could be seen through tinted glass.

Wedge ignored the fence and chose instead to penetrate from the bluff. He crawled along a row of boxwoods, clutching handfuls of grass to keep from sliding eighty feet onto Riverside Drive. He slid under wooden patios, some of which hung ten feet into the air as the bluff dropped fast below them. He stopped at the seventh condo, and swung himself onto the patio.

He rested for a moment in a wicker chair and toyed with an outside cable as if on a routine service call. No one was watching. Privacy was important to these wealthy people, they paid for it dearly, and each little terrace was shielded from the next by decorative wooden planks and all sorts of hanging vegetation. His shirt by now was sticky and clinging to his back.

The sliding glass door from the patio to the kitchen was locked, of course, a rather simple lock that slowed him for almost one minute. He picked it, leaving neither damage nor evidence, then glanced around for another look before he went in. This was the tricky part. He assumed there was a security system, probably one with contacts at every window and door. Since no one was home, it was highly probable the system would be activated. The delicate question was exactly how much noise would be made when he opened the door. Would there be a silent alert, or would he be startled with a screaming siren?

He took a breath, then carefully slid the door open. No siren greeted him. He took a quick look at the monitor above the door, then stepped inside.

The relay immediately alerted Willis, the guard at

the gate, who heard a frantic though not very loud beeping sound from his monitoring screen. He looked at the red light blinking at Number 7, home of Lee Booth, and he waited for it to stop. Mrs. Booth tripped her alarm at least twice a month, which was about the average for the flock he guarded. He checked his clipboard and noticed that Mrs. Booth had left at nine-fifteen. But she occasionally had sleepovers, usually men, and now she had her nephew staying with her, and so Willis watched the red light for forty-five seconds until it stopped blinking and fixed itself in a permanent ON position.

This was unusual, but no need to panic. These people lived behind walls and paid for around-the-clock armed guards, so they were not serious about their alarm systems. He quickly dialed Mrs. Booth's number, and there was no answer. He punched a button and set in motion a recorded 911 call requesting police assistance. He opened the key drawer and selected one for Number 7, then left the gatehouse and walked quickly across the parking lot to see about Mrs. Booth's unit. He unfastened his holster so he could grab his revolver, just in case.

Rollie Wedge stepped into the gatehouse and saw the open key drawer. He took a set, marked for Unit 7, along with a card with the alarm code and instructions, and for good measure he also grabbed keys and cards for Numbers 8 and 13, just to baffle old Willis and the cops.

TWENTY-SIX

THEY WENT to the cemetery first, to pay their respects to the dead. It covered two small hills on the edge of Clanton, one lined with elaborate tombstones and monuments where prominent families had buried themselves together, over time, and had their names carved in heavy granite. The second hill was for the newer graves, and as time had passed in Mississippi the tombstones had grown smaller. Stately oaks and elms shaded most of the cemetery. The grass was trimmed low and the shrubs were neat. Azaleas were in every corner. Clanton placed a priority on its memories.

It was a lovely Saturday, with no clouds and a slight breeze that had started during the night and chased away the humidity. The rains were gone for a while, and the hillsides were lush with greenery and wildflowers. Lee knelt by her mother's headstone and placed a small bouquet of flowers under her name. She closed her eyes as Adam stood behind her and stared at the grave. Anna Gates Cayhall, September 3, 1922–September 18, 1977. She was fifty-five when she died, Adam calculated, so he was thirteen, still living in blissful ignorance somewhere in Southern California.

She was buried alone, under a single headstone, and this in itself had presented some problems. Mates for life are usually buried side by side, at least in the South, with the first one occupying the first slot under a double headstone. Upon each visit to the deceased, the survivor gets to see his or her name already carved and just waiting.

"Daddy was fifty-six when Mother died," Lee explained as she took Adam's hand and inched away from the grave. "I wanted him to bury her in a plot where he could one day join her, but he refused. I guess he figured he still had a few years left, and he might remarry."

"You told me once that she didn't like Sam."

"I'm sure she loved him in a way, they were together for almost forty years. But they were never close. As I grew older I realized she didn't like to be around him. She confided in me at times. She was a simple country girl who married young, had babies, stayed home with them, and was expected to obey her husband. And this was not unusual for those times. I think she was a very frustrated woman."

"Maybe she didn't want Sam next to her for eternity."

"I thought about that. In fact, Eddie wanted them separated and buried at opposite ends of the cemetery."

"Good for Eddie."

"He wasn't joking either."

"How much did she know about Sam and the Klan?"

"I have no idea. It was not something we discussed. I remember she was humiliated after his arrest. She even stayed with Eddie and you guys for a while because the reporters were bothering her."

"And she didn't attend any of his trials."

"No. He didn't want her to watch. She had a problem with high blood pressure, and Sam used that as an excuse to keep her away from it."

They turned and walked along a narrow lane through the old section of the cemetery. They held hands and looked at the tombstones they were passing. Lee pointed to a row of trees across the street on another hill. "That's where the blacks are buried," she said. "Under those trees. It's a small cemetery."

"You're kidding? Even today?"

"Sure, you know, keep 'em in their place. These people couldn't stand the idea of a Negro lying amongst their ancestors."

Adam shook his head in disbelief. They climbed the hill and rested under an oak. The rows of graves spread peacefully beneath them. The dome of the Ford County Courthouse glittered in the sun a few blocks away.

"I played here as a little girl," she said quietly. She pointed to her right, to the north. "Every Fourth of July the city celebrates with a fireworks display, and the best seats in the house are here in the cemetery. There's a park down there, and that's where they shoot from. We'd load up our bikes and come to town to watch the parade and swim in the city pool and play with our friends. And right after dark, we'd all gather around here, in the midst of the dead, and sit on these tombstones to watch the fireworks. The men would stay by their trucks where the beer and whiskey were hidden, and the women would lie on quilts and tend to the babies. We would run and romp and ride bikes all over the place."

"Eddie?"

"Of course. Eddie was just a normal little brother, pesky as hell sometimes, but very much a boy. I miss him, you know. I miss him very much. We weren't close for many years, but when I come back to this town I think of my little brother."

"I miss him too."

"He and I came here, to this very spot, the night he graduated from high school. I had been in Nashville for two years, and I came back because he wanted me to watch him graduate. We had a bottle of cheap wine, and I think it was his first drink. I'll never forget it. We sat here on Emil Jacob's tombstone and sipped wine until the bottle was empty."

"What year was it?"

"Nineteen sixty-one, I think. He wanted to join the Army so he could leave Clanton and get away from Sam. I didn't want my little brother in the Army, and we discussed it until the sun came up."

"He was pretty confused?"

"He was eighteen, probably as confused as most kids who've just finished high school. Eddie was terrified that if he stayed in Clanton something would happen to him, some mysterious genetic flaw would surface and he'd become another Sam. Another Cayhall with a hood. He was desperate to run from this place."

"But you ran as soon as you could."

"I know, but I was tougher than Eddie, at least at the age of eighteen. I couldn't see him leaving home so young. So we sipped wine and tried to get a handle on life."

"Did my father ever have a handle on life?"

"I doubt it, Adam. We were both tormented by our father and his family's hatred. There are things I hope you never learn, stories that I pray remain untold. I guess I pushed them away, while Eddie couldn't."

She took his hand again and they strolled into the sunlight and down a dirt path toward the newer section of the cemetery. She stopped and pointed to a row of small headstones. "Here are your great-grandparents, along with aunts, uncles, and other assorted Cayhalls."

Adam counted eight in all. He read the names and dates, and spoke aloud the poetry and Scriptures and farewells inscribed in granite.

"There are lots more out in the country," Lee said. "Most of the Cayhalls originated around Karaway, fifteen miles from here. They were country people, and they're buried behind rural churches."

"Did you come here for these burials?"

"A few. It's not a close family, Adam. Some of these people had been dead for years before I knew about it."

"Why wasn't your mother buried here?"

"Because she didn't want to be. She knew she was about to die, and she picked the spot. She never considered herself a Cayhall. She was a Gates."

"Smart woman."

Lee pulled a handful of weeds from her grandmother's grave, and rubbed her fingers over the name of Lydia Newsome Cayhall, who died in 1961 at the age of seventy-two. "I remember her well," Lee said, kneeling on the grass. "A fine Christian woman. She'd roll over in her grave if she knew her third son was on death row."

"What about him?" Adam asked, pointing to Lydia's husband, Nathaniel Lucas Cayhall, who died in 1952 at the age of sixty-four. The fondness left Lee's face. "A mean old man," she said. "I'm sure he'd be proud of Sam. Nat, as he was known, was killed at a funeral."

"A funeral?"

"Yes. Traditionally, funerals were social occasions around here. They were preceded by long wakes with lots of visiting and eating. And drinking. Life was hard in the rural South, and often the funerals turned into drunken brawls. Nat was very violent, and he picked a fight with the wrong men just after a funeral service. They beat him to death with a stick of wood."

"Where was Sam?"

"Right in the middle of it. He was beaten too, but

survived. I was a little girl, and I remember Nat's funeral. Sam was in the hospital and couldn't attend."

"Did he get retribution?"

"Of course."

"How?"

"Nothing was ever proven, but several years later the two men who'd beaten Nat were released from prison. They surfaced briefly around here, then disappeared. One body was found months later next door in Milburn County. Beaten, of course. The other man was never found. The police questioned Sam and his brothers, but there was no proof."

"Do you think he did it?"

"Sure he did. Nobody messed with the Cayhalls back then. They were known to be half-crazy and mean as hell."

They left the family gravesites and continued along the path. "So, Adam, the question for us is, where do we bury Sam?"

"I think we should bury him over there, with the blacks. That would serve him right."

"What makes you think they'd want him?"

"Good point."

"Seriously."

"Sam and I have not reached that point yet."

"Do you think he'll want to be buried here? In Ford County?"

"I don't know. We haven't discussed it, for obvious reasons. There's still hope."

"How much hope?"

"A trace. Enough to keep fighting."

They left the cemetery on foot, and walked along a tranquil street with worn sidewalks and ancient oaks. The homes were old and well painted, with long porches and cats resting on the front steps. Children raced by on bikes and skateboards, and old people rocked in their porch swings and waved slowly. "These are my old stomping grounds, Adam," Lee said as they walked aimlessly along. Her hands were stuck deep in denim pockets, her eyes moistened with memories that were at once sad and pleasant. She looked at each house as if she'd stayed there as a child and could remember the little girls who'd been her friends. She could hear the giggles and laughs, the silly games and the serious fights of ten-year-olds.

"Were those happy times?" Adam asked.

"I don't know. We never lived in town, so we were known as country kids. I always longed for one of these houses, with friends all around and stores a few blocks away. The town kids considered themselves to be a bit better than us, but it wasn't much of a problem. My best friends lived here, and I spent many hours playing in these streets, climbing these trees. Those were good times, I guess. The memories from the house in the country are not pleasant."

"Because of Sam?"

An elderly lady in a flowered dress and large straw hat was sweeping around her front steps as they approached. She glanced at them, then she froze and stared. Lee slowed then stopped near the walkway to the house. She looked at the old woman, and the old woman looked at Lee. "Mornin', Mrs. Langston," Lee said in a friendly drawl.

Mrs. Langston gripped the broom handle and stiffened her back, and seemed content to stare.

"I'm Lee Cayhall. You remember me," Lee drawled again.

As the name Cayhall drifted across the tiny lawn, Adam caught himself glancing around to see if anyone else heard it. He was prepared to be embarrassed if the name fell on other ears. If Mrs. Langston remembered Lee, it was not apparent. She managed a polite nod of

the head, just a quick up and down motion, rather
awkward as if to say "Good morning to you. Now
move along."

"Nice to see you again," Lee said, and began walking away. Mrs. Langston scurried up the steps and disappeared inside. "I dated her son in high school," Lee
said, shaking her head in disbelief.

"She was thrilled to see you."

"She was always sort of wacky," Lee said without
conviction. "Or maybe she's afraid to talk to a
Cayhall. Afraid of what the neighbors might say."

"I think it might be best if we go incognito for the
rest of the day. What about it?"

"It's a deal."

They passed other folks puttering in their flower
beds and waiting for the mailman, but they said nothing. Lee covered her eyes with sunshades. They zig-
zagged through the neighborhood in the general direction of the central square, chatting about Lee's old
friends and where they were now. She kept in touch
with two of them, one in Clanton and one in Texas.
They avoided family history until they were on a street
with smaller, wood-framed houses stacked tightly together. They stopped at the corner, and Lee nodded at
something down the street.

"You see the third house on the right, the little
brown one there?"

"Yes."

"That's where you lived. We could walk down there
but I see people moving about."

Two small children played with toy guns in the front
yard and someone was swinging on the narrow front
porch. It was a square house, small, neat, perfect for a
young couple having babies.

Adam had been almost three when Eddie and Evelyn
disappeared, and as he stood on the corner he tried

desperately to remember something about the house. He couldn't.

"It was painted white back then, and of course the trees were smaller. Eddie rented it from a local real estate agent."

"Was it nice?"

"Nice enough. They hadn't been married long. They were just kids with a new child. Eddie worked in an auto parts store, then he worked for the state highway department. Then he took another job."

"Sounds familiar."

"Evelyn worked part-time in a jewelry store on the square. I think they were happy. She was not from here, you know, and so she didn't know a lot of people. They kept to themselves."

They walked by the house and one of the children aimed an orange machine gun at Adam. There were no memories of the place to be evoked at that moment. He smiled at the child and looked away. They were soon on another street with the square in sight.

Lee was suddenly a tour guide and historian. The Yankees had burned Clanton in 1863, the bastards, and after the war, General Clanton, a Confederate hero whose family owned the county, returned, with only one leg, the other one lost somewhere on the battlefield at Shiloh, and designed the new courthouse and the streets around it. His original drawings were on the wall upstairs in the courthouse. He wanted lots of shade so he planted oaks in perfect rows around the new courthouse. He was a man of vision who could see the small town rising from the ashes and prospering, so he designed the streets in an exact square around the courthouse common. They had walked by the great man's grave, she said, just a moment ago, and she would show it to him later.

There was a struggling mall north of town and a row

of discount supermarkets to the east, but the people of Ford County still enjoyed shopping around the square on Saturday morning, she explained as they strolled along the sidewalk next to Washington Street. Traffic was slow and the pedestrians were even slower. The buildings were old and adjoining, filled with lawyers and insurance agents, banks and cafés, hardware stores and dress shops. The sidewalk was covered with canopies, awnings, and verandas from the offices and stores. Creaky fans hung low and spun sluggishly. They stopped in front of an ancient pharmacy, and Lee removed her sunglasses. "This was a hangout," she explained. "There was a soda fountain in the back with a jukebox and racks of comic books. You could buy an enormous cherry sundae for a nickel, and it took hours to eat it. It took even longer if the boys were here."

Like something from a movie, Adam thought. They stopped in front of a hardware store, and for some reason examined the shovels and hoes and rakes leaning against the window. Lee looked at the battered double doors, opened and held in place by bricks, and thought of something from her childhood. But she kept it to herself.

They crossed the street, hand in hand, and passed a group of old men whittling wood and chewing tobacco around the war memorial. She nodded at a statue and informed him quietly that this was General Clanton, with both legs. The courthouse was not open for business on Saturdays. They bought colas from a machine outside and sipped them in a gazebo on the front lawn. She told the story of the most famous trial in the history of Ford County, the murder trial of Carl Lee Hailey in 1984. He was a black man who shot and killed two rednecks who'd raped his little daughter. There were marches and protests by blacks on one side and Klansmen on the other, and the National Guard actually camped out here, around the courthouse, to keep the peace. Lee had driven down from Memphis one day to watch the spectacle. He was acquitted by an all-white jury.

Adam remembered the trial. He'd been a junior at Pepperdine, and had followed it in the papers because it was happening in the town of his birth.

When she was a child, entertainment was scarce, and trials were always well attended. Sam had brought her and Eddie here once to watch the trial of a man accused of killing a hunting dog. He was found guilty and spent a year in prison. The county was split—the city folks were against the conviction for such a lowly crime, while the country folks placed a higher value on good beagles. Sam had been particularly happy to see the man sent away.

Lee wanted to show him something. They walked around the courthouse to the rear door where two water fountains stood ten feet apart. Neither had been used in years. One had been for whites, the other for blacks. She remembered the story of Rosia Alfie Gatewood, Miss Allie as she was known, the first black person to drink from the white fountain and escape without injury. Not long after that, the water lines were disconnected.

They found a table in a crowded café known simply as The Tea Shoppe, on the west side of the square. She told stories, all of them pleasant and most of them funny, as they ate BLT's and french fries. She kept her sunglasses on, and Adam caught her watching the people.

THEY LEFT CLANTON after lunch, and after a leisurely walk back to the cemetery. Adam drove, and Lee pointed this way and that until they were on a county highway running through small, neat farms with cows grazing the hillsides. They passed occasional pockets of white trash—dilapidated double-wide trailers with junk cars strewn about—and they passed rundown shotgun houses still inhabited by poor blacks. But the hilly countryside was pretty, for the most part, and the day was beautiful.

She pointed again, and they turned onto a smaller, paved road that snaked its way deeper into the sticks. They finally stopped in front of an abandoned white frame house with weeds shooting from the porch and ivy swarming into the windows. It was fifty yards from the road, and the gravel drive leading to it was gullied and impassable. The front lawn was overgrown with Johnsongrass and cocklebur. The mailbox was barely visible in the ditch beside the road.

"The Cayhall estate," she mumbled, and they sat for a long time in the car and looked at the sad little house.

"What happened to it?" Adam finally asked.

"Oh, it was a good house. Didn't have much of a chance, though. The people were a disappointment." She slowly removed her sunglasses and wiped her eyes. "I lived here for eighteen years, and I couldn't wait to leave it."

"Why is it abandoned?"

She took a deep breath, and tried to arrange the story. "I think it was paid for many years ago, but Daddy mortgaged it to pay the lawyers for his last trial. He, of course, never came home again, and at some point the bank foreclosed. There are eighty acres around it, and everything was lost. I haven't been back here since the foreclosure. I asked Phelps to buy it, and he said no. I couldn't blame him. I really didn't want to own it myself. I heard later from some friends here that it was rented several times, and I guess eventually abandoned. I didn't know if the house was still standing."

"What happened to the personal belongings?"

"The day before the foreclosure, the bank allowed me to go in and box up anything I wanted. I saved some things—photo albums, keepsakes, yearbooks, Bibles, some of Mother's valuables. They're in storage in Memphis."

"I'd like to see them."

"The furniture was not worth saving, not a decent piece of anything. My mother was dead, my brother had just committed suicide, and my father had just been sent to death row, and I was not in the mood to keep a lot of memorabilia. It was a horrible experience, going through that dirty little house and trying to salvage objects that might one day bring a smile. Hell, I wanted to burn everything. Almost did."

"You're not serious."

"Of course I am. After I'd been here for a couple of hours, I decided to just burn the damned house and everything in it. Happens all the time, right? I found an old lantern with some kerosene in it, and I set it on the kitchen table and talked to it as I boxed stuff up. It would've been easy."

"Why didn't you?"

"I don't know. I wish I'd had the guts to do it, but I remember worrying about the bank and the foreclosure and, well, arson is a crime, isn't it? I remember laughing at the idea of going off to prison where I'd be with Sam. That's why I didn't strike a match. I was afraid I'd get in trouble and go to prison."

The car was hot now, and Adam opened his door. "I want to look around," he said, getting out. They picked their way down the gravel drive, stepping over gullies two feet wide. They stopped at the front porch and looked at the rotting boards.

"I'm not going in there," she said firmly, and pulled her hand away from his. Adam studied the decaying porch and decided against stepping on it. He walked along the front of the house, looking at the broken windows with vines disappearing inside. He followed the drive around the house, and Lee tagged along.

The backyard was shaded by old oaks and maples, and the ground was bare in places where the sun was kept out. It stretched for an eighth of a mile down a slight incline until it stopped at a thicket. The plot was surrounded by woods in the distance.

She took his hand again, and they walked to a tree beside a wooden shed that, for some reason, was in much better condition than the house. "This was my tree," she said, looking up at the branches. "My own pecan tree." Her voice had a slight quiver.

"It's a great tree."

"Wonderful for climbing. I'd spend hours here, sitting in those branches, swinging my feet and resting my chin on a limb. In the spring and summer, I'd climb about halfway up, and no one could see me. I had my own little world up there."

She suddenly closed her eyes and covered her mouth with a hand. Her shoulders trembled. Adam placed his arm around her and tried to think of something to say.

"This is where it happened," she said after a moment. She bit her lip and fought back tears. Adam said nothing.

"You asked me once about a story," she said with clenched teeth as she wiped her cheeks with the backs of her hands. "The story of Daddy killing a black man." She nodded toward the house. Her hands shook so she stuck them in her pockets.

A minute passed as they stared at the house, neither wanting to speak. The only rear door opened onto a small, square porch with a railing around it. A delicate breeze ruffled the leaves above them and made the only sound.

She took a deep breath, then said, "His name was Joe Lincoln, and he lived down the road there with his family." She nodded at the remnants of a dirt trail that ran along the edge of a field, then disappeared into the woods. "He had about a dozen kids."

"Quince Lincoln?" Adam asked.

"Yeah. How'd you know about him?"

"Sam mentioned his name the other day when we were talking about Eddie. He said Quince and Eddie were good friends when they were kids."

"He didn't talk about Quince's father, did he?"

"No."

"I didn't think so. Joe worked here on the farm for us, and his family lived in a shotgun house that we also owned. He was a good man with a big family, and like most poor blacks back then they just barely survived. I knew a couple of his kids, but we weren't friends like Quince and Eddie. One day the boys were playing here in the backyard, it was summertime and we weren't in school. They got into an argument over a small toy, a Confederate Army soldier, and Eddie accused Quince of stealing it. Typical boy stuff, you know. I think they were eight or nine years old. Daddy happened to walk by, over there, and Eddie ran to him and told how Quince had stolen the toy. Quince emphatically denied it. Both boys were really mad and on the verge of tears. Sam, typically, flew into a rage and cursed Quince, calling him all sorts of names like 'thieving little nigger' and 'sorry little nigger bastard.' Sam demanded the soldier, and Quince started crying. He kept saying he didn't have it, and Eddie kept saying he did. Sam grabbed the boy, shook him real hard, and started slapping him on the butt. Sam was yelling and screaming and cursing, and Quince was crying and pleading.

They went around the yard a few times with Sam shaking him and hitting him. Quince finally pulled free, and ran home. Eddie ran into our house, and Daddy followed him inside. A moment later, Sam stepped through the door there, with a walking cane, which he carefully laid on the porch. He then sat on the steps and waited patiently. He smoked a cigarette and watched the dirt road. The Lincoln house was not far away, and, sure enough, within a few minutes Joe came running out of the trees there with Quince right behind him. As he got close to the house, he saw Daddy waiting on him, and he slowed to a walk. Daddy yelled over his shoulder, 'Eddie! Come here! Watch me whip this nigger!'"

She began walking very slowly to the house, then stopped a few feet from the porch. "When Joe was right about here, he stopped and looked at Sam. He said something like 'Quince says you hit him, Mr. Sam.' To which my father replied something like 'Quince is a thieving little nigger, Joe. You should teach your kids not to steal.' They began to argue, and it was obvious there was going to be a fight. Sam suddenly jumped from the porch, and threw the first punch. They fell to the ground, right about here, and fought like cats. Joe was a few years younger and stronger, but Daddy was so mean and angry that the fight was pretty even. They struck each other in the face and cursed and kicked like a couple of animals." She stopped the narrative and looked around the yard, then she pointed to the back door. "At some point, Eddie stepped onto the porch to watch it. Quince was standing a few feet away, yelling at his father. Sam made a dash for the porch and grabbed the walking cane, and the matter got out of hand. He beat Joe in the face and head until he fell to his knees, and he poked him in the stomach and groin until he could barely move. Joe looked at Quince and yelled for him to run get the shotgun. Quince took off. Sam stopped the beating, and turned to Eddie. 'Go get my shotgun,' he said. Eddie froze, and Daddy yelled at him again. Joe was on the ground, on all fours, trying to collect himself, and just as he was about to stand, Sam beat him again and knocked him down. Eddie went inside and Sam walked to the porch. Eddie returned in a matter of seconds with a shotgun, and Daddy made him go inside. The door closed."

Lee walked to the porch and sat on the edge of it. She buried her face in her hands, and cried for a long time. Adam stood a few feet away, staring at the ground, listening to the sobs. When she finally looked at him, her eyes were glazed, her mascara was running, her nose was dripping. She wiped her face with her hands, then rubbed them on her jeans. "I'm sorry," she whispered.

"Finish it, please," he said quickly.

She breathed deeply for a moment, then wiped her eyes some more. "Joe was just over there," she said, pointing to a spot in the grass not far from Adam. "He'd made it to his feet, and he turned and saw Daddy with the gun. He glanced around in the direction of his house, but there was no sign of Quince and his gun. He turned back to Daddy, who was standing right here, on the edge of the porch. Then my dear sweet father slowly raised the gun, hesitated for a second, looked around to see if anyone was watching, and pulled the trigger. Just like that. Joe fell hard and never moved."

"You saw this happen, didn't you?"

"Yes, I did."

"Where were you?"

"Over there." She nodded, but didn't point. "In my pecan tree. Hidden from the world."

"Sam couldn't see you?"

"No one could see me. I watched the whole thing." She covered her eyes again and fought back tears. Adam eased onto the porch and sat beside her.

She cleared her throat and looked away. "He watched Joe for a minute, ready to shoot again if necessary. But Joe never moved. He was quite dead. There was some blood around his head on the grass, and I could see it from the tree. I remember digging my fingernails into the bark to keep from falling, and I remember wanting to cry but being too scared. I didn't want him to hear me. Quince appeared after a few minutes. He'd heard the shot, and he was crying by the time I saw him. Just running like crazy and crying, and when he saw his father on the ground he started screaming like any child would've done. My father raised the gun again, and for a second I knew he was about to shoot the boy. But Quince threw Joe's shotgun to the ground and ran to his father. He was bawling and wailing. He wore a light-colored shirt, and soon it was covered with blood. Sam eased to the side and picked up Joe's shotgun, then he went inside with both guns."

She stood slowly and took several measured steps. "Quince and Joe were right about here," she said, marking the spot with her heel. "Quince held his father's head next to his stomach, blood was everywhere, and he made this strange moaning sound, like the whimper of a dying animal." She turned and looked at her tree. "And there I was, sitting up there like a little bird, crying too. I hated my father so badly at that moment."

"Where was Eddie?"

"Inside the house, in his room with the door locked." She pointed to a window with broken panes and a shutter missing. "That was his room. He told me later that he looked outside when he heard the shot, and he saw Quince clutching his father. Within minutes, Ruby Lincoln came running up with a string of children behind her. They all collapsed around Quince and Joe, and, God, it was horrible. They were screaming and weeping and yelling at Joe to get up, to please not die on them.

"Sam called an ambulance. He also called one of his brothers, Albert, and a couple of neighbors. Pretty soon there was a crowd in the backyard. Sam and his gang stood on the porch with their guns and watched the mourners, who dragged the body under that tree over there." She pointed to a large oak. "The ambulance arrived after an eternity, and took the body away. Ruby and her children walked back to their house, and my father and his buddies had a good laugh on the porch."

"How long did you stay in the tree?"

"I don't know. As soon as everybody was gone, I climbed down and ran into the woods. Eddie and I had a favorite place down by a creek, and I knew he would come looking for me. He did. He was scared and out of breath; told me all about the shooting, and I told him that I'd seen it. He didn't believe me at first, but I gave him the details. We were both scared to death. He reached in his pocket and pulled out something. It was the little Confederate soldier he and Quince had fought over. He'd found it under his bed, and so he decided on the spot that everything was his fault. We swore each other to secrecy. He promised he would never tell anyone that I had witnessed the killing, and I promised I would never tell anyone that he'd found the soldier. He threw it in the creek."

"Did either of you ever tell?"

She shook her head for a long time.

"Sam never knew you were in the tree?" Adam asked.

"Nope. I never told my mother. Eddie and I talked about it occasionally over the years, and as time passed we just sort of buried it away. When we returned to the house, our parents were in the middle of a huge fight. She was hysterical and he was wild-eyed and crazy. I think he'd hit her a few times. She grabbed us and told us to get in the car. As we were backing out of the driveway, the sheriff pulled up. We drove around for a while, Mother in the front seat, and Eddie and I in the back, both of us too scared to talk. She didn't know what to say. We assumed he would be taken to jail, but when we parked in the driveway he was sitting on the front porch as if nothing had happened."

"What did the sheriff do?"

"Nothing, really. He and Sam talked for a bit. Sam showed him Joe's shotgun and explained how it was a simple matter of self-defense. Just another dead nigger."

"He wasn't arrested?"

"No, Adam. This was Mississippi in the early fifties. I'm sure the sheriff had a good laugh about it, patted Sam on the back, and told him to be a good boy, and then left. He even allowed Sam to keep Joe's shotgun."

"That's incredible."

"We were hoping he'd go to jail for a few years."

"What did the Lincolns do?"

"What could they do? Who would listen to them? Sam forbade Eddie from seeing Quince, and to make sure the boys didn't get together, he evicted them from their house."

"Good God!"

"He gave them one week to get out, and the sheriff arrived to fulfill his sworn duties by forcing them out of the house. The eviction was legal and proper, Sam assured Mother. It was the only time I thought she might leave him. I wish she had."

"Did Eddie ever see Quince?"

"Years later. When Eddie started driving, he started looking for the Lincolns. They had moved to a small community on the other side of Clanton, and Eddie found them there. He apologized and said he was sorry a hundred times. But they were never friends again. Ruby asked him to leave. He told me they lived in a run-down shack with no electricity."

She walked to her pecan tree and sat against its trunk. Adam followed and leaned against it. He looked down at her, and thought of all the years she'd been carrying this burden. And he thought of his father, of his anguish and torment, of the indelible scars he'd borne to his death. Adam now had the first clue to his father's destruction, and he wondered if the pieces might someday fit together. He thought of Sam, and as he glanced at the porch he could see a younger man with a gun and hatred in his face. Lee was sobbing quietly.

"What did Sam do afterward?"

She struggled to control herself. "The house was so quiet for a week, maybe a month, I don't know. But it seemed like years before anyone spoke over dinner. Eddie stayed in his room with the door locked. I would hear him crying at night, and he told me again and again how much he hated his father. He wanted him dead. He wanted to run away from home. He blamed himself for everything. Mother became concerned, and she spent a lot of time with him. As for me, they thought I was off playing in the woods when it happened. Shortly after Phelps and I married, I secretly began seeing a psychiatrist. I tried to work it out in therapy, and I wanted Eddie to do the same. But he wouldn't listen. The last time I talked to Eddie before he died, he mentioned the killing. He never got over it."

"And you got over it?"

"I didn't say that. Therapy helped, but I still wonder what would've happened if I had screamed at Daddy before he pulled the trigger. Would he have killed Joe with his daughter watching? I don't think so."

"Come on, Lee. That was forty years ago. You can't blame yourself."

"Eddie blamed me. And he blamed himself, and we blamed each other until we were grown. We were children when it happened, and we couldn't run to our parents. We were helpless."

Adam could think of a hundred questions about the killing of Joe Lincoln. The subject was not likely to be raised again with Lee, and he wanted to know everything that happened, every small detail. Where was Joe buried? What happened to his shotgun? Was the shooting reported in the local paper? Was the case presented to a grand jury? Did Sam ever mention it to his children? Where was her mother during the fight? Did she hear the argument and the gunshot? What happened to Joe's family? Did they still live in Ford County?

"Let's burn it, Adam," she said strongly, wiping her face and glaring at him.

"You're not serious."

"Yes I am! Let's burn the whole damned place, the house, the shed, this tree, the grass and weeds. It won't take much. Just a couple of matches here and there. Come on."

"No, Lee."

"Come on."

Adam bent over gently and took her by the arm. "Let's go, Lee. I've heard enough for one day."

She didn't resist. She too had had enough for one day. He helped her through the weeds, around the house, over the ruins of the driveway, and back to the car.

They left the Cayhall estate without a word. The road turned to gravel, then stopped at the intersection of a highway. Lee pointed to the left, then closed her eyes as if trying to nap. They bypassed Clanton and stopped at a country store near Holly Springs. Lee said she needed a cola, and insisted on getting it herself. She returned to the car with a six-pack of beer and offered a bottle to Adam. "What's this?" he asked.

"Just a couple," she said. "My nerves are shot. Don't let me drink more than two, okay. Only two."

"I don't think you should, Lee."

"I'm okay," she insisted with a frown, and took a drink.

Adam declined and sped away from the store. She drained two bottles in fifteen minutes, then went to sleep. Adam placed the sack in the backseat, and concentrated on the road.

He had a sudden desire to leave Mississippi, and longed for the lights of Memphis.

TWENTY-SEVEN

EXACTLY ONE WEEK earlier, he had awakened with a fierce headache and a fragile stomach, and had been forced to face the greasy bacon and oily eggs of Irene Lettner. And in the past seven days, he'd been to the courtroom of Judge Slattery, and to Chicago, Greenville, Ford County, and Parchman. He'd met the governor, and the Attorney General. He hadn't talked to his client in six days.

To hell with his client. Adam had sat on the patio watching the river traffic and sipping decaffeinated coffee until 2 A.M. He swatted mosquitoes and struggled with the vivid images of Quince Lincoln grasping at his father's body while Sam Cayhall stood on the porch and admired his handiwork. He could hear the muted laughter of Sam and his buddies on the narrow porch as Ruby Lincoln and her children fell around the corpse and eventually dragged it across the yard to the shade of a tree. He could see Sam on the front lawn with both shotguns explaining to the sheriff exactly how the crazy nigger was about to kill him, and how he acted reasonably and in self-defense. The sheriff was quick to see Sam's point, of course. He could hear the whispers of the tormented children, Eddie and Lee, as they blamed themselves and struggled with the horror of Sam's deed. And he cursed a society so willing to ignore violence against a despised class.

He'd slept fitfully, and at one point had sat on the edge of his bed and declared to himself that Sam could find another lawyer, that the death penalty might in fact be appropriate for some people, notably his grand-father, and that he would return to Chicago immediately and change his name again. But that dream passed, and when he awoke for the last time the sunlight filtered through the blinds and cast neat lines across his bed. He contemplated the ceiling and crown molding along the walls for half an hour as he remembered the trip to Clanton. Today, he hoped, would be a late Sunday with a thick newspaper and strong coffee. He would go to the office later in the afternoon. His client had seventeen days.

Lee had finished a third beer after they arrived at the condo, then she'd gone to bed. Adam had watched her carefully, half-expecting a wild binge or sudden slide into an alcoholic stupor. But she'd been very quiet and composed, and he heard nothing from her during the night.

He finished his shower, didn't shave, and walked to the kitchen where the syrupy remains of the first pot of coffee awaited him. Lee had been up for some time. He called her name, then walked to her bedroom. He quickly checked the patio, then roamed through the condo. She was not there. The Sunday paper was stacked neatly on the coffee table in the den.

He fixed fresh coffee and toast, and took his breakfast on the patio. It was almost nine-thirty, and thankfully the sky was cloudy and the temperature was not suffocating. It would be a good Sunday for office work. He read the paper, starting with the front section.

Perhaps she'd run to the store or something. Maybe she'd gone to church. They hadn't yet reached the point of leaving notes for each other. But there'd been no talk of Lee going anywhere this morning.

He'd eaten one piece of toast with strawberry jam when his appetite suddenly vanished. The front page of the Metro section carried another story on Sam

Cayhall, with the same picture from ten years ago. It was a chatty little summary of the past week's developments, complete with a chronological chart giving the important dates in the history of the case. A cute question mark was left dangling by the date of August 8, 1990. Would there be an execution then? Evidently, Todd Marks had been given unlimited column inches by the editors because the story contained almost nothing new. The disturbing part was a few quotes from a law professor at Ole Miss, an expert in constitutional matters who'd worked on many death penalty cases. The learned professor was generous with his opinions, and his bottom line was that Sam's goose was pretty much cooked. He'd studied the file at length, had followed it for many years in fact, and was of the opinion that there was basically nothing left for Sam to do. He explained that in many death penalty cases, miracles can sometimes be performed at the last moment because usually the inmate has suffered from mediocre legal representation, even during his appeals. In those cases, experts such as himself can often pull rabbits out of hats because they're just so damned brilliant, and thus able to create issues ignored by lesser legal minds. But, regrettably, Sam's case was different because he had been competently represented by some very fine lawyers from Chicago.

Sam's appeals had been handled skillfully, and now the appeals had run their course. The professor, evidently a gambling man, gave five to one odds the execution would take place on August 8. And for all of this, the opinions and the odds, he got his picture in the paper.

Adam was suddenly nervous. He'd read dozens of death cases in which lawyers at the last minute grabbed ropes they'd never grabbed before, and convinced judges to listen to new arguments. The lore of capital litigation was full of stories about latent legal issues undiscovered and untapped until a different lawyer with a fresh eye entered the arena and captured a stay. But the law professor was right. Sam had been lucky. Though Sam despised the lawyers at Kravitz & Bane, they had provided superb representation. Now there was nothing left but a bunch of desperate motions, the gangplank appeals, as they were known.

He flung the paper on the wooden deck and went inside for more coffee. The sliding door beeped, a new sound from a new security system installed last Friday after the old one malfunctioned and some keys mysteriously disappeared. There was no evidence of a break-in. Security was tight at the complex. And Willis didn't really know how many sets of keys he kept for each unit. The Memphis police decided the sliding door had been left unlocked and slipped open somehow. Adam and Lee had not worried about it.

He inadvertently struck a glass tumbler next to the sink, and it shattered as it hit the floor. Bits of glass bounced around his bare feet, and he tiptoed gingerly to the pantry to get a broom and dustpan. He carefully swept the debris, without bloodshed, into a neat pile and dumped it into a wastebasket under the sink. Something caught his attention. He slowly reached into the black plastic garbage bag, and felt his way through warm coffee grounds and broken glass until he found a bottle and pulled it out. It was an empty pint of vodka.

He raked the coffee grounds from it and studied the label. The trash basket was small and normally emptied every other day, sometimes once a day. It was now half-filled. The bottle had not been there long. He opened the refrigerator and looked for the remaining three bottles of beer from yesterday's six-pack. She'd had two en route back to Memphis, then one at the condo. He did not remember where they had been stored, but they were not in the refrigerator. Nor in the trash in the kitchen, den, bathrooms, or bedrooms. The more he searched the more determined he became to find the bottles. He inspected the pantry, the broom closet, the linen closet, the kitchen cabinets. He went through her closets and drawers, and felt like a thief and a cheat but pressed on because he was scared.

They were under her bed, empty of course, and carefully hidden in an old Nike shoe box. Three empty bottles of Heineken stacked neatly together, as if they were to be shipped somewhere as a gift. He sat on the floor and examined them. They were fresh, with a few drops still rolling around the bottoms.

He guessed her weight to be around a hundred and thirty pounds, and her height at five feet six or seven. She was slender but not too thin. Her body couldn't handle much booze. She'd gone to bed early, around nine, then at some point sneaked around the condo fetching beer and vodka. Adam leaned against the wall, his mind racing wildly. She'd given much thought to the hiding of the green bottles, but she knew she'd get caught. She had to know Adam would look for them later. Why hadn't she been more careful with the empty pint bottle? Why was it hidden in the trash, and the beer bottles tucked away under her bed?

Then he realized he was attempting to track a rational mind, instead of a drunk one. He closed his eyes and tapped the back of his head against the wall. He'd taken her to Ford County, where they looked at graves and relived a nightmare, and where she'd worn sunglasses to hide her face. For two weeks now, he'd been demanding family secrets and yesterday he'd been kicked in the face with a few. He needed to know, he'd told himself. He wasn't certain why, but he just felt as if he had to know the reasons his family was strange and violent and hateful.

And now, it occurred to him for the first time, perhaps this was much more complicated than the casual telling of family stories. Perhaps this was painful for everyone involved. Maybe his selfish interest in closeted skeletons wasn't as important as Lee's stability.

He slid the shoe box back to its original position, then threw the vodka bottle in the wastebasket for the second time. He dressed quickly and left the building. He asked the gate man about Lee. According to a sheet of paper on his clipboard, she'd left almost two hours ago, at eight-ten.

IT WAS CUSTOMARY for lawyers at Kravitz & Bane in Chicago to spend Sunday at the office, but evidently the practice was frowned upon in Memphis. Adam had the place entirely to himself. He locked his door anyway, and was soon lost in the murky legal world of federal habeas corpus practice.

His concentration, though, was difficult and only lasted for short intervals. He worried about Lee, and he hated Sam. It would be difficult to look at him again, probably tomorrow, through the metal screen at the Row. He was frail and bleached and wrinkled, and by all rights entitled to a little sympathy from someone. Their last discussion had been about Eddie, and when it ended Sam had asked him to leave the family stuff outside the Row. He had enough on his mind at the moment. It wasn't fair to confront a condemned man with his ancient sins.

Adam was not a biographer, nor a genealogist. He hadn't been trained in sociology or psychiatry, and, frankly, he was, at the moment, quite weary of further expeditions into the cryptic history of the Cayhall family. He was simply a lawyer, a rather green one, but an advocate nonetheless whose client needed him.

It was time to practice law and forget the folklore.

At eleven-thirty, he dialed Lee's number and listened to the phone ring. He left a message on the recorder, telling her where he was and would she please call. He called again at one, and at two. No answer. He was preparing an appeal when the phone rang.

Instead of Lee's pleasant voice, he heard the clipped words of the Honorable F. Flynn Slattery. "Yes, Mr. Hall, Judge Slattery here. I've carefully considered this matter, and I'm denying all relief, including your request for a stay of execution," he said, almost with a trace of cheer. "Lots of reasons, but we won't go into them. My clerk will fax you my opinion right now, so you'll have it in a moment."

"Yes sir," Adam said.

"You'll need to appeal as soon as possible, you know. I suggest you do so in the morning."

"I'm working on the appeal now, Your Honor. In fact, it's almost finished."

"Good. So you were expecting this."

"Yes sir. I started working on the appeal right after I left your office on Tuesday." It was tempting to take a shot or two at Slattery. He was, after all, two hundred miles away. But he was also, after all, a federal judge. Adam was very aware that one day very soon he might need His Honor again.

"Good day, Mr. Hall." And with that, Slattery hung up.

Adam walked around the table a dozen times, then watched the light rain on the Mall below. He swore quietly about federal judges in general and Slattery in particular, then returned to his computer where he stared at the screen and waited for inspiration.

He typed and read, researched and printed, looked from his windows and dreamed of miracles until it was dark. He had killed several hours with footless piddling, and one reason he worked until eight o'clock was to give Lee plenty of time to return to the condo.

There was no sign of her. The security guard said she had not returned. There was no message on the recorder, other than his. He dined on microwave popcorn, and watched two movies on video. The idea of calling Phelps Booth was so repugnant he nearly shuddered at the thought.

He thought of sleeping on the sofa in the den so he would hear her if she came home, but after the last movie he retired to his room upstairs and closed the door.

TWENTY-EIGHT

THE EXPLANATION for yesterday's disappearance was slow in coming, but sounded plausible by the time she finished with it. She'd been at the hospital all day, she said as she moved slowly around the kitchen, with one of her kids from the Auburn House. Poor little girl was only thirteen, baby number one but of course there would be others, and she had gone into labor a month early. Her mother was in jail and her aunt was off selling drugs, and she had no one else to turn to. Lee'd held her hand throughout the complicated delivery. The girl was fine and the baby was okay, and now there was another unwanted little child in the Memphis ghettos.

Lee's voice was scratchy and her eyes were puffy and red. She said she'd returned a few minutes after one, and she would've called earlier but they were in the labor room for six hours and the delivery room for two. St. Peter's Charity Hospital is a zoo, especially the maternity wing, and, well, she just couldn't get to a phone.

Adam sat in his pajamas at the table, sipping coffee and studying the paper as she talked. He hadn't asked for the explanation. He tried his best to act unconcerned about her. She insisted on cooking breakfast: scrambled eggs and canned biscuits. And she was doing a good job of busying herself in the kitchen as she talked and avoided eye contact.

"What's the kid's name?" he asked seriously as if he was deeply concerned with Lee's story.

"Uh, Natasha. Natasha Perkins."

"And she's only thirteen?"

"Yes. Her mother is twenty-nine. Can you believe it? A twenty-nine-year-old grandmother."

Adam shook his head in disbelief. He happened to be looking at the small section of the *Memphis Press* where it registered the county's vital records. Marriage licenses. Divorce petitions. Births. Arrests. Deaths. He scanned the list of yesterday's births as if he were checking scores, and found no record of a new mother named Natasha Perkins.

Lee finished her struggle with the canned biscuits. She placed them on a small platter along with the eggs and served them, then sat at the other end of the table, as far away from Adam as possible. "*Bon appétit*," she said with a forced smile. Her cooking was already a rich source of humor.

Adam smiled as if everything were fine. They needed humor at this moment, but wit failed them. "Cubs lost again," he said, taking a bite of eggs and glancing at the folded newspaper.

"The Cubs always lose, don't they?"

"Not always. You follow baseball?"

"I hate baseball. Phelps turned me against every sport known to man."

Adam grinned and read the paper. They ate without talking for a few minutes, and the silence grew heavy. Lee punched the remote and the television on the counter came on and created noise. They were both suddenly interested in the weather, which was again hot and dry. She played with her food, nibbling on a half-baked biscuit and pushing the eggs around her plate. Adam suspected her stomach was feeble at the moment.

He finished quickly and took his plate to the kitchen sink. He sat again at the table to finish the paper. She was staring at the television, anything to keep her eyes away from her nephew.

"I'll probably go see Sam today," he said. "I haven't been in a week."

Her gaze fell to a spot somewhere in the middle of the table. "I wish we hadn't gone to Clanton Saturday," she said.

"I know."

"It was not a good idea."

"I'm sorry, Lee. I insisted on going, and it was not a good idea. I've insisted on a lot of things, and maybe I've been wrong."

"It's not fair—"

"I know it's not fair. I realize now that it's not a simple matter of learning family history."

"It's not fair to him, Adam. It's almost cruel to confront him with these things when he has only two weeks to live."

"You're right. And it's wrong to make you relive them."

"I'll be fine." She said this as if she certainly wasn't fine now, but there might be a bit of hope for the future.

"I'm sorry, Lee. I'm truly sorry."

"It's okay. What will you and Sam do today?"

"Talk, primarily. The local federal court ruled against us yesterday, and so we'll appeal this morning. Sam likes to talk legal strategies."

"Tell him I'm thinking about him."

"I will."

She pushed her plate away and cuddled her cup with both hands. "And ask him if he wants me to come see him."

"Do you really want to?" Adam asked, unable to conceal his surprise.

"Something tells me I should. I haven't seen him in many years."

"I'll ask him."

"And don't mention Joe Lincoln, okay, Adam? I never told Daddy what I saw."

"You and Sam never mentioned the killing?"

"Never. It became well known in the community. Eddie and I grew up with it and carried it as a burden, but, to be honest, Adam, it was not a big deal to the neighbors. My father killed a black man. It was 1950, and it was Mississippi. It was never discussed in our house."

"So Sam makes it to his grave without being confronted with the killing?"

"What do you accomplish by confronting him? It was forty years ago."

"I don't know. Maybe he'll say he was sorry."

"To you? He apologizes to you, and that makes everything okay? Come on, Adam, you're young and you don't understand. Leave it alone. Don't hurt the old man anymore. Right now, you're the only bright spot in his pathetic life."

"Okay, okay."

"You have no right to ambush him with the story of Joe Lincoln."

"You're right. I won't. I promise."

She stared at him with bloodshot eyes until he looked at the television, then she quickly excused herself and disappeared through the den. Adam heard the bathroom door close and lock. He eased across the carpet and stood in the hallway, listening as she heaved and vomited. The toilet flushed, and he ran upstairs to his room to shower and change.

BY 10 A.M., Adam had perfected the appeal to the Fifth Circuit Court of Appeals in New Orleans. Judge

Slattery had already faxed a copy of his order to the clerk of the Fifth Circuit, and Adam faxed his appeal shortly after arriving at the office. He Fed-Exed the original by overnight.

He also had his first conversation with the Death Clerk, a full-time employee of the United States Supreme Court who does nothing but monitor the final appeals of all death row inmates. The Death Clerk often works around the clock as executions go down to the wire. E. Garner Goodman had briefed Adam on the machinations of the Death Clerk and his office, and it was with some reluctance that Adam placed the first call.

The clerk's name was Richard Olander, a rather efficient sort who sounded quite tired early Monday morning. "We've been expecting this," he said to Adam, as if the damned thing should've been filed some time ago. He asked Adam if this was his first execution.

"Afraid so," Adam said. "And I hope it's my last."

"Well, you've certainly picked a loser," Mr. Olander said, then explained in tedious detail exactly how the Court expected the final appeals to be handled. Every filing from this point forward, until the *end,* regardless of where it's filed or what it's about, must also simultaneously be filed with his office, he stated flatly as if reading from a textbook. In fact, he would immediately fax to Adam a copy of the Court's rules, all of which had to be meticulously followed up until the very *end.* His office was on call, around the clock, he repeated more than once, and it was essential that they receive copies of everything. That was, of course, if Adam wanted his client to have a fair hearing with the Court. If Adam didn't care, then, well, just follow the rules haphazardly and his client would pay for it.

Adam promised to follow the rules. The Supreme

Court had become increasingly weary of the endless claims in death cases, and wanted to have all motions and appeals in hand to expedite matters. Adam's appeal to the Fifth Circuit would be scrutinized by the justices and their clerks long before the Court actually received the case from New Orleans. The same would be true for all his eleventh-hour filings. The Court would then be able to grant immediate relief, or deny it quickly.

So efficient and speedy was the Death Clerk that the Court had recently been embarrassed by denying an appeal before it was actually filed.

Then Mr. Olander explained that his office had a checklist of every conceivable last minute appeal and motion, and he and his quite able staff monitored each case to see if all possible filings took place. And if a lawyer somewhere missed a potential issue, then they would actually notify the lawyer that he should pursue the forgotten claim. Did Adam desire a copy of their checklist?

No, Adam explained that he already had a copy. E. Garner Goodman had written the book on gangplank appeals.

Very well, said Mr. Olander. Mr. Cayhall had sixteen days, and, of course, a lot can happen in sixteen days. But Mr. Cayhall had been ably represented, in his humble opinion, and the matter had been thoroughly litigated. He would be surprised, he ventured, if there were additional delays.

Thanks for nothing, Adam thought.

Mr. Olander and his staff were watching a case in Texas very closely, he explained. The execution was set for a day before Sam's, but, in his opinion, there was a likely chance for a stay. Florida had one scheduled for two days after Mr. Cayhall's. Georgia had two set for a week later, but, well, who knows. He or someone on

his staff would be available at all hours, and he himself
would personally be by the phone for the twelve-hour
period leading up to the execution.

Just call anytime, he said, and ended the conversation with a terse promise to make things as easy as
possible for Adam and his client.

Adam slammed the phone down and stalked around
his office. His door was locked, as usual, and the hallway was busy with eager Monday morning gossip. His
face had been in the paper again yesterday, and he did
not want to be seen. He called the Auburn House and
asked for Lee Booth, but she was not in. He called her
condo, and there was no answer. He called Parchman,
and told the officer at the front gate to expect him
around one.

He went to his computer and found one of his current projects, a condensed, chronological history of
Sam's case.

THE LAKEHEAD COUNTY JURY convicted Sam on
February 12, 1981, and two days later handed him a
verdict of death. He appealed directly to the Mississippi Supreme Court, claiming all sorts of grievances
with the trial and the prosecution but taking particular
exception to the fact that the trial occurred almost
fourteen years after the bombing. His lawyer, Benjamin
Keyes, argued vehemently that Sam was denied a
speedy trial, and that he was subjected to double jeopardy, being tried three times for the same crime. Keyes
presented a very strong argument. The Mississippi Supreme Court was bitterly divided over these issues, and
on July 23, 1982, handed down a split decision af-
firming Sam's conviction. Five justices voted to affirm,
three to reverse, and one abstained.

Keyes then filed a petition for writ of certiorari with
the U.S. Supreme Court, which, in effect, asked that

Court to review Sam's case. Since the Supreme Court grants "cert" on such a small number of cases, it was somewhat of a surprise when, on March 4, 1983, the Court agreed to review Sam's conviction.

The U.S. Supreme Court split almost as badly as Mississippi's on the issue of double jeopardy, but nonetheless reached the same conclusion. Sam's first two juries had been hopelessly deadlocked, hung up by the shenanigans of Clovis Brazelton, and thus Sam was not protected by the double jeopardy clause of the Fifth Amendment. He was not acquitted by either of the first two juries. Each had been unable to reach a verdict, so reprosecution was quite constitutional. On September 21, 1983, the U.S. Supreme Court ruled six to three that Sam's conviction should stand. Keyes immediately filed some motions requesting a rehearing, but to no avail.

Sam had hired Keyes to represent him during the trial and on appeal to the Mississippi Supreme Court, if necessary. By the time the U.S. Supreme Court affirmed the conviction, Keyes was working without getting paid. His contract for legal representation had expired, and he wrote Sam a long letter and explained that it was now time for Sam to make other arrangements. Sam understood this.

Keyes also wrote a letter to an ACLU lawyer-friend of his in Washington, who in turn wrote a letter to his pal E. Garner Goodman at Kravitz & Bane in Chicago. The letter landed on Goodman's desk at precisely the right moment. Sam was running out of time and was desperate. Goodman was looking for a pro bono project. They swapped letters, and on December 18, 1983, Wallace Tyner, a partner in the white-collar criminal defense section of Kravitz & Bane, filed a petition seeking postconviction relief with the Mississippi Supreme Court.

Tyner alleged many errors in Sam's trial, including the admission into evidence of the gory pictures of the bodies of Josh and John Kramer. He attacked the selection of the jury, and claimed that McAllister systematically picked blacks over whites. He claimed a fair trial was not possible because the social environment was far different in 1981 than in 1967. He maintained the venue selected by the trial judge was unfair. He raised yet again the issues of double jeopardy and speedy trial. In all, Wallace Tyner and Garner Goodman raised eight separate issues in the petition. They did not, however, maintain that Sam had suffered because of ineffective trial counsel, the primary claim of all death row inmates. They had wanted to, but Sam wouldn't allow it. He initially refused to sign the petition because it attacked Benjamin Keyes, a lawyer Sam was fond of.

On June 1, 1985, the Mississippi Supreme Court denied all of the postconviction relief requested. Tyner again appealed to the U.S. Supreme Court, but cert was denied. He then filed Sam's first petition for writ of habeas corpus and request for a stay of execution in federal court in Mississippi. Typically, the petition was quite thick, and contained every issue already raised in state court.

Two years later, on May 3, 1987, the district court denied all relief, and Tyner appealed to the Fifth Circuit in New Orleans, which in due course affirmed the lower court's denial. On March 20, 1988, Tyner filed a petition for a rehearing with the Fifth Circuit, which was also denied. On September 3, 1988, Tyner and Goodman again trekked to the Supreme Court and asked for cert. A week later, Sam wrote the first of many letters to Goodman and Tyner threatening to fire them.

The U.S. Supreme Court granted Sam his last stay on May 14, 1989, pursuant to a grant of certiorari being given in a Florida case the Court had decided to hear. Tyner argued successfully that the Florida case raised similar issues, and the Supreme Court granted stays in several dozen death cases around the country.

Nothing was filed in Sam's case while the Supreme Court delayed and debated the Florida case. Sam, however, had begun his own efforts to rid himself of Kravitz & Bane. He filed a few clumsy motions himself, all of which were quickly denied. He did succeed, however, in obtaining an order from the Fifth Circuit that effectively terminated the pro bono services of his lawyers. On June 29, 1990, the Fifth Circuit allowed him to represent himself, and Garner Goodman closed the file on Sam Cayhall. It wasn't closed for long.

On July 9, 1990, the Supreme Court vacated Sam's stay. On July 10, the Fifth Circuit vacated Sam's stay, and on the same day the Mississippi Supreme Court set his execution date for August 8, four weeks away.

After nine years of appellate warfare, Sam now had sixteen days to live.

TWENTY-NINE

THE ROW was quiet and still as another day dragged itself toward noon. The diverse collection of fans buzzed and rattled in the tiny cells, trying valiantly to push around air that grew stickier by the moment.

The early television news had been filled with excited reports that Sam Cayhall had lost his latest legal battle. Slattery's decision was trumpeted around the state as if it were indeed the final nail in the coffin. A Jackson station continued its countdown, only sixteen days to go. Day Sixteen! it said in bold letters under the same old photo of Sam. Bright-eyed reporters with heavy makeup and no knowledge of the law spouted at the cameras with fearless predictions: "According to our sources, Sam Cayhall's legal options are virtually gone. Many people believe that his execution will take place, as scheduled, on August 8." Then on to sports and weather.

There was much less talk on the Row, less yelling back and forth, fewer kites being floated along the cells. There was about to be an execution.

Sergeant Packer smiled to himself as he shuffled along Tier A. The bitching and griping that was so much a part of his daily work had almost disappeared. Now, the inmates were concerned with appeals and their lawyers. The most common request in the past two weeks had been to use the phone to call a lawyer.

Packer did not look forward to another execution, but he did enjoy the quiet. And he knew it was only temporary. If Sam got a stay tomorrow, the noise would increase immediately.

He stopped in front of Sam's cell. "Hour out, Sam."

Sam was sitting on his bed, typing and smoking as usual. "What time is it?" he asked, placing the typewriter to his side and standing.

"Eleven."

Sam turned his back to Packer and stuck his wrists through the opening in his door. Packer carefully cuffed them together. "You out by yourself?" he asked.

Sam turned with his hands behind him. "No. Henshaw wants to come out too."

"I'll get him," Packer said, nodding at Sam then nodding at the end of the tier. The door opened, and Sam slowly followed him past the other cells. Each inmate was leaning on the bars with hands and arms dangling through, each watching Sam closely as he walked by.

They made their way through more bars and more hallways, and Packer unlocked an unpainted metal door. It opened to the outside, and the sunlight burst through. Sam hated this part of his hour out. He stepped onto the grass and closed his eyes tightly as Packer uncuffed him, then opened them slowly as they focused and adjusted to the painful glow of the sun.

Packer disappeared inside without a word, and Sam stood in the same spot for a full minute as lights flashed and his head pounded. The heat didn't bother him because he lived with it, but the sunlight hit like lasers and caused a severe headache each time he was allowed to venture from the dungeon. He could easily afford a pair of cheap sunglasses, similar to Packer's, but of course that would be too sensible. Sunglasses were not on the approved list of items an inmate could own.

He walked unsteadily through the clipped grass, looking through the fence to the cotton fields beyond. The recreation yard was nothing more than a fenced-in plot of dirt and grass with two wooden benches and a basketball hoop for the Africans. It was known to guards and prisoners alike as the bullpen. Sam had stepped it off carefully a thousand times, and had compared his measurements with those of other inmates. The yard was fifty-one feet long and thirty-six feet wide. The fence was ten feet tall and crowned with another eighteen inches of razor wire. Beyond the fence was a stretch of grass that ran a hundred feet or so to the main fence, which was watched by the guards in the towers.

Sam walked in a straight line next to the fence, and when it stopped he turned ninety degrees and continued his little routine, counting every step along the way. Fifty-one feet by thirty-six. His cell was six by nine. The law library, the Twig, was eighteen by fifteen. His side of the visitors' room was six by thirty. He'd been told the Chamber Room was fifteen by twelve, and the chamber itself was a mere cube barely four feet wide.

During the first year of his confinement, he had jogged around the edges of the yard, trying to sweat and give his heart a workout. He'd also tossed shots at the basketball hoop, but quit when he went days without making one. He had eventually quit exercising, and for years had used this hour to do nothing but enjoy the freedom from his cell. At one time, he'd fallen into the habit of standing at the fence and staring past the fields to the trees where he imagined all sorts of things. Freedom. Highways. Fishing. Food. Sex occasionally. He could almost picture his little farm in Ford County not far over there between two small patches of woods. He would dream of Brazil or Argentina or some other laid-back hiding place where he should be living with a new name.

And then he'd stopped the dreaming. He'd stopped gazing through the fence as if a miracle would take him away. He walked and smoked, almost always by himself. His most rigorous activity was a game of checkers.

The door opened again, and Hank Henshaw walked through it. Packer uncuffed him as he squinted furiously and looked at the ground. He rubbed his wrists as soon as they were free, then stretched his back and legs. Packer walked to one of the benches and placed a worn cardboard box on it.

The two inmates watched Packer until he left the yard, then they walked to the bench and assumed their positions astraddle the wooden plank with the box between them. Sam carefully placed the checkerboard on the bench as Henshaw counted the checkers.

"My turn to be red," Sam said.

"You were red last time," Henshaw said, staring at him.

"I was black last time."

"No, I was black last time. It's my turn to be red."

"Look, Hank. I've got sixteen days, and if I want to be red, then I get to be red."

Henshaw shrugged and conceded. They arranged their checkers meticulously.

"I guess you get the first move," Henshaw said.

"Of course." Sam slid a checker to a vacant square, and the match was on. The midday sun baked the ground around them and within minutes their red jumpsuits stuck to their backs. They both wore rubber shower shoes with no socks.

Hank Henshaw was forty-one, now a resident of the Row for seven years but not expected to ever see the gas chamber. Two crucial errors had been made at trial, and Henshaw had a decent chance of getting reversed and freed from the Row.

"Bad news yesterday," he said as Sam pondered the next move.

"Yes, things are lookin' pretty grim, wouldn't you say?"

"Yeah. What does your lawyer say?" Neither of them looked up from the checkerboard.

"He says we have a fightin' chance."

"What the hell does that mean?" Henshaw asked as he made a move.

"I think it means they're gonna gas me, but I'll go down swinging."

"Does the kid know what he's doing?"

"Oh yeah. He's sharp. Runs in the blood, you know."

"But he's awfully young."

"He's a smart kid. Great education. Number two in his law class at Michigan, you know. Editor of the law review."

"What does that mean?"

"Means he's brilliant. He'll think of something."

"Are you serious, Sam? Do you think it's gonna happen?"

Sam suddenly jumped two black checkers, and Henshaw cursed. "You're pitiful," Sam said with a grin. "When was the last time you beat me?"

"Two weeks ago."

"You liar. You haven't beat me in three years."

Henshaw made a tentative move, and Sam jumped him again. Five minutes later, the game was over with Sam victorious again. They cleared the board, and started over.

AT NOON, Packer and another guard appeared with handcuffs, and the fun was over. They were led to their cells where lunch was in progress. Beans, peas, mashed potatoes, and several slices of dry toast. Sam ate less than a third of the bland food on his plate, and waited patiently for a guard to come after him. He held a pair of clean boxer shorts and a bar of soap. It was time to bathe.

The guard arrived and led Sam to a small shower at the end of the tier. By court order, death row inmates were allowed five quick showers a week, whether they needed them or not, as the guards liked to say.

Sam showered quickly, washing his hair twice with the soap and rinsing himself in the warm water. The shower itself was clean enough, but used by all fourteen inmates on the tier. Thus, the rubber shower shoes remained on the feet. After five minutes, the water stopped, and Sam dripped for a few more minutes as he stared at the moldy tiled walls. There were some things about the Row that he would not miss.

Twenty minutes later, he was loaded into a prison van and driven a half a mile to the law library.

Adam was waiting inside. He removed his coat and rolled up his sleeves as the guards uncuffed Sam and left the room. They greeted each other and shook hands. Sam quickly took a seat and lit a cigarette. "Where've you been?" he asked.

"Busy," Adam said, sitting across the table. "I had an unexpected trip to Chicago last Wednesday and Thursday."

"Anything to do with me?"

"You could say that. Goodman wanted to review the case, and there were a couple of other matters."

"So Goodman's still involved?"

"Goodman is my boss right now, Sam. I have to report to him if I want to keep my job. I know you hate him, but he's very concerned about you and your case. Believe it or not, he does not want to see you gassed."

"I don't hate him anymore."

"Why the change of heart?"

"I don't know. When you get this close to death, you do a lot of thinking."

Adam was anxious to hear more, but Sam let it pass. Adam watched him smoke and tried not to think about Joe Lincoln. He tried not to think of Sam's father being beaten in a drunken brawl at a funeral, and he tried to ignore all the other miserable stories Lee had told him in Ford County. He tried to block these things from his mind, but he couldn't.

He had promised her he would not mention any more nightmares from the past. "I guess you've heard about our latest defeat," he said as he pulled papers from his briefcase.

"It didn't take long, did it?"

"No. A rather quick loss, but I've already appealed to the Fifth Circuit."

"I've never won in the Fifth Circuit."

"I know. But we can't select our review court at this point."

"What can we do at this point?"

"Several things. I bumped into the governor last Tuesday after a meeting with the federal judge. He wanted to talk in private. He gave me his private phone numbers and invited me to call and talk about the case. Said he had doubts about the extent of your guilt."

Sam glared at him. "Doubts? He's the only reason I'm here. He can't wait to see me executed."

"You're probably right, but—"

"You promised not to talk to him. You signed an agreement with me expressly prohibiting any contact with that fool."

"Relax, Sam. He grabbed me outside the judge's office."

"I'm surprised he didn't call a press conference to talk about it."

"I threatened him, okay. I made him promise not to talk."

"Then you're the first person in history to silence that bastard."

"He's open to the idea of clemency."

"He told you this?"

"Yes."

"Why? I don't believe it."

"I don't know why, Sam. And I don't really care. But how can it hurt? What's the danger in requesting a clemency hearing? So he gets his picture in the paper. So the TV cameras chase him around some more. If there's a chance he'll listen, then why should you care if he gets some mileage from it?"

"No. The answer is no. I will not authorize you to request a clemency hearing. Hell no. A thousand times no. I know him, Adam. He's trying to suck you into his game plan. It's all a sham, a show for the public. He'll grieve over this until the very end, milking it for all he can. He'll get more attention than I will, and it's my execution."

"So what's the harm?"

Sam slapped the table with the palm of his hand. "Because it won't do any good, Adam! He will not change his mind."

Adam scribbled something on a legal pad and let a moment pass. Sam eased back in his seat, and lit another cigarette. His hair was still wet and he combed it back with his fingernails.

Adam placed his pen on the table and looked at his client. "What do you want to do, Sam? Quit? Throw in the towel? You think you know so damned much law, tell me what you want to do."

"Well, I've been thinking about it."

"I'm sure you have."

"The lawsuit on its way to the Fifth Circuit has merit, but it doesn't look promising. There's not much left, as I see things."

"Except Benjamin Keyes."

"Right. Except Keyes. He did a fine job for me at trial and on appeal, and he was almost a friend. I hate to go after him."

"It's standard in death cases, Sam. You always go after the trial lawyer and claim ineffective assistance of counsel. Goodman told me he wanted to do it, but you refused. It should've been done years ago."

"He's right about that. He begged me to do it, but I said no. I guess it was a mistake."

Adam was on the edge of his seat taking notes. "I've studied the record, and I think Keyes made a mistake when he didn't put you on the stand to testify."

"I wanted to talk to the jury, you know. I think I've already told you that. After Dogan testified, I thought it was essential for me to explain to the jury that I did in fact plant the bomb, but there was no intent to kill anyone. That's the truth, Adam. I didn't intend to kill anyone."

"You wanted to testify, but your lawyer said no."

Sam smiled and looked at the floor. "Is that what you want me to say?"

"Yes."

"I don't have much of a choice, do I?"

"No."

"Okay. That's the way it happened. I wanted to testify, but my lawyer wouldn't allow it."

"I'll file first thing in the morning."

"It's too late, isn't it?"

"Well, it's certainly late, and this issue should've been raised a long time ago. But what's there to lose?"

"Will you call Keyes and tell him?"

"If I have time. I'm really not concerned with his feelings at the moment."

"Then neither am I. To hell with him. Who else can we attack?"

"The list is rather short."

Sam jumped to his feet and began pacing along the table in measured steps. The room was eighteen feet long. He walked around the table, behind Adam, and along each of the four walls, counting as he went. He stopped and leaned against a shelf of books.

Adam finished some notes and watched him carefully. "Lee wants to know if she can come visit," he said.

Sam stared at him, then slowly returned to his seat across the table. "She wants to?"

"I think so."

"I'll have to think about it."

"Well, hurry."

"How's she doing?"

"Pretty fair, I guess. She sends her love and prayers, and she thinks about you a lot these days."

"Do people in Memphis know she's my daughter?"

"I don't think so. It hasn't been in the papers yet."

"I hope they keep it quiet."

"She and I went to Clanton last Saturday."

Sam looked at him sadly, then gazed at the ceiling. "What did you see?" he asked.

"Lots of things. She showed me my grandmother's grave, and the plot with the other Cayhalls."

"She didn't want to be buried with the Cayhalls, did Lee tell you that?"

"Yes. Lee asked me where you wanted to be buried."

"I haven't decided yet."

"Sure. Just let me know when you make the decision. We walked through the town, and she showed me the house we lived in. We went to the square and sat in the gazebo on the courthouse lawn. The town was very busy. People were packed around the square."

"We used to watch fireworks in the cemetery."

"Lee told me all about it. We ate lunch at The Tea Shoppe, and took a drive in the country. She took me to her childhood home."

"It's still there?"

"Yeah, it's abandoned. The house is run-down and the weeds have taken over. We walked around the place. She told me lots of stories of her childhood. Talked a lot about Eddie."

"Does she have fond memories?"

"Not really."

Sam crossed his arms and looked at the table. A minute passed without a word. Finally, Sam asked, "Did she tell you about Eddie's little African friend, Quince Lincoln?"

Adam nodded slowly, and their eyes locked together. "Yes, she did."

"And about his father, Joe?"

"She told me the story."

"Do you believe her?"

"I do. Should I?"

"It's true. It's all true."

"I thought so."

"How did you feel when she told you the story? I mean, how did you react to it?"

"I hated your guts."

"And how do you feel now?"

"Different."

Sam slowly rose from his seat and walked to the end of the table where he stopped and stood with his back to Adam. "That was forty years ago," he mumbled, barely audible.

"I didn't come here to talk about it," Adam said, already feeling guilty.

Sam turned and leaned on the same bookshelf. He crossed his arms and stared at the wall. "I've wished a thousand times it hadn't happened."

"I promised Lee I wouldn't bring it up, Sam. I'm sorry."

"Joe Lincoln was a good man. I've often wondered what happened to Ruby and Quince and the rest of the kids."

"Forget it, Sam. Let's talk about something else."

"I hope they're happy when I'm dead."

THIRTY

AS ADAM drove past the security station at the main gate the guard waved, as if by now he was a regular customer. He waved back as he slowed and pushed a button to release his trunk. No paperwork was required for visitors to leave, only a quick look in the trunk to make sure no prisoners had caught a ride. He turned onto the highway, heading south, away from Memphis, and calculated that this was his fifth visit to Parchman. Five visits in two weeks. He had a suspicion that the place would be his second home for the next sixteen days. What a rotten thought.

He was not in the mood to deal with Lee tonight. He felt some responsibility for her relapse into alcohol, but by her own admission this had been a way of life for many years. She was an alcoholic, and if she chose to drink there was nothing he could do to stop her. He would be there tomorrow night, to make coffee and conversation. Tonight, he needed a break.

It was mid-afternoon, the heat emanated from the asphalt highway, the fields were dusty and dry, the farm implements languid and slow, the traffic light and sluggish. Adam pulled to the shoulder and raised the convertible top. He stopped at a Chinese grocery in Ruleville and bought a can of iced tea, then sped along a lonely highway in the general direction of Greenville. He had an errand to run, probably an unpleasant one, but something he felt obligated to do. He hoped he had the courage to go through with it.

He stayed on the back roads, the small paved county routes, and zipped almost aimlessly across the Delta. He got lost twice, but worked himself out of it. He arrived in Greenville a few minutes before five, and cruised the downtown area in search of his target. He passed Kramer Park twice. He found the synagogue, across the street from the First Baptist Church. He parked at the end of Main Street, at the river where a levee guarded the city. He straightened his tie and walked three blocks along Washington Street to an old brick building with the sign Kramer Wholesale hanging from a veranda above the sidewalk in front of it. The heavy glass door opened to the inside, and the ancient wooden floors squeaked as he walked on them. The front part of the building had been preserved to resemble an old-fashioned retail store, with glass counters in front of wide shelves that ran to the ceiling. The shelves and counters were filled with boxes and wrappings of food products sold years ago, but now extinct. An antique cash register was on display. The little museum quickly yielded to modern commerce. The rest of the huge building was renovated and gave the appearance of being quite efficient. A wall of paned glass cut off the front foyer, and a wide carpeted hallway ran down the center of the building and led, no doubt, to offices and secretaries, and somewhere in the rear there had to be a warehouse.

Adam admired the displays in the front counters. A young man in jeans appeared from the back and asked, "Can I help you?"

Adam smiled, and was suddenly nervous. "Yes, I'd like to see Mr. Elliot Kramer."

"Are you a salesman?"

"No."

"Are you a buyer?"

"No."

The young man was holding a pencil and had things on his mind. "Then, may I ask what you need?"

"I need to see Mr. Elliot Kramer. Is he here?"

"He spends most of his time at the main warehouse south of town."

Adam took three steps toward the guy and handed him a business card. "My name is Adam Hall. I'm an attorney from Chicago. I really need to see Mr. Kramer."

He took the card and studied it for a few seconds, then he looked at Adam with a great deal of suspicion. "Just a minute," he said, and walked away.

Adam leaned on a counter and admired the cash register. He had read somewhere in his voluminous research that Marvin Kramer's family had been prosperous merchants in the Delta for several generations. An ancestor had made a hasty exit from a steamboat at the port in Greenville, and decided to call it home. He opened a small dry goods store, and one thing led to another. Throughout the ordeal of Sam's trials, the Kramer family was repeatedly described as wealthy.

After twenty minutes of waiting, Adam was ready to leave, and quite relieved. He'd made the effort. If Mr. Kramer didn't want to meet with him, there was nothing he could do about it.

He heard footsteps on the wooden floor, and turned around. An elderly gentleman stood with a business card in his hand. He was tall and thin, with wavy gray hair, dark brown eyes with heavy shadows under them, a lean, strong face, which at the moment was not smiling. He stood erect, no cane to aid him, no eyeglasses to help him see. He scowled at Adam, but said nothing.

For an instant, Adam wished he'd left five minutes ago. Then he asked himself why he was there to begin with. Then he decided to go for it anyway. "Good afternoon," he said, when it was obvious the gentleman would not speak. "Mr. Elliot Kramer?"

Mr. Kramer nodded in the affirmative, but nodded ever so slowly as if challenged by the question.

"My name is Adam Hall. I'm an attorney from Chicago. Sam Cayhall is my grandfather, and I represent him." It was obvious Mr. Kramer had already figured this out, because Adam's words didn't faze him. "I would like to talk to you."

"Talk about what?" Mr. Kramer said in a slow drawl.

"About Sam."

"I hope he rots in hell," he said, as if he was already certain of Sam's eternal destination. His eyes were so brown they were almost black.

Adam glanced at the floor, away from the eyes, and tried to think of something noninflammatory. "Yes sir," he said, very much aware that he was in the Deep South where politeness went a long way. "I understand how you feel. I don't blame you, but I just wanted to talk to you for a few minutes."

"Does Sam send his apologies?" Mr. Kramer asked. The fact that he referred to him simply as Sam struck Adam as odd. Not Mr. Cayhall, not Cayhall, just Sam, as if the two were old friends who'd been feuding and now it was time to reconcile. Just say you're sorry, Sam, and everything's fine.

The thought of a quick lie raced through Adam's mind. He could lay it on thick, say how terrible Sam felt in these his last days and how he desperately wanted forgiveness. But Adam couldn't bring himself to do it. "Would it make any difference?" he asked.

Mr. Kramer carefully placed the card in his shirt pocket, and began what would become a long stare past Adam and through the front window. "No," he said, "it wouldn't make any difference. It's something

that should've been done long ago." His words were
accented with the heavy drip of the Delta, and even
though their meanings were not welcome, their sounds
were very soothing. They were slow and thoughtful,
uttered as if time meant nothing. They also conveyed
the years of suffering, and the hint that life had ceased
long ago.

"No, Mr. Kramer. Sam does not know I'm here, so
he does not send his apologies. But I do."

The gaze through the window and into the past did
not flinch or waver. But he was listening.

Adam continued, "I feel the obligation to at least
say, for myself and Sam's daughter, that we're terribly
sorry for all that's happened."

"Why didn't Sam say it years ago?"

"I can't answer that."

"I know. You're new."

Ah, the power of the press. Of course Mr. Kramer
had been reading the papers like everyone else.

"Yes sir. I'm trying to save his life."

"Why?"

"Many reasons. Killing him will not bring back your
grandsons, nor your son. He was wrong, but it's also
wrong for the government to kill him."

"I see. And you think I've never heard this before?"

"No sir. I'm sure you've heard it all. You've seen it
all. You've felt it all. I can't imagine what you've been
through. I'm just trying to avoid it myself."

"What else do you want?"

"Could you spare five minutes?"

"We've been talking for three minutes. You have two
more." He glanced at his watch as if to set a timer,
then eased his long fingers into the pockets of his
pants. His eyes returned to the window and the street
beyond it.

"The Memphis paper quoted you as saying you

wanted to be there when they strapped Sam Cayhall in
the gas chamber; that you wanted to look him in the
eyes."

"That's an accurate quote. But I don't believe it'll
ever happen."

"Why not?"

"Because we have a rotten criminal justice system.
He's been coddled and protected in prison for almost
ten years now. His appeals go on and on. You're filing
appeals and pulling strings at this very moment to keep
him alive. The system is sick. We don't expect justice."

"I assure you he's not being coddled. Death row is a
horrible place. I just left it."

"Yeah, but he's alive. He's living and breathing and
watching television and reading books. He's talking to
you. He's filing lawsuits. And when and if death gets
near, he'll have plenty of time to make plans for it. He
can say his good-byes. Say his prayers. My grandsons
didn't have time to say good-bye, Mr. Hall. They
didn't get to hug their parents and give them farewell
kisses. They were simply blown to bits while they were
playing."

"I understand that, Mr. Kramer. But killing Sam will
not bring them back."

"No, it won't. But it'll make us feel a helluva lot
better. It'll ease a lot of pain. I've prayed a million
times that I'll live long enough to see him dead. I had a
heart attack five years ago. They had me strapped to
machines for two weeks, and the one thing that kept
me alive was my desire to outlive Sam Cayhall. I'll be
there, Mr. Hall, if my doctors allow it. I'll be there to
watch him die, then I'll come home and count my
days."

"I'm sorry you feel this way."

"I'm sorry I do too. I'm sorry I ever heard the name
Sam Cayhall."

Adam took a step backward and leaned on the counter near the cash register. He stared at the floor, and Mr. Kramer stared through the window. The sun was falling to the west, behind the building, and the quaint little museum was growing dimmer.

"I lost my father because of this," Adam said softly.

"I'm sorry. I read where he had committed suicide shortly after the last trial."

"Sam has suffered too, Mr. Kramer. He wrecked his family, and he wrecked yours. And he carries more guilt than you or I could ever imagine."

"Perhaps he won't be as burdened when he's dead."

"Perhaps. But why don't we stop the killing?"

"How do you expect me to stop it?"

"I read somewhere that you and the governor are old friends."

"Why is it any of your business?"

"It's true, isn't it?"

"He's a local boy. I've known him for many years."

"I met him last week for the first time. He has the power to grant clemency, you know."

"I wouldn't count on that."

"I'm not. I'm desperate, Mr. Kramer. I have nothing to lose at this point, except my grandfather. If you and your family are hell-bent on pushing for the execution, then the governor will certainly listen to you."

"You're right."

"And if you decided you didn't want an execution, I think the governor might listen to that as well."

"So it's all up to me," he said, finally moving. He walked in front of Adam and stopped near the window. "You're not only desperate, Mr. Hall, you're also naive."

"I won't argue that."

"It's nice to know I have so much power. If I had

known this before now, your grandfather would've been dead years ago."

"He doesn't deserve to die, Mr. Kramer," Adam said as he walked to the door. He hadn't expected to find sympathy. It was important only for Mr. Kramer to see him and know that other lives were being affected.

"Neither did my grandsons. Neither did my son."

Adam opened the door, and said, "I'm sorry for the intrusion, and I thank you for your time. I have a sister, a cousin, and an aunt, Sam's daughter. I just wanted you to know that Sam has a family, such as it is. We will suffer if he dies. If he's not executed, he'll never leave prison. He'll simply wilt away and die someday very soon of natural causes."

"You will suffer?"

"Yes sir. It's a pathetic family, Mr. Kramer, filled with tragedy. I'm trying to avoid another one."

Mr. Kramer turned and looked at him. His face bore no expression. "Then I feel sorry for you."

"Thanks again," Adam said.

"Good day, sir," Mr. Kramer said without a smile.

Adam left the building and walked along a shaded street until he was in the center of town. He found the memorial park, and sat on the same bench not far from the bronze statue of the little boys. After a few minutes, though, he was tired of the guilt and memories, and he walked away.

He went to the same café a block away, drank coffee, and toyed with a grilled cheese. He heard a Sam Cayhall conversation several tables away, but couldn't discern what exactly was being said.

He checked into a motel and called Lee. She sounded sober, and maybe a bit relieved that he would not be there tonight. He promised to return tomorrow evening. By the time it was dark, Adam had been asleep for half an hour.

THIRTY-ONE

ADAM DROVE through downtown Memphis in the predawn hours, and was locked in his office by 7 A.M. By eight, he'd talked to E. Garner Goodman three times. Goodman, it seemed, was wired and also having trouble sleeping. They discussed at length the issue of Keyes's representation at trial. The Cayhall file was filled with memos and research about what went wrong at trial, but little of it placed blame on Benjamin Keyes.

But that had been many years ago, when the gas chamber seemed too distant to worry about. Goodman was pleased to hear that Sam now felt he should've testified at trial, and that Keyes had stopped him. Goodman was skeptical of the truth at this point, but he would take Sam's word for it.

Both Goodman and Adam knew the issue should've been raised years ago, and that to do so now was a long shot at best. Law books were getting thicker by the week with Supreme Court decisions barring legitimate claims because they weren't timely filed. But it was a real issue, one always examined by the courts, and Adam got excited as he drafted and redrafted the claim and swapped faxes with Goodman.

Again, the claim would first be filed under the post-conviction relief statutes in state court. He hoped for a quick denial there so he could immediately run to federal court.

At ten, he faxed his final draft to the clerk of the Mississippi Supreme Court, and also faxed a copy of it to the attention of Breck Jefferson in Slattery's office. Faxes also went to the clerk of the Fifth Circuit in New Orleans. Then he called the Death Clerk at the Supreme Court, and told Mr. Olander what he was doing. Mr. Olander instructed him to immediately fax a copy to Washington.

Darlene knocked on the door, and Adam unlocked it. He had a visitor waiting in the reception area, a Mr. Wyn Lettner. Adam thanked her, and a few minutes later walked down the hall and greeted Lettner, who was alone and dressed like a man who owned a trout dock. Deck shoes, fishing cap. They exchanged pleasantries: fish were biting, Irene was fine, when was he coming back to Calico Rock?

"I'm in town on business, and I just wanted to see you for a few minutes," he said in a low whisper with his back to the receptionist.

"Sure," Adam whispered. "My office is down the hall."

"No. Let's take a walk."

They rode the elevator to the lobby, and stepped from the building onto the pedestrian mall. Lettner bought a bag of roasted peanuts from a pushcart vendor, and offered Adam a handful. He declined. They walked slowly north toward city hall and the federal building. Lettner alternately ate the peanuts and tossed them to the pigeons.

"How's Sam?" he finally asked.

"He has two weeks. How would you feel if you had two weeks?"

"Guess I'd be praying a lot."

"He's not at that point yet, but it won't be long."

"Is it gonna happen?"

"It's certainly being planned. There's nothing in writing to stop it."

Lettner threw a handful of peanuts into his mouth.

"Well, good luck to you. Since you came to see me, I've found myself pulling for you and ol' Sam."

"Thanks. And you came to Memphis to wish me luck?"

"Not exactly. After you left, I thought a lot about Sam and the Kramer bombing. I looked at my personal files and records—stuff I haven't thought about in years. It brought back a lot of memories. I called a few of my old buddies and we told war stories about the Klan. Those were the days."

"I'm sorry that I missed them."

"Anyway, I thought of a few things that maybe I should've told you."

"Such as?"

"There's more to the Dogan story. You know he died a year after he testified."

"Sam told me."

"He and his wife were killed when their house blew up. Some kind of propane leak in the heater. House filled up with gas, and something ignited it. Went off like a bomb, a huge fireball. Buried them in sandwich bags."

"Sad, but so what?"

"We never believed it was an accident. The crime lab boys down there tried to reconstruct the heater. A lot of it was destroyed, but they were of the opinion it had been rigged to leak."

"How does this affect Sam?"

"It doesn't affect Sam."

"Then why are we talking about it?"

"It might affect you."

"I really don't follow."

"Dogan had a son, a kid who joined the Army in 1979 and was sent to Germany. At some point in the summer of 1980, Dogan and Sam were indicted again by the circuit court in Greenville, and shortly thereafter it became widely known that Dogan had agreed to testify against Sam. It was a big story. In October of 1980, Dogan's son went AWOL in Germany. Vanished." He crunched on some peanuts and tossed the hulls to a covey of pigeons. "Never found him either. Army searched high and low. Months went by. Then a year. Dogan died not knowing what happened to the kid."

"What happened to him?"

"Don't know. To this day, he's never turned up."

"He died?"

"Probably. There was no sign of him."

"Who killed him?"

"Maybe the same person who killed his parents."

"And who might that be?"

"We had a theory, but no suspect. We thought at the time that the son was grabbed before the trial as a warning to Dogan. Perhaps Dogan knew secrets."

"Then why kill Dogan after the trial?"

They stopped under a shade tree and sat on a bench in Court Square. Adam finally took some peanuts.

"Who knew the details of the bombing?" Lettner asked. "All the details."

"Sam. Jeremiah Dogan."

"Right. And who was their lawyer in the first two trials?"

"Clovis Brazelton."

"Would it be safe to assume Brazelton knew the details?"

"I suppose. He was active in the Klan, wasn't he?"

"Yep, he was a Klucker. That makes three—Sam, Dogan, and Brazelton. Anybody else?"

Adam thought for a second. "Perhaps the mysterious accomplice."

"Perhaps. Dogan's dead. Sam wouldn't talk. And Brazelton died many years ago."

"How'd he die?"

"Plane crash. The Kramer case made him a hero down there, and he was able to parlay his fame into a very successful law practice. He liked to fly, so he bought himself a plane and buzzed around everywhere trying lawsuits. A real big shot. He was flying back from the Coast one night when the plane disappeared from radar. They found his body in a tree. The weather was clear. The FAA said there'd been some type of engine failure."

"Another mysterious death."

"Yep. So everybody's dead but Sam, and he's getting close."

"Any link between Dogan's death and Brazelton's?"

"No. They were years apart. But the theory includes the scenario that the deaths were the work of the same person."

"So who's at work here?"

"Someone who's very concerned about secrets. Could be Sam's mysterious accomplice, John Doe."

"That's a pretty wild theory."

"Yes, it is. And it's one with absolutely no proof to support it. But I told you in Calico Rock that we always suspected Sam had help. Or perhaps Sam was merely a helper for John Doe. At any rate, when Sam screwed up and got caught, John Doe vanished. Perhaps he's been at work eliminating witnesses."

"Why would he kill Dogan's wife?"

"Because she happened to be in bed with him when the house blew up."

"Why would he kill Dogan's son?"

"To keep Dogan quiet. Remember, when Dogan testified his son had been missing for four months."

"I've never read anything about the son."

"It was not well known. It happened in Germany. We advised Dogan to keep it quiet."

"I'm confused. Dogan didn't finger anybody else at trial. Only Sam. Why would John Doe kill him afterward?"

"Because he still knew secrets. And because he testified against another Klansman."

Adam cracked two shells and dropped the peanuts in front of a single, fat pigeon. Lettner finished the bag and threw another handful of hulls on the sidewalk near a water fountain. It was almost noon, and dozens of office workers hurried through the park in pursuit of the perfect thirty-minute lunch.

"You hungry?" Lettner asked, glancing at his watch.

"No."

"Thirsty? I need a beer."

"No. How does John Doe affect me?"

"Sam's the only witness left, and he's scheduled to be silenced in two weeks. If he dies without talking, then John Doe can live in peace. If Sam doesn't die in two weeks, then John Doe is still anxious. But if Sam starts talking, then somebody might get hurt."

"Me?"

"You're the one trying to find the truth."

"You think he's out there?"

"Could be. Or he might be driving a cab in Montreal. Or maybe he never existed."

Adam glanced over both shoulders with exaggerated looks of fear.

"I know it sounds crazy," Lettner said.

"John Doe is safe. Sam ain't talking."

"There's a potential danger, Adam. I just wanted you to know."

"I'm not scared. If Sam gave me John Doe's name right now, I'd scream it in the streets and file motions by the truckload. And it wouldn't do any good. It's too late for new theories of guilt or innocence."

"What about the governor?"

."I doubt it."

"Well, I want you to be careful."

"Thanks, I guess."

"Let's get a beer."

I've got to keep this guy away from Lee, Adam thought. "It's five minutes before noon. Surely you don't start this early."

"Oh, sometimes I start with breakfast."

JOHN DOE sat on a park bench with a newspaper in front of his face and pigeons around his feet. He was eighty feet away, so he couldn't hear what they were saying. He thought he recognized the old man with Adam as an FBI agent whose face had appeared in the newspapers years ago. He would follow the guy and find out who he was and where he lived.

Wedge was getting bored with Memphis, and this suited him fine. The kid worked at the office and drove to Parchman and slept at the condo, and seemed to be spinning his wheels. Wedge followed the news carefully. His name had not been mentioned. No one knew about him.

THE NOTE on the counter was dated properly. She had given the time as 7:15 P.M. It was Lee's handwriting, which was not neat to begin with but was even sloppier now. She said she was in bed with what appeared to be the flu. Please don't disturb. She'd been to the doctor who told her to sleep it off. For added effect, a prescription bottle from a local pharmacy was sitting nearby next to a half-empty glass of water. It had today's date on it.

Adam quickly checked the wastebasket under the sink—no sign of booze.

He quietly put a frozen pizza in the microwave and went to the patio to watch the barges on the river.

THIRTY-TWO

THE FIRST KITE of the morning arrived shortly after breakfast as Sam stood in his baggy boxer shorts and leaned through the bars with a cigarette. It was from Preacher Boy, and it brought bad news. It read:

Dear Sam:
The dream is finished. The Lord worked on me last night and finally showed me the rest of it. I wish he hadn't done it. There's a lot to it, and I'll explain it all if you want. Bottom line is that you'll be with him shortly. He told me to tell you to get things right with him. He's waiting. The journey will be rough, but the rewards will be worth it. I love you.
                                        Brother Randy

Bon voyage, Sam mumbled to himself as he crumpled the paper and threw it on the floor. The kid was slowly deteriorating, and there was no way to help him. Sam had already prepared a series of motions to be filed at some uncertain point in the future when Brother Randy was thoroughly insane.

He saw Gullitt's hands come through the bars next door.

"How you doin', Sam?" Gullitt finally asked.

"God's upset with me," Sam said.

"Really?"

"Yeah. Preacher Boy finished his dream last night."

"Thank God for that."

"It was more like a nightmare."

"I wouldn't worry too much about it. Crazy bastard has dreams when he's wide awake. They said yesterday he's been crying for a week."

"Can you hear him?"

"No. Thank God."

"Poor kid. I've done some motions for him, just in case I leave this place. I want to leave them with you."

"I don't know what to do with them."

"I'll leave instructions. They're to be sent to his lawyer."

Gullitt whistled softly. "Man oh man, Sam. What am I gonna do if you leave? I ain't talked to my lawyer in a year."

"Your lawyer is a moron."

"Then help me fire him, Sam. Please. You fired yours. Help me fire mine. I don't know how to do it."

"Then who'll represent you?"

"Your grandson. Tell him he can have my case."

Sam smiled, then he chuckled. And then he laughed at the idea of rounding up his buddies on the Row and delivering their hopeless cases to Adam.

"What's so damned funny?" Gullitt demanded.

"You. What makes you think he'll want your case?"

"Come on, Sam. Talk to the kid for me. He must be smart if he's your grandson."

"What if they gas me? Do you want a lawyer who's just lost his first death row client?"

"Hell, I can't be particular right now."

"Relax, J.B. You have years to go."

"How many years?"

"At least five, maybe more."

"You swear?"

"You have my word. I'll put it in writing. If I'm wrong, you can sue me."

"Real funny, Sam. Real funny."

A door clicked open at the end of the hall, and heavy footsteps came their way. It was Packer, and he stopped in front of number six. "Mornin', Sam," he said.

"Mornin', Packer."

"Put your reds on. You have a visitor."

"Who is it?"

"Somebody who wants to talk to you."

"Who is it?" Sam repeated as he quickly slipped into his red jumpsuit. He grabbed his cigarettes. He didn't care who the visitor was or what he wanted. A visit by anyone was a welcome relief from his cell.

"Hurry up, Sam," Packer said.

"Is it my lawyer?" Sam asked as he slid his feet into the rubber shower shoes.

"No." Packer handcuffed him through the bars, and the door to his cell opened. They left Tier A and headed for the same little room where the lawyers always waited.

Packer removed the handcuffs and slammed the door behind Sam, who focused on the heavyset woman seated on the other side of the screen. He rubbed his wrists for her benefit and took a few steps to the seat opposite her. He did not recognize the woman. He sat down, lit a cigarette, and glared at her.

She scooted forward in her chair, and nervously said, "Mr. Cayhall, my name is Dr. Stegall." She slipped a business card through the opening. "I'm the psychiatrist for the State Department of Corrections."

Sam studied the card on the counter in front of him. He picked it up and examined it suspiciously. "Says here your name is N. Stegall. Dr. N. Stegall."

"That's correct."

"That's a strange name, N. I've never met a woman named N. before."

The small, anxious grin disappeared from her face,

and her spine stiffened. "It's just an initial, okay. There
are reasons for it."

"What's it stand for?"

"That's really none of your business."

"Nancy? Nelda? Nona?"

"If I wanted you to know, I would've put it on the
card, now wouldn't I?"

"I don't know. Must be something horrible, whatever it is. Nick? Ned? I can't imagine hiding behind an
initial."

"I'm not hiding, Mr. Cayhall."

"Just call me S., okay?"

Her jaws clenched and she scowled through the
screen. "I'm here to help you."

"You're too late, N."

"Please call me Dr. Stegall."

"Oh, well, in that case you can call me Lawyer
Cayhall."

"Lawyer Cayhall?"

"Yes. I know more law than most of the clowns who
sit over there where you are."

She managed a slight, patronizing smile, then said,
"I'm supposed to consult you at this stage of the proceedings to see if I can be of any assistance. You don't
have to cooperate if you don't want."

"Thank you so much."

"If you need to talk to me, or if you need any medication now or later, just let me know."

"How about some whiskey?"

"I can't prescribe that."

"Why not?"

"Prison regulations, I guess."

"What can you prescribe?"

"Tranquilizers, Valium, sleeping pills, things like
that."

"For what?"

"For your nerves."

"My nerves are fine."

"Are you able to sleep?"

Sam thought for a long moment. "Well, to be honest, I am having a little trouble. Yesterday I slept off and on for no more than twelve hours. Usually I'm good for fifteen or sixteen."

"Twelve hours?"

"Yeah. How often do you get over here to death row?"

"Not very often."

"That's what I thought. If you knew what you were doing, you'd know that we average about sixteen hours a day."

"I see. And what else might I learn?"

"Oh, lots of things. You'd know that Randy Dupree is slowly going insane, and no one around here cares about him. Why haven't you been to see him?"

"There are five thousand inmates here, Mr. Cayhall. I—"

"Then leave. Go away. Go tend to the rest of them. I've been here for nine and a half years and never met you. Now that y'all are about to gas me, you come running over with a bagful of drugs to calm my nerves so I'll be sweet and gentle when you kill me. Why should you care about my nerves and my sleeping habits? You're working for the state and the state is working like hell to execute me."

"I'm doing my job, Mr. Cayhall."

"Your job stinks, Ned. Get a real job where you can help people. You're here right now because I've got thirteen days and you want me to go in peace. You're just another flunkie for the state."

"I didn't come here to be abused."

"Then get your big ass out of here. Leave. Go and sin no more."

She jumped to her feet and grabbed her briefcase. "You have my card. If you need anything, let me know."

"Sure, Ned. Don't sit by the phone." Sam stood and walked to the door on his side. He banged it twice with the palm of his hand, and waited with his back to her until Packer opened it.

ADAM WAS PACKING his briefcase in preparation for a quick trip to Parchman when the phone rang. Darlene said it was urgent. She was right.

The caller identified himself as the clerk of the Fifth Circuit Court of Appeals in New Orleans, and was remarkably friendly. He said the Cayhall petition attacking the constitutionality of the gas chamber had been received on Monday, had been assigned to a three-judge panel, and that the panel wanted to hear oral argument from both sides. Could he be in New Orleans at 1 P.M. tomorrow, Friday, for the oral argument?

Adam almost dropped the phone. Tomorrow? Of course, he said after a slight hesitation. One o'clock sharp, the clerk said, then explained that the court did not normally hear oral argument in the afternoon. But because of the urgency of this matter, the court had scheduled a special hearing. He asked Adam if he'd ever argued before the Fifth Circuit before.

Are you kidding? Adam thought. A year ago I was studying for the bar exam. He said no, in fact he had not, and the clerk said he would immediately fax to Adam a copy of the court's rules governing oral argument. Adam thanked him profusely, and hung up.

He sat on the edge of the table and tried to collect his thoughts. Darlene brought the fax to him, and he asked her to check the flights to New Orleans.

Had he caught the attention of the court with his

issues? Was this good news, or just a formality? In his brief career as a lawyer, he had stood alone before the bench to argue a client's position on only one occasion. But Emmitt Wycoff had been seated nearby, just in case. And the judge had been a familiar one. And it had happened in downtown Chicago, not far from his office. Tomorrow he would walk into a strange courtroom in a strange city and try to defend an eleventh-hour plea before a panel of judges he'd never heard of.

He called E. Garner Goodman with the news. Goodman had been to the Fifth Circuit many times, and as he talked Adam relaxed. It was neither good news nor bad, in Goodman's opinion. The court was obviously interested in the lawsuit, but they'd heard it all before. Both Texas and Louisiana had sent similar constitutional claims to the Fifth Circuit in recent years.

Goodman assured him that he could handle the arguments. Just be prepared, he said. And try to relax. It might be possible for him to fly to New Orleans and be there, but Adam said no. He said he could do it alone. Keep in touch, Goodman said.

Adam checked with Darlene, then locked himself in his office. He memorized the rules for oral argument. He studied the lawsuit attacking the gas chamber. He read briefs and cases. He called Parchman and left word for Sam that he would not be there today.

HE WORKED UNTIL DARK, then made the dreaded trip to Lee's condo. The same note was sitting on the counter, untouched and still declaring that she was in bed with the flu. He eased around the apartment and saw no signs of movement or life during the day.

Her bedroom door was slightly opened. He tapped on it while pushing. "Lee," he called out gently into the darkness. "Lee, are you all right?"

There was movement in the bed, though he couldn't see what it was. "Yes, dear," she said. "Come in."

Adam slowly sat on the edge of the bed and tried to focus on her. The only light was a faint beam from the hallway. She pushed herself up and rested on the pillows. "I'm better," she said with a scratchy voice. "How are you, dear?"

"I'm fine, Lee. I'm worried about you."

"I'll be okay. It's a wicked little virus."

The first pungent vapor wafted from the bedsheets and covers, and Adam wanted to cry. It was the reeking odor of stale vodka or gin or sour mash, or maybe a combination of everything. He couldn't see her eyes in the murky shadows, only the vague outline of her face. She was wearing a dark shirt of some sort.

"What type of medication?" he asked.

"I don't know. Just some pills. The doctor said it'll last for a few days, then quickly disappear. I feel better already."

Adam started to say something about the oddity of a flu-like virus in late July, but let it pass. "Are you able to eat?"

"No appetite, really."

"Is there anything I can do?"

"No, dear. How have you been? What day is it?"

"It's Thursday."

"I feel like I've been in a cave for a week."

Adam had two choices. He could play along with the wicked little virus act and hope she stopped the drinking before it got worse. Or he could confront her now and make her realize she was not fooling him. Maybe they would fight, and maybe this was what you were supposed to do with drunks who'd fallen off the wagon. How was he supposed to know what to do?

"Does your doctor know you're drinking?" he asked, holding his breath.

There was a long pause. "I haven't been drinking," she said, almost inaudible.

"Come on, Lee. I found the vodka bottle in the wastebasket. I know the other three bottles of beer disappeared last Saturday. You smell like a brewery right now. You're not fooling anyone, Lee. You're drinking heavily, and I want to help."

She sat straighter, and pulled her legs up to her chest. Then she was still for a long time. Adam glanced at her silhouette. Minutes passed. The apartment was deathly quiet.

"How's my dear father?" she muttered. Her words were sluggish, but still bitter.

"I didn't see him today."

"Don't you think we'll be better off when he's dead?"

Adam looked at her silhouette. "No, Lee, I don't. Do you?"

She was silent and still for at least a minute. "You feel sorry for him, don't you?" she finally asked.

"Yes, I do."

"Is he pitiful?"

"Yes, he is."

"What does he look like?"

"A very old man, with plenty of gray hair that's always oily and pulled back. He has a short gray beard. Lots of wrinkles. His skin is very pale."

"What does he wear?"

"A red jumpsuit. All death row inmates wear the same thing."

Another long pause as she thought about this. Then she said, "I guess it's easy to feel sorry for him."

"It is for me."

"But you see, Adam, I've never seen him the way you see him. I saw a different person."

"And what did you see?"

She adjusted the blanket around her legs, then grew still again. "My father was a person I despised."

"Do you still despise him?"

"Yes. Very much so. I think he should go ahead and die. God knows he deserves it."

"Why does he deserve it?"

This prompted another spell of silence. She moved slightly to her left and took a cup or glass from the nightstand. She sipped slowly, as Adam watched her shadows. He didn't ask what she was drinking.

"Does he talk to you about the past?"

"Only when I ask questions. We've talked about Eddie, but I promised we wouldn't do it again."

"He's the reason Eddie's dead. Does he realize this?"

"Maybe."

"Did you tell him? Did you blame him for Eddie?"

"No."

"You should have. You're too easy on him. He needs to know what he's done."

"I think he does. But you said yourself it's not fair to torment him at this point of his life."

"How about Joe Lincoln? Did you talk to him about Joe Lincoln?"

"I told Sam that you and I went to the old family place. He asked me if I knew about Joe Lincoln. I said that I did."

"Did he deny it?"

"No. He showed a lot of remorse."

"He's a liar."

"No. I think he was sincere."

Another long pause as she sat motionless. Then, "Has he told you about the lynching?"

Adam closed his eyes and rested his elbows on his knees. "No," he mumbled.

"I didn't think so."

"I don't want to hear it, Lee."

"Yes you do. You came down here full of questions about the family and about your past. Two weeks ago you just couldn't get enough of the Cayhall family misery. You wanted all the blood and gore."

"I've heard enough," he said.

"What day is it?" she asked.

"It's Thursday, Lee. You've already asked once."

"One of my girls was due today. Her second child. I didn't call the office. I guess it's the medication."

"And the alcohol."

"All right, dammit. So I'm an alcoholic. Who can blame me? Sometimes I wish I had the guts to do what Eddie did."

"Come on, Lee. Let me help you."

"Oh, you've already helped a great deal, Adam. I was fine, nice and sober until you arrived."

"Okay. I was wrong. I'm sorry. I just didn't realize—" His words trailed off, then quit.

She moved slightly and Adam watched as she took another sip. A heavy silence engulfed them as minutes passed. The rancid smell emanated from her end of the bed.

"Mother told me the story," she said quietly, almost whispering. "She said she'd heard rumors about it for years. Long before they married she knew he'd helped lynch a young black man."

"Please, Lee."

"I never asked him about it, but Eddie did. We had whispered about it for many years, and finally one day Eddie just up and confronted him with the story. They had a nasty fight, but Sam admitted it was true. It really didn't bother him, he said. The black kid had allegedly raped a white girl, but she was white trash and many people doubted if it was really a rape. This is according to Mother's version. Sam was fifteen or so at the time, and a bunch of men went down to the jail, got the black kid, and took him out in the woods. Sam's father, of course, was the ringleader, and his brothers were involved."

"That's enough, Lee."

"They beat him with a bullwhip, then hung him from a tree. My dear father was right in the middle of it. He couldn't really deny it, you know, because somebody took a picture of it."

"A photograph?"

"Yeah. A few years later the photo found its way into a book about the plight of Negroes in the Deep South. It was published in 1947. My mother had a copy of it for years. Eddie found it in the attic."

"And Sam's in the photograph."

"Sure. Smiling from ear to ear. They're standing under the tree and the black guy's feet are dangling just above their heads. Everybody's having a ball. Just another nigger lynching. There are no credits with the photo, no names. The picture speaks for itself. It's described as a lynching in rural Mississippi, 1936."

"Where's the book?"

"Over there in the drawer. I've kept it in storage with other family treasures since the foreclosure. I got it out the other day. I thought you might want to see it."

"No. I do not want to see it."

"Go ahead. You wanted to know about your family. Well, there they are. Grandfather, great-grandfather, and all sorts of Cayhalls at their very best. Caught in the act, and quite proud of it."

"Stop it, Lee."

"There were other lynchings, you know."

"Shut up, Lee. Okay? I don't want to hear any more."

She leaned to her side and reached for the night-stand.

"What are you drinking, Lee?"

"Cough syrup."

"Bullshit!" Adam jumped to his feet and walked through the darkness to the nightstand. Lee quickly gulped the last of the liquid. He grabbed the glass from her hand and sniffed the top of it. "This is bourbon."

"There's more in the pantry. Would you get it for me?"

"No! You've had more than enough."

"If I want it, I'll get it."

"No you won't, Lee. You're not drinking any more tonight. Tomorrow I'll take you to the doctor, and we'll get some help."

"I don't need help. I need a gun."

Adam placed the glass on the dresser and switched on a lamp. She shielded her eyes for a few seconds, then looked at him. They were red and puffy. Her hair was wild, dirty, and unkempt.

"Not a pretty sight, huh," she said, slurring her words, and looking away.

"No. But we'll get help, Lee. We'll do it tomorrow."

"Get me a drink, Adam. Please."

"No."

"Then leave me alone. This is all your fault, you know. Now leave, please. Go on to bed."

Adam grabbed a pillow from the center of the bed and threw it against the door. "I'm sleeping here tonight," he said, pointing at the pillow. "I'm locking the door, and you're not leaving this room."

She glared at him, but said nothing. He switched off the lamp, and the room was completely dark. He pressed the lock on the knob and stretched out on the carpet against the door. "Now sleep it off, Lee."

"Go to bed, Adam. I promise I won't leave the room."

"No. You're drunk, and I'm not moving. If you try

to open this door, I'll physically put you back in the bed."

"That sounds sort of romantic."

"Knock it off, Lee. Go to sleep."

"I can't sleep."

"Try it."

"Let's tell Cayhall stories, okay, Adam? I know a few more lynching stories."

"Shut up, Lee!" Adam screamed, and she was suddenly quiet. The bed squeaked as she wiggled and flipped and got herself situated. After fifteen minutes, she was subdued. After thirty minutes, the floor became uncomfortable and Adam rolled from side to side.

Sleep came in brief naps, interrupted by long periods of staring at the ceiling and worrying about her, and about the Fifth Circuit. At one point during the night he sat with his back to the door and stared through the darkness in the direction of the drawer. Was the book really there? He was tempted to sneak over and get it, then ease into the bathroom to look for the picture. But he couldn't risk waking her. And he didn't want to see it.

THIRTY-THREE

H E FOUND a pint of bourbon hidden behind a box of saltines in the pantry, and emptied it in the sink. It was dark outside. Sunlight was an hour away. He made the coffee strong, and sipped it on the sofa while he rehearsed the arguments he would present in a few hours in New Orleans.

He reviewed his notes on the patio at dawn, and by seven he was in the kitchen making toast. No sign of Lee. He didn't want a confrontation, but one was necessary. He had things to say, and she had apologies to make, and he rattled plates and forks on the counter. The volume was increased for the morning news.

But there was no movement from her part of the condo. After he showered and dressed, he gently turned the knob to her door. It was locked. She had sealed herself in her cave, and prevented the painful talk of the morning after. He wrote a note and explained that he would be in New Orleans today and tonight, and he would see her tomorrow. He said he was sorry for now, and they would talk about it later. He pleaded with her not to drink.

The note was placed on the counter where she couldn't miss it. Adam left the condo and drove to the airport.

The direct flight to New Orleans took fifty-five minutes. Adam drank fruit juice and tried to sit comfortably to soothe his stiff back. He'd slept less than three hours on the floor by the door, and vowed not to do it again. By her own admission, she'd been through recovery three times over the years, and if she couldn't stay off the booze by herself there was certainly nothing he could do to help. He would stay in Memphis until this miserable case was over, and if his aunt couldn't stay sober, then he could manage things from a hotel room.

He fought himself to forget about her for the next few hours. He needed to concentrate on legal matters, not lynchings and photographs and horror stories from the past; not his beloved aunt and her problems.

The plane touched down in New Orleans, and suddenly his concentration became sharper. He mentally clicked off the names of dozens of recent death penalty cases from the Fifth Circuit and the U.S. Supreme Court.

The hired car was a Cadillac sedan, one arranged by Darlene and charged to Kravitz & Bane. It came with a driver, and as Adam relaxed in the rear seat he conceded that life in a big firm did indeed have certain advantages. Adam had never been to New Orleans before, and the drive from the airport could've taken place in any city. Just traffic and expressways. The driver turned onto Poydras Street by the Superdome, and suddenly they were downtown. He explained to his passenger that the French Quarter was a few blocks away, not far from Adam's hotel. The car stopped on Camp Street, and Adam stepped onto the sidewalk in front of a building simply called the Fifth Circuit Court of Appeals. It was an impressive structure, with Greek columns and lots of steps leading to the front entrance.

He found the clerk's office on the main floor, and asked for the gentleman he'd spoken to, a Mr. Feriday. Mr. Feriday was as sincere and courteous in person as he'd been on the phone. He properly registered Adam, and explained some of the rules of the court. He asked Adam if he wanted a quick tour of the place. It was almost noon, the place was not busy, and it was the perfect time for a look around. They headed for the courtrooms, passing along the way various offices of the judges and staff.

"The Fifth Circuit has fifteen judges," Mr. Feriday explained as they walked casually over marble floors, "and their offices are along these hallways. Right now the court has three vacancies, and the nominations are tied up in Washington." The corridors were dark and quiet, as if great minds were at work behind the broad wooden doors.

Mr. Feriday went first to the En Banc courtroom, a large, intimidating stage with fifteen chairs sitting snugly together in a half-circle in the front of the room. "Most of the work here is assigned to three-judge panels. But occasionally the entire body sits en banc," he explained quietly, as if still in awe of the spectacular room. The bench was elevated well above the rest of the room, so that the lawyers at the podium below looked upward as they pleaded. The room was marble and dark wood, heavy drapes and a huge chandelier. It was ornate but understated, old but meticulously maintained, and as Adam inspected it he felt quite frightened. Only rarely does the entire court sit en banc, Mr. Feriday explained again as if he were instructing a first-year student of the law. The great civil rights decisions of the sixties and seventies took place right here, he said with no small amount of pride. Portraits of deceased justices hung behind the bench.

As beautiful and stately as it was, Adam hoped he never saw it again, at least not as a lawyer representing a client. They walked down the hall to the West Courtroom, which was smaller than the first but just as intimidating. This is where the three-judge panels operate, Mr. Feriday explained as they walked past the seats in the spectators' section, through the bar and to the podium. The bench again was elevated, though not as lofty or as long as En Banc.

"Virtually all oral arguments take place in the morning, beginning at nine," Mr. Feriday said. "Your case is a bit different because it's a death case that's going down to the wire." He pointed a crooked finger at the seats in the back. "You'll need to be seated out there a few minutes before one, and the clerk will call the case. Then you come through the bar and sit right here at counsel table. You'll go first, and you have twenty minutes."

Adam knew this, but it was certainly nice to be walked through it.

Mr. Feriday pointed to a device on the podium that resembled a traffic light. "This is the timer," he said gravely. "And it is very important. Twenty minutes, okay. There are horrific stories of long-winded lawyers who ignored this. Not a pretty sight. The green is on when you're talking. The yellow comes on when you want your warning—two minutes, five minutes, thirty seconds, whatever. When the red comes on, you simply stop in mid-sentence and go sit down. It's that simple. Any questions?"

"Who are the judges?"

"McNeely, Robichaux, and Judy." He said this as if Adam personally knew all three. "There's a waiting room over there, and there's a library on the third floor. Just be here about ten minutes before one. Any more questions?"

"No sir. Thanks."

"I'm in my office if you need me. Good luck." They shook hands. Mr. Feriday left Adam standing at the podium.

AT TEN MINUTES BEFORE ONE, Adam walked through the massive oak doors of the West Courtroom for the second time, and found other lawyers preparing for battle. On the first row behind the bar, Attorney General Steve Roxburgh and his cluster of assistants were huddled together plotting tactics. They hushed when Adam walked in, and a few nodded and tried to smile. Adam sat by himself along the aisle and ignored them.

Lucas Mann was seated on their side of the courtroom, though several rows behind Roxburgh and his boys. He casually read a newspaper, and waved to Adam when their eyes met. It was good to see him. He was starched from head to toe in wrinkle-free khaki, and his tie was wild enough to glow in the dark. It was obvious Mann was not intimidated by the Fifth Circuit and its trappings, and equally as obvious that he was keeping his distance from Roxburgh. He was only the attorney for Parchman, only doing his job. If the Fifth Circuit granted a stay and Sam didn't die, Lucas Mann would be pleased. Adam nodded and smiled at him.

Roxburgh and his gang rehuddled. Morris Henry, Dr. Death, was in the middle of it, explaining things to lesser minds.

Adam breathed deeply and tried to relax. It was quite difficult. His stomach was churning and his feet twitched, and he kept telling himself that it would last for only twenty minutes. The three judges couldn't kill him, they could only embarrass him, and even that could last for only twenty minutes. He could endure anything for twenty minutes. He glanced at his notes, and to calm himself he tried to think of Sam—not Sam the racist, the murderer, the lynch mob thug, but Sam the client, the old man wasting away on death row who was entitled to die in peace and dignity. Sam was about to get twenty minutes of this court's valuable time, so his lawyer had to make the most of it.

A heavy door thudded shut somewhere, and Adam

jumped in his seat. The court crier appeared from behind the bench and announced that this honorable
court was now in session. He was followed by three
figures in flowing black robes—McNeely, Robichaux,
and Judy, each of whom carried files and seemed to be
totally without humor or goodwill. They sat in their
massive leather chairs high up on the shiny, dark oak-
paneled bench, and looked down upon the courtroom.
The case of *State of Mississippi v. Sam Cayhall* was
called, and the attorneys were summoned from the
back of the room. Adam nervously walked through the
swinging gate in the bar, and was followed by Steve
Roxburgh. The Assistant Attorney Generals kept their
seats, as did Lucas Mann and a handful of spectators.
Most of these, Adam would later learn, were reporters.

The presiding judge was Judy, the Honorable T. Ei-
leen Judy, a young woman from Texas. Robichaux was
from Louisiana, and in his late fifties. McNeely looked
to be a hundred and twenty, and was also from Texas.
Judy made a brief statement about the case, then asked
Mr. Adam Hall from Chicago if he was ready to proceed. He stood nervously, his knees rubber-like, his
bowels jumping, his voice high and nervous, and he
said that, yes, in fact he was ready to go. He made it to
the podium in the center of the room and looked up,
way up, it seemed, at the panel behind the bench.

The green light beside him came on, and he assumed
correctly this meant to get things started. The room
was silent. The judges glared down at him. He cleared
his throat, glanced at the portraits of dead honorables
hanging on the wall, and plunged into a vicious attack
on the gas chamber as a means of execution.

He avoided eye contact with the three of them, and
for five minutes or so was allowed to repeat what he'd
already submitted in his brief. It was post-lunch, in the

heat of the summer, and it took a few minutes for the judges to shrug off the cobwebs.

"Mr. Hall, I think you're just repeating what you've already said in your brief," Judy said testily. "We're quite capable of reading, Mr. Hall."

Mr. Hall took it well, and thought to himself that this was his twenty minutes, and if he wanted to pick his nose and recite the alphabet, then he should be allowed to do so. For twenty minutes. As green as he was, Adam had heard this comment before from an appellate judge. It happened while he was in law school and watching a case being argued. It was standard fare in oral argument.

"Yes, Your Honor," Adam said, carefully avoiding any reference to gender. He then moved on to discuss the effects of cyanide gas on laboratory rats, a study not included in his brief. The experiments had been conducted a year ago by some chemists in Sweden for the purpose of proving that humans do not die instantly when they inhale the poison. It had been funded by a European organization working to abolish the death penalty in America.

The rats went into seizures and convulsed. Their lungs and hearts stopped and started erratically for several minutes. The gas burst blood vessels throughout their bodies, including their brains. Their muscles quivered uncontrollably. They salivated and squeaked.

The obvious point of the study was that the rats did not die quickly, but in fact suffered a great deal. The tests were conducted with scientific integrity. Appropriate doses were given to the small animals. On the average, it took almost ten minutes for death to occur. Adam labored over the details, and as he warmed to his presentation his nerves settled a bit. The judges were not only listening, but seemed to be enjoying this discussion of dying rats.

Adam had found the study in a footnote to a recent North Carolina case. It was in the fine print, and had not been widely reported.

"Now, let me get this straight," Robichaux interrupted in a high-pitched voice. "You don't want your client to die in the gas chamber because it's a cruel way to go, but are you telling us you don't mind if he's executed by lethal injection?"

"No, Your Honor. That's not what I'm saying. I do not want my client executed by any method."

"But lethal injection is the least offensive?"

"All methods are offensive, but lethal injection seems to be the least cruel. There's no doubt the gas chamber is a horrible way to die."

"Worse than being bombed? Blown up by dynamite?"

A heavy silence fell over the courtroom as Robichaux's words settled in. He had emphasized the word "dynamite," and Adam struggled for something appropriate. McNeely shot a nasty look at his colleague on the other side of the bench.

It was a cheap shot, and Adam was furious. He controlled his temper, and said firmly, "We're talking about methods of execution, Your Honor, not the crimes that send men to death row."

"Why don't you want to talk about the crime?"

"Because the crime is not an issue here. Because I have only twenty minutes, and my client has only twelve days."

"Perhaps your client shouldn't have been planting bombs?"

"Of course not. But he was convicted of his crime, and now he faces death in the gas chamber. Our point is that the chamber is a cruel way to execute people."

"What about the electric chair?"

"The same argument applies. There have been some

hideous cases of people suffering terribly in the chair before they died."

"What about a firing squad?"

"Sounds cruel to me."

"And hanging?"

"I don't know much about hanging, but it too sounds awfully cruel."

"But you like the idea of lethal injection?"

"I didn't say I like it. I believe I said it was not as cruel as the other methods."

Justice McNeely interrupted and asked, "Mr. Hall, why did Mississippi switch from the gas chamber to lethal injection?"

This was covered thoroughly in the lawsuit and the brief, and Adam sensed immediately that McNeely was a friend. "I've condensed the legislative history of the law in my brief, Your Honor, but it was done principally to facilitate executions. The legislature admitted it was an easier way to die, and so to sidestep constitutional challenges such as this one it changed the method."

"So the State has effectively admitted that there is a better way to execute people?"

"Yes sir. But the law took effect in 1984, and applies only to those inmates convicted afterward. It does not apply to Sam Cayhall."

"I understand that. You're asking us to strike down the gas chamber as a method. What happens if we do? What happens to your client and those like him who were convicted prior to 1984? Do they fall through the cracks? There is no provision in the law to execute them by lethal injection."

Adam was anticipating the obvious question. Sam had already asked it. "I can't answer that, Your Honor, except to say that I have great confidence in the Mississippi Legislature's ability and willingness to pass a new law covering my client and those in his position."

Judge Judy inserted herself at this point. "Assuming they do, Mr. Hall, what will you argue when you return here in three years?"

Thankfully, the yellow light came on, and Adam had only one minute remaining. "I'll think of something," he said with a grin. "Just give me time."

"We've already seen a case like this, Mr. Hall," Robichaux said. "In fact, it's cited in your brief. A Texas case."

"Yes, Your Honor. I'm asking the court to reconsider its decision on this issue. Virtually every state with a gas chamber or an electric chair has switched to lethal injection. The reason is obvious."

He had a few seconds left, but decided it was a good place to stop. He didn't want another question. "Thank you," he said, and walked confidently back to his seat. It was over. He had held his breakfast, and performed quite well for a rookie. It would be easier the next time.

Roxburgh was wooden and methodical, and thoroughly prepared. He tried a few one-liners about rats and the crimes they commit, but it was a dismal effort at humor. McNeely peppered him with similar questions about why the states were rushing to lethal injection. Roxburgh stuck to his guns, and recited a long line of cases where the various federal circuits had endorsed death by gas, electricity, hanging, and firing squads. The established law was on his side, and he made the most of it. His twenty minutes raced by, and he returned to his seat as quickly as Adam had.

Judge Judy talked briefly about the urgency of this matter, and promised a ruling within days. Everyone rose in unison, and the three judges disappeared from the bench. The court crier declared matters to be in recess until Monday morning.

Adam shook hands with Roxburgh and made it through the doors before a reporter stopped him. He was with a paper in Jackson, and just had a couple of questions. Adam was polite, but declined comment. He then did the same for two more reporters. Roxburgh, typically, had things to say, and as Adam walked away, the reporters surrounded the Attorney General and shoved recorders near his face.

Adam wanted to leave the building. He stepped into the tropical heat, and quickly covered his eyes with sunglasses. "Have you had lunch?" a voice asked from close behind. It was Lucas Mann, in aviator sunglasses. They shook hands between the columns.

"I couldn't eat," Adam admitted.

"You did fine. It's quite nerve-racking, isn't it?"

"Yes, it is. Why are you here?"

"It's part of my job. The warden asked me to fly down and watch the argument. We'll wait until there's a ruling before we start preparations. Let's go eat."

Adam's driver stopped the car at the curb, and they got in.

"Do you know the city?" Mann asked.

"No. This is my first visit."

"The Bon Ton Café," Mann told the driver. "It's a wonderful old place just around the corner. Nice car."

"The benefits of working for a wealthy firm."

LUNCH BEGAN with a novelty—raw oysters on the half shell. Adam had heard of them before, but had never been tempted. Mann artfully demonstrated the proper blending of horseradish, lemon juice, Tabasco, and cocktail sauce, then dropped the first oyster into the mixture. It was then delicately placed on a cracker and eaten in one bite. Adam's first oyster slid off the cracker and onto the table, but his second slid properly down his throat.

"Don't chew it," Mann instructed. "Just let it slither down." The next ten slithered down, and not soon enough for Adam. He was happy when the dozen shells on his plate were empty. They sipped Dixie beer and waited for shrimp remoulade.

"I saw where you're claiming ineffective assistance of counsel," Mann said, nibbling on a cracker.

"I'm sure we'll be filing everything from now on."

"The supreme court didn't waste any time with it."

"No, they didn't. Seems as if they're tired of Sam Cayhall. I'll file it in district court today, but I don't expect any relief from Slattery."

"I wouldn't either."

"What are my odds, with twelve days to go?"

"Getting slimmer by the day, but things are wildly unpredictable. Probably still around fifty-fifty. A few years back we came very close with Stockholm Turner. With two weeks to go, it looked certain. With a week to go, there was simply nothing else for him to file. He had a decent lawyer, but the appeals had run. He was given his last meal, and—"

"And his conjugal visit, with two prostitutes."

"How'd you know?"

"Sam told me all about it."

"It's true. He got a last minute stay, and now he's years away from the chamber. You never know."

"But what's your gut feeling?"

Mann took a long drink of beer and leaned backward as two large platters of shrimp remoulade were placed before them. "I don't have gut feelings when it comes to executions. Anything can happen. Just keep filing writs and appeals. It becomes a marathon. You can't give up. The lawyer for Jumbo Parris collapsed with twelve hours to go, and was in a hospital bed when his client went down."

Adam chewed on a boiled shrimp and washed it down with beer. "The governor wants me to talk to him. Should I?"

"What does your client want?"

"What do you think? He hates the governor. He has forbidden me to talk to him."

"You have to ask for a clemency hearing. That's standard practice."

"How well do you know McAllister?"

"Not very well. He's a political animal with great ambitions, and I wouldn't trust him for a minute. He does, however, have the power to grant clemency. He can commute the death sentence. He can impose life, or he can set him free. The statute grants broad discretionary authority to the governor. He'll probably be your last hope."

"God help us."

"How's the remoulade?" Mann asked with a mouthful.

"Delicious."

They busied themselves with eating for a while. Adam was thankful for the company and conversation, but decided to limit the talk to appeals and strategy. He liked Lucas Mann, but his client did not. As Sam would say, Mann worked for the state and the state was working to execute him.

A LATE AFTERNOON FLIGHT would have taken him back to Memphis by six-thirty, long before dark. And once there he could've killed an hour or so at the office before returning to Lee's. But he wasn't up to it. He had a fancy room in a modern hotel by the river, paid for without question by the boys at Kravitz &

Bane. All expenses were covered. He'd never seen the French Quarter.

And so he awoke at six after a three-hour nap brought on by three Dixies for lunch and a bad night's rest. He was lying across the bed with his shoes on, and he studied the ceiling fan for half an hour before he moved. The sleep had been heavy.

Lee did not answer the phone. He left a message on her recorder, and hoped she was not drinking. And if she was, then he hoped she'd locked herself in her room where she couldn't hurt anyone. He brushed his teeth and hair, and rode an elevator to the spacious lobby where a jazz band performed for happy hour. Five-cent oysters on the half shell were being hawked from a corner bar.

He walked in the sweltering heat along Canal Street until he came to Royal, where he took a right and was soon lost in a throng of tourists. Friday night was coming to life in the Quarter. He gawked at the strip clubs, trying desperately for a peek inside. He was stopped cold by an open door that revealed a row of male strippers on a stage—men who looked like beautiful women. He ate an egg roll on a stick from a Chinese carryout. He stepped around a wino vomiting in the street. He spent an hour at a small table in a jazz club, listening to a delightful combo and sipping a four-dollar beer. When it was dark, he walked to Jackson Square and watched the artists pack up their easels and leave. The street musicians and dancers were out in force in front of an old cathedral, and he clapped for an amazing string quartet comprised of Tulane students. People were everywhere, drinking and eating and dancing, enjoying the festiveness of the French Quarter.

He bought a dish of vanilla ice cream, and headed for Canal. On another night and under far different circumstances, he might be tempted to take in a strip show, sitting in the rear, of course, where no one could see him, or he might hang out in a trendy bar looking for lonely, beautiful women.

But not tonight. The drunks reminded him of Lee, and he wished he'd returned to Memphis to see her. The music and laughter reminded him of Sam, who at this very moment was sitting in a humid oven, staring at the bars and counting the days, hoping and perhaps praying now that his lawyer might work a miracle. Sam would never see New Orleans, never again eat oysters or red beans and rice, never taste a cold beer or a good coffee. He would never hear jazz or watch artists paint. He would never again fly on a plane or stay in a nice hotel. He would never fish or drive or do a thousand things free people take for granted.

Even if Sam lived past August 8, he would simply continue the process of dying a little each day.

Adam left the Quarter and walked hurriedly to his hotel. He needed rest. The marathon was about to begin.

THIRTY-FOUR

THE GUARD NAMED TINY handcuffed Sam and led him off Tier A. Sam carried a plastic bag filled tightly with the last two weeks' worth of fan mail. For most of his career as a death row inmate, he had averaged a handful of letters a month from supporters—Klansmen and their sympathizers, racial purists, anti-Semites, all types of bigots. For a couple of years he had answered these letters, but with time had grown weary of it. What was the benefit? To some he was a hero, but the more he swapped words with his admirers the wackier they became. There were a lot of nuts out there. The idea had crossed his mind that perhaps he was safer on the Row than in the free world.

Mail had been declared to be a right by the federal court, not a privilege. Thus, it could not be taken away. It could, however, be regulated. Each letter was opened by an inspector unless the envelope clearly was from an attorney. Unless an inmate was under mail censorship, the letters were not read. They were delivered to the Row in due course and dispensed to the inmates. Boxes and packages were also opened and inspected.

The thought of losing Sam was frightening to many fanatics, and his mail had picked up dramatically since the Fifth Circuit lifted his stay. They offered their unwavering support, and their prayers. A few offered money. Their letters tended to run long as they invariably blasted Jews and blacks and liberals and other conspirators. Some bitched about taxes, gun control, the national debt. Some delivered sermons.

Sam was tired of the letters. He was averaging six per day. He placed them on the counter as the handcuffs were removed, then asked the guard to unlock a small door in the screen. The guard shoved the plastic bag through the door and Adam took it on the other side. The guard left, locking the door behind.

"What's this?" Adam asked, holding the bag.

"Fan mail." Sam took his regular seat and lit a cigarette.

"What am I supposed to do with it?"

"Read it. Burn it. I don't care. I was cleaning my cell this morning and the stuff got in the way. I understand you were in New Orleans yesterday. Tell me about it."

Adam placed the letters on a chair, and sat across from Sam. The temperature outside was a hundred and two, and not much cooler inside the visitors' room. It was Saturday, and Adam was dressed in jeans, loafers, and a very light cotton polo. "The Fifth Circuit called Thursday, and said they wanted to hear from me on Friday. I went down, dazzled them with my brilliance, and flew back to Memphis this morning."

"When do they rule?"

"Soon."

"A three-judge panel?"

"Yes."

"Who?"

"Judy, Robichaux, and McNeely."

Sam contemplated the names for a moment. "McNeely's an old warrior who'll help us. Judy's a conservative bitch, oops, sorry, I mean a conservative Female-American, a Republican appointee. I doubt if she'll help. I'm not familiar with Robichaux. Where's he from?"

"Southern Louisiana."

"Ah, a Cajun-American."

"I guess. He's a hard-ass. He won't help."

"Then we'll lose by two to one. I thought you said you dazzled them with your brilliance."

"We haven't lost yet." Adam was surprised to hear Sam speak with such familiarity about the individual judges. But then, he'd been studying the court for many years.

"Where's the ineffective counsel claim?" Sam asked.

"Still in district court here. It's a few days behind the other."

"Let's file something else, okay."

"I'm working on it."

"Work fast. I've got eleven days. There's a calendar on my wall, and I spend at least three hours a day staring at it. When I wake up in the morning I make a big X over the date for the day before. I've got a circle around August 8. My X's are getting closer to the circle. Do something."

"I'm working, okay. In fact, I'm developing a new theory of attack."

"Attaboy."

"I think we can prove you're mentally unbalanced."

"I've been considering that."

"You're old. You're senile. You're too calm about this. Something must be wrong. You're unable to comprehend the reason for your execution."

"We've been reading the same cases."

"Goodman knows an expert who'll say anything for a fee. We're considering bringing him down here to examine you."

"Wonderful. I'll pull out my hair and chase butterflies around the room."

"I think we can make a hard run at a mental incompetency claim."

"I agree. Go for it. Let's file lots of things."

"I'll do it."

Sam puffed and pondered for a few minutes. They were both sweating, and Adam needed fresh air. He needed to get into his car with the windows up and turn the air on high.

"When are you coming back?" Sam asked.

"Monday. Listen, Sam, this is not a pleasant subject, but we need to address it. You're gonna die one of these days. It might be on August 8, or it might be five years from now. At the rate you're smoking, you can't last for long."

"Smoking is not my most pressing health concern."

"I know. But your family, Lee and I, need to make some burial arrangements. It can't be done overnight."

Sam stared at the rows of tiny triangles in the screen. Adam scribbled on a legal pad. The air conditioner spewed and hissed, accomplishing little.

"Your grandmother was a fine lady, Adam. I'm sorry you didn't know her. She deserved better than me."

"Lee took me to her grave."

"I caused her a lot of suffering, and she bore it well. Bury me next to her, and maybe I can tell her I'm sorry."

"I'll take care of it."

"Do that. How will you pay for the plot?"

"I can handle it, Sam."

"I don't have any money, Adam. I lost it years ago, for reasons that are probably obvious. I lost the land and the house, so there are no assets to leave behind."

"Do you have a will?"

"Yes. I prepared it myself."

"We'll look at it next week."

"You promise you'll be here Monday."

"I promise, Sam. Can I bring you anything?"

Sam hesitated for a second and almost seemed embarrassed. "You know what I'd really like?" he asked with a childish grin.

"What? Anything, Sam."

"When I was a kid, the greatest thrill in life was an Eskimo Pie."

"An Eskimo Pie?"

"Yeah, it's a little ice cream treat on a stick. Vanilla, with a chocolate coating. I ate them until I came to this place. I think they still make them."

"An Eskimo Pie?" Adam repeated.

"Yeah. I can still taste it. The greatest ice cream in the world. Can you imagine how good one would taste right now in this oven?"

"Then, Sam, you shall have an Eskimo Pie."

"Bring more than one."

"I'll bring a dozen. We'll eat 'em right here while we sweat."

SAM'S SECOND VISITOR on Saturday was not expected. He stopped at the guard station by the front gate, and produced a North Carolina driver's license with his picture on it. He explained to the guard that he was the brother of Sam Cayhall, and had been told he could visit Sam on death row at his convenience between now and the scheduled execution. He had talked to a Mr. Holland somewhere deep in Administration yesterday, and Mr. Holland had assured him the visitation rules were relaxed for Sam Cayhall. He could visit anytime between 8 A.M. and 5 P.M., any day of the week. The guard stepped inside and made a phone call.

Five minutes passed as the visitor sat patiently in his rented car. The guard made two more calls, then copied the registration number of the car onto her clipboard. She instructed the visitor to park a few feet away, lock his car, and wait by the guard station. He did so, and within a few minutes a white prison van appeared. An armed uniformed guard was behind the wheel, and he motioned for the visitor to get in.

The van was cleared through the double gates at MSU, and driven to the front entrance where two other guards waited. They frisked him on the steps. He was carrying no packages or bags.

They led him around the corner and into the empty visitors' room. He took a seat near the middle of the screen. "We'll get Sam," one of the guards said. "Take about five minutes."

Sam was typing a letter when the guards stopped at his door. "Let's go, Sam. You have a visitor."

He stopped typing and stared at them. His fan was blowing hard and his television was tuned to a baseball game. "Who is it?" he snapped.

"Your brother."

Sam gently placed the typewriter on the bookshelf and grabbed his jumpsuit. "Which brother?"

"We didn't ask any questions, Sam. Just your brother. Now come on."

They handcuffed him and he followed them along the tier. Sam once had three brothers, but his oldest had died of a heart attack before Sam was sent to prison. Donnie, the youngest at age sixty-one, now lived near Durham, North Carolina. Albert, age sixty-seven, was in bad health and lived deep in the woods of rural Ford County. Donnie sent the cigarettes each month, along with a few dollars and an occasional note. Albert hadn't written in seven years. A spinster aunt had written until her death in 1985. The rest of the Cayhalls had forgotten Sam.

It had to be Donnie, he said to himself. Donnie was the only one who cared enough to visit. He hadn't seen him in two years, and he stepped lighter as they neared the door to the visitors' room. What a pleasant surprise.

Sam stepped through the door and looked at the man sitting on the other side of the screen. It was a face he didn't recognize. He glanced around the room, and confirmed it was empty except for this visitor, who at the moment was staring at Sam with a cool and even gaze. The guards watched closely as they sprung the handcuffs, so Sam smiled and nodded at the man. Then he stared at the guards until they left the room and shut the door. Sam sat opposite his visitor, lit a cigarette, and said nothing.

There was something familiar about him, but he couldn't identify him. They watched each other through the opening in the screen.

"Do I know you?" Sam finally asked.

"Yes," the man answered.

"From where?"

"From the past, Sam. From Greenville and Jackson and Vicksburg. From the synagogue and the real estate office and the Pinder home and Marvin Kramer's."

"Wedge?"

The man nodded slowly, and Sam closed his eyes and exhaled at the ceiling. He dropped his cigarette and slumped in his chair. "God, I was hoping you were dead."

"Too bad."

Sam glared wildly at him. "You son of a bitch," he said with clenched teeth. "Son of a bitch. I've hoped and dreamed for twenty-three years that you were dead. I've killed you a million times myself, with my bare hands, with sticks and knives and every weapon known to man. I've watched you bleed and I've heard you scream for mercy."

"Sorry. Here I am, Sam."

"I hate you more than any person has ever been

hated. If I had a gun right now I'd blow your sorry ass to hell and back. I'd pump your head full of lead and laugh until I cried. God, how I hate you."

"Do you treat all your visitors like this, Sam?"

"What do you want, Wedge?"

"Can they hear us in here?"

"They don't give a damn what we're saying."

"But this place could be wired, you know."

"Then leave, fool, just leave."

"I will in a minute. But first I just wanted to say that I'm here, and I'm watching things real close, and I'm very pleased that my name has not been mentioned. I certainly hope this continues. I've been very effective at keeping people quiet."

"You're very subtle."

"Just take it like a man, Sam. Die with dignity. You were with me. You were an accomplice and a conspirator, and under the law you're just as guilty as me. Sure I'm a free man, but who said life is fair. Just go on and take our little secret to your grave, and no one gets hurt, okay?"

"Where have you been?"

"Everywhere. My name's not really Wedge, Sam, so don't get any ideas. It was never Wedge. Not even Dogan knew my real name. I was drafted in 1966, and I didn't want to go to Vietnam. So I went to Canada and came back to the underground. Been there ever since. I don't exist, Sam."

"You should be sitting over here."

"No, you're wrong. I shouldn't, and neither should you. You were an idiot for going back to Greenville. The FBI was clueless. They never would've caught us. I was too smart. Dogan was too smart. You, however, happened to be the weak link. It would've been the last bombing too, you know, with the dead bodies and all. It was time to quit. I fled the country and would've never returned to this miserable place. You would've gone home to your chickens and cows. Who knows what Dogan would've done. But the reason you're sitting over there, Sam, is because you were a dumbass."

"And you're a dumbass for coming here today."

"Not really. No one would believe you if you started screaming. Hell, they all think you're crazy anyway. But just the same, I'd rather keep things the way they are. I don't need the hassle. Just accept what's coming, Sam, and do it quietly."

Sam carefully lit another cigarette, and thumped the ashes in the floor. "Leave, Wedge. And don't ever come back."

"Sure. I hate to say it, Sam, but I hope they gas you."

Sam stood and walked to the door behind him. A guard opened it, and took him away.

THEY SAT IN THE REAR of the cinema and ate popcorn like two teenagers. The movie was Adam's idea. She'd spent three days in her room, with the virus, and by Saturday morning the binge was over. He had selected a family restaurant for dinner, one with quick food and no alcohol on the menu. She'd devoured pecan waffles with whipped cream.

The movie was a western, politically correct with the Indians as the good guys and the cowboys as scum. All pale faces were evil and eventually killed. Lee drank two large Dr Peppers. Her hair was clean and pulled back over her ears. Her eyes were clear and pretty again. Her face was made up and the wounds of the past week were hidden. She was as cool as ever in jeans and cotton button-down. And she was sober.

Little had been said about last Thursday night when Adam slept by the door. They had agreed to discuss it later, at some distant point in the future when she could handle it. That was fine with him. She was walking a shaky tightrope, teetering on the edge of another plunge into the blackness of dipsomania. He would protect her from torment and distress. He would make things pleasant and enjoyable. No more talk of Sam and his killings. No more talk of Eddie. No more Cayhall family history.

She was his aunt, and he loved her dearly. She was fragile and sick, and she needed his strong voice and broad shoulders.

THIRTY-FIVE

PHILLIP NAIFEH awoke in the early hours of Sunday morning with severe chest pains, and was rushed to the hospital in Cleveland. He lived in a modern home on the grounds at Parchman with his wife of forty-one years. The ambulance ride took twenty minutes, and he was stable by the time he entered the emergency room on a gurney.

His wife waited anxiously in the corridor as the nurses scurried about. She had waited there before, three years earlier with the first heart attack. A somber-faced young doctor explained that it was a mild one, that he was quite steady and secure and resting comfortably with the aid of medication. He would be monitored diligently for the next twenty-four hours, and if things went as expected he'd be home in less than a week.

He was absolutely forbidden from getting near Parchman, and could have nothing to do with the Cayhall execution. Not even a phone call from his bed.

SLEEP WAS BECOMING a battle. Adam habitually read for an hour or so in bed, and had learned in law school that legal publications were marvelous sleeping aids. Now, however, the more he read the more he worried. His mind was burdened with the events of the past two weeks—the people he'd met, the things he'd learned, the places he'd been. And his mind raced wildly with what was to come.

He slept fitfully Saturday night, and was awake for

long stretches of time. When he finally awoke for the last time, the sun was up. It was almost eight o'clock. Lee had mentioned the possibility of another foray into the kitchen. She had once been quite good with sausage and eggs, she'd said, and anybody could handle canned biscuits, but as he pulled up his jeans and slipped on a tee shirt, he could smell nothing.

The kitchen was quiet. He called her name as he examined the coffeepot—half full. Her bedroom door was open and the lights were off. He quickly checked every room. She was not on the patio sipping coffee and reading the paper. A sick feeling came over him and grew worse with each empty room. He ran to the parking lot—no sign of her car. He stepped barefoot across the hot asphalt and asked the security guard when she'd left. He checked a clipboard, and said it had been almost two hours ago. She appeared to be fine, he said.

He found it on a sofa in the den, a three-inch stack of news and ads known as the Sunday edition of the *Memphis Press*. It had been left in a neat pile with the Metro section on top. Lee's face was on the front of this section, in a photo taken at a charity ball years earlier. It was a close-up of Mr. and Mrs. Phelps Booth, all smiles for the camera. Lee was smashing in a strapless black dress. Phelps was decorated fashionably in black tie. They seemed to be a wonderfully happy couple.

The story was Todd Marks's latest exploitation of the Cayhall mess, and with each report the series was becoming more tabloid-like. It started friendly enough, with a weekly summary of the events swirling around the execution. The same voices were heard—McAllister's, Roxburgh's, Lucas Mann's, and Naifeh's steady "no comments." Then it turned mean-spirited quickly as it gleefully exposed Lee Cayhall Booth:

prominent Memphis socialite, wife of important banker Phelps Booth of the renowned and rich Booth family, community volunteer, aunt of Adam Hall, and, believe it or not, daughter of the infamous Sam Cayhall!

The story was written as if Lee herself were guilty of a terrible crime. It quoted alleged friends, unnamed of course, as being shocked to learn her true identity. It talked about the Booth family and its money, and pondered how a blue blood such as Phelps could stoop to marry into a clan such as the Cayhalls. It mentioned their son Walt, and again quoted unnamed sources who speculated about his refusal to return to Memphis. Walt had never married, it reported breathlessly, and lived in Amsterdam.

And then, worst of all, it quoted another nameless source and told the story of a charity event not too many years ago at which Lee and Phelps Booth were present and sat at a table near Ruth Kramer. The source had also been at the dinner, and distinctly remembered where these people had sat. The source was a friend of Ruth's and an acquaintance of Lee's, and was just plain shocked to learn that Lee had such a father.

A smaller photo of Ruth Kramer accompanied the story. She was an attractive woman in her early fifties.

After the sensational uncovering of Lee, the story went on to summarize Friday's oral argument in New Orleans and the latest maneuverings of the Cayhall defense.

Taken as a whole, it was sleazy narrative that accomplished nothing except that it pushed the daily murder summaries onto the second page.

Adam threw the paper on the floor and sipped coffee. She had awakened on this warm Sunday, clean and sober for the first time in days, probably in much better spirits, and had settled on the sofa with a fresh cup of coffee and the paper. Within minutes she'd been slapped in the face and kicked in the stomach, and now she'd left again. Where did she go during these times? Where was her sanctuary? Certainly she stayed away from Phelps. Maybe she had a boyfriend somewhere who took her in and gave her comfort, but that was doubtful. He prayed she wasn't driving the streets aimlessly with a bottle in her hand.

No doubt, things were hopping around the Booth estates this morning. Their dirty little secret was out, plastered on the front page for the world to see. How would they cope with the humiliation? Imagine, a Booth marrying and producing offspring with such white trash, and now everyone knew. The family might never recover. Madame Booth was certainly distressed, and probably bedridden by now.

Good for them, Adam thought. He showered and changed clothes, then lowered the top on the Saab. He didn't expect to see Lee's maroon Jaguar on the deserted streets of Memphis, but he drove around anyway. He started at Front Street near the river, and with Springsteen blaring from the speakers he randomly made his way east, past the hospitals on Union, through the stately homes of midtown, and back to the projects near Auburn House. Of course he didn't find her, but the drive was refreshing. By noon, the traffic had resumed, and Adam went to the office.

SAM'S ONLY GUEST on Sunday was again an unexpected one. He rubbed his wrists when the handcuffs were removed, and sat across the screen from the gray-haired man with a jolly face and a warm smile.

"Mr. Cayhall, my name is Ralph Griffin, and I'm the chaplain here at Parchman. I'm new, so we haven't met."

Sam nodded, and said, "Nice to meet you."

"My pleasure. I'm sure you knew my predecessor."

"Ah yes, the Right Reverend Rucker. Where is he now?"

"Retired."

"Good. I never cared for him. I doubt if he makes it to heaven."

"Yes, I've heard he wasn't too popular."

"Popular? He was despised by everyone here. For some reason we didn't trust him. Don't know why. Could be because he was in favor of the death penalty. Can you imagine? He was called by God to minister to us, yet he believed we should die. Said it was in the Scriptures. You know, the eye for an eye routine."

"I've heard that before."

"I'm sure you have. What kind of preacher are you? What denomination?"

"I was ordained in a Baptist church, but I'm sort of nondenominational now. I think the Lord's probably frustrated with all this sectarianism."

"He's frustrated with me too, you know."

"How's that?"

"You're familiar with Randy Dupree, an inmate here. Just down the tier from me. Rape and murder."

"Yes. I've read his file. He was a preacher at one time."

"We call him Preacher Boy, and he's recently acquired the spiritual gift of interpreting dreams. He also sings and heals. He'd probably play with snakes if they allowed it. You know, take up the serpents, from the book of Mark, sixteenth chapter, eighteenth verse. Anyway, he just finished this long dream, took over a month, sort of like a mini-series, and it eventually was revealed to him that I will in fact be executed, and that God is waiting for me to clean up my act."

"It wouldn't be a bad idea, you know. To get things in order."

"What's the rush? I have ten days."

"So you believe in God?"

"Yes, I do. Do you believe in the death penalty?"

"No, I don't."

Sam studied him for a while, then said, "Are you serious?"

"Killing is wrong, Mr. Cayhall. If in fact you are guilty of your crime, then you were wrong to kill. It's also wrong for the government to kill you."

"Hallelujah, brother."

"I've never been convinced that Jesus wanted us to kill as a punishment. He didn't teach that. He taught love and forgiveness."

"That's the way I read the Bible. How in hell did you get a job here?"

"I have a cousin in the state senate."

Sam smiled and chuckled at this response. "You won't last long. You're too honest."

"No. My cousin is the chairman of the Committee on Corrections, and rather powerful."

"Then you'd better pray he gets reelected."

"I do every morning. I just wanted to stop by and introduce myself. I'd like to talk to you during the next few days. I'd like to pray with you if you want. I've never been through an execution before."

"Neither have I."

"Does it scare you?"

"I'm an old man, Reverend. I'll be seventy in a few months, if I make it. At times, the thought of dying is quite pleasant. Leaving this godforsaken place will be a relief."

"But you're still fighting."

"Sure, though sometimes I don't know why. It's like a long bout with cancer. You gradually decline and

grow weak. You die a little each day, and you reach the
point where death would be welcome. But no one
really wants to die. Not even me."

"I've read about your grandson. That must be heart-
warming. I know you're proud of him."

Sam smiled and looked at the floor.

"Anyway," the reverend continued, "I'll be around.
Would you like for me to come back tomorrow?"

"That would be nice. Let me do some thinking,
okay?"

"Sure. You know the procedures around here, don't
you? During your last few hours you're allowed to
have only two people present. Your lawyer and your
spiritual adviser. I'll be honored to stay with you."

"Thanks. And can you find the time to talk to Randy
Dupree? The poor kid is cracking up, and he really
needs help."

"I'll do it tomorrow."

"Thanks."

ADAM WATCHED a rented movie by himself, with
the phone nearby. There had been no word from Lee.
At ten, he made two calls to the West Coast. The first
was to his mother in Portland. She was subdued, but
glad to hear from him, she said. She did not ask about
Sam, and Adam did not offer. He reported that he was
working hard, that he was hopeful, and that he would,
in all likelihood, return to Chicago in a couple of
weeks. She'd seen a few stories in the papers, and she
was thinking about him. Lee was fine, Adam said.

The second call was to his younger sister, Carmen, in
Berkeley. A male voice answered the phone in her
apartment, Kevin somebody if Adam remembered correctly, a steady companion for several years now. Carmen was soon on the phone, and seemed anxious to
hear about events in Mississippi. She too had followed

the news closely, and Adam put an optimistic spin on things. She was worried about him down there in the midst of all those horrible Kluckers and racists. Adam insisted he was safe, things were quite peaceful, actually. The people were surprisingly gentle and laid-back. He was staying at Lee's and they were making the best of it. To Adam's surprise, she wanted to know about Sam—what was he like, his appearance, his attitude, his willingness to talk about Eddie. She asked if she should fly down and see Sam before August 8, a meeting Adam had not contemplated. Adam said he would think about it, and that he would ask Sam.

He fell asleep on the sofa, with the television on.

At three-thirty Monday morning, he was awakened by the phone. A voice he'd never heard before crisply identified himself as Phelps Booth. "You must be Adam," he said.

Adam sat up and rubbed his eyes. "Yes, that's me."

"Have you seen Lee?" Phelps asked, neither calm nor urgent.

Adam glanced at a clock on the wall above the television. "No. What's the matter?"

"Well, she's in trouble. The police called me about an hour ago. They picked her up for drunk driving at eight-twenty last night, and took her to jail."

"Oh no," Adam said.

"This is not the first time. She was taken in, refused the breath test of course, and was put in the drunk tank for five hours. She listed my name on the paperwork, so the cops called me. I ran downtown to the jail, and she had already posted bail and walked out. I thought maybe she'd called you."

"No. She was not here when I woke up yesterday morning, and this is the first thing I've heard. Who would she call?"

"Who knows? I hate to start calling her friends and waking them up. Maybe we should just wait."

Adam was uncomfortable with his sudden inclusion into the decision making. These people had been married, for better or for worse, for almost thirty years, and they had obviously been through this before. How was he supposed to know what to do? "She didn't drive away from the jail, did she?" he asked timidly, certain of the answer.

"Of course not. Someone picked her up. Which brings up another problem. We need to get her car. It's in a lot by the jail. I've already paid the towing charges."

"Do you have a key?"

"Yes. Can you help me get it?"

Adam suddenly remembered the newspaper story with the smiling photo of Phelps and Lee, and he also remembered his speculation about the Booth family's reaction to it. He was certain most of the blame and venom had been directed at him. If he'd stayed in Chicago, none of this would've happened.

"Sure. Just tell me what—"

"Go wait by the guardhouse. I'll be there in ten minutes."

Adam brushed his teeth and laced up his Nikes, and spent fifteen minutes chatting about this and that with Willis, the guard, at the gate. A black Mercedes, the longest model in history, approached and stopped. Adam said good-bye to Willis, and got in the car.

They shook hands because it was the polite thing to do. Phelps was dressed in a white jogging suit and wore a Cubs cap. He drove slowly on the empty street. "I guess Lee has told you some things about me," he said, without a trace of concern or regret.

"A few things," Adam said carefully.

"Well, there's a lot to tell, so I'm not going to ask what subjects she's covered."

A very good idea, Adam thought. "It's probably best if we just talk about baseball or something. I take it you're a Cubs fan."

"Always a Cubs fan. You?"

"Sure. This is my first season in Chicago, and I've been to Wrigley a dozen times. I live pretty close to the park."

"Really. I go up three or four times a year. I have a friend with a box. Been doing it for years. Who's your favorite player?"

"Sandberg, I guess. How about you?"

"I like the old guys. Ernie Banks and Ron Santo. Those were the good days of baseball, when the players had loyalty and you knew who'd be on your team from one year to the next. Now, you never know. I love the game, but greed's corrupted it."

It struck Adam as odd that Phelps Booth would denounce greed. "Maybe, but the owners wrote the book on greed for the first hundred years of baseball. What's wrong with the players asking for all the money they can get?"

"Who's worth five million a year?"

"Nobody. But if rock stars make fifty, what's wrong with baseball players making a few million? It's entertainment. The players are the game, not the owners. I go to Wrigley to see the players, not because the *Tribune* happens to be the current owner."

"Yeah, but look at ticket prices. Fifteen bucks to watch a game."

"Attendance is up. The fans don't seem to mind."

They drove through downtown, deserted at four in the morning, and within minutes were near the jail. "Listen, Adam, I don't know how much Lee has told you about her drinking problem."

"She told me she's an alcoholic."

"Definitely. This is the second drunk driving charge. I was able to keep the first out of the papers, but I don't know about this. She's suddenly become an item around town. Thank heaven she hasn't hurt anybody." Phelps stopped the car at a curb near a fenced lot. "She's been in and out of recovery half a dozen times."

"Half a dozen. She told me she'd been through treatment three times."

"You can't believe alcoholics. I know of at least five times in the past fifteen years. Her favorite place is a swanky little abuse center called Spring Creek. It's on a river a few miles north of the city, real nice and peaceful. It's for the wealthy only. They get dried out and pampered. Good food, exercise, saunas, you know, all the bells and whistles. It's so damned nice I think people want to go there. Anyway, I have a hunch she'll turn up there later today. She has some friends who'll help her get checked in. She's well known around the place. Sort of a second home."

"How long will she stay there?"

"It varies. The minimum is a week. She has stayed as long as a month. Costs two thousand bucks a day, and of course they send me the bills. But I don't mind. I'll pay any amount to help her."

"What am I supposed to do?"

"First, we try to find her. I'll get my secretaries on the phones in a few hours, and we'll track her down. She's fairly predictable at this point, and I'm sure she'll turn up in a detox ward, probably at Spring Creek. I'll start pulling strings in a few hours and try to keep it out of the paper. It won't be easy, in light of everything else that's been printed recently."

"I'm sorry."

"Once we find her, you need to go see her. Take

some flowers and candy. I know you're busy, and I know what's ahead for the next, uh—"

"Nine days."

"Nine days. Right. Well, try to see her. And, when the thing down at Parchman is over, I suggest you go back to Chicago, and leave her alone."

"Leave her alone?"

"Yeah. It sounds harsh, but it's necessary. There are many reasons for her many problems. I'll admit I'm one of the reasons, but there's lots of stuff you don't know. Her family is another reason. She adores you, but you also bring back nightmares and a lot of suffering. Don't think bad of me for saying this. I know it hurts, but it's the truth."

Adam stared at the chain-link fence across the sidewalk next to his door.

"She was sober once for five years," Phelps continued. "And we thought she'd stay that way forever. Then Sam was convicted, and then Eddie died. When she returned from his funeral, she fell into the black hole, and I thought many times that she'd never get out. It's best for her if you stay away."

"But I love Lee."

"And she loves you. But you need to adore her from a distance. Send her letters and cards from Chicago. Flowers for her birthday. Call once a month and talk about movies and books, but stay away from the family stuff."

"Who'll take care of her?"

"She's almost fifty years old, Adam, and for the most part she's very independent. She's been an alcoholic for many years, and there's nothing you or I can do to help her. She knows the disease. She'll stay sober when she wants to stay sober. You're not a good influence. Nor am I. I'm sorry."

Adam breathed deeply and grabbed the door latch.

"I'm sorry, Phelps, if I've embarrassed you and your family. It was not intentional."

Phelps smiled and placed a hand on Adam's shoulder. "Believe it or not, my family is in many ways more dysfunctional than yours. We've been through worse."

"That, sir, is difficult to believe."

"It's true." Phelps handed him a key ring and pointed to a small building inside the fence. "Check in there, and they'll show you the car."

Adam opened the door and got out. He watched the Mercedes ease away and disappear. As Adam walked through a gate in the fence, he couldn't shake the unmistakable feeling that Phelps Booth actually still loved his wife.

THIRTY-SIX

RETIRED COLONEL George Nugent was barely ruffled by the news of Naifeh's heart attack. The old guy was doing quite well by Monday morning, resting comfortably and out of danger, and what the hell he was only months away from retirement anyway. Naifeh was a good man, but past his usefulness and hanging on simply to bolster his pension. Nugent was considering a run for the head position if he could get his politics straight.

Now, however, he was pressed with a more critical matter. The Cayhall execution was nine days away, actually only eight because it was scheduled for one minute after midnight on Wednesday of next week, which meant that Wednesday counted as another day though only one minute of it was used. Tuesday of next week was actually the last day.

On his desk was a shiny leather-bound notebook with the words Mississippi Protocol printed professionally on the front. It was his masterpiece, the result of two weeks of tedious organizing. He'd been appalled at the haphazard guides and outlines and checklists thrown together by Naifeh for previous executions. It was a wonder they'd actually been able to gas anyone. But now there was a plan, a detailed and carefully arranged blueprint that included everything, in his opinion. It was two inches thick and a hundred and eighty pages long, and of course had his name all over it.

Lucas Mann entered his office at fifteen minutes after

eight, Monday morning. "You're late," Nugent snapped, now a man in charge of things. Mann was just a simple lawyer. Nugent was the head of an execution team. Mann was content with his work. Nugent had aspirations, which in the past twenty-four hours had been bolstered considerably.

"So what," Mann said as he stood by a chair facing the desk. Nugent was dressed in his standard dark olive pants with no wrinkles and heavily starched dark olive shirt with gray T-shirt underneath. His boots gleamed with heavily buffed polish. He marched to a point behind his desk. Mann hated him.

"We have eight days," Nugent said as if this were known only to him.

"I think it's nine," Mann said. Both men were standing.

"Next Wednesday doesn't count. We have eight working days left."

"Whatever."

Nugent sat stiffly in his chair. "Two things. First, here is a manual I've put together for executions. A protocol. From A to Z. Completely organized, indexed, cross-indexed. I'd like for you to review the statutes contained herein and make sure they're current."

Mann stared at the black binder but did not touch it.

"And second, I'd like a report each day on the status of all appeals. As I understand it, there are no legal impediments as of this morning."

"That's correct, sir," Mann answered.

"I'd like something in writing first thing each morning with the updates."

"Then hire yourself a lawyer, sir. You're not my boss, and I'll be damned if I'll write a little brief for your morning coffee. I'll let you know if something happens, but I won't push paper for you."

Ah, the frustrations of civilian life. Nugent longed

for the discipline of the military. Damned lawyers. "Very well. Will you please review the protocol?"

Mann flipped it open and turned a few pages. "You know, we've managed four executions without all this."

"I find that very surprising, frankly."

"Frankly, I don't. We've become quite efficient, I'm sad to say."

"Look, Lucas, I don't relish this," Nugent said wistfully. "Phillip asked me to do it. I hope there's a stay. I really do. But if not, then we must be prepared. I want this to run smoothly."

Mann acknowledged the obvious lie, and picked up the manual. Nugent had yet to witness an execution, and he was counting hours, not days. He couldn't wait to see Sam strapped in the chair, sniffing gas.

Lucas nodded and left the office. In the hallway, he passed Bill Monday, the state executioner, no doubt headed to Nugent's for a quiet pep talk.

ADAM ARRIVED at the Twig shortly before 3 P.M. The day had begun with the panic over Lee's drunk driving mess, and had not improved.

He had been sipping coffee at his desk, nursing a headache and trying to do some research, when in the span of ten minutes Darlene brought a fax from New Orleans and a fax from the district court. He'd lost twice. The Fifth Circuit upheld the decision of the federal court on Sam's claim that the gas chamber was unconstitutional because it was cruel and obsolete, and the district court denied the claim that Benjamin Keyes had performed ineffectively at trial. The headache had suddenly been forgotten. Within an hour, the Death Clerk, Mr. Richard Olander, had called from Washington inquiring about Adam's plans to appeal, and he also wanted to know what other filings might be con-

templated by the defense. He told Adam that there
were only eight working days to go, you know, as if
Adam had to be reminded. Thirty minutes after
Olander's call, a clerk at the death desk of the Fifth
Circuit called and asked Adam when he planned to ap-
peal the district court's ruling.

Adam had explained to both death clerks at both
courts that he was perfecting his appeals as quickly as
possible, and he would try to file by the end of the day.
When he stopped to think about it, it was a little un-
nerving practicing law with such an audience. At this
moment of the process, there were courts and justices
watching to see what he would do next. There were
clerks calling and asking what he might be contemplating. The reason was obvious and disheartening. They
weren't concerned with whether or not Adam would
seize the magical issue that would prevent an execution. They were concerned only about logistics. The
death clerks had been instructed by their superiors to
monitor the waning days so the courts could rule
quickly, usually against the inmate. These justices did
not enjoy reading briefs at three in the morning. They
wanted copies of all last minute filings on their desks
long before the appeals officially arrived.

Phelps had called him at the office just before noon
with the news that Lee had not been found. He had
checked every detox and recovery facility within a hundred miles, and no one had admitted a Lee Booth. He
was still searching, but was very busy now with meetings and such.

Sam arrived at the prison library thirty minutes later
in a somber mood. He'd heard the bad news at noon
on television, on the Jackson station that was counting
down the days. Only nine more. He sat at the table and
stared blankly at Adam. "Where are the Eskimo Pies?"
he asked sadly, like a small child who wanted candy.

Adam reached under the table and retrieved a small styrofoam cooler. He placed it on the table and opened it. "They almost confiscated these at the front gate. Then the guards picked through and threatened to throw them out. So, enjoy."

Sam grabbed one, admired it for a long second, then carefully peeled off the wrapper. He licked the chocolate coating, then took a massive bite. He chewed it slowly with his eyes closed.

Minutes later, the first Eskimo Pie was gone, and Sam started on the second. "Not a good day," he said, licking the edges.

Adam slid some papers to him. "Here are both decisions. Short, to the point, and strongly against us. You don't have a lot of friends on these courts, Sam."

"I know. At least the rest of the world adores me. I don't wanna read that crap. What do we do next?"

"We're gonna prove you're too crazy to execute, that because of your advanced age you don't fully comprehend the nature of your punishment."

"Won't work."

"You liked the idea Saturday. What's happened?"

"It won't work."

"Why not?"

"Because I'm not insane. I know full well why I'm being executed. You're doing what lawyers do best—dreaming up offbeat theories, then finding wacky experts to prove them." He took a large bite of ice cream and licked his lips.

"You want me to quit?" Adam snapped.

Sam pondered his yellow fingernails. "Maybe," he said, quickly running his tongue across a finger.

Adam slid into the seat next to him, as opposed to his usual lawyerly position across the table, and studied him closely. "What's the matter, Sam?"

"I don't know. I've been thinking."

"I'm listening."

"When I was very young, my best friend was killed in a car wreck. He was twenty-six, had a new wife, new child, new house, his whole life in front of him. Suddenly, he was dead. I've outlived him by forty-three years. My oldest brother died when he was fifty-six. I've outlived him by thirteen years. I'm an old man, Adam. A very old man. I'm tired. I feel like giving it up."

"Come on, Sam."

"Look at the advantages. It takes the pressure off you. You won't be forced to spend the next week running crazy and filing useless claims. You won't feel like a failure when it's over. I won't spend my last days praying for a miracle, but instead I can get my things in order. We can spend more time together. It'll make a lot of people happy—the Kramers, McAllister, Roxburgh, eighty percent of the American people who favor the death penalty. It'll be another glorious moment for law and order. I can go out with a little dignity, instead of looking like a desperate man who's afraid to die. It's really quite appealing."

"What's happened to you, Sam? Last Saturday you were still ready to fight the bear."

"I'm tired of fighting. I'm an old man. I've had a long life. And what if you're successful in saving my skin? Where does that leave me? I'm not going anyplace, Adam. You'll go back to Chicago and bury yourself in your career. I'm sure you'll come down whenever you can. We'll write letters and send cards. But I have to live on the Row. You don't. You have no idea."

"We're not quitting, Sam. We still have a chance."

"It's not your decision." He finished the second Eskimo Pie and wiped his mouth with a sleeve.

"I don't like you like this, Sam. I like it when you're mad and nasty and fighting."

"I'm tired, okay?"

"You can't let them kill you. You have to fight to the bitter end, Sam."

"Why?"

"Because it's wrong. It's morally wrong for the state to kill you, and that's why we can't give up."

"But we're gonna lose anyway."

"Maybe. Maybe not. But you've been fighting for almost ten years. Why quit with a week to go?"

"Because it's over, Adam. This thing has finally run its course."

"Perhaps, but we can't quit. Please don't throw in the towel. Hell, I'm making progress. I've got these clowns on the run."

Sam offered a gentle smile and a patronizing gaze.

Adam inched closer and placed his hand on Sam's arm. "I've thought of several new strategies," he said in earnest. "In fact, tomorrow we've got an expert coming to examine you."

Sam looked at him. "What kind of expert?"

"A shrink."

"A shrink?"

"Yeah. From Chicago."

"I've already talked to a shrink. It didn't go well."

"This guy's different. He works for us and he'll say that you've lost your mental faculties."

"You're assuming I had them when I got here."

"Yes, we're assuming that. This psychiatrist will examine you tomorrow, then he'll quickly prepare a report to the effect that you're senile and insane and just a blithering idiot, and who knows what else he'll say."

"How do you know he'll say this?"

"Because we're paying him to say it."

"Who's paying him?"

"Kravitz & Bane, those dedicated Jewish-Americans in Chicago you hate, but who've been busting their asses to keep you alive. It's Goodman's idea, actually."

"Must be a fine expert."

"We can't be too particular at this point. He's been used by some of the other lawyers in the firm on various cases, and he'll say whatever we want him to say. Just act bizarre when you talk to him."

"That shouldn't be too difficult."

"Tell him all the horror stories about this place. Make it sound atrocious and deplorable."

"No problem there."

"Tell him how you've deteriorated over the years, and how it's especially hard on a man your age. You're by far the oldest one here, Sam, so tell him how it's affected you. Lay it on thick. He'll fix up a compelling little report, and I'll run to court with it."

"It won't work."

"It's worth a try."

"The Supreme Court allowed Texas to execute a retarded boy."

"This ain't Texas, Sam. Every case is different. Just work with us on this, okay?"

"Us? Who is us?"

"Me and Goodman. You said you didn't hate him anymore, so I figured I'd let him in on the fun. Seriously, I need help. There's too much work for only one lawyer."

Sam scooted his chair away from the table, and stood. He stretched his arms and legs, and began pacing along the table, counting steps as he went.

"I'll file a petition for cert to the Supreme Court in the morning," Adam said as he looked at a checklist on his legal pad. "They probably won't agree to hear it, but I'll do it anyway. I'll also finish the appeal to the Fifth Circuit on the ineffectiveness claim. The shrink will be here tomorrow afternoon. I'll file the mental competency claim Wednesday morning."

"I'd rather go peacefully, Adam."

"Forget it, Sam. We're not quitting. I talked to Carmen last night, and she wants to come see you."

Sam sat on the edge of the table and watched the floor. His eyes were narrow and sad. He puffed and blew smoke at his feet. "Why would she want to do that?"

"I didn't ask why, nor did I suggest it. She brought it up. I told her I'd ask you."

"I've never met her."

"I know. She's your only granddaughter, Sam, and she wants to come."

"I don't want her to see me like this," he said, waving at his red jumpsuit.

"She won't mind."

Sam reached into the cooler and took another Eskimo Pie. "Do you want one?" he asked.

"No. What about Carmen?"

"Let me think about it. Does Lee still want to visit?"

"Uh, sure. I haven't talked to her in a couple of days, but I'm sure she wants to."

"I thought you were staying with her."

"I am. She's been out of town."

"Let me think about it. Right now I'm against it. I haven't seen Lee in almost ten years, and I just don't want her to remember me like this. Tell her I'm thinking about it, but right now I don't think so."

"I'll tell her," Adam promised, uncertain if he would see her anytime soon. If she had in fact sought treatment, she would undoubtedly be secluded for several weeks.

"I'll be glad when the end comes, Adam. I'm really sick of all this." He took a large bite of ice cream.

"I understand. But let's put it off for a while."

"Why?"

"Why? It's obvious. I don't want to spend my entire legal career encumbered with the knowledge that I lost my first case."

"That's not a bad reason."

"Great. So we're not quitting?"

"I guess not. Bring on the shrink. I'll act as loony as possible."

"That's more like it."

LUCAS MANN was waiting for Adam at the front gate of the prison. It was almost five, the temperature still hot and the air still sticky. "Gotta minute?" he asked through the window of Adam's car.

"I guess. What's up?"

"Park over there. We'll sit under the shade."

They walked to a picnic table by the Visitors Center, under a mammoth oak with the highway in view not far away. "A couple of things," Mann said. "How's Sam? Is he holding up okay?"

"As well as can be expected. Why?"

"Just concerned, that's all. At last count, we had fifteen requests for interviews today. Things are heating up. The press is on its way."

"Sam is not talking."

"Some want to talk to you."

"I'm not talking either."

"Fine. We have a form that Sam needs to sign. It gives us written authorization to tell the reporters to get lost. Have you heard about Naifeh?"

"I saw it in the paper this morning."

"He'll be okay, but he can't supervise the execution. There's a nut named George Nugent, an assistant superintendent, who'll coordinate everything. He's a commandant. Retired military and all, a real gung-ho type."

"It really makes no difference to me. He can't carry out the death warrant unless the courts allow it."

"Right. I just wanted you to know who he was."

"I can't wait to meet him."

"One more thing. I have a friend, an old buddy from law school who now works in the governor's administration. He called this morning, and it seems as if the governor is concerned about Sam's execution. According to my friend, who no doubt was told by the governor to solicit me to speak to you, they would like to conduct a clemency hearing, preferably in a couple of days."

"Are you close to the governor?"

"No. I despise the governor."

"So do I. So does my client."

"That's why my friend was recruited to call and lean on me. Allegedly, the governor is having serious doubts about whether Sam should be executed."

"Do you believe it?"

"It's doubtful. The governor's reputation was made at the expense of Sam Cayhall, and I'm certain he's fine-tuning his media plan for the next eight days. But what is there to lose?"

"Nothing."

"It's not a bad idea."

"I'm all for it. My client, however, has given me strict orders not to request such a hearing."

Mann shrugged as if he really didn't care what Sam did. "It's up to Sam then. Does he have a will?"

"Yes."

"How about burial arrangements?"

"I'm working on them. He wants to be buried in Clanton."

They started walking toward the front gate. "The body goes to a funeral home in Indianola, not far from here. It'll be released to the family there. All visitation ends four hours before the scheduled execution. From that point on, Sam can have only two people with him —his lawyer and his spiritual adviser. He also needs to select his two witnesses, if he so chooses."

"I'll speak to him."

"We need his approved list of visitors between now and then. It's usually family and close friends."

"That'll be a very short list."

"I know."

THIRTY-SEVEN

EVERY OCCUPANT of the Row knew the procedure, though it had never been reduced to writing. The veterans, including Sam, had endured four executions over the past eight years, and with each the procedure had been followed with small variations. The old hands talked and whispered among themselves, and they were usually quick to dispense descriptions of the last hours to the new guys, most of whom arrived at the Row with muted questions about how it's done. And the guards liked to talk about it.

The last meal was to be taken in a small room near the front of the Row, a room referred to simply as the front office. It had a desk and some chairs, a phone and an air conditioner, and it was in this room that the condemned man received his last visitors. He sat and listened as his lawyers tried to explain why things were not developing as planned. It was a plain room with locked windows. The last conjugal visit was held here, if in fact the inmate was up to it. Guards and administrators loitered in the hallway outside.

The room was not designed for the last hours, but when Teddy Doyle Meeks became the first in many years to be executed in 1982, such a room was suddenly needed for all sorts of purposes. It once belonged to a lieutenant, then a case manager. It had no other name except for the front office. The phone on the desk was the last one used by the inmate's lawyer when he received the final word that there would be no more stays, no more appeals. He then made the long walk back to Tier A, to the far end where his client waited in the Observation Cell.

The Observation Cell was nothing more than a regular cell on Tier A, just eight doors down from Sam. It was six by nine, with a bunk, a sink, and a toilet, just like Sam's, just like all the others. It was the last cell on the tier, and the nearest to the Isolation Room, which was next to the Chamber Room. The day before the execution, the inmate was to be taken for the last time from his cell and placed in Observation. His personal belongings were to be moved too, which was usually a quick task. There he waited. Usually, he watched his own private drama on television as the local television stations monitored his last ditch appeals. His lawyer waited with him, seated on the flimsy bed, in the dark cell, watching the news reports. The lawyer ran back and forth to the front office. A minister or spiritual adviser was also allowed in the cell.

The Row would be dark and deathly quiet. Some of the inmates would hover above their televisions. Others would hold hands and pray through the bars. Others would lie on their beds and wonder when their time would come. The outside windows above the hallway were all closed and bolted. The Row was locked down. But there were voices between the tiers, and there were lights from the outside. For men who sit for hours in tiny cells, seeing and hearing everything, the flurry of strange activity was nerve-racking.

At eleven, the warden and his team would enter Tier A and stop at the Observation Cell. By now, the hope of a last minute stay was virtually exhausted. The inmate would be sitting on his bed, holding hands with his lawyer and his minister. The warden would announce that it was time to go to the Isolation Room. The cell door would clang and open, and the inmate would step into the hallway. There would be shouts of support and reassurance from the other inmates, many of whom would be in tears. The Isolation Room is no more than twenty feet from the Observation Cell. The inmate would walk through the center of two rows of armed and bulky security guards, the largest the warden could find. There was never any resistance. It wouldn't do any good.

The warden would lead the inmate into a small room, ten feet by ten, with nothing in it except a foldaway bed. The inmate would sit on the bed with his lawyer by his side. At this point, the warden, for some baffling reason, would feel the need to spend a few moments with the inmate, as if he, the warden, were the last person the inmate wanted to chat with. The warden eventually would leave. The room would be quiet except for an occasional bang or knock from the room next door. Prayers were normally completed at this point. There were just minutes to go.

Next door to the Isolation Room was the Chamber Room itself. It was approximately fifteen feet by twelve, with the gas chamber in the center of it. The executioner would be hard at work while the inmate prayed in isolation. The warden, the prison attorney, the doctor, and a handful of guards would be making preparations. There would be two telephones on the wall for the last minute clearance. There was a small room to the left where the executioner mixed his solutions. Behind the chamber was a series of three windows, eighteen inches by thirty, and covered for the moment by black drapes. On the other side of the windows was the witness room.

At twenty minutes before midnight, the doctor would enter the Isolation Room and attach a stethoscope to the inmate's chest. He would leave, and the warden would enter to take the condemned man to see the chamber.

The Chamber Room was always filled with people, all anxious to help, all about to watch a man die. They would back him into the chamber, strap him in, close the door, and kill him.

It was a fairly straightforward procedure, varied a bit to accommodate the individual case. For example, Buster Moac was in the chair with half the straps in place when the phone rang in the Chamber Room. He went back to the Isolation Room and waited six miserable hours until they came for him again. Jumbo Parris was the smartest of the four. A longtime drug user before he made it to the Row, he began asking the psychiatrist for Valium days before his execution. He chose to spend his last hours alone, no lawyer or minister, and when they came to fetch him from the Observation Cell, he was stoned. He had evidently stockpiled the Valium, and had to be dragged to the Isolation Room where he slept in peace. He was then dragged to the chamber and given his final dosage.

It was a humane and thoughtful procedure. The inmate remained in his cell, next to his pals, up to the very end. In Louisiana, they were removed from the Row and placed in a small building known as the Death House. They spent their final three days there, under constant supervision. In Virginia, they were moved to another city.

Sam was eight doors from the Observation Cell, about forty-eight feet. Then another twenty feet to the Isolation Room, then another twelve feet to the chamber. From a point in the center of his bed, he'd calculated many times that he was approximately eighty-five feet from the gas chamber.

And he made the calculation again Tuesday morning as he carefully made an X on his calendar. Eight days. It was dark and hot. He had slept off and on and spent most of the night sitting in front of his fan. Breakfast and coffee were an hour away now. This would be day number 3,449 on the Row, and the total did not include time spent in the county jail in Greenville during his first two trials. Only eight more days.

His sheets were soaked with sweat, and as he lay on the bed and watched the ceiling for the millionth time he thought of death. The actual act of dying would not be too terrible. For obvious reasons, no one knew the exact effects of the gas. Maybe they would give him an extra dose so he'd be dead long before his body twitched and jerked. Maybe the first breath would knock him senseless. At any rate, it wouldn't take long, he hoped. He'd watched his wife shrivel and suffer greatly from cancer. He'd watched kinfolks grow old and vegetate. Surely, this was a better way to go.

"Sam," J. B. Gullitt whispered, "you up?"

Sam walked to his door and leaned through the bars. He could see Gullitt's hands and forearms. "Yeah. I'm up. Can't seem to sleep." He lit the first cigarette of the day.

"Me neither. Tell me it's not gonna happen, Sam."

"It's not gonna happen."

"You serious?"

"Yeah, I'm serious. My lawyer's about to unload the heavy stuff. He'll probably walk me outta here in a coupla weeks."

"Then why can't you sleep?"

"I'm so excited about gettin' out."

"Have you talked to him about my case?"

"Not yet. He's got a lot on his mind. As soon as I get out, we'll go to work on your case. Just relax. Try and get some sleep."

Gullitt's hands and forearms slowly withdrew, then his bed squeaked. Sam shook his head at the kid's ignorance. He finished the cigarette and thumped it down the hall, a breach of the rules that would earn him a violation report. As if he cared.

He carefully took his typewriter from the shelf. He had things to say and letters to write. There were people out there he needed to speak to.

GEORGE NUGENT entered the Maximum Security Unit like a five-star general and glared disapprovingly at the hair and then at the unshined boots of a white security guard. "Get a haircut," he growled, "or I'll write you up. And work on those boots."

"Yes sir," the kid said, and almost saluted.

Nugent jerked his head and nodded at Packer, who led the way through the center of the Row to Tier A. "Number six," Packer said as the door opened.

"Stay here," Nugent instructed. His heels clicked as he marched along the tier, gazing with disdain into each cell. He stopped at Sam's, and peered inside. Sam was stripped to his boxers, his thin and wrinkled skin gleaming with sweat as he pecked away. He looked at the stranger staring at him through the bars, then returned to his work.

"Sam, my name is George Nugent."

Sam hit a few keys. The name was not familiar, but Sam assumed he worked somewhere up the ladder since he had access to the tiers. "What do you want?" Sam asked without looking.

"Well, I wanted to meet you."

"My pleasure, now shove off."

Gullitt to the right and Henshaw to the left were suddenly leaning through the bars, just a few feet from Nugent. They snickered at Sam's response.

Nugent glared at them, and cleared his throat. "I'm an assistant superintendent, and Phillip Naifeh has placed me in charge of your execution. There are a few things we need to discuss."

Sam concentrated on his correspondence, and cursed when he hit a wrong key. Nugent waited. "If I could have a few minutes of your valuable time, Sam."

"Better call him Mr. Cayhall," Henshaw added helpfully. "He's a few years older than you, and it means a lot to him."

"Where'd you get those boots?" Gullitt asked, staring at Nugent's feet.

"You boys back away," Nugent said sternly. "I need to talk to Sam."

"Mr. Cayhall's busy right now," Henshaw said. "Perhaps you should come back later. I'll be happy to schedule an appointment for you."

"Are you some kinda military asshole?" Gullitt asked.

Nugent stood stiffly and glanced to his right and to his left. "I'm ordering you two to get back, okay. I need to speak to Sam."

"We don't take orders," Henshaw said.

"And what're you gonna do about it?" Gullitt asked. "Throw us in solitary? Feed us roots and berries? Chain us to the walls? Why don't you just go ahead and kill us?"

Sam placed his typewriter on the bed, and walked to the bars. He took a long drag, and shot smoke through them in the general direction of Nugent. "What do you want?" he demanded.

"I need a few things from you."

"Such as?"

"Do you have a will?"

"That's none of your damned business. A will is a private document to be seen only if it's probated, and it's probated only after a person dies. That's the law."

"What a dumbass!" Henshaw shrieked.

"I don't believe this," Gullitt offered. "Where did Naifeh find this idiot?" he asked.

"Anything else?" Sam asked.

Nugent's face was changing colors. "We need to know what to do with your things."

"It's in my will, okay."

"I hope you're not going to be difficult, Sam."

"It's Mr. Cayhall," Henshaw said again.

"Difficult?" Sam asked. "Why would I be difficult? I intend to cooperate fully with the state while it goes about its business of killing me. I'm a good patriot. I would vote and pay taxes if I could. I'm proud to be an American, an Irish-American, and at this moment I'm still very much in love with my precious state, even though it plans to gas me. I'm a model prisoner, George. No problems out of me."

Packer was thoroughly enjoying this as he waited at the end of the tier. Nugent stood firm.

"I need a list of the people you want to witness the execution," he said. "You're allowed two."

"I'm not giving up yet, George. Let's wait a few days."

"Fine. I'll also need a list of your visitors for the next few days."

"Well, this afternoon I have this doctor coming down from Chicago, you see. He's a psychiatrist, and he's gonna talk to me and see how nutty I really am, then my lawyers will run to court and say that you, George, can't execute me because I'm crazy. He'll have time to examine you, if you want. It won't take long."

Henshaw and Gullitt horselaughed, and within seconds most of the other inmates on the tier were chiming in and cackling loudly. Nugent took a step backward and scowled up and down the tier. "Quiet!" he demanded, but the laughter increased. Sam continued puffing and blowing smoke through the bars. Catcalls and insults could be heard amid the ruckus.

"I'll be back," Nugent shouted angrily at Sam.

"He shall return!" Henshaw yelled, and the commotion grew even louder. The commandant stormed away, and as he marched swiftly to the end of the hall, shouts of "Heil Hitler" rang through the tier.

Sam smiled at the bars for a moment as the noise died, then returned to his position on the edge of the bed. He took a bite of dry toast, a sip of cold coffee. He resumed his typing.

THE AFTERNOON DRIVE to Parchman was not a particularly pleasant one. Garner Goodman sat in the front seat as Adam drove, and they talked strategy and brainstormed about the last minute appeals and procedures. Goodman planned to return to Memphis over the weekend, and be available during the last three days. The psychiatrist was Dr. Swinn, a cold, unsmiling man in a black suit. He had wild, bushy hair, dark eyes hidden behind thick glasses, and was completely incapable of small talk. His presence in the backseat was discomfiting. He did not utter a single word from Memphis to Parchman.

The examination had been arranged by Adam and Lucas Mann to take place in the prison hospital, a remarkably modern facility. Dr. Swinn had very plainly informed Adam that neither he nor Goodman could be present during his evaluation of Sam. And this was perfectly fine with Adam and Goodman. A prison van met them at the front gate, and carried Dr. Swinn to the hospital deep inside the farm.

Goodman had not seen Lucas Mann in several years. They shook hands like old friends, and immediately lapsed into war stories about executions. The conversation was kept away from Sam, and Adam appreciated it.

They walked from Mann's office across a parking lot to a small building behind the administration complex.

The building was a restaurant, designed along the lines of a neighborhood tavern. Called The Place, it served basic food to the office workers and prison employees. No alcohol. It was on state property.

They drank iced tea and talked about the future of capital punishment. Both Goodman and Mann agreed that executions would soon become even more commonplace. The U.S. Supreme Court was continuing its swing to the right, and it was weary of the endless appeals. Ditto for the lower levels of the federal judiciary. Plus, American juries were becoming increasingly reflective of society's intolerance of violent crime. There was much less sympathy for death row inmates, a much greater desire to fry the bastards. Fewer federal dollars were being spent to fund groups opposed to the death penalty, and fewer lawyers and their firms were willing to make the enormous pro bono commitments. The death row population was growing faster than the number of lawyers willing to take capital cases.

Adam was quite bored with the conversation. He'd read and heard it a hundred times. He excused himself and found a pay phone in a corner. Phelps was not in, a young secretary said, but he'd left a message for Adam: no word from Lee. She was scheduled to be in court in two weeks; maybe she'd turn up then.

DARLENE typed Dr. Swinn's report while Adam and Garner Goodman worked on the petition to accompany it. The report was twenty pages long in rough draft, and sounded like soft music. Swinn was a hired gun, a prostitute who'd sell an opinion to the highest bidder, and Adam detested him and his ilk. He roamed the country as a professional testifier, able to say this today and that tomorrow, depending on who had the deepest pockets. But for the moment, he was their whore, and he was quite good. Sam was suffering from advanced senility. His mental faculties had eroded to the point where he did not know and appreciate the nature of his punishment. He lacked the requisite competence to be executed, and therefore the execution would not serve any purpose. It was not an entirely unique legal argument, nor had the courts exactly embraced it. But, as Adam found himself saying every day, what was there to lose? Goodman seemed to be more than a little optimistic, primarily because of Sam's age. He could not recall an execution of a man over the age of fifty.

They, Darlene included, worked until almost eleven.

THIRTY-EIGHT

GARNER GOODMAN did not return to Chicago Wednesday morning, but instead flew to Jackson, Mississippi. The flight took thirty minutes, hardly time for a cup of coffee and an unthawed croissant. He rented a car at the airport and drove straight to the state capitol. The legislature was not in session, and there were plenty of parking places on the grounds. Like many county courthouses rebuilt after the Civil War, the capitol defiantly faced south. He stopped to admire the war monument to Southern women, but spent more time studying the splendid Japanese magnolias at the bottom of the front steps.

Four years earlier, during the days and hours prior to the Maynard Tole execution, Goodman had made this same journey on two occasions. There was a different governor then, a different client, and a different crime. Tole had murdered several people in a two-day crime spree, and it had been quite difficult to arouse sympathy for him. He hoped Sam Cayhall was different. He was an old man who'd probably die within five years anyway. His crime was ancient history to many Mississippians. And on and on.

Goodman had been rehearsing his routine all morning. He entered the capitol building and once again marveled at its beauty. It was a smaller version of the U.S. Capitol in Washington, and no expense had been spared. It had been built in 1910 with prison labor. The state had used the proceeds from a successful lawsuit against a railroad to construct itself this monument.

He entered the governor's office on the second floor and handed his card to the lovely receptionist. The governor was not in this morning, she said, and did he have an appointment? No, Goodman explained pleasantly, but it was very important, and would it be possible for him to see Mr. Andy Larramore, chief counsel for the governor?

He waited as she made several calls, and half an hour later Mr. Larramore presented himself. They made their introductions and disappeared into a narrow hallway that ran through a maze of small offices. Larramore's cubbyhole was cluttered and disorganized, much like the man himself. He was a small guy with a noticeable bend at the waist and absolutely no neck. His long chin rested on his chest, and when he talked his eyes, nose, and mouth all squeezed together tightly. It was a horrible sight. Goodman couldn't tell if he was thirty or fifty. He had to be a genius.

"The governor is speaking to a convention of insurance agents this morning," Larramore said, holding an itinerary as if it were a piece of fine jewelry. "And then he visits a public school in the inner city."

"I'll wait," Goodman said. "It's very important, and I don't mind hanging around."

Larramore placed the sheet of paper aside, and folded his hands on the table. "What happened to that young fellow, Sam's grandson?"

"Oh, he's still lead counsel. I'm the director of pro bono for Kravitz & Bane, so I'm here to assist him."

"We're monitoring this thing very closely," Larramore said, his face wrinkling fiercely in the center, then relaxing at the end of each sentence. "Looks like it will go down to the wire."

"They always do," Goodman said. "How serious is the governor about a clemency hearing?"

"I'm sure he'll entertain the idea of a hearing. The granting of clemency is an entirely different matter. The statute is very broad, as I'm sure you know. He can commute the death sentence and instantly parole the convict. He can commute it to life in prison, or something less than that."

Goodman nodded. "Will it be possible for me to see him?"

"He's scheduled to return here at eleven. I'll speak to him then. He'll probably eat lunch at his desk, so there may be a gap around one. Can you be here?"

"Yes. This must be kept quiet. Our client is very much opposed to this meeting."

"Is he opposed to the idea of clemency?"

"We have seven days to go, Mr. Larramore. We're not opposed to anything."

Larramore crinkled his nose and exposed his upper teeth, and picked up the itinerary again. "Be here at one. I'll see what I can do."

"Thanks." They chatted aimlessly for five minutes, then Larramore was besieged by a series of urgent phone calls. Goodman excused himself and left the capitol. He paused again at the Japanese magnolias and removed his jacket. It was nine-thirty, and his shirt was wet under the arms and sticking to his back.

He walked south in the general direction of Capitol Street, four blocks away and considered to be the main street of Jackson. In the midst of the buildings and traffic of downtown, the governor's mansion sat majestically on manicured grounds and faced the capitol. It was a large antebellum home surrounded by gates and fences. A handful of death penalty opponents had gathered on the sidewalk the night Tole was executed and yelled at the governor. Evidently, he had not heard them. Goodman stopped on the sidewalk and remembered the mansion. He and Peter Wiesenberg had walked hurriedly through a gate to the left of the main drive with their last plea, just hours before Tole was gassed. The governor at that time was having a late dinner with important people, and had become quite irritated with their interruption. He denied their final request for clemency, then, in the finest Southern tradition, invited them to stay for dinner.

They'd politely declined. Goodman explained to His Honor that they had to hurry back to Parchman to be with their client as he died. "Be careful," the governor had told them, then returned to his dinner party.

Goodman wondered how many protestors would be standing on this spot in a few short days, chanting and praying and burning candles, waving placards, and yelling at McAllister to spare old Sam. Probably not very many.

There has seldom been a shortage of office space in the central business district in Jackson, and Goodman had little trouble finding what he wanted. A sign directed his attention to vacant footage on the third floor of an ugly building. He inquired at the front desk of a finance company on the ground level, and an hour later the owner of the building arrived and showed him the available space. It was a dingy two-room suite with worn carpet and holes in the wallboard. Goodman walked to the lone window and looked at the front of the capitol building three blocks away. "Perfect," he said.

"It's three hundred a month, plus electricity. Rest room's down the hall. Six-month minimum."

"I need it for only two months," Goodman said, reaching into his pocket and withdrawing a neatly folded collection of cash.

The owner looked at the money, and asked, "What kind of business are you in?"

"Marketing analysis."

"Where are you from?"

"Detroit. We're thinking about establishing a branch in this state, and we need this space to get started. But for only two months. All cash. Nothing in writing. We'll be out before you know it. Won't make a sound."

The owner took the cash and handed Goodman two keys, one for the office, the other for the entrance on Congress Street. They shook hands and the deal was closed.

Goodman left the dump and returned to his car at the capitol. Along the way he chuckled at the scheme he was pursuing. The idea was Adam's brainchild, another long shot in a series of desperate plots to save Sam. There was nothing illegal about it. The cost would be slight, and who cared about a few dollars at this point? He was, after all, Mr. Pro Bono at the firm, the source of great pride and self-righteousness among his peers. Nobody, not even Daniel Rosen, would question his expenditures for a little rent and a few phones.

AFTER THREE WEEKS as a death row lawyer, Adam was beginning to yearn for the predictability of his office in Chicago, if, in fact, he still had an office. Before ten o'clock Wednesday, he had finished a claim for postconviction relief. He had talked with various court clerks four times, then with a court administrator. He had talked with Richard Olander in Washington twice concerning the habeas claim attacking the gas chamber, and he had talked with a clerk at the death desk at the Fifth Circuit in New Orleans regarding the ineffectiveness claim.

The claim alleging Sam's lack of mental competence

was now in Jackson, by fax with the original to follow by Fed-Ex, and Adam was forced to politely beg the court's administrator to speed things up. Hurry up and deny it, he said, though not in those words. If a stay of execution was forthcoming, it would in all likelihood be issued by a federal judge.

Each new claim brought with it a scant new ray of hope, and, as Adam was quickly learning, also the potential for another loss. A claim had to clear four obstacles before it was extinguished—the Mississippi Supreme Court, the federal district court, the Fifth Circuit, and the U.S. Supreme Court—so the odds were against success, especially at this stage of the appeals. Sam's bread and butter issues had been litigated thoroughly by Wallace Tyner and Garner Goodman years ago. Adam was now filing the crumbs.

The clerk at the Fifth Circuit doubted if the court would care to indulge in another oral argument, especially since it appeared that Adam would be filing new claims every day. The three-judge panel would probably consider only the briefs. Conference calls would be used if the judges wished to hear his voice.

Richard Olander called again to say the Supreme Court had received Adam's petition for cert, or request to hear the case, and that it had been assigned. No, he did not think the Court would care to hear oral argument. Not this late in the game. He also informed Adam that he had received by fax a copy of the new claim of mental incompetency, and that he would monitor it through the local courts. Interesting, he said. He asked again what new claims Adam might be contemplating, but Adam wouldn't say.

Judge Slattery's law clerk, Breck Jefferson, he of the permanent scowl, called to inform Adam that His Honor had received by fax a copy of the new claim filed with the Mississippi Supreme Court, and frankly

His Honor didn't think much of it but would nonetheless give it full consideration once it arrived in their court.

Adam took a little satisfaction in the knowledge that he had managed to keep four very different courts hopping at the same time.

At eleven, Morris Henry, the infamous Dr. Death in the Attorney General's office, called to inform Adam that they had received the latest round of gangplank appeals, as he enjoyed calling them, and Mr. Roxburgh himself had assigned a dozen lawyers to produce the responding paperwork. Henry was nice enough on the phone, but the call had made its point—we have lots of lawyers, Adam.

The paperwork was being generated by the pound now, and the small conference table was covered with neat stacks of it. Darlene was in and out of the office constantly—making copies, delivering phone messages, fetching coffee, proofreading briefs and petitions. She'd been trained in the tedious field of government bonds, so the detailed and voluminous documents did not intimidate her. She confessed more than once that this was an exciting change from her normal drudgery. "What's more exciting than a looming execution?" Adam asked.

Even Baker Cooley managed to tear himself away from the latest updates in federal banking regulations and popped in for a look.

Phelps called around eleven to ask if Adam wanted to meet for lunch. Adam did not, and begged off by blaming deadlines and cranky judges. Neither had heard from Lee. Phelps said she'd disappeared before, but never for more than two days. He was worried and thinking about hiring a private investigator. He'd keep in touch.

"There's a reporter here to see you," Darlene said,

handing him a business card declaring the presence of Anne L. Piazza, correspondent for *Newsweek*. She was the third reporter who'd contacted the office on Wednesday. "Tell her I'm sorry," Adam said with no regret.

"I did that already, but I thought that since it was *Newsweek* you might wanna know."

"I don't care who it is. Tell her the client's not talking either."

She left in a hurry as the phone was ringing. It was Goodman, reporting from Jackson that he was to see the governor at one. Adam brought him up to date on the flurry of activity and phone calls.

Darlene delivered a deli sandwich at twelve-thirty. Adam ate it quickly, then napped in a chair as his computer spewed forth another brief.

GOODMAN FLIPPED through a car magazine as he waited alone in the reception area next to the governor's office. The same pretty secretary worked on her nails between phone calls at her switchboard. One o'clock came and went without comment. Same for one-thirty. The receptionist, now with glorious peach nails, apologized at two. No problem, said Goodman with a warm smile. The beauty of a pro bono career was that labor was not measured by time. Success meant helping people, regardless of hours billed.

At two-fifteen, an intense young woman in a dark suit appeared from nowhere and walked to Goodman. "Mr. Goodman, I'm Mona Stark, the governor's chief of staff. The governor will see you now." She smiled correctly, and Goodman followed her through a set of double doors and into a long, formal room with a desk at one end and a conference table far away at the other.

McAllister was standing by the window with his

jacket off, tie loosened, sleeves up, very much the be-
leaguered and overworked servant of the people.
"Hello, Mr. Goodman," he said with a hand thrust
forward and teeth flashing brilliantly.

"Governor, my pleasure," Goodman said. He had
no briefcase, no standard lawyer accessories. He
looked as if he'd simply passed by on the street and
decided to stop and meet the governor.

"You've met Mr. Larramore and Ms. Stark," McAllister said, waving a hand at each.

"Yes. We've met. Thanks for seeing me on such short
notice." Goodman tried to match his dazzling smile,
but it was hopeless. At the moment, he was most humble and appreciative just to be in this great office.

"Let's sit over here," the governor said, waving at
the conference table and leading the way. The four of
them sat on separate sides of the table. Larramore and
Mona withdrew pens and were poised for serious note-
taking. Goodman had nothing but his hands in front of
him.

"I understand there've been quite of lot of filings in
the past few days," McAllister said.

"Yes sir. Just curious, have you been through one of
these before?" Goodman asked.

"No. Thankfully."

"Well, this is not unusual. I'm certain we'll be filing
petitions until the last moment."

"Can I ask you something, Mr. Goodman?" the governor said sincerely.

"Certainly."

"I know you've handled many of these cases. What's
your prediction at this point? How close will it get?"

"You never know. Sam's a bit different from most
inmates on death row because he's had good lawyers—
good trial counsel, then superb appellate work."

"By you, I believe."

Goodman smiled, then McAllister smiled, then Mona managed a grin. Larramore remained hunched over his legal pad, his face contorted in furious concentration.

"That's right. So Sam's major claims have already been ruled on. What you're seeing now are the desperate moves, but they often work. I'd say fifty-fifty, today, seven days away."

Mona quickly recorded this on paper as if it carried some enormous legal significance. Larramore had written every word so far.

McAllister thought about it for a few seconds. "I'm a little confused, Mr. Goodman. Your client does not know we're meeting. He's opposed to the idea of a clemency hearing. You want this meeting kept quiet. So why are we here?"

"Things change, Governor. Again, I've been here many times before. I've watched men count down their last days. It does strange things to the mind. People change. As the lawyer, I have to cover every base, every angle."

"Are you asking for a hearing?"

"Yes sir. A closed hearing."

"When?"

"What about Friday?"

"In two days," McAllister said as he gazed through a window. Larramore cleared his throat, and asked, "What sort of witnesses do you anticipate?"

"Good question. If I had names, I'd give them to you now, but I don't. Our presentation will be brief."

"Who will testify for the state?" McAllister asked Larramore, whose moist teeth glistened as he pondered. Goodman looked away.

"I'm certain the victims' family will want to say something. The crime is usually discussed. Someone from the prison might be needed to discuss the type of inmate he's been. These hearings are quite flexible."

"I know more about the crime than anyone," McAllister said, almost to himself.

"It's a strange situation," Goodman confessed. "I've had my share of clemency hearings, and the prosecutor is usually the first witness to testify against the defendant. In this case, you were the prosecutor."

"Why do you want the hearing closed?"

"The governor has long been an advocate of open meetings," Mona added.

"It's really best for everyone," Goodman said, much like the learned professor. "It's less pressure on you, Governor, because it's not exposed and you don't have a lot of unsolicited advice. We, of course, would like for it to be closed."

"Why?" McAllister asked.

"Well, frankly, sir, we don't want the public to see Ruth Kramer talking about her little boys." Goodman watched them as he delivered this. The real reason was something else altogether. Adam was convinced that the only way to talk Sam into a clemency hearing was to promise him it would not be a public spectacle. If such a hearing was closed, then Adam could maybe convince Sam that McAllister would be prevented from grandstanding.

Goodman knew dozens of people around the country who would gladly come to Jackson on a moment's notice to testify on Sam's behalf. He had heard these people make some persuasive, last minute arguments against death. Nuns, priests, ministers, psychologists, social workers, authors, professors, and a couple of former death row inmates. Dr. Swinn would testify about how dreadfully Sam was doing these days, and he would do an excellent job of trying to convince the governor that the state was about to kill a vegetable.

In most states, the inmate has a right to a last minute clemency hearing, usually before the governor. In Mississippi, however, the hearing was discretionary.

"I guess that makes sense," the governor actually said.

"There's enough interest already," Goodman said, knowing that McAllister was giddy with dreams of the forthcoming media frenzy. "It will benefit no one if the hearing is open."

Mona, the staunch open meetings advocate, frowned even harder and wrote something in block letters. McAllister was deep in thought.

"Regardless of whether it's open or closed," he said, "there's no real reason for such a hearing unless you and your client have something new to add. I know this case, Mr. Goodman. I smelled the smoke. I saw the bodies. I cannot change my mind unless there's something new."

"Such as?"

"Such as a name. You give me the name of Sam's accomplice, and I'll agree to a hearing. No promise of clemency, you understand, just a regular clemency hearing. Otherwise, this is a waste of time."

"Do you believe there was an accomplice?" Goodman asked.

"We were always suspicious. What do you think?"

"Why is it important?"

"It's important because I make the final decision, Mr. Goodman. After the courts are finished with it, and the clock ticks down next Tuesday night, I'm the only person in the world who can stop it. If Sam deserves the death penalty, then I have no problem sitting by while it happens. But if he doesn't, then the execution should be stopped. I'm a young man. I do not want to be haunted by this for the rest of my life. I want to make the right decision."

"But if you believe there was an accomplice, and you obviously do, then why not stop it anyway?"

"Because I want to be sure. You've been his lawyer for many years. Do you think he had an accomplice?"

"Yes. I've always thought there were two of them. I don't know who was the leader and who was the follower, but Sam had help."

McAllister leaned closer to Goodman and looked into his eyes. "Mr. Goodman, if Sam will tell me the truth, then I will grant a closed hearing, and I will consider clemency. I'm not promising a damned thing, you understand, only that we'll have the hearing. Otherwise, there's nothing new to add to the story."

Mona and Larramore scribbled faster than court reporters.

"Sam says he's telling the truth."

"Then forget the hearing. I'm a busy man."

Goodman sighed in frustration, but kept a smile in place. "Very well, we'll talk to him again. Can we meet here again tomorrow?"

The governor looked at Mona, who consulted a pocket calendar and began shaking her head as if tomorrow was hopelessly filled with speeches and appearances and meetings. "You're booked," she said in a commanding tone.

"What about lunch?"

Nope. Wouldn't work. "You're speaking to the NRA convention."

"Why don't you call me?" Larramore offered.

"Good idea," the governor said, standing now and buttoning his sleeves.

Goodman stood and shook hands with the three. "I'll call if something breaks. We are requesting a hearing as soon as possible, regardless."

"The request is denied unless Sam talks," said the governor.

"Please put the request in writing, sir, if you don't mind," Larramore asked.

"Certainly."

They walked Goodman to the door, and after he left the office McAllister sat in his official chair behind his desk. He unbuttoned his sleeves again. Larramore excused himself and went to his little room down the hall.

Ms. Stark studied a printout while the governor watched the rows of buttons blink on his phone. "How many of these calls are about Sam Cayhall?" he asked. She moved a finger along a column.

"Yesterday, you had twenty-one calls regarding the Cayhall execution. Fourteen in favor of gassing him. Five said to spare him. Two couldn't make up their minds."

"That's an increase."

"Yeah, but the paper had that article about Sam's last ditch efforts. It mentioned the possibility of a clemency hearing."

"What about the polls?"

"No change. Ninety percent of the white people in this state favor the death penalty, and about half the blacks do. Overall, it's around eighty-four percent."

"Where's my approval?"

"Sixty-two. But if you pardon Sam Cayhall, I'm sure it'll drop to single digits."

"So you're against the idea."

"There's absolutely nothing to gain, and much to lose. Forget polls and numbers, if you pardon one of those thugs up there you'll have the other fifty sending lawyers and grandmothers and preachers down here begging for the same favor. You have enough on your mind. It's foolish."

"Yeah, you're right. Where's the media plan?"

"I'll have it in an hour."

"I need to see it."

"Nagel's putting the final touches on it. I think you should grant the request for a clemency hearing anyway. But hold it Monday. Announce it tomorrow. Let it simmer over the weekend."

"It shouldn't be closed."

"Hell no! We want Ruth Kramer crying for the cameras."

"It's my hearing. Sam and his lawyers will not dictate its conditions. If they want it, they'll do it my way."

"Right. But keep in mind, you want it too. Tons of coverage."

GOODMAN SIGNED a three-month lease for four cellular phones. He used a Kravitz & Bane credit card and deftly dodged the barrage of questions by the chirpy young salesman. He went to a public library on State Street and found a reference table filled with phone books. Judging by their thickness, he selected those of the larger Mississippi towns, places like Laurel, Hattiesburg, Tupelo, Vicksburg, Biloxi, and Meridian. Then he picked the thinner ones—Tunica, Calhoun City, Bude, Long Beach, West Point. At the information desk, he converted bills to quarters, and spent two hours copying pages from the phone books.

He went merrily about his work. No one would've believed the natty little man with bushy gray hair and bow tie was in fact a partner in a major Chicago firm with secretaries and paralegals at his beck and call. No one would've believed he earned over four hundred thousand dollars a year. And he couldn't have cared less. E. Garner Goodman was happy with his work. He was trying his best to save another soul from being legally killed.

He left the library and drove a few blocks to the

Mississippi College School of Law. A professor there by the name of John Bryan Glass taught criminal procedure and law, and also had begun publishing scholarly articles against the death penalty. Goodman wanted to make his acquaintance, and to see if maybe the professor had a few bright students interested in a research project.

The professor was gone for the day, but scheduled to teach a 9 A.M. class on Thursday. Goodman checked out the law school's library, then left the building. He drove a few blocks to the Old State Capitol Building, just killing time, and took an extended tour of it. It lasted for thirty minutes, half of which was spent at the Civil Rights Exhibit on the ground floor. He asked the clerk in the gift shop about a bed and breakfast, and she suggested the Millsaps-Buie House, about a mile down the street. He found the lovely Victorian mansion just where she'd said, and took the last vacant room. The house was immaculately restored with period pieces and furnishings. The butler fixed him a Scotch and water, and he took it to his room.

THIRTY-NINE

THE AUBURN HOUSE opened for business at eight. A feeble and dispirited security guard in a bad uniform unlocked the gate across the drive, and Adam was the first person into the parking lot. He waited in his car for ten minutes until another parked nearby. He recognized the woman as the counselor he'd met in Lee's office two weeks earlier. He stopped her on the sidewalk as she was entering a side door. "Excuse me," he said. "We've met before. I'm Adam Hall. Lee's nephew. I'm sorry, but I don't remember your name."

The lady held a worn briefcase in one hand and a brown lunch bag in the other. She smiled and said, "Joyce Cobb. I remember. Where's Lee?"

"I don't know. I was hoping you might know something. You haven't heard from her?"

"No. Not since Tuesday."

"Tuesday? I haven't talked to her since Saturday. Did you talk to her Tuesday?"

"She called here, but I didn't talk to her. It was the day they ran that drunk driving story in the paper."

"Where was she?"

"She never said. She asked for the administrator, said she would be out for a while, had to get some help, stuff like that. Never said where she was or when she was coming back."

"What about her patients?"

"We're covering for her. It's always a struggle, you know. But we'll manage."

"Lee wouldn't forget these girls. Do you think maybe she's talked to them this week?"

"Look, Adam, most of these girls don't have phones, okay? And Lee certainly would not go into the projects. We're seeing her girls, and I know they haven't talked to her."

Adam took a step back and looked at the gate. "I know. I need to find her. I'm really worried."

"She'll be okay. She did this once before, and everything worked out." Joyce was suddenly in a hurry to get inside. "If I hear something, I'll let you know."

"Please do. I'm staying at her place."

"I know."

Adam thanked her, and drove away. By nine, he was at the office, buried in paper.

COLONEL NUGENT sat at the end of a long table in the front of a room filled with guards and staff people. The table was on a slight platform twelve inches above the rest of the room, and behind it on the wall was a large chalkboard. A portable podium sat in a corner. The chairs along the table to his right were empty, so that the guards and staff sitting in the folding chairs could see the faces of the more important ones on Nugent's left. Morris Henry from the Attorney General's office was there, thick briefs lying before him. Lucas Mann sat at the far end taking notes. Two assistant superintendents were next to Henry. A flunkie from the governor's office was next to Lucas.

Nugent glanced at his watch, then began his little pep talk. He referred to his notes, and aimed his comments at the guards and staff. "As of this morning, August 2, all stays have been lifted by the various courts, and there's nothing to stop the execution. We are proceeding as if it will take place as planned, at one minute after midnight next Wednesday. We have six

full days to prepare, and I am determined for this thing
to take place smoothly, without a hitch.

"The inmate has at least three petitions and appeals
currently working their way through the various
courts, and, of course, there's no way to predict what
might happen. We are in constant contact with the Attorney General's office. In fact, Mr. Morris Henry is
here with us today. It is his opinion, and an opinion
shared by Mr. Lucas Mann, that this thing will go
down to the wire. A stay could be granted at any moment, but that looks doubtful. We have to be ready
regardless. The inmate is also expected to request a
clemency hearing from the governor, but, frankly, that
is not expected to be successful. From now until next
Wednesday, we will be in a state of preparedness."

Nugent's words were strong and clear. He had center stage, and was obviously enjoying every moment of
it. He glanced at his notes, and continued. "The gas
chamber itself is being prepared. It's old and it hasn't
been used in two years, so we're being very careful
with it. A representative of the manufacturer arrives
this morning, and will conduct tests today and tonight.
We'll go through a complete rehearsal of the execution
over the weekend, probably Sunday night, assuming
there's no stay. I have collected the lists of volunteers
for the execution team, and I'll make that determination this afternoon.

"Now, we're being inundated with requests from the
media for all sorts of things. They want to interview
Mr. Cayhall, his lawyer, our lawyer, the warden, the
guards, other inmates on the row, the executioner, everybody. They want to witness the execution. They
want pictures of his cell and the chamber. Typical media silliness. But we must deal with it. There is to be no
contact with any member of the press unless I first approve it. That goes for every employee of this institu-

tion. No exceptions. Most of these reporters are not from around here, and they get their jollies making us look like a bunch of ignorant rednecks. So don't talk to them. No exceptions. I'll issue the appropriate releases when I deem necessary. Be careful with these people. They're vultures.

"We're also expecting trouble from the outside. As of about ten minutes ago, the first group of Ku Klux Klansmen arrived at the front gate. They were directed to the usual spot between the highway and the administration building where the protests take place. We've also heard that other such groups will be here shortly, and it appears as if they plan to protest until this thing is over. We'll watch them closely. They have the right to do this, so long as it's peaceful. Though I wasn't here for the last four executions, I've been told that groups of death penalty supporters usually show up and raise hell. We plan to keep these two groups separated, for obvious reasons."

Nugent couldn't sit any longer, and stood stiffly at the end of the table. All eyes were on him. He studied his notes for a second.

"This execution will be different because of Mr. Cayhall's notoriety. It will attract a lot of attention, a lot of media, a lot of other loonies. We must act professionally at all times, and I will not tolerate any breach of the rules of conduct. Mr. Cayhall and his family are entitled to respect during these last few days. No off-color comments about the gas chamber or the execution. I will not stand for it. Any questions?"

Nugent surveyed the room and was quite pleased with himself. He'd covered it all. No questions. "Very well. We'll meet again in the morning at nine." He dismissed them, and the room emptied hurriedly.

* * *

GARNER GOODMAN caught Professor John Bryan
Glass as he was leaving his office and heading for a
lecture. The class was forgotten as the two stood in the
hallway and swapped compliments. Glass had read all
of Goodman's books, and Goodman had read most of
Glass's recent articles condemning the death penalty.
The conversation quickly turned to the Cayhall mess,
and specifically to Goodman's pressing need for a
handful of trustworthy law students who could assist
with a quick research project over the weekend. Glass
offered his help, and the two agreed to have lunch in a
few hours to pursue the matter.

Three blocks from the Mississippi College School of
Law, Goodman found the small and cramped offices of
Southern Capital Defense Group, a quasi federal
agency with small, cramped offices in every state in the
Death Belt. The director was a young, black, Yale-edu-
cated lawyer named Hez Kerry, who had forsaken the
riches of the big firms and dedicated his life to abolish-
ing the death penalty. Goodman had met him on two
prior occasions at conferences. Though Kerry's Group,
as it was referred to, did not directly represent every
inmate on death row, it did have the responsibility of
monitoring every case. Hez was thirty-one years old
and aging quickly. The gray hair was evidence of the
pressure of forty-seven men on death row.

On a wall above the secretary's desk in the foyer was
a small calendar, and across the top of it someone had
printed the words BIRTHDAYS ON DEATH ROW.
Everybody got a card, nothing more. The budget was
tight, and the cards were usually purchased with
pocket change collected around the office.

The group had two lawyers working under Kerry's
supervision, and only one full-time secretary. A few
students from the law school worked several hours a
week, for free.

Goodman talked with Hez Kerry for more than an hour. They planned their movements for next Tuesday —Kerry himself would camp out at the clerk's office at the Mississippi Supreme Court. Goodman would stay at the governor's office. John Bryan Glass would be recruited to sit in the Fifth Circuit's satellite office in the federal courthouse in Jackson. One of Goodman's former associates at Kravitz & Bane now worked in Washington, and he had already agreed to wait at the Death Clerk's desk. Adam would be left to sit on the Row with the client and coordinate the last minute calls.

Kerry agreed to participate in Goodman's market analysis project over the weekend.

At eleven, Goodman returned to the governor's office in the state capitol, and handed to Lawyer Larramore a written request for a clemency hearing. The governor was out of the office, very busy these days, and he, Larramore, would see him just after lunch. Goodman left his phone number at the Millsaps-Buie House, and said he would call in periodically.

He then drove to his new office, now supplied with the finest rental furniture available on two months' lease, cash of course. The folding chairs were leftovers from a church fellowship hall, according to the markings under the seats. The rickety tables too had seen their share of potluck suppers and wedding receptions.

Goodman admired his hastily assembled little hole-in-the-wall. He took a seat, and on a new cellular phone he called his secretary in Chicago, Adam's office in Memphis, his wife at home, and the governor's hotline.

BY 4 P.M. Thursday, the Mississippi Supreme Court still had not denied the claim based on Sam's alleged mental incompetence. Almost thirty hours had passed since Adam filed it. He'd made a nuisance of himself calling the court's clerk. He was tired of explaining the obvious—he needed an answer, please. There was not the slightest trace of optimism that the court was actually considering the merits of the claim. The court, in Adam's opinion, was dragging its feet and delaying his rush to federal court. At this point, relief in the state supreme court was impossible, he felt.

He wasn't exactly on a roll in the federal courts either. The U.S. Supreme Court had not ruled on his request to consider the claim that the gas chamber was unconstitutional. The Fifth Circuit was sitting on his ineffectiveness of counsel claim.

Nothing was moving on Thursday. The courts were just sitting there as if these were ordinary lawsuits to be filed and assigned and docketed, then continued and delayed for years. He needed action, preferably a stay granted at some level, or if not a stay then an oral argument, or a hearing on the merits, or even a denial so he could move on to the next court.

He paced around the table in his office and listened for the phone. He was tired of pacing and sick of the phone. The office was littered with the debris of a dozen briefs. The table was blanketed with disheveled piles of paper. Pink and yellow phone messages were stuck along one bookshelf.

Adam suddenly hated the place. He needed fresh air. He told Darlene he was going for a walk, and left the building. It was almost five, still bright and very warm. He walked to the Peabody Hotel on Union, and had a drink in a corner of the lobby near the piano. It was his first drink since Friday in New Orleans, and although he enjoyed it he worried about Lee. He looked for her in the crowd of conventioneers flocking around the registration desk. He watched the tables in the lobby fill up with well-dressed people, hoping that for some reason she would appear. Where do you hide when you're fifty years old and running from life?

A man with a ponytail and hiking boots stopped and stared, then walked over. "Excuse me, sir. Are you Adam Hall, the lawyer for Sam Cayhall?"

Adam nodded.

The man smiled, obviously pleased that he'd recognized Adam, and walked to his table. "I'm Kirk Kleckner with the *New York Times*." He laid a business card in front of Adam. "I'm here covering the Cayhall execution. Just arrived, actually. May I sit down?"

Adam waved at the empty seat across the small round table. Kleckner sat down. "Lucky to find you here," he said, all smiles. He was in his early forties with a rugged, globe-trotting journalist look—scruffy beard, sleeveless cotton vest over a denim shirt, jeans. "Recognized you from some pictures I studied on the flight down."

"Nice to meet you," Adam said dryly.

"Can we talk?"

"About what?"

"Oh, lots of things. I understand your client will not give interviews."

"That's correct."

"What about you?"

"The same. We can chat, but nothing for the record."

"That makes it difficult."

"I honestly don't care. I'm not concerned with how difficult your job may be."

"Fair enough." A pliant young waitress in a short skirt stopped by long enough to take his order. Black coffee. "When did you last see your grandfather?"

"Tuesday."

"When will you see him again?"

"Tomorrow."

"How is he holding up?"

"He's surviving. The pressure is building, but he's taking it well, so far."

"What about you?"

"Just having a ball."

"Seriously. Are you losing sleep, you know, things like that?"

"I'm tired. Yeah, I'm losing sleep. I'm working lots of hours, running back and forth to the prison. It'll go down to the wire, so the next few days will be hectic."

"I covered the Bundy execution in Florida. Quite a circus. His lawyers went days without sleep."

"It's difficult to relax."

"Will you do it again? I know this is not your specialty, but will you consider another death case?"

"Only if I find another relative on death row. Why do you cover these things?"

"I've written for years on the death penalty. It's fascinating. I'd like to interview Mr. Cayhall."

Adam shook his head and finished his drink. "No. There's no way. He's not talking to anyone."

"Will you ask him for me?"

"No."

The coffee arrived. Kleckner stirred it with a spoon. Adam watched the crowd. "I interviewed Benjamin Keyes yesterday in Washington," Kleckner said. "He said he wasn't surprised that you're now saying he made mistakes at trial. He said he figured it was coming."

At the moment, Adam didn't care about Benjamin Keyes or any of his opinions. "It's standard. I need to run. Nice to meet you."

"But I wanted to talk about—"

"Listen, you're lucky you caught me," Adam said, standing abruptly.

"Just a couple of things," Kleckner said as Adam walked away.

Adam left the Peabody, and strolled to Front Street near the river, passing along the way scores of well-dressed young people very much like himself, all in a hurry to go home. He envied them; whatever their vocations or careers, whatever their pressures at the moment, they weren't carrying burdens as heavy as his.

He ate a sandwich at a delicatessen, and by seven was back in his office.

THE RABBIT had been trapped in the woods at Parchman by two of the guards, who named him Sam for the occasion. He was a brown cottontail, the largest of the four captured. The other three had already been eaten.

Late Thursday night, Sam the rabbit and his handlers, along with Colonel Nugent and the execution team, entered the Maximum Security Unit in prison vans and pickups. They drove slowly by the front and around the bullpens on the west end. They parked by a square redbrick building attached to the southwest corner of MSU.

Two white metal doors without windows led to the interior of the square building. One, facing south, opened to a narrow room, eight feet by fifteen, where the witnesses sat during the execution. They faced a series of black drapes that, when opened, revealed the rear of the chamber itself, just inches away.

The other door opened into the Chamber Room, a fifteen-by-twelve room with a painted concrete floor. The octagonal-shaped gas chamber sat squarely in the middle, glowing smartly from a fresh coat of silver enamel varnish and smelling like the same. Nugent had inspected it a week earlier and ordered a new paint job. The death room, as it was also known, was spotless and sanitized. The black drapes over the windows behind the chamber were pulled.

Sam the rabbit was left in the bed of a pickup while a small guard, about the same height and weight as Sam Cayhall, was led by two of his larger colleagues into the Chamber Room. Nugent strutted and inspected like General Patton—pointing and nodding and frowning. The small guard was pushed gently into the chamber first, then joined by the two guards who turned him around and eased him into the wooden chair. Without a word or a smile, neither a grin nor a joke, they strapped his wrists first with leather bands to the arms of the chair. Then his knees, then his ankles. Then one lifted his head up an inch or two and held it in place while the other managed to buckle the leather head strap.

The two guards stepped carefully from the chamber, and Nugent pointed to another member of the team, who stepped forward as if to say something to the condemned.

"At this point, Lucas Mann will read the death warrant to Mr. Cayhall," Nugent explained like an amateur movie director. "Then I will ask if he has any last words." He pointed again, and a designated guard closed the heavy door to the chamber and sealed it.

"Open it," Nugent barked, and the door came open. The small guard was set free.

"Get the rabbit," Nugent ordered. One of the handlers retrieved Sam the rabbit from the pickup. He sat innocently in a wire cage that was handed to the same two guards who'd just left the chamber. They carefully placed him in the wooden chair, then went about their task of strapping in an imaginary man. Wrists, knees, ankles, head, and the rabbit was ready for the gas. The two guards left the chamber.

The door was shut and sealed, and Nugent signaled

for the executioner, who placed a canister of sulfuric acid into a tube that ran into the bottom of the chamber. He pulled a lever, a clicking sound occurred, and the canister made its way to the bowl under the chair.

Nugent stepped to one of the windows and watched intently. The other members of the team did likewise. Petroleum jelly had been smeared around the edges of the windows to prevent seepage.

The poisonous gas was released slowly, and a faint mist of visible vapors rose from under the chair and drifted upward. At first, the rabbit didn't react to the steam that permeated his little cell, but it hit him soon enough. He stiffened, then hopped a few times, banging into the sides of his cage; then he went into violent convulsions, jumping and jerking and twisting frantically. In less than a minute, he was still.

Nugent smiled as he glanced at his watch. "Clear it," he ordered, and a vent at the top of the chamber was opened, releasing the gas.

The door from the Chamber Room to the outside was opened, and most of the execution team walked out for fresh air or a smoke. It would be at least fifteen minutes before the chamber could be opened and the rabbit removed. Then they had to hose it down and clean up. Nugent was still inside, watching everything. So they smoked and had a few laughs.

Less than sixty feet away, the windows above the hallway of Tier A were open. Sam could hear their voices. It was after ten and the lights were off, but in every cell along the tier two arms protruded from the bars as fourteen men listened in dark silence.

A death row inmate lives in a six-by-nine cell for twenty-three hours a day. He hears everything—the strange clicking sound of a new pair of boots in the hallway; the unfamiliar pitch and accent of a different voice; the faraway hum of a lawn mower or weedeater.

And he can certainly hear the opening and closing of the door to the Chamber Room. He can hear the satisfied and important chuckles of the execution team.

Sam leaned on his forearms and watched the windows above the hallway. They were practicing for him out there.

FORTY

BETWEEN THE WESTERN EDGE of Highway 49 and the front lawn of the administrative buildings of Parchman, a distance of fifty yards, there was a grassy strip of land that was smooth and noticeable because it was once a railroad track. It was where the death penalty protestors were corralled and monitored at every execution. They invariably arrived, usually small groups of committed souls who sat in folding chairs and held homemade placards. They burned candles at night and sang hymns during the final hours. They sang hymns, offered prayers, and wept when the death was announced.

A new twist had occurred during the hours preceding the execution of Teddy Doyle Meeks, a child rapist and killer. The somber, almost sacred protest had been disrupted by carloads of unruly college students who suddenly appeared without warning and had a delightful time demanding blood. They drank beer and played loud music. They chanted slogans and heckled the shaken death protestors. The situation deteriorated as the two groups exchanged words. Prison officials moved in and restored order.

Maynard Tole was next, and during the planning of his execution another section of turf on the other side of the main drive was designated for the death penalty proponents. Extra security was assigned to keep things peaceful.

When Adam arrived Friday morning, he counted seven Ku Klux Klansmen in white robes. Three were engaged in some attempt at synchronized protest, a casual walking along the edge of the grassy strip near the highway with posters strung over their shoulders. The other four were erecting a large blue and white canopy. Metal poles and ropes were scattered on the ground. Two ice chests sat next to several lawn chairs. These guys were planning to stay awhile.

Adam stared at them as he rolled to a stop at the front gate of Parchman. He lost track of time as he watched the Kluckers for minutes. So this was his heritage, his roots. These were the brethren of his grandfather and his grandfather's relatives and ancestors. Were some of these figures the same ones who'd been recorded on film and edited by Adam into the video about Sam Cayhall? Had he seen them before?

Impulsively Adam opened the door of his car and got out. His coat and briefcase were in the rear seat. He began walking slowly in their direction, and stopped near their ice chests. Their placards demanded freedom for Sam Cayhall, a political prisoner. Gas the real criminals, but release Sam. For some reason, Adam was not comforted by their demands.

"What do you want?" demanded one with a sign draped over his chest. The other six stopped what they were doing and stared.

"I don't know," Adam said truthfully.

"Then what are you looking at?"

"I'm not sure."

Three others joined the first, and they stepped together near Adam. Their robes were identical—white and made of a very light fabric with red crosses and other markings. It was almost 9 A.M., and they were already sweating. "Who the hell are you?"

"Sam's grandson."

The other three crowded behind the others, and all

seven examined Adam from a distance of no more than five feet. "Then you're on our side," one said, relieved.

"No. I'm not one of you."

"That's right. He's with that bunch of Jews from Chicago," another said for the edification of the rest, and this seemed to stir them up a bit.

"Why are you people here?" Adam asked.

"We're trying to save Sam. Looks like you're not gonna do it."

"You're the reason he's here."

A young one with a red face and rows of sweat on his forehead took the lead and walked even closer to Adam. "No. He's the reason we're here. I wasn't even born when Sam killed those Jews, so you can't blame it on me. We're here to protest his execution. He's being persecuted for political reasons."

"He wouldn't be here had it not been for the Klan. Where are your masks? I thought you people always hid your faces."

They twitched and fidgeted as a group, uncertain what to do next. He was, after all, the grandson of Sam Cayhall, their idol and champion. He was the lawyer trying to save a most precious symbol.

"Why don't you leave?" Adam asked. "Sam doesn't want you here."

"Why don't you go to hell?" the young one sneered.

"How eloquent. Just leave, okay. Sam's worth much more to you dead than alive. Let him die in peace, then you'll have a wonderful martyr."

"We ain't leavin'. We'll be here till the end."

"And what if Sam asks you to leave? Will you go then?"

"No," he sneered again, then glanced over his shoulders at the others who all seemed to agree that they would, in fact, not leave. "We plan to make a lot of noise."

"Great. That'll get your pictures in the papers. That's what this is about, isn't it? Circus clowns in funny costumes always attract attention."

Car doors slammed somewhere behind Adam, and as he looked around he saw a television crew making a speedy exit from a van parked near his Saab.

"Well, well," he said to the group. "Smile, fellas. This is your big moment."

"Go to hell," the young one snapped angrily. Adam turned his back to them and walked toward his car. A hurried reporter with a cameraman in tow rushed to him.

"Are you Adam Hall?" she asked breathlessly. "Cayhall's lawyer?"

"Yes," he said without stopping.

"Could we have a few words?"

"No. But those boys are anxious to talk," he said, pointing over his shoulder. She walked along beside him while the cameraman fumbled with his equipment. Adam opened his car door, then slammed it as he turned the ignition.

Louise, the guard at the gate, handed him a numbered card for his dashboard, then waved him through.

PACKER WENT THROUGH the motions of the obligatory frisk inside the front door of the Row. "What's in there?" he asked, pointing to the small cooler Adam held in his left hand.

"Eskimo Pies, Sergeant. Would you like one?"

"Lemme see." Adam handed the cooler to Packer, who flipped open the top just long enough to count half a dozen Eskimo Pies, still frozen under a layer of ice.

He handed the cooler back to Adam, and pointed to the door of the front office, a few feet away. "Y'all will be meetin' in here from now on," he explained. They stepped into the room.

"Why?" Adam asked as he looked around the room. There was a metal desk with a phone, three chairs, and two locked file cabinets.

"That's just the way we do things. We lighten up some as the big day gets close. Sam gets to have his visitors here. No time limit either."

"How sweet." Adam placed his briefcase on the desk and picked up the phone. Packer left to fetch Sam.

The kind lady in the clerk's office in Jackson informed Adam that the Mississippi Supreme Court had denied, just minutes ago, his client's petition for postconviction relief on the grounds that he was mentally incompetent. He thanked her, said something to the effect that this was what he expected and that it could've been done a day earlier, then asked her to fax a copy of the court's decision to his office in Memphis, and also to Lucas Mann's office at Parchman. He called Darlene in Memphis and told her to fax the new petition to the federal district court, with copies faxed to the Fifth Circuit and to Mr. Richard Olander's rather busy death desk at the Supreme Court in Washington. He called Mr. Olander to inform him it was coming, and was told that the U.S. Supreme Court had just denied cert on Adam's claim that the gas chamber was unconstitutional.

Sam entered the front office without handcuffs while Adam was on the phone. They shook hands quickly, and Sam took a seat. Instead of a cigarette, he opened the cooler and removed an Eskimo Pie. He ate it slowly while listening as Adam talked with Olander. "U.S. Supreme Court just denied cert," Adam whispered to Sam with his hand over the receiver.

Sam smiled oddly and studied some envelopes he'd brought with him.

"The Mississippi Supreme Court also turned us down," Adam explained to his client as he punched more numbers. "But that was to be expected. We're filing it in federal court right now." He was calling the Fifth Circuit to check the status of the ineffective counsel claim. The clerk in New Orleans informed him that no action had been taken that morning. Adam hung up and sat on the edge of the desk.

"Fifth Circuit is still sitting on the ineffectiveness claim," he reported to his client, who knew the law and the procedure and was absorbing it like a learned attorney. "All in all, not a very good morning."

"The Jackson TV station this morning said I've requested a clemency hearing from the governor," Sam said, between bites. "Certainly this can't be true. I didn't approve it."

"Relax, Sam. It's routine."

"Routine my ass. I thought we had an agreement. They even had McAllister on the tube talking about how he was grieving over his decision about a clemency hearing. I warned you."

"McAllister is the least of our problems, Sam. The request was a formality. We don't have to participate."

Sam shook his head in frustration. Adam watched him closely. He wasn't really angry, nor did he really care what Adam had done. He was resigned, almost defeated. The little bit of bitching came naturally. A week earlier he would've lashed out.

"They practiced last night, you know. They cranked up the gas chamber, killed a rat or something, everything worked perfectly and so now everyone's excited about my execution. Can you believe it? They had a dress rehearsal for me. The bastards."

"I'm sorry, Sam."

"Do you know what cyanide gas smells like?"

"No."

"Cinnamon. It was in the air last night. The idiots didn't bother to close the windows on our tier, and I got a whiff of it."

Adam didn't know if this was true or not. He knew the chamber was vented for several minutes after an execution and the gas escaped into the air. Surely it couldn't filter onto the tiers. Maybe Sam had heard stories about the gas from the guards. Maybe it was just part of the lore. He sat on the edge of the desk, casually swinging his feet, staring at the pitiful old man with the skinny arms and oily hair. It was such a horrible sin to kill an aged creature like Sam Cayhall. His crimes were committed a generation ago. He had suffered and died many times in his six-by-nine cell. How would the state benefit by killing him now?

Adam had things on his mind, not the least of which was perhaps their last gasping effort. "I'm sorry, Sam," he said again, very compassionately. "But we need to talk about some items."

"Were there Klansmen outside this morning? The television had a shot of them here yesterday."

"Yes. I counted seven a few minutes ago. Full uniforms except for the masks."

"I used to wear one of those, you know," he said, much like a war veteran bragging to little boys.

"I know, Sam. And because you wore one, you're now sitting here on death row with your lawyer counting the hours before they strap you in the gas chamber. You should hate those silly fools out there."

"I don't hate them. But they have no right to be here. They abandoned me. Dogan sent me here, and when he testified against me he was the Imperial Wizard of Mississippi. They gave me not one dime for legal fees. They forgot about me."

"What do you expect from a bunch of thugs? Loyalty?"

"I was loyal."

"And look where you are, Sam. You should denounce the Klan and ask them to leave, to stay away from your execution."

Sam fiddled with his envelopes, then placed them carefully in a chair.

"I told them to leave," Adam said.

"When?"

"Just a few minutes ago. I exchanged words with them. They don't give a damn about you, Sam, they're just using this execution because you'll make such a marvelous martyr, someone to rally around and talk about for years to come. They'll chant your name when they burn crosses, and they'll make pilgrimages to your gravesite. They want you dead, Sam. It's great PR."

"You confronted them?" Sam asked, with a trace of amusement and pride.

"Yeah. It was no big deal. What about Carmen? If she's coming, she needs to make travel arrangements."

Sam took a thoughtful puff. "I'd like to see her, but you've gotta warn her about my appearance. I don't want her to be shocked."

"You look great, Sam."

"Gee thanks. What about Lee?"

"What about her?"

"How's she doing? We get newspapers in here. I saw her in the Memphis paper last Sunday, then I read about her drunk driving charge on Tuesday. She's not in jail, is she?"

"No. She's in a rehab clinic," Adam said as if he knew exactly where she was.

"Can she come visit?"

"Do you want her to?"

"I think so. Maybe on Monday. Let's wait and see."

"No problem," Adam said, wondering how in the

world he could find her. "I'll talk to her over the weekend."

Sam handed Adam one of the envelopes, unsealed. "Give this to the people up front. It's a list of approved visitors from now until then. Go ahead, open it."

Adam looked at the list. There were four names. Adam, Lee, Carmen, and Donnie Cayhall. "Not a very long list."

"I have lots of relatives, but I don't want them here. They haven't visited me in nine and a half years, so I'll be damned if they'll come draggin' in here at the last minute to say good-bye. They can save it for the funeral."

"I'm getting all kinds of requests from reporters and journalists for interviews."

"Forget it."

"That's what I've told them. But there's one inquiry that might interest you. There's a man named Wendall Sherman, an author of some repute who's published four or five books and won some awards. I haven't read any of his work, but he checks out. He's legitimate. I talked to him yesterday by phone, and he wants to sit with you and record your story. He seemed to be very honest, and said that the recording could take hours. He's flying to Memphis today, just in case you say yes."

"Why does he want to record me?"

"He wants to write a book about you."

"A romance novel?"

"I doubt it. He's willing to pay fifty thousand dollars up front, with a percentage of the royalties later on."

"Great. I get fifty thousand a few days before I die. What shall I do with it?"

"I'm just relaying the offer."

"Tell him to go to hell. I'm not interested."

"Fine."

"I want you to draw up an agreement whereby I assign all rights to my life story to you, and after I'm gone you do whatever the hell you want with it."

"It wouldn't be a bad idea to record it."

"You mean—"

"Talk into a little machine with little tapes. I can get one for you. Sit in your cell and talk about your life."

"How boring." Sam finished the Eskimo Pie and tossed the stick in the wastebasket.

"Depends on how you look at it. Things seem rather exciting now."

"Yeah, you're right. A pretty dull life, but the end was sensational."

"Sounds like a best seller to me."

"I'll think about it."

Sam suddenly jumped to his feet, leaving the rubber shower shoes under his chair. He loped across the office in long strides, measuring and smoking as he went. "Thirteen by sixteen and a half," he mumbled to himself, then measured some more.

Adam made notes on a legal pad and tried to ignore the red figure bouncing off the walls. Sam finally stopped and leaned on a file cabinet. "I want you to do me a favor," he said, staring at a wall across the room. His voice was much lower. He breathed slowly.

"I'm listening," Adam said.

Sam took a step to the chair and picked up an envelope. He handed it to Adam and returned to his position against the file cabinet. The envelope was turned over so that Adam could not see the writing on it.

"I want you to deliver that," Sam said.

"To whom?"

"Quince Lincoln."

Adam placed it to his side on the desk, and watched Sam carefully. Sam, however, was lost in another world. His tired eyes stared blankly at something on the wall across the room. "I've worked on it for a week," he said, his voice almost hoarse, "but I've thought about it for forty years."

"What's in the letter?" Adam asked slowly.

"An apology. I've carried the guilt for many years, Adam. Joe Lincoln was a good and decent man, a good father. I lost my head and killed him for no reason. And I knew before I shot him that I could get by with it. I've always felt bad about it. Real bad. There's nothing I can do now except say that I'm sorry."

"I'm sure it'll mean something to the Lincolns."

"Maybe. In the letter I ask them for forgiveness, which I believe is the Christian way of doing things. When I die, I'd like to have the knowledge that I tried to say I'm sorry."

"Any idea where I might find him?"

"That's the hard part. I've heard through family that the Lincolns are still in Ford County. Ruby, his widow, is probably still alive. I'm afraid you'll just have to go to Clanton and start asking questions. They have an African sheriff, so I'd start with him. He probably knows all the Africans in the county."

"And if I find Quince?"

"Tell him who you are. Give him the letter. Tell him that I died with a lot of guilt. Can you do that?"

"I'll be happy to. I'm not sure when I can do it."

"Wait until I'm dead. You'll have plenty of time once this is over."

Sam again walked to the chair, and this time picked up two envelopes. He handed them to Adam, and began pacing slowly, back and forth across the room. The name of Ruth Kramer was typed on one, no address, and Elliot Kramer on the other. "Those are for the Kramers. Deliver them, but wait until the execution is over."

"Why wait?"

"Because my motives are pure. I don't want them to think I'm doing this to arouse sympathy in my dying hours."

Adam placed the Kramer letters next to Quince Lincoln's—three letters, three dead bodies. How many more letters would Sam crank out over the weekend? How many more victims were out there?

"You're sure you're about to die, aren't you, Sam?"

He stopped by the door and pondered this for a moment. "The odds are against us. I'm getting prepared."

"We still have a chance."

"Sure we do. But I'm getting ready, just in case. I've hurt a lot of people, Adam, and I haven't always stopped to think about it. But when you have a date with the grim reaper, you think about the damage you've done."

Adam picked up the three envelopes and looked at them. "Are there others?"

Sam grimaced and looked at the floor. "That's all, for now."

THE JACKSON PAPER on Friday morning carried a front-page story about Sam Cayhall's request for a clemency hearing. The story included a slick photo of Governor David McAllister, a bad one of Sam, and lots of self-serving comments by Mona Stark, the governor's chief of staff, all to the effect that the governor was struggling with the decision.

Since he was a real man of the people, a regular servant to all Mississippians, McAllister had installed an expensive telephone hotline system shortly after he was elected. The toll-free number was plastered all over the state, and his constituents were constantly barraged with public service ads to use the People's Hotline. Call the governor. He cared about your opinions. Democracy at its finest. Operators were standing by.

And because he had more ambition than fortitude, McAllister and his staff tracked the phone calls on a daily basis. He was a follower, not a leader. He spent serious money on polls, and had proven adept at quietly discovering the issues that bothered people, then jumping out front to lead the parade.

Both Goodman and Adam suspected this. McAllister seemed too obsessed with his destiny to launch new initiatives. The man was a shameless vote-counter, so they had decided to give him something to count.

Goodman read the story early, over coffee and fruit, and by seven-thirty was on the phone with Professor John Bryan Glass and Hez Kerry. By eight, three of Glass's students were sipping coffee from paper cups in the grungy temporary office. The marketing analysis was about to begin.

Goodman explained the scheme and the need for secrecy. They were breaking no laws, he assured them, just manipulating public opinion. The cellular phones were on the tables, along with pages of phone numbers Goodman had copied on Wednesday. The students were a little apprehensive, but nonetheless anxious to begin. They would be paid well. Goodman demonstrated the technique with the first call. He dialed the number.

"People's Hotline," a pleasant voice answered.

"Yes, I'm calling about the story in this morning's paper, the one about Sam Cayhall," Goodman said slowly in his best imitation of a drawl. It left a lot to be desired. The students were very amused.

"And your name is?"

"Yes, I'm Ned Lancaster, from Biloxi, Mississippi," Goodman replied, reading from the phone lists. "And I voted for the governor, a fine man," he threw in for good measure.

"And how do you feel about Sam Cayhall?"

"I don't think he should be executed. He's an old man who's suffered a lot, and I want the governor to give him a pardon. Let him die in peace up there at Parchman."

"Okay. I'll make sure the governor knows about your call."

"Thank you."

Goodman pushed a button on the phone, and took a bow before his audience. "Nothing to it. Let's get started."

The white male selected a phone number. His conversation went something like this: "Hello, this is Lester Crosby, from Bude, Mississippi. I'm calling about the execution of Sam Cayhall. Yes ma'am. My number? It's 555-9084. Yes, that's right, Bude, Mississippi, down here in Franklin County. That's right. Well, I don't think Sam Cayhall ought to be sent to the gas chamber. I'm just opposed to it. I think the governor should step in and stop this thing. Yes ma'am, that's right. Thank you." He smiled at Goodman, who was punching another number.

The white female was a middle-aged student. She was from a small town in a rural section of the state, and her accent was naturally twangy. "Hello, is this the governor's office? Good. I'm calling about the Cayhall story in today's paper. Susan Barnes. Decatur, Mississippi. That's right. Well, he's an old man who'll probably die in a few years anyway. What good will it do for the state to kill him now? Give the guy a break. What? Yes, I want the governor to stop it. I voted for the governor, and I think he's a fine man. Yes. Thank you too."

The black male was in his late twenties. He simply informed the hotline operator that he was a black Mississippian, very much opposed to the ideas Sam Cayhall and the Klan promoted, but nonetheless opposed to the execution. "The government does not have the right to determine if someone lives or dies," he said. He did not favor the death penalty under any circumstances.

And so it went. The calls poured in from all over the state, one after the other, each from a different person with a different logic for stopping the execution. The students became creative, trying assorted accents and novel reasonings. Occasionally, their calls would hit busy signals, and it was amusing to know that they had jammed the hotline. Because of his crisp accent, Goodman assumed the role of the outsider, sort of a traveling death penalty abolitionist who bounced in from all over the country with a dazzling array of ethnic aliases and strange locales.

Goodman had worried that McAllister might be paranoid enough to trace the calls to his hotline, but had decided that the operators would be too busy.

And busy they were. Across town, John Bryan Glass canceled a class and locked the door to his office. He had a delightful time making repeated calls under all sorts of names. Not far from him, Hez Kerry and one of his staff attorneys were also bombarding the hotline with the same messages.

ADAM HURRIED to Memphis. Darlene was in his office, trying vainly to organize the mountain of paperwork. She pointed to a stack nearest his computer. "The decision denying cert is on top, then the decision from the Mississippi Supreme Court. Next to it is the petition for writ of habeas corpus to be filed in federal district court. I've already faxed everything."

Adam removed his jacket and threw it on a chair. He looked at a row of pink telephone messages tacked to a bookshelf. "Who are these people?"

"Reporters, writers, quacks, a couple are other lawyers offering their assistance. One is from Garner Goodman in Jackson. He said the market analysis is going fine, don't call. What is the market analysis?"

"Don't ask. No word from the Fifth Circuit?"

"No."

Adam took a deep breath and eased into his chair.

"Lunch?" she asked.

"Just a sandwich, if you don't mind. Can you work tomorrow and Sunday?"

"Of course."

"I need for you to stay here all weekend, by the phone and the fax. I'm sorry."

"I don't mind. I'll get a sandwich."

She left, closing the door behind her. Adam called Lee's condo, and there was no answer. He called the Auburn House, but no one had heard from her. He called Phelps Booth, who was in a board meeting. He called Carmen in Berkeley and told her to make arrangements to fly to Memphis on Sunday.

He looked at the phone messages, and decided none were worth returning.

AT ONE O'CLOCK, Mona Stark spoke to the press loitering around the governor's office in the capitol. She said that after much deliberation, the governor had decided to grant a clemency hearing on Monday at 10 A.M., at which time the governor would listen to the issues and appeals, and make a fair decision. It was an awesome responsibility, she explained, this weighing of life or death. But David McAllister would do what was just and right.

FORTY-ONE

PACKER WENT TO THE CELL at five-thirty Saturday morning, and didn't bother with the handcuffs. Sam was waiting, and they quietly left Tier A. They walked through the kitchen where the trustees were scrambling eggs and frying bacon. Sam had never seen the kitchen, and he walked slowly, counting his steps, checking the dimensions. Packer opened a door and motioned for Sam to hurry and follow. They stepped outside, into the darkness. Sam stopped and looked at the square brick room to his right, the little building that housed the gas chamber. Packer pulled his elbow, and they walked together to the east end of the row where another guard was watching and waiting. The guard handed Sam a large cup of coffee, and led him through a gate into a recreation yard similar to the bullpens on the west end of the Row. It was fenced and wired, with a basketball goal and two benches. Packer said he would return in an hour, and left with the guard.

Sam stood in place for a long time, sipping the hot coffee and absorbing the landscape. His first cell had been on Tier D, on the east wing, and he'd been here many times before. He knew the exact dimensions— fifty-one feet by thirty-six. He saw the guard in the tower sitting under a light and watching him. Through the fences and over the tops of the rows of cotton, he could see the lights of other buildings. He slowly walked to a bench and sat down.

How thoughtful of these kind people to grant his

request to see one final sunrise. He hadn't seen one in nine and a half years, and at first Nugent said no. Then Packer intervened, and explained to the colonel that it was okay, no security risk at all, and what the hell, the man was supposed to die in four days. Packer would take responsibility for it.

Sam stared at the eastern sky, where a hint of orange was peeking through scattered clouds. During his early days on the Row, when his appeals were fresh and unresolved, he had spent hours remembering the glorious humdrum of everyday life, the little things like a warm shower every day, the companionship of his dog, extra honey on his biscuits. He actually believed back then that one day he would again be able to hunt squirrels and quail, to fish for bass and bream, to sit on the porch and watch the sun come up, to drink coffee in town, and drive his old pickup wherever he wanted. His goal during those early fantasies on the Row had been to fly to California and find his grandchildren. He had never flown.

But the dreams of freedom had died long ago, driven away by the tedious monotony of life in a cell, and killed by the harsh opinions of many judges.

This would be his final sunrise, he truly believed that. Too many people wanted him dead. The gas chamber was not being used often enough. It was time for an execution, dammit, and he was next in line.

The sky grew brighter and the clouds dissipated. Though he was forced to watch this magnificent act of nature through a chain-link fence, it was satisfying nonetheless. Just a few more days and the fences would be gone. The bars and razor wire and prison cells would be left for someone else.

TWO REPORTERS smoked cigarettes and drank machine coffee as they waited by the south entrance to the capitol early Saturday morning. Word had been leaked that the governor would spend a long day at the office, struggling with the Cayhall thing.

At seven-thirty, his black Lincoln rolled to a stop nearby, and he made a quick exit from it. Two well-dressed bodyguards escorted him to the entrance, with Mona Stark a few steps behind.

"Governor, do you plan to attend the execution?" the first reporter asked hurriedly. McAllister smiled and raised his hands as if he'd love to stop and chat but things were much too critical for that. Then he saw a camera hanging from the other reporter's neck.

"I haven't made a decision yet," he answered, stopping just for a second.

"Will Ruth Kramer testify at the clemency hearing on Monday?"

The camera was raised and ready. "I can't say right now," he answered, smiling into the lens. "Sorry, guys, I can't talk now."

He entered the building and rode the elevator to his office on the second floor. The bodyguards assumed their positions in the foyer, behind morning newspapers.

Lawyer Larramore was waiting with his updates. He explained to the governor and Ms. Stark that there had been no changes in the various Cayhall petitions and appeals since 5 P.M. yesterday. Nothing had happened overnight. The appeals were becoming more desperate, and the courts would deny them more quickly, in his opinion. He had already spoken with Morris Henry at the AG's office, and, in the learned judgment of Dr. Death, there was now an 80 percent chance that the execution would take place.

"What about the clemency hearing on Monday? Any word from Cayhall's lawyers?" McAllister asked.

"No. I asked Garner Goodman to stop by at nine

this morning. Thought we'd talk to him about it. I'll be in my office if you need me."

Larramore excused himself. Ms. Stark was performing her morning ritual of scanning the dailies from around the state and placing them on the conference table. Of the nine papers she monitored, the Cayhall story was on the front page of eight. The announcement of a clemency hearing was of special interest Saturday morning. Three of the papers carried the same AP photo of the Klansmen roasting idly under the fierce August sun outside of Parchman.

McAllister removed his coat, rolled up his sleeves, and began peering over the papers. "Get the numbers," he said tersely.

Mona left the office, and returned in less than a minute. She carried a computer printout, which obviously bore dreadful news.

"I'm listening," he said.

"The calls stopped around nine last night, last one was at nine-o-seven. The total for the day was four hundred and eighty-six, and at least ninety percent voiced strong opposition to the execution."

"Ninety percent," McAllister said in disbelief. He was no longer in shock, though. By noon yesterday, the hotline operators had reported an unusual number of calls, and by one Mona was analyzing printouts. They had spent much of yesterday afternoon staring at the numbers, contemplating the next move. He had slept little.

"Who are these people?" he said, staring through a window.

"Your constituents. The calls are coming from all over the state. The names and numbers appear to be legitimate."

"What was the old record?"

"I don't know. Seems like we had around a hundred

one day when the legislature gave itself another pay raise. But nothing like this."

"Ninety percent," he mumbled again.

"And there's something else. There were lots of other calls to various numbers in this office. My secretary took a dozen or so."

"All for Sam, right?"

"Yes, all opposed to the execution. I've talked to some of our people, and everybody got nailed yesterday. And Roxburgh called me at home last night and said that his office had been besieged with calls against the execution."

"Good. I want him to sweat too."

"Do we close the hotline?"

"How many operators work on Saturday and Sunday?"

"Only one."

"No. Leave it open today. Let's see what happens today and tomorrow." He walked to another window and loosened his tie. "When does the polling start?"

"Three this afternoon."

"I'm anxious to see those numbers."

"They could be just as bad."

"Ninety percent," he said, shaking his head.

"Over ninety percent," Mona corrected him.

THE WAR ROOM was littered with pizza boxes and beer cans, evidence of a long day of market analysis. A tray of fresh doughnuts and a row of tall paper coffee cups now awaited the analysts, two of whom had just arrived with newspapers. Garner Goodman stood at the window with a new pair of binoculars, watching the capitol three blocks away, and paying particular attention to the windows of the governor's office. During a moment of boredom yesterday, he'd gone to a mall in search of a bookstore. He'd found the binoculars in the window of a leather shop, and throughout the afternoon they'd had great fun trying to catch the governor pondering through his windows, no doubt wondering where all those damned calls were coming from.

The students devoured the doughnuts and newspapers. There was a brief but serious discussion about some obvious procedural deficiencies in Mississippi's postconviction relief statutes. The third member of the shift, a first-year student from New Orleans, arrived at eight, and the calls started.

It was immediately apparent that the hotline was not as efficient as the day before. It was difficult to get through to an operator. No problem. They used alternate numbers—the switchboard at the governor's mansion, the lines to the cute little regional offices he'd established, amid great fanfare, around the state so that he, a common man, could stay close to the people.

The people were calling.

Goodman left the office and walked along Congress Street to the capitol. He heard the sounds of a loudspeaker being tested, and then saw the Klansmen. They were organizing themselves, at least a dozen in full parade dress, around the monument to Confederate women at the base of the front steps to the capitol. Goodman walked by them, actually said hello to one, so that when he returned to Chicago he could say he talked to some real Kluckers.

The two reporters who'd waited for the governor were now on the front steps watching the scene below. A local television crew arrived as Goodman entered the capitol.

The governor was too busy to meet with him, Mona Stark explained gravely, but Mr. Larramore could spare a few minutes. She looked a bit frazzled, and this pleased Goodman greatly. He followed her to Larramore's office where they found the lawyer on the phone. Goodman hoped it was one of his calls. He obediently took a seat. Mona closed the door and left them.

"Good morning," Larramore said as he hung up.

Goodman nodded politely, and said, "Thanks for the hearing. We didn't expect the governor to grant one, in light of what he said on Wednesday."

"He's under a lot of pressure. We all are. Is your client willing to talk about his accomplice?"

"No. There's been no change."

Larramore ran his fingers through his sticky hair and shook his head in frustration. "Then what's the purpose of a clemency hearing? The governor is not going to budge on this, Mr. Goodman."

"We're working on Sam, okay. We're talking to him. Let's plan on going through with the hearing on Monday. Maybe Sam will change his mind."

The phone rang and Larramore snatched it angrily. "No, this is not the governor's office. Who is this?" He scribbled down a name and phone number. "This is the governor's legal department." He closed his eyes and shook his head. "Yes, yes, I'm sure you voted for the governor." He listened some more. "Thank you, Mr. Hurt. I'll tell the governor you called. Yes, thanks."

He returned the receiver to the phone. "So, Mr. Gilbert Hurt from Dumas, Mississippi, is against the execution," he said, staring at the phone, dazed. "The phones have gone crazy."

"Lots of calls, huh?" Goodman asked, sympathetically.

"You wouldn't believe."

"For or against?"

"About fifty-fifty, I'd say," Larramore said. He took the phone again and punched in the number for Mr.

Gilbert Hurt of Dumas, Mississippi. No one answered. "This is strange," he said, hanging up again. "The man just called me, left a legitimate number, now there's no answer."

"Probably just stepped out. Try again later." Goodman hoped he wouldn't have the time to try again later. In the first hour of the market analysis yesterday, Goodman had made a slight change in technique. He had instructed his callers to first check the phone numbers to make certain there was no answer. This prevented some curious type such as Larramore or perhaps a nosy hotline operator from calling back and finding the real person. Odds were the real person would greatly support the death penalty. It slowed things a bit for the market analysts, but Goodman felt safer with it.

"I'm working on an outline for the hearing," Larramore said, "just in case. We'll probably have it in the House Ways and Means Committee Room, just down the hall."

"Will it be closed?"

"No. Is this a problem?"

"We have four days left, Mr. Larramore. Everything's a problem. But the hearing belongs to the governor. We're just thankful he's granted one."

"I have your numbers. Keep in touch."

"I'm not leaving Jackson until this is over."

They shook hands quickly and Goodman left the office. He sat on the front steps for half an hour and watched the Klansmen get organized and attract the curious.

FORTY-TWO

THOUGH HE'D WORN a white robe and a pointed hood as a much younger man, Donnie Cayhall kept his distance from the lines of Klansmen patrolling the grassy strip near the front gate of Parchman. Security was tight, with armed guards watching the protestors. Next to the canopy where the Klansmen gathered was a small group of skinheads in brown shirts. They held signs demanding freedom for Sam Cayhall.

Donnie watched the spectacle for a moment, then followed the directions of a security guard and parked along the highway. His name was checked at the guardhouse, and a few minutes later a prison van came for him. His brother had been at Parchman for nine and a half years, and Donnie had tried to visit at least once a year. But the last visit had been two years ago, he was ashamed to admit.

Donnie Cayhall was sixty-one, the youngest of the four Cayhall brothers. All had followed the teachings of their father and joined the Klan in their teens. It had been a simple decision with little thought given to it, one expected by the entire family. Later he had joined the Army, fought in Korea, and traveled the world. In the process, he had lost interest in wearing robes and burning crosses. He left Mississippi in 1961, and went to work for a furniture company in North Carolina. He now lived near Durham.

Every month for nine and a half years, he had shipped to Sam a box of cigarettes and a small amount of cash. He'd written a few letters, but neither he nor Sam was interested in correspondence. Few people in Durham knew he had a brother on death row.

He was frisked inside the front door, and shown to the front office. Sam was brought in a few minutes later, and they were left alone. Donnie hugged him for a long time, and when they released each other both had moist eyes. They were of similar height and build, though Sam looked twenty years older. He sat on the edge of the desk and Donnie took a chair nearby.

Both lit cigarettes and stared into space.

"Any good news?" Donnie finally asked, certain of the answer.

"No. None. The courts are turning everything down. They're gonna do it, Donnie. They're gonna kill me. They'll walk me to the chamber and gas me like an animal."

Donnie's face fell to his chest. "I'm sorry, Sam."

"I'm sorry too, but, dammit, I'll be glad when it's over."

"Don't say that."

"I mean it. I'm tired of living in a cage. I'm an old man and my time has come."

"But you don't deserve to be killed, Sam."

"That's the hardest part, you know. It's not that I'm gonna die, hell, we're all dying. I just can't stand the thought of these jackasses getting the best of me. They're gonna win. And their reward is to strap me in and watch me choke. It's sick."

"Can't your lawyer do something?"

"He's trying everything, but it looks hopeless. I want you to meet him."

"I saw his picture in the paper. He doesn't resemble our people."

"He's lucky. He looks more like his mother."

"Sharp kid?"

Sam managed a smile. "Yeah, he's pretty terrific. He's really grieving over this."

"Will he be here today?"

"Probably. I haven't heard from him. He's staying with Lee in Memphis," Sam said with a touch of pride. Because of him, his daughter and his grandson had become close and were actually living together peacefully.

"I talked to Albert this morning," Donnie said. "He says he's too sick to come over."

"Good. I don't want him here. And I don't want his kids and grandkids here either."

"He wants to pay his respects, but he can't."

"Tell him to save it for the funeral."

"Come on, Sam."

"Look, no one's gonna cry for me when I'm dead. I don't want a lot of false pity before then. I need something from you, Donnie. And it'll cost a little money."

"Sure. Anything."

Sam pulled at the waist of his red jumpsuit. "You see this damned thing. They're called reds, and I've worn them every day for almost ten years. This is what the State of Mississippi expects me to wear when it kills me. But, you see, I have the right to wear anything I want. It would mean a lot if I die in some nice clothes."

Donnie was suddenly hit with emotion. He tried to speak, but words didn't come. His eyes were wet and his lip quivered. He nodded, and managed to say, "Sure, Sam."

"You know those work pants called Dickies? I wore them for years. Sort of like khakis."

Donnie was still nodding.

"A pair of them would be nice, with a white shirt of some sort, not a pullover but one with buttons on it. Small shirt, small pants, thirty-two in the waist. A pair of white socks, and some kind of cheap shoes. Hell, I'll just wear them once, won't I? Go to Wal-Mart or some place and you can probably get the whole thing for less than thirty bucks. Do you mind?"

Donnie wiped his eyes and tried to smile. "No, Sam."

"I'll be a dude, won't I?"

"Where will you be buried?"

"Clanton, next to Anna. I'm sure that'll upset her peaceful rest. Adam's taking care of the arrangements."

"What else can I do?"

"Nothing. If you'll just get me a change of clothes."

"I'll do it today."

"You're the only person in the world who's cared about me all these years, do you know that? Aunt Barb wrote me for years before she died, but her letters were always stiff and dry, and I figured she was doing it so she could tell her neighbors."

"Who the hell was Aunt Barb?"

"Hubert Cain's mother. I'm not even sure she's related to us. I hardly knew her until I arrived here, then she started this awful correspondence. She was just all tore up by the fact that one of her own had been sent to Parchman."

"May she rest in peace."

Sam chuckled, and was reminded of an ancient childhood story. He told it with great enthusiasm, and minutes later both brothers were laughing loudly. Donnie was reminded of another tale, and so it went for an hour.

BY THE TIME Adam arrived late Saturday afternoon, Donnie had been gone for hours. He was taken to the front office, where he spread some papers on the desk. Sam was brought in, his handcuffs removed, and the door was closed behind them. He held more envelopes, which Adam noticed immediately.

"More errands for me?" he asked suspiciously.

"Yeah, but they can wait until it's over."

"To whom?"

"One is to the Pinder family I bombed in Vicksburg. One is to the Jewish synagogue I bombed in Jackson. One is to the Jewish real estate agent, also in Jackson. There may be others. No hurry, since I know you're busy right now. But after I'm gone, I'd appreciate it if you'd take care of them."

"What do these letters say?"

"What do you think they say?"

"I don't know. That you're sorry, I guess."

"Smart boy. I apologize for my deeds, repent of my sins, and ask them to forgive me."

"Why are you doing this?"

Sam stopped and leaned on a file cabinet. "Because I sit in a little cage all day. Because I have a typewriter and plenty of paper. I'm bored as hell, okay, so maybe I want to write. Because I have a conscience, not much of one, but it's there, and the closer I get to death the guiltier I feel about the things I've done."

"I'm sorry. They'll be delivered." Adam circled something on his checklist. "We have two appeals left. The Fifth Circuit is sitting on the ineffectiveness claim. I expected something by now, but there's been no movement for two days. The district court has the mental claim."

"It's all hopeless, Adam."

"Maybe, but I'm not quitting. I'll file a dozen more petitions if I have to."

"I'm not signing anything else. You can't file them if I don't sign them."

"Yes I can. There are ways."

"Then you're fired."

"You can't fire me, Sam. I'm your grandson."

"We have an agreement saying I can fire you whenever I want. We put it in writing."

"It's a flawed document, drafted by a decent jailhouse lawyer, but fatally defective nonetheless."

Sam huffed and puffed and began striding again on his row of tiles. He made half a dozen passes in front of Adam, his lawyer now, tomorrow, and for the remainder of his life. He knew he couldn't fire him.

"We have a clemency hearing scheduled for Monday," Adam said, looking at his legal pad and waiting for the explosion. But Sam took it well and never missed a step.

"What's the purpose of the clemency hearing?" he asked.

"To appeal for clemency."

"Appeal to whom?"

"The governor."

"And you think the governor will consider granting me clemency?"

"What's there to lose?"

"Answer the question, smartass. Do you, with all your training, experience, and judicial brilliance, seriously expect this governor to entertain ideas of granting me clemency?"

"Maybe."

"Maybe my ass. You're stupid."

"Thank you, Sam."

"Don't mention it." He stopped directly in front of Adam and pointed a crooked finger at him. "I've told you from the very beginning that I, as the client and as such certainly entitled to some consideration, will have nothing to do with David McAllister. I will not appeal to that fool for clemency. I will not ask him for a pardon. I will have no contact with him, whatsoever. Those are my wishes, and I made this very plain to you, young man, from day one. You, on the other hand, as the lawyer, have ignored my wishes and gone about your merry business doing whatever the hell you wanted. You are the lawyer, nothing more or less. I, on the other hand, am the client, and I don't know what they taught you in your fancy law school, but I make the decisions."

Sam walked to an empty chair and picked up another envelope. He handed it to Adam, and said, "This is a letter to the governor requesting him to cancel the clemency hearing on Monday. If you refuse to get it canceled, then I will make copies of this and give it to the press. I will embarrass you, Garner Goodman, and the governor. Do you understand?"

"Plain enough."

Sam returned the envelope to the chair, and lit another cigarette.

Adam made another circle on his list. "Carmen will be here Monday. I'm not sure about Lee."

Sam eased to a chair and sat down. He did not look at Adam. "Is she still in rehab?"

"Yes, and I'm not sure when she'll get out. Do you want her to visit?"

"Let me think about it."

"Think fast, okay."

"Funny, real funny. My brother Donnie stopped by earlier. He's my youngest brother, you know. He wants to meet you."

"Was he in the Klan?"

"What kind of question is that?"

"It's a simple yes or no question."

"Yes. He was in the Klan."

"Then I don't want to meet him."

"He's not a bad guy."

"I'll take your word for it."

"He's my brother, Adam. I want you to meet my brother."

"I have no desire to meet new Cayhalls, Sam, especially ones who wore robes and hoods."

"Oh, really. Three weeks ago you wanted to know everything about the family. Just couldn't get enough of it."

"I surrender, okay? I've heard enough."

"Oh, there's lots more."

"Enough, enough. Spare me."

Sam grunted and smiled smugly to himself. Adam glanced at his legal pad, and said, "You'll be happy to know that the Kluckers outside have now been joined by some Nazis and Aryans and skinheads and other hate groups. They're all lined along the highway, waving posters at cars passing by. The posters, of course, demand the freedom of Sam Cayhall, their hero. It's a regular circus."

"I saw it on television."

"They're also marching in Jackson around the state capitol."

"This is my fault?"

"No. It's your execution. You're a symbol now. About to become a martyr."

"What am I supposed to do?"

"Nothing. Just go ahead and die, and they'll all be happy."

"Aren't you an asshole today."

"Sorry, Sam. The pressure's getting to me."

"Throw in the towel. I have. I highly recommend it."

"Forget it. I've got these clowns on the run, Sam. I have not yet begun to fight."

"Yeah, you've filed three petitions, and a total of seven courts have turned you down. Zero for seven. I hate to see what'll happen when you really get cranked up." Sam said this with a wicked smile, and the humor found its mark. Adam laughed at it, and both breathed a bit easier. "I have this great idea for a lawsuit after you're gone," he said, feigning excitement.

"After I'm gone?"

"Sure. We'll sue them for wrongful death. We'll name McAllister, Nugent, Roxburgh, the State of Mississippi. We'll bring in everybody."

"It's never been done," Sam said, stroking his beard, as if deep in thought.

"Yeah, I know. Thought of it all by myself. We might not win a dime, but think of the fun I'll have harassing those bastards for the next five years."

"You have my permission to file it. Sue them!"

The smiles slowly disappeared and the humor was gone. Adam found something else on his checklist. "Just a couple more items. Lucas Mann asked me to ask you about your witnesses. You're entitled to have two people in the witness room, in case this gets that far."

"Donnie doesn't want to do it. I will not allow you to be there. I can't imagine anybody else who'd want to see it."

"Fine. Speaking of them, I have at least thirty requests for interviews. Virtually every major paper and news magazine wants access."

"No."

"Fine. Remember that writer we discussed last time, Wendall Sherman? The one who wants to record your story on tape and—"

"Yeah. For fifty thousand bucks."

"Now it's a hundred thousand. His publisher will put up the money. He wants to get everything on tape, watch the execution, do extensive research, then write a big book about it."

"No."

"Fine."

"I don't want to spend the next three days talking about my life. I don't want some stranger poking his nose around Ford County. And I don't particularly need a hundred thousand dollars at this point in my life."

"Fine with me. You once mentioned the clothing you wanted to wear—"

"Donnie's taking care of it."

"Okay. Moving right along. Barring a stay, you're allowed to have two people with you during your final hours. Typically, the prison has a form for you to sign designating these people."

"It's always the lawyer and the minister, right?"

"That's correct."

"Then it's you, and Ralph Griffin, I guess."

Adam filled the names in on a form. "Who's Ralph Griffin?"

"The new minister here. He's opposed to the death penalty, can you believe it? His predecessor thought we should all be gassed, in the name of Jesus, of course."

Adam handed the form to Sam. "Sign here."

Sam scribbled his name and handed it back.

"You're entitled to a last conjugal visit."

Sam laughed loudly. "Come on, son. I'm an old man."

"It's on the checklist, okay. Lucas Mann whispered to me the other day that I should mention it to you."

"Okay. You've mentioned it."

"I have another form here for your personal effects. Who gets them?"

"You mean my estate?"

"Sort of."

"This is morbid as hell, Adam. Why are we doing this now?"

"I'm a lawyer, Sam. We get paid to sweat the details. It's just paperwork."

"Do you want my things?"

Adam thought about this for a moment. He didn't want to hurt Sam's feelings, but at the same time he couldn't imagine what he'd do with a few ragged old garments, worn books, portable television, and rubber shower shoes. "Sure," he said.

"Then they're yours. Take them and burn them."

"Sign here," Adam said, shoving the form under his face. Sam signed it, then jumped to his feet and started pacing again. "I really want you to meet Donnie."

"Sure. Whatever you want," Adam said, stuffing his legal pad and the forms into his briefcase. The nitpicking details were now complete. The briefcase seemed much heavier.

"I'll be back in the morning," he said to Sam.

"Bring me some good news, okay."

COLONEL NUGENT strutted along the edge of the highway with a dozen armed prison guards behind him. He glared at the Klansmen, twenty-six at last count, and he scowled at the brown-shirted Nazis, ten in all. He stopped and stared at the group of skinheads mingling next to the Nazis. He swaggered around the edge of the grassy protest strip, pausing for a moment to speak to two Catholic nuns sitting under a large umbrella, as far away from the other demonstrators as possible. The temperature was one hundred degrees, and the nuns were broiling under the shade. They sipped ice water, their posters resting on their knees and facing the highway.

The nuns asked him who he was and what he wanted. He explained that he was the acting warden for the prison, and that he was simply making sure the demonstration was orderly.

They asked him to leave.

FORTY-THREE

ERHAPS IT WAS BECAUSE it was Sunday, or maybe it was the rain, but Adam drank his morning coffee in unexpected serenity. It was still dark outside, and the gentle dripping of a warm, summer shower on the patio was mesmerizing. He stood in the open door and listened to the splashing of the raindrops. It was too early for traffic on Riverside Drive below. There were no noises from the tugboats on the river. All was quiet and peaceful.

And there wasn't a heckuva lot to be done this day, Day Three before the execution. He would start at the office, where another last minute petition had to be organized. The issue was so ridiculous Adam was almost embarrassed to file it. Then he would drive to Parchman and sit with Sam for a spell.

It was unlikely there would be movement by any court on Sunday. It was certainly possible since the death clerks and their staffs were on call when an execution was looming. But Friday and Saturday had passed without rulings coming down, and he expected the same inactivity today. Tomorrow would be much different, in his untrained and untested opinion.

Tomorrow would be nothing but frenzy. And Tuesday, which of course was scheduled to be Sam's last day as a breathing soul, would be a nightmare of stress.

But this Sunday morning was remarkably calm. He had slept almost seven hours, another recent record.

His head was clear, his pulse normal, his breathing relaxed. His mind was uncluttered and composed.

He flipped through the Sunday paper, scanning the headlines but reading nothing. There were at least two stories about the Cayhall execution, one with more pictures of the growing circus outside the prison gate. The rain stopped when the sun came up, and he sat in a wet rocker for an hour scanning Lee's architectural magazines. After a couple of hours of peace and tranquility, Adam was bored and ready for action.

There was unfinished business in Lee's bedroom, a matter Adam had tried to forget but couldn't. For ten days now, a silent battle had raged in his soul over the book in her drawer. She'd been drunk when she told him about the lynching photo, but it was not the delirious talk of an addict. Adam knew the book existed. There was a real book with a real photo of a young black man hanging by a rope, and somewhere under his feet was a crowd of proud white people, mugging for the camera, immune from prosecution. Adam had mentally pieced the picture together, adding faces, sketching the tree, drawing the rope, adding titles to the space under it. But there were some things he didn't know, he couldn't visualize. Was the dead man's face perceptible? Was he wearing shoes, or barefoot? Was a very young Sam easily recognizable? How many white faces were in the photo? And how old were they? Any women? Any guns? Blood? Lee said he'd been bullwhipped. Was the whip in the photo? He had imagined the picture for days now, and it was time to finally look in the book. He couldn't wait until later. Lee might make a triumphant return. She might move the book, hide it again. He planned to spend the next two or three nights here, but that could change with one phone call. He could be forced to rush to Jackson or sleep in his car at Parchman. Such routine matters as lunch and dinner and sleeping were suddenly unpredictable when your client had less than a week to live.

This was the perfect moment, and he decided that he was now ready to face the lynch mob. He walked to the front door and scanned the parking lot, just to make sure she hadn't decided to drop in. He actually locked the door to her bedroom, and pulled open the top drawer. It was filled with her lingerie, and he was embarrassed for this intrusion.

The book was in the third drawer, lying on top of a faded sweatshirt. It was thick and bound in green fabric—*Southern Negroes and the Great Depression*. Published in 1947 by Toffler Press, Pittsburgh. Adam clutched it and sat on the edge of her bed. The pages were immaculate and pristine, as if the book had never been handled or read. Who in the Deep South would read such a book anyway? And if the book had been in the Cayhall family for several decades, then Adam was positive it had never been read. He studied the binder and pondered what set of circumstances brought this particular book into the custody of the Sam Cayhall family.

The book had three sections of photos. The first was a series of pictures of shotgun houses and ramshackle sheds where blacks were forced to live on plantations. There were family portraits on front porches with dozens of children, and there were the obligatory shots of farm workers stooped low in the fields picking cotton.

The second section was in the center of the book, and ran for twenty pages. There were actually two lynching photos, the first a horribly gruesome scene with two robed and hooded Kluckers holding rifles and posing for the camera. A badly beaten black man swung from a rope behind them, his eyes half open, his face pulverized and bloody. KKK lynching, Central Mississippi, 1939, explained the caption under it, as if these rituals could be defined simply by locale and time.

Adam gaped at the horror of the picture, then turned the page to find the second lynching scene, this one almost tame compared to the first. The lifeless body at the end of the rope could be seen only from the chest down. The shirt appeared to be torn, probably by the bullwhip, if in fact one had been used. The black man was very thin, his oversized pants drawn tightly at the waist. He was barefoot. No blood was visible.

The rope that held his body could be seen tied to a lower branch in the background. The tree was large with bulky limbs and a massive trunk.

A festive group had gathered just inches under his dangling feet. Men, women, and boys clowned for the camera, some striking exaggerated poses of anger and manliness—hard frowns, fierce eyes, tight lips, as if they possessed unlimited power to protect their women from Negro aggression; others smiled and seemed to be giggling, especially the women, two of whom were quite pretty; a small boy held a pistol and aimed it menacingly at the camera; a young man held a bottle of liquor, twisted just so to reveal the label. Most of the group seemed quite joyous that this event had occurred. Adam counted seventeen people in the group, and every single one was staring at the camera without shame or worry, without the slightest hint a wrong had been committed. They were utterly immune from prosecution. They had just killed another human, and it was painfully obvious they had done so with no fear of the consequences.

This was a party. It was at night, the weather was warm, liquor was present, pretty women. Surely they'd brought food in baskets and were about to throw quilts on the ground for a nice picnic around the tree.

Lynching in rural Mississippi, 1936, read the caption.

Sam was in the front row, crouched and resting on a knee between two other young men, all three posing hard for the camera. He was fifteen or sixteen, with a slender face that was trying desperately to appear dangerous—lip curled, eyebrows pinched, chin up. The cocky braggadocio of a boy trying to emulate the more mature thugs around him.

He was easy to spot because someone had drawn, in faded blue ink, a line across the photo to the margin where the name Sam Cayhall was printed in block letters. The line crossed the bodies and faces of others and stopped at Sam's left ear. Eddie. It had to be Eddie. Lee said that Eddie had found this book in the attic, and Adam could see his father hiding in the darkness, weeping over the photograph, identifying Sam by pointing the accusatory arrow at his head.

Lee also had said that Sam's father was the leader of this ragtag little mob, but Adam couldn't distinguish him. Perhaps Eddie couldn't either because there were no markings. There were at least seven men old enough to be Sam's father. How many of these people were Cayhalls? She'd also said that his brothers were involved, and perhaps one of the younger men resembled Sam, but it was impossible to tell for certain.

He studied the clear, beautiful eyes of his grandfather, and his heart ached. He was just a boy, born and reared in a household where hatred of blacks and others was simply a way of life. How much of it could be blamed on him? Look at those around him, his father, family, friends and neighbors, all probably honest, poor, hardworking people caught for the moment at the end of a cruel ceremony that was commonplace in their society. Sam didn't have a chance. This was the only world he knew.

How would Adam ever reconcile the past with the present? How could he fairly judge these people and their horrible deed when, but for a quirk of fate, he would've been right there in the middle of them had he been born forty years earlier?

As he looked at their faces, an odd comfort engulfed him. Though Sam was obviously a willing participant, he was only one member of the mob, only partly guilty. Clearly, the older men with the stern faces had instigated the lynching, and the rest had come along for the occasion. He looked at the photo, it was inconceivable to think that Sam and his younger buddies had initiated this brutality. Sam had done nothing to stop it. But maybe he had done nothing to encourage it.

The scene produced a hundred unanswered questions. Who was the photographer, and how did he happen to be there with his camera? Who was the young black man? Where was his family, his mother? How'd they catch him? Had he been in jail and released by the authorities to the mob? What did they do with his body when it was over? Was the alleged rape victim one of the young women smiling at the camera? Was her father one of the men? Her brothers?

If Sam was lynching at such an early age, what could be expected of him as an adult? How often did these folks gather and celebrate like this in rural Mississippi?

How in God's world could Sam Cayhall have become anything other than himself? He never had a chance.

SAM WAITED PATIENTLY in the front office, sipping coffee from a different pot. It was strong and rich, unlike the watered-down brew they served the inmates each morning. Packer had given it to him in a large paper cup. Sam sat on the desk with his feet on a chair. The door opened and Colonel Nugent marched inside with Packer behind. The door was closed. Sam stiffened and snapped off a smart salute.

"Good morning, Sam," Nugent said somberly. "How you doing?"

"Fabulous. You?"

"Getting by."

"Yeah, I know you gotta lot on your mind. This is tough on you, trying to arrange my execution and making sure it goes real smooth. Tough job. My hat's off to you."

Nugent ignored the sarcasm. "Need to talk to you about a few things. Your lawyers now say you're crazy, and I just wanted to see for myself how you're doing."

"I feel like a million bucks."

"Well, you certainly look fine."

"Gee thanks. You look right spiffy yourself. Nice boots."

The black combat boots were sparkling, as usual. Packer glanced down at them and grinned.

"Yes," Nugent said, sitting in a chair and looking at a sheet of paper. "The psychiatrist said you're uncooperative."

"Who? N.?"

"Dr. Stegall."

"That big lard-ass gal with an incomplete first name? I've talked to her only once."

"Were you uncooperative?"

"I certainly hope so. I've been here for almost ten years, and she finally trots her big ass over here when I've got one foot in the grave to see how I'm getting along. All she wanted to do was give me some dope so I'll be stoned when you clowns come after me. Makes your job easier, doesn't it."

"She was only trying to help."

"Then God bless her. Tell her I'm sorry. It'll never

happen again. Write me up with an RVR. Put it in my file."

"We need to talk about your last meal."

"Why is Packer in here?"

Nugent glanced at Packer, then looked at Sam. "Because it's procedure."

"He's here to protect you, isn't he? You're afraid of me. You're scared to be left alone with me in this room, aren't you, Nugent? I'm almost seventy years old, feeble as hell, half dead from cigarettes, and you're afraid of me, a convicted murderer."

"Not in the least."

"I'd stomp your ass all over this room, Nugent, if I wanted to."

"I'm terrified. Look, Sam, let's get down to business. What would you like for your last meal?"

"This is Sunday. My last meal is scheduled for Tuesday night. Why are you bothering me with it now?"

"We have to make plans. You can have anything, within reason."

"Who's gonna cook it?"

"It'll be prepared in the kitchen here."

"Oh, wonderful! By the same talented chefs who've been feeding me hog slop for nine and a half years. What a way to go!"

"What would you like, Sam? I'm trying to be reasonable."

"How about toast and boiled carrots? I'd hate to burden them with something new."

"Fine, Sam. When you decide, tell Packer here and he'll notify the kitchen."

"There won't be a last meal, Nugent. My lawyer will unload the heavy artillery tomorrow. You clowns won't know what hit you."

"I hope you're right."

"You're a lying sonofabitch. You can't wait to walk

me in there and strap me down. You're giddy with the thought of asking me if I have any last words, then nodding at one of your gophers to lock the door. And when it's all over, you'll face the press with a sad face and announce that 'As of twelve-fifteen, this morning, August 8, Sam Cayhall was executed in the gas chamber here at Parchman, pursuant to an order of the Circuit Court of Lakehead County, Mississippi.' It'll be your finest hour, Nugent. Don't lie to me."

The colonel never looked from the sheet of paper. "We need your list of witnesses."

"See my lawyer."

"And we need to know what to do with your things."

"See my lawyer."

"Okay. We have numerous requests for interviews from the press."

"See my lawyer."

Nugent jumped to his feet and stormed from the office. Packer caught the door, waited a few seconds, then calmly said, "Sit tight, Sam, there's someone else to see you."

Sam smiled and winked at Packer. "Then get me some more coffee, would you, Packer?"

Packer took the cup, and returned with it a few minutes later. He also handed Sam the Sunday paper from Jackson, and Sam was reading all sorts of stories about his execution when the chaplain, Ralph Griffin, knocked and entered.

Sam placed the paper on the desk and inspected the minister. Griffin wore white sneakers, faded jeans, and a black shirt with a white clerical collar. "Mornin', Reverend," Sam said, sipping his coffee.

"How are you, Sam?" Griffin asked as he pulled a chair very near the desk and sat in it.

"Right now my heart's filled with hate," Sam said gravely.

"I'm sorry. Who's it directed at?"

"Colonel Nugent. But I'll get over it."

"Have you been praying, Sam?"

"Not really."

"Why not?"

"What's the hurry? I have today, tomorrow, and Tuesday. I figure you and I'll be doing lots of praying come Tuesday night."

"If you want. It's up to you. I'll be here."

"I want you to be with me up to the last moment, Reverend, if you don't mind. You and my lawyer. Y'all are allowed to sit with me during the last hours."

"I'd be honored."

"Thanks."

"What exactly do you want to pray about, Sam?"

Sam took a long drink of coffee. "Well, first of all, I'd like to know that when I leave this world, all the bad things I've done have been forgiven."

"Your sins?"

"That's right."

"God expects us to confess our sins to him and ask for forgiveness."

"All of them? One at a time?"

"Yes, the ones we can remember."

"Then we'd better start now. It'll take a while."

"As you wish. What else would you like to pray for?"

"My family, such as it is. This will be hard on my grandson, and my brother, and maybe my daughter. There won't be a lot of tears shed for me, you understand, but I would like for them to be comforted. And I'd like to say a prayer for my friends here on the Row. They'll take it hard."

"Anyone else?"

"Yeah. I want to say a good prayer for the Kramers, especially Ruth."

"The family of the victims?"

"That's right. And also the Lincolns."

"Who are the Lincolns?"

"It's a long story. More victims."

"This is good, Sam. You need to get this off your chest, to cleanse your soul."

"It'll take years to cleanse my soul, Reverend."

"More victims?"

Sam sat the cup on the desk and gently rubbed his hands together. He searched the warm and trusting eyes of Ralph Griffin. "What if there are other victims?" he asked.

"Dead people?"

Sam nodded, very slowly.

"People you've killed?"

Sam kept nodding.

Griffin took a deep breath, and contemplated matters for a moment. "Well, Sam, to be perfectly honest, I wouldn't want to die without confessing these sins and asking God for forgiveness."

Sam kept nodding.

"How many?" Griffin asked.

Sam slid off the desk and eased into his shower shoes. He slowly lit a cigarette, and began pacing back and forth behind Griffin's chair. The reverend changed positions so he could watch and hear Sam.

"There was Joe Lincoln, but I've already written a letter to his family and told them I was sorry."

"You killed him?"

"Yes. He was an African. Lived on our place. I always felt bad about it. It was around 1950."

Sam stopped and leaned on a file cabinet. He spoke to the floor, as if in a daze. "And there were two men, white men, who killed my father at a funeral, many

years ago. They served some time in jail, and when
they got out, me and my brothers waited patiently. We
killed both of them, but I never felt that bad about it,
to be honest. They were scum, and they'd killed our
father."

"Killing is always wrong, Sam. You're fighting your
own legal killing right now."

"I know."

"Did you and your brothers get caught?"

"No. The old sheriff suspected us, but he couldn't
prove anything. We were too careful. Besides, they
were real lowlifes, and nobody cared."

"That doesn't make it right."

"I know. I always figured they deserved what they
got, then I was sent to this place. Life has new meaning
when you're on death row. You realize how valuable it
is. Now I'm sorry I killed those boys. Real sorry."

"Anybody else?"

Sam walked the length of the room, counting each
step, and returned to the file cabinet. The minister
waited. Time meant nothing right now.

"There were a couple of lynchings, years ago," Sam
said, unable to look Griffin in the eyes.

"Two?"

"I think. Maybe three. No, yes, there were three, but
at the first one I was just a kid, a small boy, and all I
did was watch, you know, from the bushes. It was
Klan lynching, and my father was involved in it, and
me and my brother Albert sneaked into the woods and
watched it. So that doesn't count, does it?"

"No."

Sam's shoulders sank against the wall. He closed his
eyes and lowered his head. "The second one was a regular mob. I was about fifteen, I guess, and I was right
in the middle of it. A girl got raped by an African, at
least she said it was a rape. Her reputation left a lot to

be desired, and two years later she had a baby that was half African. So who knows? Anyway, she pointed the finger, we got the boy, took him out, and lynched him. I was as guilty as the rest of the mob."

"God will forgive you, Sam."

"Are you sure?"

"I'm positive."

"How many murders will he forgive?"

"All of them. If you sincerely ask forgiveness, then he'll wipe the slate clean. It's in the Scriptures."

"That's too good to be true."

"What about the other lynching?"

Sam began shaking his head, back and forth, eyes closed. "Now, I can't talk about that one, preacher," he said, exhaling heavily.

"You don't have to talk to me about it, Sam. Just talk to God."

"I don't know if I can talk to anybody about it."

"Sure you can. Just close your eyes one night, between now and Tuesday, while you're in your cell, and confess all these deeds to God. He'll instantly forgive you."

"Just doesn't seem right, you know. You kill someone, then in a matter of minutes God forgives you. Just like that. It's too easy."

"You must be truly sorry."

"Oh, I am. I swear."

"God forgets about it, Sam, but man does not. We answer to God, but we also answer to the laws of man. God will forgive you, but you suffer the consequences according to the dictates of the government."

"Screw the government. I'm ready to check outta here anyway."

"Well, let's make sure you're ready, okay?"

Sam walked to the desk and sat on the corner next to Griffin. "You stick close, okay, Reverend? I'll need some help. There's some bad things buried in my soul. It might take some time to get them out."

"It won't be hard, Sam, if you're really ready."

Sam patted him on the knee. "Just stick close, okay?"

FORTY-FOUR

THE FRONT OFFICE was filled with blue smoke when Adam entered. Sam was puffing away on the desk, reading about himself in the Sunday paper. Three empty coffee cups and several candy wrappers littered the desk. "You've made yourself at home, haven't you?" Adam said, noticing the debris.

"Yeah, I've been here all day."

"Lots of guests?"

"I wouldn't call them guests. The day started with Nugent, so that pretty well ruined things. The minister stopped by to see if I've been praying. I think he was depressed when he left. Then the doctor came by to make sure I'm fit enough to kill. Then my brother Donnie stopped by for a short visit. I really want you to meet him. Tell me you've brought some good news."

Adam shook his head and sat down. "No. Nothing's changed since yesterday. The courts have taken the weekend off."

"Do they realize Saturdays and Sundays count? That the clock doesn't stop ticking for me on the weekends?"

"It could be good news. They could be considering my brilliant appeals."

"Maybe, but I suspect the honorable brethren are more likely at their lake homes drinking beer and cooking ribs. Don't you think?"

"Yeah, you're probably right. What's in the paper?"

"Same old rehash of me and my brutal crime, pictures of those people out front demonstrating, comments from McAllister. Nothing new. I've never seen such excitement."

"You're the man of the hour, Sam. Wendall Sherman and his publisher are now at a hundred and fifty thousand, but the deadline is six o'clock tonight. He's in Memphis, sitting with his tape recorders, just itching to get down here. He says he'll need at least two full days to record your story."

"Great. What exactly am I supposed to do with the money?"

"Leave it to your precious grandchildren."

"Are you serious? Will you spend it? I'll do it if you'll spend it."

"No. I'm just kidding. I don't want the money, and Carmen doesn't need it. I couldn't spend it with a clear conscience."

"Good. Because the last thing I wanna do between now and Tuesday night is to sit with a stranger and talk about the past. I don't care how much money he has. I'd rather not have a book written about my life."

"I've already told him to forget it."

"Attaboy." Sam eased to his feet and began walking back and forth across the room. Adam took his place on the edge of the desk and read the sports section of the Memphis paper.

"I'll be glad when it's over, Adam," Sam said, still walking, talking with his hands. "I can't stand this waiting. I swear I wish it was tonight." He was suddenly nervous and irritable, his voice louder.

Adam placed the paper to his side. "We're gonna win, Sam. Trust me."

"Win what!" he snapped angrily. "Win a reprieve? Big deal! What do we gain from that? Six months? A year? You know what that means? It means we'll get to do this again someday. I'll go through the whole damned ritual again—counting days, losing sleep, plotting last minute strategies, listening to Nugent or some other fool, talking to the shrink, whispering to the chaplain, being patted on the ass and led up here to this cubbyhole because I'm special." He stopped in front of Adam and glared down at him. His face was angry, his eyes wet and bitter. "I'm sick of this, Adam! Listen to me! This is worse than dying."

"We can't quit, Sam."

"We? Who the hell is we? It's my neck on the line, not yours. If I get a stay, then you'll go back to your fancy office in Chicago and get on with your life. You'll be the hero because you saved your client. You'll get your picture in *Lawyer's Quarterly,* or whatever you guys read. The bright young star who kicked ass in Mississippi. Saved his grandfather, a wretched Klucker, by the way. Your client, on the other hand, is led back to his little cage where he starts counting days again." Sam threw his cigarette on the floor and grabbed Adam by the shoulders. "Look at me, son. I can't go through this again. I want you to stop everything. Drop it. Call the courts and tell them we're dismissing all the petitions and appeals. I'm an old man. Please allow me to die with dignity."

His hands were shaking. His breathing was labored. Adam searched his brilliant blue eyes, surrounded with layers of dark wrinkles, and saw a stray tear ease out of one corner and fall slowly down his cheek until it vanished in the gray beard.

For the first time, Adam could smell his grandfather. The strong nicotine aroma mixed with an odor of dried perspiration to form a scent that was not pleasant. It was not repulsive, though, the way it would have been if radiated by a person with access to plenty of soap and hot water, air conditioning, and deodorant. After the second breath, it didn't bother Adam at all.

"I don't want you to die, Sam."

Sam squeezed his shoulders harder. "Why not?" he demanded.

"Because I've just found you. You're my grandfather."

Sam stared for a second longer, then relaxed. He released Adam and took a step backward. "I'm sorry you found me like this," he said, wiping his eyes.

"Don't apologize."

"But I have to. I'm sorry I'm not a better grandfather. Look at me," he said, glancing down at his legs. "A wretched old man in a red monkey suit. A convicted murderer about to be gassed like an animal. And look at you. A fine young man with a beautiful education and a bright future. Where in the world did I go wrong? What happened to me? I've spent my life hating people, and look what I have to show for it. You, you don't hate anybody. And look where you're headed. We have the same blood. Why am I here?"

Sam slowly sat in a chair, put his elbows on his knees, and covered his eyes. Neither moved or spoke for a long time. The occasional voice of a guard could be heard in the hall, but the room was quiet.

"You know, Adam, I'd rather not die in such an awful way," Sam said hoarsely with his fists resting on his temples, still looking blankly at the floor. "But death itself doesn't worry me now. I've known for a long time that I would die here, and my biggest fear was dying without knowing anyone would care. That's an awful thought, you know. Dying and nobody cares. There's nobody to cry and grieve, to mourn properly at the funeral and burial. I've had dreams where I saw my body in a cheap wooden casket lying in the funeral home in Clanton, and not a soul was in the room with me. Not even Donnie. In the same dream, the preacher chuckled through the funeral service because it was just the two of us, all alone in the chapel, rows and rows of empty pews. But that's different now. I know somebody cares about me. I know you'll be sad when I die because you care, and I know you'll be there when I'm buried to make sure it's done properly. I'm really ready to go now, Adam. I'm ready."

"Fine, Sam, I respect that. And I promise I'll be here to the bitter end, and I'll grieve and mourn, and after it's over I'll make sure you're buried properly. No one's gonna screw around with you, Sam, as long as I'm here. But, please, look at it through my eyes. I have to give it my best shot, because I'm young and I have the rest of my life. Don't make me leave here knowing I could've done more. It's not fair to me."

Sam folded his arms across his chest and looked at Adam. His pale face was calm, his eyes still wet. "Let's do it this way," he said, his voice still low and pained. "I'm ready to go. I'll spend tomorrow and Tuesday making final preparations. I'll assume it's gonna happen at midnight Tuesday, and I'll be ready for it. You, on the other hand, play it like a game. If you can win it, good for you. If you lose it, I'll be ready to face the music."

"So you'll cooperate?"

"No. No clemency hearing. No more petitions or appeals. You have enough junk floating around out there to keep you busy. Two issues are still alive. I'm not signing any more petitions."

Sam stood, his decrepit knees popping and wobbling. He walked to the door and leaned on it. "What about Lee?" he asked softly, reaching for his cigarettes.

"She's still in rehab," Adam lied. He was tempted to blurt out the truth. It seemed childish to be lying to Sam in these declining hours of his life, but Adam still held a strong hope that she would be found before Tuesday. "Do you want to see her?"

"I think so. Can she get out?"

"It may be difficult, but I'll try. She's sicker than I first thought."

"She's an alcoholic?"

"Yes."

"Is that all? No drugs?"

"Just alcohol. She told me she's had a problem for many years. Rehab is nothing new."

"Bless her heart. My children didn't have a chance."

"She's a fine person. She's had a rough time with her marriage. Her son left home at an early age and never returned."

"Walt, right?"

"Right," Adam answered. What a heartbroken bunch of people. Sam was not even certain of the name of his grandson.

"How old is he?"

"I'm not sure. Probably close to my age."

"Does he even know about me?"

"I don't know. He's been gone for many years. Lives in Amsterdam."

Sam picked up a cup from the desk and took a drink of cold coffee. "What about Carmen?" he asked.

Adam glanced at his watch. "I pick her up at the Memphis airport in three hours. She'll be here in the morning."

"That just scares the hell outta me."

"Relax, Sam. She's a great person. She's smart, ambitious, pretty, and I've told her all about you."

"Why'd you do that?"

"Because she wants to know."

"Poor child. Did you tell her what I look like?"

"Don't worry about it, Sam. She doesn't care what you look like."

"Did you tell her I'm not some savage monster?"

"I told her you were a sweetheart, a real dear, sort of

a delicate little fella with an earring, ponytail, limp wrist, and these cute little rubber shower shoes that you sort of glide in."

"You kiss my ass!"

"And that you seemed to be a real favorite of the boys here in prison."

"You're lying! You didn't tell her all that!" Sam was grinning, but half serious, and his concern was amusing. Adam laughed, a bit too long and a bit too loud, but the humor was welcome. They both chuckled and tried their best to seem thoroughly amused by their own wit. They tried to stretch it out, but soon the levity passed and gravity sank in. Soon they were sitting on the edge of the desk, side by side, feet on separate chairs, staring at the floor while heavy clouds of tobacco smoke boiled above them in the motionless air.

There was so much to talk about, yet there was little to say. The legal theories and maneuverings had been beaten to death. Family was a subject they'd covered as much as they'd dared. The weather was good for no more than five minutes of conjecture. And both men knew they would spend much of the next two and a half days together. Serious matters could wait. Unpleasant subjects could be shoved back just a bit longer. Twice Adam glanced at his watch and said he'd best be going, and both times Sam insisted he stay. Because when Adam left, they would come for him and take him back to his cell, his little cage where the temperature was over a hundred. Please stay, he begged.

LATE THAT NIGHT, well after midnight, long after Adam had told Carmen about Lee and her problems, and about Phelps and Walt, about McAllister and Wyn Lettner, and the theory of the accomplice, hours after they'd finished a pizza and discussed their mother and father and grandfather and the whole pathetic bunch,

Adam said the one moment he'd never forget was the two of them sitting there on the desk, passing time in silence as an invisible clock ticked away, with Sam patting him on the knee. It was like he had to touch me in some affectionate way, he explained to her, like a good grandfather would touch a small loved one.

Carmen had heard enough for one night. She'd been on the patio for four hours, suffering through the humidity and absorbing the desolate oral history of her father's family.

But Adam had been very careful. He'd hit the peaks and skipped the woeful valleys—no mention of Joe Lincoln or lynchings or sketchy hints of other crimes. He portrayed Sam as a violent man who made terrible mistakes and was now burdened with remorse. He had toyed with the idea of showing her his video of Sam's trials, but decided against it. He would do it later. She could handle only so much in one night. At times, he couldn't believe the things he'd heard in the past four weeks. It would be cruel to hit her with all of it in one sitting. He loved his sister dearly. They had years to discuss the rest of the story.

FORTY-FIVE

MONDAY, AUGUST 6, 6 A.M. Forty-two hours to go. Adam entered his office and locked the door.

He waited until seven, then called Slattery's office in Jackson. There was no answer, of course, but he was hoping for a recorded message that might direct him to another number that might lead to someone down there who could tell him something. Slattery was sitting on the mental claim; just ignoring it as if it were simply another little lawsuit.

He called information and received the home number for F. Flynn Slattery, but decided not to bother him. He could wait until nine.

Adam had slept less than three hours. His pulse was pounding, his adrenaline was pumping. His client was now down to the last forty-two hours, and dammit, Slattery should quickly rule one way or the other. It wasn't fair to sit on the damned petition when he could be racing off to other courts with it.

The phone rang and he lunged for it. The Death Clerk from the Fifth Circuit informed him that the court was denying the appeal of Sam's claim of ineffective assistance of counsel. It was the opinion of the court that the claim was procedurally barred. It should've been filed years ago. The court did not get to the merits of the issue.

"Then why'd the court sit on it for a week?" Adam demanded. "They could've reached this nitpicking decision ten days ago."

"I'll fax you a copy right now," the clerk said.

"Thanks. I'm sorry, okay."

"Keep in touch, Mr. Hall. We'll be right here waiting on you."

Adam hung up, and went to find coffee. Darlene arrived, tired, haggard, and early, at seven-thirty. She brought the fax from the Fifth Circuit, along with a raisin bagel. Adam asked her to fax to the U.S. Supreme Court the petition for cert on the ineffectiveness claim. It had been prepared for three days, and Mr. Olander in Washington had told Darlene that the Court was already reviewing it.

Darlene then brought two aspirin and a glass of water. His head was splitting as he packed most of the Cayhall file into a large briefcase and a cardboard box. He gave Darlene a list of instructions.

Then he left the office, the Memphis branch of Kravitz & Bane, never to return.

COLONEL NUGENT waited impatiently for the tier door to open, then rushed into the hallway with eight members of his select execution team behind him. They swarmed into the quietness of Tier A with all the finesse of a Gestapo squad—eight large men, half in uniform, half plainclothed, following a strutting little rooster. He stopped at cell six, where Sam was lying on his bed, minding his own business. The other inmates were instantly watching and listening, their arms hanging through the bars.

"Sam, it's time to go to the Observation Cell," Nugent said as if he were truly bothered by this. His men lined the wall behind him, under the row of windows.

Sam slowly eased himself from the bed, and walked to the bars. He glared at Nugent, and asked, "Why?"

"Because I said so."

"But why move me eight doors down the tier? What purpose does it serve?"

"It's procedure, Sam. It's in the book."

"So you don't have a good reason, do you?"

"I don't need one. Turn around."

Sam walked to his sink and brushed his teeth for a long time. Then he stood over his toilet and urinated with his hands on his hips. Then he washed his hands, as Nugent and his boys watched and fumed. Then he lit a cigarette, stuck it between his teeth, and eased his hands behind his back and through the narrow opening in the door. Nugent slapped the cuffs on his wrists, and nodded at the end of the tier for the door to be opened. Sam stepped onto the tier. He nodded at J. B. Gullitt, who was watching in horror and ready to cry. He winked at Hank Henshaw.

Nugent took his arm and walked him to the end of the hall, past Gullitt and Loyd Eaton and Stock Turner and Harry Ross Scott and Buddy Lee Harris, and, finally, past Preacher Boy, who at the moment was lying on his bed, facedown, crying. The tier ran to a wall of iron bars, identical to those on the front of the cells, and the wall had a heavy door in the center of it. On the other side was another group of Nugent's goons, all watching quietly and loving every moment of it. Behind them was a short, narrow hallway that led to the Isolation Room. And then to the chamber.

Sam was being moved forty-eight feet closer to death. He leaned against the wall, puffing, watching in stoic silence. This was nothing personal, just part of the routine.

Nugent walked back to cell six and barked orders. Four of the guards entered Sam's cell and began grabbing his possessions. Books, typewriter, fan, television, toiletries, clothing. They held the items as if they were contaminated and carried them to the Observation

Cell. The mattress and bedding were rolled up and moved by a burly plainclothed guard who accidentally stepped on a dragging sheet and ripped it.

The inmates watched this sudden flurry of activity with a saddened curiosity. Their cramped little cells were like additional layers of skin, and to see one so unmercifully violated was painful. It could happen to them. The reality of an execution was crashing in; they could hear it in the heavy boots shuffling along the tier, and in the stern muted voices of the death team. The distant slamming of a door would've barely been noticed a week ago. Now, it was a jolting shock that rattled the nerves.

The officers trooped back and forth with Sam's assets until cell six was bare. It was quick work. They arranged things in his new home without the slightest care.

None of the eight worked on the Row. Nugent had read somewhere in Naifeh's haphazard notes that the members of the execution team should be total strangers to the inmate. They should be pulled from the other camps. Thirty-one officers and guards had volunteered for this duty. Nugent had chosen only the best.

"Is everything in?" he snapped at one of his men.

"Yes sir."

"Very well. It's all yours, Sam."

"Oh thank you, sir," Sam sneered as he entered the cell. Nugent nodded to the far end of the hall, and the door closed. He walked forward and grabbed the bars with both hands. "Now, listen, Sam," he said gravely. Sam was leaning with his back to the wall, looking away from Nugent. "We'll be right here if you need anything, okay. We moved you down here to the end so we can watch you better. All right? Is there anything I can do for you?"

Sam continued to look away, thoroughly ignoring him.

"Very well." He backed away, and looked at his men. "Let's go," he said to them. The tier door opened less than ten feet from Sam, and the death team filed out. Sam waited. Nugent glanced up and down the hall, then stepped from the tier.

"Hey, Nugent!" Sam suddenly yelled. "How 'bout taking these handcuffs off!"

Nugent froze and the death team stopped.

"You dumbass!" Sam yelled again as Nugent scurried backward, fumbling for keys, barking orders. Laughter erupted along the tier, loud horselaughs and guffaws and boisterous catcalls. "You can't leave me handcuffed!" Sam screamed into the hallway.

Nugent was at Sam's door, gritting his teeth, cursing, finally getting the right key. "Turn around," he demanded.

"You ignorant sonofabitch!" Sam yelled through the bars directly into the colonel's red face, which was less than two feet away. The laughter roared even louder.

"And you're in charge of my execution!" Sam said angrily, and rather loudly for the benefit of others. "You'll probably gas yourself!"

"Don't bet on it," Nugent said tersely. "Now turn around."

Someone, either Hank Henshaw or Harry Ross Scott, yelled out, "Barney Fife!" and instantly the chant reverberated along the tier:

"Barney Fife! Barney Fife! Barney Fife!"

"Shut up!" Nugent yelled back.

"Barney Fife! Barney Fife!"

"Shut up!"

Sam finally turned around and stuck out his hands so Nugent could reach them. The cuffs came off, and the colonel quick-stepped it through the tier door.

"Barney Fife! Barney Fife! Barney Fife!" they chanted in perfect unison until the door clanged shut and the hallway was empty again. Their voices died suddenly, the laughter was gone. Slowly, their arms disappeared from the bars.

Sam stood facing the hall and glared at the two guards who were watching him from the other side of the tier door. He spent a few minutes organizing the place—plugging in the fan and television, stacking his books neatly as if they would be used, checking to see if the toilet flushed and the water ran. He sat on the bed and inspected the torn sheet.

This was his fourth cell on the Row, and undoubtedly the one he would occupy for the briefest period of time. He reminisced about the first two, especially the second, on Tier B, where his close friend Buster Moac had lived next door. One day they came for Buster and brought him here, to the Observation Cell, where they watched him around the clock so he wouldn't commit suicide. Sam had cried when they took Buster away.

Virtually every inmate who made it this far also made it to the next stop. And then to the last.

GARNER GOODMAN was the first guest of the day in the splendid foyer of the governor's office. He actually signed the guestbook, chatted amiably with the pretty receptionist, and just wanted the governor to know that he was available. She was about to say something else when the phone buzzed on her switchboard. She punched a button, grimaced, listened, frowned at Goodman who looked away, then thanked the caller. "These people." She sighed.

"Beg your pardon," Goodman offered, ever the innocent.

"We've been swamped with calls about your client's execution."

"Yes, it's a very emotional case. Seems as if most people down here are in favor of the death penalty."

"Not this one," she said, recording the call on a pink form. "Almost all of these calls are opposed to his execution."

"You don't say. What a surprise."

"I'll inform Ms. Stark you're here."

"Thank you." Goodman took his familiar seat in the foyer. He glanced through the morning papers again. On Saturday, the daily paper in Tupelo made the mistake of beginning a telephone survey to gauge public opinion on the Cayhall execution. A toll-free number was given on the front page with instructions, and, of course, Goodman and his team of market analysts had bombarded the number over the weekend. The Monday edition ran the results for the first time, and they were astounding. Of three hundred and twenty calls, three hundred and two were opposed to the execution. Goodman smiled to himself as he scanned the paper.

Not too far away, the governor was sitting at the long table in his office and scanning the same papers. His face was troubled. His eyes were sad and worried.

Mona Stark walked across the marbled floor with a cup of coffee. "Garner Goodman's here. Waiting in the foyer."

"Let him wait."

"The hotline's already flooded."

McAllister calmly looked at his watch. Eleven minutes before nine. He scratched his chin with his knuckles. From 3 P.M. Saturday until 8 P.M. Sunday, his pollster had called over two hundred Mississippians. Seventy-eight percent favored the death penalty, which was not surprising. However, of the same sample polled, fifty-one percent believed Sam Cayhall should not be executed. Their reasons varied. Many felt he was simply too old to face it. His crime had been committed twenty-three years ago, in a generation different from today's. He would die in Parchman soon enough anyway, so leave him alone. He was being persecuted for political reasons. Plus, he was white, and McAllister and his pollsters knew that factor was very important, if unspoken.

That was the good news. The bad news was contained in a printout next to the newspapers. Working with only one operator, the hotline received two hundred and thirty-one calls on Saturday, and one hundred and eighty on Sunday. A total of four hundred and eleven. Over ninety-five percent opposed the execution. Since Friday morning, the hotline had officially recorded eight hundred and ninety-seven calls about old Sam, with a strong ninety percent plus opposed to his execution. And now the hotline was hopping again.

There was more. The regional offices were reporting an avalanche of calls, almost all opposed to Sam dying. Staff members were coming to work with stories of long weekends with the phones. Roxburgh had called to say his lines had been flooded.

The governor was already tired. "There's something at ten this morning," he said to Mona without looking at her.

"Yes, a meeting with a group of Boy Scouts."

"Cancel it. Give my apologies. Reschedule it. I'm not in the mood for any photographs this morning. It's best if I stay here. Lunch?"

"With Senator Pressgrove. You're supposed to discuss the lawsuit against the universities."

"I can't stand Pressgrove. Cancel it, and order some chicken. And, on second thought, bring in Goodman."

She walked to the door, disappeared for a minute, and returned with Garner Goodman. McAllister was standing by the window, staring at the buildings downtown. He turned and flashed a weary smile. "Good morning, Mr. Goodman."

They shook hands and took seats. Late Sunday afternoon, Goodman had delivered to Larramore a written request to cancel the clemency hearing, pursuant to their client's rather strident demands.

"Still don't want a hearing, huh?" the governor said with another tired smile.

"Our client says no. He has nothing else to add. We've tried everything." Mona handed Goodman a cup of black coffee.

"He has a very hard head. Always has, I guess. Where are the appeals right now?" McAllister was so sincere.

"Proceeding as expected."

"You've been through this before, Mr. Goodman. I haven't. What's your prediction, as of right now?"

Goodman stirred his coffee and pondered the question. There was no harm in being honest with the governor, not at this point. "I'm one of his lawyers, so I lean toward optimism. I'd say seventy percent chance of it happening."

The governor thought about this for a while. He could almost hear the phones ringing off the walls. Even his own people were getting skittish. "Do you know what I want, Mr. Goodman?" he asked sincerely.

Yeah, you want those damned phones to stop ringing, Goodman thought to himself. "What?"

"I'd really like to talk to Adam Hall. Where is he?"

"Probably at Parchman. I talked to him an hour ago."

"Can he come here today?"

"Yes, in fact he was planning on arriving in Jackson this afternoon."

"Good. I'll wait for him."

Goodman suppressed a smile. Perhaps a small hole had ruptured in the dam.

Oddly, though, it was on a different, far more unlikely front where the first hint of relief surfaced.

SIX BLOCKS AWAY in the federal courthouse, Breck Jefferson entered the office of his boss, the Honorable F. Flynn Slattery, who was on the phone and rather perturbed at a lawyer. Breck held a thick petition for writ of habeas corpus, and a legal pad filled with notes.

"Yes?" Slattery barked, slamming down the phone.

"We need to talk about Cayhall," Breck said somberly. "You know we've got his petition alleging mental incompetence."

"Let's deny it and get it outta here. I'm too busy to worry with it. Let Cayhall take it to the Fifth Circuit. I don't want that damned thing lying around here."

Breck looked troubled, and his words came slower. "But there's something you need to take a look at."

"Aw, come on, Breck. What is it?"

"He may have a valid claim."

Slattery's face fell and his shoulders slumped. "Come on. Are you kidding? What is it? We have a trial starting in thirty minutes. There's a jury waiting out there."

Breck Jefferson had been the number-two student in his law class at Emory. Slattery trusted him implicitly. "They're claiming Sam lacks the mental competence to face an execution, pursuant to a rather broad Mississippi statute."

"Everybody knows he's crazy."

"They have an expert who's willing to testify. It's not something we can ignore."

"I don't believe this."

"You'd better look at it."

His Honor massaged his forehead with his fingertips. "Sit down. Let me see it."

* * *

"JUST A FEW MORE MILES," Adam said as they sped toward the prison. "How you doing?"

Carmen had said little since they left Memphis. Her first journey into Mississippi had been spent looking at the vastness of the Delta, admiring the lushness of its miles of cotton and beans, watching in amazement as crop dusters bounced along the tops of the fields, shaking her head at the clusters of impoverished shacks. "I'm nervous," she admitted, not for the first time. They had talked briefly about Berkeley and Chicago and what the next years might bring. They had said nothing about their mother or father. Sam and his family were likewise neglected.

"He's nervous too."

"This is bizarre, Adam. Rushing along this highway in this wilderness, hurrying to meet a grandfather who's about to be executed."

He patted her firmly on the knee. "You're doing the right thing." She wore oversized chinos, hiking boots, a faded red denim shirt. Very much the grad student in psychology.

"There it is." He suddenly pointed ahead. On both sides of the highway, cars had parked bumper to bumper. Traffic was slow as people walked toward the prison.

"What's all this?" she asked.

"This is a circus."

They passed three Klansmen walking on the edge of the pavement. Carmen stared at them, then shook her head in disbelief. They inched forward, going slightly faster than the people hurrying to the demonstrations. In the middle of the highway in front of the entrance, two state troopers directed traffic. They motioned for Adam to turn right, which he did. A Parchman guard pointed to an area along a shallow road ditch.

They held hands and walked to the front gate, pausing for a moment to stare at the dozens of robed Klansmen milling about in front of the prison. A fiery speech was being delivered into a megaphone that malfunctioned every few seconds. A group of brownshirts stood shoulder to shoulder, holding signs and facing the traffic. No fewer than five television vans were parked on the other side of the highway. Cameras were everywhere. A news helicopter circled above.

At the front gate, Adam introduced Carmen to his new pal Louise, the guard who took care of the paperwork. She was nervous and frazzled. There'd been an altercation or two between the Kluckers and the press and the guards. Things were dicey at the moment, and not likely to improve, in her opinion.

A uniformed guard escorted them to a prison van, and they hurriedly left the front entrance.

"Unbelievable," Carmen said.

"It gets worse each day. Wait till tomorrow."

The van slowed as they eased along the main drive, under the large shade trees and in front of the neat, white houses. Carmen watched everything.

"This doesn't look like a prison," she said.

"It's a farm. Seventeen thousand acres. Prison employees live in those houses."

"With children," she said, looking at bicycles and scooters lying in the front yards. "It's so peaceful. Where are the prisoners?"

"Just wait."

The van turned to the left. The pavement stopped and the dirt road began. Just ahead was the Row.

"See the towers there?" Adam pointed. "The fences and the razor wire?" She nodded.

"That's the Maximum Security Unit. Sam's home for the past nine and a half years."

"Where's the gas chamber?"

"In there."

Two guards looked inside the van, then waved it through the double gates. It stopped near the front door where Packer was waiting. Adam introduced him to Carmen, who by now was barely able to speak. They stepped inside, where Packer frisked them gently. Three other guards watched. "Sam's already in there," Packer said, nodding to the front office. "Go on in."

Adam took her hand and clenched it tightly. She nodded and they walked to the door. He opened it.

Sam was sitting on the edge of the desk, as usual. His feet were swinging under him and he was not smoking. The air in the room was clear and cool. He glanced at Adam, then looked at Carmen. Packer closed the door behind them.

She released Adam's hand and walked to the desk, looking Sam squarely in the eyes. "I'm Carmen," she said softly. Sam eased from the desk. "I'm Sam, Carmen. Your wayward grandfather." He drew her to him and they embraced.

It took a second or two for Adam to realize Sam had shaved his beard. His hair was shorter and looked much neater. His jumpsuit was zipped to the neck.

Sam squeezed her shoulders and examined her face. "You're as pretty as your mother," he said hoarsely. His eyes were moist and Carmen was fighting back tears.

She bit her lip and tried to smile.

"Thanks for coming," he said, trying to grin. "I'm sorry you had to find me like this."

"You look great," she said.

"Don't start lying, Carmen," Adam said, breaking the ice. "And let's stop the crying before it gets outta hand."

"Sit down," Sam said to her, pointing to a chair. He sat next to her, holding her hand.

"Business first, Sam," Adam said as he leaned on the desk. "Fifth Circuit turned us down early this morning. So we're off to greener pastures."

"Your brother here is quite a lawyer," Sam said to Carmen. "He gives me this same news every day."

"Of course, I don't have much to work with," Adam said.

"How's your mother?" Sam asked her.

"She's fine."

"Tell her I asked about her. I remember her as a fine person."

"I will."

"Any word on Lee?" Sam asked him.

"No. Do you want to see her?"

"I think so. But if she can't make it, I'll understand."

"I'll see what I can do," Adam said confidently. His last two phone calls to Phelps had not been returned. Frankly, he didn't have time at the moment to look for Lee.

Sam leaned closer to her. "Adam tells me you're studying psychology."

"That's right. I'm in grad school at Cal Berkeley. I'll—"

A sharp knock on the door interrupted the conversation. Adam opened it slightly, and saw the anxious face of Lucas Mann. "Excuse me for a minute," he said to Sam and Carmen, and stepped into the hall.

"What's up?" he asked.

"Garner Goodman's looking for you," Mann said, almost in a whisper. "He wants you in Jackson immediately."

"Why? What's going on?"

"Looks like one of your claims has found its mark."

Adam's heart stopped. "Which one?"

"Judge Slattery wants to talk about the mental incompetence. He's scheduled a hearing for five this afternoon. Don't say anything to me, because I might be a witness for the state."

Adam closed his eyes and gently tapped his head against the wall. A thousand thoughts swirled wildly through his brain. "Five this afternoon. Slattery?"

"Hard to believe. Look, you need to move fast."

"I need a phone."

"There's one in there," Mann said, nodding to the door behind Adam. "Look, Adam, it's none of my business, but I wouldn't tell Sam. This is still a long shot, and there's no sense getting his hopes up. If it were my decision, I'd wait until the hearing is over."

"You're right. Thanks, Lucas."

"Sure. I'll see you in Jackson."

Adam returned to the room, where the discussion had drifted to life in the Bay Area. "It's nothing," Adam said with a frown, and went casually to the phone. He ignored their quiet talk as he punched the numbers.

"Garner, it's Adam. I'm here with Sam. What's up?"

"Get your ass down here, old boy," Goodman said calmly. "Things are moving."

"I'm listening." Sam was describing his first and only trip to San Francisco, decades ago.

"First, the governor wants to talk privately with you. He seems to be suffering. We're wearing his ass out with the phones, and he's feeling the heat. More important, Slattery, of all people, is hung up on the mental claim. I talked with him thirty minutes ago, and he's just thoroughly confused. I didn't help matters. He wants a hearing at five this afternoon. I've already talked to Dr. Swinn, and he's on standby. He'll land in Jackson at three-thirty and be ready to testify."

"I'm on my way," Adam said with his back to Sam and Carmen.

"Meet me at the governor's office."

Adam hung up. "Just getting the appeals filed," he explained to Sam, who at the moment was totally indifferent. "I need to get to Jackson."

"What's the hurry?" Sam asked, like a man with years to live and nothing to do.

"Hurry? Did you say hurry? It's ten o'clock, Sam, on Monday. We have exactly thirty-eight hours to find a miracle."

"There won't be any miracles, Adam." He turned to Carmen, still holding her hand. "Don't get your hopes up, dear."

"Maybe—"

"No. It's my time, okay. And I'm very ready. I don't want you to be sad when it's over."

"We need to go, Sam," Adam said, touching his shoulder. "I'll be back either late tonight or early in the morning."

Carmen leaned over and kissed Sam on the cheek. "My heart is with you, Sam," she whispered.

He hugged her for a second, then stood by the desk. "You take care, kid. Study hard and all that. And don't think badly of me, okay? I'm here for a reason. It's nobody's fault but mine. There's a better life waiting on me outside this place."

Carmen stood and hugged him again. She was crying as they left the room.

FORTY-SIX

B Y NOON, Judge Slattery had fully embraced the gravity of the moment, and though he tried hard to conceal it, he was enjoying immensely this brief interval in the center of the storm. First, he had dismissed the jury and lawyers in the civil trial pending before him. He had twice talked to the clerk of the Fifth Circuit in New Orleans, then to Justice McNeely himself. The big moment had come a few minutes after eleven when Supreme Court Justice Edward F. Allbright called from Washington to get an update. Allbright was monitoring the case by the hour. They talked law and theory. Neither man was opposed to the death penalty, and both had particular problems with the Mississippi statute in question. They were concerned that it could be abused by any death row inmate who could pretend to be insane and find a wacky doctor to play along.

The reporters quickly learned that a hearing of some type was scheduled, and they not only flooded Slattery's office with calls but parked themselves in his receptionist's office. The U.S. marshal was called to disperse the reporters.

The secretary brought messages by the minute. Breck Jefferson dug through countless law books and scattered research over the long conference table. Slattery talked to the governor, the Attorney General, Garner Goodman, dozens of others. His shoes were under his massive desk. He walked around it, holding the receiver with a long cord, thoroughly enjoying the madness.

IF SLATTERY'S OFFICE was hectic, then the Attorney General's was pure chaos. Roxburgh had gone ballistic with the news that one of Cayhall's shots in the dark had hit a target. You fight these bears for ten years, up and down the appellate ladders, out of one courtroom and into another, battling the creative legal minds of the ACLU and similar outfits, producing along the way enough paperwork to destroy a rain forest, and right when you've got him in your sights, he files a ton of gangplank appeals and one of them gets noticed by a judge somewhere who just happens to be in a tender mood.

He had stormed down the hall to the office of Morris Henry, Dr. Death himself, and together they hastily had assembled a team of their best criminal boys. They met in a large library with rows and stacks of the latest books. They reviewed the Cayhall petition and the applicable law, and they plotted strategy. Witnesses were needed. Who had seen Cayhall in the last month? Who could testify about the things he said and did? There was no time for one of their doctors to examine him. He had a doctor, but they didn't. This was a significant problem. To get their hands on him with a reputable doctor, the state would be forced to ask for time. And time meant a stay of execution. A stay was out of the question.

The guards saw him every day. Who else? Roxburgh called Lucas Mann, who suggested that he talk to Colonel Nugent. Nugent said he'd seen Sam just hours earlier, and, yes, of course, he would be happy to testify. Son of a bitch wasn't crazy. He was just mean. And Sergeant Packer saw him every day. And the prison psychiatrist, Dr. N. Stegall, had met with Sam, and she could testify. Nugent was anxious to help. He also suggested the prison chaplain. And he would think about others.

Morris Henry organized a hit squad of four lawyers to do nothing but dig for dirt on Dr. Anson Swinn. Find other cases he'd been involved in. Talk to other lawyers around the country. Locate transcripts of his testimony. The guy was nothing but a hired mouthpiece, a professional testifier. Get the goods to discredit him.

Once Roxburgh had the attack planned and others doing the work, he rode the elevator to the lobby of the building to chat with the press.

ADAM PARKED in a vacant spot on the grounds of the state capitol. Goodman was waiting under a shade tree with his jacket off and sleeves rolled up, his paisley bow tie perfect. Adam quickly introduced Carmen to Mr. Goodman.

"The governor wants to see you at two. I just left his office, for the third time this morning. Let's walk to our place," he said, waving toward downtown. "It's just a coupla blocks."

"Did you meet Sam?" Goodman asked Carmen.

"Yes. This morning."

"I'm glad you did."

"What's on the governor's mind?" Adam asked. They were walking much too slow to suit him. Relax, he told himself. Just relax.

"Who knows? He wants to meet with you privately. Maybe the market analysis is getting to him. Maybe he's planning a media stunt. Maybe he's sincere. I can't read him. He does look tired, though."

"The phone calls are getting through?"

"Splendidly."

"No one's suspicious?"

"Not yet. Frankly, we're hitting them so fast and so hard I doubt they have time to trace calls."

Carmen shot a blank look at her brother, who was too preoccupied to see it.

"What's the latest from Slattery?" Adam asked as they crossed a street, pausing for a minute in silence to watch the demonstration under way on the front steps of the capitol.

"Nothing since ten this morning. His clerk called you in Memphis, and your secretary gave him my number here. That's how they found me. He told me about the hearing, and said Slattery wants the lawyers in his chamber at three to plan things."

"What does this mean?" Adam asked, desperate for his mentor to say that they were on the brink of a major victory.

Goodman sensed Adam's anxiety. "I honestly don't know. It's good news, but no one knows how permanent it is. Hearings at this stage are not unusual."

They crossed another street and entered the building. Upstairs, the temporary office was buzzing as four law students rattled away on cordless phones. Two were sitting with their feet on the table. One stood in the window and talked earnestly. One was pacing along the far wall, phone stuck to her head. Adam stood by the door and tried to absorb the scene. Carmen was hopelessly confused.

Goodman explained things in a loud whisper. "We're averaging about sixty calls an hour. We dial more than that, but the lines stay jammed, obviously. We're responsible for the jamming, and this keeps other people from getting through. It was much slower over the weekend. The hotline used only one operator." He delivered this summary like a proud plant manager showing off the latest in automated machinery.

"Who are they calling?" Carmen asked.

A law student stepped forward and introduced himself to Adam, and then to Carmen. He was having a ball, he said.

"Would you like something to eat?" Goodman asked. "We have some sandwiches." Adam declined.

"Who are they calling?" Carmen asked again.

"The governor's hotline," Adam replied, without explanation. They listened to the nearest caller as he changed his voice and read a name from a phone list. He was now Benny Chase from Hickory Flat, Mississippi, and he had voted for the governor and didn't think Sam Cayhall should be executed. It was time for the governor to step forward and take care of this situation.

Carmen cut her eyes at her brother, but he ignored her.

"These four are law students at Mississippi College," Goodman explained further. "We've used about a dozen students since Friday, different ages, whites and blacks, male and female. Professor Glass has been most helpful in finding these people. He's made calls too. So have Hez Kerry and his boys at the Defense Group. We've had at least twenty people calling."

They pulled three chairs to the end of a table and sat down. Goodman found soft drinks in a plastic cooler, and sat them on the table. He continued talking in a low voice. "John Bryan Glass is doing some research as we speak. He'll have a brief prepared by four. Hez Kerry is also at work. He's checking with his counterparts in other death states to see if similar statutes have been used recently."

"Kerry is the black guy?" Adam said.

"Yeah, he's the director of the Southern Capital Defense Group. Very sharp."

"A black lawyer busting his butt to save Sam."

"It makes no difference to Hez. It's just another death case."

"I'd like to meet him."

"You will. All these guys will be at the hearing."

"And they're working for free?" Carmen asked.

"Sort of. Kerry is on salary. Part of his job is to monitor every death case in this state, but since Sam has private lawyers Kerry is off the hook. He's donating his time, but it's something he wants to do. Professor Glass is on salary at the law school, but this is definitely outside the scope of his employment there. We're paying these students five bucks an hour."

"Who's paying them?" she asked.

"Dear old Kravitz & Bane."

Adam grabbed a nearby phone book. "Carmen needs to get a flight out of here this afternoon," he said, flipping to the yellow pages.

"I'll take care of it," Goodman said, taking the phone book. "Where to?"

"San Francisco."

"I'll see what's available. Look, there's a little deli around the corner. Why don't you two get something to eat? We'll walk to the governor's office at two."

"I need to get to a library," Adam said, looking at his watch. It was almost one o'clock.

"Go eat, Adam. And try to relax. We'll have time later to sit down with the brain trust and talk strategy. Right now, you need to relax and eat."

"I'm hungry," Carmen said, anxious to be alone with her brother for a few minutes. They eased from the room, and closed the door behind them.

She stopped him in the shabby hallway before they reached the stairs. "Please explain that to me," she insisted, grabbing his arm.

"What?"

"That little room in there."

"It's pretty obvious, isn't it?"

"Is it legal?"

"It's not illegal."

"Is it ethical?"

Adam took a deep breath and stared at the wall. "What are they planning to do with Sam?"

"Execute him."

"Execute, gas, exterminate, kill, call it what you want. But it's murder, Carmen. Legal murder. It's wrong, and I'm trying to stop it. It's a dirty business, and if I have to bend a few ethics, I don't care."

"It stinks."

"So does the gas chamber."

She shook her head and held her words. Twenty-four hours earlier she'd been eating lunch with her boyfriend at a sidewalk café in San Francisco. Now, she wasn't sure where she was.

"Don't condemn me for this, Carmen. These are desperate hours."

"Okay," she said, and headed down the stairs.

THE GOVERNOR and the young lawyer were alone in the vast office, in the comfortable leather chairs, their legs crossed and feet almost touching. Goodman was rushing Carmen to the airport to catch a flight. Mona Stark was nowhere in sight.

"It's strange, you know, you're the grandson, and you've known him for less than a month." McAllister's words were calm, almost tired. "But I've known him for many years. In fact, he's been a part of my life for a long time. And I've always thought that I'd look forward to this day. I've wanted him to die, you know, to be punished for killing those boys." He flipped his bangs and gently rubbed his eyes. His words were so genuine, as if two old friends were catching up on the gossip. "But now I'm not so sure. I have to tell you, Adam, the pressure's getting to me."

He was either being brutally honest, or he was a talented actor. Adam couldn't tell. "What will the state prove if Sam dies?" Adam asked. "Will this be a better place to live when the sun comes up Wednesday morning and he's dead?"

"No. But then you don't believe in the death penalty. I do."

"Why?"

"Because there has to be an ultimate punishment for murder. Put yourself in Ruth Kramer's position, and you'd feel differently. The problem you have, Adam, and people like you, is that you forget about the victims."

"We could argue for hours about the death penalty."

"You're right. Let's skip it. Has Sam told you anything new about the bombing?"

"I can't divulge what Sam's told me. But the answer is no."

"Maybe he acted alone, I don't know."

"What difference would it make today, the day before the execution?"

"I'm not sure, to be honest. But if I knew that Sam was only an accomplice, that someone else was responsible for the killings, then it would be impossible for me to allow him to be executed. I could stop it, you know. I could do that. I'd catch hell for it. It would hurt me politically. The damage could be irreparable, but I wouldn't mind. I'm getting tired of politics. And I don't enjoy being placed in this position, the giver or taker of life. But I could pardon Sam, if I knew the truth."

"You believe he had help. You've told me that already. The FBI agent in charge of the investigation believes it too. Why don't you act on your beliefs and grant clemency?"

"Because we're not certain."

"So, one word from Sam, just one name thrown out here in the final hours, and, bingo, you take your pen and save his life?"

"No, but I might grant a reprieve so the name could be investigated."

"It won't happen, Governor. I've tried. I've asked so often, and he's denied so much, that it's not even discussed anymore."

"Who's he protecting?"

"Hell if I know."

"Perhaps we're wrong. Has he ever given you the details of the bombing?"

"Again, I can't talk about our conversations. But he takes full responsibility for it."

"Then why should I consider clemency? If the criminal himself claims he did the crime, and acted alone, how am I supposed to help him?"

"Help him because he's an old man who'll die soon enough anyway. Help him because it's the right thing to do, and deep down in your heart you want to do it. It'll take guts."

"He hates me, doesn't he?"

"Yes. But he could come around. Give him a pardon and he'll be your biggest fan."

McAllister smiled and unwrapped a peppermint. "Is he really insane?"

"Our expert says he is. We'll do our best to convince Judge Slattery."

"I know, but really? You've spent hours with him. Does he know what's happening?"

At this point, Adam decided against honesty. McAllister was not a friend, and not at all trustworthy. "He's pretty sad," Adam admitted. "Frankly, I'm surprised any person can keep his mind after a few months on death row. Sam was an old man when he got there, and he's slowly deteriorated. That's one reason he's declined all interviews. He's quite pitiful."

Adam couldn't tell if the governor believed this, but he certainly absorbed it.

"What's your schedule tomorrow?" McAllister asked.

"I have no idea. It depends on what happens in Slattery's court. I had planned to spend most of the day with Sam, but I might be running around filing last minute appeals."

"I gave you my private number. Let's keep in touch tomorrow."

SAM TOOK THREE BITES of pinto beans and some of the corn bread, then placed the tray at the end of his bed. The same idiot guard with the blank face watched him through the bars of the tier door. Life was bad enough in these cramped cubicles, but living like an animal and being watched was unbearable.

It was six o'clock, time for the evening news. He was anxious to hear what the world was saying about him. The Jackson station began with the breaking story of a last minute hearing before Federal Judge F. Flynn Slattery. The report cut to the outside of the federal courthouse in Jackson where an anxious young man with a microphone explained that the hearing had been delayed a bit as the lawyers wrangled in Slattery's office. He tried his best to briefly explain the issue. The defense was now claiming that Mr. Cayhall lacked sufficient mental capacity to understand why he was being executed. He was senile and insane, claimed the defense, which would call a noted psychiatrist in this last ditch effort to stop the execution. The hearing was expected to get under way at any moment, and no one knew when a decision might be reached by Judge Slattery. Back to the anchorwoman, who said that, meanwhile, up at the state penitentiary at Parchman, all systems were go for the execution. Another young man with a microphone was suddenly on the screen, standing somewhere near the front gate of the prison, describing the increased security. He pointed to his right, and the camera panned the area near the highway where a regular carnival was happening. The highway patrol was out in force, directing traffic and keeping a wary eye on an assemblage of several dozen Ku Klux Klansmen. Other protestors included various groups of white supremacists and the usual death penalty abolitionists, he said.

The camera swung back to the reporter, who now had with him Colonel George Nugent, acting superintendent for Parchman, and the man in charge of the execution. Nugent grimly answered a few questions, said things were very much under control, and if the courts gave the green light then the execution would be carried out according to the law.

Sam turned off the television. Adam had called two hours earlier and explained the hearing, so he was prepared to hear that he was senile and insane and God knows what else. Still, he didn't like it. It was bad enough waiting to be executed, but to have his sanity slandered so nonchalantly seemed like a cruel invasion of privacy.

The tier was hot and quiet. The televisions and radios were turned down. Next door, Preacher Boy softly sang "The Old Rugged Cross," and it was not unpleasant.

In a neat pile on the floor against the wall was his new outfit—a plain white cotton shirt, Dickies, white socks, and a pair of brown loafers. Donnie had spent an hour with him during the afternoon.

He turned off the light and relaxed on the bed. Thirty hours to live.

THE MAIN COURTROOM in the federal building was packed when Slattery finally released the lawyers from his chamber for the third time. It was the last of a series of heated conferences that had dragged on for most of the afternoon. It was now almost seven.

They filed into the courtroom and took their places behind the appropriate tables. Adam sat with Garner Goodman. In a row of chairs behind them were Hez Kerry, John Bryan Glass, and three of his law students. Roxburgh, Morris Henry, and a half dozen assistants crowded around the state's table. Two rows behind them, behind the bar, sat the governor with Mona Stark on one side and Larramore on the other.

The rest of the crowd was primarily reporters—no cameras were allowed. There were curious spectators, law students, other lawyers. It was open to the public. In the back row, dressed comfortably in a sports coat and tie, was Rollie Wedge.

Slattery made his entrance and everyone stood for a moment. "Be seated," he said into his microphone. "Let's go on the record," he said to the court reporter. He gave a succinct review of the petition and the applicable law, and outlined the parameters of the hearing. He was not in the mood for lengthy arguments and pointless questions, so move it along, he told the lawyers.

"Is the petitioner ready?" he asked in Adam's direction. Adam stood nervously, and said, "Yes sir. The petitioner calls Dr. Anson Swinn."

Swinn stood from the first row and walked to the witness stand where he was sworn in. Adam walked to the podium in the center of the courtroom, holding his notes and pushing himself to be strong. His notes were typed and meticulous, the result of some superb research and preparation by Hez Kerry and John Bryan Glass. The two, along with Kerry's staff, had devoted the entire day to Sam Cayhall and this hearing. And they were ready to work all night and throughout tomorrow.

Adam began by asking Swinn some basic questions about his education and training. Swinn's answers were accented with the crispness of the upper Midwest, and this was fine. Experts should talk differently and travel great distances in order to be highly regarded. With his black hair, black beard, black glasses, and black suit, he indeed gave the appearance of an ominously brilliant master of his field. The preliminary questions were short and to the point, but only because Slattery had already reviewed Swinn's qualifications and ruled that he could in fact testify as an expert. The state could attack his credentials on cross-examination, but his testimony would go into the record.

With Adam leading the way, Swinn talked about his two hours with Sam Cayhall on the previous Tuesday. He described his physical condition, and did so with such relish that Sam sounded like a corpse. He was quite probably insane, though insanity was a legal term, not medical. He had difficulty answering even basic questions like What did you eat for breakfast? Who is in the cell next to you? When did your wife die? Who was your lawyer during the first trial? And on and on.

Swinn very carefully covered his tracks by repeatedly telling the court that two hours simply was not enough time to thoroughly diagnose Mr. Cayhall. More time was needed.

In his opinion, Sam Cayhall did not appreciate the fact that he was about to die, did not understand why he was being executed, and certainly didn't realize he was being punished for a crime. Adam gritted his teeth to keep from wincing at times, but Swinn was certainly convincing. Mr. Cayhall was completely calm and at ease, clueless about his fate, wasting away his days in a six-by-nine cell. It was quite sad. One of the worst cases he'd encountered.

Under different circumstances, Adam would've been horrified to place on the stand a witness so obviously full of bull. But at this moment, he was mighty proud of this bizarre little man. Human life was at stake.

Slattery was not about to cut short the testimony of Dr. Swinn. This case would be reviewed instantly by the Fifth Circuit and perhaps the U.S. Supreme Court, and he wanted no one from above second-guessing him. Goodman suspected this, and Swinn had been prepped to ramble. So with the court's indulgence, Swinn launched into the likely causes of Sam's problems. He described the horrors of living in a cell twenty-three hours a day; of knowing the gas chamber is a stone's throw away; of being denied companionship, decent food, sex, movement, plenty of exercise, fresh air. He'd worked with many death row inmates around the country and knew their problems well. Sam, of course, was much different because of his age. The average death row inmate is thirty-one years old, and has spent four years waiting to die. Sam was sixty when he first arrived at Parchman. Physically and mentally, he was not suited for it. It was inevitable he would deteriorate.

Swinn was under Adam's direct examination for forty-five minutes. When Adam had exhausted his questions, he sat down. Steve Roxburgh strutted to the podium, and stared at Swinn.

Swinn knew what was coming, and he was not the least bit concerned. Roxburgh began by asking who was paying for his services, and how much he was charging. Swinn said Kravitz & Bane was paying him two hundred dollars an hour. Big deal. There was no jury in the box. Slattery knew that all experts get paid, or they couldn't testify. Roxburgh tried to chip away at Swinn's professional qualifications, but got nowhere. The man was a well-educated, well-trained, experienced psychiatrist. So what if he decided years ago he could make more money as an expert witness. His qualifications weren't diminished. And Roxburgh was not about to argue medicine with a doctor.

The questions grew even stranger as Roxburgh began asking about other lawsuits in which Swinn had testified. There was a kid who was burned in a car wreck in Ohio, and Swinn had given his opinion that the child was completely mentally disabled. Hardly an extreme opinion.

"Where are you going with this?" Slattery interrupted loudly.

Roxburgh glanced at his notes, then said, "Your Honor, we're attempting to discredit this witness."

"I know that. But it's not working, Mr. Roxburgh. This court knows that this witness has testified in many trials around the country. What's the point?"

"We are attempting to show that he is willing to state some pretty wild opinions if the money is right."

"Lawyers do that every day, Mr. Roxburgh."

There was some very light laughter in the audience, but very reserved.

"I don't want to hear it," Slattery snapped. "Now move on."

Roxburgh should've sat down, but the moment was too rich for that. He moved to the next minefield, and began asking questions about Swinn's examination of Sam. He went nowhere. Swinn fielded each question with a fluid answer that only added to his testimony on direct examination. He repeated much of the sad description of Sam Cayhall. Roxburgh scored no points, and once thoroughly trounced, finally went to his seat. Swinn was dismissed from the stand.

The next and last witness for the petitioner was a surprise, though Slattery had already approved him. Adam called Mr. E. Garner Goodman to the stand.

Goodman was sworn, and took his seat. Adam asked about his firm's representation of Sam Cayhall, and Goodman briefly outlined the history of it for the record. Slattery already knew most of it. Goodman smiled when he recalled Sam's efforts to fire Kravitz & Bane.

"Does Kravitz & Bane represent Mr. Cayhall at this moment?" Adam asked.

"Indeed we do."

"And you're here in Jackson at this moment working on the case?"

"That's correct."

"In your opinion, Mr. Goodman, do you believe Sam Cayhall has told his lawyers everything about the Kramer bombing?"

"No I do not."

Rollie Wedge sat up a bit and listened intently.

"Would you please explain?"

"Certainly. There has always been strong circum-stantial evidence that another person was with Sam Cayhall during the Kramer bombing, and the bomb-ings that preceded it. Mr. Cayhall always refused to discuss this with me, his lawyer, and even now will not cooperate with his attorneys. Obviously, at this point in this case, it is crucial that he fully divulge everything to his lawyers. And he is unable to do so. There are facts we should know, but he won't tell us."

Wedge was at once nervous and relieved. Sam was holding fast, but his lawyers were trying everything.

Adam asked a few more questions, and sat down.

Roxburgh asked only one. "When was the last time you spoke with Mr. Cayhall?"

Goodman hesitated and thought about the answer. He honestly couldn't remember exactly when. "I'm not sure. It's been two or three years."

"Two or three years? And you're his lawyer?"

"I'm one of his lawyers. Mr. Hall is now the principal lawyer on this case, and he's spent innumerable hours with the client during the last month."

Roxburgh sat down, and Goodman returned to his seat at the table.

"We have no more witnesses, Your Honor," Adam said for the record.

"Call your first witness, Mr. Roxburgh," Slattery said.

"The state calls Colonel George Nugent," Roxburgh announced. Nugent was found in the hallway, and escorted to the witness stand. His olive shirt and pants were wrinkle-free. The boots were gleaming. He stated for the record who he was and what he was doing. "I was at Parchman an hour ago," he said, looking at his watch. "Just flew down on the state helicopter."

"When did you last see Sam Cayhall?" Roxburgh asked.

"He was moved to the Observation Cell at nine this morning. I spoke with him then."

"Was he mentally alert, or just drooling over in the corner like an idiot?"

Adam started to jump and object, but Goodman grabbed his arm.

"He was extremely alert," Nugent said eagerly. "Very sharp. He asked me why he was being moved from his cell to another one. He understood what was happening. He didn't like it, but then Sam doesn't like anything these days."

"Did you see him yesterday?"

"Yes."

"And was he able to speak, or just lying around like a vegetable?"

"Oh, he was quite talkative."

"What did you talk about?"

"I had a checklist of things I needed to cover with Sam. He was very hostile, even threatened me with bodily harm. He's a very abrasive person with a sharp tongue. He settled down a bit, and we talked about his last meal, his witnesses, what to do with his personal effects. Things such as that. We talked about the execution."

"Is he aware he is about to be executed?"

Nugent burst into laughter. "What kind of question is that?"

"Just answer it," Slattery said without a smile.

"Of course he knows. He knows damned well what's going on. He's not crazy. He told me the execution would not take place because his lawyers were about to unload the heavy artillery, as he put it. They've planned all this." Nugent waved both hands at the entire courtroom.

Roxburgh asked about prior meetings with Sam, and Nugent spared no details. He seemed to remember every word Sam had uttered in the past two weeks, especially the biting sarcasm and caustic remarks.

Adam knew it was all true. He huddled quickly with Garner Goodman, and they decided to forgo any cross-examination. Little could be gained from it.

Nugent marched down the aisle and out of the courtroom. The man had a mission. He was needed at Parchman.

The state's second witness was Dr. N. Stegall, psychiatrist for the Department of Corrections. She made her way to the witness stand as Roxburgh conferred with Morris Henry.

"State your name for the record," Slattery said.

"Dr. N. Stegall."

"Ann?" His Honor asked.

"No. N. It's an initial."

Slattery looked down at her, then looked at Roxburgh who shrugged as if he didn't know what to say.

The judge eased even closer to the edge of his bench, and peered down at the witness stand. "Look, Doctor, I didn't ask for your initial, I asked for your name. Now, you state it for the record, and be quick about it."

She jerked her eyes away from his, cleared her throat, and reluctantly said, "Neldeen."

No wonder, thought Adam. Why hadn't she changed it to something else?

Roxburgh seized the moment and asked her a rapid series of questions about her qualifications and training. Slattery had already deemed her fit to testify.

"Now, Dr. Stegall," Roxburgh began, careful to avoid any reference to Neldeen, "when did you meet with Sam Cayhall?"

She held a sheet of paper that she looked at. "Thursday, July 26."

"And the purpose of this visit?"

"As part of my job, I routinely visit death row inmates, especially those with executions approaching. I provide counseling and medication, if they request it."

"Describe Mr. Cayhall's mental condition?"

"Extremely alert, very bright, very sharp-tongued, almost to the point of being rude. In fact, he was quite rude to me, and he asked me not to come back."

"Did he discuss his execution?"

"Yes. In fact, he knew that he had thirteen days to go, and he accused me of trying to give him medication so he wouldn't be any trouble when his time came. He also expressed concern for another death row inmate,

Randy Dupree, who Sam thinks is deteriorating mentally. He was most concerned about Mr. Dupree, and chastised me for not examining him."

"In your opinion, is he suffering from any form of decreased mental capacity?"

"Not at all. His mind is very sharp."

"No further questions," Roxburgh said, and sat down.

Adam walked purposefully to the podium. "Tell us, Dr. Stegall, how is Randy Dupree doing?" he asked at full volume.

"I, uh, I haven't had a chance to see him yet."

"Sam told you about him eleven days ago, and you haven't bothered to meet with him."

"I've been busy."

"How long have you held your present job?"

"Four years."

"And in four years how many times have you talked to Sam Cayhall?"

"Once."

"You don't care much for the death row inmates, do you, Dr. Stegall?"

"I certainly do."

"How many men are on death row right now?"

"Well, uh, I'm not sure. Around forty, I think."

"How many have you actually talked to? Give us a few names."

Whether it was fear or anger or ignorance, no one could tell. But Neldeen froze. She grimaced and cocked her head to one side, obviously trying to pull a name from the air, and obviously unable to do so. Adam allowed her to hang for a moment, then said, "Thank you, Dr. Stegall." He turned and walked slowly back to his chair.

"Call your next witness," Slattery demanded.

"The state calls Sergeant Clyde Packer."

Packer was fetched from the hallway and led to the front of the courtroom. He was still in uniform, but the gun had been removed. He swore to tell the truth, and took his seat on the witness stand.

Adam was not surprised at the effect of Packer's testimony. He was an honest man who simply told what he'd seen. He'd known Sam for nine and a half years, and he was the same today as he was when he first arrived. He typed letters and law papers all day long, read many books, especially legal ones. He typed writs for his buddies on the Row, and he typed letters to wives and girlfriends for some of the guys who couldn't spell. He chain-smoked because he wanted to kill himself before the state got around to it. He loaned money to friends. In Packer's humble opinion, Sam was as mentally alert now as he'd been nine and a half years earlier. And his mind was very quick.

Slattery leaned a bit closer to the edge of the bench when Packer described Sam's checkers games with Henshaw and Gullitt.

"Does he win?" His Honor asked, interrupting.

"Almost always."

Perhaps the turning point of the hearing came when Packer told the story of Sam wanting to see a sunrise before he died. It happened late last week when Packer was making his rounds one morning. Sam had quietly made the request. He knew he was about to die, said he was ready to go, and that he'd like to sneak out early one morning to the bullpen on the east end and see the sun come up. So Packer took care of it, and last Saturday Sam spent an hour sipping coffee and waiting for the sun. Afterward, he was very grateful.

Adam had no questions for Packer. He was excused, and left the courtroom.

Roxburgh announced that the next witness was Ralph Griffin, the prison chaplain. Griffin was led to the stand, and looked uncomfortably around the court-room. He gave his name and occupation, then glanced warily at Roxburgh.

"Do you know Sam Cayhall?" Roxburgh asked.

"I do."

"Have you counseled him recently?"

"Yes."

"When did you last see him?"

"Yesterday. Sunday."

"And how would you describe his mental state?"

"I can't."

"I beg your pardon."

"I said I can't describe his mental condition."

"Why not?"

"Because right now I'm his minister, and anything he says or does in my presence is strictly confidential. I can't testify against Mr. Cayhall."

Roxburgh stalled for a moment, trying to decide what to do next. It was obvious neither he nor his learned underlings had given any thought to this situation. Perhaps they'd just assumed that since the chaplain was working for the state, then he'd cooperate with them. Griffin waited expectantly for an assault from Roxburgh.

Slattery settled the matter quickly. "A very good point, Mr. Roxburgh. This witness should not be here. Who's next?"

"No further witnesses," the Attorney General said, anxious to leave the podium and get to his seat.

His Honor scribbled some notes at length, then looked at the crowded courtroom. "I will take this matter under advisement and render an opinion, probably early in the morning. As soon as my decision is ready, we will notify the attorneys. You don't need to hang around here. We'll call you. Court's adjourned."

Everyone stood and hurried for the rear doors.

Adam caught the Reverend Ralph Griffin and thanked him, then he returned to the table where Goodman, Hez Kerry, Professor Glass, and the students were waiting. They huddled and whispered until the crowd was gone, then left the courtroom. Someone mentioned drinks and dinner. It was almost nine.

Reporters were waiting outside the door to the courtroom. Adam threw out a few polite no-comments and kept walking. Rollie Wedge eased behind Adam and Goodman as they inched through the crowded hallway. He vanished as they left the building.

Two groups of cameras were ready outside. On the front steps, Roxburgh was addressing one batch of reporters, and not far away on the sidewalk, the governor was holding forth. As Adam walked by, he heard McAllister say that clemency was being considered, and that it would be a long night. Tomorrow would be even tougher. Would he attend the execution? someone asked. Adam couldn't hear the reply.

THEY MET at Hal and Mal's, a popular downtown restaurant and watering hole. Hez found a large table in a corner near the front and ordered a round of beer. A blues band was cranked up in the back. The dining room and bar were crowded.

Adam sat in a corner, next to Hez, and relaxed for the first time in hours. The beer went down fast and calmed him. They ordered red beans and rice, and chatted about the hearing. Hez said he'd performed wonderfully, and the law students were full of compliments. The mood was optimistic. Adam thanked them for their help. Goodman and Glass were at the far end of the table, lost in a conversation about another death row case. Time passed slowly, and Adam attacked his dinner when it arrived.

"This is probably not a good time to bring this up,"

Hez said out of the corner of his mouth. He wanted no one to hear but Adam. The band was even louder now.

"I guess you'll go back to Chicago when this is over," he said, looking at Goodman to make sure he was still engaged with Glass.

"I guess so," Adam said, without conviction. He'd had little time to think past tomorrow.

"Well, just so you'll know, there's an opening in our office. One of my guys is going into private practice, and we're looking for a new lawyer. It's nothing but death work, you know."

"You're right," Adam said quietly. "This is a lousy time to bring it up."

"It's tough work, but it's satisfying. It's also heart-breaking. And necessary." Hez chewed on a bite of sausage, and washed it down with beer. "The money is lousy, compared with what you're making with the firm. Tight budget, long hours, lots of clients."

"How much?"

"I can start you at thirty thousand."

"I'm making sixty-two right now. With more on the way."

"I've been there. I was making seventy with a big firm in D.C. when I gave it up to come here. I was on the fast track to a partnership, but it was easy to quit. Money's not everything."

"You enjoy this?"

"It grows on you. It takes strong moral convictions to fight the system like this. Just think about it."

Goodman was now looking their way. "Are you driving to Parchman tonight?" he asked loudly.

Adam was finishing his second beer. He wanted a third, but no more. Exhaustion was rapidly setting in. "No. I'll wait until we hear something in the morning."

They ate and drank and listened to Goodman and

Glass and Kerry tell war stories of other executions. The beer flowed, and the atmosphere went from optimism to outright confidence.

SAM LAY in the darkness and waited for midnight. He'd watched the late news and learned that the hearing was over, and that the clock was still ticking. There was no stay. His life was in the hands of a federal judge.

At one minute after midnight, he closed his eyes and said a prayer. He asked God to help Lee with her troubles, to be with Carmen, and to give Adam the strength to survive the inevitable.

He had twenty-four hours to live. He folded his hands over his chest, and fell asleep.

FORTY-SEVEN

NUGENT WAITED until exactly seven-thirty to close the door and start the meeting. He walked to the front of the room, and surveyed his troops. "I just left MSU," he said somberly. "The inmate is awake and alert, not at all the blithering zombie we read about in the paper this morning." He paused and smiled and expected everyone to admire his humor. It went undetected.

"In fact, he's already had his breakfast, and is already bitching about wanting his recreation time. So at least something is normal around here. There's no word from the federal court in Jackson, so this thing is on schedule unless we hear otherwise. Correct, Mr. Mann?"

Lucas was sitting at the table across the front of the room, reading the paper and trying to ignore the colonel. "Right."

"Now, there are two areas of concern. First is the press. I've assigned Sergeant Moreland here to handle these bastards. We're gonna move them to the Visitors Center just inside the front gate, and try to keep them pinned down there. We're gonna surround them with guards, and just dare them to venture about. At four this afternoon, I'll conduct the lottery to see which reporters get to watch the execution. As of yesterday, there were over a hundred names on the request list. They get five seats.

"The second problem is what's happening outside the gate. The governor has agreed to assign three dozen troopers for today and tomorrow, and they'll be here shortly. We have to keep our distance from these nuts, especially the skinheads, sumbitches are crazy, but at the same time we have to maintain order. There were two fights yesterday, and things could've deteriorated rapidly if we hadn't been watching. If the execution takes place, there could be some tense moments. Any questions?"

There were none.

"Very well. I'll expect everyone to act professionally today, and carry this out in a responsible manner. Dismissed." He snapped off a smart salute, and proudly watched them leave the room.

SAM STRADDLED THE BENCH with the checkerboard in front of him, and waited patiently for J. B. Gullitt to enter the bullpen. He sipped the stale remains of a cup of coffee.

Gullitt stepped through the door, and paused as the handcuffs were removed. He rubbed his wrists, shielded his eyes from the sun, and looked at his friend sitting alone. He walked to the bench and took his position across the board.

Sam never looked up.

"Any good news, Sam?" Gullitt asked nervously. "Tell me it won't happen."

"Just move," Sam said, staring at the checkers.

"It can't happen, Sam," he pleaded.

"It's your turn to go first. Move."

Gullitt slowly lowered his eyes to the board.

THE PREVAILING THEORY of the morning was that the longer Slattery sat on the petition, the greater the likelihood of a stay. But this was the conventional wisdom of those who were praying for a reprieve. No word had come by 9 A.M., nothing by 9:30.

Adam waited in Hez Kerry's office, which had become the operations center during the past twenty-four hours. Goodman was across town supervising the relentless hounding of the governor's hotline, a task he seemed to savor. John Bryan Glass had parked himself outside Slattery's office.

In the event Slattery denied a stay, they would immediately appeal to the Fifth Circuit. The appeal was completed by nine, just in case. Kerry had also prepared a petition for cert to the U.S. Supreme Court if the Fifth Circuit turned them down. The paperwork was waiting. Everything was waiting.

To occupy his mind, Adam called everyone he could think of. He called Carmen in Berkeley. She was asleep and fine. He called Lee's condo, and, of course, there was no answer. He called Phelps's office and talked to a secretary. He called Darlene to tell her he had no idea when he might return. He called McAllister's private number, but got a busy signal. Perhaps Goodman had it jammed too.

He called Sam and talked about the hearing last night, with special emphasis on the Reverend Ralph Griffin. Packer had testified too, he explained, and told only the truth. Nugent, typically, was an ass. He told Sam he would be there around noon. Sam asked him to hurry.

By eleven, Slattery's name was being cursed and defamed with righteous fervor. Adam had had enough. He called Goodman and said he was driving to Parchman. He said farewell to Hez Kerry, and thanked him again.

Then he raced away, out of the city of Jackson, north on Highway 49. Parchman was two hours away if he drove within the speed limit. He found a talk radio station that promised the latest news twice an hour, and listened to an interminable discussion about casino gambling in Mississippi. There was nothing new on the Cayhall execution at the eleven-thirty newsbreak.

He drove eighty and ninety, passing on yellow lines and on curves and over bridges. He sped through speed zones in tiny towns and hamlets. He was uncertain what drew him to Parchman with such speed. There wasn't much he could do once he got there. The legal maneuverings had been left behind in Jackson. He would sit with Sam and count the hours. Or maybe they would celebrate a wonderful gift from federal court.

He stopped at a roadside grocery near the small town of Flora for gas and fruit juice, and he was driving away from the pumps when he heard the news. The bored and listless talk show host was now filled with excitement as he relayed the breaking story in the Cayhall case. United States District Court Judge F. Flynn Slattery had just denied Cayhall's last petition, his claim to be mentally incompetent. The matter would be appealed to the Fifth Circuit within the hour. Sam Cayhall had just taken a giant step toward the Mississippi gas chamber, the host said dramatically.

Instead of punching the accelerator, Adam slowed to a reasonable speed and sipped his drink. He turned off the radio. He cracked his window to allow the warm air to circulate. He cursed Slattery for many miles, talking vainly at the windshield and dragging up all sorts of vile names. It was now a little past noon. Slattery, in all fairness, could've ruled five hours ago. Hell, if he had guts he could've ruled last night. They could be in front of the Fifth Circuit already. He cursed Breck Jefferson also, for good measure.

Sam had told him from the beginning that Mississippi wanted an execution. It was lagging behind Louisiana and Texas and Florida; even Alabama and Georgia and Virginia were killing at a more enviable rate. Something had to be done. The appeals were endless. The criminals were coddled. Crime was rampant. It was time to execute somebody and show the rest of the country that this state was serious about law and order.

Adam finally believed him.

He stopped the swearing after a while. He finished the drink and threw the bottle over the car and into a ditch, in direct violation of Mississippi laws against littering. It was difficult to express his present opinions of Mississippi and its laws.

He could see Sam sitting in his cell, watching the television, hearing the news.

Adam's heart ached for the old man. He had failed as a lawyer. His client was about to die at the hands of the government, and there wasn't a damned thing he could do about it.

THE NEWS electrified the army of reporters and cameramen now sprawled about the small Visitors Center just inside the front gate. They gathered around portable televisions and watched their stations in Jackson and Memphis. At least four shot live segments from Parchman while countless others milled around the area. Their little section of ground had been cordoned off by ropes and barricades, and was being watched closely by Nugent's troops.

The racket increased noticeably along the highway when the news spread. The Klansmen, now a hundred strong, began chanting loudly in the direction of the administration buildings. The skinheads and Nazis and Aryans hurled obscenities at anyone who would listen to them. The nuns and other silent protestors sat under umbrellas and tried to ignore their rowdy neighbors.

Sam heard the news as he was holding a bowl of

turnip greens, his final meal before his last meal. He stared at the television, watched the scenes switch from Jackson to Parchman and back again. A young black lawyer he'd never heard of was talking to a reporter and explaining what he and the rest of the Cayhall defense team would do next.

His friend Buster Moac had complained that there were so damned many lawyers involved with his case in the last days that he couldn't keep up with who was on his side and who was trying to kill him. But Sam was certain Adam was in control.

He finished the turnip greens, and placed the bowl on the tray at the foot of his bed. He walked to the bars and sneered at the blank-faced guard watching him from behind the tier door. The hall was silent. The televisions were on in every cell, all turned low and being watched with morbid interest. Not a single voice could be heard, and that in itself was extremely rare.

He pulled off his red jumpsuit for the last time, wadded it up and threw it in a corner. He kicked the rubber shower shoes under his bed, never to see them again. He carefully placed his new outfit on the bed, arranged it just so, then slowly unbuttoned the short-sleeved shirt and put it on. It fit nicely. He slid his legs into the stiff work khakis, pulled the zipper up and buttoned the waist. The pants were two inches too long, so he sat on the bed and turned them up into neat, precise cuffs. The cotton socks were thick and soothing. The shoes were a bit large but not a bad fit.

The sensation of being fully dressed in real clothes brought sudden, painful memories of the free world. These were the pants he'd worn for forty years, until he'd been incarcerated. He'd bought them at the old dry goods store on the square in Clanton, always keeping four or five pair in the bottom drawer of his large dresser. His wife pressed them with no starch, and after a half dozen washings they felt like old pajamas. He wore them to work and he wore them to town. He wore them on fishing trips with Eddie, and he wore them on the porch swinging little Lee. He wore them to the coffee shop and to Klan meetings. Yes, he'd even worn them on that fateful trip to Greenville to bomb the office of the radical Jew.

He sat on his bed and pinched the sharp creases under his knees. It had been nine years and six months since he had worn these pants. Only fitting, he guessed, that he should now wear them to the gas chamber.

They'd be cut from his body, placed in a bag, and burned.

ADAM STOPPED FIRST at Lucas Mann's office. Louise at the front gate had given him a note saying it was important. Mann closed the door behind him and offered a seat. Adam declined. He was anxious to see Sam.

"The Fifth Circuit received the appeal thirty minutes ago," Mann said. "I thought you might want to use my phone to call Jackson."

"Thanks. But I'll use the one at the Row."

"Fine. I'm talking to the AG's office every half hour, so if I hear something I'll give you a call."

"Thanks." Adam was fidgeting.

"Does Sam want a last meal?"

"I'll ask him in a minute."

"Fine. Give me a call, or just tell Packer. What about witnesses?"

"Sam will have no witnesses."

"What about you?"

"No. He won't allow it. We agreed on it a long time ago."

"Fine. I can't think of anything else. I have a fax and

a phone, and things may be a bit quieter in here. Feel free to use my office."

"Thanks," Adam said, stepping from the office. He drove slowly to the Row and parked for the last time in the dirt lot next to the fence. He walked slowly to the guard tower and placed his keys in the bucket.

Four short weeks ago he had stood there and watched the red bucket descend for the first time, and he'd thought how crude but effective this little system was. Only four weeks! It seemed like years.

He waited for the double gates, and met Tiny on the steps.

Sam was already in the front office, sitting on the edge of the desk, admiring his shoes. "Check out the new threads," he said proudly when Adam entered.

Adam stepped close and inspected the clothing from shoes to shirt. Sam was beaming. His face was clean-shaven. "Spiffy. Real spiffy."

"A regular dude, aren't I?"

"You look nice, Sam, real nice. Did Donnie bring these?"

"Yeah. He got them at the dollar store. I started to order some designer threads from New York, but what the hell. It's only an execution. I told you I wouldn't allow them to kill me in one of those red prison suits. I took it off a while ago, never to wear one again. I have to admit, Adam, it was a good feeling."

"You've heard the latest?"

"Sure. It's all over the news. Sorry about the hearing."

"It's in the Fifth Circuit now, and I feel good about it. I like our chances there."

Sam smiled and looked away, as if the little boy were telling his grandfather a harmless lie. "They had a black lawyer on television at noon, said he was working for me. What the hell's going on?"

"That was probably Hez Kerry." Adam placed his briefcase on the desk and sat down.

"Am I paying him too?"

"Yeah, Sam, you're paying him at the same rate you're paying me."

"Just curious. That screwball doctor, what's his name, Swinn? He must've done a number on me."

"It was pretty sad, Sam. When he finished testifying, the entire courtroom could see you floating around your cell, scratching your teeth and peeing on the floor."

"Well, I'm about to be put out of my misery." Sam's words were strong and loud, almost defiant. There was not a trace of fear. "Look, I have a small favor to ask of you," he said, reaching for yet another envelope.

"Who is it this time?"

Sam handed it to him. "I want you to take this to the highway by the front gate, and I want you to find the leader of that bunch of Kluckers out there, and I want you to read it to him. Try and get the cameras to film it, because I want people to know what it says."

Adam held it suspiciously. "What does it say?"

"It's quick and to the point. I ask them all to go home. To leave me alone, so that I can die in peace. I've never heard of some of those groups, and they're getting a lot of mileage out of my death."

"You can't make them leave, you know."

"I know. And I don't expect them to. But the television makes it appear as if these are my friends and cronies. I don't know a single person out there."

"I'm not so sure it's a good idea right now," Adam said, thinking out loud.

"Why not?"

"Because as we speak, we're telling the Fifth Circuit that you're basically a vegetable, incapable of putting together thoughts like this."

Sam was suddenly angry. "You lawyers," he sneered. "Don't you ever give up? It's over, Adam, stop playing games."

"It's not over."

"As far as I'm concerned it is. Now, take the damned letter and do as I say."

"Right now?" Adam asked, looking at his watch. It was one-thirty.

"Yes! Right now. I'll be waiting here."

ADAM PARKED by the guardhouse at the front gate, and explained to Louise what he was about to do. He was nervous. She gave a leery look at the white envelope in his hand, and yelled for two uniformed guards to walk over. They escorted Adam through the front gate and toward the demonstration area. Some reporters covering the protestors recognized Adam, and immediately flocked to him. He and the guards walked quickly along the front fence, ignoring their questions. Adam was scared but determined, and more than a little comforted by his newly found bodyguards.

He walked directly to the blue and white canopy that marked the headquarters for the Klan, and by the time he stopped, a group of white-robes was waiting for him. The press encircled Adam, his guards, the Klansmen. "Who's in charge here?" Adam demanded, holding his breath.

"Who wants to know?" asked a burly young man with a black beard and sunburned cheeks. Sweat dripped from his eyebrows as he stepped forward.

"I have a statement here from Sam Cayhall," Adam said loudly, and the circle compressed. Cameras clicked. Reporters shoved microphones and recorders into the air around Adam.

"Quiet," someone yelled.

"Get back!" one of the guards snapped.

A tense group of Klansmen, all in matching robes but most without the hoods, packed tighter together in front of Adam. He recognized none of them from his last confrontation on Friday. These guys did not look too friendly.

The racket stopped along the grassy strip as the crowd pushed closer to hear Sam's lawyer.

Adam pulled the note from the envelope and held it with both hands. "My name is Adam Hall, and I'm Sam Cayhall's lawyer. This is a statement from Sam," he repeated. "It's dated today, and addressed to all members of the Ku Klux Klan, and to the other groups demonstrating on his behalf here today. I quote: 'Please leave. Your presence here is of no comfort to me. You're using my execution as a means to further your own interests. I do not know a single one of you, nor do I care to meet you. Please go away immediately. I prefer to die without the benefit of your theatrics.'"

Adam glanced at the stern faces of the Klansmen, all hot and dripping with perspiration. "The last paragraph reads as follows, and I quote: 'I am no longer a member of the Ku Klux Klan. I repudiate that organization and all that it stands for. I would be a free man today had I never heard of the Ku Klux Klan.' It's signed by Sam Cayhall." Adam flipped it over and thrust it toward the Kluckers, all of whom were speechless and stunned.

The one with the black beard and sunburned cheeks lunged at Adam in an attempt to grab the letter. "Gimme that!" he yelled, but Adam yanked it away. The guard to Adam's right stepped forward quickly and blocked the man, who pushed the guard. The guard shoved him back, and for a few terrifying seconds Adam's bodyguards scuffled with a few of the Kluckers. Other guards had been watching nearby, and within seconds they were in the middle of the shoving match. Order was restored quickly. The crowd backed away.

Adam smirked at the Kluckers. "Leave!" Adam shouted. "You heard what he said! He's ashamed of you!"

"Go to hell!" the leader yelled back.

The two guards grabbed Adam and led him away before he stirred them up again. They moved rapidly toward the front gate, knocking reporters and cameramen out of the way. They practically ran through the entrance, past another line of guards, past another swarm of reporters, and finally to Adam's car.

"Don't come back up here, okay?" one of the guards pleaded with him.

MCALLISTER'S OFFICE was known to have more leaks than an old toilet. By early afternoon, Tuesday, the hottest gossip in Jackson was that the governor was seriously considering clemency for Sam Cayhall. The gossip spread rapidly from the capitol to the reporters outside where it was picked up by other reporters and onlookers and repeated, not as gossip, but as solid rumor. Within an hour of the leak, the rumor had risen to the level of near fact.

Mona Stark met in the rotunda with the press and promised a statement by the governor at a later hour. The courts were not finished with the case, she explained. Yes, the governor was under tremendous pressure.

FORTY-EIGHT

IT TOOK THE FIFTH CIRCUIT less than three hours to bump the last of the gangplank appeals along to the U.S. Supreme Court. A brief telephone conference was held at three. Hez Kerry and Garner Goodman raced to Roxburgh's office across from the state capitol building. The Attorney General had a phone system fancy enough to hook up himself, Goodman, Kerry, Adam and Lucas Mann at Parchman, Justice Robichaux in Lake Charles, Justice Judy in New Orleans, and Justice McNeely in Amarillo, Texas. The three-judge panel allowed Adam and Roxburgh to make their arguments, then the conference was disbanded. At four o'clock, the clerk of the court called all parties with the denial, and faxes soon followed. Kerry and Goodman quickly faxed the appeal to the U.S. Supreme Court.

Sam was in the process of receiving his last physical exam when Adam finished his short chat with the clerk. He slowly hung up the phone. Sam was scowling at the young, frightened doctor who was taking his blood pressure. Packer and Tiny stood nearby, at the request of the doctor. With five people present, the front office was crowded.

"Fifth Circuit just denied," Adam said solemnly. "We're on our way to the Supreme Court."

"Not exactly the promised land," Sam said, still staring at the doctor.

"I'm optimistic," Adam said halfheartedly for the benefit of Packer.

The doctor quickly placed his instruments in his bag. "That's it," he said, heading for the door.

"So I'm healthy enough to die?" Sam asked.

The doctor opened the door and left, followed by Packer and Tiny. Sam stood and stretched his back, then began pacing slowly across the room. The shoes slipped on his heels and affected his stride. "Are you nervous?" he asked with a nasty smile.

"Of course. And I guess you're not."

"The dying cannot be worse than the waiting. Hell, I'm ready. I'd like to get it over with."

Adam almost said something trite about their reasonable chances in the Supreme Court, but he was not in the mood to be rebuked. Sam paced and smoked and was not in a talkative mood. Adam, typically, got busy with the telephone. He called Goodman and Kerry, but their conversations were brief. There was little to say, and no optimism whatsoever.

COLONEL NUGENT stood on the porch of the Visitors Center and asked for quiet. Assembled before him on the lawn was the small army of reporters and journalists, all anxiously awaiting the lottery. Next to him on a table was a tin bucket. Each member of the press wore an orange numbered button dispensed by the prison administration as credentials. The mob was unusually quiet.

"According to prison regulations, there are eight seats allotted to members of the press," Nugent explained slowly, his words carrying almost to the front gate. He was basking in the spotlight. "One seat is allotted to the AP, one to the UPI, and one to the Mississippi Network. That leaves five to be selected at random. I'll pull five numbers from this bucket, and if one of them corresponds to your credentials, then it's your lucky day. Any questions?"

Several dozen reporters suddenly had no questions. Many of them pulled at their orange badges to check their numbers. A ripple of excitement went through the group. Nugent dramatically reached into the bucket and pulled out a slip of paper. "Number four-eight-four-three," he announced, with all the skill of a seasoned bingo caller.

"Here you go," an excited young man called back, tugging at his lucky badge.

"Your name?" Nugent yelled.

"Edwin King, with the *Arkansas Gazette*."

A deputy warden next to Nugent wrote down the name and paper. Edwin King was admired by his colleagues.

Nugent quickly called the other four numbers and completed the pool. A noticeable ebb of despair rolled through the group as the last number was called out. The losers were crushed. "At exactly eleven, two vans will pull up over there." Nugent pointed to the main drive. "The eight witnesses must be present and ready. You will be driven to the Maximum Security Unit to witness the execution. No cameras or recorders of any type. You will be searched once you arrive there. Sometime around twelve-thirty, you will reboard the vans and return to this point. A press conference will then be held in the main hall of the new administration building, which will be opened at 9 P.M. for your convenience. Any questions?"

"How many people will witness the execution?" someone asked.

"There will be approximately thirteen or fourteen people in the witness room. And in the Chamber Room, there will be myself, one minister, one doctor, the state executioner, the attorney for the prison, and two guards."

"Will the victims' family witness the execution?"

"Yes. Mr. Elliot Kramer, the grandfather, is scheduled to be a witness."

"How about the governor?"

"By statute, the governor has two seats in the witness room at his discretion. One of those seats will go to Mr. Kramer. I have not been told whether the governor will be here."

"What about Mr. Cayhall's family?"

"No. None of his relatives will witness the execution."

Nugent had opened a can of worms. The questions were popping up everywhere, and he had things to do. "No more questions. Thank you," he said, and walked off the porch.

DONNIE CAYHALL arrived for his last visit a few minutes before six. He was led straight to the front office, where he found his well-dressed brother laughing with Adam Hall. Sam introduced the two.

Adam had carefully avoided Sam's brother until now. Donnie, as it turned out, was clean and neat, well groomed and dressed sensibly. He also resembled Sam, now that Sam had shaved, cut his hair, and shed the red jumpsuit. They were the same height, and though Donnie was not overweight, Sam was much thinner.

Donnie was clearly not the hick Adam had feared. He was genuinely happy to meet Adam and proud of the fact that he was a lawyer. He was a pleasant man with an easy smile, good teeth, but very sad eyes at the moment. "What's it look like?" he asked after a few minutes of small talk. He was referring to the appeals.

"It's all in the Supreme Court."

"So there's still hope?"

Sam snorted at this suggestion.

"A little," Adam said, very much resigned to fate. There was a long pause as Adam and Donnie searched for less sensitive matters to discuss. Sam really didn't care. He sat calmly in a chair, legs crossed, puffing away. His mind was occupied with things they couldn't imagine.

"I stopped by Albert's today," Donnie said.

Sam's gaze never left the floor. "How's his prostate?"

"I don't know. He thought you were already dead."

"That's my brother."

"I also saw Aunt Finnie."

"I thought she was already dead," Sam said with a smile.

"Almost. She's ninety-one. Just all tore up over what's happened to you. Said you were always her favorite nephew."

"She couldn't stand me, and I couldn't stand her. Hell, I didn't see her for five years before I came here."

"Well, she's just plain crushed over this."

"She'll get over it."

Sam's face suddenly broke into a wide smile, and he started laughing. "Remember the time we watched her go to the outhouse behind Grandmother's, then peppered it with rocks? She came out screaming and crying."

Donnie suddenly remembered, and began to shake with laughter. "Yeah, it had a tin roof," he said between breaths, "and every rock sounded like a bomb going off."

"Yeah, it was me and you and Albert. You couldn't have been four years old."

"I remember though."

The story grew and the laughter was contagious. Adam caught himself chuckling at the sight of these two old men laughing like boys. The one about Aunt Finnie and the outhouse led to one about her husband,

Uncle Garland, who was mean and crippled, and the laughs continued.

SAM'S LAST MEAL was a deliberate snub at the fingerless cooks in the kitchen and the uninspired rations they'd tormented him with for nine and a half years. He requested something that was light, came from a carton, and could be found with ease. He had often marveled at his predecessors who'd ordered seven-course dinners—steaks and lobster and cheesecake. Buster Moac had consumed two dozen raw oysters, then a Greek salad, then a large rib eye and a few other courses. He'd never understood how they summoned such an appetite only hours before death.

He wasn't the least bit hungry when Nugent knocked on the door at seven-thirty. Behind him was Packer, and behind Packer was a trustee holding a tray. In the center of the tray was a large bowl with three Eskimo Pies in it, and to the side was a small thermos of French Market coffee, Sam's favorite. The tray was placed on the desk.

"Not much of a dinner, Sam," Nugent said.

"Can I enjoy it in peace, or will you stand there and pester me with your idiot talk?"

Nugent stiffened and glared at Adam. "We'll come back in an hour. At that time, your guest must leave, and we'll return you to the Observation Cell. Okay?"

"Just leave," Sam said, sitting at the desk.

As soon as they were gone, Donnie said, "Damn, Sam, why didn't you order something we could enjoy? What kind of a last meal is this?"

"It's my last meal. When your time comes, order what you want." He picked up a fork and carefully scraped the vanilla ice cream and chocolate covering off the stick. He took a large bite, then slowly poured the coffee into the cup. It was dark and strong with a rich aroma.

Donnie and Adam sat in the chairs along a wall, watching Sam's back as he slowly ate his last meal.

THEY'D BEEN ARRIVING since five o'clock. They came from all over the state, all driving alone, all riding in big four-door cars of varied colors with elaborate seals and emblems and markings on the doors and fenders. Some had racks of emergency lights across the roof. Some had shotguns mounted on the screens above the front seats. All had tall antennas swinging in the wind.

They were the sheriffs, each elected in his own county to protect the citizenry from lawlessness. Most had served for many years, and most had already taken part in the unrecorded ritual of the execution dinner.

A cook named Miss Mazola prepared the feast, and the menu never varied. She fried large chickens in animal fat. She cooked black-eyed peas in ham hocks. And she made real buttermilk biscuits the size of small saucers. Her kitchen was in the rear of a small cafeteria near the main administration building. The food was always served at seven, regardless of how many sheriffs were present.

Tonight's crowd would be the largest since Teddy Doyle Meeks was put to rest in 1982. Miss Mazola anticipated this because she read the papers and everybody knew about Sam Cayhall. She expected at least fifty sheriffs.

They were waved through the front gates like dignitaries, and they parked haphazardly around the cafeteria. For the most part they were big men, with earnest stomachs and voracious appetites. They were famished after the long drive.

Their banter was light over dinner. They ate like

hogs, then retired outside to the front of the building where they sat on the hoods of their cars and watched it grow dark. They picked chicken from their teeth and bragged on Miss Mazola's cooking. They listened to their radios squawk, as if the news of Cayhall's death would be transmitted at any moment. They talked about other executions and heinous crimes back home, and about local boys on the Row. Damned gas chamber wasn't used enough.

They stared in amazement at the hundreds of demonstrators near the highway in front of them. They picked their teeth some more, then went back inside for chocolate cake.

It was a wonderful night for law enforcement.

FORTY-NINE

DARKNESS BROUGHT an eerie quiet to the highway in front of Parchman. The Klansmen, not a single one of whom had considered leaving after Sam asked them to, sat in folding chairs and on the trampled grass, and waited. The skinheads and like-minded brethren who'd roasted in the August sun sat in small groups and drank ice water. The nuns and other activists had been joined by a contingent from Amnesty International. They lit candles, said prayers, hummed songs. They tried to keep their distance from the hate groups. Pick any other day, another execution, another inmate, and those same hateful people would be screaming for blood.

The calm was broken momentarily when a pickup load of teenagers slowed near the front entrance. They suddenly began shouting loudly and in unison, "Gas his ass! Gas his ass! Gas his ass!" The truck squealed tires and sped away. Some of the Klansmen jumped to their feet, ready for battle, but the kids were gone, never to return.

The imposing presence of the highway patrol kept matters under control. The troopers stood about in groups, watching the traffic, keeping close watch on the Klansmen and the skinheads. A helicopter made its rounds above.

GOODMAN FINALLY CALLED a halt to the market analysis. In five long days, they had logged over two thousand calls. He paid the students, confiscated the cellular phones, and thanked them profusely. None of them seemed willing to throw in the towel, so they walked with him to the capitol where another candle-light vigil was under way on the front steps. The governor was still in his office on the second floor.

One of the students volunteered to take a phone to John Bryan Glass, who was across the street at the Mississippi Supreme Court. Goodman called him, then called Kerry, then called Joshua Caldwell, an old friend who'd agreed to wait at the Death Clerk's desk in Washington. Goodman had everyone in place. All the phones were working. He called Adam. Sam was finishing his last meal, Adam said, and didn't wish to talk to Goodman. But he did want to say thanks for everything.

WHEN THE COFFEE and ice cream were gone, Sam stood and stretched his legs. Donnie had been quiet for a long time. He was suffering and ready to go. Nugent would come soon, and he wanted to say good-bye now.

There was a spot where Sam had spilled ice cream on his new shirt, and Donnie tried to remove it with a cloth napkin. "It's not that important," Sam said, watching his brother.

Donnie kept wiping. "Yeah, you're right. I'd better go now, Sam. They'll be here in a minute."

The two men embraced for a long time, patting each other gently on the back. "I'm so sorry, Sam," Donnie said, his voice shaking. "I'm so sorry."

They pulled apart, still clutching each other's shoulders, both men with moist eyes but no tears. They would not dare cry before each other. "You take care," Sam said.

"You too. Say a prayer, Sam, okay?"

"I will. Thanks for everything. You're the only one who cared."

Donnie bit his lip and hid his eyes from Sam. He shook hands with Adam, but could not utter a word. He walked behind Sam to the door, then left them.

"No word from the Supreme Court?" Sam asked out of nowhere, as if he suddenly believed there was a chance.

"No," Adam said sadly.

He sat on the desk, his feet swinging beneath him. "I really want this to be over, Adam," he said, each word carefully measured. "This is cruel."

Adam could think of nothing to say.

"In China, they sneak up behind you and put a bullet through your head. No last bowl of rice. No farewells. No waiting. Not a bad idea."

Adam looked at his watch for the millionth time in the past hour. Since noon, there had been gaps when hours seemed to vanish, then suddenly time would stop. It would fly, then it would crawl. Someone knocked on the door. "Come in," Sam said faintly.

The Reverend Ralph Griffin entered and closed the door. He'd met with Sam twice during the day, and was obviously taking this hard. It was his first execution, and he'd already decided it would be his last. His cousin in the state senate would have to find him another job. He nodded at Adam and sat by Sam on the desk. It was almost nine o'clock.

"Colonel Nugent's out there, Sam. He said he's waiting on you."

"Well, then, let's not go out. Let's just sit here."

"Suits me."

"You know, preacher, my heart has been touched these past few days in ways I never dreamed possible. But, for the life of me, I hate that jerk out there. And I can't overcome it."

"Hate's an awful thing, Sam."

"I know. But I can't help it."

"I don't particularly like him either, to be honest."

Sam grinned at the minister and put his arm around him. The voices outside grew louder, and Nugent barged into the room. "Sam, it's time to go back to the Observation Cell," he said.

Adam stood, his knees weak with fear, his stomach in knots, his heart racing wildly. Sam, however, was unruffled. He jumped from the desk. "Let's go," he said.

They followed Nugent from the front office into the narrow hallway where some of the largest guards at Parchman were waiting along the wall. Sam took Adam by the hand, and they walked slowly together with the reverend trailing behind.

Adam squeezed his grandfather's hand, and ignored the faces as they walked by. They went through the center of the Row, through two sets of doors, then through the bars at the end of Tier A. The tier door closed behind them, and they followed Nugent past the cells.

Sam glanced at the faces of the men he'd known so well. He winked at Hank Henshaw, nodded bravely at J. B. Gullitt who had tears in his eyes, smiled at Stock Turner. They were all leaning through the bars, heads hung low, fear stamped all over their faces. Sam gave them his bravest look.

Nugent stopped at the last cell and waited for the door to be opened from the end of the tier. It clicked loudly, then rolled open. Sam, Adam, and Ralph entered, and Nugent gave the signal to close the door.

The cell was dark, the solitary light and television both off. Sam sat on the bed between Adam and the reverend. He leaned on his elbows with his head hanging low.

Nugent watched them for a moment, but could think of nothing to say. He'd be back in a couple of hours, at eleven, to take Sam to the Isolation Room. They all knew he was coming back. It seemed too cruel at this moment to tell Sam he was leaving, but that he would return. So he stepped away and left through the tier door where his guards were waiting and watching in the semidarkness. Nugent walked to the Isolation Room where a foldaway cot had been installed for the prisoner's last hour. He walked through the small room, and stepped into the Chamber Room where final preparations were being made.

The state executioner was busy and very much in control. He was a short, wiry man named Bill Monday. He had nine fingers and would earn five hundred dollars for his services if the execution took place. By statute, he was appointed by the governor. He was in a tiny closet known simply as the chemical room, less than five feet from the gas chamber. He was studying a checklist on a clipboard. Before him on the counter was a one-pound can of sodium cyanide pellets, a nine-pound bottle of sulfuric acid, a one-pound container of caustic acid, a fifty-pound steel bottle of anhydrous ammonia, and a five-gallon container of distilled water. To his side on another, smaller counter were three gas masks, three pair of rubber gloves, a funnel, hand soap, hand towels, and a mop. Between the two counters was an acid mixing pot mounted on a two-inch pipe that ran into the floor, under the wall, and resurfaced next to the chamber near the levers.

Monday had three checklists, actually. One contained instructions for mixing the chemicals: the sulfuric acid and distilled water would be mixed to obtain approximately a 41 percent concentration; the caustic soda solution was made by dissolving one pound of caustic acid in two and a half gallons of water; and there were a couple of other brews that had to be mixed to clean the chamber after the execution. One list included all the necessary chemicals and supplies. The third list was the procedure to follow during an actual execution.

Nugent spoke to Monday; all was proceeding as planned. One of Monday's assistants was smearing petroleum jelly around the edges of the chamber's windows. A plainclothed member of the execution team was checking the belts and straps on the wooden chair. The doctor was fiddling with his EKG monitor. The door was open to the outside, where an ambulance was already parked.

Nugent glanced at the checklists once more, though he'd memorized them long ago. In fact, he'd even rewritten one other checklist, a suggested chart to record the execution. The chart would be used by Nugent, Monday, and Monday's assistant. It was a numbered, chronological list of the events of the execution: water and acid mixed, prisoner enters chamber, chamber door locked, sodium cyanide enters acid, gas strikes prisoner's face, prisoner apparently unconscious, prisoner certainly unconscious, movements of prisoner's body, last visible movement, heart stopped, respiration stopped, exhaust valve opened, drain valves opened, air valve opened, chamber door opened, prisoner removed from chamber, prisoner pronounced dead. Beside each was a blank line to record the time elapsed from the prior event.

And there was an execution list, a chart of the twenty-nine steps to be taken to begin and complete the task. Of course, the execution list had an appendix, a list of the fifteen things to do in the step-down, the last of which was to place the prisoner in the ambulance.

Nugent knew every step on every list. He knew how

to mix the chemicals, how to open the valves, how long to leave them open, and how to close them. He knew it all.

He stepped outside to speak to the ambulance driver and get some air, then he walked back through the Isolation Room to Tier A. Like everyone else, he was waiting for the damned Supreme Court to rule one way or the other.

He sent the two tallest guards onto the tier to close the windows along the top of the outside wall. Like the building, the windows had been there for thirty-six years and they did not shut quietly. The guards pushed them up until they slammed, each one echoing along the tier. Thirty-five windows in all, every inmate knew the exact number, and with each closing the tier became darker and quieter.

The guards finally finished and left. The Row was now locked down—every inmate in his cell, all doors secured, all windows closed.

Sam had begun shaking with the closing of the windows. His head dropped even lower. Adam placed an arm around his frail shoulders.

"I always liked those windows," Sam said, his voice low and hoarse. A squad of guards stood less than fifteen feet away, peering through the tier door like kids at the zoo, and Sam didn't want his words to be heard. It was hard to imagine Sam liking anything about this place. "Used to, when it came a big rain the water would splash on the windows, and some of it would make it inside and trickle down to the floor. I always liked the rain. And the moon. Sometimes, if the clouds were gone, I could stand just right in my cell and catch a glimpse of the moon through those windows. I always wondered why they didn't have more windows around here. I mean, hell—sorry, preacher—but if they're determined to keep you in a cell all day, why shouldn't you be able to see outdoors? I never understood that. I guess I never understood a lot of things. Oh well." His voice trailed off, and he didn't speak again for a while.

From the darkness came the mellow tenor of Preacher Boy singing "Just a Closer Walk with Thee." It was quite pretty.

> Just a closer walk with Thee,
> Grant it, Jesus, is my plea,
> Daily walking close to Thee . . .

"Quiet!" a guard yelled.

"Leave him alone!" Sam yelled back, startling both Adam and Ralph. "Sing it, Randy," Sam said just loud enough to be heard next door. Preacher Boy took his time, his feelings obviously wounded, then began again.

A door slammed somewhere, and Sam jumped. Adam squeezed his shoulder, and he settled down. His eyes were lost somewhere in the darkness of the floor.

"I take it Lee wouldn't come," he said, his words haunted.

Adam thought for a second, and decided to tell the truth. "I don't know where she is. I haven't talked to her in ten days."

"Thought she was in a rehab clinic."

"I think she is too, but I just don't know where. I'm sorry. I tried everything to find her."

"I've thought about her a lot these past days. Please tell her."

"I will." If Adam saw her again, he would struggle to keep from choking her.

"And I've thought a lot about Eddie."

"Look, Sam, we don't have long. Let's talk about pleasant things, okay?"

"I want you to forgive me for what I did to Eddie."

"I've already forgiven you, Sam. It's taken care of. Carmen and I both forgive you."

Ralph lowered his head next to Sam's, and said, "Perhaps there are some others we should think about too, Sam."

"Maybe later," Sam said.

The tier door opened at the far end of the hallway, and footsteps hurried toward them. Lucas Mann, with a guard behind him, stopped at the last cell and looked at the three shadowy figures huddled together on the bed. "Adam, you have a phone call," he said nervously. "In the front office."

The three shadowy figures stiffened together. Adam jumped to his feet, and without a word stepped from the cell as the door opened. His belly churned violently as he half-ran down the tier. "Give 'em hell, Adam," J. B. Gullitt said as he raced by.

"Who is it?" Adam asked Lucas Mann, who was beside him, step for step.

"Garner Goodman."

They weaved through the center of MSU and hurried to the front office. The receiver was lying on the desk. Adam grabbed it and sat on the desk. "Garner, this is Adam."

"I'm at the capitol, Adam, in the rotunda outside the governor's office. The Supreme Court just denied all of our cert petitions. There's nothing left up there."

Adam closed his eyes and paused. "Well, I guess that's the end of that," he said, and looked at Lucas Mann. Lucas frowned and dropped his head.

"Sit tight. The governor's about to make an announcement. I'll call you in five minutes." Goodman was gone.

Adam hung up the phone and stared at it. "The Supreme Court turned down everything," he reported to

Mann. "The governor's making a statement. He'll call back in a minute."

Mann sat down. "I'm sorry, Adam. Very sorry. How's Sam holding up?"

"Sam is taking this much better than I am, I think."

"It's strange, isn't it? This is my fifth one, and I'm always amazed at how calmly they go. They give up when it gets dark. They have their last meal, say goodbye to their families, and become oddly placid about the whole thing. Me, I'd be kicking and screaming and crying. It would take twenty men to drag me out of the Observation Cell."

Adam managed a quick smile, then noticed an open shoe box on the desk. It was lined with aluminum foil with a few broken cookies in the bottom. It had not been there when they left an hour earlier. "What's that?" he asked, not really curious.

"Those are the execution cookies."

"The execution cookies?"

"Yeah, this sweet little lady who lives down the road bakes them every time there's an execution."

"Why?"

"I don't know. In fact, I have no idea why she does it."

"Who eats them?" Adam asked, looking at the remaining cookies and crumbs as if they were poison.

"The guards and trustees."

Adam shook his head. He had too much on his mind to analyze the purpose of a batch of execution cookies.

FOR THE OCCASION, David McAllister changed into a dark navy suit, freshly starched white shirt, and dark burgundy tie. He combed and sprayed his hair, brushed his teeth, then walked into his office from a side door. Mona Stark was crunching numbers.

"The calls finally stopped," she said, somewhat relieved.

"I don't want to hear it," McAllister said, checking his tie and teeth in a mirror. "Let's go."

He opened the door and stepped into the foyer where two bodyguards met him. They flanked him as he walked into the rotunda where bright lights were waiting. A throng of reporters and cameras pressed forward to hear the announcement. He stepped to a makeshift stand with a dozen microphones wedged together. He grimaced at the lights, waited for quiet, then spoke.

"The Supreme Court of the United States has just denied the last appeals from Sam Cayhall," he said dramatically, as if the reporters hadn't already heard this. Another pause as the cameras clicked and the microphones waited. "And so, after three jury trials, after nine years of appeals through every court available under our Constitution, after having the case reviewed by no less than forty-seven judges, justice has finally arrived for Sam Cayhall. His crime was committed twenty-three years ago. Justice may be slow, but it still works. I have been called upon by many people to pardon Mr. Cayhall, but I cannot do so. I cannot overrule the wisdom of the jury that sentenced him, nor can I impose my judgment upon that of our distinguished courts. Neither am I willing to go against the wishes of my friends the Kramers." Another pause. He spoke without notes, and it was immediately obvious he'd worked on these remarks for a long time. "It is my fervent hope that the execution of Sam Cayhall will help erase a painful chapter in our state's tortured history. I call upon all Mississippians to come together from this sad night forward, and work for equality. May God have mercy on his soul."

He backed away as the questions flew. The body-

guards opened a side door, and he was gone. They
darted down the stairs and out the north entrance
where a car was waiting. A mile away, a helicopter was
also waiting.

Goodman walked outside and stood by an old cannon, aimed for some reason at the tall buildings downtown. Below him, at the foot of the front steps, a large
group of protestors held candles. He called Adam with
the news, then he walked through the people and the
candles and left the capitol grounds. A hymn started as
he crossed the street, and for two blocks it slowly
faded away. He drifted for a while, then walked
toward Hez Kerry's office.

FIFTY

THE WALK BACK to the Observation Cell was much longer than before. Adam made it alone, by now on familiar terrain. Lucas Mann disappeared somewhere in the labyrinth of the Row.

As Adam waited before a heavy barred door in the center of the building, he was immediately aware of two things. First, there were many more people hanging around now—more guards, more strangers with plastic badges and guns on their hips, more stern-faced men with short-sleeved shirts and polyester ties. This was a happening, a singular phenomenon too thrilling to be missed. Adam speculated that any prison employee with enough pull and enough clout just had to be on the Row when Sam's death sentence was carried out.

The second thing he realized was that his shirt was soaked and the collar was sticking to his neck. He loosened his tie as the door clicked loudly, then slid open under the hum of a hidden electric motor. A guard somewhere in the maze of concrete walls and windows and bars was watching and punching the right buttons. He stepped through, still pulling on the knot of his tie and the button under it, and walked to the next barrier, a wall of bars leading to Tier A. He patted his forehead, but there was no sweat. He filled his lungs with muggy, dank air.

With the windows shut, the tier was now suffocating. Another loud click, another electric hum, and he stepped into the thin hallway, which Sam had told him was seven and a half feet wide. Three dingy sets of fluorescent bulbs cast dim shadows on the ceiling and floor. He pushed his heavy feet past the dark cells, all filled with brutal murderers, each one now praying or meditating, a couple even crying.

"Good news, Adam?" J. B. Gullitt pleaded from the darkness.

Adam didn't answer. Still walking, he glanced up at the windows with their various shades of paint splattered around the ancient panes, and was struck by the question of how many lawyers before him had made this final walk from the front office to the Observation Cell to inform a dying man that the last thin shred of hope was now gone. This place had a rich history of executions, and so he concluded that many others had suffered along this trail. Garner Goodman himself had carried the final news to Maynard Tole, and this gave Adam a much needed shot of strength.

He ignored the curious stares of the small mob standing and gawking at him at the end of the tier. He stopped at the last cell, waited, and the door obediently opened.

Sam and the reverend were still sitting low on the bed, heads nearly touching in the darkness, whispering. They looked up at Adam, who sat next to Sam and placed his arm around his shoulders, shoulders that now seemed even frailer. "The Supreme Court just denied everything," he said very softly, his voice on the verge of cracking. The reverend exhaled a painful moan. Sam nodded as if this was certainly expected. "And the governor just denied clemency."

Sam tried to raise his shoulders bravely, but power failed him. He slumped even lower.

"Lord have mercy," Ralph Griffin said.

"Then it's all over," Sam said.

"There's nothing left," Adam whispered.

Excited murmurings could be heard from the death squad squeezed together at the end of the tier. This thing would happen after all. A door slammed somewhere behind them, in the direction of the chamber, and Sam's knees jerked together.

He was silent for a moment—one minute or fifteen, Adam couldn't tell. The clock was still lurching and stopping.

"I guess we oughta pray now, preacher," Sam said.

"I reckon so. We've waited long enough."

"How do you wanna do it?"

"Well, Sam, just exactly what do you want to pray about?"

Sam pondered this for a moment, then said, "I'd like to make sure God's not angry with me when I die."

"Good idea. And why do you think God might be angry with you?"

"Pretty obvious, isn't it?"

Ralph rubbed his hands together. "I guess the best way to do this is to confess your sins, and ask God to forgive you."

"All of them?"

"You don't have to list them all, just ask God to forgive everything."

"Sort of a blanket repentance."

"Yeah, that's it. And it'll work, if you're serious."

"I'm serious as hell."

"Do you believe in hell, Sam?"

"I do."

"Do you believe in heaven?"

"I do."

"Do you believe that all Christians go to heaven?"

Sam thought about this for a long time, then nodded slightly before asking, "Do you?"

"Yes, Sam. I do."

"Then I'll take your word for it."

"Good. Trust me on this one, okay?"

"It seems too easy, you know. I just say a quick prayer, and everything's forgiven."

"Why does that bother you?"

"Because I've done some bad things, preacher."

"We've all done bad things. Our God is a God of infinite love."

"You haven't done what I've done."

"Will you feel better if you talk about it?"

"Yeah, I won't ever feel right unless I talk about it."

"I'm here, Sam."

"Should I leave for a minute?" Adam asked. Sam clutched his knee. "No."

"We don't have a lot of time, Sam," Ralph said, glancing through the bars.

Sam took a deep breath, and spoke in a low monotone, careful that only Adam and Ralph could hear. "I killed Joe Lincoln in cold blood. I've already said I was sorry."

Ralph was mumbling something to himself as he listened. He was already in prayer.

"And I helped my brothers kill those two men who murdered our father. Frankly, I've never felt bad about it until now. Human life seems a whole lot more valuable these days. I was wrong. And I took part in a lynching when I was fifteen or sixteen. I was just part of a mob, and I probably couldn't have stopped it if I'd tried. But I didn't try, and I feel guilty about it."

Sam stopped. Adam held his breath and hoped the confession was over. Ralph waited and waited, and finally asked, "Is that it, Sam?"

"No. There's one more."

Adam closed his eyes and braced for it. He was dizzy and wanted to vomit.

"There was another lynching. A boy named Cletus. I

can't remember his last name. A Klan lynching. I was eighteen. That's all I can say."

This nightmare will never end, Adam thought.

Sam breathed deeply and was silent for several minutes. Ralph was praying hard. Adam just waited.

"And I didn't kill those Kramer boys," Sam said, his voice shaking. "I had no business being there, and I was wrong to be involved in that mess. I've regretted it for many years, all of it. It was wrong to be in the Klan, hating everybody and planting bombs. But I didn't kill those boys. There was no intent to harm anyone. That bomb was supposed to go off in the middle of the night when no one would be anywhere near it. That's what I truly believed. But it was wired by someone else, not me. I was just a lookout, a driver, a flunky. This other person rigged the bomb to go off much later than I thought. I've never known for sure if he intended to kill anyone, but I suspect he did."

Adam heard the words, received them, absorbed them, but was too stunned to move.

"But I could've stopped it. And that makes me guilty. Those little boys would be alive today if I had acted differently after the bomb was planted. Their blood is on my hands, and I've grieved over this for many years."

Ralph gently placed a hand on the back of Sam's head. "Pray with me, Sam." Sam covered his eyes with both hands and rested his elbows on his knees.

"Do you believe Jesus Christ was the son of God; that he came to this earth, born of a virgin, lived a sinless life, was persecuted, and died on the cross so that we might have eternal salvation? Do you believe this, Sam?"

"Yes," he whispered.

"And that he arose from the grave and ascended into heaven?"

"Yes."

"And that through him all of your sins are forgiven? All the terrible things that burden your heart are now forgiven. Do you believe this, Sam?"

"Yes, yes."

Ralph released Sam's head, and wiped tears from his eyes. Sam didn't move, but his shoulders were shaking. Adam squeezed him even tighter.

Randy Dupree started whistling another stanza of "Just a Closer Walk with Thee." His notes were clear and precise, and they echoed nicely along the tier.

"Preacher," Sam said as his back stiffened, "will those little Kramer boys be in heaven?"

"Yes."

"But they were Jews."

"All children go to heaven, Sam."

"Will I see them up there?"

"I don't know. There's a lot about heaven we don't know. But the Bible promises that there will be no sorrow when we get there."

"Good. Then I hope I see them."

The unmistakable voice of Colonel Nugent broke the calm. The tier door clanged, rattled, and opened. He marched five feet to the door of the Observation Cell. Six guards were behind him. "Sam, it's time to go to the Isolation Room," he said. "It's eleven o'clock."

The three men stood, side by side. The cell door opened, and Sam stepped out. He smiled at Nugent, then he turned and hugged the reverend. "Thanks," he said.

"I love you, brother!" Randy Dupree yelled from his cell, not ten feet away.

Sam looked at Nugent, and asked, "Could I say good-bye to my friends?"

A deviation. The manual plainly said that the prisoner was to be taken directly from the Observation

Cell to the Isolation Room, with nothing being mentioned about a final promenade down the tier. Nugent was dumbstruck, but after a few seconds rallied nicely. "Sure, but make it quick."

Sam took a few steps and clasped Randy's hands through the bars. Then he stepped to the next cell and shook hands with Harry Ross Scott.

Ralph Griffin eased past the guards and left the tier. He found a dark corner and wept like a child. He would not see Sam again. Adam stood in the door of the cell, near Nugent, and together they watched Sam work his way down the hallway, stopping at each cell, whispering something to each inmate. He spent the most time with J. B. Gullitt, whose sobs could be heard.

Then he turned and walked bravely back to them, counting steps as he went, smiling at his pals along the way. He took Adam by the hand. "Let's go," he said to Nugent.

There were so damned many guards packed together at the end of the tier that it was a tight squeeze just to get by them. Nugent went first, then Sam and Adam. The mass of human congestion added several degrees to the temperature and several layers to the stuffy air. The show of force was necessary, of course, to subdue a reluctant prisoner, or perhaps to scare one into submission. It seemed awfully silly with a little old man like Sam Cayhall.

The walk from one room to another took only seconds, a distance of twenty feet, but Adam winced with every painful step. Through the human tunnel of armed guards, through the heavy steel door, into the small room. The door on the opposite wall was shut. It led to the chamber.

A flimsy cot had been hauled in for the occasion. Adam and Sam sat on it. Nugent closed the door, and knelt before them. The three of them were alone. Adam again placed his arm around Sam's shoulders.

Nugent was wearing a terribly pained expression. He placed a hand on Sam's knee, and said, "Sam, we're gonna get through this together. Now—"

"You goofy fool," Adam blurted, amazed at this remarkable utterance.

"He can't help it," Sam said helpfully to Adam. "He's just stupid. He didn't even realize it."

Nugent felt the sharp rebuke, and tried to think of something proper to say. "I'm just trying to get through this, okay?" he said to Adam.

"Why don't you just leave?" Adam said.

"You know something, Nugent?" Sam asked. "I've read tons of law books. And I've read pages and pages of prison regulations. And nowhere have I read anything that requires me to spend my last hour with you. No law, statute, regulation, nothing."

"Just get the hell out of here," Adam said, ready to strike if necessary.

Nugent jumped to his feet. "The doctor will enter through that door at eleven-forty. He'll stick a stethoscope to your chest, then leave. At eleven fifty-five, I will enter, also through that door. At that time, we'll go into the Chamber Room. Any questions?"

"No. Leave," Adam said, waving at the door. Nugent made a quick exit.

Suddenly, they were alone. With an hour to go.

TWO IDENTICAL PRISON VANS rolled to a stop in front of the Visitors Center, and were boarded by the eight lucky reporters and one lone sheriff. The law allowed, but did not require, the sheriff of the county where the crime was committed to witness the execution.

The man who was the sheriff of Washington County

in 1967 had been dead for fifteen years, but the current sheriff was not about to miss this event. He had informed Lucas Mann earlier in the day that he fully intended to invoke the power of the law. Said he felt like he owed it to the people of Greenville and Washington County.

Mr. Elliot Kramer was not present at Parchman. He had planned the trip for years, but his doctor intervened at the last moment. His heart was weak and it was just too risky. Ruth Kramer had never thought seriously of witnessing the execution. She was at home in Memphis, sitting with friends, waiting for it to end.

There would be no members of the victims' family present to witness the killing of Sam Cayhall.

The vans were heavily photographed and filmed as they left and disappeared on the main drive. Five minutes later, they stopped at the gates of MSU. Everyone was asked to step outside, where they were checked for cameras and recorders. They reboarded the vans and were cleared through the gates. The vans drove through the grass along the front of MSU, then around the bullpens on the west end, then stopped very near the ambulance.

Nugent himself was waiting. The reporters stepped from the vans and instinctively began looking wildly around, trying to grasp it all to record later. They were just outside a square redbrick building that was somehow attached to the low, flat structure that was MSU. The little building had two doors. One was closed, the other was waiting for them.

Nugent was not in the mood for nosy reporters. He hurriedly guided them through the open door. They stepped into a small room where two rows of folding chairs were waiting, facing an ominous panel of black drapes.

"Take a seat, please," he said rudely. He counted

eight reporters, one sheriff. Three seats were empty. "It is now eleven-ten," he said dramatically. "The prisoner is in the Isolation Room. Before you here, on the other side of these curtains, is the Chamber Room. He will be brought in at five minutes before twelve, strapped in, the door locked. The curtains will be opened at exactly midnight, and when you see the chamber the prisoner will already be inside it, less than two feet from the windows. You will see only the back of his head. I didn't design this, okay? It should take about ten minutes before he is pronounced dead, at which time the curtains will be closed and you'll return to the vans. You'll have a long wait, and I'm sorry this room has no air conditioning. When the curtains open, things will happen quickly. Any questions?"

"Have you talked to the prisoner?"

"Yes."

"How's he holding up?"

"I'm not getting into all that. A press conference is planned at one, and I'll answer those questions then. Right now I'm busy." Nugent left the witness room and slammed the door behind him. He walked quickly around the corner, and entered the Chamber Room.

"WE HAVE LESS than an hour. What would you like to talk about?" Sam asked.

"Oh, lots of things. Most of it unpleasant, though."

"It's kinda hard to have an enjoyable conversation at this point, you know."

"What are you thinking right now, Sam? What's going through your mind?"

"Everything."

"What are you afraid of?"

"The smell of the gas. Whether or not it's painful. I don't want to suffer, Adam. I hope it's quick. I want a big whiff of it, and maybe I'll just float away. I'm not afraid of death, Adam, but right now I'm afraid of dying. I just wish it was over. This waiting is cruel."

"Are you ready?"

"My hard little heart is at peace. I've done some bad things, son, but I feel like God might give me a break. I certainly don't deserve one."

"Why didn't you tell me about the man who was with you?"

"It's a long story. We don't have much time."

"It could've saved your life."

"No, nobody would've believed it. Think about it. Twenty-three years later I suddenly change my story and blame it all on a mystery man. It would've been ridiculous."

"Why'd you lie to me?"

"I have reasons."

"To protect me?"

"That's one of them."

"He's still out there, isn't he?"

"Yes. He's close by. In fact, he's probably out front with all the other loonies right now. Just watching. You'd never see him, though."

"He killed Dogan and his wife?"

"Yes."

"And Dogan's son?"

"Yes."

"And Clovis Brazelton?"

"Probably. He's a very talented killer, Adam. He's deadly. He threatened me and Dogan during the first trial."

"Does he have a name?"

"Not really. I wouldn't tell you anyway. You can never breathe a word of this."

"You're dying for someone else's crime."

"No. I could've saved those little boys. And God

knows I've killed my share of people. I deserve this, Adam."

"No one deserves this."

"It's far better than living. If they took me back to my cell right now and told me I'd stay there until I died, you know what I'd do?"

"What?"

"I'd kill myself."

After spending the last hour in a cell, Adam couldn't argue with this. He could not begin to comprehend the horror of living twenty-three hours a day in a tiny cage.

"I forgot my cigarettes," Sam said, patting his shirt pocket. "I guess this is a good time to quit."

"Are you trying to be funny?"

"Yeah."

"It's not working."

"Did Lee ever show you the book with my lynching picture in it?"

"She didn't show it to me. She told me where it was, and I found it."

"You saw the picture."

"Yes."

"A regular party, wasn't it?"

"Pretty sad."

"Did you see the other picture of the lynching, one page over?"

"Yes. Two Kluckers."

"With robes and hoods and masks."

"Yes, I saw it."

"That was me and Albert. I was hiding behind one of the masks."

Adam's senses were beyond the point of shock. The gruesome photograph flashed through his mind, and he tried to purge it. "Why are you telling me this, Sam?"

"Because it feels good. I've never admitted it before,

and there's a certain relief in facing the truth. I feel better already."

"I don't want to hear any more."

"Eddie never knew it. He found that book in the attic, and somehow figured out I was in the other party photo. But he didn't know I was one of the Kluckers."

"Let's not talk about Eddie, okay?"

"Good idea. What about Lee?"

"I'm mad at Lee. She skipped out on us."

"It would've been nice to see her, you know. That hurts. But I'm so glad Carmen came."

Finally, a pleasant subject. "She's a fine person," Adam said.

"A great kid. I'm very proud of you, Adam, and of Carmen. Y'all got the good genes from your mother. I'm so lucky to have two wonderful grandchildren."

Adam listened and didn't try to respond. Something banged next door, and they both jumped.

"Nugent must be playing with his gadgets in there," Sam said, his shoulders vibrating again. "You know what hurts?"

"What?"

"I've been thinking a lot about this, really flogging myself the last couple of days. I look at you, and I look at Carmen, and I see two bright young people with open minds and hearts. You don't hate anybody. You're tolerant and broad-minded, well educated, ambitious, going places without the baggage I was born with. And I look at you, my grandson, my flesh and blood, and I ask myself, Why didn't I become something else? Something like you and Carmen? It's hard to believe we're actually related."

"Come on, Sam. Don't do this."

"I can't help it."

"Please, Sam."

"Okay, okay. Something pleasant." His voice trailed

off and he leaned over. His head was low and hanging almost between his legs.

Adam wanted an in-depth conversation about the mysterious accomplice. He wanted to know it all—the real details of the bombing, the disappearance, how and why Sam got caught. He also wanted to know what might become of this guy, especially since he was out there, watching and waiting. But these questions would not be answered, so he let them pass. Sam would take many secrets to his grave.

THE ARRIVAL of the governor's helicopter created a stir along the front entrance of Parchman. It landed on the other side of the highway where another prison van waited. With a bodyguard on each elbow and Mona Stark racing behind, McAllister scampered into the van. "It's the governor!" someone yelled. The hymns and prayers stopped momentarily. Cameras raced to film the van, which raced through the front gate and disappeared.

Minutes later, it stopped near the ambulance behind MSU. The bodyguards and Ms. Stark remained in the van. Nugent met the governor and escorted him into the witness room where he took a seat in the front row. He nodded at the other witnesses, all sweating profusely by now. The room was an oven. Black mosquitoes bounced along the walls. Nugent asked if there was anything he could fetch for the governor.

"Popcorn," McAllister cracked, but no one laughed. Nugent frowned and left the room.

"Why are you here?" a reporter asked immediately.

"No comment," McAllister said smugly.

The ten of them sat in silence, staring at the black drapes and anxiously checking their watches. The nervous chatter had ended. They avoided eye contact, as if they were ashamed to be participants in such a macabre event.

Nugent stopped at the door of the gas chamber and consulted a checklist. It was eleven-forty. He told the doctor to enter the Isolation Room, then he stepped outside and gave the signal for the guards to be removed from the four towers around MSU. The odds of escaping gas injuring a tower guard after the execution were minuscule, but Nugent loved the details.

THE KNOCK on the door was faint indeed, but at the moment it sounded as if a sledgehammer were being used. It cracked through the silence, startling both Adam and Sam. The door opened. The young doctor stepped in, tried to smile, dropped to one knee, and asked Sam to unbutton his shirt. A round stethoscope was stuck to his pale skin, with a short wire left hanging to his belt.

The doctor's hands shook. He said nothing.

FIFTY-ONE

AT ELEVEN-THIRTY, Hez Kerry, Garner Goodman, John Bryan Glass, and two of his students stopped their idle talk and held hands around the cluttered table in Kerry's office. Each offered a silent prayer for Sam Cayhall, then Hez voiced one for the group. They sat in their seats, deep in thought, deep in silence, and said another short one for Adam.

THE END CAME QUICKLY. The clock, sputtering and braking for the last twenty-four hours, suddenly roared ahead.

For a few minutes after the doctor left, they shared a light, nervous chatter as Sam walked twice across the small room, measuring it, then leaned on the wall opposite the bed. They talked about Chicago, and Kravitz & Bane, and Sam couldn't imagine how three hundred lawyers existed in the same building. There was a jittery laugh or two, and a few tense smiles as they waited for the next dreaded knock.

It came at precisely eleven fifty-five. Three sharp raps, then a long pause. Nugent waited before barging in.

Adam immediately jumped to his feet. Sam took a deep breath, and clenched his jaws. He pointed a finger at Adam. "Listen to me," he said firmly. "You can walk in there with me, but you cannot stay."

"I know. I don't want to stay, Sam."

"Good." The crooked finger dropped, the jaws

slackened, the face sank. Sam reached forward and took Adam by the shoulders. Adam pulled him close and hugged him gently.

"Tell Lee I love her," Sam said, his voice breaking. He pulled away slightly and looked Adam in the eyes. "Tell her I thought about her to the very end. And I'm not mad at her for not coming. I wouldn't want to come here either if I didn't have to."

Adam's head nodded quickly, and he struggled not to cry. Anything, Sam, anything.

"Say hello to your mom. I always liked her. Give my love to Carmen, she's a great kid. I'm sorry about all this, Adam. It's a terrible legacy for you guys to carry."

"We'll do fine, Sam."

"I know you will. I'll die a very proud man, son, because of you."

"I'll miss you," Adam said, the tears now running down his cheeks.

The door opened and the colonel stepped in. "It's time now, Sam," he said sadly.

Sam faced him with a brave smile. "Let's do it!" he said strongly. Nugent went first, then Sam, then Adam. They stepped into the Chamber Room, which was packed with people. Everyone stared at Sam, then immediately looked away. They were ashamed, thought Adam. Ashamed to be here taking part in this nasty little deed. They wouldn't look at Adam.

Monday, the executioner, and his assistant were along the wall next to the chemical room. Two uniformed guards were crowded next to them. Lucas Mann and a deputy warden were near the door. The doctor was busy to the immediate right, adjusting his EKG and trying to appear calm.

And in the center of the room, now surrounded by the various participants, was the chamber, an octagonal-shaped tube with a gleaming fresh coat of silver paint. Its door was open, the fateful wooden chair just waiting, a row of covered windows behind it.

The door to the outside of the room was open, but there was no draft. The room was like a sauna, everyone was drenched with sweat. The two guards took Sam and led him into the chamber. He counted the steps—only five of them from the door to the chamber—and suddenly he was inside, sitting, looking around the men to find Adam. The men's hands moved rapidly.

Adam had stopped just inside the door. He leaned on the wall for strength, his knees spongy and weak. He stared at the people in the room, at the chamber, at the floor, the EKG. It was all so sanitary! The freshly painted walls. The sparkling concrete floors. The doctor with his machines. The clean, sterile little chamber with its glowing luster. The antiseptic smell from the chemical room. Everything so spotless and hygienic. It should've been a clinic where people went to get themselves healed.

What if I vomit on the floor, right here at the feet of the good doctor, what would that do for your disinfected little room, Nugent? How would the manual treat that, Nugent, if I just lost it right here in front of the chamber? Adam clutched his stomach.

Straps on Sam's arms, two of them for each, then two more for the legs, over the shiny new Dickies, then the hideous head brace so he wouldn't hurt himself when the gas hit. There now, all buckled down, and ready for the vapors. All neat and tidy, spotless and germ-free, no blood to be shed. Nothing to pollute this flawless, moral killing.

The guards backed out of the narrow door, proud of their work.

Adam looked at him sitting in there. Their eyes met, and for an instant Sam closed his.

The doctor was next. Nugent said something to him, but Adam couldn't hear the words. He stepped inside and rigged the wire running from the stethoscope. He was quick with his work.

Lucas Mann stepped forward with a sheet of paper. He stood in the door of the chamber. "Sam, this is the death warrant. I'm required by law to read it to you."

"Just hurry," Sam grunted without opening his lips.

Lucas lifted the piece of paper, and read from it: "Pursuant to a verdict of guilty and a sentence of death returned against you by the Circuit Court of Washington County on February 14, 1981, you are hereby condemned to die by lethal gas in the gas chamber at the Mississippi State Penitentiary at Parchman. May God have mercy on your soul." Lucas backed away, then reached for the first of two phones mounted on the wall. He called his office to see if there were any miraculous last minute delays. There were none. The second phone was a secured line to the Attorney General's office in Jackson. Again, all systems were go. It was now thirty seconds after midnight, Wednesday, August 8. "No stays," he said to Nugent.

The words bounced around the humid room and crashed in from all directions. Adam glanced at his grandfather for the last time. His hands were clenched. His eyes were closed tightly, as if he couldn't look at Adam again. His lips were moving, as if he had just one more quick prayer.

"Any reason why this execution should not proceed?" Nugent asked formally, suddenly craving solid legal advice.

"None," Lucas said with genuine regret.

Nugent stood in the door of the chamber. "Any last words, Sam?" he asked.

"Not for you. It's time for Adam to leave."

"Very well." Nugent slowly closed the door, its thick

rubber gasket preventing noise. Silently, Sam was now locked up, and buckled down. He closed his eyes tightly. Just please hurry.

Adam eased behind Nugent, who was still facing the chamber door. Lucas Mann opened the door to the outside, and both men made a quick exit. Adam glanced back at the room for the last time. The executioner was reaching for a lever. His assistant was inching to the side to catch a glimpse. The two guards were jockeying for position so they could watch the old bastard die. Nugent and the deputy warden and the doctor were crowded along the other wall, all inching closer, heads bobbing up and over, each fearful he might miss something.

The ninety-degree heat outside seemed much cooler. Adam walked to the end of the ambulance and leaned on it for a second.

"Are you all right?" Lucas asked.

"No."

"Just take it easy."

"You're not gonna witness it?"

"No. I've seen four. That's enough for me. This one's especially difficult."

Adam stared at the white door in the center of the brick wall. Three vans were parked nearby. A group of guards smoked and whispered by the vans. "I'd like to leave," he said, afraid that he was about to be sick.

"Let's go." Lucas grabbed his elbow and led him to the first van. He said something to a guard, who jumped into the front seat. Adam and Lucas sat on a bench in the center of it.

Adam knew at that precise moment his grandfather was in the chamber gasping for breath, his lungs seared with burning poison. Just over there, in that little red-brick building, right now, he's sucking it in, trying to swallow as much as possible, hoping to simply float away to a better world.

He began to cry. The van moved around the recreation yards and through the grass in front of the Row. He covered his eyes, and cried for Sam, for his suffering at this moment, for the despicable way he was being forced to die. He looked so pitiful sitting there in his new clothes being tied down like an animal. He cried for Sam and the last nine and a half years he'd spent staring through bars, trying to catch a glimpse of the moon, wondering if anyone out there cared about him. He cried for the whole wretched Cayhall family and their miserable history. And he cried for himself, for his anguish at this moment, for the loss of a loved one, for his failure to stop this madness.

Lucas patted him gently on the shoulder and the van rolled and stopped, then rolled and stopped again. "I'm sorry," he said more than once.

"This your car?" Lucas asked as they stopped outside the gate. The dirt parking lot was filled to capacity. Adam yanked the door handle and stepped out without a word. He could say thanks later.

He sped along the gravel trail, between the rows of cotton, until he came to the main drive. He drove quickly to the front entrance, slowing only briefly as he weaved around two barricades, then stopped at the front gate so a guard could check his trunk. To his left was the swarm of reporters. They were on their feet, waiting anxiously for word from the Row. Mini-cams were ready.

There was no one in his trunk, and he was waved around another barricade, almost hitting a guard who wasn't moving fast enough. He stopped at the highway, and paused to look at the candlelight vigil under way to his right. Hundreds of candles. And a hymn in progress somewhere down the way.

He sped away, past state troopers loitering about, enjoying the break in the action. He sped past cars parked on the shoulders for two miles, and soon Parchman was behind him. He pushed the turbo, and was soon doing ninety.

He headed north for some reason, though he had no intention of going to Memphis. Towns like Tutwiler, Lambert, Marks, Sledge, and Crenshaw flew by. He rolled the windows down and the warm air swirled around the seats. The windshield was peppered with large bugs and insects, the plague of the Delta, he'd learned.

He just drove, with no particular destination. This trip had not been planned. He'd given no thought to where he would go immediately after Sam died, because he never truly believed it would happen. Maybe he'd be in Jackson now, drinking and celebrating with Garner Goodman and Hez Kerry, getting plastered because they'd pulled a rabbit out of the hat. Maybe he'd be at the Row, still on the phone trying desperately to get the details of a last minute stay that would later become permanent. Maybe a lot of things.

He wouldn't dare go to Lee's, because she might actually be there. Their next meeting would be a nasty one, and he preferred to postpone it. He decided to find a decent motel. Spend the night. Try and sleep. Figure things out tomorrow after the sun was up. He raced through dozens of hamlets and towns, none with a room for rent. He slowed considerably. One highway led to another. He was lost but didn't care. How can you be lost when you don't know where you're going? He recognized towns on road signs, turned this way then that way. An all-night convenience store caught his attention on the outskirts of Hernando, not far from Memphis. There were no cars parked in front. A middle-aged lady with jet-black hair was behind the counter, smoking, smacking gum, and talking on the phone. Adam went to the beer cooler and grabbed a six-pack.

"Sorry, hon, can't buy beer after twelve."

"What?" Adam demanded, reaching into his pocket.

She didn't like his snarl. She carefully laid the phone next to the cash register. "We can't sell beer here after midnight. It's the law."

"The law?"

"Yes. The law."

"Of the State of Mississippi?"

"That's correct," she said smartly.

"Do you know what I think of the laws of this state right now?"

"No, dear. And I honestly don't care."

Adam flipped a ten-dollar bill on the counter and carried the beer to his car. She watched him leave, then stuck the cash in her pocket and went back to the phone. Why bother the cops over a six-pack of beer?

He was off again, going south on a two-lane highway, obeying the speed limit and gulping the first beer. Off again in pursuit of a clean room with a free continental breakfast, pool, cable, HBO, kids stay free.

Fifteen minutes to die, fifteen minutes to vent the chamber, ten minutes to wash it down with ammonia. Spray the lifeless body, deader than hell, according to the young doctor and his EKG. Nugent pointing here and there—get the gas masks, get the gloves, get those damned reporters back on the vans and out of here.

Adam could see Sam in there, head fallen to one side, still strapped under those enormous leather buckles. What color was his skin now? Surely not the pale whiteness of the past nine and a half years. Surely the gas turned his lips purple and his flesh pink. The chamber is now clear, all is safe. Enter the chamber, Nugent says, unbuckle him. Take the knives. Cut off the cloth-

ing. Did his bowels loosen? Did his bladder leak? They
always do. Be careful. Here, here's the plastic bag. Put
the clothes in here. Spray the naked body.

Adam could see the new clothes—the stiff khakis,
the oversized shoes, the spotless white socks. Sam had
been so proud to wear real clothes again. Now they
were rags in a green garbage sack, handled like venom
and soon to be burned by a trustee.

Where are the clothes, the blue prison pants and
white T-shirt? Get them. Enter the chamber. Dress the
corpse. No shoes are necessary. No socks. Hell, he's
just going to the funeral home. Let the family worry
about dressing him for a decent burial. Now the
stretcher. Get him out of there. Into the ambulance.

Adam was near a lake somewhere, over a bridge,
through a bottom, the air suddenly damp and cool.
Lost again.

FIFTY-TWO

THE FIRST GLINT of sunrise was a pink halo over a hill above Clanton. It strained through the trees, and was soon turning to yellow, then to orange. There were no clouds, nothing but brilliant colors against the dark sky.

There were two unopened beers sitting in the grass. Three empty cans had been tossed against a nearby headstone. The first empty can was still in the car.

The dawn was breaking. Shadows fell toward him from the rows of other gravestones. The sun itself was soon peeking at him from behind the trees.

He'd been there for a couple of hours, though he'd lost track of time. Jackson and Judge Slattery and Monday's hearing were years ago. Sam had died minutes ago. Or was he dead? Had they already done their dirty act? Time was still playing games.

He hadn't found a motel, not that he'd looked very hard. He'd found himself near Clanton, then was drawn here where he'd located the headstone of Anna Gates Cayhall. Now he rested against it. He'd drunk the warm beer and thrown the cans at the largest monument within range. If the cops found him here and took him to jail, he wouldn't care. He'd been in a cell before. "Yeah, just got out of Parchman," he'd tell his cellmates, his rap partners. "Just walked out of death row." And they'd leave him alone.

Evidently, the cops were occupied elsewhere. The graveyard was secure. Four little red flags had been staked out next to his grandmother's plot. Adam noticed them as the sun rose to the east. Another grave to be dug.

A car door closed somewhere behind him, but he didn't hear it. A figure walked toward him, but he didn't know it. It moved slowly, searching the cemetery, cautiously looking for something.

The snapping of a twig startled Adam. Lee was standing beside him, her hand on her mother's headstone. He looked at her, then looked away.

"What are you doing here?" he asked, too numb to be surprised.

She gently lowered herself first to her knees, then she sat very close to him. her back pressed to her mother's engraved name. She wrapped her arm around his elbow.

"Where the hell have you been, Lee?"

"In treatment."

"You could've called, dammit."

"Don't be angry, Adam, please. I need a friend." She leaned her head on his shoulder.

"I'm not sure I'm your friend, Lee. What you did was terrible."

"He wanted to see me, didn't he?"

"He did. You, of course, were lost in your own little world, self-absorbed as usual. No thought given to others."

"Please, Adam, I've been in treatment. You know how weak I am. I need help."

"Then get it."

She noticed the two cans of beer, and Adam quickly tossed them away. "I'm not drinking," she said, pitifully. Her voice was sad and hollow. Her pretty face was tired and wrinkled.

"I tried to see him," she said.

"When?"

"Last night. I drove to Parchman. They wouldn't let me in. Said it was too late."

Adam lowered his head and softened considerably. He would accomplish nothing by cursing her. She was an alcoholic, struggling to overcome demons he hoped he would never meet. And she was his aunt, his beloved Lee. "He asked about you at the very end. He asked me to tell you he loved you, and that he wasn't angry because you didn't come see him."

She started crying very quietly. She wiped her cheeks with the backs of her hands, and cried for a long time.

"He went out with a great deal of courage and dignity," Adam said. "He was very brave. He said his heart was right with God, and that he hated no one. He was terribly remorseful for the things he'd done. He was a champ, Lee, an old fighter who was ready to move on."

"You know where I've been?" she asked between sniffles, as if she'd heard nothing he said.

"No. Where?"

"I've been to the old home place. I drove there from Parchman last night."

"Why?"

"Because I wanted to burn it. And it burned beautifully. The house and the weeds around it. One huge fire. All up in smoke."

"Come on, Lee."

"It's true. I almost got caught, I think. I might've passed a car on the way out. I'm not worried, though. I bought the place last week. Paid thirteen thousand dollars to the bank. If you own it, then you can burn it, right? You're the lawyer."

"Are you serious?"

"Go look for yourself. I parked in front of a church a mile away to wait for the fire trucks. They never came. The nearest house is two miles away. No one saw the fire. Drive out and take a look. There's nothing left but the chimney and a pile of ashes."

"How—"

"Gasoline. Here, smell my hands." She shoved them under his nose. They bore the acrid, undeniable smell of gasoline.

"But why?"

"I should've done it years ago."

"That doesn't answer the question. Why?"

"Evil things happened there. It was filled with demons and spirits. Now they're gone."

"So they died with Sam?"

"No, they're not dead. They've gone off to haunt someone else."

It would be pointless to pursue this discussion, Adam decided quickly. They should leave, maybe return to Memphis where he could get her back into recovery. And maybe therapy. He would stay with her and make sure she got help.

A dirty pickup truck entered the cemetery through the iron gates of the old section, and puttered slowly along the concrete path through the ancient monuments. It stopped at a small utility shed in a corner of the lot. Three black men slowly scooted out and stretched their backs.

"That's Herman," she said.

"Who?"

"Herman. Don't know his last name. He's been digging graves here for forty years."

They watched Herman and the other two across the valley of tombstones. They could barely hear their voices as the men deliberately went about their preparations.

Lee stopped the sniffling and crying. The sun was well above the treeline, its rays hitting directly in their faces. It was already warm. "I'm glad you came," she said. "I know it meant a lot to him."

"I lost, Lee. I failed my client, and now he's dead."

"You tried your best. No one could save him."

"Maybe."

"Don't punish yourself. Your first night in Memphis, you told me it was a long shot. You came close. You put up a good fight. Now it's time to go back to Chicago and get on with the rest of your life."

"I'm not going back to Chicago."

"What?"

"I'm changing jobs."

"But you've been a lawyer for only a year."

"I'll still be a lawyer. Just a different kind of practice."

"Doing what?"

"Death penalty litigation."

"That sounds dreadful."

"Yes, it does. Especially at this moment in my life. But I'll grow into it. I'm not cut out for the big firms."

"Where will you practice?"

"Jackson. I'll be spending more time at Parchman."

She rubbed her face and pulled back her hair. "I guess you know what you're doing," she said, unable to hide the doubt.

"Don't bet on it."

Herman was walking around a battered yellow backhoe parked under a shade tree next to the shed. He studied it thoughtfully while another man placed two shovels in its bucket. They stretched again, laughed about something, and kicked the front tires.

"I have an idea," she said. "There's a little café north of town. It's called Ralph's. Sam took me—"

"Ralph's?"

"Yeah."

"Sam's minister was named Ralph. He was with us last night."

"Sam had a minister?"

"Yes. A good one."

"Anyway, Sam would take me and Eddie there on our birthdays. Place has been here for a hundred years. We'd eat these huge biscuits and drink hot cocoa. Let's go see if it's open."

"Now?"

"Yeah." She was excited and getting to her feet. "Come on. I'm hungry."

Adam grabbed the headstone and pulled himself up. He hadn't slept since Monday night, and his legs were heavy and stiff. The beer made him dizzy.

In the distance, an engine started. It echoed unmuffled through the cemetery. Adam froze. Lee turned to see it. Herman was operating the backhoe, blue smoke boiling from the exhaust. His two co-workers were in the front bucket with their feet hanging out. The backhoe lunged in low gear, then started along the drive, very slowly past the rows of graves. It stopped and turned.

It was coming their way.

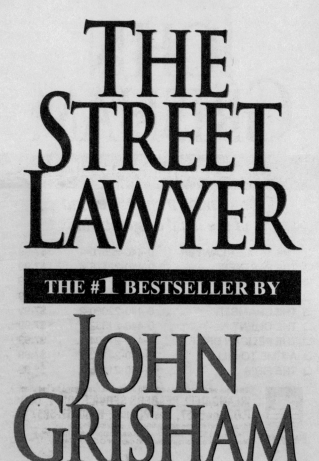